TWO BOOKS IN ONE SPECIAL VOLUME

SEA TO SHINING SEA

INTO THE LONG DARK NIGHT

Michael Phillips

BETHANY HOUSE PUBLISHERS
MINNEAPOLIS, MINNESOTA 55438

Cover by Dan Thornberg
Bethany House Publishers staff artist.

Published by Bethany House Publishers
A Ministry of Bethany Fellowship, Inc.
6820 Auto Club Road, Minneapolis, Minnesota 55438

Printed in the United States of America
First Combined Hardcover Edition for Christian Herald Family Bookshelf: 1992

Library of Congress Cataloging-in-Publication Data

Phillips, Michael R., 1946—
    Sea to shining sea / Michael Phillips
    p. cm.— (The Journals of Corrie Belle Hollister ; bk 5)
    1. United States—History—Civil War, 1861-1865—Fiction.
    I. Title. II. Series: Phillips, Michael R., 1946—
Journals of Corrie Belle Hollister ; 5.
PS3566.H492S4   1992
813'.54—dc20   92-15197
ISBN 1-55661-227-3   CIP

SEA TO
SHINING SEA

SEA TO SHINING SEA

MICHAEL PHILLIPS

Cover by Dan Thornberg,
Bethany House Publishers staff artist.

Published by Bethany House Publishers
A Ministry of Bethany Fellowship, Inc.
6820 Auto Club Road, Minneapolis, Minnesota 55438

Printed in the United States of America

Library of Congress Cataloging-in-Publication Data

Phillips, Michael R., 1946–
    Sea to shining sea / Michael Phillips
        p.   cm. — (The Journals of Corrie Belle Hollister ; bk. 5)
    1. United States—History—Civil War, 1861–1865—Fiction.
    I. Title. II. Series: Phillips, Michael R., 1946–
Journals of Corrie Belle Hollister ; 5.
PS3566.H492S4   1992
813'.54—dc20   92–15197
ISBN 1–55661–227–3   CIP

To Judith Pella,

the greatest writing partner a fellow author
could wish for, with deep gratitude and
prayers for your best in all the future holds.
Thank you for allowing me
to be part of your life!

CONTENTS

CHAPTER 1

SAN FRANCISCO AGAIN

The setting was unbelievable!

When I first walked into the huge ballroom of the Montgomery Hotel at Pa's side, I could not take in all the magnificence of the place. Under the bright lights of chandeliers, the men sauntered around in expensive blacuits, and the women in long gowns. Waiters carried food and drinks about on silver trays, and hundreds of important people milled together in that gigantic fancy room.

All I could think was, *What are we doing here?*

But we *were* there. And as we walked in, I think Pa sensed my nervousness.

"Come on, buck up, Corrie," he whispered down to me, placing a reassuring hand on my arm. "They invited us. And you're every bit the lady any of these other women are."

He patted my hand. "So don't you go willowy on me or faint or nothin'," he added. "I'm just as nervous as you are."

When the invitation had come a month earlier for Pa and me to attend the Republican reception in June of 1860 at the Montgomery Hotel in San Francisco, at first I didn't think too much of it. But a few days later Pa said, "We oughta go to that shindig, Corrie. It's not every day a couple of country locals like us get the chance to mix with important folks. What do you think?"

"You really want to, Pa?"

"Sure, just so long as you come too."

"I don't know why they invited me," I said. "You're mayor of a town. But why me?"

"Because you're a prominent young lady writer," said Pa. "Ain't no big mystery in that."

11

"Maybe it was Jessie Fremont's doing," I suggested. "She and Mr. Fremont probably know every important Republican in California. Maybe they told somebody about me before they left for the East."

"Never hurts to know high-up people," said Pa with a wink. "Anyhow, what do you think—you up for a trip to San Francisco?"

And so there we were. Pa in his new suit, fresh-shaved, looked as handsome and important as ever a man could. And I wore my new dress—yellow, with ruffles and a sash, and my hair fixed up with a matching ribbon in it. We walked into the ballroom of the Montgomery Hotel to join all the men who would play a leading role in the upcoming national election of 1860.

"Hey, Hollister!" called out a voice. We both turned to see Carl Denver hurrying our way. He greeted us and shook our hands. "Come with me," he said. "There's someone I want you to meet."

Before we could say much in reply, Mr. Denver had us in tow, steering us through the crowd. Then all of a sudden we were face-to-face with one of the tallest, most handsome men I had ever seen.

"Cal," said Mr. Denver, "I want you to meet two friends of mine from up in Miracle Springs—this is Corrie Hollister and her father, Drummond Hollister, the mayor of Miracle. Corrie, Hollister . . . meet Cal Burton, an important fellow here in San Francisco these days."

Pa shook the man's hand. I just stood there watching and listening to him laugh at Mr. Denver's words.

"Come on now, Carl," he said, "you shouldn't lie to these good people. I'm no more important than the shoeshine boy on the street outside."

"Don't let his modesty fool you," said Mr. Denver, turning to me and speaking as if it were confidential. "Cal works for Leland Stanford, and from what I hear, he is moving up fast. You keep your eye on him, Corrie. He might get you a story or two that'll make you famous."

"A story—what are you talking about, Carl?" said Burton, turning away from Pa and toward us.

"Corrie here's a writer, Cal—you know, California's woman reporter."

"Why, of course!" he said. "Now I remember you telling me about her." He took my hand, but instead of giving it a manly shake, he just held it softly for a moment.

My heart started beating fast, and I could feel my face reddening all the way up the back of my neck and cheeks. My eyes had been following my hand as it was swallowed up in his. And now I found myself slowly glancing up as he released it. His eyes bored straight into mine.

I'm embarrassed to admit it, but the touch of his hand, the look in his eyes, and his smile made me feel a little light-headed for the rest of the evening. I'm sure Pa noticed, especially when he caught me staring in Mr. Burton's direction a couple of times. But he was nice enough not to say anything about it.

He was too busy anyway, meeting people and listening to speeches. I met a lot of other people too, but as I think back on the evening, I only remember a few of the names. Cal Burton did take me to meet his boss, the important railroad man and politician, Mr. Stanford. I couldn't say I actually spoke to him, because he was busy talking with some important Republicans about the election and slavery and the need for railroad development in California.

I wish I could recall more of the things I heard everyone talking about, because those were important times for California's future. The election, the railroad, and slavery were the subjects on everyone's minds and the topics of every conversation.

But I don't remember very much, because I couldn't keep my eyes off Cal Burton, and I couldn't keep down the fluttering in my chest. I thought everybody in the huge ballroom must have been able to hear the pounding of my pulse, although nobody seemed to pay much attention.

Cal was tall, with straight light-brown hair, parted in the middle and coming down over his forehead almost to his eyebrows, then falling around the sides just above his ears. He wore a fancy suit, light brown like his hair, and a ruffled shirt and polished boots. What a figure he cut, with those blue eyes that contrasted with the brown of his hair and suit and the tan of his face! He had a friendly smile and a warm tone, yet a thoughtfulness that made his brow crinkle when he was thinking about what to say.

Altogether, Cal Burton had a lively, interesting, intelligent, pleasant face. How could I help giving it a second, or even a third look?

I heard Pa's voice at my side. "He's going to get a headache if you keep looking at him like that!"

"Oh, Pa!" I said, blushing again. "I was just—"

"I know what you was doing, Corrie," Pa added. "And there's nothin' wrong with admitting you like the looks of a good-looking young man." He gave me a smile. "You just might want to not be so obvious about it."

"I didn't know I was."

Pa chuckled. "Everybody in the place is gonna know if you don't pull those eyes of yours back inside your head! Now come on, what do you say you and I go over and hear what some of those men in the fancy suits are saying about the election?"

CHAPTER 2

THE PRESIDENTIAL ELECTION OF 1860

As much as I had been interested in the election of 1856 because of my involvement with the Fremonts, the election of 1860 was a far more important one for the future of the whole nation. Mr. Fremont's being halfway a Californian had stirred up California quite a bit. But now even larger issues were at stake. Everything had grown more serious and heated, and even though it mostly had to do with the South and slavery, Californians were mighty interested too.

Slavery had been an issue for a long time. Pa said he remembered them talking about it back in the East when he was in his teen years. There had been preachers and politicians talking out against it and trying to get it abolished for a lot of years. But there was never anything they could do about it. Throughout the 1850s, although the debate had gotten pretty heated, the government in Washington had been almost completely controlled by the South. The southern states had kept the northern states from making any changes. And the border states were usually more sympathetic with the South, since most of them allowed slavery too.

So even though there had been growing opposition to slavery all through the 1850s, there had been nothing any of the northern politicians could do about it. I had just been growing up during those years, and hadn't known or cared much about it. But now it was 1860, and I *was* interested. So I asked people lots of questions to find out all I could. And gradually toward the end of the decade that had just passed, it began to look as if a change might be coming.

15

For one thing, Abraham Lincoln was becoming more and more well known, especially after the famous debates with Stephen Douglas in 1858 when they'd both been running for Congress in Illinois. Lincoln was known to be antislavery, and his abolitionist views made southern politicians angry.

Meanwhile, the country just kept growing, just like Miracle Springs and Sacramento and San Francisco and all of California had grown.

But the westward expansion meant that most new states were in areas where there was no slavery. Minnesota became a state in 1858, and then Oregon in 1859. Counting California too, there were eighteen northern and western states, while the southern and border regions had only fifteen. The southerners who had been in control for all that time started to get nervous because there weren't any new places for slavery to expand. Westward lay the Nebraska Territory and the Dakota Territory and the Colorado Territory and the Washington Territory and the Utah and Nevada and New Mexico territories. And all of those places, if they ever did become states, weren't very likely to side with the powerful slave men from the South.

All these things combined to make the year of 1860, and the election which would be held in November, one of the most important years in the whole history of our country.

Only a month before Pa and I went to San Francisco, the leaders of the Republican party had nominated Abraham Lincoln of Illinois to be their candidate for president of the United States. Against him would be running the man he already knew so well from his home state—Stephen A. Douglas.

Southerners realized the fate of slavery if Lincoln were elected, especially now that the number of slave states was in a minority. They were determined to defeat him!

That's what some of the men were discussing that evening at the Montgomery. The speeches were all about the future of the Union, they called it, and the reasons why all God-fearing and slavery-hating Californians had to do everything they could to work for Mr. Lincoln's election in California. And it wouldn't be easy—there were many more Democrats in California than Republicans.

Mr. Thomas Starr King made a speech that stirred everybody up about the need to support the northern states, even though we were so far out west. He was the pastor of the Unitarian church in San Francisco, but had only recently arrived from Boston where the man introducing him said he had been a famous preacher and lecturer. He had come from the East only a month or two earlier, and he made it sound as if debate was heated back East over which direction the nation was going to go. As for the election, however, he said he still wasn't sure how much to involve himself, being a minister.

Other men at the Montgomery were talking about issues not directly having to do with the disputes between North and South, but having to do with the future of California itself, and what the election would mean out here.

Economics and money and growth were the issues they were talking about—travel and gold and population changes and the expansion of the railroad both up and down the state and toward the East. Communication with the East was a major concern. Even though Oregon up to the north was now a state too, there had still always been the feeling that we were isolated from the rest of the country, and that the states in the West weren't as important as the other states.

Of course, nobody here believed that! To listen to them talk, California was the *most* important state! But they wanted everybody else to know it too.

The Pony Express had just started up two months earlier. At least now mail and news didn't take so long to reach back and forth across the huge continent. News used to take three weeks by the fastest stagecoaches to get across the plains and mountains and prairies from Missouri to California. Now it took only nine or ten days from St. Joseph to Sacramento! Since there were telegraph lines from there to the big cities on the East Coast, the whole country was separated from each other by less than two weeks as far as news was concerned.

Mr. Stanford was talking about this very issue. "Mail is one thing," he said, "but *people* are another. Getting *people* quickly back and forth between California and the East—*that's* what it will take before California can truly stand up and fully take its place alongside the other states of these great United States of America."

"Horses and stagecoaches," Mr. Stanford said, "are the transportation and communication methods of the past. But the future lies with machines and inventions." He went on to make a speech about how the equality and impact of full statehood could be achieved only by a railroad line stretching all the way across the country.

While I was listening to all this, I felt a touch on my arm. "Miss Hollister," a voice said, "I wonder if I might have a word with you."

CHAPTER 3

AN UNEXPECTED PROPOSITION

I turned, and my heart took off racing again at the sight of Cal Burton!

I glanced toward Pa, and before I knew it I was walking across the room at Mr. Burton's side. I was afraid to look at him and at the same time unable to keep my eyes off him.

"There's somebody I want you to talk to," he said as he led me through the maze of people. In another minute I was standing in the middle of a small group of four or five men. One of them began talking to me, but I forgot his name as soon as I'd been told, and I remember only about half of what he said, even though it turned out to be a conversation that changed the whole course of my life.

"I heard about you from Cal here," the man was saying, "and of course I'm on close terms with your editor, Ed Kemble. So I'm not altogether unaware of the role you played on behalf of our Republican party four years ago."

"I didn't do anything that did any good," I said, finally finding my voice.

"Perhaps not," the man went on. "You may have considered all that happened a waste of time and energy, but I would disagree with you."

"The story I wrote about Mr. Fremont was killed," I said.

"True enough. Your article was never printed. But what would you say if I told you I had read it?"

"I don't know," I replied. "I'm not sure I would believe you."

19

The man laughed, and all the others in the small group listening to our conversation followed his lead. It was the first time I had seen Cal Burton laugh, and I enjoyed the sound of it. His even white teeth and broad smile gave me a whole new reason to like his looks. But the man was still talking to me, so I had to do my best to pay attention.

"Well, I have," he said. "I should have known from reading your words that you would be a plain-talking young lady, even if it means calling an important man a liar to his face!"

He chuckled again, but as I started to tell him I hadn't meant anything by it, he held up his hand and spoke again.

"Don't worry, Miss Hollister," he said. "I took no offense at what you said. I admire a woman who's not afraid to speak her mind in front of men. Especially a young pretty one like you."

I blushed immediately. It was an awful embarrassment!

I'm not pretty and you know it, I said to him in my mind. But outwardly I just glanced down at the floor for a minute. My first reaction was that he was probably poking fun at me like Uncle Nick always did. But then I realized he hadn't been doing that at all. Neither he nor any of the other men seemed to make light of his words a bit. I recovered myself and looked up. His face was serious, and I could see that he'd meant what he'd said.

"I'm very earnest, Miss Hollister, in what I say. You see, my friends consider me a pretty straightforward man myself. So I recognize honesty and fearlessness for the virtues they are. A lot of folks who are involved in politics do so much double-talking you can't tell what they're saying. Most of them aren't saying much worth listening to. But I've always been of a mind to speak out what's on my heart, and then people can do what they want with your words. Wouldn't you agree that's the best way of going about it when you have something to say?"

"I reckon so," I answered.

"That's another thing I like about you, Miss Hollister. You don't try to put on airs. You're a country girl and you never try to hide it. You speak honestly, you speak out as the young lady you are, and as far as I can tell, you aren't much afraid of anyone or worried what they'll think." He paused and looked me straight in the eye. "Would you say that is an accurate representation of yourself?" he asked after a moment.

"I . . . I don't know," I said, stumbling a little. The man certainly was straightforward, I'll say that for him! "I wouldn't say I'm not afraid of anything. But I guess you're right about speaking my mind honestly. My minister back home, and my mother—my stepmother, I should say—"

"That would be Almeda Parrish, would it not?" he interrupted.

"Almeda Parrish *Hollister*," I corrected him.

"Yes, of course. I knew of Mrs. Parrish before I had heard of either you or your father. A woman with a fine reputation. But I don't suppose you need me to sing her praises, do you?"

I smiled and shook my head.

"And I read some of your articles about the Miracle Springs election, the whole feud between your family and that skunk of a banker Royce. You see, I do some checking to make sure of myself before I become involved with anyone. I make a habit of going into things with my eyes open."

"I can see that," I said.

"I admire your stepmother, and I have been keeping an eye on your father as well. He strikes me as a man California might hear more from one day."

"He's here," I said eagerly, "if you would like to meet him."

The man chuckled again. "Of course he's here. I'm the one who arranged for both of you to be invited! I have every intention of speaking with your father before the night is done. But right now I'm speaking with you, and we were talking about your work for the Fremont cause four years ago, and the bravery you displayed in uncovering that story. Printed or not, it was a fine piece of work, and a courageous thing to do. But a great many things have changed since 1856. Our party was just in its infancy then, and John Fremont did not have the nationwide strength to stand up against Buchanan. Even had your article made it into the *Alta*, it is doubtful it would have had much of an impact, and it would have been too late even to be picked up in the East. Therefore, what I want to talk with you about, Miss Hollister, is not your work of the past, but what you might do for the Republican party in the future."

He stopped, looking at me intently.

"I'm not sure I understand you," I said. "I don't know much about politics. I haven't paid much attention since then. Except for what my pa does as mayor, that is."

"I'm not concerned how much you know of what used to be. This is a new day, Miss Hollister. This election of 1860 is the one that's going to change the direction of this nation forever. Don't any of the rest of you tell John what I've said," he warned, glancing around at the other men in the small group before turning his eyes back to me. "But John Fremont, as much as I admire the man, represents the Republican party of the past. He was an explorer, after all. That is how he will be remembered. But the future, both of our party and of this country, lies with the man from Illinois who is heading our presidential ticket this year. I'm sure you've heard of Abraham Lincoln, Miss Hollister?"

"Of course," I answered. "There was already talk about him in 1856."

"Well, I am convinced his time has finally come, and that he is the man to take our country forward—into the new decade, into the future, and away from the Democratic control that has dominated Washington for the past thirty years."

He stopped again, still looking at me with an almost inquisitive expression.

"I'm not sure I understand," I said finally. "You're probably right about everything you say. But I don't see what it has to do with me."

"Simple, Miss Hollister. I want to enlist your support in the cause. I want you to help us with the campaign, in even a more active way than you did for John Fremont four years ago."

"Help . . . in what way? How could I possibly help?"

"Writing articles on Mr. Lincoln's behalf. Perhaps even taking to the stump once in a while. Women might not be able to vote, but men sure pay attention when a woman speaks out!"

"The stump . . . what do you mean?"

"Speaking, Miss Hollister. Giving speeches to go along with your writing, helping us raise money and votes for the Republican ticket in November."

"You're talking about speechmaking—me?" I exclaimed.

"That's exactly what I'm talking about," he replied with a broad smile. "I want you on our side."

CHAPTER 4

WONDERING WHAT TO DO

The rest of the evening was lost in a blur.

There was music and more discussions and a few other speeches and refreshments. I stayed close to Pa. There weren't but a handful of other women present, and I'm sure no one as young as I was. But Cal Burton seemed to be keeping an eye on me. He was very polite and not the least bit forward; he treated me as if I was the most important person there.

As Pa and I walked back to Miss Sandy Bean's Boarding House from the downtown district, the night fog had rolled in and a chill was in the air. But my face felt hot, even more so in the brisk night, and I felt so full and alive that I could hardly keep from skipping up the walk. I tried my best to keep it under control, but I know Pa couldn't help but notice.

He walked along beside me, the sound of his boots clumping along the boards of the walkways and thudding dully on the hard-packed dirt of the streets we crossed, talking and smiling and laughing lightly with me. He didn't do a thing to make me feel foolish for being . . . well, just for being the way a young woman sometimes is!

Before we parted for the night, Pa took me in his arms, gave me a tight squeeze, then said, "You're some lady, Corrie Belle. You do your pa right proud, whether it's ridin' a horse in the woods or at some fancy big-city political gathering."

Then he kissed me good-night and sent me into my room.

The next morning we left Miss Bean's and caught the steamer across the bay and up the river to Sacramento. As we moved out across the water, although it was still early, some of the fog had lifted back to reveal a portion of the city in bright sunlight. It was different than any time I'd left the city before. Instead of being anxious to get home, there was a lump in the pit of my stomach, pulling at me and making me wish I could stay. Pa seemed to know I was full of new and unaccustomed thoughts, and neither of us said much during the quiet boat ride across the bay.

About halfway across, a small cloud of lingering fog drifted by and settled down on top of the boat. With the sun gone, suddenly a chill came over me. I shivered and turned away from the railing, then sat down on a nearby bench with a sigh.

The fog seemed to fit my mood perfectly, although I didn't even know what my mood was. A cloud had settled over my spirits just as the fog had engulfed the boat in its white, quiet chill. Pa stayed at the railing, leaning over, looking down into the water as it splashed rhythmically by. I was so absorbed in my own thoughts that I was hardly aware that he had a lot on his mind, too.

It was still pretty early in the day, and as the river narrowed and we lost sight of the city, we went inside and took some seats next to a window. We floated along awhile in silence. Then all of a sudden, without hardly even thinking what I was saying, I blurted out:

"Well, Pa, do you think I ought to do it?"

"Do what?" he said, glancing over at me. He had no idea what I could be talking about.

"Get involved with the election," I answered. "You know, try to help Mr. Lincoln get elected."

"My daughter, the speechmaker!" said Pa with the first smile I'd seen on his face all day.

"Come on, Pa! You know I'll never be that kind of person. Maybe I'll just write some, like I did about the election before."

"It'd be sure to help the Republican cause," he said. "You ain't just a curiosity no more. You saw the byline Kemble put on your article last winter about the flood of California's rivers— *Corrie Belle Hollister, California's Woman Reporter.*"

"That doesn't mean much."

"Sure it does! You're not just a kid wantin' to write any more. You're just about Kemble's most famous reporter."

"But not the best paid!" I said, trying to laugh.

"You're still a woman, and you can't expect to get close to what a man does. But if Kemble knows what's good for him, he'll keep you happy. That's just what I told him too, last night."

"Pa, you didn't!"

"'Course I did. It's the truth, too. He's got all kinds of men writin' for his paper. There are hundreds of men writing for the papers in San Francisco and Sacramento. But there's only one woman. And you're it, and he's got you. So I told him he'd better treat you like the important young lady you are or else I'd tell you to take your writing someplace else."

"Pa, that's downright embarrassing."

"It's the truth."

"What did he say?"

"Aw, you know Kemble. He flustered some, but he didn't deny a word of it. That fellow Cal Burton was listening too, and he gave Kemble a few words to back up what I'd said besides."

I glanced away. I didn't want Pa to see the red in my cheeks just from the mention of Cal's name. He kept right on talking, but I'm sure he knew. Pa usually knew most things I was thinking . . . more than he liked to let on.

"I tell you, Corrie, you shouldn't underestimate yourself. You just might have the chance to influence this election. You know that folks pay attention to what you write—men as well as women. You wanted to be a writer, and you've done it. You just might be able to help elect the first Republican president this country's ever had."

"My writing's not that important. You just think so because you're my Pa."

"Well, I got a right to be proud! If you ask me, there's not a better person they could get to stand up and tell folks they oughta vote for Mr. Lincoln for president. When folks hear your name, they're all gonna know who you are. *Corrie Belle Hollister*. Why, maybe nobody thought nothing of it back in '55 when you wrote about the blizzard. But now when folks see those words above a piece of writing, they know they'd better pay attention, because *the* woman newspaper writer of California is speaking to them. And they're gonna know your name just as well if you're speaking out to a crowd of people."

"I'm not so sure," I said. "I don't know if I want to do that anyway. It sounds pretty frightening to me, getting up in front of a bunch of men. What if they yell at me or don't listen or say rude things?"

"Then you yell right back at them and tell 'em to shut their mouths and pay attention. Ain't that what Almeda'd do if a group of rowdy men got rude at her?"

I smiled at the thought. That was exactly what Almeda would do.

"Besides, if word got out that you were gonna be someplace, I got no doubt there'd be plenty of women there too, and they'd keep the men quiet."

"I don't know—"

"You got a duty to your country, Corrie. Maybe when me and Nick was fighting the Mexicans back in '47, it wasn't all that patriotic a thing. We were just a couple of men not knowing what to do with ourselves. We didn't know much about all the disputes with President Polk. But you see, now you've got a chance to do something and know it's important at the same time."

"I'd like to hear about the Mexican war, Pa."

"Ask Almeda about it."

"Almeda?" I said. "Why her? *You're* the one who fought in it."

"Nick and I may have fought in it, but we didn't know anything of what it was about. Your pa wasn't much of a literate man back in those days, I'm sorry to say, Corrie. Almeda told me what I was really fighting for."

"What was it, then, you and Uncle Nick were fighting for? Wasn't it just to keep the Mexicans from taking our territory?"

"That's the way Polk and the Democrats would like to tell it. But according to Almeda, that wasn't it at all. It was actually the other way around—we were taking *their* territory in the Southwest, just like we've been doing from the Indians in the North."

"So what *were* you fighting for?"

"You sure you want to know? It ain't too pleasant a notion."

"Of course I want to know."

"We were fighting for slavery, Corrie—nothing less than just that. Even in California like we were, that's what it was about."

"But . . . how could it have been about slavery way back then, Pa?"

"The southerners have been trying to hedge their bets for a long time. Grabbing up all that land in the Southwest, all the way from Texas to California. You see, that was the Democrats' way to get their hands on lots of new territory that would become slave states someday. Polk wasn't no fool. He was a southerner himself, and he saw the handwriting on the wall. They knew clear back then that slavery didn't have much of a chance unless they got lots of new slave states eventually."

"That's what Almeda says?"

"She gets downright hot in her breeches about slavery. Being a northerner herself, and a woman mighty full of strong ideas, she hates the very thought of it. She says that we attacked the Mexicans and forced the war ourselves, even though the government was saying they attacked us and we were only defending the cause of freedom. Hoots, that's just exactly what Nick and I was told when we joined up."

"How does she know all that?"

"She says it comes from reading what she calls between the lines, reading what nobody says but what's there if you know how to look for it."

I was quiet a while, thinking about all he'd said.

"But you see, Corrie," Pa went on, "that's all the more reason for you maybe to help Mr. Lincoln. Back then, without knowing it, I helped the South and the Democrats. Now you can do something about it on the other side."

"It still doesn't seem as if I'd make much of a difference."

"I'm telling you, Corrie, people aren't just listening to you out of curiosity. You're writing news that's important. You know as well as I do what Kemble said, that folks back East read your articles on the flooding and it was their way of finding out what was happening here. News, Corrie, not just curiosity writing. You're a genuine newspaper reporter whose words are being read from the Pacific all the way to the Atlantic. You're making a way for a lot of women who never figured they could do anything in this man's world. You're doing it, and they're proud of you—just like I am."

"You make it sound so important, Pa," I said.

"Maybe I am your pa, but I still say it *is* important. Your articles are sure more important than anything that weasel O'Flaridy's ever done!"

I laughed at the thought of Robin's condescension toward me the first time we met in Mr. Kemble's office.

"I'm glad to see you can laugh," said Pa. "You were downright furious with him over the Fremont article. Whatever became of him? I haven't heard you mention his name in more than a year."

"Mr. Kemble told me he left the *Alta* and went back East somewhere. St. Louis, I think it was at first. He always did have big ambitions, and I know it stuck in his craw that I was getting more well known than he. He couldn't abide getting outdone by a woman, and I think he wanted to get out of here and make a name for himself."

"Well, he can make his name however he pleases, but I'm proud of my own Corrie's name and what she's done with it. And I think you oughta do what the man asked you to do and help out the Republicans to get Mr. Lincoln elected."

I was quiet for a minute or so, thinking about what Pa'd said.

"But how do I know if it's the right thing?" I asked after a bit.

"You mean whether Lincoln's the right man to be president?" said Pa.

"That too, but mainly whether it's the right thing for *me* to do. I mean, just because something's there to do, and just because somebody *else* thinks I ought to do it, that doesn't necessarily make it right, does it?"

I paused. Pa didn't say anything but just kept looking over at me, and then I continued.

"I knew for a long time that I wanted to write. It was something I wanted to do inside *myself*, whether anybody else cared, or whether anybody else ever read anything I wrote. But then when something like this comes along, from the outside, so to speak, and not from inside myself, it's an altogether different thing. I just can't do something because somebody wants me to. There's got to be a rightness about it."

"I hadn't given a thought myself to the idea of running for mayor until Almeda and Avery and Nick and the rest of you all talked me into it."

"But after a bit, didn't you start thinking it was the right thing for *you* to do too, no matter what we thought?"

"Sure. I wouldn't have done it otherwise."

"That's what I mean, Pa. Even if Mr. Lincoln is the right man, I can't do it because anyone else thinks I should. It's still got to be right for *me*."

"Well, then, do you think Mr. Lincoln's the man who ought to be the country's president?"

"I don't guess there's any doubt about that. Slavery's no good, and like the man said, it's time the southern states didn't control things as they have for so long."

"So then, there's your place to start thinking about it. At least you're in agreement with the cause they're talking about. You sure couldn't do it if that weren't true. Now all you have to do is decide if it's something *you* want to do, that you feel is *right* for you to do."

"Sometimes that's not an easy thing to know."

We were both silent a while. Finally Pa reached over and took my hand, then bowed his head and closed his eyes right there on the steamer.

"God," he prayed out loud, "me and Corrie here, we've got some things to decide about our future, and about what we ought to do about some things. And we ain't altogether sure in our own minds what's best. So we ask you right now to help us, and to guide us in what we do. We need your help, God, to keep us walkin' right along the path you want us on. Neither of us want to be anywhere else but right where you'd have us. So show us where that is."

He looked up and opened his eyes. "Amen," I added.

Again we sat in silence for a while as we floated along.

"You just never know where something's going to lead you," I said at length.

Pa nodded.

"Just like starting to write and getting that first article published in the *Alta*, or walking into the *Gold Nugget*, looking for Uncle Nick that day and having you walk out instead. Things have a way of piling onto each other. Something you do today can change the whole direction of your life."

"Makes you think about being careful before you jump into something new, don't it?" said Pa. "Whether it's writing or may-oring or anything else."

"Yeah, I reckon that's what I'm thinking now. If I say that I'll write and maybe even talk to some folks about voting for Abraham Lincoln and Hannibal Hamlin, who can tell what it might mean in my life a year from now, or even five years from now? It might change things as much as writing that first article did."

"You heard what all them men in San Francisco were saying," said Pa. "This year of 1860 is just about the most important year this country's ever faced. So I reckon you're right. If this election's the most important in a long spell, then it's bound to have some effect on your life too."

"That's what I'm thinking, Pa. But how do you know what to do when you can't see up ahead what that effect might be?"

"You can't see into the future, that's for sure, Corrie."

"I know," I laughed. "Sometimes I'd like to, though."

"Well, look at it this way—if this election is gonna help decide which direction the nation's going from now on, maybe you can't see into the future, but you might have a hand in helping decide it."

"But electing either Lincoln or Douglas could change my life as much as it's sure to change the country one way or the other."

"Yep, I figure it could."

I let out a sigh. "I don't suppose there's much else to do but wait for God to show me something," I said finally.

"I reckon he will," said Pa.

"I hope so."

"If you're looking for it, he won't leave you in doubt for too long a spell about what to do."

CHAPTER 5

THE ROCK OF CHANGING CIRCUMSTANCES

We rode along for fifteen or twenty minutes without saying anything more. Outside, the rolling landscape passed slowly, reminding me of the time I'd first made the leisurely trip down the river with Almeda.

It seemed so long ago now!

The country was shrinking; California was shrinking. Stagecoaches ran daily to most places north from Sacramento. The Pony Express delivered mail in record time; rail lines were being laid down all over the country, and the national election seemed so much closer and important than ever before! I felt I was being stretched, so that the whole country was part of my life, my world.

Just the thought that my writing went all the way from the Pacific to the Atlantic was enough to make me stop and wonder what God was doing with me. Nobody paid any attention to what a woman did, and yet people *were* reading my words all the way back there in the East, as well as at home in Miracle Springs. It was sometimes more than I could imagine!

"You know, Corrie," Pa said after a while, "I've got a future to be thinking about too."

I looked up from the midst of my daydreaming. "You mean whether to keep being mayor?"

"There's that too," answered Pa. "But plenty more besides."

"What, Pa? You sound as if it's something serious."

Pa sighed and looked out the window thoughtfully.

"Is there something wrong?" I asked.

31

He gave a little laugh, although there wasn't anything comical in the sound of it.

"Wrong, Corrie?" he said wistfully. "No. I was just reflecting on all the changes that come even when you're not looking for them. Life has a way of bringing things to you and plopping them smack in your way so there's no way you can avoid them. You may be thinking you're heading down one road toward some- where, but then all of a sudden a giant rock falls in the middle of your path. And you figure, that's okay, you'll just walk around it. But in getting past it, without realizing it, you change directions, and then all of a sudden you're going along a different path toward someplace different. You never knew there was someplace differ- ent to go, but you're headed there, and you never set foot on the first road you was on again."

"You're going to have to try again, Pa," I said. "I don't suppose I'm used to hearing you philosophize about life quite like that."

Pa burst out laughing so hard he couldn't stop. Several of the other people in the boat turned their heads to see what the joke was.

"I must've been around you and Almeda and Avery too much," he said finally, still half laughing. "Or too long trying to make sense of being mayor to that town of miners, farmers, ranch- ers, and kids!"

"But I still want to know what you meant by the road with the big rock falling in the middle of it."

"Well, for example, Nick and I coming west, we didn't plan on all that trouble we got into. I always figured on farming my land and raising my family in what you'd call a normal way. Then all of a sudden, the rock of circumstances fell—the robbery, the shooting. Suddenly Nick and I were running from the law and heading west.

"That's what I mean, Corrie. There we were on a new path toward someplace we never figured on going. We never set foot on the first road again. I've been out West ever since, never saw your ma again. It was a long time before I could even think about Aggie without getting pretty stirred up inside. You know that, 'cause I shed my share of tears with you after finding out she was gone. You understand? A change comes out of nowhere—you don't see it coming, you don't expect it, you ain't done nothing to plan for it . . . but your life will never be the same again."

"Now I see, Pa."

"Same thing that day you and the rest of the kids showed up in Miracle. I stumbled out of the *Gold Nugget* and there the five of you was standing there, with Almeda wagging her tongue at me. And *wham*—my life took off in a new direction!

"I guess we get blindsided by circumstances every now and then. So when one of them big boulders slams down in front of you, it makes pretty good sense to look things over a spell before you start off either moving around it or in a new direction. You never know what tomorrow's gonna bring, and you just might never get back to the same place again."

"Like that man asking me if I'd help with the election?"

"Exactly like that. You see, that's a big rock in your path. It's not anything bad, like me and Nick's getting into trouble. Why, it's a real opportunity for you—might be the best thing that ever came along. But you just can't ever know ahead of time what might come next on account of it. That's why you gotta stop and take a good look at things and at the decisions you make. If you say yes to the man, it might change everything for you, Corrie. It might not . . . but then it *might*. You just can't know for sure."

As I watched Pa and listened to him, I realized that his being a father and a husband for the second time in his life, the mayor of a growing community, and a man who took his faith in God more seriously than most men did—all that had changed Pa *inside* more than even he realized. Just to hear him talk amazed me when I thought back to those first couple of years after the kids and I came to California. He might talk about the boulder and his and Uncle Nick's coming out West and being mayor, but I could see that the most important new path Drummond Hollister was walking along was deep inside his heart and mind, and maybe didn't have as much to do with all those other things as he might think.

"It's the same with the country, Corrie," Pa went on, "or with a town, a community, a family. Things come up, and then things change. Everything around here for two hundred miles is the way it is because a man named Marshall found a pretty little rock in a mountain stream up in the hills. And Miracle Springs became what it did 'cause our friend Alkali Jones found a piece of the same kind of rock in the creek up behind our place."

"According to him, at least," I said with a smile.

"You're right there, Corrie!" laughed Pa. "But *somebody* found gold there anyhow, including Tad when he was just a little runt. And then all of a sudden everything's changed.

"And this election—all those men back there were saying how important it is for the future of the country. Why, who can tell, we might look back someday and say that the election of 1860, and whoever becomes the new president next year, steered the whole country off in a new direction. You just never know what might be around the corner, and so you oughta be watching and paying attention as best you can."

Again he fell silent and gazed out the window for a while.

"I see what you are saying, Pa," I said. "And I'm sure going to take your advice and try to think carefully through what's best for me to do. If it's going to change the direction of my future, it can't be something I do without thinking and praying. But I don't think you were really talking about my decision, were you, Pa, when you first said it? There's something else on your mind, isn't there?"

He sighed, then and turned his head back and looked at me.

"Can't ever fool you, can I?"

"You said you had your future to be thinking about," I said, "more than just mayoring."

"Yeah, I guess I did say that, didn't I?"

"Yes, you did. So, what is it you've been beating around the bush to try to tell me about?"

Pa took a deep breath. "Do you know who that man was who asked you about helping out with the election?" he asked.

"I got introduced to him," I answered, "but I forgot his name."

"His name's Alexander Dalton."

"That's right, now I remember. But I'd never heard of him, Pa."

"He's not the kind of man people do hear of. Crocker and Hopkins and Stanford and Fremont—they're the public men, the famous, the names folks hear about. Lincoln and Douglas—

they're the ones running for president. But back behind men like that there are always other folks making things happen that nobody ever sees. Kingmakers, they're called. They'll never be kings themselves, but they hold power to *make* kings. You see what I mean?"

I nodded. "So, is Mr. Dalton like that—a kingmaker?"

"That's exactly what he is," replied Pa. "He's just about one of the most important men in all the West, even though he's practically unknown except by the people who need to know him. Fremont, Stanford—he's helped make them the important men they are."

"So that's why he was the one talking to me about getting involved."

"He's the top Republican in California, Corrie—the chairman of the Republican party for all of California and Oregon. It's his job to make sure Lincoln carries the state."

"Is that all he does?"

Pa chuckled. "Not by a long shot, Corrie! He's got to see to all kinds of business besides just presidential politics."

"Like what?"

"California politics, the state's future, all the kinds of things politicians think about. He's got to raise money for the party, he's got to see to the state's growth, he's got to make decisions about who does what, who's in charge of what. He's the one more than anyone else who has power to get people elected to committees and even to the Congress in Washington. Leastways, if the Republican party keeps growing like it has, he'll be doing all those things. The way I hear it, he's just about the second most influential man in Sacramento behind Governor Downey."

"You sound like you know him, Pa."

"I've met him a time or two. He's always at the mayors' conferences I got to go to. He knows everybody. He's made speeches to us about all the plans to get California split up into different states."

"So what does it all have to do with us, Pa?"

"It's got to do with you 'cause he asked you to help with the election, Corrie. He's trying to get Lincoln elected."

"But what about you?"

"Well, daughter of mine, you weren't the only Hollister that Dalton talked to last night," said Pa.

"I didn't see you with him," I said.

"It wasn't a long conversation," Pa replied. "And it was private. He took me outside for a minute."

"It sounds secretive—why, Pa?"

"Some things are best not made public until the right time, Corrie. You know how fellas like Royce can twist and turn things to their own advantage if you're not careful."

"Now you've got me dying of curiosity, Pa! What did Dalton say?"

"Well . . . he asked me to run for the state legislature in Sacramento come November."

CHAPTER 6

A SURPRISE IN SACRAMENTO

"Pa, that's wonderful!" I exclaimed. "Are you going to do it?"

"I don't know, Corrie. I've got lots to think about, just like you. God's bound to cause a heap of changes, like I was saying, we can't see now. It's not something you can do lightly. Naturally I gotta talk and pray with Almeda about it."

"Would you have to move to Sacramento, Pa?"

"I reckon most of the men do, but there ain't no way I'd leave Miracle. I'm not about to pack up everyone to go live in a city. And there's sure no way I'd move there myself or with just me and Almeda, and leave everyone."

"I could take care of the kids, Pa. Zack and I are adults. With Emily and Mike married and down in Auburn, that only leaves Becky and Tad. They're fifteen and seventeen. We can take care of ourselves. You and Almeda can take little Ruth with you to Sacramento and you can become a famous politician. If we have any problems, there's Uncle Nick and Aunt Katie across the stream."

"No, I'm not gonna split up my family for nobody, not for Alexander Dalton, not for my own future, not even for California. Besides, what if you decide to do what he wants *you* to do? Then you'd be gone a lot, too."

"Zack's twenty-one. He's a grown man."

"You know as well as I do that he's itching to be off wherever a horse'll carry him. He and Little Wolf are gone half the time as it is. No, Corrie, if I decide to run, and even if I win, then they'll just have to settle for a congressman who represents his people as best he can by staying with those people and going into Sacramento whenever he has to."

"I wonder how long it'll be before the train comes up that far?"

"I doubt if that'll be for years. There's lots of other places in California growing faster than us. I'm sure I'd have to travel by horse or stagecoach for a good while yet."

"Did Mr. Dalton say why he wanted you to run?" I asked.

A sheepish look came over Pa's face. I'd never seen anything quite like it in his expression before.

"Aw, he did, but you know them politicians—they're always saying things that aren't true to get things how they want them."

"What did he say, Pa?"

"Aw, he just said he and other folks in Sacramento'd been keeping their eyes on me ever since I got elected mayor, and some of them figured I was the kind of man they needed in the capitol to help set the direction for the state in the coming years."

"Of course you're the kind of man the state needs!" I said. I leaned over and gave him a hug. "Pa, I am so proud of you."

Neither of us had noticed the steamer slowing down as we approached the dock at Sacramento.

"Looks like we're to the halfway point," said Pa. "We'll have to decide on our futures later."

We got up and left the boat, walking into the bright warm sunlight of Sacramento in early afternoon. San Francisco was always much cooler, but here in Sacramento, summer was on the way.

If we had come by horseback or had left a wagon or buckboard in Sacramento, we might have made it home by late that same night. But we had taken the stage down, and the return stage north left early in the morning, so we'd have to stay over.

We got our bags and Pa hired a buckboard to drive us to Miss Baxter's Boarding House. We always stayed with her whenever we were in the city. By this time, with her keeping tabs on us and all the changes that had come in our family since we first arrived in California with Captain Dixon eight years earlier, she was as good a family friend as we had anywhere in the city.

Once we got ourselves situated at her place, we went out for a walk. Pa said he wanted to show me the statehouse where the legislature and governor had their offices, and where California's government was run from. Since we had all afternoon, we decided to go on foot. As we walked I could tell easily enough that Pa was thinking about what it would be like for him to be involved in what went on in that building. At one point Pa stopped and pointed to a construction site. "See that?" he said. "That's the big new domed capitol they're just beginning." Little did I know how much he would be involved in that building.

We walked for quite a while, back toward the downtown section of town. The day had become warmer and we were enjoying ourselves, talking about what the future might hold for us. As we crossed the street between the post office and station, in the distance I noticed a lady who caught my attention.

"Pa, doesn't that woman coming this way look like Katie?" I asked. "Or am I just imagining it?"

"There *was* something about her that struck me as familiar," Pa replied. He eyed her a little closer as we walked. "If I didn't know better, I'd swear she could pass for Katie's twin sister!"

My curiosity got the best of me. As she approached, I stopped and addressed her.

"Excuse me, but would you happen to know a lady named Katie Morgan Hollister, who lives in Miracle Springs?"

The woman's face lit up. "I sure do," she said. "Katie is my older sister."

"What!" I exclaimed. "But . . . how can—but . . . what are you—"

The woman laughed at my confusion, and the sound of her laughter left no more doubt that she was related to Katie.

"My name is Edie," she said, "Edie Simpson. Edie *Morgan* Simpson, that is. My husband died two months ago, so I decided to come out to pay Katie a surprise visit while I try to decide what's to become of my life. I take it you know Katie."

"I'm the man she came out here to marry," interjected Pa with a laugh. "Drummond Hollister's the name, ma'am, and this is my daughter Corrie."

"Corrie Belle Hollister, of course! I know your name from Katie's letters. And, Drummond, I am so pleased to meet you too. Katie speaks highly of you both." She extended her hand and gave us each a firm handshake. "How are Katie and Nick?"

"Couldn't be better, ma'am," said Pa. "Erich's gonna turn five next month, and little baby Anne—what is she, Corrie?" he said, turning to me. "A year by now?"

"Fourteen months," I said. "She was born last April, and she just started walking three weeks ago."

"I can't wait to see Katie and meet her family!" said Edie brightly.

"She doesn't know you're coming, ma'am?" asked Pa.

"No. I thought about sending her a letter by Pony Express, telling about Mr. Simpson's passing. But then I thought I might as well just come and see her in person."

"When did you get here?"

"Only this morning."

"How did you come—by ship to San Francisco?" I asked.

"I came overland by the Butterfield coach."

"The ox-bow route, huh?" said Pa.

"Yes, and I felt every bump in the whole punishing trip. I certainly got my $225 worth, and I must say I am very glad to be here at last."

She paused and laughed again. "I took the train to St. Louis. From there the coach went south through Texas, then New Mexico and to Fort Yuma. Luckily the only Indian attack was nearby and the driver outran them to the fort. Then the way led to Los Angeles and north to Sacramento. I arrived only an hour ago. I was just on my way out to locate a suitable lodging for the night."

"Well, think no more about it, ma'am," said Pa. "If you'll show me where your bags are, I'll get them for you. Then we'll get us a ride back to our boardinghouse. You can stay with us tonight, and we'll be off to Miracle bright and early in the morning."

CHAPTER 7

BACK HOME IN MIRACLE SPRINGS

It was late the next afternoon when the stage pulled into Miracle Springs.

We got out, and just in the time it took Pa to get our bags down off the top and walk across the street to the Mine and Freight, half a dozen people came up to greet us and ask about our trip.

"Afternoon to you, Mayor Hollister," said the man in charge of the stage office when he came out to meet the stage. He'd been in town only about a year and still acted as if Pa was about the most important man for miles. I reckon in a way he was, but Pa's old friends still just called him Drum like they always had. But even as they said it, there was a hint of a different tone to it. They knew that Pa had become something special.

As we walked across the street to the office, Edie said, "My goodness, I knew my sister's brother-in-law was the mayor, but I didn't expect *this* much attention. They act like you're a celebrity around here!"

Pa just laughed.

Above the building stood a big sign that read: *Hollister-Parrish Mine and Freight Company*, a change Almeda had insisted on even though she still ran the business pretty much herself, with my help. The *Hollister* on the sign didn't mean me, of course, but Pa.

My little half-sister, Ruth, was three years old, and she was a handful, so Almeda didn't spend nearly so much time in town as she once did. I came into the office on most days; Pa helped out

41

now and then, and Marcus Weber and Mr. Ashton took care of everything else. Almeda wouldn't have needed to come in at all, but she usually made the ride into town once or twice a week, when Pa or I would stay home with Ruth. She was too much of a businesswoman to be content always being at home.

But times had changed in Miracle Springs in the ten years Almeda had been there. There wasn't as much mining and freighting business to be done nowadays, even though Mr. Royce had closed down his competing enterprise. Mining itself had slacked off a lot; most of the men had all the equipment they needed, and Miracle Springs had become less of a gold-rush mining town, and more of a regular community made up of all kinds of people and families.

The business was still called the Mine and Freight, but Almeda and I had gradually started carrying a wider range of goods and merchandise. Now it resembled a general store for all the kinds of work men around the area did—farmers and ranchers as well as miners. We had wood tools and plows and barbed-wire and wagon parts and hand tools, even some harness and saddle equipment and seeds—lots of different things people needed. We were careful not to order goods that any of the other merchants carried; Almeda had strong feelings about such things as loyalty and competition. But if there were things folks needed they couldn't get someplace else, we found a way to get what they needed.

Pa and Uncle Nick still worked the mine several days a week, but not like they once did. They still dug gold out of it, and Alkali Jones was always talking about hitting another rich vein just a little ways farther into the side of the mountain. "Dang if there ain't a whole new lode in there, Drum," I had heard him say again and again. "I can smell it, *hee, hee, hee!*"

Whether Pa or Uncle Nick believed him, I don't know, but the persistence with which he trusted his "gold-sniffer," as he sometimes called his nose, usually brought out a wisecrack or two from Uncle Nick, and a sly wink in our direction from Pa. But he loved Mr. Jones—partly like a brother, partly like a trusted friend, even like a father. He would never do anything to hurt his feelings. Whenever the word *mayor* was used in Alkali Jones's hearing, we'd hear his high cackling *hee, hee, hee!* sooner or later.

He still couldn't get used to *dad-blamed ol' Drum being mayor to nothin' but a hill of prairie dogs! Hee, hee, hee!*

Pa and Uncle Nick didn't need to mine. The business did well enough along with the original strike to keep our whole little community of two families fed. But mining was so much in their blood that there was no way they could keep themselves from doing it. I suppose Alkali Jones's predictions of a new vein drove all the men to keep going deep down inside. Hope could be a powerful force. So Pa and Uncle Nick kept poking and picking and sometimes blasting away, and little bits of gold kept tumbling down the stream.

Pa mayored about as much as Almeda kept shop, though most of it was folks coming to him rather than him doing much of anything. He had no office in town. People knew where to find him when they wanted.

"Hey, Marcus," said Pa, sticking his head inside the livery out behind the office, "you got a wagon and a couple horses you could hitch up for us?"

"Yes sir, Mister Hollister," said a beaming Marcus Weber, coming out to greet us. "Your wife's gonna be glad to see you."

"Why's that, Marcus?"

"Little Ruth, she done took a fever."

Pa's face wrinkled in concern as he threw a couple of the bags in the back of one of the wagons. "Anything serious?" he asked.

"I dunno. Miz Almeda, she was just in here a minute yesterday, on her way to the Doc's."

"Hmm . . . then we better get out there as soon as we can," said Pa. "Corrie, why don't you and Edie go back to the stage office and get the rest of the bags. I'll give Marcus a hand with the horses and wagon."

By the time we got back, he and Mr. Weber nearly had the wagon ready to go. We climbed aboard. In two or three minutes, we were off and rumbling through the streets of Miracle and out of town toward the claim.

As much as I could with the bouncing and racket of the horses and wagon, I told Edie about the town—how it had grown and what it was like when we first came in 1852. We'd already told her all about the Gold Nugget and us five kids showing up and

Almeda going in to fetch Pa, thinking he was dead and that it was Uncle Nick inside. But now I had a chance to show her everything firsthand. In many ways the town was different than back then—bigger, less raucous, fewer saloons, more stores.

Mr. Royce still had the only bank in town. Pa and the town council had denied Finchwood another petition a year after the first, so they finally decided to open their new bank in Oroville instead. Mr. Royce had lowered the interest rate on all the loans he held to four and a half percent to match Finchwood's. Maybe he wasn't making as much profit as he once did, but folks were much more kindly disposed toward him, and you could tell from his face that he was a happier man for it, too. So nothing more had come of the "Hollister-Parrish Bank."

"It's so different than a city or town in the East," said Edie as we bounced over the bridge and out of town. "So much more primitive."

"You should have seen Miracle Springs eight years ago!" I said.

"Don't get me wrong, Corrie. It looks like a lovely town. Especially compared with some of the rough places the stagecoach went through!" She shook her head at the memory. "My, oh, my! Some of the things I saw! The territories and towns across the plains are called the frontier for good reason—every man carrying a gun! At least Miracle Springs appears to be more civilized than those places. But you really should see the East someday, Corrie."

"We came from the East," I said.

"Oh, where?"

"New York. But only the country part. I've never seen the city."

"Ah, New York is indeed the city of cities!"

"What about Washington?" I asked.

"I've never been there," replied Edie. "There's nothing there but the government. Why would you want to visit Washington?"

"I'm interested in politics," I answered. "I sometimes write about it in my articles."

"You *write* about politics! Good heavens, that kind of foolishness is for men, don't you know that, Corrie? What could a young woman like you possibly have to do with politics? We can't even vote!"

"I'm still interested in what happens to our country."

"The men will decide everything, so what difference does it make what we think about it?"

"But aren't you interested?"

"Not in men's affairs."

"What about slavery?"

"What about it?"

"Don't you think it's wrong?"

"How could it be wrong when half the country has slaves? It's not a moral issue of right and wrong, Corrie. It's just part of the economics of the country. It's how things are, that's all."

"That doesn't make it right," I insisted.

"That's what the northerners are always trying to do—make it a matter of right and wrong. But it's just different cultures. Slavery is part of the South. Northerners have no right to condemn something they know nothing about."

For someone who wasn't interested in politics, Edie seemed to have some definite ideas about slavery. And I wasn't sure I altogether liked the sound of them.

"You make it sound like northerners belong to a different country," I said. "Is there really that much difference?"

"When you live in the South, Corrie, there is. The North is a different country—and not a friendly one."

"You live in the South?"

"Of course. Virginia has always been a slave state, and always will be. My husband, the late Mr. Simpson, worked for a large landowner and had dealings with slaves all the time. It's just how things are in the South, and always have been."

"But . . . but doesn't slavery seem wrong to you?" I said again.

"I told you before, it's not a matter of right or wrong. Besides, slavery's in the Bible. Nobody in the Bible ever said it was wrong."

CHAPTER 8

MIXED HOMECOMING

I'd been so engrossed in the conversation with Edie that I hadn't even noticed that we were approaching the claim.

Suddenly there were Tad and Becky running toward us, followed by Almeda carrying Ruth. I expected to see Zack come out of the barn any second, but he never did.

We jumped down, and there were hugs and greetings and questions. Pa kissed Almeda and stretched his long arms around her and Ruth all at once. "How's my little daughter?" he asked, looking from one to the other. "Marcus said she wasn't feeling too well." He felt her forehead with his big rough palm.

"She was so hot yesterday," said Almeda. "I was worried and took her in to see Doc Shoemaker. "He thinks it might have been a spider bite."

"How is she?" said Pa, looking concerned. "She does feel warm."

"Better today. She's cooled off considerably and seems to be getting some of her spunk back."

All this time Edie had been standing beside the wagon. A brief silence followed, and Pa seemed to suddenly remember our passenger. He turned back toward her and motioned her forward. "But I plumb forgot our guest! Almeda, you'll never guess who we picked up in Sacramento," he said. "This here's Katie's sister! Edie, meet my wife, Almeda."

Almeda came forward and greeted her warmly. "Surely there is some logical explanation," she said, laughing. "This must be more than an accidental meeting."

46

Edie told about her husband's death and her decision to come for a visit, followed by her version of running into me and Pa in Sacramento. "So where do Katie and Nick live?" she said, looking around.

"Not more than a quarter mile upstream," answered Pa. "Come on everyone, into the wagon. Let's get Edie on to her reunion with her sister!"

We all scrambled back in. Pa gave Edie a lift up into the back with us kids, then took Almeda's hand and helped her up to the seat beside him, with Ruth in her lap. Then he clucked to the two horses, and off we lurched up the road alongside the creek toward the mine, where we would cross over into the woods on the other side.

What a reunion it was! I don't think I'd ever seen Aunt Katie so much at a loss for words. She was so surprised she didn't know whether to laugh or cry, so instead she just stood there with a look of silent disbelief on her face. By the time we left them half an hour later, the two sisters were talking so fast we could hardly understand them. Pa gave Uncle Nick a smile, almost as if to say, *You're gonna have your hands full now with two Virginia women.* Uncle Nick watched us go with a shrug and look that said, *What do I do now?*

When we got back to our place, Tad handed our two bags down to Pa, and we all went inside.

"Well, tell us all about San Francisco and the fancy gathering you two important Hollisters went to," said Almeda, pouring Pa a cup of coffee from the pot on the stove. "We've all been praying for you, and we're anxious to hear how God answered. So . . . did anything exciting happen while you were there?"

Pa and I glanced at each other. Pa gave me a wink, and I burst out laughing.

"What is it?" said Almeda with a curious smile. "*Something* must have happened!"

"Naw, nothing much," said Pa, "not unless you count getting asked to help Honest Abe Lincoln get elected and run for state legislature all within the same hour."

"What!" exclaimed Almeda. "Who asked . . . somebody asked *you*?"

48

"There was a man named Dalton," I put in. "I didn't know who he was at first, but Pa told me later that he was the most important Republican in the state. He asked me to help with the election in November."

"Help . . . how?"

"Writing . . . I don't know," I answered. "I'm not quite sure what he wanted."

"Corrie's being modest," added Pa. "I told you, Corrie, that you're an important person in this state. There was even some talk," he said, turning to Almeda, "of her making speeches on behalf of the Republican ticket."

"Corrie, that's wonderful! What do you think—are you going to do it?"

"I don't know," I shrugged. "Pa and I talked about it, and prayed together. We were both saying how you never know where something's going to lead. But Pa's news is even bigger! They asked him to run for the legislature in Sacramento!"

"Drummond!" exclaimed Almeda. "Is it true?"

"I reckon they figure there ain't no harm in asking," answered Pa noncommittally. "So ask they did."

"What did you say?"

"I didn't say anything. Just like Corrie, I said I'd think about it. I ain't about to pick up stakes and disrupt my family again. So I don't rightly see as how I could do it. But I didn't tell them anything definite."

"My husband and daughter—the politicians!" laughed Almeda. "I can hardly believe it!"

"You started it with all your notions of running for mayor!" joked Pa. "Now look what you landed me into!"

"And giving me that journal," I added in fun.

"You two aren't fooling anybody. You love every bit of it, and you both know it!"

"Corrie, tell Almeda about the new friend you met there."

"Oh, Pa, why'd you have to bring that up?" I said, blushing.

"What's this?" asked Almeda and Becky at the same time.

"Just some important young man who took a fancy to Corrie."

"Pa, he did not!" I said.

"Don't lie, Corrie," teased Pa. "You should have seen them,

Becky," he went on, "together nearly the whole evening. Why, Corrie deserted me, and I was alone for most of the reception."

"Pa! Now it's you who's lying."

"Well, maybe exaggerating just a tad."

"I want to know all about him," said Almeda.

"There's nothing to tell. He's a friend of Mr. Denver's, and he's the one who took me to meet Mr. Dalton, that's all. I'm sure he was just doing what he was supposed to do and nothing more. I'll probably never see him again."

Finally Pa figured I'd had enough of the ribbing, and he turned toward Almeda. "Where's Zack?"

Her face fell and the room suddenly got silent.

"Zack and Almeda had a big argument, Pa," said Tad finally.

"Is that true?" said Pa, his forehead crinkling as he turned toward Almeda.

She nodded. "I'm afraid so, Drummond."

"What about?"

"Something he wanted to do. I told him he'd have to wait until you got back and talk it over with you."

"What was so all-fired important that it couldn't wait a couple of days?" asked Pa.

"I don't know what got into him. He just exploded. I've never seen him like that before. He stormed away, talking nonsense about always having to go along with what everyone else wanted and nobody ever asking him what *he* thought. I don't know where it all came from, but from the sound of it, it must have been pent up a long time."

"I'll take his breeches off and tan his hide but good when he gets home!" said Pa. It was clear he was angry.

"Don't do anything rash, Drum. Zack's not a boy anymore."

"He's *my* boy!"

"He's your son. But he's grown, and whatever this storm is that's built up inside him, it's not something to be taken lightly."

"What was it he got in his head to do?"

"He said he was going to join the Pony Express, Pa," said Tad.

"That true, Almeda?"

"That's pretty much the gist of it. They were offering good money, he said, and he and Little Wolf had both decided to go.

There were some openings between Nevada and Utah."

"What about Lame Pony? What does he think?"

"I haven't seen him since. It only happened two days ago."

"And Zack hasn't come back?"

Almeda shook her head.

"He's probably up the hill at Jack's. I'll ride out there and see what's up."

CHAPTER 9

FATHER AND SON

None of us saw Zack for five days.

Pa went up to Jack Lame Pony's, but neither he nor Little Wolf knew where Zack had gone. Little Wolf couldn't tell him much more than Almeda had, that a fellow they had met had offered the boys jobs with the new mail delivery service and that they had talked about taking him up on his offer. Then Zack had gone home to tell Almeda about it, and that was the last anyone had seen of him.

Then as we were talking, Zack came walking through the door. We hadn't even heard the sound of a horse riding up.

I don't know where he'd been, but he looked dirty and unshaven. He gave me a little nod of greeting, but he didn't smile, and he tried to pretend Pa wasn't there. He probably knew what was coming.

"Where you been, son?" said Pa.

"Out riding," muttered Zack.

"Where?"

"Just around," said Zack, shuffling toward the kitchen area to see if there was anything to eat.

"I was a mite surprised to come home and find you gone," said Pa. "When I'm away I expect you to look after the family."

Zack said nothing. He picked up a piece of bread and bit into it.

"You don't figure you owe no responsibility to the family, is that it?"

Zack mumbled something, but I couldn't make it out.

51

"What's that you say?"

"I said it ain't my family no more."

"What do you mean by that?" Pa's tone was stern. It was easy to tell that he was getting riled.

"What should you care what I do? You all got your own plans. Corrie's got her writing, and you all think she's pretty great at everything she does. And you're busy being the town's important man. There ain't nothing Almeda can't do for herself. What do any of you need me for?"

"When I'm not here, I want you keeping a watch over things, that's what," said Pa, his voice icy. Zack hadn't looked at any of us straight in the face since walking in. If he was embarrassed about running off, he didn't show it. He just looked mad. I could feel the tension between him and Pa hanging in the air.

"Zack, please," said Almeda in a pleading tone, "I don't want—"

"You don't need me, Almeda. Don't try to pretend."

"Zack, that's not true," she said, turning to him with tender eyes full of anguish. "You know that I do need you—"

"Almeda," Zack said, cutting her off again, "you don't have to try to make me feel good anymore like you did when I was a boy."

"That's no way to talk to your mother, boy!" said Pa. By now he was storming mad.

"She ain't my mother!"

"She's my wife and a woman, and that means you better learn to talk to her with respect in your voice, unless you want my belt around that hind end of yours!"

"So you still think I'm a little kid too?"

"You're my son, and I'll whip you if I need to."

Becky and Tad stared at the two of them; it was all I could do to keep from bursting out crying. To suddenly have two of the people you love most in all the world arguing and yelling at each other was too horrible even to describe.

Zack turned away and laughed—a bitter, awful laugh.

"You find something funny in that?" asked Pa.

"Yeah," retorted Zack, spinning around and leveling that bitter-looking grin on Pa. "I'm twenty-one years old. I'm taller than you. I can ride a horse better than anyone for miles. But you still think of me as a little kid. You don't even know what it's like for me. I got a life of my own to live, and you don't even know the kinds of things I'm thinking about. Everything's about Corrie and Almeda or your being mayor or the Mine and Freight. You got no time for me—you never had. What do you care what I do? You just expect me to be around to take care of things so you can leave whenever you want."

"What's that supposed to mean?"

"You figure out what it means."

"None of that matters. You're not going to the Pony Express without my say-so. Whatever you may think, I'm still your pa. And I still got a right to tell you what you can and can't do."

Zack stared straight into his face, and the next words out of his mouth were so biting I could almost feel them slicing straight into Pa's heart.

"You never knew what it was like for me," said Zack. "You never knew the times I cried myself to sleep when I was a kid, hoping you'd come home. I was frightened without a father. I got teased and made fun of something awful 'cause I was little, and sometimes I came home with bruises and a black eye from trying to defend myself. I used to dream how good it would be to come home to feel the arms of a pa to hold me. I'd beg God to help us find you. But we never did, and I had to grow up alone like that. You'll never know how much you hurt Ma, and how she'd cry sometimes when she didn't know I was watching. She kept loving you and kept praying for you—always asking God to protect you and watch over you. But I finally quit praying, because I was sick of being disappointed."

Zack stopped for a second, trembling with emotion. Then he added, "So I don't reckon you got a right to call yourself my father no more. You may be my pa. But I figure I'm old enough to decide for myself what I want!"

Zack's words came so fast and were so unexpected that Pa didn't know what to do. I know Pa was hurt by what Zack had said, but his response came out as anger.

"However mixed up a job I done of it, I'm your pa whether you like it or not!"

"I'm stuck here with nothing but women and babies and little kids," Zack shot back. "You can go off and do whatever you want, and you figure I got nothing of my own that matters?"

"You got no right to talk about your mother and sisters that way. You apologize to them, or you're gonna feel that belt like I told you!"

"Ha! Your belt ain't gonna come anywhere near my rump! And I ain't apologizing to nobody! It's true, everything I said. I said to myself a long time ago I was getting out of here first chance I got. God knows I spent my muscles and blistered my hands working that mine for you all these years. You don't know how many days I sweated all day long, aching inside just for you to smile at me once and say I'd done a good day's work. But I might as well not even been there, for all you ever noticed! I don't reckon you'll figure you owe me anything for it. Well, that's fine with me. But all that's over with. I met a guy, and he's got a place arranged for me in the Pony Express. And I don't care if Little Wolf's changed his mind, I'm gonna take it. It's the chance I been waiting for to get out of this place!"

He turned and strode toward the door, still without looking at any of the rest of us. But Pa was closer, and took two giant steps and cut him off. He laid a strong hand on Zack's shoulder.

"No you're not, son," he said. "You ain't goin' nowhere without my leave. Now you get back in here, and we'll sit down and talk about it."

"I'm not talking about nothing," retorted Zack. "I've listened to all the rest of you long enough. Nobody ever seemed much interested in talking to me before. Now I'm going, whether you like it or not."

"And I'm telling you you're not."

"It's too late. I signed the papers. I start my first run next week."

"Then I'll go talk to this fella and unsign them."

Zack laughed again.

"You're not leaving home, Zack! You hear me, son? You got duties to this family."

Zack's eyes squinted ever so slightly, and his next words weren't loud but they cut deep.

"Is that how it was when *you* left Ma?" he said icily. "Duties to the family!" He laughed again. "*You* talk to *me* about duty to the family? Where were you all those years when I needed a pa? Even after we'd come all the way across the country to find you, you didn't want us. You denied you even knew us!"

Zack's back was to me as he spoke, and I could see Pa's grip on my brother's shoulder loosen. Pa unconsciously took half a step backward, as if Zack's words had been a physical blow across Pa's face. The rest of us stood in stunned silence to hear Zack accuse Pa like that.

"Well," he went on, "you talk about duty all you want, but I figure I've already about done as much as you ever did. You ran out on us, and even now you're always gone somewhere or another, but still you figure I'll do for you what you never did for me. Well, I tell you, I ain't gonna do it no more! If I go ride for the Pony Express, at least I ain't leaving a wife and five kids like you done!"

He wrested free of Pa's hand. As he did, Almeda approached, her eyes full of tears, and stretched out a hand and gently placed it on his shoulder.

"Oh, Zack," she pleaded, "if only I could make you see how much we all—"

But Zack, still backing his way free of Pa, either didn't hear her tender words of love or misunderstood her gesture. For whatever reason, as her hand touched him, thinking she intended to restrain him further, he reached up and in a swift motion threw her hand off him and took a step toward the door.

Seeing him rebuke Almeda so rudely was all Pa needed to jolt him awake from his stunned silence. Zack's reaction could not have been more ill-chosen.

Pa's eye's inflamed with rage. He leaped forward and struck Zack across the jaw. Yet even as Zack fell, Pa realized what he'd done and pulled back.

His cheek red from the blow and his body trembling, Zack slowly rose. "It's no secret where your loyalties lie," he said. "Everything for the women, but you won't lift a finger unless it's *against* your own son!"

He turned, opened the door, and stalked off, slamming it behind him. Pa half stumbled back into a chair, mortified at what he'd done. His face was white as a sheet.

The house was silent. The next sound we heard was Zack's horse galloping away.

CHAPTER 10

PA AND TAD

The silence, the tension, the uncertainty the rest of that day and the next was so thick and strong that we all walked around in a numbed state of sadness. Besides Pa, I think Zack's leaving was hardest on Tad. He had been a devoted son to Pa and a loving younger brother to Zack. And now suddenly the two idols of his world had nearly come to blows. He moped around in silence.

Pa managed to keep busy in the barn, going to town a lot, fixing things. He worked harder at the mine than I'd seen him work in three years, taking out his frustration on the rocks.

By the end of the second day, I sensed a gradual change come over Pa, and I was glad to see it. Zack was gone, and how long it would be before we might see him again, no one could tell. But instead of allowing it to destroy what was still left, Pa began to draw Tad closer. I suppose if good can come out of such a problem, it was good to see Pa trying to make use of what time was left him with his youngest son to build up the relationship so he didn't hurt him like he had done to Zack.

Of course Tad had been involved in the mine ever since he had found the huge nugget that had changed everything for our family. But on the second day after Zack's leaving, instead of just walking up to the mine to pound away by himself, Pa said, "Say, Tad, how about you and me seeing if we can dig any gold out of that hill today?"

Tad was still feeling pretty low, but he went with Pa. I don't know if the two of them talked much, and if they did I doubt they talked about the one person who was most on their minds. But they both came back, sweating and tired and dirty, in much better spirits than before. Hard work has a way of clearing out both the mind and the heart when they're cluttered up with feelings that are hard to understand.

The next day they cleaned out the barn together and repaired a section of the corral. Almeda and I could see that Pa was doing what he could to help ease Tad's pain and at the same time trying to give them both something—not to *take* the place of Zack, but maybe *in* the place of Zack's being there. That something was each other.

The two of them kept busy all week—busy, active, working hard, and tired. If they were going to keep thinking about Zack, they were going to have to do it in the midst of work and exercise! They got more gold out of the mountain and stream than they had in any week for three years, prompting Alkali Jones to fairly burst at the seams with his predictions of a new lode *just waitin' to spill out all over the dad-blamed valley, hee, hee, hee!*

The barn and grounds hadn't looked so tidy for a long time. They even took the wagon out into the woods and got started on next winter's firewood supply when summer hadn't even officially begun yet. At week's end, the two of them mounted up and went up into the mountains overnight—the first time Pa had ever gone hunting alone with Tad—and they came back the next afternoon with two bucks slung over the pack mules. For the first time since Zack's leaving, I saw a smile on Tad's face as he was telling us about stalking the one that he himself had shot.

"He was too far away to get a clean shot when we first spotted him," Tad said, his eyes gleaming. "So we had to work our way through the brush and trees to get closer without spooking him."

"You shoulda seen him," said Pa proudly. "He took dead aim right into the flank below his shoulder. One shot was all it needed. The big creature dropped where he stood without twitching a muscle. I've never seen such a shot!"

Tad went on excitedly telling about how they ran across the second one. I glanced over at Pa, watching him quietly. I could tell from the look in his eyes that he knew his efforts all week had paid off, that Tad felt better about Zack. Pa couldn't know it yet, but his efforts accomplished far more than just helping Tad deal with the loss of his brother. The two of them were closer than they had ever been, and were fast friends from that day on.

I knew the pain over Zack, and what Zack had said, went further inside Pa than he was letting on. Almeda knew, too, how deeply he felt it. But Pa was the kind of man who had to sort things out by himself for a spell before he was ready to talk. I was sure he would let us know what he was feeling once he was ready. In the meantime, he seemed to be putting his efforts into helping Tad figure out his frustrations.

Whatever Zack might have said, I saw a loving, unselfish man when I looked at Pa. And I wished Zack could see, as I did, how Pa had been a good father to all of us—at least once we'd arrived in California.

When we first came to California, Zack carried a chip around on his shoulder against Pa for a while, but I thought he'd gotten over all that years ago.

But I guess I was wrong. All it took for me to forgive Pa was to talk with him a few times and see how his own heart ached over the past. I had seen Pa cry and pray and grow, and I knew what kind of man he was—deep down, on the inside. But maybe he and Zack had never talked that way.

As I thought about Zack, I realized that when a person isn't able to forgive someone, a little seed of anger will eventually sprout and grow until branches and roots and leaves of bitterness come bursting out somewhere.

With Zack, apparently the forgiveness didn't get finished, and now he was gone. And Pa was feeling one of the deepest pains a man can feel on account of it.

Meanwhile, other things kept us from thinking only about Zack. The Sunday after Pa and Tad got back from their hunting trip, Aunt Katie and Uncle Nick invited all of us to their place to eat and to have a family visit with them and Edie.

That day suddenly put Zack into the background of our thoughts for a while, and got me thinking about the dilemma of my decision all over again.

CHAPTER 11

A HEATED DISCUSSION
ABOUT SLAVERY

After dinner was over, Almeda and Aunt Katie put Ruth and Anne down to sleep; then the rest of us got to talking.

Pa had been telling Uncle Nick and Aunt Katie about our trip to San Francisco and about my conversation with Mr. Dalton.

"So, are you going to do it, Corrie?" Uncle Nick asked me.

"I don't know," I answered. "I'm just waiting to see what might come of it. I said to the Lord that if it was something he wanted me to pursue, then he'd have to make something happen so I'd know it."

"How could he do that?" asked Edie.

"He has lots of ways," I replied. "I just want to make sure I don't do something *myself*. If I just patiently wait, then there's no danger of making a decision all on my own. When he wants me to move a certain way, maybe in some new direction, then he'll make sure I get the message. He'll send someone or some circumstance to give me a nudge."

"That sounds like a rather passive approach to life," said Edie. "I thought all you Californians were pioneers who didn't wait for anybody but went out and did whatever you wanted to do!"

We all laughed.

"Is that what easterners think of Californians?" asked Almeda.

"That's what I thought before I became one myself!" said Katie.

"I don't mean I just sit by and don't do anything," I said to Edie. "I go on about my life as usual. But in making important decisions, I want to be sure I wait for the Lord to have some say in it, too."

"So if the Lord gives you the nudge you're talking about," Uncle Nick asked again, "then do you figure you'll do it?"

"I like what they're saying about Mr. Lincoln," I said. "It seems important for the country that he get elected. I suppose I'm thinking that maybe I ought to try to help."

"If he wins in November, the whole South will rise up against it," put in Edie abruptly. "A Lincoln victory will destroy the nation."

A moment of silence followed. I think we were all a bit shocked at her strong statement, and no one had expected it of her.

"Is it really that serious?" Almeda asked after a moment.

"Before he died, my husband used to say that if the Republicans nominated Lincoln, and if the country elected him, the South would never stand for it. It's not just the slavery issue, he said, but the whole southern way of life."

"How can that way of life be justified when it is based on such a horrid thing as human beings enslaving others of their kind?" Almeda asked. "In Christ's own words, he came to set people free."

"That is an ideal not necessarily found in this life, Almeda. That's the mistake abolitionists always make—quoting the Bible and talking about God's hatred of slavery when there is nothing of the kind to be found in the Holy Scriptures."

Almeda's strong feelings surfaced. "You cannot mean you actually believe slavery to be just!" she said. "How can there be any doubt, for a serious-minded Christian, that slavery is wrong?"

"There are Christians in the South just as well as in the North."

"They cannot honestly deceive themselves into thinking slavery is *right*! It goes against every truth of the Bible."

"Abraham had slaves. The Ten Commandments mention slavery twice without disapproving of it. Jesus never uttered a word condemning slavery, although it was widespread in the world at the time he lived. Paul told slaves to obey their masters, and even returned a runaway slave to his master."

"It sounds like you met someone who knows her Bible as well as you do, Almeda," chuckled Uncle Nick.

"All of what you said may be true, Edie," said Pa, "but be honest with us. Do people in the South, God-fearing people especially—do they really believe slavery is right, deep down in their hearts?"

"I can't speak for everyone, Drummond. All I know is that church leaders and preachers all through the South are just as staunch *for* slavery as the abolitionists are against it."

"What do you think, Katie?" Pa asked.

Katie hesitated a moment, weighing, I think, how she should answer when the debate was between her own sister and her upbringing in Virginia and her new family, which had no firsthand exposure to the issue at hand.

"You have to realize," she said at length, "that slavery was common practice when I was growing up. We were all taught to accept it as the natural order of things between the races—even, some said, for the good of the Negro people. Since coming to California six years ago, I've hardly thought about it. All the disputes between the states and all the arguments over whether slavery is right or wrong—that's risen to new heights since I left. I don't even know what I think."

"Have you read *Uncle Tom's Cabin*?" I asked Edie.

"Certainly not. Harriet Beecher Stowe is hated in Virginia! That book is full of falsehoods from cover to cover!"

"I have read that its portrayal of slavery is quite accurate," said Almeda.

"Then you must be listening to a northern abolitionist. Everyone in the South knows the book for what it is—a pack of lies."

"I want to know something," I asked. "Why did you say that if Mr. Lincoln wins it will destroy the country?"

"Because he has been speaking out against slavery for two years, ever since he ran against Douglas for the Senate in '58. My husband and the men he worked with say Lincoln is sure to attempt to free the slaves. To do so would ruin the South economically. That's why the southern states would never go along with it."

"What would they do?"

"There is already talk circulating around Virginia of withdrawing from the United States and forming a new country if Lincoln wins."

A few gasps went around the room, including one from Katie herself. We all sat in stunned silence a minute. Because of my articles, we always got the *Alta*. We had read of the growing dispute over slavery between the northern and southern states, and had even seen the word *secession* more than once. But somehow it hadn't struck root exactly how serious the division was until Edie began talking about the Southern states *forming a new country*.

Uncle Nick broke the heavy silence with a laugh. He was probably the least well read of any of us, and the idea of two separate countries, a slave South and a free North, struck him as absolutely preposterous.

"That's the craziest thing I ever heard!" he said. "There's nothing in the South that could keep a country together. The South would die without the North!"

I could see Edie getting ready to give Uncle Nick a sharp reply, but Pa spoke up first.

"Don't be too sure of that, Nick," he said. "You know about the big collapse of the banks in New York two years ago and all the financial crises it caused." Pa had read more of the newspapers that came to me than I realized!

"Not much. Didn't hurt us here."

"Well, it hurt the North, and it still hasn't recovered all the way. But the South is booming. Their cotton helped save the northern banks. They can sell all they want in Europe. I tell you, Nick, there's folks saying the South is stronger financially than the North."

"There you go sounding like a politician again!" laughed Uncle Nick. "Where do you get all that stuff, Drum?"

"Well, I figure if I'm gonna have a daughter that writes for the paper, I might as well read it."

"I've read that too," said Almeda. "The North needs the South, not the other way around. If the South were to pull out, they would have plenty of resources. The cotton crop would support it."

"Exactly!" agreed Edie. "Without the South, the North would perish. If Lincoln dared to tamper with slavery, he would be cutting the throat of the very North he thinks he loves so much. The future of the United States lies south of the Mason-Dixon line."

Again there was silence for a while. At last Katie spoke. "After all this, Corrie," she said, "do you *still* think you'll support Lincoln?"

"I don't know," I said with a sigh. "I suppose there's more to the decision than I thought at first."

CHAPTER 12

I QUESTION MYSELF

It was a hard dilemma.

Now all of a sudden the slavery issue wasn't two thousand miles distant but right in my own backyard, even right in my own family. It had hardly occurred to me before that Katie had, indeed, come from a slave state. We had never talked about it. But now Edie's arrival, and her strong views on the subject, brought the debate closer to home.

In spite of everything she said, in my own heart and mind I couldn't see how slavery could be anything but wrong. It couldn't be right to treat other people the way slaves were treated! I was in agreement with Mr. Lincoln.

But what if it was true that his election could spell ruin to the country? What if his election caused an even more serious rift between North and South than already existed? Did I want to be part of contributing to that? What would it all mean to California?

I found myself wondering about my responsibility as a writer and a Christian in a lot of new ways. If people really were paying attention to what I said, I had to be sure of myself when I put my pen to the paper. What if I said something wrong, something that readers believed and took action on? I would be responsible for misleading them.

Always before, I'd written about things because I was interested in them. That's why I started writing—because it was something I wanted to do for myself. I wanted to express my thoughts and feelings. And there were so many things I wanted to explore! Writing seemed the natural way to express what was inside me, to communicate, even to grow as a person. That's what my journal was to begin with—just a diary of my own thoughts and feelings. It had never been meant for anybody else.

I reflected on Ma, on things she'd said to me. I had always been a reader and more quiet than outgoing. She'd made no secret of thinking I'd probably never get married. She figured I ought to read and write and keep a diary so I could be a teacher when I got older and no man would have me.

I had done what Ma said, even though I sometimes ached when I realized it took her dying to get me started. Writing in my diary back then had been a way of letting the pain out.

I was twenty-three now, and I had books and books of diaries and journals! That first beautiful book Almeda had given me, with *The Journal of Corrie Belle Hollister* stamped across the front of it, had been the first of many such volumes I had filled with memories and recollections and drawings over the years.

At first Pa and Uncle Nick had kidded me about always writing down what I was thinking. But once the articles started, and payments of two, and then four, and then even eight dollars started to come in for things I'd written, they realized maybe it was a worthwhile thing for me to be doing, after all. But even then it was just *my* writing.

Then gradually my writing started getting bigger than just *my* own personal, private thoughts. Especially as I'd written about the two elections back in 1856, I had thought a lot about truth and trying to tell the truth to people. Even from men like Derrick Gregory and Mr. Royce, I had learned a thing or two about truth and being fair. I tried to learn from everybody I met, although men like that probably had no idea they were helping to teach me and show me things, even by their deceit.

Yet I don't think it ever really struck me that anything I might say was important . . . not *really* important. I was trying to learn about truth and being a good reporter, but I figured that it was still mostly for me. Robin O'Flaridy still looked down on me, even after the '56 elections; my story had never appeared, and Mr. Fremont had lost the election. Nothing I had done or said *had* been that important, and I had gone back to writing about people and floods and how things were in California now that the gold rush was slowing down.

Mr. Kemble kept telling me that my articles were getting a wider audience in the East on account of a woman reporter being so unusual, but I didn't think much about it. I knew of plenty of women authors and it didn't seem so unusual. Julia Ward Howe wrote poems, and Harriet Beecher Stowe and Louisa May Alcott wrote, too. I didn't see what was so unusual about what I did. After all, Mrs. Alcott's poems and stories were being published in the *Atlantic Monthly*.

"None of those women are writing for newspapers, Corrie," Mr. Kemble said to me. "That's what I'm trying to tell you. Newspapers influence people. All those other women are just writing stories. They can get as famous as you please, but they're not going to be taken as seriously as a nonfiction *news* reporter."

"*Uncle Tom's Cabin* has influenced a lot of people," I said.

"It's sold a million copies," he replied. "But it's still just a story."

"You can't say Mrs. Stowe isn't an influential writer."

"She is indeed. Her book probably has started more fights and brawls and arguments than any book ever published in this country. But she's still just a novelist. You, on the other hand, Corrie Belle Hollister—*you* are more than a novelist. You are a newspaper reporter. And while it may be true that when you first came in here with little stories about leaves and blizzards and apple seeds and new schools and colorful people you had met, tricking me into thinking you were a man—"

I glanced up at him, but the little curl of his lip and twinkle in his eye told me he was just having fun with me. He never lost an opportunity to remind me of my first byline: *C.B.* Hollister.

"As I was saying," he went on, "at first I may have published some of your stories as a lark, just for the novelty of showing up some of the other papers with something by a young woman. But I've got to admit you surprised me. You kept at it. You didn't back down from me, or from the odds that were against you, not from anything. You proved yourself to be quite a tenacious, plucky young woman, Corrie. In the process, I'll be darned if you didn't start writing some pretty fair stories and getting yourself quite a following of readers—women *and* men."

He stopped and looked me over as he did from time to time,

kind of like he was thinking the whole thing through all over again, wondering how he'd gotten himself into the fix of having a woman on his staff.

"So that's why," he went on after a minute, "you're different, Corrie. Your name might not be as famous as Mrs. Stowe's. A hundred years from now nobody'll know the name Corrie Hollister, because newspapers get thrown away, while books don't. But right now, people are listening to what you say, Corrie. I tell you, you've got an influence that you don't realize."

His words kept coming back to me as I debated with myself about what I ought to do, especially after all Edie Simpson had said. It was more than just journal writing now.

What if . . . *what if* something I said or wrote really did influence the election? Even if I caused only one or two people to vote differently than they might have otherwise, it was still a sobering responsibility.

I did a lot of talking to the Lord about it in the days after Pa and I got back from San Francisco, running the pros and cons through my mind, and always remembering Pa's words on the boat. *You never know what might be around the corner, and so you ought to be watching and paying attention as best you can.* I knew Pa was doing the same thing, both about his decision and about Zack's leaving.

Ordinarily I would have talked to him or Almeda. But with slavery and the North-South dispute and the heated difference of opinion about Mr. Lincoln, I thought this was a decision I had to make alone—just between me and the Lord.

After the discussion at Uncle Nick and Aunt Katie's, I was growing more and more sure that slavery was wrong and should be abolished. But I saw more clearly now that there might be consequences—not only to my decision, but to the whole outcome of the election—that no one could predict. It might even mean disputes in our own family.

In my heart I found myself wanting to do it. I wanted my writing to *matter* for the sake of truth. If Mr. Lincoln and the antislavery people and the Republican party represented that truth, then I wanted to be part of helping people know it. But I had to be sure. So I found myself telling the Lord that I wouldn't do anything further, and that if I was supposed to get any more involved, he would have to make it clear by having somebody contact *me*, or by sending along some circumstance I couldn't ignore. I didn't want to initiate anything more all by myself.

If I never heard again from Mr. Dalton or anybody else from the Republican party, I would take that as God's way of saying no.

The dilemma of whether I should get involved with the election wasn't the only question my mind was wrestling with since hearing Katie's sister's views on slavery. But it was probably the easiest one to resolve.

In the meantime, I found myself thinking a lot about something Pa had told me about Davy Crockett. They had both fought in the Mexican War, and everyone who fought in California admired the men who died in the same cause at the Alamo.

Davy Crockett had been a congressman from Tennessee before he went to Texas, and I had read that Mr. Crockett always told folks in Washington he had based his life on the saying, *Be sure you're right, then go ahead*. I found myself reflecting on those words every day.

I kept saying to myself, "Don't go ahead until you're sure you're right."

I was pretty certain the *cause* was right. Now I just had to wait to see if involving myself in it was what God wanted me to do. Figuring that out, as well as waiting, was the hardest part of all.

CHAPTER 13

A VISIT WITH THE RUTLEDGES

I found myself coming away from that afternoon at Uncle Nick and Aunt Katie's with a heaviness in my heart, a confusion—not about the slavery issue alone, but rather how there could be so many different views on the same thing. I wanted to talk with someone about it, but I didn't feel that Almeda or Pa would be the right persons. I respected them as much as ever, but maybe because they'd been part of the discussion, and I knew that Almeda herself held pretty strong opinions on things, I wanted to get an outside, unbiased perspective.

Since it was a spiritual question even more than something to do with issues, I thought of Rev. Rutledge. As a pastor, he not only ought to have answers to spiritual questions, but by now I knew that he didn't usually voice outspoken views on issues people normally differed about. When it came to the Bible, he said what he had to say without fear and without backing down. But he never took sides about politics or on decisions facing the community. Pa would sometimes get riled when he wanted Rev. Rutledge's support for something the town council was getting ready to vote on.

The Rutledges had become our good friends, and we had grown to feel a great deal of respect for Rev. Rutledge since his first awkward days in Miracle Springs. He had changed nearly as much as Pa had. His teaching and his sermons and his outlook on life and Scripture and what being a Christian meant had been important in forming the person I'd grown up to be. There was a lot of Almeda in me, and a lot of Pa. But there were big chunks of Harriet and Avery Rutledge, too. They both had influenced me in different ways.

So on the Monday after the dinner and discussion, I found myself saddling up my horse and riding down into Miracle Springs for a visit with them. School had been out for a week, and I knew that Rev. Rutledge usually spent Mondays at home, so I hoped to find them both there.

Harriet opened the door. "Corrie, hello! It's nice to see you!"

"I wondered if I might talk with you," I said. "Both of you, I mean. Is the Reverend at home?"

"Yes . . . yes, he is. Come in, Corrie—Avery, we have a visitor," she called out as she led me inside and closed the door.

I followed her into their sitting room, where Rev. Rutledge was just rising from his chair, a copy of the *Alta* in his hand.

"Corrie, welcome," he said, giving me a warm handshake. "Harriet and I always enjoy your visits."

"Thank you," I said. "I've come to ask you about something that is troubling me . . . I hope you don't mind."

"Of course not. Troubled souls are in my line of work," he said with a laugh.

"It's not my soul that's troubled, only my mind."

"I was only jesting. You can feel free to share anything with me, with both of us if you like."

"I would like both your opinions," I said, glancing back at the former Miss Stansberry, whom I still sometimes had a hard time calling by her first name. "It's not what you'd call a spiritual problem, but there's something about being a Christian I don't understand as well as I'd like."

"Well, we've been through a lot of growing together, Corrie, you and I, and your whole family," said Rev. Rutledge. "You've spent lots of hours in this house talking and praying with Harriet and me, and it wouldn't surprise me if we've learned just as much from you as you might have from either of us."

"That could hardly be," I said, "when I sit and listen to your sermons on most Sundays. I've learned more from listening to you talk about the Scriptures than you can imagine."

"The best sermons aren't to be found in church, Corrie."

"How do you mean?"

"Do you remember what the apostle Peter said in his first letter? 'Ye also, as lively stones, are being built up a spiritual house.' He's saying that *we* are the building blocks and bricks of the house that God is building. Then the apostle Paul wrote to the Corinthians about our being *living* epistles or letters. 'Ye are our epistle written in our hearts, known and read by all men . . . written not with ink, but with the Spirit of the living God, written not in tables of stone, but in fleshy tables of the heart.' " He paused, then added, "Do you see the connection I'm trying to make?"

"I always like it better when you tell me instead of my trying to guess," I answered with a smile.

He laughed. "People can be stones and letters, according to the Scriptures—*living* stones and letters. In the same way, *people* can be sermons too. And living people-sermons are far more powerful than anything a preacher says in church. I suppose the point I am attempting to make is that *you* make a better sermon just by your life than any thousand sermons I may preach."

"That's nice of you to say, but I'm not sure I believe it," I said. "When you preach, people listen to what you have to say. Nobody pays that much attention to people going around just living."

"Oh, I think you're wrong about that, Corrie. As a matter of fact, I think it is exactly the reverse. People sit quietly when I'm preaching. But most of them aren't really listening, not deep down in their hearts. You might be, and a few others. But most people don't know how to *really* listen and absorb what another person is saying. There's an art to listening that most folks don't know too much about."

"I suppose you're right. But then, what about when people aren't in church?"

"People look as if they're listening in church, when they're really not. In the same way, out in the midst of life, people look as if they're not paying that much attention, but they really *are*. In other words, people listen far more to the living people-sermons around them every day than you would ever know to look at them."

"Hmm . . . I hadn't thought of that."

"Tell me, has Almeda influenced your life?"

"You know she has, in a thousand ways."

"Why is that, do you think? Is it because of the things she's *said* to you, or the person she *is*?"

"Of course it's the second, although she's taught me a lot too."

"Certainly she has. But it's the *living* sermon she *is* that's gone the deepest inside you, isn't it? Her words go only so far as she lives them out. What do you think my sermons would mean to you if you never saw my words at work in what I tried to do in the rest of my life?"

"Not much," I admitted.

"How much did you listen to me when I first came?"

I laughed.

"There, you see. And when *did* my sermons start getting into you?"

"You're right," I smiled. "When I saw the real *you*, when I saw you and Pa trying to form a real relationship."

"That's right. That's the living stone, the living epistle—the real-life sermon at work. So I stick by what I said to begin with— the best sermons aren't to be found in church, and your life is as dynamic a sermon as I'll ever preach. One that people are watching and observing and listening to all the time."

"Do you really think so?"

"You listen to me, Corrie; the Lord has placed you in many situations where you are constantly being a living epistle, a flesh-and-blood sermon to the people you rub shoulders with. You have more influence for him than you realize—and I don't mean only because you write. The person you are is the living sermon. You can believe me—people *are* listening to it!"

I didn't say anything more for a minute. That word *influence* had come up again, and I couldn't help wondering if what Rev. Rutledge had said had any bearing on the decision I was facing.

CHAPTER 14

TRYING TO GET TO THE BOTTOM OF TRUTH

"Would you like some tea?" asked Harriet as the room fell silent for a few moments.

"Yes, thank you," I replied, looking up again.

"What I meant to say a while ago," said Rev. Rutledge as his wife went to the stove, "is that we've been through a great deal together, and it's always a pleasure to talk and share with you about anything that is on your mind."

"I appreciate it," I replied.

"So . . . what is troubling you?"

I drew in a long breath of air, then let it out slowly. "It's hard to put into words exactly," I said finally. "We had a family talk yesterday—you knew that Aunt Katie's sister was here for a visit?"

"Yes, I met her yesterday. They were in church."

"She and Katie are from Virginia."

"Right. That's what I understand."

"Well, we all got to talking about slavery and the dispute over it between the North and the South, and I came away confused."

"About whether slavery is right or wrong?"

"Not exactly that. What I found bothering me as I went to bed last night was that all—on *both* sides—think they're right, and they've got passages out of the Bible and seemingly religious reasons for thinking what they do. How can people look at the very same thing and then think completely opposite ways about it?"

"That's been going on for centuries, Corrie. People look at things differently."

"You'd think at least Christian people would be of one mind."

"That's never been the case. Christians have had some of the world's most bitter arguments."

"It doesn't seem right."

"No doubt it isn't. But it still happens."

"Why?"

"I suppose besides looking at things differently, people also have motives of self that get mixed in with what they believe. So the stands they take on things have as much to do with what they *want* as what they believe."

"Christians ought to be able to separate the two, and take their own wants out of it."

"Perhaps they ought to be able to, but not many people can do that—even Christians."

"What about truth? Can there be something that's true down underneath everything? It seems like people ought to be trying to find it if there is."

"It always comes back to truth for you, doesn't it, Corrie?" Rev. Rutledge smiled.

"I think about it a lot. If a writer doesn't have a grasp of the truth, it doesn't seem like there's much to write about. At least that's how I've come to see it."

"Ever since that sermon I preached years ago about Jesus and Pilate."

"You sure got me started thinking with that one!"

"Yes, and apparently you haven't stopped since."

"That's another thing a writer's got to do—keep thinking."

"I'll take your word for it, not being a writer myself."

"It shouldn't be any different for a preacher."

"I suppose you're right."

Harriet came in with a tray of tea and cups. She served us, then sat down herself.

"Well, I don't care if people have always differed and argued, it seems to me that if there's such a thing as truth and right and wrong, Christians especially ought to feel the same about it. I don't understand how two people can both be Christians and believe the exact opposite. One thing can't be right and wrong at the same time. There's no sense to it!"

"Something like slavery?" asked the minister.

"Not just slavery, but that's as good an example as there is. Edie said that Abraham had slaves, and slavery is mentioned in the Ten Commandments, and then she said that according to the Bible, slavery is right. Almeda quoted the verse about being made free and then said that slavery went *against* the truths of the Bible. There they are—both Christians and yet saying the very opposite thing. Doesn't one of them have to be wrong? *Is* there a right and wrong about it?"

"Is it just slavery you're trying to understand, Corrie?" asked Harriet.

"No, I don't suppose it is," I answered. "I do have to decide if I'm going to write any articles about this election between Mr. Douglas and Mr. Lincoln. I suppose that comes down to the North-South dispute and the question of slavery in the end. But right now I'm trying to understand how two Christians can look at the same thing and see it so differently."

A silence filled the small room, and we all took a sip of our tea. I could tell Rev. Rutledge was thinking hard. That was one of the reasons I liked to talk to him, because he didn't give an answer until he had thought about it first.

"You're right about one thing, Corrie," he said at last. "There *has* to be such a thing as right and wrong. Otherwise the Bible and its whole message is meaningless. There has to be such a thing as truth, which is the opposite of falsehood."

"That's what I believe, too. Then why isn't it more clear?"

"Because people get in the way. They don't always see as clearly as they should. Their vision gets foggy and blurred, and then truth and right and wrong get muddled up in the process."

"Mixing in, like you said before, what they *want* to believe?"

"That's it exactly."

"Then if people are going by what they *want* to think instead of trying to get at what truth is, how do you ever get to the bottom of it? It seems like all you'd do is end up debating your different viewpoints."

"That's all most people do end up doing. To answer your question, if you're talking to a person who views things only through his *own* blurry vision of what he himself *wants* to be true, then you probably can't get to the bottom of a question like slavery. You just each tell the other what you think and leave it at that."

"But there we are back at the question I asked to begin with— how *do* you get at what the truth is if you don't know yourself and you want to talk to other Christians about it?"

"The first thing you have to do, I suppose, is talk and pray things over with people who also want to get down to the underneath layer, down to where truth is, even below what they themselves might want or not want. You can't get too far in a discussion unless you share that much at least."

"That's why I like to talk to the two of you," I said. "I know you want to get to things down at that level just like I do."

"I hope I do," sighed Rev. Rutledge. "But it's difficult, Corrie. Every one of us has personal biases and preferences and wants and tendencies that we can't ever escape. Laying those down, even for the sake of trying to find truth, is not an easy thing to do. I constantly try to put *myself* in the background so I can be on the lookout for something deeper."

He paused, but then went on after a moment.

"There is another way of looking at it too, Corrie," he said. "There are two different kinds of truth you can be looking for. Or perhaps I should say two different kinds of right and wrong."

"I don't quite understand that, but I'll keep listening," I said.

He laughed. "Let me see if I can explain it. I've only been thinking this through recently myself. First, there's the kind of right and wrong that's absolute, that's clear in the Bible. It's always the same, it's the same for everybody in every situation. There's no variation to it. Right is right and wrong is wrong. Lying is like that—it's always wrong. Murder, stealing, hatred—those things are always wrong. And of course, in the same way there are right things too that are *always* right, true things that are *always* true. It is true that God made the world. It is true that Jesus Christ lived and died for our sins. It is true that man cannot live meaningfully apart from God. It is true that people are supposed to treat one another with kindness and love. All those things are true no matter what anyone says. If somebody says differently—that God didn't make the world or that it's all right to be cruel—then he would be wrong. These are the kinds of things I call 'absolute' truth or 'absolute' right and wrong. There's no question about them."

"I understand all that. Then, what's the second kind?"

"Well, that's the one I've been wrestling through in my own mind lately. I haven't come up with a good name for it yet. It has to do with things that *aren't* absolute, where the Bible *doesn't* necessarily give a clear view on it, or maybe doesn't say anything at all about it. For example, is it *right* for your father to be mayor of Miracle Springs?"

"I hope so!" I said.

"So do I. And I think it is. But do you remember how the whole thing came about? It was Almeda who got involved first, and yet in the end she decided it was the wrong thing for her to do. You see, running for mayor isn't something you can say is right *or* wrong. It might be either."

"Almeda didn't think it was what God wanted for her."

"Exactly. Because of that it would have been wrong for her to do it, yet at the same time it could be *right* for your father."

"The same thing being right and wrong all at the same time. That could get a mite confusing."

"Once I started looking around, I found so many examples of this I'd never noticed before. Is rain a good or a bad thing? Both. It depends on the situation. Too much and you have a flood, too little and there's a drought. Is it right or wrong for a young lady to be a journalist? It might be either, depending on whether God wanted her to be or not."

I smiled.

"Harriet and I, of course, think that God *has* led you all along the way you've come, and we are very proud of you. That was just an example."

"I see."

"Personal decisions, like writing or being a mayor, are easy enough to see. But there are all kinds of things in the Bible that aren't black and white either. Does everybody come to God in the same way? Is there a *right* form of salvation? Those kinds of questions are very perplexing to a man in my occupation, as you can imagine. Nicodemus came to Jesus by night and the Lord told him about being born again. Paul was blinded by a great light.

God spoke to Moses in a bush. Timothy and St. Mark grew up under believing parents. So many differences! There may not be any question about murder, stealing, and lying. But what about all the deep things St. Paul wrote about in his letters? There are so many interpretations about what he meant. Does hell last forever? Will we know each other in heaven as we do now? Is the devil a real being? What does it mean to be dead to sin? Oh, Corrie, you can't imagine all the questions and issues ministers get involved talking and thinking about where there are no clear biblical answers!"

"What do you do to keep from getting confused?" I asked.

Rev. Rutledge laughed loudly. "I *don't* keep from getting confused!" he said. "I talk to my wife, and we both get more confused than ever!"

They both laughed.

"You see, Corrie," Rev. Rutledge went on in a minute, "as long as you keep a balanced perspective on such things, you can't go too far wrong. I am aware that I don't know too much about heaven and hell. But I am perfectly content not to know, because I realize we're not supposed to know such things perfectly. God didn't make them clear in the same way he made lying and stealing and murder clear. Some things are supposed to be absolute, others aren't. Where people go wrong is in adopting some personal view on one of the non-absolute things, and then saying that people who disagree with them are wrong."

"So if we were talking about heaven," I said, "I might say, 'I think we'll know each other there,' and you might say, 'I don't think we'll know each other there,' but neither of us could say the other one was wrong."

"We could say that we disagreed, but we couldn't know absolute right or wrong about it because the Bible doesn't make it clear."

"Hmm . . . that is interesting," I said. "Then it comes down to whether a certain question is absolute, like lying and stealing; or not absolute, like being mayor or what heaven will be like."

"That's what it comes down to, all right—what things fit into which category. That's where most people go wrong and start arguing with other people—they assume *their* views are more absolute than someone else's."

"But there *are* absolutes where someone *is* right and someone *is* wrong?"

"Yes. And on such issues Christians must not waver from the truth. But on all the other wide range of things, we have to give each other freedom to think without criticizing."

A long pause followed. Finally I spoke up again.

"Which kind of question do you think slavery is?" I asked. "Is it right or wrong in an absolute way, and everybody ought to feel the same about it? Or is it right for the South but maybe wrong for the North, and each side ought to respect the other's view?"

"Ah, Corrie, you've landed right in the middle of the hornet's nest with that question!"

"The whole future of the country may depend on the answer," I insisted.

"That may well be, which is why slavery is such a divisive issue. Of course, I personally find the very notion of slavery abhorrent, contrary to everything I see mirrored in the life of Jesus. Yet . . . I know there are Christians, and ministers, in the South who do not see it so. The Baptists, the Methodists, and the Presbyterians have already split over the question, their southern factions believing just as strongly *in* the validity of slavery as their northern counterparts believing it is wrong."

"How can that be?" I said in frustration, back again to the original quandary that had brought me to the Rutledges in the first place.

"People on both sides heatedly and righteously consider it an absolute issue with an absolute right and truth at the bottom of it—their *own*! Neither side will admit to anything except that the other side is absolutely in the wrong."

"What do you think? Is slavery one of the absolute issues, where there *is* a positive right and a positive wrong?"

A long silence followed. At last Rev. Rutledge exhaled a long sigh. I could tell he had already thought long and hard on the very question I had posed but without coming any nearer a conclusion than I had.

"I wish I knew, Corrie," he said almost wearily. "I truly wish I knew." Again he paused, then added, "And I fear for our country unless God somehow reveals *his* mind on the matter to large groups of people on both sides . . . and soon."

CHAPTER 15

A TALK WITH PA

In spite of his activity with Tad, Pa could not help but be weighed down by Zack's leaving and by the angry words he himself had spoken. Both Almeda and I knew him well enough to see that beneath the surface he was struggling hard to come to terms with what had happened.

A few days later I found him alone on the far side of the corral checking a hoof on one of the ponies. I walked up behind him.

"Made any decision about Sacramento, Pa?" I asked.

He slowly set the pony's foot back down onto the dirt, then straightened up. The weary and downcast look on his face made him seem ten years older than he was. The loose shoe was the furthest thing from his mind.

"Sacramento?" he repeated, forcing a slight chuckle. "To tell you the truth, Corrie, I hadn't hardly thought about it for a week. What about you? Got any idea what you aim to do yet?"

"No," I shrugged. "I've been thinking about it, but I don't suppose I'm any closer to knowing what God wants me to do than when we came back from San Francisco."

"I reckon getting away from all the hubbub of the city does slow the pace a mite. I suppose that's why I like it here. I couldn't abide living in no city. That's one thing I think I've decided. Whatever comes, I don't aim to leave Miracle. Zack's right about one thing. I was a fool to leave the only other home I ever had."

"He didn't say that, Pa."

"He didn't have to say those words. He may as well have said it. And even if he didn't say it, it's true anyhow, and I don't intend to make the same mistake twice. I've got a home now, and I'm gonna keep it, even if it means I turn my back on everything any other man would give his eyeteeth for. No, I don't suppose I've thought about it much, but I don't reckon there's much else to do now but say no."

"Zack's just all mixed up now, Pa," I said. "You can't plan your whole future on one outburst."

"It goes a lot deeper than just the other day, Corrie. Couldn't you tell? It had been building up inside the boy for years, and I never knew it. I don't know how I could have been such a blind fool!"

He turned away and leaned over the rail fence. I knew what he was fighting against. I walked toward him and laid my hand gently on his shoulder. He didn't say anything, and after a minute I pulled away, then climbed up and sat down on the top rail of the fence, looking up toward the mine.

"Doesn't seem to me like you ought to blame yourself, Pa," I said after a minute or two.

"How can I not blame myself? Don't seem like there's anybody else I can rightly blame."

"He'll cool off and come back, Pa."

"I ain't so sure, Corrie. You saw that look in his eye. He was determined. And it's sure he's not just a kid anymore. I got a feeling we might not see him for a spell."

"Are you afraid for him?"

"No, that ain't it."

"Like you said, he's not a kid. He's old enough to take care of himself. He's been away before, just like I have. You never seemed too worried about me, and Zack's a man."

"I'm not worried about him, Corrie. Sure, I know Zack's every bit the man I was at his age. He's made of better stuff inside, too. But I can't help feeling a heap of guilt for the things he said. I haven't been the pa to him I should have been. He's right about me running out on you kids and your ma. My life isn't one to be altogether proud of. The boy's got every right to hate me. I deserve it."

He stopped and let out a long sigh.

"But even when he said what he did," Pa went on, "telling me how he'd hurt and saying nothing but what was the truth about me, like a blame fool I just got angry at him. . . ."

Finally Pa's voice broke slightly at the memory of the blow he had given his son.

"God, oh, God . . . how could I?" he said in a more forlorn tone than I'd ever heard. "Telling him I'd take the belt to him! No wonder he was mad. He had a right to be. How could I have been so blind all this time to what he was feeling and thinking?"

He stopped. It was quiet for a minute, Pa breathing in deeply, but kind of unsteadily.

"Zack was always one to keep things inside, more than me, Pa," I said. "When we first came here, he was trying to be more a man than he was. Then he took to hanging around you and Uncle Nick all the time, wanting to be grown up."

"He did grow up too," said Pa. "I don't know why I didn't let him know better how I felt about him."

"You tried, Pa."

"Not enough. But a man just gets so busy and involved with his *own* affairs that he doesn't even know what his kids are thinking. They grow up so blamed fast; suddenly they're adults and they're holding things inside them that you done. But there's no way you can go back and make it right to them."

He paused a moment, then looked up at me earnestly.

"You got anything you're holding inside about anything I've done or said, Corrie?" he asked. "It'd kill me to find out something I oughta know but not find out till it's too late."

"I don't think so, Pa," I answered with a smile. "Nothing I know of at least. You've been about the finest pa a girl could have, and I love you, Pa."

He looked away. There were tears in his eyes, both from what I'd said and from the hurt over Zack.

"Pa," I said, "I feel bad, too. I was guilty of taking Zack for granted myself. I figured Zack felt just like I did about being a Christian, but maybe he had a more independent streak in him than I did. You and I talked about your past, and you confided in me and we prayed together. I suppose I was able to put it behind me more than he did. It made me love you more, but I guess people can react to the same situation in opposite ways, and so what drew me closer to you, he resented. It's not your fault. You can't lash out at yourself for Zack's holding things against you."

"If he had a right to . . . if it was for mistakes I made."

"You said it yourself, Pa—he's grown up now, just like I have, and so he's got to be responsible himself for his reactions. That's part of growing up too, it seems to me."

"Maybe you're right. But how does a man keep from feeling guilty over not giving his own son all of him he might have?"

Neither of us had seen Almeda walking slowly toward us as we'd been talking. She came closer and heard the last of Pa's question. He glanced up, then reached out his hand and drew her toward him.

"Still wrestling with Zack, Drummond?" she said.

Pa sighed and nodded his head. I knew they'd talked a lot about it already.

The three of us were silent for a while; then Almeda began to pray softly. "Oh, Father," she said, "I ask for a special pouring down of your grace for my husband. Comfort his father's heart and ease his pain over his son."

She stopped. There was nothing else to pray. Her simple words had expressed what both of us were feeling right then toward Pa. I was praying silently myself, not knowing what I could say. Then to my surprise I heard Pa's voice.

"God," he prayed in a raspy, quiet voice, "watch over my son. Wherever he is right now, take care of him. Even if he doesn't think I care about him, Lord, show him that you care for him. And if you can, help him to see that I do too. Bring him back to us safe, Lord."

"Amen," Almeda added softly.

Again it was silent for a while. At last Pa and Almeda headed off toward the creek, Pa's arm still around her shoulder, talking softly together.

CHAPTER 16

SURPRISE VISITOR

The summer progressed. July was hotter than June. August was hotter than July. We heard no word from Zack.

"What are you gonna do, Corrie?" Pa asked me one day at breakfast. "That paper of yours is getting fuller and fuller of election news all the time, and I still haven't seen your name in it anywhere."

"Are you going to write for Lincoln or Douglas?" asked Tad around a mouthful of warm biscuit.

"She wouldn't support a Democrat," said Becky. "You'd never go against Mr. Fremont's party, would you, Corrie?"

All summer, Katie and Edie had kept political issues stirred up to such an extent that even Becky and Tad were aware of what was happening. We'd managed to stay clear of any arguing about it again, although Edie and Almeda kept a cool distance from each other because of their strong views on the two opposite sides of the slavery question. I'd never really thought much about Almeda being a "northerner" before. But even ten years in California couldn't take the Bostonian out of her, any more than Edie's recent trip west could take the Virginian out of her.

"I don't know, Becky," I answered. "I suppose I might be able to support a Democrat someday if he was the right man. But not this year. As far as I can see, Mr. Lincoln's the best man to be president."

"Then why don't you write an article saying so and send it in to Kemble?" asked Pa.

"I'm still a little confused over how Christians can feel so differently about the same thing."

"They do, though, so why don't you just jump into it and give 'em *your* two cents' worth?"

"What if I'm not right?"

"Do you have to be right to speak your mind?"

"It seems like if I'm going to advise people what to do, and tell them how they ought to feel and how they ought to vote, then I *have* to be right. I couldn't do it otherwise."

"Do you still have doubts about how you feel, Corrie?" asked Almeda.

I thought for a while. "No, I don't suppose I do," I answered finally. "I guess down inside I *do* think I know that slavery is wrong. It's just knowing whether I'm supposed to say that in public, and tell people they ought to vote for Mr. Lincoln—that's the thing I'm still unsure about."

"How are you going to know that?" asked Pa.

"I guess I'm waiting for some sign from the Lord, something that tells me he's urging me one way or the other. You've always said to me, Almeda," I said, turning toward her, "that when in doubt about what to do, it never hurts to wait."

"God never will discipline us for going too slowly." Almeda smiled. "I've had to learn that the hard way. We can get ourselves into plenty of trouble by going too fast, but not from holding back waiting for God's guidance."

"What kind of a sign, Corrie?" asked Tad. "Is God gonna say something to you in a dream or something?"

I laughed. "I don't know, Tad. I doubt it. Just circumstances, probably. I feel like I know what's right, and even what I'd like to do. But I also feel like I need to wait until he brings something to me, rather than me going out to do something myself."

"Well, I hope he does it pretty soon," said Pa. "If you wait much longer without making up your mind, the election's gonna come and go and leave you behind altogether."

"If that happens, then I'll just figure I wasn't supposed to do anything in the first place, and everything will be fine."

After breakfast I decided to saddle up Raspberry and go for a long ride. Somehow the day reminded me of the one more than two years earlier when I had ridden up to the top of Fall Creek

Mountain on my twenty-first birthday. It had been a while since I had a good long ride, and somehow the questions at breakfast put me in a reflective mood.

The sun was well up as I headed off east, and the earth was already warming up fast. I never got tired of the smell of sugar pines under the beating of the sun's rays. Especially if there'd been rain anytime recently, and the earth underneath a bed of fallen pine needles was moist, the fragrance of the warming dirt, the dead leaves and needles and cones, and the live breathing trees were to me the very smell of heaven itself.

It hadn't rained today, of course, because it was the first week of August, but the smell was almost as wonderful. The rugged, rough-textured bark of the trees, cracked and splitting, oozed the translucent sticky pitch that ran up and down the trunks. It was precious to me, as were all things of the forest, as indications of the fingerprints of God when he made the world.

I had been thinking for a year or more about the first chapter of Romans, and found myself almost daily awakening to its truth, that God's invisible being really was clearly visible and obvious in everything around me—that is, if I had eyes to see him.

The world tells us what God is like. But most folks don't take that truth deep enough to allow the world to really speak actively to their hearts and minds about God's character. I found myself forgetting it sometimes, too. At such times, the world around me only spoke quietly, not with the vibrant reality that the bark was speaking to me today about his creativity.

More and more I thought that God intends for the world to really *speak* to us—loudly, constantly, every day. I believed that God means for our surroundings to be a very close-up way of us getting information about him. The world God made with his own hands should speak to us just as directly and actively as the words of Jesus himself.

As I rode through the woods and meadows, I found all these thoughts running through my mind as they had many times before. I found myself thinking about the barn back at home, and how much it could tell a stranger about Pa, if that stranger took it upon himself to look past the surface appearances of things— how orderly Pa kept his tools, how he lined up the spare saddles, the stables, the feeding troughs, the wagon and buggy, the loft for hay and straw. To a casual observer, none of these things would be especially noticeable. But since I had heard Pa talk about why he had done such and such and question aloud how he should build this part or where he ought to put that, I saw evidences of Pa's personality everywhere as I looked around the barn.

I saw Almeda's personality at home and in her office at the Mine and Freight in town, too—how she kept her desk, the pictures on the walls, the books in the bookcase, how she organized the whole business. She was *there,* just as Pa was in the barn— even if neither of them happened to be there in person. The barn, the office, the house—they all reflected both characters and personalities because they had put so much of themselves *into* them, maybe even without knowing it.

In the same way, the whole world is like God's office, his barn, the room where he lives. His desk and walls and rooms are full of things that are shouting about the person he is. It's up to us to try to discover what those characteristics of his personality are. Every tiniest detail of the universe is full of energetic life.

The bear and the ant *both* reflect the God who made them— the bear, his power and magnificence; the ant, his energy and productivity and unceasing labor.

The sun and the moon *both* are pictures of God—the heat and brightness and life-sustaining force of the sun, and the reflected light that God's being is able to give, even in the darkness when the fullness of his presence is turned away for a time.

The world could no more keep quiet about the nature of God than could Pa's barn or Almeda's office about them. The world is shouting at us, so loudly that in most people's ears it sounds like silence. The thunder of his voice is so huge and so deep that it rumbles past them in awesome silence. They hear nothing.

I reined Raspberry in, slowed to a stop, then dismounted. I hadn't gone far, probably not more than an hour from home, not nearly as far up into the mountains as I had that day two years before.

Most of the ground was brown under the scorching summer's sun. Where snow had lain six months earlier, now the dirt was hard-packed, with dried mountain grasses blowing gently in the rising breeze. Among the trees all was still and quiet. The only sounds were those of the birds overhead and the buzzing of bees and flies and other tiny flying creatures.

I left Raspberry tethered to a pine branch and walked through a thicket of trees into an open meadow. I felt full, happy, over-flowing with life. Thinking about God all the way up as I had ridden had filled me with a sense of how good he had been to me.

Suddenly I found myself running . . . running across the grass as fast as I could, running toward nowhere, but urged on by a feeling inside I could not keep back. I wanted to scale the heights of the hills under my feet, I wanted to run and climb to the peaks of the world, I wanted to shout and sing and laugh and cry all at once!

On I ran, my heart pounding, my legs beginning to tire. But the weariness just made me want to run all the more! I wanted to exhaust myself, to run until I dropped!

At last I could not go another step.

I lifted my hands into the air and threw my head back, gazing upward into the empty expanse of blue. Two or three white, bil-lowing clouds hung there in the midst of it, lazily working their way across the sky. I felt great throbbing prayers inside me, yet I had no words to say. There was only a sense that God was nearby, and even that he was looking down on me right then. A closeness came over me that I had never felt before, as if his great arms of love were wrapping themselves around me, even as I stood there all alone in the middle of that meadow, hands held upward toward the sky.

Slowly I dropped my hands back to my sides and turned around and began walking down the way I had run. I was crying, although I did not know when the tears had begun to flow.

I don't think I'd ever been happier in my life than in that moment. I *knew* God my Father was with me, that he loved me, that his tender arms were about me, and that I was his.

"God," I said softly, "I want nothing more than to be your daughter . . . to be completely yours. Oh, God—take away from me any other ambitions or motives or desires than just to let you be my Father every moment. Let me be content that you care for me, as content as I am right now."

All at once the prayers that I hadn't been able to pray a few moments earlier began to bubble up out of me in an endless spring. Thoughts and prayers and feelings tumbled together from out of my heart and mind. Such a desire swept through me to be nothing more, to do nothing more, than what God himself wanted for me. Any anxieties I may have had over the future or what to do vanished. I *knew* God would direct my pathway, as one of my favorite proverbs promised.

I felt so thankful, so appreciative to God for all he had done for me—for the love of life, for the sense of his presence with me, for the peacefulness he had given me. What poured out of me was unspoken thankfulness, and a calm knowing that he *would* direct my steps, that he would keep my life in his hands, and that he would show me what I was to do and when.

I rode Raspberry back toward town and arrived at the house sometime shortly after noon. My spirit was still calm, and I could not have been more unprepared for the surprise that awaited me the moment I walked in the door of the house.

There, talking to Pa, sat Cal Burton!

CHAPTER 17

THE INVITATION

Inside, my knees went weak, and a lump shot up from somewhere down in my stomach up to my throat. Flushed from the exercise of the ride, I knew my face went immediately pale. A faintness swept over me, even as Pa jumped up the moment he saw me come in.

"Look who's here from San Francisco, Corrie!" he said.

I hardly needed Pa to point it out to me! Even in my state of perturbation, I knew well enough who it was!

I took his hand, feeling a slight tremble go through me at the touch, and said, "Mr. Burton . . . but I don't understand . . . what are you doing here?" Never had my voice sounded so high and squeaky! And I had never sounded so stupid in all my life.

He laughed. "I know it must come as a surprise, and I apologize for coming all this way to see you without warning."

"Don't say another word about it," Pa said boisterously. "You're welcome anytime, with or without warning. Out this far from the city we don't stand too much on ceremony."

As Pa was responding to Mr. Burton's apology, I immediately decided that he had come to see Pa. It must have something to do with them wanting him to run for the legislature in Sacramento.

"So are you going to do it, Pa?" I said, turning to him.

"Do what?"

"Run for the legislature."

"What are you talking about, Corrie Belle? What's me running for office got to do with anything?"

"Isn't that what you two were talking about?"

"I don't know where you got a notion like that," laughed Pa. "We were just sitting here passing the time till *you* got back."

The blank look of confusion on my face must have been more humorous than I intended it to be because both men laughed.

"I'm sorry," said Mr. Burton. "I was speaking to you a moment ago, not your father. It's *you* I came all this way to see."

My heart fluttered all over again! "Me?" I squeaked. "What would you want to see me for?"

Pa laughed again. He was really enjoying my discomfort! "Corrie, you just go get yourself a drink of water, then come and sit down with us. Cal here's got to talk to you."

I did as Pa said, and a minute or two later the three of us were seated.

I glanced from one to the other of them. Mr. Burton spoke first.

"What I came for, Corrie," he said, "was to ask you again, on behalf of Mr. Dalton in San Francisco, if you would consider helping us with the Lincoln campaign."

I stared back blankly at him.

"I have been thinking about it," I said finally. "But I just hadn't decided yet what I ought to do."

"Mr. Dalton thought you might not have taken his words seriously before, and felt a personal visit from me might persuade you. Let me assure you, he was quite serious. He . . . we all, that is, would very much like you to be part of the Republican campaign team."

The color began coming back into my cheeks. I didn't know what to think!

"What . . . what would I do?"

"We were sure you'd ask that. I've already spoken to your editor, Mr. Kemble, about your writing a couple articles in favor of Mr. Lincoln from a woman's point of view. Then we would like to include you among the speakers at a public assembly to be held in Sacramento four days from now. A woman has never addressed such a gathering, in this campaign at least, and Mr. Dalton feels you could have a great influence. My instructions were to convince you to say yes, and to bring you back to Sacramento with me."

I sat staring, trying to take in his words.

"Don't just sit there, Corrie," Pa said finally. "The man's talking to you."

"I . . . I don't know what to say," I stammered.

"Say the only thing you can say, Corrie," said Mr. Burton. "I was instructed not to take no for an answer. The Republican party will pay your coach fare and put you up in a nice hotel. The trip won't cost you a cent."

"Well, I have been praying about what to do."

"And do you have reservations?"

"No, not exactly."

"Then it's all settled."

"I'll have to talk to my mother and father," I said.

"Of course. I understand." He rose and shook Pa's hand. "I'm going to ride back into town. I'm supposed to see the banker Royce for Carl, and I'll be at the boardinghouse if you should need me. Otherwise, perhaps I'll drop back by later this afternoon."

"And join us for supper," suggested Pa.

"But, your wife. . . ?" hesitated Mr. Burton.

"My wife will be delighted when I tell her," insisted Pa. "Now it's my turn not to take no for an answer!"

They both laughed, and it was agreed.

CHAPTER 18

EMBARRASSMENT ENOUGH
TO LAST A LIFETIME

I *had* been praying about it, like I'd said. But now that the moment of decision had come and I was face-to-face with it, I felt nervous and uncertain all over again. Of course, how much of that had to do with the election and how much had to do with Cal Burton himself, it was impossible for a twenty-three-year-old girl like me to know.

I couldn't help being a little taken with him. He was just about the finest-looking man a girl like me'd ever set eyes on. And so nice—how could I keep from liking him?

As much as I tried to concentrate on things like the election and what I ought to do as a writer, my mind kept filling up with Cal Burton. I wanted to say yes just because of him. All kinds of doubts would rise up, reminding me that I wasn't pretty, that a man like him would never look twice at me. I'd take to looking in a mirror and fiddling with my hair without even realizing I was doing it. When I suddenly woke up to the fact that I was daydreaming the day away, I could hardly stand what I saw in the glass and would turn away in disgust.

One time Pa chanced by the open door of my room and saw me standing there like an idiot, turned sideways, looking at myself. I caught his reflection in the mirror as he walked by, mortified to have him see me like that. I got so flushed my skin burned, and I turned away from the mirror and ran outside. Pa never said a word, but he knew well enough what I was thinking about.

All the rest of that day I wandered about in a daze, trying to concentrate, trying to pray, trying to be rational about it. But it was useless. I'd never figured myself to be overly emotional as women were sometimes said to be. I thought my head was sitting pretty level on my shoulders.

But after this day I didn't know! As close as I'd felt to God that very morning, suddenly he might as well have been a thousand miles away. I couldn't stand it, but I couldn't help it either.

I had to talk to Almeda! But when she got back from town about an hour after Mr. Burton had left, I couldn't get up the gumption to tell her. I had always talked to her about everything, but this was different. I couldn't help being embarrassed for how I was feeling.

Cal Burton came back some time between four and five in the afternoon. I was wandering around aimlessly near the corral when I heard his rented buggy approaching. I had been working in the garden and rubbing Raspberry down, and I was positively filthy from head to foot. I quickly ran into the barn, hoping he wouldn't see me. He reined in the horses in front of the house and went inside. I watched the house for a few minutes from one of the barn windows, being careful to keep out of sight.

A little later, the door opened and Pa and Mr. Burton came out. They were talking away like old friends. Pa really seemed to like Mr. Burton. It was the happiest I'd seen him since Zack left.

Suddenly I realized they were heading straight for the barn! I jumped back from the window and hurriedly ran back into the back part of the building where it was darkest, frantically trying not to make any noises that would give me away. I was just crouching down behind two bales of hay in the far corner of the barn when I heard Pa and Mr. Burton enter by the opposite door. I held my breath and hoped the hay didn't make me sneeze!

"Corrie!" I heard Pa's voice call out. "Corrie . . . you in here?"

A brief silence followed.

"Blamed if she wasn't around just a few minutes ago," I heard Pa say. I thought I heard his footstep coming nearer. He *had* to know where I was! It would be awful if they found me like I was! What would I say? But I hadn't answered Pa's call, so now there was nothing I could do but make *sure* they didn't see me!

Silently I hunched down even more, lowering my face into my dress so if any part of me did show, at least my hair would blend in with the hay and straw around me. Why had I hidden? Now I was really in a pickle!

I heard Pa's footsteps going one way and the other, looking about. "Corrie!" he called out again. I felt like such a deceiver for not answering, but I couldn't make myself say anything now!

Pretty soon they turned and headed back out. "Can't imagine where she went," Pa said. "But come on, Cal, I'll show you the mine, and take you up to see my brother-in-law. Corrie'll be along soon enough. The two of you can talk about your business later."

These last words were faint, because by now they were outside and walking up the stream toward the mine. Slowly I crept out of my hiding place and tiptoed toward the window. I peeked carefully around the edge of it. There they were, thirty yards away, their backs to me, in animated conversation, Pa seemingly telling him all about the mining operation, which Mr. Burton seemed interested in by his questions and gestures.

I stepped back inside the barn and breathed a big sigh of relief. Then first it struck me what I must look like. I was sweating like a horse, my hair was all messed up and hanging all over everywhere, my dress was dirty and had pieces of straw and hay stuck to it all over. I was a mess! Whether I was pretty or not, I was certainly in no condition to meet a man like Cal Burton!

I sneaked back to the window and peeked around the edge. There they still were, almost at the mine now. I needed to go clean up, but I was dying to know what they were saying! What if they were talking about me?

Pa turned and led the way toward the creek. They crossed the bridge and in another minute were out of sight, walking through the trees toward Uncle Nick and Aunt Katie's. Without even thinking what I was doing, suddenly I left the barn and hurryed after them, keeping out of sight behind trees and brush, just in case one of them should glance back in my direction.

I made it all the way to the bridge, then stopped. I couldn't hear their voices any longer.

Quickly I ran across the bridge, then ducked out of sight off the pathway again. From there I slowly made my way through the trees toward the clearing, moving from tree to tree, glancing around to make sure no one else was coming who could see me. I slipped around behind the house. Everything was quiet, but I knew they were inside. I crept out from my hiding place and ran to the house, kneeling down behind one of the back windows.

I was safe there. Even if someone came to the window and looked out, they couldn't see me. That side of the house faced the forest, which was close by and generally darker than the front. I strained my ears to listen.

"All this way to talk to our future Congressman, eh, Drum?" I heard Uncle Nick say.

"No, he didn't come to see me. I already told you, I'm not at all sure what I'm gonna do."

I heard a woman's voice next, either Aunt Katie's or Edie's.

"He came to see Corrie, of course," Pa answered whoever it was. "And to take her back to Sacramento with him."

Some exclamations went around, followed by some laughter. How mortifying. They *were* talking about me!

Uncle Nick must have made a joke, although I was glad I didn't hear it. Some more laughter and comments went around the room. "I'm sure Corrie will keep her head," said Katie.

Cal Burton was the next to speak. "It's all for the good of the party, I assure you," he said. "They genuinely want her involved, as they do her father, I might add. I promise to take good care of her."

"It's your chance to be a famous man, Drum," said Uncle Nick, going back to the subject of Pa's running for office.

"That's the last thing I want," said Pa. The laughter had faded from his voice, and I figured he might be thinking about all the things Zack had said. The conversation gradually subsided, and I couldn't hear everything. The next thing I did hear seemed to be Cal Burton talking to Aunt Katie and her sister. Edie had apparently said something about having recently come from the East.

"What's it been like there?" Mr. Burton asked her.

Edie laughed. Her voice had an edge to it just like Katie's, and I could hear her distinctly. "How do you mean?" she said. "Between my husband dying and political tensions, I can't say it was an altogether pleasant time for me before coming here."

"I suppose what I meant was more the weather, the scenery. It's been some time since I saw spring come out in that region, and your mentioning Virginia flooded me with memories."

"Why?" asked Katie, drawing into the conversation. "*You're* not from there, are you?"

"No, but close by. Roanoke Rapids, North Carolina, actually."

"I would never have known! What happened to your accent?"

"A casualty of coming west to California!" he laughed.

"And *you* are working for the Republicans?" put in Edie in astonishment.

"You have to take the opportunities that come your way, you know."

I had hardly paused to consider why their three voices sounded so clear. With the next words Katie uttered I suddenly knew—they had been gradually moving closer to the window I was crouched below outside.

"Is it only me, or is it rather hot in here?" said Katie.

When I heard her hand on the window latch. I panicked and ran. But it was too late!

"Why Corrie Hollister," I heard behind me. "What in heaven's name are you doing out there?"

I stopped and turned, trying to look as though nothing was wrong. "Oh . . . I was just coming around the back of the house," I said lamely. "I heard you talking and couldn't help listening."

"Eavesdropping!" said Katie with pretended annoyance. "Shame on you, Corrie!"

There stood Cal Burton right behind Katie, along with Edie, looking out the window at me where I stood like the mooncalf I was! I was so glad the trees kept the light dim. I would have died for him to see me in the state I was in!

"Well, Corrie, don't just stand there," said Katie. "You were coming in, weren't you?"

"I . . . was . . . I mean I didn't want to—"

"Come on around to the door, Corrie," she insisted. "As I understand it, this man came all the way from the big city to see you."

I hastily tried to think of some way to squirm out of the awkwardness and get out of there. But by now Pa realized what the ruckus was about. He came outside as I walked slowly around the side of the house.

"Where you been, Corrie?" he said. "I've been looking high and low for you."

"Just around and about, Pa."

"Well, come on in. Cal's back."

"No, I have to go back home and take a bath before supper, Pa."

"At least come in and say hello."

"Oh, Pa, I'd rather—"

"Come in and be sociable a minute," interrupted Pa. "You can clean yourself up later."

I knew there was no way out of it, so I sighed silently and went into the house with Pa. He may not have minded my dirty dress and mussed hair, but Uncle Nick wasn't about to miss the chance for kidding. For once I wished he'd have kept his humor to himself. Usually I didn't mind, but this time it hurt.

"Corrie Belle," he said, "you're a mess! You look like you just stepped out from wrestling with a dad-blamed hog!"

"Nick! Haven't you got any sense in your head?" Aunt Katie rebuked him sharply. "Now's not the time for saying such things."

I was grateful for Katie's standing up for me, especially since it gave me a quick second to blink back the tears.

"I think your niece looks just as nice as can be, Mr. Belle," said Cal Burton to Uncle Nick. Hearing his voice say such a thing took my breath away for an instant, and I almost forgot the mess I was in. "Hello again, Corrie," he added, turning to face me and holding out his hand.

I shook it, daring a quick glance up into his face. His eyes were looking straight at me. I glanced away almost as fast as I'd looked up.

"Honest, hard-working, robust beauty, Mr. Belle," he said, turning again to Uncle Nick. "Not the kind of thing you see too much in the city, you can take it from me. I'll take a handsome young lady from the country like this anytime!"

"Oh, Corrie," whispered Aunt Katie behind her hand, but loud enough so that she made sure everyone in the room heard her, "you better snatch up this fellow while you can! Men like that don't come along but once in a lifetime!"

Now my face *was* red! I couldn't stand it, being the center of everyone's talk. But everybody just stood there looking at me in my dirt-smeared dress. I could hardly keep the tears back now. It was awful to be stuck there like that!

"So, where have you been, Corrie," asked Pa, "to get such a mess all over you? We got a guest for dinner."

"I know, Pa," I said, trying to stay calm. "I was rubbing down Raspberry. I guess the time got going too fast for me." I wiped the back of my hand across my eyes.

Pa laughed. "You just smeared a streak of dirt across your forehead," he said. "Here," he added, reaching into his pocket for a handkerchief, "you can wipe it off with this."

Suddenly, without even realizing what I was doing, I spun around and ran for the door. I made for the woods as fast as I could, tears streaming down my cheeks.

CHAPTER 19

LEARNING TO LOOK FOR THE LORD'S DOORS

Somehow I managed to get through the horrid day.

After a long cry I went back home, got water for a hot bath, with Almeda's help, and was probably halfway presentable by the time Pa and Cal Burton got back down from Uncle Nick's. Almeda and I talked a little, but I think both of us realized if we talked *too* much about what had happened, I'd start bawling like a baby all over again. So she just loved me as best she could, and let me take my bath and get dressed by myself.

Pa felt bad for what he'd done, I knew that. I did my best to look at him in a way that would tell him I didn't hold anything against him, and that I knew it was my own fault. I didn't want him to have to worry about anything he'd said to me on top of his heartache over Zack.

Cal Burton kept being just as nice as he could be all evening, treating me as if nothing out of the ordinary had happened at all. But I kept my eyes away from his. Down inside I was just too mortified over having behaved like a ridiculous little schoolgirl.

"So, Miss Hollister, what about going to Sacramento to work for Mr. Lincoln?" he asked.

"I've been thinking about it," I said, "but I haven't had the chance to talk with Pa and Almeda yet."

He smiled into my eyes—a smile that almost made me forget how foolish I'd been. "I understand," he said. "I can stay for another day at the boardinghouse in town, and we can discuss it again tomorrow." Then he and Pa spent most of the rest of the evening talking about politics. As interested as I'd been before, I just couldn't seem to concentrate on what they were talking about. I sat there silent the whole time, my mind muddled up with Mr. Burton's eyes, his smile, his deep resonant voice. Then I'd think about running out of Uncle Nick and Aunt Katie's that afternoon, with a dirty dress and crying, with everybody staring after me! It was a miracle I didn't cry again just thinking about it! I did shed a few more tears later, though, lying in bed trying desperately to go to sleep and put the day behind me at last.

I felt just as stupid the next morning, but at least a night's sleep put some distance between the present and my inane behavior. The sun shining into my room helped cheer my spirits somewhat. Besides, whatever I felt like, I had to make a decision about what to do.

I got dressed and walked out. Almeda was just taking the water for Pa's coffee off the stove. I walked toward her. She put the kettle down and drew me to her in a warm embrace. We stood there for a long time without saying a word. I wrapped my arms tightly about her waist and buried my face in her neck. It felt so good to know I was loved no matter what I did!

"What should I do, Almeda?" I said finally, slowly pulling away from her and sitting down.

"About yesterday, or about going to Sacramento?"

"I don't think there's *anything* I can do about yesterday!" I laughed halfheartedly. "No, I mean, should I go?"

"What are you feeling about it?"

"After yesterday it's hard to know. I thought I had things more or less worked out about the election. I was even beginning to look forward to writing something. Now I'm confused again."

"Do you feel the Lord prompting you to go?"

"Oh, I don't know!" I wailed in frustration. "I can't even concentrate enough to pray or to ask the Lord what to do! I don't know why, but it seems like a big decision. I have the feeling that whatever I decide, the results will be with me a long time, maybe for the rest of my life. But God might as well be a thousand miles away for any feeling I have of his presence."

"Do you think he really *is* a thousand miles away, Corrie?" Almeda asked.

"No, I know he hasn't gone anywhere. You've taught me better than that. I know you can't depend on your feelings. God is near, he is still with me—I know that. I just don't feel him, that's all."

Almeda smiled. "I'm so glad to hear you say that, Corrie," she said. "It doesn't concern me to hear you say the Lord seems distant as long as you know he *really* is still right beside you."

"I know it, at least in my head," I answered. "But not feeling him, not hearing his voice anywhere makes a decision that much harder. How can I *know* what his will is?"

"Could he be speaking to you in ways you're not used to?"

"How do you mean?"

"God doesn't always speak to us by giving us a strong urging or compelling to do something. The older we grow as Christians, the more he actually may *not* give us those strong inward voices telling us what he wants us to do."

"Why is that?"

"I have an idea," Almeda answered. "But it's only my own personal theory, nothing I've found in the Bible or anywhere." She gave a little laugh. "So if I answer your question, you can't hold me to it if someday the Lord shows us I'm wrong."

"Agreed," I said.

"Okay, here it is." She paused, took a breath, then launched in. "When we're young, either in age or young as a Christian, there are many things we don't know. Young people have to learn about life. And when you decide to give your heart to the Lord, there are many, many things you have to learn about what life with him is like. The Lord has to tutor us, for a while, helping us learn new habits, new attitudes, new ways of looking at things. He has to train us spiritually. He has to teach us to stand, then walk, then move forward as Christians. In the same way that a parent has to train a child in the ways of life in the world, our Father has to train us in the ways of life in his kingdom. Until we get our spiritual bearings, that training has to be very direct, very close, very personal. There is so much we don't know and that he needs to teach us."

She stopped, and a thoughtful look passed over her face. Then she laughed again.

"Oh, Corrie!" she said. "If you could have seen me that first year or two I was married to Mr. Parrish. There was so much I had to learn, not just about being a Christian, but about being a wife, about living a normal existence. Every day was a new learning experience!

"You see, that's what I am getting at. Both my heavenly Father and Mr. Parrish together contributed to that remaking process in me. But eventually I did change. Eventually I learned the new ways. And now, after all these years, I am truly an altogether new and changed person. I have matured in many ways. As a Christian, as a daughter of God, although he is still with me always—inside my heart and right beside me—I no longer require the same kind of training I did back then. I am God's daughter, but I am also a grown woman. I think God treats me in many cases like an adult rather than a child. Whereas, at first he had to show me *everything*, and had to take my hand and literally guide me through every step of life, he doesn't have to do that anymore. He has trained me, and in the same way that a parent gradually releases a child to walk on his own, I think God begins to release us—not to walk independently of him, but to walk beside him as he has shown us without his having to direct every single move we make. In obedience to him, we walk along the path he has given us to walk, without having to stop to consider every step. Does that make sense?"

"I think so," I said.

"It's very difficult to explain what I mean," Almeda went on. "I don't mean to sound as though I think I want to walk independently, or that I think God isn't there with every step I take. I do try to bring him into all aspects of my life, even more than I did at the beginning. But the more we mature as Christians, the more of our decisions he leaves in *our* hands—knowing that we are walking along the road he has placed us in, and according to the ways and habits and attitudes that he has trained into us."

"In other words," I said, "he might be leaving part of the decision of what I should do in *my* hands?"

"Exactly. If he *didn't* want you to write, I am confident he would let you know it very clearly, and I am equally confident you would obey his voice. But since he *has* led you into writing in the past, I think he will very often let *you* make the decision yourself as to what specific things you write about. He may give you a stronger sense of leading at some times than others. But there will also be times when he will trust you to go either way when you're facing a particular decision, and he will make *either* one work out for the best."

"Hmm . . . that is a new way to look at it."

"God is our Father, of course. We must look to him for *everything*. We can't breathe a single breath without him. We can't take a step without him. Yet it is one of the many paradoxes of the Christian life that he also entrusts to us a sort of partnership with him. As we walk along *with* him, keeping our hand tightly in his, it is as if he says to us, 'My son, my daughter, I have trained you and taught you and placed my life and spirit inside you. Now go . . . walk in the confidence of your sonship. I will always be at your side; if you err or misstep, my hand will be right there to help you up and guide you back into the middle of the path. But until then, walk on with the boldness that comes from having my Spirit inside you.'"

"Do you think that applies to big decisions too?" I asked. "Things like whether or not I should get involved in this election?"

"I think we always have to pray and ask the Father for his specific guidance," replied Almeda. "Then the time comes when we must make a decision."

"And if we don't seem to hear a definite answer?"

She thought a minute, then answered. "There are two ways, it seems to me, in which God can answer our prayers and direct us. He can open doors, or he can close doors. If we're standing still, facing a fork in the road, facing a decision to be made, he can either open a door going in one direction or close the door going in the other. Or, if we don't happen to see the fork, or don't see *any* possibilities clearly, it has always seemed best to me to keep moving and praying until he either opens or closes a door. I've even prayed something like this sometimes: 'Lord, I don't know for sure if this is the way you want me to go. It *seems* to be best right now, and I *think* this is what you want, so I'm going to keep moving cautiously ahead until you say otherwise. Please, Lord, if this is not what you want me to do, slam the door shut in my face.' "

"Is that what you did before the election four years ago?" I asked.

"I suppose it was something like that, although there was, as I now look back on it, an ample supply of my own wishful thinking involved in what I *thought* was God's leading. Yes, I thought I was going in the right direction, so I moved ahead. But then when God made some things clear in my thinking about my relationship with your father, I knew he was closing the door."

"And so maybe Cal Burton's coming like he has is the Lord's way of opening the door to what I've been in doubt about all this time."

"It wouldn't surprise me a bit," said Almeda.

"I've been thinking about Davy Crockett's saying, 'Be sure you're right, then go ahead.' Maybe I've been expecting the Lord to be more direct than he wants to be."

"There's wisdom in that motto," said Almeda. "Yet on the other hand, we don't always have the luxury of being absolutely sure before we *have* to go ahead. In the absence of any positive leading by God, sometimes we have to launch out according to what circumstances seem to be saying, and prayerfully trust God to open and close doors as we go along."

Both of us were quiet a minute or two, until the door opened behind us and Pa walked in. Almeda glanced up, then her face fell.

"Oh, Drummond!" she exclaimed. "I'm afraid I let your coffee get cold."

"What'd you go and do a thing like that for, woman?" barked Pa, throwing me a wink.

"Corrie and I were talking. I'm sorry."

"Cold coffee from your hand is better than a hot cup from anyone else's," said Pa, walking to Almeda and giving her a kiss.

She handed him the cup. He took a long swallow, then nodded in satisfaction. "Yep . . . not bad at all!"

"So, what do you think, Corrie?" asked Pa. "You recovered from your embarrassing little runaround yesterday?"

"Oh, Pa, don't remind me!" I said. "Mr. Burton probably thinks I'm a complete ninny!"

"Don't bet on it, Corrie. I walked him out to his buggy last night and we chatted awhile. He thinks a lot of you. Seems like all them high-up fellas in Sacramento do."

"No more than they think of you, Pa," I said.

"Naw, Corrie. A man like me ain't that unusual. If I turn down their offer, they'll just get someone else. Who knows, maybe Franklin Royce'll run instead of me! But you—that's different! If you turn them down, who else are they going to get? Ain't too many young women like my daughter Corrie Belle around!"

"Cut it out, Pa," I said. "I was a complete fool yesterday, and you know it."

"Doesn't make me love you any less, or make me any less proud of you. So . . . you decided yet?"

"I don't know, Pa."

"Seems to me that Cal's coming with a direct invitation like he brought—seems like that's just exactly the sign from the Lord you were waiting for."

I glanced over at Almeda.

"An open door?" I suggested.

"Looks like one to me," said Pa, taking another drink of his coffee. "If you ask me, I say you oughta do it!"

CHAPTER 20

MY DECISION

I took Pa's advice.

I may have been twenty-three, but I still figured my pa was about as dependable a man as there could be. Even if he hadn't been my pa, I would have heeded his words. His being my father made it all the more important to listen to him and obey him as fully as I could. I'd had plenty of independence at times in the past, but the older I got, the more I found myself wanting to trust his way of looking at things.

Besides, I *wanted* to do it. I was interested in politics. I knew by now that I was against slavery, and that I did want Mr. Lincoln to win the election—maybe not as much as I had Mr. Fremont four years earlier, but enough to be able to speak out and tell folks that's how I felt.

So Pa's words gave me the nudge forward I needed—a nudge, as it turned out, that would make a mighty big difference in my life.

I left the next day on the midmorning stage south to Sacramento. Pa and Almeda and Becky and Tad took me to town to see me off. I was dressed in the traveling suit Almeda had Mrs. Gianni make for me. She said it would help to save my two fancy dresses for special occasions if I had something just to travel in. It was of dark brown patterned wool on the bottom, with a loose white muslin blouse with a short wool wraparound cape if it should be chilly.

When Cal Burton took my hand to help me up into the stage, I nearly wilted, even though my heart was pounding rapidly inside my chest. I tried not to show anything on my face, but sat down, then looked out at my family while Mr. Burton took the seat next to me. They were all smiling and waving and saying their farewells to me as if I were going to be gone a month instead of just four or five days.

"Don't you worry about a thing, Mrs. Hollister," Mr. Burton said through the open window. "I'll make sure your daughter is well taken care of."

"We stopped worrying about Corrie four years ago," laughed Pa, "when she took to gallivanting off all over California by herself on horseback!"

"What's this?" he said, glancing over at me.

"A long story," I answered.

"I want to hear about it. What is your father talking about?"

"The *last* time I got mixed up in an election," I said, laughing. "I hope this one turns out better than that."

The stage jerked into motion. I leaned outside again, and they all waved. I kept looking back, waving as we picked up speed down the main street of Miracle Springs. Something about this departure was different than any other before, even though I had gone a lot farther than Sacramento in the past. Probably the difference had something to do with the man sitting next to me inside the stagecoach.

As we pulled out of town and headed south, I could not keep from thinking of the awful scene after Aunt Katie discovered me outside her window, and wondering if Cal Burton would say something about it. I didn't know *what* I was going to talk to him about the whole way!

I shouldn't have worried. He treated me with complete respect and kindness, never referred to the incident at Uncle Nick's, and was so easy to talk with I soon forgot my nervousness and began to converse more freely than I imagined possible with a relative stranger. He asked me about my involvement with the Fremont-Buchanan election, and I told him about my adventures in Sonora and Mariposa, and what had happened with my story in the end.

"I never could help feeling less important than the other people around whenever I was in the city," I said. "And everything that happened back then only made it worse."

"From what I've heard, you've stood your ground against Kemble more than once, and even made him back down a time or two."

I couldn't keep from smiling at the memory.

"That doesn't sound like a timid country girl to me."

"I suppose you're right," I said. "I did do that. But down inside, someone like me still can't help feeling kind of out of place in a big city and around important goings-on. Like that gathering in San Francisco that Pa and I went to in June."

"You seemed perfectly at ease to me."

"Oh no—I was so nervous!"

"Why?"

"I guess because I'm not used to all the big-city fancy ways. I'm more at home on the back of a horse than in a frilly dress."

"You could have fooled me. You looked as elegant that evening as any young woman I could imagine."

I blushed and glanced down at my lap. Nobody had ever used the word *elegant* about *me* before! The very thought of me being elegant would have made me laugh if I hadn't been so embarrassed at the words.

"So tell me, did you ever get to meet the Fremonts after all you tried to do on their behalf?" Mr. Burton asked.

"Yes. Ankelita Carter arranged for me to meet them when they came to California after the election."

"I imagine they were very appreciative of your efforts."

"They were very nice to me," I said. "Jessie Fremont's a writer too, and so she seemed interested in all I was doing."

"And Colonel Fremont?"

"He said he had mentioned my name to some of his friends as someone to 'get on your side when the chips are down.' I laughed at first, and didn't think anything more about it. But now I find myself wondering if it might be true, after all."

"I imagine if Colonel Fremont said he told people about Corrie Hollister, then he probably did exactly that. He and Lincoln were talked about in connection with each other for a while. You can never tell where your name might be getting around. Kemble told me that just about everything you write nowadays finds its way into print in the East. It must make you very proud to have accomplished so much as a woman, especially at such a young age."

"I guess I never really stopped to think about it," I said. "It never crossed my mind to think that I had *accomplished* anything."

"The women of this country would likely disagree. Someday they'll look back on you as a pioneer of a different kind than Daniel Boone, and John Fremont when he first explored the West."

"Me, a pioneer?" I said.

"Of course. You mark my words, the day will come when people will remember your name and be proud of you for what you did."

"Mr. Burton," I asked after a minute, "do you think it is because of something Mr. Fremont may have said that Mr. Dalton asked me to help with the election?"

"I never heard anything to that effect. It's possible, of course. But as influential as he was in helping to form the Republican party and make it a viable alternative to the southern Democrats, the party has begun to move in different directions than those of John Fremont himself. He does not have the influence he once did, as fond as you may be of him. Although you may not know it, your editor, Ed Kemble, thinks more highly of you than he probably lets on in your hearing. Word about Corrie Hollister has gotten around San Francisco and Sacramento without any help from John Fremont."

He paused, then looked over at me earnestly. "There is one other thing I have to reply to about your question," he said. "If we are going to be friends, as I hope we will, you are going to have to call me Cal. I'm only twenty-five. That can't be more than a year or two older than you. If I've taken the liberty to call you Corrie instead of Miss Hollister, the least you can do is drop the Mister."

"I'll try," I said shyly.

"If you ever meet my father, you can use Mr. Burton again. But not until then . . . agreed?"

"Agreed," I nodded with a smile.

CHAPTER 21

A RIDE NOT TO FORGET

We rode for some time without talking again. Cal spoke to a man and woman in the opposite seat, who were on their way from Reno to Sacramento. They, too, had spent the night in Miracle Springs.

When he turned to me again, he seemed to have returned to the subject we had been discussing earlier. "Do you really feel ill at ease in the city, Corrie?" he asked.

"Just when I have to pretend I'm something I'm not," I answered.

"Why would you want to be other than you are?"

"I don't suppose I do. But when you're in the city, around people in fancy clothes who know how the city works and are doing important things, a country person like me can't help but feel that Robin O'Flaridy had it right all along when he said I was just a bumpkin from the sticks."

"O'Flaridy?"

"Never mind," I laughed.

"He really had the nerve to call you that?"

"Robin had enough nerve to do plenty more besides that! Yet sometimes that's exactly how I do feel—especially around important people. When I'm at home and can be all by myself and write, I don't have to worry about what anyone thinks of me. I can be free with my thoughts and let them flow out onto the paper. But something like what we're going to Sacramento to do—that makes me real nervous. It makes me wish I was more used to the city and its ways so I didn't feel like a bumpkin."

"Let me tell you something, Corrie," he said seriously. "Don't ever wish to be something different than exactly the person you are. I've been in a lot of cities, and I've known many city people. But I don't know that I've ever met a family quite like yours, or a young lady quite like you, or a man quite like your father."

He stopped, then turned and looked out the window at the passing scenery. The silence lasted a long time. When he finally turned back toward me, I could see a wistfulness in his eyes, a far-off look—almost longing for something or a painful memory out of his past. I knew he'd gone somewhere far away and was now struggling to bring his mind back to the present.

Until that moment, Cal Burton had seemed so high above me, so confident and sure of himself, mingling with important people, a friend of politicians and assistant to Mr. Stanford, one of California's most influential men. All of a sudden, in the brief second when he turned back from the window and his eyes met mine, he was an ordinary person just like me, and in that instant I momentarily forgot about all of the things that made us so different. All of a sudden he did seem to be *Cal* to me rather than *Mister* Burton.

"No, Corrie," he said with a sigh, "don't ever leave Miracle Springs, or your family. It's too special a treasure. Wherever you go, whatever you do, however many people you meet, and however many big cities you visit, don't change. Don't let Miracle Springs and the country and that homestead by the creek you love so much—don't let it get away from you. You can stand tall alongside anybody, no matter how big or important they may seem to you. You've got something just as important down inside, whether anybody sees it right off or not."

I didn't know how to respond, so I kept quiet.

"So you've got nothing to be nervous about," he added after a moment. "When we get to Sacramento, you just be who you are, and that will be enough for anybody."

"I'll do my best," I replied.

"So tell me," Cal said, brightening up again with that wide smile of his, "what's it like to write? How do you do it? How'd you ever get started writing for the *Alta*, anyway?"

"I started out just keeping a journal," I said. "I wrote down things I felt, things I thought about. I just did it for myself at first."

"How'd you start writing for the newspaper, then?"

I told him about the blizzard of '55 and the story I wrote about it. "After that," I said, "I just kept doing it a little more, thinking of things to write about, getting braver about sending things to Mr. Kemble."

"And getting braver about facing him and speaking up to him, too, from what I understand."

"What do you mean—how do you know about that?"

"Dalton had me do some checking up on you," Cal answered. "Kemble was half mad, half proud of you when he told me about your facing him down and arm-twisting him into paying you eight dollars for an article he wanted to buy for a dollar."

I laughed. "How I could have been so brash back then?" I said. "At nineteen, to think I should get paid what a man did. I don't know whether it was bravery or stupidity!"

"It must have worked. You made a name for yourself. You've written a lot of articles, Kemble likes you, and you've made a little money at it, I would imagine."

"Forty-three dollars, altogether," I said.

"Is that all?" exclaimed Cal. "I would have thought it would be hundreds!"

"I got only eight dollars that once. Most of the time Mr. Kemble still pays me between two and six dollars an article, and I've written only fourteen or fifteen articles he's published. Some of them are so short I get only a dollar."

"Then you must not write for the money."

"Oh no, it's not that at all."

"What then?"

I had to stop and think a minute. "It's a lot of things," I said finally. "People, nature, thoughts, ideas, feelings . . . I don't know if I could really explain it, but what's inside me has to come out in words. When I think something or notice something or have some kind of an insight about the world, to be able to communicate that to someone else is the greatest feeling on earth."

"Are you an intellectual, Corrie Hollister?" Cal asked, with a serious and pensive look on his face. For an instant I thought he might be poking fun at me, but then I realized he honestly was trying to figure out more about me.

"An intellectual?" I repeated in surprise. "You must be joking!"

"You're certainly a thinker, almost a philosopher in a way."

"A philosopher! That's even more strange to hear you say. Didn't you hear me a few minutes ago—some people think I'm a bumpkin from nowhere."

"Ah, but they don't know you like I am beginning to," replied Cal, his eyes open wide in a knowing expression. "But you don't deny that you're a thinker, do you?"

"I don't suppose I could be a writer without being a thinker at the same time," I answered finally.

"There—you see . . . a philosopher! A philosopher is just someone who thinks and has his own way of looking at things and then writes them down for other people to think about too. Isn't that what you do, in your own personal Corrie-Belle-Hollister-from-Miracle-Springs sort of way?"

"Maybe you're right. But I don't think of it like that. I just look at things, at the world, to observe people. Then I write about what I see, describe it, and maybe try to figure out what it means."

"Tell me what *you* mean."

"Maybe it's just from living in the country. But I have this feeling that everything is supposed to *mean* something. There are two ways we can look at something—just as it is on the surface or on two levels at once—what it looks like *and* what it is saying about life and the world. Do you know what I mean? Don't you have the feeling that the whole world is talking to you all the time if you just had sharp enough hearing to listen?"

"I've never thought of it before."

"Oh, but it is!"

"Give me an example."

I thought for a minute. "There's the creek outside our house. Sometimes I lie awake in my bed at night and just listen to it singing and babbling away down the hill toward the town in the dark. Or sometimes I sit beside it on a sunny day, with my feet in the water, watching for an hour as the clear water tumbles and splashes over the rocks. I love that creek! And don't you see why? It's so much more than just water. Its splashy, wet noises are constantly bringing messages down from the mountains—telling tales of snow and winter, of secret places where it has been, under the hills where huge vaults of gold exist that no man has ever seen, telling about falls it has cascaded over and about the fish and otters that play in its deep pools. Oh, it's got so much to tell if you only stop and listen to its voice. But best of all, when you kneel down and put your lips to it in the early spring when it's icy cold, and you drink in a mouthful, then it tells about life itself and how God made it, such a simple thing to look at, as the very sustainer of everything that lives and grows. The water that comes down that creek is nothing short of a miracle."

Cal laughed. "You are indeed able to see a great deal in things that most people look right past."

"But that's not nearly all," I said enthusiastically. "If there has been a heavy snow up in the mountains and then a week of warm weather comes, the stream will grow and grow, almost hourly, until it thunders and roars and rushes down with foamy swiftness. Then the stream can tell stories about the science of water itself—how it is gathered up into the sky from the ocean, to wait and accumulate together in clouds, finally to descend back to the earth in snows and rains, hitting the earth and soaking into it and wandering to and fro in streams and springs, sometimes pausing in lakes, until it finds its way back to the ocean again. I sometimes think of all these mysteries as I sit and watch and listen to the water as I did yesterday."

"Now I know I was not mistaken!"

"About what?"

"About your being a philosopher."

"Nonsense!" I replied. "It's all there for anyone to see. That's what I love so much about the country, about life. *Everything* is just as full of marvels and secret mysteries as the stream. Just the other day I was looking at the bark on the pine trees in the woods and found myself thinking about the mysteries of how the trees grow and gather nourishment from the ground. Nothing is without a meaning, almost a personality—*if* you know how to look for it and what you are looking for."

"And what is the meaning, the mystery, the significance of it all, Corrie?"

"Why, that God made it, of course."

"I don't see what is so mysterious about that. Everybody believes that. Everything has to be *made* somehow, by someone."

"The mystery is in what it tells us about God. He put himself into every tiniest thing."

"Even an ugly old gray rock?"

"Of course. His hand can't touch anything without leaving his fingerprints behind—even on the simplest of rocks."

"Hmm . . . you do have a way of looking at things differently than most people. Is this how you write, too?"

"I don't know," I laughed.

"Have you ever written about streams and pine trees?"

"No. I just think about things when I'm watching them. Sometimes they find their way into things I write, but mostly they just get into my journal where nobody else sees them."

"You mentioned your journal before—tell me about it."

"I keep journals of things I do and think about. Sometimes I draw pictures in it or respond to books I've read. When I'm writing in my journal, I don't have to be as careful as if I'm writing an article, so I just let it be as personal as I want."

"You said journals. How many journals do you have?"

"I've filled up five—no, let's see . . . yes, five. I just started my sixth book in the almost eight years I've been keeping a journal."

He drew in a sigh, then turned to glance out the window. The pause in conversation suddenly made me realize how much I'd forgotten my nervousness and how much talking I'd been doing. A fresh wave of embarrassment swept over me.

"I can hardly believe it. I must have babbled on for ten or fifteen miles!"

"Please, don't fret about it," said Cal, turning slowly back to face me. His voice was soft and reflective. "I enjoy listening to you, Corrie. It takes me back to a simpler time in my own life when some of those things were important to me, too."

"Did you once live in the country?" I asked.

"A long time ago," he answered, and again that same wistful look filled his eyes and I heard the longing in his voice that I had detected earlier.

"I'd love to hear about it," I said.

A long silence followed. I could see a look of pain cross his face, and he turned to gaze outside for a while again. When he finally spoke, it was only to close the door into himself that he had opened just for an instant, and only a crack.

"Maybe someday, Corrie," he said slowly. "But I don't think I'm up to it right now."

CHAPTER 22

TRUTH OR OPPORTUNITY

We were just coming to Auburn, where the stage stopped for half an hour to pick up one more passenger, get the mail, and give the passengers time for coffee and food if anyone wanted it. Cal asked me if I'd like to join him in the restaurant for something to eat, but I said I'd rather just walk around and stretch my legs. After I'd answered him, I realized I was a little hungry, yet somehow I'd thought maybe he'd rather be alone after the way our conversation had ended. I opened my bag and pulled out the apple I'd brought along and munched on it as I walked up and down the main street of Auburn.

When we climbed back into the stage, Cal's gaiety had returned. It was more crowded now, but he was just as genial as ever, talking to the others, helping the elderly lady who had gotten on at Auburn to adjust to the bumps and noises, and speaking to me again in a way that put me completely at ease.

We talked back and forth, gradually working our way around to the reason for the ride in the first place.

"What am I supposed to say when we get there?" I asked him. "I've never made a speech before in my life."

"Are you nervous?"

"Of course. How could I not be?"

"Don't worry about a thing, Corrie. All you have to do is be yourself and people will love you."

"I've got to do a little more than that," I said. "I have to say *something*."

"Sure, but it hardly matters *what* you say. What the people

119

are coming out to see is a woman standing up there—and a pretty one!—with the men. Standing up and saying, 'Vote for Lincoln.' "

I don't know what got into me, but suddenly I lost my shyness and out of my mouth popped the words, "Come on, Cal. I'm not pretty, and you shouldn't lie like that."

The instant I said it, I wanted to retract the words! But he just laughed. "You are something, Corrie Hollister!" he said, still laughing. "Not afraid to speak your mind one bit. But you won't object if I disagree with you, will you? You're going to stand up there and folks are going to say to themselves, 'There's one beautiful young woman, and I'm going to listen to what she has to say!' So there, Corrie—like it or not. I'm not taking back a word of it!"

Now I was embarrassed again!

"But is it really true that it doesn't matter how good a speech I make?" I asked, trying to turn the discussion back toward Sacramento.

"Doesn't matter a bit. We want you there because of who you are, that's all. Dalton and the others know you're not a speech-maker."

"There's a big difference between speaking in front of people and writing down thoughts on paper when you're all alone," I said.

We bounced along for a while, then Cal asked me, "Why are you interested in politics, Corrie? How did you get involved in the first place?"

I stopped to think. "I suppose it was my mother's decision to run for mayor of Miracle Springs," I answered after a bit. "Actually, she's my stepmother—Almeda, you know. And it turned out she *didn't* run, but my pa did instead. It all happened in 1856, and we were so involved in it as a family, how could I help but be interested? So I wrote a few articles about the Miracle Springs election. Then with the presidential election going on at the same time, and Mr. Fremont being a Californian, well, I just kind of got drawn into it."

"But why did you *stay* interested? Why did you get *so* involved with the Fremont cause as to risk your life and do all you did, especially when you'd never met the man?"

"I don't know; I suppose it seemed the right thing to do."

"The *right* thing?"

"Yes. The more I found out about everything, the more I knew I had to stand up for the truth, and to write the truth so that people would know how things *really* were."

"Truth . . . hmm."

"For me there's no other reason to write at all. That's what everything's about—all of life, in fact."

"Like the Miracle Springs Creek?" suggested Cal.

"Yes," I said. "The creek, the election in '56, what kind of person I want to be. It's all about truth. The creek's got truth in it, if you know where to look for it. It seems to me that life's about learning to be a true person. That's what being a Christian is to me—not knowing a lot of religious things, but becoming a *true* person, a true daughter of God. That's what my writing's about too—learning to find life's good things, life's *right* things, life's *true* things—and then writing about them in a way folks can understand, in a way that gets down inside them. Whether I'm writing about creeks or trees or politics, I've got to make sure inside myself that it's *truth* I'm writing about."

Cal was very thoughtful for a minute. "An unusual approach to political reporting," he said at length. "And so," he added, "have you satisfied yourself that supporting Lincoln is the right and true thing to do?"

"I had to spend a lot of time thinking and praying about it," I answered. "It wasn't an easy decision. But, yes, I'm satisfied now that it's what I'm supposed to do, and so I'll give myself to stand up for the truth as I see it just as much as I did before with Mr. Fremont. What about you? Isn't that why you're in favor of Mr. Lincoln?"

Cal thought for a moment. Then a smile spread across his face. "My boss, Mr. Stanford, would not take it too kindly if I didn't," he said. "He is one of California's leading Republicans!"

"Why did you go to work for him," I asked, "if it wasn't because you believed in what he stood for?"

"Leland Stanford believes in himself," laughed Cal, "and his businesses and his railroad and making money."

"But surely you believe in *him*?"

122

"Of course I do. But I'm afraid it's on a more pragmatic level than because he stands for the truth. I hope you won't hate me, Corrie, but I believe in Mr. Stanford because I believe he represents the future, and therefore offers me the greatest opportunity to be in step with the future when it comes. Truth doesn't seem to me as important in this case as who holds the key to the future. Does Leland Stanford, or does former governor Latham, or does Congressman Burch with his idea of a separate California republic, or do the Breckinridge southern Democrats, or does Governor Downey, or does the state's new golden-tongued orator Thomas Starr King? Where does the future lie, Corrie? That seems to me the question. That is why I have cast my lot with Mr. Stanford and his cause. He'll be governor one day, mark my words. His railroad will span the continent. He may one day even live in the White House. And I want to be standing beside him if he does!"

"What about Mr. Lincoln? Do you believe in him in the same way?" I asked.

Cal's face turned thoughtful. "I can't say as I do, Corrie," he answered. "I think the North is very weak, both politically and economically. In a financial battle between North and South, the southern states would win hands down. With regard to the future of this nation, I do not see the North leading the way. For now it seems to me that the West is where the true future exists."

"For now?"

"Change that. Let me just say I came to the West because I saw the future moving in this direction."

We rode along for a while in silence. The three other passengers were occasionally making some attempts to carry on a conversation, but I think they were mostly listening to us. Whenever Cal and I stopped talking, it generally quieted down as if they were waiting for us to continue. Finally I picked the discussion up again.

"Is it all right if I ask you the same question you asked me?" I said. "Why did *you* get involved in politics?"

"A fair enough question," answered Cal. "I'll see if I can give you as straightforward an answer as you gave me."

He paused, thought for a minute, then went on. "The answer is very simple really—politics has been in my family as long as I have. Does the name Stephens mean anything to you?"

I shook my head.

"It's my mother's maiden name. My uncle, her brother, spent sixteen years in Congress in Washington, until just last year, and had served six terms in his state legislature before that. He is such a political creature that his very name raises images of the founding of the country itself—Alexander Hamilton Stephens."

"So it was in your blood?"

"In more ways than one. And I began to love it early in my life. I was only eight when my uncle packed his bags for Washington, but I remember it as distinctly as if it were yesterday. When we went up to visit him there, the sense of power the place exuded got into me and I knew I wanted to be part of it someday too. My uncle was a Whig. But he was a pragmatic man too, and he taught me to look for opportunity wherever and however it came. And so now here I am working for the new Republican party, which didn't even exist eight years ago."

He laughed at the thought.

"Don't you see, Corrie? It's all about opportunity! That's what politics represents to me. It's where the power is, where the future is. That's why my uncle said to me, 'Cal, the future's in the West. If you want a life in politics that'll take you to the top, seek it in California. That's where tomorrow's leaders are going to come from.' So I took his advice, and here I am!"

"You're involved in politics and with Mr. Stanford for where they will *take* you?"

"Do I detect a slightly negative tone?"

"I just wanted to know," I answered. "I never thought of that before, at least in relation to myself. I don't envision my writing *taking me* anywhere—at least not in the way you mean it."

"Your reputation is growing in importance. That doesn't mean anything to you?"

"I never think about it. I want to grow *inside*, as a person. But I never think about becoming important."

"Well, I do. I want to *be* somebody. I want my life to count. Don't you see, Corrie? People like you and me, young men and women with ideas and enthusiasm, we're going to be tomorrow's leaders of the country. Doesn't that excite you? Don't you want to be part of it?"

"I've never thought of it. What about what you said two hours ago about the simpler life? You told me never to leave the simple country life behind. It even sounded as if you wished you could go back to it yourself. Now you're saying that I ought to want to be important."

"I grew up in the country too," said Cal. "I suppose part of me looks back on my childhood with a kind of longing. But once the lure of politics began to get hold of me, with all the opportunities it afforded, I vowed to myself that I would use every opportunity, every situation, to the fullest."

"To the fullest . . . in what way?"

"For where it could take me, what it could do for me—for taking advantage of the opportunity in whatever ways I was able."

I fell silent, and we didn't pick up the same conversation again. Cal had certainly given me a lot to think about. We were both on our way to Sacramento to be involved in Mr. Lincoln's campaign together, and yet our reasons and motives seemed very different.

CHAPTER 23

SPEECHMAKING IN SACRAMENTO

They had offered to put me up in a big hotel in Sacramento, but I said I preferred to stay with Miss Baxter in her boarding-house.

The meeting was scheduled for the afternoon after we arrived. I must have taken an hour to get ready. Just pulling the dress over my head and trying to button the buttons with my trembling fingers was so hard I finally had to ask Miss Baxter to help me. The dress was a light brown cotton, with full sleeves, navy piping around the collar and lapels, and a matching navy ribbon around the waist. I wished Almeda had been there to help me get it all just right and brush my hair and tie it up with its ribbon. But Miss Baxter was a fine substitute. It was so nice to have a woman there to share the anxious moments with me!

Cal came to pick me up in a fancy buggy and complimented me on how I looked. But I was still dreadfully nervous.

A platform had been built downtown near the capital buildings and decorated with red, white, and blue banners. Flags were flying, and a band was playing peppy patriotic songs. Quite a crowd had already gathered, and wagons and buggies were still pulling up. It reminded me of the festive day in Miracle Springs back in '52, but one look around told me this was a much bigger and more important event. All the men were dressed in expensive suits, and just the looks on their faces told me they were probably important men in California's politics.

Most of them were, too. Cal introduced me to more than a

125

dozen people that day, and I can hardly remember a single one of them. I was so nervous before and so relieved after my brief time up on the platform that my mind was blank of everything else.

There were going to be speeches on behalf of all three of the candidates for president. In addition to me, Mr. Stanford and some other of his friends, Mr. Dalton and a famous orator named Edward D. Baker, all spoke for Abraham Lincoln. The Republicans were in the minority in California, as they were in the rest of the country. Up until this time, in the national elections California had always sided with the party that favored slavery. But now in 1860, when the line came to be drawn so clearly between North and South, and between slavery and antislavery, the Republicans hoped to break this record and bring California around and make it a free, pro-Union Republican state.

The split of the Democratic party, Cal told me, would help more than anything to make this possible. After the nomination of Stephen Douglas by the moderate wing of the party, the southern faction set up John Breckinridge as a candidate as well. On this day in Sacramento, many prominent Californians came out in favor of both men.

Governor Downey gave a speech in support of Douglas. I was surprised at how many famous western politicians were in favor of the southern cause and slavery. Former governor Latham supported Breckinridge, although he wasn't there that day because he was now serving in the U.S. Senate representing California. California's other senator, William Gwin, formerly from Mississippi, did happen to be present, and spoke on behalf of the southern cause and candidate Breckinridge. John Weller, also speaking for Breckinridge, actually brought up the issue of the South seceding from the Union. I couldn't believe slavery could be so important to the South that they would actually try to start a new country rather than to see the slaves set free.

I had my journal with me and I tried to write down some of what was said. But all the newspapers told about the speeches anyway, and I got copies the next day so I could read them over again. Weller said this: "I do not know whether Lincoln will be elected or not. I will personally urge every Californian to vote instead for John C. Breckinridge of the Southern Democratic party. I do know this, that if our efforts fail and if Lincoln is elected, and if he attempts to carry out his doctrines, the South will surely withdraw from the Union. And I should consider them less than men if they did not."

One speech got the biggest applause and was written up in all the newspapers of the state during the next few days—the one delivered by Edward Baker. He had been defeated a year before as candidate for Congress and then had gone up to Oregon where he had been elected to the Senate from the new state. He had come down to California and had been called upon to speak on behalf of the Republican party, freedom, and the election of Abraham Lincoln. People said afterward it was one of the greatest political speeches ever delivered in California. Baker said:

> Where the feet of my youth were planted, there, by Freedom, my feet shall stand. I will walk beneath her banner. I will glory in her strength. I have watched her, in history, struck down on a hundred chosen fields of battle. I have seen her friends fly from her. I have seen her foes gather round her. I have seen them bind her to the stake. I have seen them give her ashes to the winds, regathering them again that they might scatter them yet more widely. But when they turned to exult, I have seen her again meet them, face-to-face, resplendent in complete steel and brandishing in her strong right hand a flaming sword, red with insufferable light. I take courage. The people gather round her. The Genius of America will at last lead her sons to freedom.

After Baker's speech I wasn't any too anxious to walk up there on that platform, with four or five hundred people standing all around listening, and open my timid little mouth to try to say something. What could I say that could compare in any way with what Mr. Baker had said?

But there was no getting around it. And eventually I heard Mr. Dalton start to introduce me. I sat there listening to him, my whole body sweating and shaking, terrified at the ordeal that was about to come.

"Ladies and gentlemen, fellow Californians," he said, "you have heard from eminent statesmen today, from senators and governors and political leaders and men of industry and commerce.

128

But I now want to introduce to you a young lady of perhaps equal
reputation in some circles, a young lady whose simple and honest
words have been read in newspapers from one shining sea of this
great land all the way to the other; a young lady who, I must tell
you, is a bit nervous about all this. She is a country girl, yet her
words ring with truth whenever she sets pen to paper. Therefore
I know what she says to you today comes directly from the heart.
Ladies and gentlemen, I give you Miss Cornelia Belle Hollister."

I stood up. I glanced at Cal, sitting beside me, and he gave me
a smile of encouragement. I walked up the steps and to the front
of the platform.

I stood there for a moment. Everyone was quiet, all eyes looking up at me, waiting.

"I've never made a speech before in my life," I began. "I don't
know if this will even qualify as one now. They told me all I had
to do was say what I felt and thought about things, and that would
be good enough. I suppose I can do that."

My voice sounded so tiny, like a little mouse! All the other
men had loud, deep voices, and I sounded like a little girl. I didn't
think the people more than ten feet away would be able to hear a
thing I said!

"I've been thinking a lot about this election," I said after clearing my throat and trying to speak up a little louder. "I had to
think about which side I'd be on and what I ought to do about it.
I can't say as I'm a Democrat or a Republican, and it hardly
matters much since I can't vote anyway."

A small wave of laughter spread among the men who were
listening. There were a good number of women there too, and by
now most of them had come forward as close to the platform as
they could. They were all watching me intently.

"I don't know Mr. Lincoln or Mr. Douglas, or Mr. Breckinridge, for that matter, who I just found out today is running too.
To tell you the truth, I don't really know too much about any of
the issues except for the issue of slavery and freedom. But if you
want a woman's point of view, that's just about the most important
issue of all. And that's the one I spent nearly all my time thinking
over when it came to this election.

"The conclusion I came to is that freedom is a mighty important thing in this country of ours. The Constitution talks about it, and I guess it seems to me that if people in the United States of America can't be free, then I don't know where else in the world freedom's going to find a place to grow. Some of the Democrats might say that the freedom the Constitution talks about doesn't apply to Negroes because they aren't people in the same way as the rest of us are, so they don't have the same right to be free. But I don't agree with that. I'm a woman, and I don't have the right to vote. But that doesn't make me feel any less of a human being, and I don't figure too many Negroes feel like they're less than human, either.

"It looks to me like freedom's a thing that's got to apply to everybody, or else it doesn't mean much. It's got to apply to women and Negroes, to rich people and poor people, to folks in California just like it does to folks in Alabama or anywhere else. Some of these men we've been listening to today have said you ought to vote for Mr. Douglas or Mr. Breckinridge because it'll be better for the South, and the whole country, or because Mr. Lincoln's made so many strong remarks about being against slavery that the South will be so mad if he gets elected, there's no telling what they might do.

"All of that doesn't seem to have anything to do with freedom, if you ask me. The Democrats have been the party that supported slavery all these years. Now the Republicans are trying to change that by standing for freedom. It seems to me that's about the most important thing of all. I don't know much about money and the economy and all that. But if folks in these United States aren't free, then it doesn't seem to me that our money means much, or the word freedom or our Constitution either.

"Four years ago I tried to write some things to help Colonel Fremont get to the White House, because he was against slavery too, just like Mr. Lincoln is. He got defeated, and I figured my efforts had been wasted.

"But now I've got a chance to try to do something again, and I hope the people of this country will do better by the cause of freedom for our people than last time. That's why I decided, after thinking about it a good long while, to support Abraham Lincoln. No, I can't vote. But if I could, I'd vote for Mr. Lincoln, and it seems to me you all ought to vote for him too."

I turned and walked back down the steps and sat down. I was sweating and trembling from head to foot. I never heard any of the applause, but Cal told me they loved it, especially all the women.

The next morning, on the *front page* of the Sacramento *Union*, I was shocked to read the headline over a two-column article: *BAKER, DOWNEY, WELLER, HOLLISTER ADDRESS SACRAMENTO ELECTORATE.* And toward the end of the article, they actually quoted from *my* speech!

CHAPTER 24

DINNER AT LIVINGSTONE'S

By the time all the festivities of the day were finished, I was exhausted, not just from having given the speech, but from everything that had followed—talking to people, shaking hands, greeting a long line of women well-wishers who treated me like some kind of hero for "the cause," as they put it, although I had no idea what cause they were talking about.

I had tried to keep smiling and stay friendly, but by the end of the afternoon I was *so* tired. Cal stayed at my side nearly the whole time, encouraging me, telling me what to do if I got confused, picking up the conversation for me if I didn't know what to say. All day long I kept meeting people, most of whom I can't even remember. But they all looked important.

Then he took me and showed me inside some of the capital buildings, including where the legislature met. "Here's where your father will be one of these days," he said, and I thought to myself that they shouldn't count on it because Pa was an independent man who was used to making up his own mind and not having anyone else do his thinking for him. But just the thought of Pa in the midst of all these fancy, dressed-up men brought a smile to my lips. I couldn't imagine *him* making a speech in front of that great big Assembly hall! And if he did, he'd no doubt shake things up once in a while!

"What's so funny, Corrie?" Cal asked.

"Oh nothing," I replied, still smiling to myself.

"You've got something on your mind. You can't hide that."

"I was just thinking about what it would be like if Pa *was* to come here," I said.

"I hope he does," replied Cal. "This place could use more men of his caliber."

Finally, around six o'clock, Cal took me to dinner at a place called Livingstone's. We drove up to the front of Livingstone's, and Cal jumped out of the buggy, took my hand, and helped me down to the street, while someone else hopped up and drove the horses around to the back. Then Cal slipped his arm through mine and led me inside. I don't know if I'd ever felt so out of place in my life! If this was what it was like to be a *lady*, I wasn't sure I liked it.

Livingstone's turned out to be a fancier restaurant than I had ever seen—even nicer than the International House, where Almeda had taken me on our first trip to San Francisco. Mingling around the front door were several men in tuxedos and women in silk dresses. The flash of diamonds caught my eye now and then. Once we were inside, I realized all the more what a glamorous place Cal had brought me to. I heard music playing from somewhere, and the waiters were dressed up to look like preachers.

I was so nervous, I felt like I was going to stumble and fall over my dress with every step. And Cal was close to me, our arms linked together, my dress brushing up alongside him, my arm and shoulder touching his as we slowly made our way to our table behind one of the fancy-dressed waiters. As I sat down, Cal went behind me and helped scoot my chair in.

I'd never been treated like this, and I hardly knew what to do! Just the thought of Robin O'Flaridy made me laugh inside at the comparison. Cal was such a fine and gentlemanly *man*! I took stock of the white linen tablecloth, the candle in the middle of the table, the wine glasses and silver, which all made me think: What is Corrie Hollister doing *here*?

I might have been California's best-known woman reporter, but I couldn't make heads or tails of the menu. Cal helped me order. I had roast lamb with some fancy kind of potatoes with cheese mixed into them. It was tasty, but I didn't have much of an appetite. I don't know if it was because of how tired I was, but I could eat only about half of what the waiter brought me.

"You stole the show today, Corrie," said Cal across the table.

"I did not," I responded. "You heard all those other men, and the clapping after Mr. Baker's speech!"

"Those men are all politicians. Edward Baker's on his way to Washington. Speechmaking is the business of men like that. I'll wager Baker's given several hundred speeches in his life—all smooth, polished, every word just as it ought to be. But *you*— your speech was different. It was from the heart . . . it was just *you*! I saw Dalton's face as he was watching."

"What . . . what was he thinking?" I asked, wondering what he meant.

"He was sitting back in his chair with just the hint of a smile on his face. He knew well and good that he'd found the right young lady."

"He didn't say anything to me afterward."

"Alexander Dalton can be a funny man at times. But he knows politics like no one in this state. And you mark my words, you will hear from him again. I tell you, Corrie, there were some people there today paying more attention to you than anyone else who got up on that platform the whole day."

"I don't believe a word of it," I said, although I looked down at my plate in embarrassment at the same time. I couldn't help feeling pride at his words. I suppose part of me knew he was just trying to make me feel good about the day, yet another part wanted to believe he was sincere and wouldn't say anything he didn't really mean.

"Well, there's nothing I can do to convince you," said Cal sincerely, "even if I do know these men and their kind better than you do." He paused, then put his fork down and looked across the table at me. "But I will tell you this, Corrie," he added, "and even if you can't believe the other, I hope you will believe this. You were not only the prettiest speaker in all of Sacramento today, in *my* humble estimation you were also the most eloquent. If Abraham Lincoln does not carry California, it will be only because the men of this state were too deaf to heed the words of his most ardent supporter."

The rest of the evening was lost in a fuzzy blur. Even as I lay in bed hours later, I could hardly recall the specifics of it in any pattern that made sense. By the time I tried to write about it in my journal as I bounced along in the stagecoach going home, it had nearly all escaped me. The feelings inside lingered, but what we had done, where we had gone, what we had seen, and the words we had spoken—I could recall none of them.

I do know that Cal showed me nearly all of Sacramento—Sutter's fort, some of the old original houses still standing from the 1840s. We got out and walked along the river just about the time the sun was setting and the half moon was coming up. Then we rode again in the buggy, for hours it seemed, until the city was dark and night sounds faintly echoed about in the distance.

It was very quiet and still when at last Cal pulled the horse up in front of Miss Baxter's. The only sounds were the crickets in the trees lining the streets. Even the occasional shouts from the saloons down in the center of town were so faint as to be drowned out by the thunderous chirping of the tiny creatures overhead.

Cal got down, tied the reins to the fence, then came over to my side, held up his hand to take mine, and helped me down to the street. I was finally getting used to such treatment, although it still brought about a fluttering sensation all through me. But I wasn't prepared for him keeping hold of my hand as he led me up to Miss Baxter's porch!

We walked toward the house slowly, in silence. When we reached the porch, Cal stopped, still grasping my hand, and turned toward me.

"Corrie," he said, "this has been one of the most pleasurable days I have spent in all my life. You are an engaging and wonderful young woman."

He looked deeply into my eyes. The light from the moon reflected from his, seeming to draw me right into them. My heart was pounding so hard, I thought the whole boardinghouse must hear, and that windows would begin opening any moment to find out what the racket was!

Then he slowly drew my hand up, bent slightly, and kissed the top of my hand as he held it between his fingers. I just stood there, compliantly watching as his lips rested for just a second on my hand. Yet inside, my heart and brain were exploding with the sounds of a thousand waves crashing against a stormy shore.

He raised his head, released my hand, and softly uttered the words, "Good-night, Corrie."

Then he turned and was gone. I remained standing on the porch, watching him bound up into the carriage seat, and briskly urge the horse into action with a flick of the rein and a click of his tongue.

I was alone, in the silent darkness of the Sacramento night. Alone with only the sound of a million crickets in my ears and ocean waves somewhere down in my heart.

I can't remember opening the door and walking inside the house, or climbing the darkened stairs to the room I always stayed in whenever I came to Sacramento. I cannot remember taking off my bonnet, nor getting out of my long dress and tossing it across the chair. Somehow I got into my night clothes, although I don't recall that, either.

When I next came to myself I was lying on my back in the soft bed, moonlight streaming through the window into the room. Just lying there. Thinking, yet not thinking. A smile on my face, my heart full, yet my mind empty. Full of feelings, yet none that could be expressed in words.

The only words I was aware of were those three that kept repeating themselves over and over and over . . . *Good-night, Corrie.*

I don't know how long I lay there. But somehow, eventually, my eyelids closed with heaviness, the sound of the waves and the crickets gradually subsided, and sleep slowly stole over me.

CHAPTER 25

THE TWO LETTERS

It seemed kind of dull at home for the next couple of weeks. I couldn't find much energy to interest myself in anything. I went on long walks and rides and pretty much kept to myself. I doubt I did anybody much good when I went into town and tried to busy myself with Mine and Freight business.

Marcus Weber looked me over with his big drooping eyes of concern every day I came in, and finally, when he couldn't stand it any longer, he burst out one day, "What in tarnation be ailin' you, Miss Corrie? Blamed if I just can't stand to see you lookin' so sad!"

I smiled, but from the reaction on his beautiful, tender black face I could tell it didn't reassure him much. "Nothing, Marcus," I said. "I am just fine. Just a little tired."

I know he wasn't convinced. He looked me over for another several seconds, with an unspoken expression of concern flooding across his humble features. He gave me a nervous fatherly hug, and I almost thought I detected a tear in one of his eyes. Then he turned and went back out to the livery. In those brief moments, I felt my heart's eyes could see down into Marcus far deeper than his mere words expressed.

It was such a revelation. I could see how much he really loved me! To be loved like that, when you realize how deep it goes into somebody *else's* heart, has to be one of the most humbling things in all of life.

Pa acted the same way, looking at me with concern, asking if I was sick, telling me I ought to be eating more or I was going to waste away. Almeda didn't say much; she just smiled at me a lot, and gave me more than my share of motherly hugs whenever she had the chance. She knew what it was, and knew that I had to work through it as best I could on my own.

A couple of letters arrived early in August that helped me get back on my feet and quit thinking so much about Cal Burton. I couldn't stop thinking about him altogether, but having something to *do* at least got my brain and hands occupied with activity.

The first was a letter to Pa from Alexander Dalton. He said the time was getting very close when Pa would have to make up his mind about whether to run or not. He stressed again his assurance that Drummond Hollister was exactly the kind of man the state of California needed, and his confidence that if Pa made up his mind soon, there would be victory in November. He would handle the whole campaign and all the details, he said. It would not cost Pa a cent. All he had to do was give his consent and perhaps make two or three speeches between Miracle Springs and Sacramento—Grass Valley and Auburn, and maybe one or two other towns besides.

The second letter was addressed to me. My heart jumped for a moment, but then settled back into place when I saw the familiar handwriting of my editor at the *Alta*. Not so long ago, a note or letter from Mr. Kemble would send me into a positive tizzy. Now I found myself opening it almost with disappointment. His words, however, were sufficient to bring a tingle to my skin.

> You always continue to astound me, Corrie Hollister. I never gave you two cents' worth of a chance of succeeding in this business, but you've been writing for me for six years and are one of the most well-known reporters I have. And now you've taken up speechmaking and politics besides! Is there anything you don't do?
>
> In any case, I have heard the reports from Sacramento where, as I understand it, you were quite impressive. My Republican friends are badgering me for an article under your byline in support of the Lincoln-Hamlin ticket. Dalton says he will pay half if I will offer you enough myself to encourage you to set your pen to paper again as you did, unfortunately in vain, for the Fremont cause. He also assures me that, for the right article, he could almost guarantee publication in

most of the major eastern cities. We would like an article of some length, which men and politicians would heed as well as the women who make up your customary readership. This is the title we would like to use: "Why Abraham Lincoln Should Be President—A Woman's Point of View."

Can you do it? We will pay you a total of ten dollars. We would need the finished article by September 15 in order to get it to the east and published within the first week or two of October.

I remain, sincerely yours,

EDWARD KEMBLE

CHAPTER 26

A BOLD DECISION

I don't know what Pa intended to do about the letter he had received, but I needed something to occupy my mind for a while, and I liked what Mr. Kemble had suggested. I started on the article right away.

I had no sooner begun when thoughts of Zack began to intrude into my mind. Maybe it was from seeing Pa wrestling with his decision, and knowing Zack was part of what he was thinking about in it all. There still had been no word from or about Zack, and even though we didn't talk about it much, we were all worried.

I couldn't help feeling personally involved. I didn't feel responsible for his leaving, but I did feel that maybe I'd let Zack down too, that a lot of the things he'd said to Pa applied to me as well. I even felt that some of what I'd done, the opportunities I'd had and the attention I'd received, all went into making him feel less important. It wasn't true, of course, but his outburst surely made it seem like that's how he felt. I thought we were about as close as a brother and sister could be, and then I found out that he was hurting about all kinds of things no one knew about. It wasn't right for him to suffer like that, and I began to feel that it was important for me to do something about it.

At first I thought of writing Zack a letter. What better way to get in touch with him? He'd have his hands on it in just a few days!

Then I realized what a stupid idea it was. He might have his hands on it, but a letter would just be stuck inside a mail pouch in his saddlebags, and he would never see it! We had no idea where he was staying, so there was no way to address a letter actually *to* him.

All the while I was working on my Lincoln article, Zack kept running through my mind. I'd see his face, first laughing, then serious. I'd see him riding on a horse like the wind. I recalled our first coming to California and how he'd tried so hard to act grown up. I remembered the pain I could see underneath the brave exterior. I remembered how he and Pa had a hard time at first, but how they had become friends—or so I'd thought. I remembered the first gun Pa gave him that Christmas and how proud Zack had been, and how much he'd loved working at the mine with the three men.

So many memories kept rising and falling into my thoughts, all now clouded over with the pain and hurt of his bitter words of anger the day he'd left.

One day a daring plan came into my mind—in its own way almost as daring, I suppose, as Zack's going off as he had. I went to talk to Pa about it.

"What would you think," I asked, "if I was to go find Zack?"

"Tarnation, girl!" he exclaimed. "How you figure on doing that?"

"I'll follow the Express route east till I get to Zack's leg."

"You're gonna ride along with the Pony Express! You're a decent rider, Corrie. But you ain't gonna keep up with *them* skinny young wild men!"

"I don't have to keep up with them, Pa," I said. "I only have to follow the route. I figure I'll go from station to station, asking as I go about Zack. Somebody's bound to know of him, and somewhere along the line I'll run into him."

Pa rubbed his chin and made like he was thinking. "It's a foolhardy enough notion for my daughter to have thought of," he said after a while, breaking into a grin.

"Is it all right, Pa?" I asked eagerly.

"'Course it ain't all right. This is crazier than any of your schemes four years ago!" Pa's tone was lighthearted, but I could tell he meant it, too.

I laughed kind of sheepishly.

"What do you want me to say?" he went on. "That I like the idea? It's dangerous out there."

"We have to find out about Zack sometime, Pa," I said.

"Yeah," Pa sighed. "And I reckon by now you *have* proved yourself, and I trust you. But I don't like the idea of you being out there alone. I don't like it for a second, and I don't see how I could do anything but try to keep you from it just like I did Zack."

"But I'd only be gone for a short time, Pa. Not like what Zack wanted to do—not to take a job."

Pa sighed. "I'm as anxious about Zack as you are. Why don't you take the stage?"

"The stage doesn't follow the same route till it gets to Wyoming."

"The wagon trail?"

"There are no wagon trains going east this late in the year. I wouldn't find anybody to hook up with that way, either. Besides, the California Trail goes north of the Express route. There's no way I can see to find him except to go straight out to Placerville and Carson City and then straight across Nevada toward Salt Lake City."

"I tell you, it's dangerous territory, Corrie. Your ma died out there from the heat. You know that better than I do. There's Indians, desert, sometimes no water."

"That was almost ten years ago, Pa. It's more civilized now. There are horse-changing stations every twenty or twenty-five miles. There are people, food, water, a place to rest. If I just told them my brother was a rider, they'd be hospitable enough, and even let me sleep the night."

Pa thought again. "Yeah, I reckon that's so," he said. "Still, I don't much like the idea of you being that far from home alone."

All of a sudden *another* wild idea struck me.

"Why don't you come with me, Pa?" I said. "Let's go find Zack together!"

Pa's face remained blank, not twitching so much as a muscle. But his eyes betrayed that somewhere deep behind them, his mind was spinning fast to take in the words I had said and to figure out what to do about them.

"You know his being gone's eating at you, Pa," I said after a minute, "just like it is me. Let's both go out there and find him and tell him we're sorry for not letting him know how we felt, and tell him we love him."

Still Pa was silent, thinking it all over. He stood there for a long time, looking out into the distance. Finally he turned to me.

"You think he'd listen to me?" he said softly, the pain and uncertainty all too clear in his voice.

"Of course he would, Pa," I said. "What son's going to turn his own pa away?"

"Seems like that's just what he wanted to do."

"Oh, Pa, no he didn't. He was just feeling pain and confusion. He didn't know what to do with it all. I think you got in the way, that's all."

"But I was the cause of it all."

"No you weren't, Pa. Kids blame their parents for all kinds of things that are really no one's fault but their *own*. They just don't want to look down inside themselves, so they blame the nearest person around."

"Did you ever do that, Corrie?" asked Pa. He and I had lots of personal talks together. But when he said those words, there was an earnestness in his voice I'd never heard before. Never in my life had I seen a man so vulnerable as Pa was at that moment, so stripped of all the barriers men usually put up to shield themselves from other people. I felt I was looking all the way to the bottom of Pa's very soul, where there was a tender human being just as capable of feelings and suffering and questions and pain and worry as any woman or any child. It's not the kind of thing most kids ever get the chance to see in their parents, but I saw it right then in my pa, and it pulled me all the deeper into him and made me love him all the more.

He was looking at me intently, almost as if he were afraid of the answer I would give him.

"When we first got here," I said, "there were a couple of times I felt hurt, Pa. But Ma had just died. I was so confused about everything, and I was only fifteen."

"Did you blame me for what happened?" Pa asked, still with the earnest, transparent, questioning probing in his eyes.

Again, I thought hard. "I can't say as there wasn't any pain, Pa," I said. "That was a hard time for all of us. But no, after we were together awhile, I never blamed you, Pa. I got to know you too well. I got to know what was inside that heart of yours. I found out how much you loved Ma, how much you loved all of us and missed us . . . and how much you loved me. How could I blame you for anything, Pa, once I really knew who you were . . . once I knew how full of love you were?"

Pa was still gazing straight at me with those manly, loving, almost pleading eyes of his. But as I was speaking they had slowly filled with tears. His lips remained unmoved, but in those sparkling eyes I could see his relief.

We just stood, holding each other's gaze for a minute. Then finally Pa did smile, and as he did he took me in his arms, drew me to him, and embraced me with a strength that almost squeezed the breath out of me.

"Thank you, Corrie," he said, his voice just the slightest bit quivery.

"Yes, Pa," I whispered.

"I'm sorry for the pain you felt."

"It's long past now."

"Not for Zack," he said.

"For me it is, Pa. And you have to remember that I know you better than he does."

"It means more to me than you can know, Corrie, that you believe in me, and don't blame me. That means more to a man than his kin can ever realize."

We stood for another minute or two in each other's arms. "I love you, Pa," I said finally.

Just a moment more we stood; then Pa withdrew his hands from around me, pulled back, and looked at me, his blinking eyes drying again. He smiled broadly.

"Then let's you and me go find Zack!" he said.

CHAPTER 27

THE PONY EXPRESS

The idea for the Pony Express came from a businessman by the name of William Russell, who hoped that the government would pay his company—Russell, Majors, and Waddell—to have mail delivered speedily coast to coast. He proposed that they be paid one thousand dollars a week for two trips in both directions. The government never did pay for the service, and the costs involved turned out to be as high as ten to fifteen thousand dollars a week instead.

Before the Pony Express began in April of 1860, mail took twenty-five days to go from the East Coast to California—*if* the stagecoach didn't break a wheel, run into snow, or get attacked by Indians! Compared with how isolated California had been from the rest of the country in the early 1800s, even that was mighty fast. But when the organizers of the Pony Express said they would take mail between St. Joseph, Missouri, and Sacramento in ten days or less, everyone was amazed and wondered if such speed was possible.

Naturally, with Zack's fondness for horses, we had been curious and had followed the development of the idea with interest. Like all the papers, the *Alta* carried detailed stories about the first few mail crossings. Even in the midst of all the political news of 1860, some of the Pony Express riders became nationally known heroes. I read all the news articles that had been written for over a year now about it. Zack had sent off for some pamphlets too, and I had saved all the articles I'd read from different papers. So now with Pa and me planning to go find him, I pulled out everything I'd accumulated and read through it again.

Actually, the idea wasn't really Russell's at all, because there had been something like the Pony Express during the Roman Empire. And in the 1200s, Kublai Khan, the emperor of China, had a huge system of communication with stations stretching all the way from China to Europe, and with as many as four hundred fresh horses at every station, and thousands and thousands of messengers.

But for the United States the idea was new. And with mountains and deserts and Indians and bandits and no roads and no station houses, it was all a pretty big undertaking for Mr. Russell's company to get started. We had been reading about it in the papers for months before the horses actually began carrying mail.

There were to be eighty expert light riders riding between eighty relay stations, and making use of four to five hundred fast and hardy top-quality Indian horses. Forty of the riders would be stretched out in a line going east, the other forty in a line going west—all of them going back and forth both ways from their home base. It turned out later that there were two hundred riders in all—eighty in the saddle at all times, and the others resting between rides and replacements.

The mail would be carried by a leather cover that fit right over the saddle, called a *mochila*. There were four pouches on all four corners of the *mochila*, each of which had a lock on it. The keys were kept only in St. Joseph and Sacramento—the two end points of the Express—and at Salt Lake City in the middle.

From California, the route of the Express went to Placerville, up over the Sierra Nevadas and down into Carson City, Nevada. From there it went straight across the high desert of the Great Basin and over the awful salt flats to Salt Lake. That was the only real city along the way, and was about a third of the whole distance. From Salt Lake the riders went gradually north up into the Rockies, past Fort Bridger, through South Pass, and to Casper, Wyoming. Then they started south, to Fort Laramie, and down onto the plains of Nebraska, following the same routes as the Mormon Trail and the Oregon Trail, down to Fort Kearny, into northeastern Kansas and to St. Joseph. The whole distance from Sacramento was 1,966 miles.

So many eager young boys wanted to join the Pony Express right at first that they could have probably been hired cheaply. But Russell, Majors, and Waddell decided to pay them over a hundred dollars a month—high pay for anybody! As time went on, though, even that much money wasn't enough to keep some of them riding for the Express!

I don't know how God-fearing the owners of the company were, but they must have had some religious beliefs, because every rider that signed on, besides being given a lightweight rifle and a Colt revolver, was also given a Bible to carry with him. Riders also received the clothes that became the "uniform" of the Pony Express—a bright red shirt and blue dungarees. I never did understand, given as much trouble as they had with the Indians, why they made the riders dress so brightly!

Before he was hired, every rider had to sign a pledge that read:

> I do hereby swear, before the Great and Living God, that during my engagement, and while I am an employee of Russell, Majors, & Waddell, I will, under no circumstances, use profane language; that I will drink no intoxicating liquors; that I will not quarrel or fight with any other employee of the firm, and that in every respect I will conduct myself honestly, be faithful to my duties, and so direct all my acts as to win the confidence of my employers. So help me God.

At least if Zack had to leave home, I was glad it was to work for a company with high standards of morality like that. I just hoped all those who signed that pledge kept to their word and lived by it!

CHAPTER 28

PA AND I TAKE TO THE TRAIL

With the history it had and the reputation the Pony Express had already gained, when Pa and I left Sacramento it was almost as if we were following in the footsteps of George Washington. It seems odd to talk about California and the West as being part of history when everything was so new out here. But if the gold rush and the Pony Express didn't make us westerners part of history, nothing ever would.

A fellow named Sam Hamilton rode the first leg between Sacramento and Sportsman's Hall. The Express left Sacramento every Tuesday and Saturday. Since we had arrived late Monday, we stayed at Miss Baxter's and decided to leave at the same time. Pa was excited, and wanted to see how long we could keep pace with him.

But Sam was a skinny little fellow, and his horse not much bigger. To give them an advantage when trying to outrun Indians, each animal's load was limited to 165 pounds—20 pounds for the mail, 25 pounds for equipment, and 120 pounds for the rider. Zack must have lied about his weight, because I knew he weighed at least 130 or 140 pounds. But little Sam Hamilton might have been only 110!

When we took off down the street out of Sacramento, Hamilton was a block ahead of me and Pa before we'd gone a mile! He glanced back, lifted his hat in final greeting, gave us a shout of *Good Luck,* and gradually disappeared in a cloud of dust. Finally Pa pulled up his horse, turned around at me laughing, and said, "We gave it a gallant effort, Corrie! But there ain't no way we're

147

gonna keep up with him for even two miles!"

"And if we keep running our horses like this," I yelled as we reined them down to a gentle canter, "they won't make it past Placerville!"

Already the dust cloud surrounding little Sam Hamilton was fading into the distance. I could hardly imagine that the mail pouch he was carrying would be in Missouri in ten days or less!

Pa and I slowed up and walked for about ten minutes, Pa breaking out in laughter every so often at how ridiculous it was for us to think we were going to keep up with the Express rider. Then we eased our two horses on into a trot. If we didn't move at a little bit of a pace, we would never get to Nevada.

We were obviously not going to make it to a station house every night, so we would spend some nights alone out on the trail. With Pa along, I felt as safe as if we had our own private detachment of Cavalry. There would not be any danger of Indian attack until well into Nevada, and we hoped by then to have had some word about Zack.

The weather proved better for us than it had been back in April for that first "Pony" run. It was beautiful climbing up high into the Sierras, although the trail was narrow and rocky in places, with huge cliffs on the edge falling away into deep gorges and canyons. I couldn't imagine how Warren Upson had made it through here at all in the snowy blizzard of that first run!

"Listen to this, Pa," I said as we sat around our campfire on our second night out. I had been reading an account of the first runs of the Express from some papers I'd brought along, keeping track of what had happened as we followed along the same route. "It was snowing here on that very first run."

"Hard to make their time in a blizzard."

"But they did it! Want me to read it to you?"

"Sure," said Pa, sipping his coffee. "I ain't going nowhere. Maybe I'll fall asleep with you reading to me!"

I began: *"Everything had been arranged on that first day for the two riders to leave St. Joseph and Sacramento at the same time, one heading east, the other heading west. . . ."*

I stopped for a second, then said, "I wonder what it was like when the two batches of mail passed each other. It must have been somewhere in Wyoming."

"Getting a little ahead of your story, ain't you?" said Pa.

"But don't you wonder if the riders stopped and chatted or if they just blew by each other with a shout and wave?"

"To tell you the truth, I never thought of it."

"How I wish I could have been there to watch it!"

"I'm gonna be sound asleep before you have that mail pouch out of Sacramento! Now you got my curiosity up—come on, read me the story, girl."

"Yes, Pa," I said with a smile. "First let me read you a short little notice out of the *Alta*."

My paper had been involved in the Pony Express right from the beginning, and we had been watching it closely all year, especially after Zack's leaving. But only the names of the most well-known riders were ever mentioned, so we had never seen anything about Zack. The April 3 edition of that year had an article on the festivities about the first rider leaving San Francisco, and that's what I read to Pa.

"The first Pony Express started yesterday afternoon, from the Alta Telegraph Company on Montgomery Street. The saddlebags were duly lettered 'Overland Pony Express,' and the horse (a wiry little animal) was dressed with miniature flags. He proceeded, just before four o'clock, to the Sacramento boat, and was loudly cheered by the crowd as he started. . . . The express matter amounted to 85 letters, which at $5 per letter gave a total receipt of $425."

"Didn't you tell me that first fellow wasn't even a Pony Express rider at all?" said Pa.

I laughed again. "He was just a messenger who worked at the paper," I answered.

James Randall told me later how much he'd wished he could go farther. But he only rode three blocks to the waterfront, and then got on the steamer for Sacramento with San Francisco's part of the mail. It was in Sacramento that the route of the Pony Express *really* started, despite Mr. Kemble's attempt to make San Francisco and the *Alta* seem like the most important parts of the whole thing!

"You ever gonna get back to that story you started out of the *Bee*?"

"I'm trying, Pa." I picked up the first paper again and finally read to Pa the whole article.

"Sam Hamilton was the first rider out of Sacramento on April 3. He rode sixty miles to the station at Sportsman's Hall, where he handed off the mochila and leather pouches to Warren 'Boston' Upson, who had to cross the treacherous Sierra Nevadas. There had just been a fresh snowfall, and a new storm was on the way. The very first day out from Sacramento proved to be one of the most dangerous. Warren found himself in the middle of a blinding blizzard crossing over the mountains, having to walk his pony on foot part of the way, and many times nearly losing the trail. At last he made it safely to his station house at Friday's Station, right on the California border.

"Robert Haslam took over next, riding across the perilous Great Basin to Fort Churchill, Nevada. This was one of the worst parts of the whole route, with many mountain ranges, rivers which often disappeared into 'sinks' in the ground and were hard to follow, and broken canyons, rocky terrain, wild animals, rattlesnakes, a critical lack of water in summer, snow in winter, and Indians besides. The long distance across Nevada and Utah was the most hazardous of all."

"Not much wonder why Zack found himself an opening there," Pa interrupted. Neither of us said it right then, but it also explained why we were so worried about him. Already, in the first five months of the Express, there had been numerous attacks reported, and several killings of station people. Some whole stations had been burned to the ground.

I put down the Sacramento paper to read the account from a Salt Lake City reporter who told about the midpoint of that first run. Many of the riders in Utah were Mormon boys who knew the difficult terrain in both directions out of Salt Lake City. Although this was not an exact halfway point, it was close enough to be considered the major intersection between eastbound and westbound mail. The first riders reached Salt Lake within two days of each other. The *Alta* later ran the article that had appeared in Salt Lake in the *Deseret News* on April 11.

The first Pony Express from the West left Sacramento at 12 P.M. on the night of the third inst., and arrived on the night of the seventh, inside of prospectus time. The roads were heavy, the weather stormy. The last seventy-five miles were made in five hours and fifteen minutes in a heavy rain.

The Express from the East left St. Joseph, Mo., at 6:30

P.M. on the evening of the third and arrived in this city at 6:25 P.M. on the evening of the ninth. The difference in time between this city and St. Joseph is something near one hour and fifteen minutes, bringing us within six days' communication with the frontier, and seven days from Washington—a result which we, accustomed to receive news three months after date, can well appreciate.

The weather has been very disagreeable and stormy for the past week and in every way calculated to retard the operation of the company, and we are informed that the Express eastward was five hours in going from this place to Snyder's Mill, a distance of twenty-five miles.

The probability is that the Express will be a little behind time in reaching Sacramento this trip, but when the weather becomes settled and the roads good, we have no doubt that they will be able to make the trip in less than ten days.

After putting down the *Alta* reprint, again I read from the *Bee* as Pa listened.

"Up through the Rockies out of Salt Lake, then through South Pass, past the famous landmark Independence Rock, and across the Platte River to Fort Laramie. This is the major stop where riders could feel a sense of civilization again. Fort Laramie is one of the major trading posts and army headquarters of the Rockies region, where trappers, Indians, emigrants, and travelers all mix with one another.

"From Fort Laramie down to the Cottonwood Springs station and into Nebraska, the riders regularly pass stagecoaches and wagon trains, as their route follows already well-worn paths. Through woodlands gradually descending down into the plains and across buffalo and antelope country, riders are again likely to encounter Indian lodges or tepee villages, until they arrive at Fort Kearny in Nebraska, which was originally built to protect travelers along the Oregon Trail.

"Across Nebraska and Kansas at this time of year, the trail is heavy with wagon trains. The Kickapoo Indians of Kansas are mostly peaceful and friendly farmers who had learned to get on very well with the white man, and thus gave the Pony Express Riders no trouble. And across the Missouri River from Kansas lay the final destination of the eastbound rider—St. Joseph!

"The first two runs arrived at their respective destinations at almost

152

the same time. From St. Joseph to Sacramento it had taken nine days and twenty-three hours—one hour ahead of schedule. The eastbound trip had taken one hour longer—exactly ten days!"

I laid down the paper. If Pa wasn't asleep yet, he would be soon. It was dark and the fire was getting a little low. Everything was quiet except for the night sounds—mostly crickets. I put a couple more pieces of wood on the fire and watched them spark and flare up. Then I settled down into my bedroll, watching the flames but reflecting back on that day when the first Pony Express rider from Missouri had reached Sacramento and then gone on to San Francisco.

What a celebration there had been that April 13! I wish we could have been there, but we heard about it as if we had been. Both the Senate and the Assembly of the legislature adjourned and the whole city turned out to welcome Sam Hamilton, returning from Sportsman's Hall, where he had been waiting for Warren Upson to return with the eastbound pouches. Sam was given a hero's welcome as he hurried to the steamer to take the mail on downriver to San Francisco. He didn't arrive there until the middle of the night, but that didn't stop the torchlight celebration, band music, fire engines, cheering, booming of cannons, and speechmaking, including one from my editor, Mr. Kemble! The people of San Francisco rejoiced, for it seemed that their isolation from the rest of the world was over.

It was a significant year for the Pony Express, with so much news going on between North and South, and over the election. The news that was carried back and forth between East and West was now less than a week and a half old, instead of nearly a month old! The news people were most excited of all. An article in the *Sacramento Union* read:

Yesterday's proceedings, impromptu though they were, will long be remembered in Sacramento. The more earnest part of the "Pony" welcome had been arranged earlier in the day. This was the cavalcade of citizens to meet the little traveler a short distance from the city and escort him into town. Accordingly, late in the day, a deputation of about eighty persons, together with a deputation of the Sacramento Hussars, assembled at the old Fort, and stretched out their lines on either side along the road along which the Express was to come.

Meanwhile, the excitement had increased all over the city. The balconies of the stores were occupied by ladies, and the roofs and sheds were taken possession of by the more agile of the opposite sex, straining to catch a glimpse of the "Pony."

At length—5:45—all this preparation was rewarded. First a cloud of rolling dust in the direction of the Fort, then a horseman, bearing a small flag, riding furiously down J Street, and then a straggling charging band of horsemen flying after him, heralding the coming of the Express; a cannon, placed on the square at Tenth Street, sent forth its noisy welcome. Amidst the firing and shouting, and waving of hats and ladies' handkerchiefs, the pony was seen coming down J Street, surrounded by about thirty of the citizen deputation. Out of this confusion emerged the Pony Express, trotting up to the door of the agency and depositing its mail in ten days from St. Joseph to Sacramento. Hip, hip, hurrah for the Pony Carrier!

CHAPTER 29

TAVISH

Zack had said he would be riding somewhere between Nevada and Utah. As Pa and I rode along over the next couple of days, we hoped we would find him before we got too far. From Sacramento to Salt Lake was about six-hundred eighty miles!

The first ad I had seen for hiring Express riders was in the *Alta* earlier that year. It read: WANTED—young, skinny, wiry fellows, not over 18. Must be expert riders, willing to risk death daily. Orphans preferred. Wages $25 a week.

Zack must have lied about his age too. I heard about one Express rider named David Jay who was only thirteen, and another named William Cody who was fifteen. I don't know why they wanted them so young. A boy that age wouldn't know how to take care of himself if his horse broke a leg or if he got captured by Indians. Of course, they didn't want them to do anything but ride, and eventually they replaced the rifle with a knife. They weren't supposed to stop to fight the Indians who chased them— only outrun them! Maybe they wanted boys who had no family and who were so young that when they got killed, no one would miss them too much.

I suppose for that much pay, a lot of boys would love the adventure of the Pony Express. A hundred dollars a month *plus* board and keep was a lot of money!

They earned it, though. They rode all day and all night, changing horses every twenty or twenty-five miles over the most desolate stretches, every ten miles where it was more civilized. The places where they just changed horses were called swing stations. Each rider would ride three or four or even five horses, and then would stop at a station house where another rider would take over. Most of the time they rode seventy-five miles, usually on three horses. That took them seven or eight hours, and by that time they were ready to stop for food and sleep.

We got to Friday's Station at the Nevada border, and then down into the Carson valley of western Nevada. At the next station house, we met "Pony Bob" Haslam. Even though he was hardly more than a boy, he was already a legend from all the adventures and narrow escapes he had riding across Nevada. We spent the night there with the station keeper. Pony Bob was expected the next day in from the east, and the man kept us up half the night telling us of Bob's exploits over the last five months. When we told him we were looking for Zack Hollister, a shadow passed over his face.

"You know Zack?" Pa asked.

"Heard of him. Don't know him, though," the man replied.

"Why did you frown when I said his name?"

"On account of where I last heard he was riding."

"Where's that?" said Pa with concern.

"Nevada-Utah border. It's hot enough to be hell over there this time of year, Mister," the man said. "And the Paiutes is nasty as ever. Can't see as how I could let you and your daughter go over there and be able to live with myself later."

"I gotta see my son," said Pa.

"You stand a better chance of seeing him if you just wait for him to come home than for the two of you to head out across the Basin."

"Surely they wouldn't hurt two people just passing through," I said.

"Look, Miss," the man said, squinting his eyes at me. "Them Paiutes has been on the warpath since last May. There's over eight thousand of them. They got guns. They'll kill anybody, no matter whether they're innocent or not. They been attacking all over Nevada. We've lost half dozen stations. I tell you, the two of you'd be dead before you was two days out."

I looked over at Pa, my eyes wide. I didn't like the sound of this!

For the next half hour or so Pa and the stationman talked about the Express and the Indians. I think the man was as anxious to have somebody to talk to as he was interested in convincing us not to go any farther into Nevada. Living out there mostly alone like they did, the two or three men at the station houses got tired of each other mighty quick and were plenty happy to see visitors— especially out in the middle of nowhere like in Nevada!

Pa later said to me that this particular fellow had talked so much because I was a pretty young lady and he was trying to impress me with every tall tale he could think up to tell. I told Pa I didn't believe a word of it, but he insisted he wasn't pulling my leg. The truth of it is that the man did have tales to tell that made my blood shiver right inside me.

Pa even told him I was a newspaper writer and that he ought to be careful what he said or it might find its way into print some-day. The man looked at me kinda funny, probably not believing Pa any more than Pa said *he* believed half his wild stories. But in any case, the man grew even more talkative after that.

"I tell you, Mister," he said after pouring each of us a cup of coffee, "if I was you, I'd turn straight around and head back the way you come. Word is them blamed Paiutes is headed this di-rection again."

"Again?" said Pa.

"Yep. They was all over here three, four months back. Major Ormsby took over a hundred men from Carson City and went out after them and was beaten back so bad they had to retreat to the city. Three weeks we was without the Express at all."

"What happened?"

"Finally the army got them back up into the mountains, helped by a snowstorm—in the middle of June, if you can believe that, little lady!" he added, turning toward me with a chuckle. "Since then it ain't been too bad at this end. But they keep raiding to the east, and like I told you, word is they been heading back this way."

I took a sip of the coffee out of the tin cup the man had handed me. I couldn't keep from wincing. It was the bitterest, foulest stuff I had ever tasted! He must've crushed the beans with a hammer and then soaked them in water for a week, then boiled the water and called it coffee! I didn't care much for coffee anyway, but that thick, black syrup was awful. Pa was a regular coffee drinker, and I saw even him grimace slightly with his first drink. But he took a big gulp, swallowed it down bravely, and even had a second cup when the man offered it a little while later.

"Yeah, it's a wonder they keep any riders between Carson and Salt Lake," the man was saying. "Most of the originals have quit or been wounded or injured by this time anyway. But they keep on finding adventure-crazy young fools who'll hire on—meaning no offense to your son, Mister—but it takes a special breed of young rapscallion to put up with the dangers those boys face every day and every night out alone on the trail."

"Zack's a good rider," said Pa. "Maybe that'll keep him outta the way of—"

"They're *all* good riders, Mister!" interrupted the man. "Them that ain't—why, they'd be dead inside o' two or three days. They don't ride for the Express unless they're the best riders this side of the Ohio valley. It ain't good riding that keeps 'em alive in this foolhardy business."

"What is it?" I asked.

"It's pluck, little lady. It's determination, it's courage, it's guts, it's bravado. It's being able to look death in the face and not blink. You ever heard of Nick Wilson?" he asked, looking back toward Pa.

Pa shook his head.

"The blamed fool had a will to live beyond what any mortal oughta have to have. They left him for dead a couple of times, but he lived to tell what happened. Takes a lot of that too—a will to live."

He looked at us, almost as if baiting us to *ask* what happened before he would continue.

"We're listening," said Pa finally, taking another sip of the horrid coffee.

"Young Nick got to the relay station at Spring Valley, but there weren't nobody there. No sign of the keeper. Everything looked in order. No sign of attack. The relay horses were grazing near the cabins. So Nick, he didn't waste no time asking questions— he just jumped off his mount and started to saddle himself up a new horse.

"All of a sudden if he didn't hear a dreadful screaming whooping war cry that's the fear of every Express rider. He pulled out his Colt and started firing at the Indians that was heading toward the corral to steal the rest of the horses. The blamed fool took off chasing them to try to scare them away! But just then, from behind a tree close by, another redskin drew aim at Nick and sent a stone-tipped arrow right at him. Nick never saw him till it was too late. The arrow hit him above his left eye, and the arrowhead went right into his skull, halfway into his head. And there Nick fell and lay, right there among the trees.

"The Indians made off with all the horses, and figured they'd killed the young kid. But two men happened along a few hours later, found him, and saw that he was still alive. They tried to get the arrow out, but couldn't. All they managed to do was loosen the shaft from the stone tip, but there the arrowhead stuck, tight as ever. Weren't nothing much they could do, so they dragged him into the shade, then rode off to the next relay station to tell somebody they had a dead rider and an untended station.

"The next morning, two men came back from the station, figuring to bury the dead rider they'd been told about. Blamed if they didn't find Nick lying there, still breathing faintly! They didn't figure he'd survive the trip, but they hoisted him up across a saddle and carried him back with them to the Ruby Valley station.

"But that kid had no hankering to die just yet. He stayed alive long enough for them to get a doctor to him. He cut out the arrowhead and bandaged up the gashing wound as best he could. He hadn't woke up since the arrow slammed into his head, and no one could figure why he kept breathing! But he did, and after a few more days he woke up and looked around and asked what all the fuss was about. I ain't lying to you, Mister, when I tell you that Nick was up and riding his stretch o' the Express line in less than two months!"

"What about his wound?" I couldn't help asking.

"Yeah, well, it weren't none too pretty, and that's a fact. Ol' Nick, he don't see too good outta that eye, and he still keeps a patch over it to hide the ugly hole. But blamed if he can't still ride with the best of 'em!"

Pa took in a deep breath, no doubt thinking of Zack. But the man hardly gave us a chance to get our wits back together before he was off again.

"Pony Bob, though," he said. "He's my favorite o' the riders. Why, that young fool, he don't know the meaning of the word fear. And he don't know the meaning of tired, neither! He's saved more lives than his own, and ridden more than his share of dangerous miles. You recollect what I was telling you about pluck, little lady?" he asked, looking at me.

I nodded.

"Well, Pony Bob's made of the stuff, I can tell ya that! Why, one time he was riding along lickety-split, and rounding a bend suddenly found himself squared off face-to-face with a war party of thirty mean, blood-thirsty Paiutes! He reined in his pony, sat there a minute, this one young kid staring back at an ambush from one of the most savage tribes west of the Sioux. I tell ya, them Paiutes has killed and massacred and burned to death more settlers and workers for the Express than all the other tribes put together!

"After sitting there a spell, that young rascal just drew out his revolver, and then just ever so slowly urged his pony on. He just stared straight back into their faces, walked right up to 'em, gun held out just beside him. And without a word being said, them Indians watched him ride right through their midst and just keep going.

"Now *that's* guts!" he said, laughing and showing what teeth he had left. "Them redskins was probably so surprised that he'd challenge them right to their faces like that, they couldn't help admiring him!"

The station tender himself was almost as good a subject for an article as anything he was telling us. His name was Claude Tavish, which he only told us after Pa asked him. He had broad shoulders and big, muscular arms, which was probably a good thing for all the work he had to do around the place—building and repairing things, blacksmithing, fixing meals for the riders, and tending their horses and getting them saddled and ready. He said he had a helper who came out the four days a week when the riders came through in both directions.

Mr. Tavish had probably been a blacksmith before, and that's how he got so strong. But now he was starting to get a little fat. His hair was getting thin, too, and gray around the edges. He didn't look as if he worried too much about what he looked like. His face had four or five days' worth of beard stubble on it, and the graying whiskers stood out on the brown face. He had a pleasant enough expression, and a nice smile except for the two or three missing teeth. But he seemed tired, from more than just the work—almost as if life itself was exhausting him.

If we could have gotten him to stop talking so much about all the Express riders he knew, I would have liked to ask him about his *own* life. I had the feeling that behind all the tales he was telling us was probably a sad story of his own—maybe a family dead, or left behind. I couldn't help but wonder why he was out here like this, all by himself in a dangerous job, at his age. It was plain he liked people by the way he wanted to visit with us. But here he was miles from anybody. He reminded me a little of how Alkali Jones might have been at fifty, but without the same gleam in his eye. His eyes did sparkle some when he was talking, but behind the sparkle was a look that made me suspect there was pain somewhere back in his past.

All the time I'd been observing *him*, he had been talking about Bob Haslam. "Fortitude, that's what he's got—enough for a dozen riders! Why, during the Paiute War, he started off his ride one day with a seventy-five-mile stretch to the Reese River Station. That's all a rider's suppose to have to do in a day, but on account of the Indian trouble, there weren't nobody to hand the mail off to, and all the horses had been requisitioned by the army to fight back the Indians. So Pony Bob, he just kept on riding, hoping for better luck fifteen miles away at Buckland's. But there his replacement refused to ride from fear of all the war parties out on the loose.

"Pony Bob had already been riding some nine or ten hours, but there wasn't no one else to carry the mail. So with a fresh horse, he took off again, an' had to pass through three more stations without finding another rider to replace him. He'd ridden 190 miles almost continuously!

"An' what should be the news awaiting him? Only that the rider from the other direction had been badly hurt in a fall. Pony

Bob got himself an hour and a half of sleep before they woke him up to make the return trip. Off he rode again, only to get to the first station that he had left several hours before to find all five of the crew murdered by Indians and all the horses stolen. He kept right on, all the way to Buckland's, where he slept nine hours, waiting for nightfall when there would be less danger from Indians. Then he continued on through the night, outrunning a party of Paiutes who spotted him once, and finally arriving back here after 380 miles!

"I tell ya, I was glad to see the lad! I made him the finest meal I knew how to make, and put him to bed and told him to sleep for a week! He'd only lost four hours from the scheduled time after riding practically four days on ten hours sleep! Quite a kid! The company gave him a special hundred-dollar prize after that."

"Sounds like he's a fellow you oughta talk to and write an article about, Corrie!" said Pa.

"You'll meet him in the morning!" said Mr. Tavish. "He's due in sometime afore noon."

"How long will he be here?" I asked.

"Day or two. If there ain't no Indian trouble, he'll ride out east again day after tomorrow evening."

"Might there be Indian trouble . . . this close to California?" I asked, growing nervous again.

"There's been reports of Paiutes scouting this way. But don't you worry none about Pony Bob. He can outrun anyone. Why, there was another time when he rode into the Dry Creek Station and found the whole staff murdered. He kept going to Cold Springs, and the station was burned down and the dead body of the station keeper lying in the ashes."

As he spoke, Mr. Tavish stopped momentarily and drew in a deep breath. "Funny how fate works, ain't it?" he said reflectively. "When I first was hired by the Express, I worked the Cold Springs Station, but then I got transferred here. Otherwise, that woulda been me laying there with a Paiute arrow sticking out of my chest."

He paused again. "But ol' Bob, he kept on riding. Wasn't nothing much else he could do, I don't reckon. When he came to Sand Creek, he told the station tender all he'd seen and managed to get him to leave with him. That night the Sand Creek Station was burned down, too.

"Those were a bad couple of months back the early part of the summer! It's better now, but there ain't no one I'd rather was coming our way than Pony Bob. If there is trouble, he'll know of it and be far enough ahead of 'em to warn us."

He stopped again, and the station room was quiet for a minute or two. I looked around and began noticing all the stuff hanging up and sitting on shelves or in crates everywhere. The floor was dirt. Several bunks were built right into the far wall, and besides the bench Pa and I were sitting on, there wasn't much else in the way of furniture. Just a table, one chair, and empty crates turned up on end for people to sit on. There was a big wood stove for cooking with shelves full of supplies—flour, sugar, coffee, cornmeal, hams and bacon, containers of dried fruit and meat, tea, coffee, beans. All around the rest of the room were scattered an assortment of other things they might need—tools, brooms, candles, blankets, buckets, medicines, borax, tin dishes, turpentine, castor oil, rubbing alcohol, even sewing supplies. The alcohol was only for treating wounds or injuries. No drinking of any liquor was allowed at any of the Pony Express stations. Of course, there were lots of guns and rifles and ammunition around too.

Outside there were a couple of other buildings—a blacksmithing forge, a stable and barn. They had to have everything on hand that might possibly be needed for any situation—Indian attack, lame horses, broken legs, loose shoes, wounds, injury. At most of the Nevada stations, the ground was so dry that there was no grass for animals to graze on, so they had to have a large supply of oats and other feed on hand, too.

"Where'd you say your boy was at?" Mr. Tavish asked Pa.

"Not sure. Far as we know, out toward Utah."

Mr. Tavish gave a low whistle. "That ain't good, Mister. He musta come in after the Indian troubles quieted down. They brought in lots of new kids in July to replace the ones that left. When'd he join up?"

"Early July. He said he'd heard there was openings out toward eastern Nevada."

"Openings is right!" laughed Mr. Tavish. "The whole blame line from Carson to Salt Lake was open! Weren't hardly nobody left."

The look on Pa's face was not a happy one. My heart sank just
to hear the stationman's words.

"Well, can't be helped now," he went on. "If your boy's alive,
he's alive. If he's dead, I'd probably have heard about it. So we'll
wait on Bob tomorrow and see if he knows anything. One thing's
for sure, Mister, you ain't gonna take the little lady here no further
east than right here. If you was fool enough to go by yourself,
there wouldn't be much I could do to stop you, though I wouldn't
give a plugged nickel for your chances out there alone. But with
a young lady—nope, I just wouldn't let you go another mile past
here."

Pa and I looked at each other. I guess this is where we'd be
spending the night!

"You ever heard of Billy Cody?" Mr. Tavish asked.

"Nope," Pa answered. I nodded my head that I had.

"What'd you hear about him?" asked Mr. Tavish.

"Only that he wasn't much older than a boy," I said.

"Cody's just like Pony Bob! Guts of a man inside the body of
a kid. I hope your brother's like that . . . for his sake. Otherwise,
even if he is still alive, he ain't likely to stay that way for long. But
let me tell you about Cody," he went on.

"They gave him an extra bit of mail one time, a box of money
that had to get through. Now the Indians, they'll attack anybody
or anything just to be ornery. But the bandits and thieves with
white skin, they're more particular. They're after loot. Well, I tell
you what happened—there'd been reports of a couple outlaws in
the region where Cody was riding. And with him having to carry
cash money, it was a dangerous situation. So Cody, he hid his
mochila and mail cases under an extra leather blanket. Then he
filled a couple of extra pouches with paper so that if he was held
up, the robbers would think they had the real thing.

"Well, sure enough, blamed if Cody didn't get stopped as he
was riding through a narrow ravine. The two bandits had guns on
him and told him to get off his horse and put his hands in the air.
He obeyed. One of the men rode closer, put away his gun, and
reached out to grab the fake mail pouches from Cody's horse. But
instead of waiting for them to take it and hope they'd leave without
discovering them to be worthless, Billy suddenly flung the whole

blanket up in the man's face, drawing his gun at the same instant, and shot the thief. The other man fled. Billy jumped on his horse and took off after him."

Mr. Tavish stopped in his story long enough to give a great laugh.

"That's the kind of kids out riding this part of the Express territory," he said. "Kids that can send grown men to flight! Yes sir, I hope the young fella you're looking for can take care of himself like that!"

I shuddered. Just the thought of Zack having to shoot at or possibly even kill someone was enough to turn my stomach. I could hardly stand the thought that he was mixed up in such a violent thing as the Pony Express seemed to be.

I knew Pa was thinking the same thing. He and Uncle Nick had run with a much rougher crowd, and had fought in the Mexican War. But I suppose it seemed different to Pa, thinking about his own son. Things he went through himself, he didn't want his kids to have to face. And however young Bill Cody and Pony Bob and all the rest of them were, to me and Pa, Zack still seemed too young to be part of all this.

CHAPTER 30

THE FRIGHT OF MY LIFE!

The rest of that night we listened to more of Claude Tavish's stories, although by the time supper was over, Pa'd managed to get him talking about something besides the Pony Express. It turned out Mr. Tavish had fought in the Mexican War too, and that kept him and Pa busy till late talking about their recollections. At least it took our minds off worrying about Zack.

I mixed up some biscuits to go with beans and a ham hock Mr. Tavish had boiling on top of the stove. He raved and raved about those biscuits, even though there wasn't anything to them that he couldn't have done himself. He didn't have any baking powder to mix in, so they were flat and hard. But he kept saying he hadn't eaten anything so good in years. "Anything tastes better if a woman's hand's gone into the making of it," he said. "A man and woman can put all the same ingredients in a bowl, and mix it up, and cook it just the same, and feed whatever it is to a passel of hungry miners or cowboys or anybody else. They'll all cuss and complain at the man for his lousy grub, but they'll rave and carry on at how wonderful the lady's food tastes. I always figured they weren't treating me none too fairly, but after tasting them biscuits of your's, little lady, I reckon I know what they been getting at all these years. There just ain't no denying that a woman's hand's got something special in it."

"They taste about the same as always to me," I said. "But thank you all the same, Mr. Tavish."

I listened with interest to the two men talk, because now every story that came out gave me new glimpses into Pa's past during

165

those years before we were together again.

"Where was you at?" Pa had asked Mr. Tavish.

"Buena Vista, where else!" answered the stationman.

"You *were* at the center of it all," said Pa. "Me and Nick never got that close to Santa Anna."

"Lucky for you! He was a mean cuss—came at us with 15,000 men. But he hadn't counted on Zachary Taylor! No sir. Us with our 5,000 just waited in the mountains for them to attack. Dreadful night, I can tell you—wind, rain, hardly no sleep. But it must have been worse for them Mexicans, because the next day we sent 'em running!"

"Tell me," asked Pa. "What did the men think of President Polk?"

"I don't know, what's to think? He was president and we was following orders," answered Tavish.

"Did they think the war was a good one? What about slavery?"

"What about it?"

"Did you talk about how what you were really fighting for was to have more slave states in the country?"

"Tarnation, no! We were just fighting the Mexicans. We didn't know what it was about. Why, did you fellers in California talk about all that?"

"No," said Pa thoughtfully. "Back then I didn't know what it was about any more than you did. I was just curious, that's all."

When we went to bed that night, I lay in my bedroll on one of those hard wooden bunks. I couldn't get right to sleep, and as I listened to Pa and Mr. Tavish snoring, all his stories about the Indians came back into my mind. I should have been more concerned for Zack, but instead I grew more and more terrified for myself! I remembered his words about how savage the Paiutes were, and how they were headed our way, and how many people they'd killed.

Then I started to realize how far out in the middle of the desert we were—twenty or twenty-five miles past Carson City—and how we were all alone. Pretty soon every little noise I heard made me jump, and I started imagining that the place was surrounded by fifty or a hundred Indians, sneaking up on us quietly in the night, to kill us!

In the distance a wolf's cry rang out. I practically jumped out of my skin! My heart was racing, and I couldn't imagine how Pa and Mr. Tavish could just sleep so calmly through it all. All sorts of little noises I hadn't noticed before seemed to be coming out of the night—creaks and groans from the cabin, an occasional whistle of wind through a crack, now and then a bird or other animal, a sound from the stables, the bark of a wild dog, and always the howl of the wolves far off in the mountains.

I had been out on the trail alone many times, but never had I been so scared as I was tonight.

Never had the morning sunshine looked so good! The wind had died down and whatever the spooky noises had been during the night, they had gone away too. The place was calm and cheery; even Mr. Tavish looked more chipper as a result of his company and the discovery of a comrade from the days before the gold rush and California's statehood. The dull, sad look in his eyes had given way to something almost like enthusiasm.

"Well, little lady, what's you and me gonna rustle up for breakfast?" he greeted me warmly. "Flapjacks?"

"We need eggs for that," I said. "And milk."

"We got no milk, but I just may be able to lay my hands on two or three eggs," he said with a wink, "*if* my hens have been the good girls they oughta have been during the night. You just wait here, and I'll go check the coop."

He disappeared outside, and returned in about three minutes, face beaming, with two brand-new eggs in each hand.

"We'll make us up the finest batch of flapjacks this side of the gold diggin's!" he announced, and immediately began taking down pans and dumping flour into a bowl. I don't know what he needed me for!

"Here, little lady," he called out after a minute. "You take over here. We want 'em to have that female touch. I gotta go draw us some water. You get 'em cooking on the griddle there. You'll find syrup and grease up there on the shelf to the right. While we're at it, what say we fry us up some bacon to go with 'em?"

I nodded and smiled my agreement. Mr. Tavish left the cabin just as Pa came back in.

"What's Tavish so all-fired beaming about?" asked Pa with a grin.

"I don't know, Pa. Talking about the war last night seemed to perk him up."

"And the presence of a young lady on the premises might have had something to do with it!" added Pa.

Whatever it was, when the stationmaster returned ten minutes later, not a speck of gray stubble was left on his clean-shaven face. He also put on a new clean shirt for breakfast. In the meantime, his young helper, a Mexican boy named Juan who lived a few miles away, had come to help him prepare for Pony Bob's arrival. By then I had a good stack of pancakes ready, with several more on the griddle. Mr. Tavish rang his bell, and the four of us gathered around the table while he offered a simple prayer of thanks. Pa and I sat down on the bench. Juan pulled up one of the crates, and Mr. Tavish took over at the stove to watch the flapjacks and the last of the sizzling bacon. He wouldn't hear of me doing any more now. I was his guest, he said.

We had barely started eating when the sounds of galloping horses caught our attention. Mr. Tavish's smile faded. There were too many horses for it to be a Pony rider!

He threw down the metal spatula with a clang onto the stove and ran to the door. He opened it for a second, then slammed it shut with a thud and pulled the iron bolt down across it.

"Indians!" he cried. "Juan . . . get the rifles and ammo!"

Even before anyone had the chance to ask him if he was serious, one of the two windows of the cabin shattered, its glass tinkling down the wall onto the dirt floor. At almost the same instant, an arrow slammed into the opposite wall.

Mr. Tavish ran to it, yanked it out of the timber, examined it for a second, then swore under his breath. "Paiutes!" The despair in his voice filled me with a dread such as I had never felt before, and hope I never ever feel again in my life!

I looked around for Pa, but there was only time enough for our eyes to meet briefly. In that second, a multitude of unspoken thoughts passed between our hearts. But there was no time even for a word, for the next instant Juan was shoving a rifle into my hand, and Mr. Tavish was showing Pa where to crouch down behind one of the windows. I took the gun without even thinking, and before I knew it I was huddled down a little ways from Pa.

Things happened so fast there was no time for me to stop and realize, *I don't want to kill anyone . . . even an Indian!*

I don't know how much time passed. It could have been an hour. It could have been five minutes for all I know. There was a lot of gunfire, both inside and outside the cabin, and several more arrows flew through the windows, both of which were broken. After one of them, I heard Pa shout, "Corrie, you keep your head down, you hear!" His voice held such a fearful yet commanding authority, I didn't dare crane my neck up any more to try to see what was going on. I'd never heard such a sound in his voice before!

The Indians must have had guns too, because there were far too many gunshots to be coming from just the three guns inside. The rifle I still held in my hand was silent!

"Use that carbine, little lady!" Mr. Tavish called out at me, but I didn't have words to answer him. I just kept lying there on the floor, trying to stay out of the way. Pa was shooting out the window at the attackers. It all seemed completely natural at the time. Only later did I realize that he was trying to *kill* someone with that gun he was firing.

"I was praying to God the whole time," he told me later, "that I *wouldn't* have to kill no one. But when his family's in danger, a man does things he might not do otherwise. And if I had to kill to keep them Indians away from you, Corrie, I would have done it and asked God if it was right or wrong later. I'd have done just about anything to keep their savage hands off you, including getting myself killed trying."

In the meantime, it seemed as if we were all going to be killed!

Thwaack! An arrow flew through the window above my head, coming at a low angle, and stuck into the adjacent wall next to me only about five feet away. Pa glanced over at it. His face was white, and he was sweating.

"I got me one . . . I got one!" shouted Juan.

"Keep down, you little fool!" yelled Tavish, who was crouched down reloading his rifle. "Just because you shoot one Indian don't give you no reason to stick your head up like that and give 'em an easy target. When you've picked off fifteen or twenty, then you can shout about it!"

His rifle reloaded, Mr. Tavish turned back to the window, one knee bent to the ground, raised the gun to his shoulder, squinted his eye along the barrel, and started firing rapidly again at our attackers, his gun resting on the bottom ledge where broken glass was strewn about.

He only got off a couple more shots; then all of a sudden Mr. Tavish screamed out in pain. I looked over just in time to see him falling backward to the floor, an arrow sticking out of his shoulder.

The gunfire in the cabin ceased. Juan and Pa looked at each other as if wondering what to do now. The next instant, however, Juan was firing from his vantage point with renewed vengeance.

"Corrie, get over and see what you can do for him!" yelled Pa.

"What do I do, Pa?"

"I don't know. See how bad it is. Get a towel or something and keep it from bleeding!"

Pa turned back to the window and started shooting again. I crept over to where Mr. Tavish lay. His shirt was torn and red, and the warm blood was dripping down and soaking into the dirt. His face was white, but he managed to give me a thin smile.

"I'm sorry, little lady," he whispered. "I didn't mean to get you mixed up in nothin' like this."

"How is . . . is it bad?" I asked.

"I'll live. Them Paiutes ain't gonna get rid of Tavish so easy, but—" He winced in pain. "Blame if it don't hurt somethin' fierce, though!"

"What should I do?" I asked. Thinking back, I realize that I didn't hear any more gunfire after that. For the next two or three minutes, the whole world centered around me and Claude Tavish. "Should I try to . . . to get the arrow out?" I asked, shuddering involuntarily even as I said the words.

"I don't know if you can," he answered, closing his eyes and breathing in a slow deep breath as if preparing himself for the ordeal. "But the thing's gotta come out."

"What should I do?"

"Look in there and see how far it's stuck in. If it didn't get all twisted or lodged against a bone, you oughta be able to yank it straight out."

I bent over a little closer, trying to see.

"Get in there with your fingers, little lady! A little blood ain't gonna hurt you. Ain't no way you're gonna find how deep it's gone unless you get in there and wipe some of the blood away and see where the tip is."

I leaned closer toward him, but I couldn't see a thing. His shirt was all red and the wooden shaft of the arrow disappeared inside it. I reached out and gingerly touched the arrow right where it went into his shirt, but the same instant pulled my hand back.

"Get in there, little lady!" This time Mr. Tavish's words were a command. "You want me to bleed to death? Get in there, and if the arrowhead ain't all the way inside, then you give it a good hard pull!"

Again I probed with my fingers, tearing at the hole in his shirt to make it bigger. There was so much blood I still couldn't see. I didn't even stop to think what I was doing at the time, but later from seeing the blood all over me, I realized that I grabbed the hem of my dress as I crouched there beside him and used it to wipe away some of the blood so that I could see the wound better.

Less than a minute had gone by since he'd fallen. The blood was still warm and wet and oozing from his shoulder. I tore a bigger hole in his shirt and wiped back the blood as best I could. Then I felt all around the arrow with my fingers. The sensation of feeling his wet bloody flesh, with the arrow sticking out, was too horrible to describe. I turned away, my stomach retching. I gagged two or three times, but luckily didn't throw up. I turned back to him, took a deep breath, gritted my teeth and lips together to keep my stomach down where it belonged, and tried to examine the wound again.

I felt all about. My hands were all bloody by this time, but by now I was determined to get the arrow out. I could feel the jagged hole the rough arrowhead had made. I forced my fingers to move around it, feeling at the base of the arrow. Down low, just at the skin line, I could feel the top end of the stone arrowhead. Feeling that hard piece of stone inside his soft flesh made me gag again.

"Is the head exposed?" asked Mr. Tavish.

"It's right at the edge of your shoulder," I said.

"It ain't all covered up?"

"No, I can feel the top of it."

"Good. You pull it out."

I shuddered again, clenched my teeth, and grabbed hold of the arrow with both hands and pulled.

My hands just slid up the shaft, but it remained as tightly lodged in Mr. Tavish's shoulder as ever.

"Blood's as slippery as grease!" he said. "Wipe off your hands first."

I grabbed at the end of my dress again, wiped off my hands as best I could, then wiped off the shaft of the arrow, trying to clean if off right down to the wound.

I clutched at it again, down low right on his skin. This time I could feel my dried hands take hold against the wood. I closed my eyes, then yanked upward for all I was worth.

Mr. Tavish let out a horrible yell, rising up off the ground as I pulled, then falling back down again. The sound of his voice made me let go. When I looked back down at his face, he was breathing rapidly in obvious pain. But the arrow was still stuck in his shoulder!

"Good girl," he whispered, though his eyes were closed. "One more time and we'll have it."

I swallowed hard, then grabbed the arrow again. This time I determined I wasn't going to let go. I pulled again, but this time when I felt the resistance of the arrow sticking into him, I held on all the tighter and gave one mighty tug.

I fell backward, the arrow in my hand.

This time Mr. Tavish hadn't screamed out, although I had felt his body rise up again as I yanked. He was lying on the floor, his eyes still closed, breathing rapidly. I can't even imagine how painful it must have been for him. I don't know why he didn't just faint from the agony of it.

"Now go over to the cupboard behind the stove," he said, still in a faint, quiet voice. "Behind the black pot there's a bottle of whiskey. You go get it . . . but keep your head down."

He must have sensed me hesitate, because I saw his eyes open a crack.

"There's alcohol there on the shelf," I said.

He forced a smile. "Don't want alcohol," he said. "I want whiskey."

Still I hesitated.

"I know . . . I know, little lady," he said. "But them rules is to keep the kids in line and not for the likes of old fellers like me. You won't tell Mr. Russell, will you? Besides, I only keep it for medicinal purposes."

I got to my feet and ran over to the cupboard. The bottle of whiskey was right where he said it was. He must have had a number of wounds to treat recently, because the bottle was less than half full. I took it back to him and pulled out the cork.

Without a moment's hesitation, Mr. Tavish reached out with his uninjured hand, took the bottle from me, and took a long swig that used up half the remaining contents in one huge swallow. Then he handed it back to me.

"Pour it into the wound," he said. "You gotta get it right in the hole, or I'll die of gangrene before the month's out!"

I put the mouth of the bottle to the hole in his shoulder and poured it in. His face twisted up in an awful look of pain. He sucked in a wincing breath through his clenched teeth, his eyes shut tight. He held his breath for what seemed like a long time, then slowly let it out in a long sigh as his body relaxed.

"Once more, Corrie," he whispered. "Pour it in again."

I did, and he winced sharply just like before, though this time it didn't seem to be quite so bad.

"Now go get a towel. Soak a piece of it in whiskey and stuff it in there and try to bandage me up as best you can so's I don't keep bleeding."

I don't know when the shooting had stopped. Like I said, I hadn't noticed anything but Mr. Tavish. But suddenly it did seem awful quiet. I stood up to go find a towel. But as I turned around, my heart sank with an altogether new terror.

There stood an Indian with a rifle pointed straight at Pa!

I stood paralyzed with fear while three or four more Paiutes climbed in through the broken windows, training their guns on the rest of us.

CHAPTER 31

THE MOST UNUSUAL BREAKFAST IN THE WORLD

They must have known they'd gotten one of us when only two guns were firing at them instead of three. Then when Juan stopped to reload, the Indian had jumped through the silent window, and the next second Pa was staring down the barrel of a Paiute gun.

Pa could have tried to shoot him, of course. But then they'd both have been dead, and there would have been a dozen more Indians following right after the first. Not only would it have been pointless, Pa didn't want to shoot anyone anyway. I saw him glance over at me, all blood-stained like I was, as he set his rifle down. I knew he would have killed to save me if he needed to. But now it looked as if we were all going to die together! And the look of futility on his face said there wasn't much he could do about it.

By now one of them had opened the door, and more Indians were pouring into the cabin, some holding bows, others rifles, talking in a strange language, making gestures and signs, looking around, taking stock of the inside of the station. They didn't seem to pay any attention to my being a woman, which I know was the main thing on Pa's mind. I don't suppose I looked all that attractive to them in the condition I was in!

A few of them started taking things—some tools and supplies, what food they could carry—while two of the others talked among themselves. Then one of them gave what sounded like an order, and another ran outside and returned a minute later with several strands of buffalo rope. He threw one of them to his companion, and the two of them grabbed Juan and Pa and started to tie them up. Then one of them approached me, grabbed at my arm, and pulled me over against one of the two support timbers in the middle of the cabin. He yanked my hands behind my back and tied me up too. He was none too gentle, and he smelled horrible. I tried not to cry out, but he hurt my wrists as he twisted the rope around them and yanked it tight.

I don't know what danger they thought Mr. Tavish was going to be in his condition, but one of them dragged him by the feet over next to me, then pulled him viciously to his feet and tied him up behind me. We could feel each other's hands but couldn't see each other.

"I'm sorry about this, little lady," Mr. Tavish groaned softly. "These blamed Pai—"

A blow across the side of his head and face put an end to whatever he had been going to say.

Meanwhile, the Indians who were taking things seemed to have gotten all they wanted out of the cabin and had left. Outside we could hear movement and rustling. The door was still open and I could see them dragging brush and bales of straw from the stables over toward the station. Out one of the windows I could see the same thing going on.

"What are they doing?" I whispered when the one who had been tying us up went over to check on the knots around Pa and Juan.

"Fixing to burn down the place," Mr. Tavish whispered back. "It's their favorite way—surround the place with kindling and firewood and set it ablaze."

"What about us?" I said in horror.

"It's the Paiute way of burning the white man at the stake. The good-for-nothin' savages!"

"They're going to leave us inside?" I gasped.

"Leave us inside to burn, take us outside and put arrows through our hearts—their kind ain't too particular how the white man dies."

"Pa!" I wailed.

"Be brave, Corrie," I heard Pa answer, even though I couldn't see him from the direction I was facing. "Just remember—this ain't the end of it. Our Father will take care of us, even if—"

He never finished. I heard a big *whack*, and I squirmed at my ropes, straining around to try to see Pa. I managed just to see him out of the corner of my eye. His head was hanging limp, a red gash from the butt of the Indian's rifle already swelling up from above his ear down into the upper part of his cheek. The blow had knocked him unconscious.

I found myself wishing they'd do the same to me. If I was going to get burned up, I'd rather be asleep!

There was still a lot of activity outside, but it looked as if they had just about got the cabin all surrounded with dry material that would ignite in just a few seconds. Then it got very quiet. The Indian who had seemed to be in charge walked out the door and was gone for two or three minutes. When he finally came back in, the look on his face was one of taking a last look around to make sure he hadn't missed anything. A handful of others followed him in, then stood back waiting. He walked slowly about, indicating now one thing, now another, with a grunt and a few words. The others picked up whatever he'd pointed to and took it outside. They grabbed up several blankets on a shelf that had been missed before, a shovel, an axe, an unopened bag of beans.

The leader walked slowly around the table, eyeing it carefully, then over to the stove, where he first noticed the flapjacks and bacon still frying away. By now the two large pancakes on the griddle were black on the bottom, and the thin strips of bacon burned to cinders. But the smell seemed to attract his attention. He glanced back at the table, then again eyed the stove, this time lifting the lid off the pot of coffee, which still sat there steaming hot. The smell seemed to appeal to him. He smiled, replaced the lid, took a tin cup from the shelf behind the stove, and poured out a cup of the black brew.

As he sipped at it, he must have thought more of it than I had the previous evening, because he smiled again, then called to his companions, apparently asking them if they wanted some. They all set down the things they'd been carrying outside and approached him, grabbing cups wherever they could find them, and pouring coffee for themselves.

The five or six Indians left in the cabin talked and laughed as they sipped at Mr. Tavish's strong coffee. Then before I even realized what was happening, they all sat down around the table, using *our* plates and eating up the flapjacks that *we* had cooked!

There they were, getting ready to burn the place down, and us along with it, and they were celebrating by eating *our* breakfast!

After some discussion, they finally figured out that the syrup was sweet and tasted good on top of the pancakes. They poured it on, then tore the pancakes in half with their fingers, picked them up, and ate them. It was the messiest breakfast I had ever seen in my life, and if I hadn't been about to die, I probably would have laughed myself silly. As it was, I didn't know whether to laugh or cry or look the other way and try to ignore their uncivilized antics.

But they were impossible to ignore. By now they were making quite a racket. The pancakes and bacon were gone in a few minutes, and they had syrup and grease all over their faces and hands. Then they got up and started rummaging all through the cabin to see if there was anything *else* they could find to eat! One of them grabbed up the bottle of syrup and drank down the rest of it, then set it back down on the table with a crash and a loud laugh. The rest were helping themselves to more coffee, spilling half of it in their haste. One had discovered a tin of dried venison, which all the rest now came and started to fight over.

Then suddenly, in the distance, a bugle sounded, followed by the pounding gallop of approaching horses.

All activity inside the cabin stopped immediately, and they looked around at one another. Immediately, I realized that the Paiutes had heard the sound, too, and were scared by it. They dropped everything and ran for the door. Within fifteen seconds, amid shouts and unintelligible cries, we heard their ponies galloping away in the opposite direction, followed by pursuing gunfire.

CHAPTER 32

PONY BOB!

It wasn't the cavalry at all who had rescued us!

Pony Bob was early in arriving on his run from the east. He'd seen signs of the Indians from far off and had ridden in shooting and firing up a storm.

He was a courageous young boy, that much we already knew, but I doubt if he really expected to scare off twenty or thirty Paiutes all by himself. But he had help that we didn't know about when we first heard him approach. All he'd been trying to do was distract the war party long enough for that help to arrive. Fortunately for everybody, he didn't have to wait for it before he got into the cabin to untie us.

We heard his horse gallop up and stop, and a few seconds later he ran inside.

"Am I glad to see you!" Mr. Tavish whispered weakly. "Get us outta these ropes, Bob!"

Pony Bob was already slicing through the cords around my hands and Mr. Tavish's with a knife. The instant I was free I ran over to Pa and threw my arms around him.

"I love you, Pa!" I said, not able to keep from crying and not the least bit embarrassed about my tears. I hardly even realized that he was still bound hand and foot and couldn't have hugged me back if he'd tried!

Pony Bob was just what I might have expected. Small, thin, six inches shorter than Zack, and with a recklessness, almost a mean streak in his young eyes. He didn't look as if he was afraid of anybody or anything. Whether it was courage that drove him,

178

or just that he didn't have anyone in this life he cared about enough to stay alive for, I couldn't tell. His face showed little trace of a beard, but his eyes had the hardness of a man of fifty. In Mr. Tavish's eyes I had seen the dull pain of loneliness; in young Bob Haslam's I saw only emptiness.

"Everyone outside!" gasped Mr. Tavish, even before Pa and Juan were free. "We gotta pull the straw away from the station. One flaming arrow and the place'll go up like a dry brushfire in a hot wind!"

He staggered outside, and with his uninjured arm began dragging back the brush and straw the Indians had piled up. In a minute all four of the rest of us had joined him.

"By now they'll know they was run off by only Bob. They'll either be back or will try to set the place off from where they're hiding!"

"In two or three minutes the army'll be here," said young Haslam.

"What?" Mr. Tavish said, breathing hard and gritting his teeth against the pain.

"Ormsby's out from Carson. He heard they'd attacked the Widow Cutt's place yesterday. I'd seen signs of the raiding party all the way in the last ten miles. I ran into his troop of men five or six miles back and told him I thought they were heading for the station. They're right behind me."

"Blamed if you ain't better'n a whole hundred cavalrymen!" said Tavish, his face flushed with fever and exertion. The next instant a shot rang out, followed by the sound of a bullet ricocheting off an iron wagon wheel next to the station house. It had come from the direction the Indians had gone.

"Them Paiutes is back!" cried Tavish. "Everyone inside!"

We rushed into the station. Pony Bob bolted the door. Pa, Juan, and Bob grabbed rifles and sent several volleys of fire out through the windows, hoping to discourage the war party from trying the same thing again. Mr. Tavish, still bleeding, made me help him get a rifle up onto the window ledge where he could rest it against his good shoulder.

But the shooting didn't last long this time.

Again we heard a bugle call, followed by thunderous hoofbeats. A minute later Major Ormsby's troop of forty men roared past after the Paiutes, who were back on their horses and making for the mountains as fast as they could. We never saw them again.

Once the cavalry had passed, Mr. Tavish sank into the one chair, and Pony Bob packed and dressed the wound.

"The army's bugle didn't sound anything like what I heard before you came," I said to Pony Bob when he had finished bandaging Mr. Tavish's shoulder.

He and Mr. Tavish laughed.

"That's because Pony Bob's weren't no army bugle, little lady. Back when the Express started, they gave every rider a horn so as to announce his coming to the station. Wasn't long before everybody knew we didn't need 'em. You can see the dust five miles away, and hear the horse's hooves a mile away, so what use was the horn? But Pony Bob, he just kept his. How come, Bob?"

"Aw, just for fun," replied Bob. "You never know when you're gonna have need of something like that."

"If the army ever heard someone trying to imitate their charge with a little tin horn like that, they'd take it from him and trample it flat!" said Mr. Tavish.

"Anyhow, the Indians believed he was a one-man cavalry charge," laughed Pa. "So I'm mighty glad you saved it, son. Say, you know a Zack Hollister?"

Pony Bob's face grew thoughtful. "Yeah, I think I heard of him," he answered after a minute. "Rides over to the east. Ain't never run into him myself, though."

"These folks come from California looking to find him," put in Mr. Tavish. "You reckon they could make it to Utah, Bob?"

"Not unless they want to go through what you've just been through every day—and that's *without* a station to hide in and no cavalry within miles."

"You reckon the Paiutes are going on the warpath again?"

"They're everywhere out there. I was lucky to make it through. You want my advice, Mister," said Pony Bob to Pa, "you'll saddle up and head for Carson and just keep right on going past the Sierras. If Zack Hollister's your kin, there ain't much you can do for him now. But if you aim to keep this pretty girl of yours alive, you'd best take my advice."

"When's the safest time to leave for Carson, you reckon?" asked Pa.

"Right now," answered Mr. Tavish. "Ormsby's driven the savages up into the hills. They won't bother nobody for some few days, and he and his men will be moving back that way, so if there was trouble, they'd be on the trail with you."

"We ought to do what they say, Pa," I said. "If we are ever going to find Zack, it doesn't seem as if this is the time to do it."

Pa thought long and hard for a few minutes. He knew we had to go back, but he was torn with wanting to find his son.

Finally he nodded. "Well then, Corrie, I reckon you and me had best saddle up our horses and get our things together."

"You could make Carson, or maybe even Friday's Station before nightfall," said Mr. Tavish.

"I'm obliged to you for everything, Tavish," said Pa, shaking the stationman's good hand. "All except for nearly getting us killed, that is!"

"You come back and visit again, Hollister," he said, smiling weakly. "And bring the little lady with you. She's a right fine nurse, along with being a cook and a newspaper writer!"

"You take care of yourself!" said Pa.

"And get a doctor to fix up your shoulder," I added, giving Mr. Tavish a one-sided hug. "I don't want to worry about anything happening to it."

Pa and I were on the trail back in the direction of Carson City in less than twenty minutes.

We rode for the rest of the morning in silence, interrupted only by Pony Bob as he passed, finishing up his run to Carson. We had probably started fifteen or twenty minutes ahead of him, but he caught up with us in no time.

We heard him coming behind us and stopped to turn around. At first all we could see was swirling dust in the middle of the desert valley floor, although the sound of the iron-clad hooves could be heard thudding loudly against the rocky trail. We squinted to watch as the cloud of dust grew steadily larger. Then a black speck began to appear in the middle of the cloud, which gradually sprouted arms and legs and came alive with movement. Across the endless level of the Carson sink, the cloud of dust grew, the now-defined horse and rider in its midst obscuring mountains and desert and sky. A show it was—magnificent to behold!

He was nearly upon us, and we watched in nothing less than awe, as if history itself resided in the four locked pouches of the *mochila* coming from the East and bound for the Pacific. Had I been able to pull out paper and pencil, to stop the motion of Pony Bob and his steed, I would have tried to capture in a drawing what I felt as he flew past. As it is, however, the scene must lodge only in my memory, for it was over in a few brief seconds.

As he thundered by, I saw the blur of four powerful black feet, Bob's arms and the reins and the bandanna around his neck all flying, and in the center of it all the huge black head of the horse, his eyes flaming, his nostrils wide to suck in all the air he could, mouth foaming, his powerful frame bulging and pulsating with muscular strength. He was by us in an instant. Only Bob's whoop of greeting, and long drawn out *Haaalllisteeeerrrrr!* lingered echoing in the wind with the suddenly retreating hoofbeats.

Like a blur, it was gone. Man and horse flew by our wide-eyed faces like a thunderstorm borne on a swift wind, then receded into the distance ahead . . . tinier, tinier, until Pony Bob disappeared in a dust cloud against the blue of the horizon. Except for the lingering whirlwind of dust, I might have believed that the whole thing had been the dreaming fancy of an overactive imagination.

But it was no dream. Pa's next words woke me out of my reverie. He had been astonished by the sight as well.

"Tarnation!" he exclaimed. "That boy does know how to ride! I reckon Tavish was right when he said they're *all* good riders!"

We rode for an hour after that without either of us saying anything. After all we'd been through, our anxiety over Zack, and even wondering where the band of Paiutes were, there was plenty to think about. I was thinking about the attack that morning, Zack, and the Indians. But Pa hadn't been thinking about those things at all I found out.

"I think I'm gonna do it, Corrie," he said after a long, long time of quiet.

"Do what, Pa?"

"Run for the legislature."

"You are? Why, Pa, that's . . . that's wonderful!" I exclaimed.

"You really think so?"

"Yes—I was hoping you would!"

"Why's that?"

"Because you're a fine man, Pa, and I want everyone to know it. What made you decide?"

"I can't rightly say," replied Pa. "Something about what happened back there just—I don't know, Corrie, it just made me think it's the right thing to do."

"Does it have anything to do with Zack?"

Pa thought for a minute. "I'm not sure. I guess I just got to figuring that everybody's gonna die sometime. We came closer than I'd like to think back there! But if I am gonna die, then I oughta have done something worth remembering before I do. Raising my kids right is probably about the most important thing a man can do, and I ain't done such a good job of that."

"Please, Pa, I don't like to hear you talk like that."

"All right, Corrie. Let's just say that *one* of my sons doesn't think much of my fathering. Maybe the rest of you still look up to me. But you're all nearly grown. Why, little Tad's gonna be a man himself in another year or two. So I figure my fathering days are nearly over—except for little Ruth, of course. Whether I've done a good or a bad job of it, maybe I oughta be looking for something else worth doing that people will remember Drummond Hollister for. You don't always get too many chances to do something important, so when one comes along, a man's gotta look at it and decide if he wants to do it, or before he knows it, the chance is gone and might never come back."

"A man *or* a woman," I added with a smile.

"Right you are there, Corrie. Which is why you've got to take your opportunities with writing and with this election, and why maybe I've got to take mine with this political thing Dalton's offering me."

"I understand, Pa."

I really did. I had been thinking along the same lines for the last couple of months—not having to do with dying or doing something important, but having to do, as Pa and Cal had both said, with taking the opportunities that came your way.

In some ways the decisions facing both Pa and me were similar too. And the choices we made were bound to have a big effect on our futures.

CHAPTER 33

A CONVERSATION IN SACRAMENTO

Things started to happen pretty fast after we got back from Nevada. Pa's decision to run for the California House of Representatives was like yanking up the boards to let the water from a stream into a sluice trough. Once the water started flowing, it rushed through fast! I know it didn't take our minds off Zack and the danger he was in, but it kept us busy enough that we didn't have to mope around and think about it.

We stopped in Sacramento long enough for Pa to meet with Mr. Dalton and tell him what he decided.

"I'm pleased to hear of your decision, Hollister," Mr. Dalton said.

"I still don't have much notion of what I'm supposed to do," Pa said sheepishly. I knew he felt awkward around smooth politicians like Alexander Dalton.

"You just leave everything to me. All you have to do is try to spread the word around your area that folks need to vote for you. Since you've already run for mayor a time or two, it ought not to be too difficult."

"We'll make up some more handbills, Pa," I suggested, "just like last time."

"Good girl!" said Mr. Dalton, giving me a gentle slap on the back. "I like how she thinks, Hollister," he added to Pa. "Political acumen must run in the family! Like I say, you just leave the rest of the territory north of Sacramento to me. I'll be in touch with you and let you know everything you need to do."

Pa nodded his head agreeably. "And as for you, young lady," he went on, turning to me, "that was some article you wrote!"

"You read it?" I asked, half embarrassed, the other half astonished.

"Did I ever! So did the rest of the state. It appeared three days ago in the *Alta,* and another half dozen papers have already picked it up. I don't suppose I should be surprised after that speech you gave here in town about freedom. Some of the people I'm in touch with are already starting to say you just might be one of the best weapons Abraham Lincoln has in this state. In fact, because of that speech of yours, the Rev. Thomas Starr King, who was in the audience that day, has decided to become even more actively involved than he had planned. He wants to work with you!"

"That's my Corrie!" exclaimed Pa proudly. I tried to hide my embarrassment. I didn't know Mr. Dalton that well, but ever since the first time we'd seen him in San Francisco I couldn't escape the feeling that he sometimes exaggerated how he said things just to make me feel good, so that I'd be more inclined to do what he might want me to do later. I suppose politicians had to do that sometimes, but I hoped what he said about Mr. King was true. I liked Mr. Dalton well enough, but I didn't like having to wonder what he *really* thought. It seemed to me a man's words ought to be exactly what they were—no more and no less. In his case, I always had the feeling they were just a little bit more than he truly meant.

Nevertheless, I was just vain enough to enjoy his compliment anyway. I hoped there was *some* truth in his words, and that my article would do some good.

"In fact," he was saying, "there are two more large rallies we've got scheduled—one right here in Sacramento and another in San Francisco. I hope you'll be able to join us both times."

I shrugged noncommittally and glanced at Pa, but the expression on his face didn't give me any help.

"I realize it's a great distance to come," he added hurriedly. "But we'll pay for all your expenses, of course, just like before. And you can know that you're having a great impact for the good of our country and its future . . . for liberty, just as you said in your speech!"

"I'll think about it," I answered him.

"I've already talked to Cal about bringing you down for them."
He paused, and when he went on I wasn't sure I liked the sly look
in his eye or the tone of his voice. "He's taking good care of you,
I understand," he said.

I nodded.

"Since you and he seemed to, ah . . . hit it off, as it were, I
took the liberty of asking Leland—that's Mr. Stanford—to allow
me to borrow young Cal now and then to help out with the election, and to make sure my favorite young newspaper writer is kept
just as happy as she can be."

Again he smiled, with a look I didn't altogether like. Now I
was sure his words said more than he meant. I knew, after all the
years he'd been involved in important things, that I *wasn't* his
favorite newspaper writer. But he'd said it just as plain as day. You
couldn't actually call something like that a lie, but it certainly
wasn't the whole truth. I didn't think Mr. Dalton was intentionally
trying to deceive me. He probably considered it a nice thing to
say. But it still wasn't the truth—the *whole* truth, anyway. I don't
suppose Alexander Dalton was the kind of man who had made
truth the same kind of priority as I had. I hoped it wasn't politics
that had made him the way he was. I didn't want Pa to get like
that if he went to Sacramento—saying one thing but always having
a slightly different meaning to it that he *didn't* say.

"You like Cal, don't you?" Mr. Dalton asked, seeing me hesitate.

"Yes," I answered, blushing a little.

"Good, good! People like to see a nice young man and woman
standing up for principles and involving themselves in the nation's
affairs. I'm very happy to hear that we'll see you again up on the
platform representing the Republican party!"

"I don't think you heard my daughter, Mr. Dalton," said Pa.
"At least, I never heard her say for sure what she was going to
do."

"Did I misunderstand?" he said, looking at me bewildered.

"I said I would think about it," I said. "And I will."

"Fine! That's all I can expect. I will have Cal get in touch with
you about the details."

CHAPTER 34

WARNING SIGNS

I *did* speak both times Mr. Dalton had told me about. How could I say no when Cal practically begged me? And why would I have *wanted* to say no, anyway? I wouldn't have turned down another chance to be with Cal.

The most memorable part of September, however, wasn't the two speeches I gave. They weren't much different than the first, although I wasn't quite so nervous even though there were more people listening. But after we were through in San Francisco, instead of going straight back home, Cal invited me down to Mr. Stanford's ranch south of San Francisco in a little town called Palo Alto.

"He raises horses," Cal said. "There's a big ranch house where you'll be very comfortable. I'll show you his estate. We'll saddle up two of his finest horses and I'll show you the peninsula. It's beautiful country!"

"I . . . I don't know," I hesitated. "I suppose it would be all right. It does sound fun." Inside, my heart was beating wildly. It sounded like a dream come true—a fairy tale!

"How will we get there?" I asked, not even knowing what I was saying.

"I've got one of Mr. Stanford's finest carriages here in the city. I'm heading back down to the estate bright and early in the morning. Say you'll join me!"

"But . . . how will I get back here, and then home?"

"Don't worry, Corrie. With a man of the world like me to take care of everything, you need have no concerns. I'll see to your every need!"

In the thrill of the moment, I totally believed him. Not until later, as I lay in bed that night, did I realize that something about his words had struck a tiny chord of dissonance somewhere inside my brain.

Just then, as we were still talking about it, Mr. Dalton walked up. He greeted me kindly, congratulated me on a job well done, as he put it, and then turned to Cal and began speaking more quietly and more seriously. It was clear they didn't intend for me to listen, but they made no particular attempt to keep me from hearing, either. Men have a way of ignoring women when they want to, and paying attention to them when they want to. And when they're ignoring them, they seem to think they're not there at all, or that their minds don't work because they're not being paid attention to. But women are generally smarter and more aware of things than men realize. In this case I *was* listening, and I found their conversation very interesting, even though I know they probably thought my head was off in the clouds someplace.

"One of Senator Gwin's *Breckinridge* people is making trouble for us down in the South," Dalton was saying. "There's talk of a *Breckinridge*-Douglas coalition to smear Lincoln, to insure that *one* of the two Democrats wins California. Apparently they've sent someone up this way to spread the lies into northern California, too."

"What's his name?" asked Cal.

"Jewks . . . Terrance Jewks."

"Where is he? How do I find him?"

"Their people are said to be putting him up someplace in the city."

"Don't worry about a thing," Cal said after a while. "I'll take care of it. If he's in one of the San Francisco hotels, I'll find him."

"You know what to do?"

"I've run into just this sort of thing with Mr. Stanford. I've got ways of handling his sort."

"Leland tells me you are very resourceful," said Mr. Dalton, a grin breaking over his face.

"My goal is to be useful," replied Cal, returning the smile.

"Nothing more?" queried Dalton. "Leland is a powerful man, a man whose star is on the rise."

The look on Cal's face told that he knew exactly what that meant.

"All the more reason for me to serve him faithfully," said Cal, "as well as the whole party. To answer your question—yes, I know what to do. And I've got just the people to do it. Believe me, Mr. Jewks will not prove troublesome. He'll wish he stayed in the South and left northern politics to the Republicans!"

"Good. I knew I could count on you," said Dalton. The two shook hands, and I was left alone with Cal again.

"What was that all about?" I asked.

"Nothing . . . nothing, Corrie, my dear. Just the details of politics."

"It didn't sound too pleasant."

"Politics sometimes gets a little messy, Corrie. You must know that. Your father is a politician."

"He's mayor of Miracle Springs," I replied. "I don't know that I'd call him a politician."

"Well, he soon will be, from what I understand," Cal persisted. "Once he's sitting in the statehouse in Sacramento, his hands will get dirty, too."

"Not Pa's," I insisted.

Cal laughed. "Don't worry, Corrie. I'm not talking about anything serious. But it can't be helped. Your pa will explain it to you someday. In the meantime, you and I don't have to worry about all that! How about me taking you out for a fancy first-class dinner and a night on the town to celebrate your speech today? Then I'll get you safe and sound back to Miss Bean's later, and pick you up tomorrow morning for Palo Alto!"

Cal made me feel special, more like a real woman than I'd ever imagined I'd feel. I don't suppose I really believed half the sweet things he said to me. Yet I wanted to believe them so badly that I convinced myself to ignore the uncomfortable warning signs.

Besides, Cal Burton was not the kind of man a girl says *no* to. And I didn't really *want* to say no, after all.

CHAPTER 35

MEMORIES ON HORSEBACK

Palo Alto was all Cal promised it would be . . . and more!

Mr. Stanford and his wife treated me as if I were the most honored guest they'd ever had on the estate. I could hardly believe that a short time ago I was out in the desolate land of Nevada nearly being burned alive by Indians, and now I was hobnobbing with one of California's wealthiest men—and, according to Cal, one of its most influential politicians too!

The Stanford estate was completely different from the primitive Fremont estate at Mariposa. Mr. Fremont was also rich, of course, but he spent so little time in California, and Mariposa was so far away from everywhere else that he never did much to fancy it up. But I could tell instantly that the Stanfords intended to live on their new estate a long time. Besides politics and railroads, Mr. Stanford loved horses, and told me it had always been a lifelong dream of his to raise them. Now that he had a place and the means to do it, he intended to make his dream come true, right there in Palo Alto.

Mr. Stanford was a good friend of John and Jessie Fremont, and once Cal explained to him my connection with the campaign of 1856, he told me many interesting things I hadn't known.

"John Fremont may have lost the election in '56," he said, "but as far as I'm concerned it was a great victory. For a man to come so close to becoming president only four years after the formation of a new party is remarkable, in my opinion, and we Republicans owe him a great debt of gratitude. We'll win this year with Lincoln, thanks to people like you throughout the country,

191

Corrie. The John Fremont campaign four years ago laid the groundwork for this year's victory."

"Was he considered as a candidate again this year?" I asked.

"By a few people. But to be honest with you, there wasn't a great deal of support for him at the convention. Lincoln represents the rising new tide of the party, Corrie, although John's name was bandied about for vice-president. I wouldn't be surprised to see him with a cabinet appointment in the new administration, however. Lincoln thinks highly of him, from what I understand."

Just then Cal walked in.

"The horses are all saddled, Corrie. Shall we head out over the hills and see what kind of adventure we can find?"

"You be sure to take her up to the top of the ridge, Cal," said Mr. Stanford. "On a clear day like this, Corrie, from up there you can see out to the Pacific to the west, down into the bay to the east, and, if it's clear as crystal like it gets after a rain, you can just make out a bit of San Francisco at the tip of the peninsula. It's the most stunning view in all of California, if you ask me. And it's right here on my estate!"

"I'll be sure she sees it," said Cal.

"I probably won't see you again, Corrie," he said. "I've got a meeting with the Crocker brothers this evening, and tomorrow I have to get up to Sacramento early to see Judah, Huntington, and Hopkins on some railroad business. But you enjoy the rest of your stay, and you let my wife or Cal here know if you need anything."

"Thank you, sir," I said. "You are very kind."

It was still fairly early in the morning when we set out. Cal led the way at a leisurely pace, westward from the house and barns, down through a grassy little valley, and then up the gradual incline at the far end. The grass was dry and brown at this time of the year, and the hills were gently rolling, with oaks scattered thinly about. The air was not hot, just pleasantly warm. There was no breeze yet.

Gradually the climb grew steeper, though still nothing like the mountains I was used to back in the foothills country around Miracle. There was no trail, but the grass was almost meadowlike. We wound around gnarled old oaks, crossed several small streams, came across little glens that interrupted the upward ascent, and if

I had let myself daydream, I could have easily thought we might crest a small rise and see the snowcapped Sierras in the distance. It was hard to believe we were actually going in the exact opposite direction.

Finally a clearing spread out before us, with a rise about four or five hundred yards farther that seemed to taper off at its crest into a flat plateau.

"There it is!" said Cal.

"What?"

"The top. That's the summit."

"The summit!" I repeated with a laugh. "That makes it sound like a mountain."

"Okay, maybe it's not a mountain peak. But it's the highest hill for thirty miles in either direction. It's the one Mr. Stanford told me to show you."

"I'll race you there!" I cried.

"You're on!" Cal yelled back, giving his horse a slap on the rump and lurching into a gallop.

I let him get about twenty yards out in front, just enough of a lead for him to look back to see me sitting at the starting point calmly. Then I dug my heels into the mare Mr. Stanford had let me pick out earlier in the morning. I had liked her looks immediately, and had tested her speed a couple times on the way up, so I was confident of what kind of mount I had under me.

By the time Cal looked back again I had closed half the distance between us, and drew alongside him before we were halfway to the top. I didn't even look over, but just leaned forward against my mare's neck and whisked by. I reached the top, reined in the mare, and was sitting calmly in the saddle regaining my breath by the time Cal galloped up alongside ten or fifteen seconds later.

"What took you so long?" I asked, grinning.

"Let me answer with a question—where did *you* learn to ride like that?" laughed Cal. "You put me to shame."

"I'm just a country girl," I answered. "I told you I've been riding for years. When you don't live in a city, you learn to ride."

"Maybe it's you who ought to be riding for the Pony Express instead of your brother!"

"I might if they let girls join," I said.

"Don't you dare! We need you too much in this campaign!"

Now that the race to the top of the hill was behind us, I had a chance to look around and see where we were.

"It's absolutely breathtaking!" I exclaimed.

Spread out, not above us as the Sierras would have been, but rather below us like a distant blue infinite carpet stretching all the way to the horizon, was the Pacific Ocean. The day was perfect. The sky was nearly as blue as the sea, with a few billows of clouds suspended lazily here and there. As we had come up over the ridge, the gentlest whisper of a breeze had met us, and now as I drew in deep breaths I could smell just the faintest hint of the ocean's fragrance.

I stretched all around in my saddle, looking down upon the long blue fingers of San Francisco's huge bay in the other direction, just as Mr. Stanford had described it. Then I turned north to see if the city itself was in view. It hadn't rained in the last several days, but it was just clear enough that I *thought* I could see fuzzy glimpses of it. If it wasn't the actual buildings of the city I saw, perhaps it was just the rounding part of the end of the peninsula, with my imagination filling in shapes where I knew the city was.

"Look over that way," said Cal, pointing northeast. "There's the mouth of the Sacramento River emptying into the bay. And Sacramento eighty miles away," he added, swinging his arm a little to the right.

As I watched Cal describing the view, I saw a subtle change come over him when he began talking about Sacramento. The capital city, it seemed, possessed a greater significance for him than all the rest.

"What is it about Sacramento that's so special to you?" I asked.

"Opportunity, Corrie," he said after a long silence. "Just like I told you before . . . opportunity."

I thought back to Pa's talk on our way to Carson City; he had said that sometimes we have to take the chances that come our way before it is too late. But I had the feeling he and Cal meant two completely different things. Pa seemed to be saying that we ought to be mindful of the opportunities God puts in our path. Cal seemed to be saying something else, although I wasn't quite sure what it was yet.

"Look around you, Corrie," Cal went on, turning in his saddle. "Look out there—what do you see?" He pointed due west.

"The ocean," I answered.

"What else do you see?"

"The sky," I said, half in question.

"What else?"

"I don't know, Cal . . . the clouds?"

"No, Corrie! Down there is the end of the land, the coast of California . . . the *end* of the country, the last piece of the United States, the edge of the whole continent!"

His face was lit up as if he had revealed the whole riddle of the universe. He kept looking at me as if expecting light to break in upon my mind at any second.

"Don't you see what that means?" he asked finally.

"Uh . . . I guess I don't," I said.

"It means the end of one kind of opportunity and the beginning of a whole new era in our country's history—a whole era of *new* opportunities!"

Again he stopped and scanned all around, at everything we could see. Slowly we began walking our horses along the plateau of the ridge.

"You see, Corrie," Cal began, "for the last century, the whole thrust of opportunity in this country was just to *get* here—to reach the Pacific. This was the frontier. It had to be explored, then tamed. Lewis and Clark, Jedediah Smith, even your own John Fremont back in his exploring days—they were men whose passion was just *getting* here, to this very place, to the Pacific coast. Then all those who came after them—trappers and traders and homesteaders and cattle ranchers, and families by wagon trains— they were coming here just to *be* here—to come west, to live, to settle, to make lives for themselves. Do you see what I mean? *Getting* west was the opportunity in itself! Then came the gold rush, and men and women poured in by the hundreds of thousands. Now California and Oregon are states, and one day Nevada and Washington will be, too. We've reached the end, the end of the frontier, Corrie. The country's come as far west as it can go. California's been tamed and settled. And here we stand, right at the very end, gazing down to where California meets the Pacific."

We rode on slowly; then he stopped and suddenly jumped down off his mount, gazing down toward the ocean below us.

"Do you know where the *next* era of opportunity lies, Corrie?" he asked.

"Where, Cal?" I said.

He hesitated just momentarily, then wheeled around, stretched his arms widely out into the air as he faced eastward, and cried, "Out there! Back where we've come from—toward the east and everywhere between this spot right here and the same spot overlooking the Atlantic coast somewhere in New York or Maryland or Georgia! It's what we *do* with this land now that we've conquered it and explored it. We've spent two hundred years just getting to this spot, Corrie. Many people shed their blood so that you and I could stand here and look out upon that expanse of blue. In the next century, fortunes are going to be made and empires are going to be built by those who lay hold of the opportunities afforded them.

"Men like Leland Stanford *came* west. That was their first opportunity. He came from Wisconsin with his four brothers and set up business in Sacramento. Getting here was his first opportunity, which he took hold of, and it made him a rich man. But he didn't stop there. Then he turned his eyes back *over* the country he had crossed, and he began to take hold of new political opportunities—the opportunity of power. He ran for governor of this state. Even though he lost, Leland Stanford is still looking for new frontiers to conquer. He came to the Pacific, but now he is seeking to *return* to the East by rail—a new opportunity. I have no doubt that he and his friends *will* one day build a railroad back to the East where they all came from, and grow even more wealthy and powerful in the process.

"Oh, Corrie, don't you see what I'm getting at? It's in the statehouses like Sacramento where these opportunities of the future originate—where the laws are made. It's there where the powerful people gather, where the money flows from. Politics, money, and influence—they are the opportunities of the *next* century! Those with vision to see such things will go far."

He turned around, his eyes glowing as he looked up at me. I sat still on the mare, listening to every word he said.

"From the Pacific to the Atlantic," I said, halfway to myself, reflecting on what he'd said a minute ago.

"Sea to sea . . . shore to shore! That's it exactly!"

"There's only one thing I don't understand, Cal," I said. "Why then do you want to have anything to do with someone like me? I'm hardly the kind of person you're talking about."

"But you are, Corrie! I knew that right from the first, when I heard about you and then when I laid eyes on you. Not only were you a beautiful young lady, all dressed up at the Montgomery Hotel in San Francisco. You also have done just what I'm talking about. You came west. The first frontier was just *getting* here and joining back up with your father and uncle. But no sooner had you done that than you turned back around and set your sights on higher goals. You started writing; you took every opportunity that you could, and now your writing is being read all the way back across the country. And the very Pony Express pouches that your brother carries across the mountains and desert have newspapers in them with *your* articles and speeches written down for folks in the East to read. You know the Fremonts and Mr. Stanford and Mr. Dalton. Don't you see, Corrie—in your own way, you're going to be an important person someday too, just like Leland Stanford!"

"That doesn't sound like me, Cal," I said.

"But it is, Corrie. You should be proud of it!"

"I never set my sights on having high goals. I never tried to *take* opportunities so I could get well known. That kind of thing never entered my mind, Cal."

"It happened all the same. And now look at you—who would deny that you're better off for all of it. For a *woman* to have done all you have, at such a young age . . . it's remarkable, Corrie! I tell you, you ought to be downright proud!"

I suppose it was idiotic of me to keep questioning him. He had been so nice to me, and a short time ago I had thought I was in love with him. Maybe I still was. I had even persuaded myself that his attentions came from feelings he perhaps shared. But I had to know.

"Is that why you want to have something to do with me?" I persisted. "Because I might be an important person someday?"

"No, of course not," he answered quickly. His voice bore a roughness, a defensiveness I had never heard before, as if such a blunt question had caught him momentarily with his guard down. It wasn't the kind of thing young women asked when men were showering them with praise.

"That is, not if you find such a motive to be offensive," he said smoothly, recovering his old composure. "I cannot deny that your accomplishments and reputation add to the charm I find so compelling about you. But even without them, I would still find you attractive above any other of the young ladies I have known. Do you believe me, Corrie?"

"I would like to."

"Then *do* believe me," he implored. His voice was so sincere; how could I possibly not believe he was in earnest? "Come, Corrie . . . get down. Walk with me." He reached up his hand and helped me down off the mare. When my feet were on the ground, however, he did not let go. My heart fluttered to feel his hand around mine, but I was too flustered to make any attempt to pull it away.

"Ah, Corrie," he said at last, "so much lies within our grasp— young persons like us, with life and opportunities and exciting new times for the country ahead of us!"

We walked on. My mind and heart were spinning in a dozen directions at once. I'd always thought of myself as rational and level-headed, but not now. Not with Cal Burton.

"Be part of it with me, Corrie," he said after a minute or two. "Let's find our opportunities together, and take advantage of them! You and I—we can be the Lewis and Clark of the next generation. You'll be a famous writer someday. And I'll—well, who knows how far we can go, Corrie, or what we can achieve! We can go back across this continent in the footsteps of Leland Stanford and men like him, and maybe even start to make our own marks in the history books of this country! What do you say, Corrie?"

I know I was being a fool, but I couldn't help asking one more time, "But . . . why me, Cal?"

"Don't you know, Corrie? Haven't you figured it out from all I've been telling you? It's because I care for you, Corrie—I care deeply. That's why, with us working together, there wouldn't be anything we couldn't do, couldn't achieve, couldn't get if we set our minds to it!''

Cal's closeness and the excitement in his tone overwhelmed me. I felt like running! I pulled my hand out of his and took off across the grass as fast as I could go.

"Hey . . . where are you off to?" called Cal behind me. I heard him start to chase after me, but I ran all the faster. I ran until I was tired, then slowed and let him catch up with me.

When he did, he threw his long arm around my shoulder and gave me a squeeze, then let go as we turned and started walking back to where the horses were nibbling at the brown grass.

We mounted back up and started slowly down the hill.

We rode down to the seashore, stopped and ran along the sandy beach, explored a watery cave, then galloped the horses miles along the sand before climbing back up inland, over the ridge of the peninsula again, and down through the woods and meadows. Even though we didn't arrive back at the Stanford estate until late in the afternoon, in spite of all the exertion and the long ride, I didn't seem to be hungry.

Dinner wasn't exactly "formal," but I did put on a different dress than the one I'd ridden in all afternoon, and Cal made his appearance in a black coat and ruffled white shirt with bow tie. He was indeed a handsome young man, and seeing him all dressed up reminded me of how taken I had been with him that night in San Francisco back in June.

When I went to bed that night, I lay awake a long time, dreaming of horses and sand and oak trees and the shining sun dancing and reflecting off the shimmering white and blue surface of the ocean. But mostly I dreamed of a tan face with brown hair flying above it in the breeze, and eyes of a blue so deep that even the sky above and the Pacific below seemed pale by comparison.

CHAPTER 36

HOW MANY STATES?

When I got back to Miracle Springs several days later, the two speeches I had made already seemed far in the past. But knowing nothing about my trip to Palo Alto, Pa and Almeda were full of questions about the political situation.

"You heard anything more from Mr. Dalton?" I asked him.

"Got a letter just yesterday," Pa answered. "He asked how the handbills that you had suggested were coming along—"

I had forgotten all about them—we were going to have to get busy in a hurry!

"*And*," Pa went on, "he said he'd arranged for me to speak at a town meeting over in Marysville next week."

"What do you think, Corrie?" asked Almeda.

"What's more important is what *you* think," I answered.

"I think it's wonderful!" she said with a big smile. "I had no idea what I was starting when I got the notion of running for mayor. Now look what it's caused—Drummond Hollister running for state office!"

In California, the presidential election of 1860 in California had as much to do with the dispute between North and South as it did anywhere else in the country. The battle for supremacy of the nation, and which region was going to hold the reins of power, *was* the election of 1860. In addition to the slavery issue itself, the election would determine who was going to direct the course of the future of the United States of America.

The South had controlled the government in Washington for thirty years. But all of a sudden, a major change seemed at hand.

But the South did not intend to give up without a fight. The battle was to be waged on November 6, 1860.

California was one of the only states, however, where the dispute over control between North and South went on *inside* the state. California was now the second biggest state next to Texas, almost nine hundred miles from top to bottom, running north and south. The top of California next to Oregon was parallel with New York, and the bottom border ran right through the middle of Mississippi, Alabama, and Georgia. It was only natural, I suppose, that there would be debate *within* California as to which side its loyalties ought to lie on.

Even during the Mexican period in California before the gold rush, there had been a spirit of sectionalism between the northern and southern halves of the state. Especially once the gold rush came, those in the south didn't like all the activity of the north. When statehood was being discussed in 1849, many southern Californians did not want to be part of the new state and proposed dividing California in half at San Luis Obispo. They wanted to be able to go on with the slow pace of their old way of life, without being forced to be part of the frantic, growing, alien north where people were pouring in and towns were growing into great metropolitan areas overnight. Those in the south felt it unfair that they should have to pay taxes and support a state government that was located in the north, and that was expensive and heavily weighted toward the needs and concerns of the north. The south was so sparsely settled, it would even have preferred not to be a state at all, just as long as it could be separate from the north.

Statehood came to the whole state, but the desire to split the state into northern and southern halves continued as a volatile issue all the way through the 1850s. A huge movement in Los Angeles and throughout the south in 1851 tried to develop enough support to break away and form a new state. In the next two years, the southern legislators in Sacramento tried to call a constitutional convention that would divide the state. But since the north controlled the state legislature, such attempts were defeated.

Finally, in 1855 a bill was finally introduced into the California Assembly that at first called for a new state named *Columbia* to be formed. Then later the bill was changed to split California into *three* states. A new state called *Colorado* would be made of the area south of San Luis Obispo. A new state called *Shasta* would be made of the far northern part bordering Oregon. And *California* would remain as the central region of the three states.

That bill never passed, but the idea for making separate states continued, and even gradually began to be supported by some northerners. Another bill was introduced in Sacramento in 1859, again for two states, and again with the separation at San Luis Obispo, creating a new territory south of that to be called *Colorado*. This time there *was* enough support for the idea to pass both the state senate and the state assembly in Sacramento.

But the legislature couldn't split the state apart all by themselves. There were two other groups of people who had to be part of the decision, too—the federal government and the people who lived in the part of California where they wanted to create a new state.

So the legislature wrote up a bill that would create a new territory to be called *Colorado*—*if* two thirds of the people in that region south of San Luis Obispo approved of the plan, and *if* the Congress in Washington, D.C., also approved. The bill passed in the state assembly 33 to 15, and in the state senate 15 to 12. Then a special election was set up late in 1859 for the people of southern California to vote themselves on whether they wanted their part of the state to be formed into a new territory called *Colorado*.

They surely did! The people south of San Luis Obispo voted 2,457 to 828 in favor of dividing California in half, and calling their half Colorado.

Therefore, in January of 1860, Governor Milton Latham formally sent the results of the bill and both votes to President James Buchanan, asking for the U.S. Congress to approve the division of California.

No approval had yet been given, however. The rest of the nation was too taken up with other momentous events that year. The election between Lincoln and Douglas and the dispute between the southern states and northern states all made a local squabble within distant California seem a little insignificant to the politicians in Washington. Not only was California far away from the rest of the country, it was made up mostly of Spanish-speaking Mexicans in the south and gold-hungry miners in the north. At least that's what Pa said folks in the East thought about us.

"What does that have to do with splitting up the state, Pa?" Tad asked when we were all sitting talking about it a couple of weeks later.

"Nothing directly, son," answered Pa. "It's only that back in Washington I reckon they figure California's a mite different than other states, and that maybe they just oughta leave it alone to do what it wants."

"But if California wants it, all they have to do is approve it," said Becky.

"Well, there are certain kinds of things where the federal government's just not anxious to interfere. It's called *states' rights*. This country got its start as a collection of independent states that pretty much did what they pleased. The government in Washington was set up just to ride herd over the whole conglomeration, while the states went on deciding things for themselves. That's why it's called the United *States* of America instead of something else."

"You sound like a politician, Pa!" laughed Becky.

"Of course he's a politician!" said Almeda. "That's what being mayor is all about."

"I mean he sounds like a speechmaker."

"Like Corrie!" said Tad.

"I'm no speechmaker, Tad," I said.

"What about it, Drummond?" said Almeda. "Did that speech you made in Marysville last week go to your head? You *are* starting to sound a little high-falutin' for the likes of simple country folk like us."

"Now you cut that out, Almeda!" joked Pa. "You all know well and good I ain't about to start sounding like no doggone politician from Sacramento or Washington. I was only trying to answer Becky's question."

"Is states' rights why there's slavery some places and it's against the law in others?" asked Tad.

"Right you are, son. That's it exactly. It's up to the states to decide for themselves."

"What about right and wrong?" I asked. "It seems as if on an issue like slavery there ought to be more to it than everybody deciding what they want to do. That's why I decided to support

Mr. Lincoln, because of right and wrong.''

"But who's to say what's right and what's wrong? You've listened to Katie and Edie, Corrie. They *don't* see anything wrong in slavery, because they were both brought up in the South. That's why the government in Washington has always stayed out of such disputes. They don't want to get into the business of deciding right and wrong, so they let the states decide whatever *they* want to do.''

"Then, why don't they let California split into two states?" asked Tad.

Pa looked at him a minute, then shook his head with a puzzled expression.

"The truth of the matter, son, is that I'm blamed if I know," he answered finally. "Maybe they just ain't got around to approving it.''

"If you're elected to the Assembly, Drummond," said Almeda, "what stand are *you* going to take?"

"On what?" asked Pa.

"On the split of California. Are you going to continue to push for it next year if President Buchanan doesn't act on the measure before the election?"

Again Pa grew thoughtful. "If I do get elected to the Assembly, which I still doubt, then I'll have to figure out what I'm gonna do about a lot of things. Right now I can't say. I can't see much reason to be against dividing it up, but I got no objections to keeping it the way it is, either."

"If they won't let California do what *it* wants to do," said Becky, "then why do they let the states do whatever they want to do about slavery? It doesn't seem fair.''

"Politics isn't always fair, girl, any more than the government always does what's *right*, like Corrie was saying. States' rights isn't a doctrine of governing that always makes things turn out fair. It just happens to be how this here country got put together in the first place. Besides, Buchanan's a Democrat and a southerner. Letting the states do whatever they want—that's just how the southerners want to keep it, so they can keep having their slaves and growing their cotton. No Democrat's gonna change that.''

"A Republican might," I suggested.

"Yeah, you're right, daughter, a Republican just might. That's why the Democrats and southerners are so all-fired worried about this election. They figure if Lincoln's elected, it just might be the end of states' rights altogether.''

"Why can't it all just keep going how it is?" asked Tad. "Some states could have slaves if they wanted, others don't have to."

"Yes, Pa," added Becky, "why can't there keep being states' rights no matter who gets elected?"

"That's what the southerners want," put in Almeda. "But Abraham Lincoln has made no secret of his revulsion toward slavery."

Pa turned to me. "Corrie," he said, "where's that paper that had your article about the election in it? Seems I recollect reading a speech of Lincoln's there."

"I'll get it, Pa," I said, jumping up.

"You see, Becky," Pa went on, "Mr. Lincoln figures we just can't keep going forever with half of the states one way, the other half the other way. He says it's tearing the country apart, making people hate each other, making it so the government can't do anything but argue and dispute and can't get on with the business of helping make the country what it ought to be. He says that we *got* to be what our name says—*united*. One way or the other— either all for slavery or all against it. We can't keep being split up like we have been. And now that there's more northern states than southern, the southerners figure that if he's elected, he's gonna try to take the *whole* country the direction he wants to go."

"Against states' rights?"

"They don't figure Mr. Lincoln cares so much for states' rights as much as he wants to do what *he* thinks is right."

Just then I returned with the paper.

"Here," said Pa, reaching out and taking it from me, "just listen to this. I'll read you part of the speech and you can see for yourselves what Mr. Lincoln says about it."

He rustled through the *Alta* till he found the speech on the second page and began to read.

> In my opinion, the agitation over the issue of slavery will not cease until a crisis shall have been reached and passed. A house divided against itself cannot stand. I believe this government cannot endure, permanently half slave and half free. I do not expect the Union to be dissolved—I do not

expect the house to fall—but I DO expect it will cease to be divided. It will become all one thing, or all the other. Either the opponents of slavery will arrest the further spread of it, and place it where the public mind shall rest in the belief that it is in the course of ultimate extinction; or its advocates will push it forward, till it shall become alike lawful in all the States, old as well as new—North as well as South.

"I didn't understand that, Pa," said Tad.

"He's just saying that it's got to be all one way or all the other. Slavery's either got to be legal everywhere throughout the whole country, or else it's got to be thrown out completely, including in the South."

"What about the states that are talking of seceding, Drummond?" asked Almeda seriously. "Do you think it could actually happen?"

"No way to know, Almeda. One thing's for sure—people can be mighty stubborn and dead set against change, whether they're right *or* wrong."

"But if some states want to secede, should they have the right to?" I asked. Ever since I had decided to get involved in the election, I'd been thinking about this question because I knew it was on Abraham Lincoln's mind. I still hadn't been able to figure out even what I thought about it.

"That's the question of 1860, girl," said Pa. "It ain't so much just about slavery, but whether states' rights gives some of the states the right to pull themselves out of the United States of America altogether. If California can't split in half without the government's permission, then can some of the southern states go off and do whatever they want to do without permission either? I don't reckon anybody knows the answer to that question yet. But if Mr. Lincoln gets elected, I don't much doubt that some of 'em are gonna put it to the test and see what comes of it."

Pa surely was sounding like a politician! From a fugitive to a gold miner to a father to a mayor . . . and now he was talking about the future of the whole country as if he was personally involved in what happened.

And as a candidate for the California State Assembly, I guess he was, at that!

CHAPTER 37

THE ELECTION APPROACHES

In a way, the question that California politicians had been debating was just a small version of the same issue politicians in the rest of the country were wrestling with.

Should California, where the interests of the northern and southern sections were much different, be one *state* or two? And should the whole country be one *nation* or two? How far did states' rights go, anyway?

Trouble had been brewing between the North and South for a long time. There had been strong outcries against slavery for almost thirty years—going clear back to the preaching of Charles Finney in the 1830s as well as that of many others. The American Anti-Slavery Society was formed in 1833. William Lloyd Garrison had begun a radical antislavery newspaper called *The Liberator* two years before that stirred up sentiments on both sides all over the country. More societies were formed. Books were written. And dozens of preachers denounced slavery from the pulpit.

But none of that could do anything to put an end to slavery. The Congress in Washington, D.C., made the laws. And since Congress was controlled all that time by the Democratic party, which was mostly made up of men from the South, they continued to uphold the right of each individual state to have slavery if it wanted—which, of course, all the southern states did.

When the Republican party formed in the early 1850s, the Democrats and southerners weren't too worried. But it grew so rapidly—with new states and territories all being more inclined toward northern interests, and with antislavery preaching continuing to grow—that by 1856 the Democrats realized they *should* be worried. Buchanan had been elected over John Fremont only by a hairsbreadth. If two of the northern states had gone for Fremont instead, he would have become president. The governor of Virginia, Edie had told us, had been thinking of secession even back then if Fremont had been elected.

Now, in 1860, southern leaders *were* worried!

In the North, there was strong and growing opposition to the hold of the South. But the southerners had no intention of giving up their power without a fight. There were growing threats throughout the year that a number of the states of the South would simply secede, or pull out of the Union. The South was financially strong, and if it had to, it would simply form its own new nation. But it would *not* give up slavery, nor give up its right to make its own decisions.

But the election of 1860 was not as simple as Democrats against Republicans, North against South, slavery against abolition. In fact, there were *four* candidates for president. Douglas, the Democrat, was not even a southerner at all. He was from Abraham Lincoln's home state of Illinois, and was the U.S. senator from Illinois. He had defeated Lincoln for that position in 1858 after their famous series of debates.

Many southerners, in fact, didn't like Douglas. He wasn't strongly enough in favor of slavery to suit them. But most Democrats, by 1860, realized that Lincoln was absolutely sure to win if they nominated a proslavery southerner to run against him. So at the Democratic convention earlier in the year, a majority had nominated the northerner Douglas, figuring that a northern candidate was their only hope against Lincoln.

That only angered the Democrats from the deep South. Win or not, they wanted a candidate who stood *for* slavery! So they organized a convention of *their* own and nominated their Democratic candidate, Buchanan's vice-president, John Breckinridge, from the slave state of Kentucky.

Now there were two Democrats running against Lincoln!

Back in the spring, a whole new party had been formed, called the Constitutional Union party. They hoped to find some middle ground between both the Democrats and the Republicans, and stood above all else simply for loyalty to the Union itself. They hoped to attract support from Union-loving conservatives in the South. The ticket for this new party was made up of two U.S. senators, one from the North, one from the South—John Bell of Tennessee for president and Edward Everett of Massachusetts for vice president.

So those were the four candidates: Lincoln for the Republicans, Douglas for the Democrats, Breckinridge for the southern Democrats, and Bell for the Constitutional Union party.

It was a hard-fought campaign. Douglas traveled up and down New England calling on people to preserve the Union and speaking against secession—sounding almost like Lincoln himself—trying to get the northern vote while retaining southern Democratic support. Even as pro-southern as he was, Breckinridge tried to convince the voters that he, too, was opposed to secession.

In California, as in the rest of the country, the Democrats had been in control, and there was a large pro-southern sentiment throughout the state. But the split of the Democratic party also split California and its leaders. Governor Downey declared his support for Douglas. Former governors Weller and Latham and Senator Gwin declared their support for Breckinridge. And Mr. Stanford and his business and railroad associates Huntington, Cole, Hopkins, and Charles and Edwin Crocker made up the most well-known of the Republican leadership within the state.

It was remarkable to me how much pro-southern, pro-slavery support there was in *northern* California. Except for the possibility that a lot of Californians had come from the South, I couldn't understand it. I hadn't understood it back in 1856, and I still didn't understand it in 1860. If the Democratic party hadn't been split in its loyalties, I don't think Mr. Lincoln would have had a ghost of a chance in California.

CHAPTER 38

NOVEMBER 6, 1860

We made up the handbills for Pa. This time it was important to distribute them not just around Miracle Springs but everywhere possible in the whole section of the state north of Sacramento in the Assembly district Pa hoped to represent. Pa was running as a Republican, and though there were several other candidates—one other Republican and three Democrats all together—we hoped that he might have a chance to win. For the flyer I wrote a story that told all about Pa and who he was, adding quotes from some people in Miracle Springs saying what a good mayor he'd been.

Then I wrote an article for the handbill, like the speech I'd given in Sacramento about freedom and the future of the country. It probably didn't have much to do with Pa and whether he'd be a good legislator or not, but I hoped it would help. I didn't want to say *too* much, because if people knew that a Hollister was writing telling people to vote for a Hollister, it might not seem altogether unbiased.

Edie was still with Aunt Katie, and in spite of our differences about slavery itself, she thought it was exciting about Pa's running for office, even as a Republican. She offered to help, and the rest of us were ready to do anything we could, too. It was a lot of work, but we split up and took handbills to all the towns for thirty or forty miles around Miracle Springs—wherever we could get to on horseback and back in a day, or to the towns Pa or I passed through on our way to Sacramento. We even gave them to Marcus Weber when he had deliveries to make.

In every town we posted a copy of the handbill up on the town announcement board, or if they didn't have one, on a post some-where near the center of town. Then the rest we'd leave at the General Store if they'd let us. Most of the folks knew something about Pa and were happy to pass out the flyers to their customers.

I didn't make any more speeches, although Pa did at a couple more towns where Mr. Dalton had made arrangements for him. He was having lots of the smaller northern newspapers print ar-ticles about Pa, too, and told us just a week before the election that Drummond Hollister was the most widely known and rec-ognized name of the five candidates.

I got several letters from Cal in the month preceding the elec-tion, although I didn't see him again. I wrote to him several times, too, and asked him about what I'd overheard between him and Mr. Dalton concerning the anti-Lincoln move in the southern por-tion of the state. *It's all taken care of, Corrie,* he wrote back in his next letter. *Forget you heard a word about it.* In fact, he expressed surprise that I remembered the incident.

It was a minor annoyance, he went on to say, *which we took care of. I have every confidence our Mr. Lincoln will carry the day in northern California.*

The long-awaited day finally came on Tuesday, November 6. Pa and Uncle Nick went to vote, but of course it was days before the ballots were all collected and counted, and two weeks before we found out what the results were throughout the rest of the country. That Pony Express rider carrying the election news was one of the most eagerly anticipated since the Express had begun. They didn't have to ride all the way to Sacramento for the news to reach us, because by that time a telegraph had been installed between San Francisco and Churchill, Nevada. The San Francisco papers carried news of the election results on November 19.

The Democratic strategy of two candidates hadn't worked. And the Independent had done much better than predicted, car-rying three states. Douglas had received the second highest num-ber of votes behind Lincoln, but only carried Missouri and split New Jersey with Lincoln. Breckinridge got only 18 percent of the total vote. But because of his strong support in the proslavery South, he carried eleven southern states.

The final votes were: Lincoln 1,866,000, Douglas 1,383,000,

Breckinridge 848,000, and Bell 593,000.

Abraham Lincoln received 40 percent of the total, not nearly a majority. But because he carried all the northern states and seventeen states in all, his electoral vote was a huge majority. The final electoral results were: Lincoln 180, Breckinridge 79, Bell 39, and Douglas 12.

Abraham Lincoln had been elected the next president of the United States!

CHAPTER 39

A DREADFUL WAY TO END A YEAR

But would the United States stay *united* for much longer? Almost immediately after the election it began to look as if the answer was no!

The South was now clearly and unmistakably the minority. The once-powerful region that had controlled the nation had been defeated. Many mixed sentiments ran through the hearts of loyal southerners—pride, honor, fear of what the North might do. And stubbornness, too. They feared that their traditional and cherished ways of life would now be destroyed, their lands taken, their fortunes and businesses ruined. Their pride had been assaulted. Many southerners felt themselves superior, and that *they* were more capable of ruling the nation no matter what the election might have said. Now the mammon-worshiping materialists of the North were in power, intent on destroying the southern culture forever, and replacing it with their Yankee ways.

Their honor was at stake. They would not, they *could* not submit to such humiliation. They must save the South, even if they had to create a whole new republic to do it!

It did not take long for the southern states to act. They had prepared for this moment for more than a year should Lincoln be elected. One month after the vote, on December 6, 1860, South Carolina voted to withdraw from the Union.

Rapidly the governors of the other southern states called special sessions of their legislatures to vote on similar measures. They wanted to act hurriedly, while a sympathetic and Democratic

James Buchanan was still president. What Abraham Lincoln might do once he took office on March 3, no one knew. And the southern states didn't want to wait to find out!

I suppose that in the South during these tense months, there was a feeling of excitement, as if they were part of a historic and honorable cause, out of which a new and noble nation was about to be born. But in the rest of the country, news of what South Carolina had done caused only gloom. Why, we all wondered, would they try to tear the country apart?

We still hoped nothing might come of it. South Carolina had always been the most radical southern state. Back in 1832 when Pa hadn't been much more than a boy, South Carolina had gotten defiant and had threatened to do the same thing. But President Jackson had answered heatedly and had said he'd send in the army if he had to. South Carolina had backed down.

Many people held the opinion that they could be forced to back down again if Buchanan would act, and act promptly. But President Buchanan's party had been defeated. He had only three months more to serve, and he had never been a swift decision maker. The result was that he did nothing, and left events to take their course. He would just wait and let the new president worry about it.

In the meantime, the South became stronger and stronger in their resolve that they would *never* back down again.

As bad as all this was, it wasn't the worst news to come to Miracle Springs as 1860 came to an end. Two weeks before Christmas, a letter arrived addressed to Pa. The handwriting was a barely legible scrawl, but his name and "Miracle Springs could be made out on the envelope. The letter inside was no easier to read. It was a single sheet of paper.

HOLISTR,

I hope this here letter gits to you. I give it to Pony Bob an tol him to give hit to the next feller an to git hit to Sacremeno an that somebudy there'd no how to git it to youe. This aint no good kin of letter to have to writ to nobudy nohow, an I hate to be the one to have to do hit. But I figger youd rather hear hit from a freen than from somebudy you never heerd of. What I got to say jis this, Holistr, an Im sorry as a man

kin be, but word came to us las week that yer sons horse come wanderin into the stashun without nary a trace o the kid. The mail was ther but no rider. Thats all we heerd. I sent Pony Bob back out ther an tol him to fin out sumthin mor, on account o youe bein my freen an all. I didnt want to writ you til we cud tell you jist what happen. But Bob he didnt git no more informashun, an nobudys heerd hide or hare o the boy sinse, and its been more na week now, an this time o yere nobudy kin live out in them hills past tu or thre days. Im sorry as kin be, but hit dont look good fer yer boy. Hits been snowin there tu. An the blame Piyutes. Give yer little lady my best, and tell her Im sorry tu.
Tavish

The whole rest of the week a spirit of gloom hovered all about the claim. When all the folks in town heard about it, a quiet settled over all of Miracle Springs. Pa was held in mighty high regard by everyone, and so was Almeda. The fact that Zack had been riding for the Pony Express had made people proud in a way. His disappearance affected everyone.

Rev. Rutledge prayed for Zack in church the next Sunday, and of course everybody came up to us to offer their sympathy and to say they'd be praying for all of us.

Mr. Royce was among them. "I'm sorry to hear about the boy, Hollister," he said, shaking Pa's hand. "I really mean that."

"I know you do, Franklin," replied Pa.

"The kid had spunk. Almost as much as your girl there," he added, glancing toward me with as much of a smile as Franklin Royce was ever likely to give anyone. "He was the one who saved my money and your wife's property back when the Dutch Flat gang was causing so much trouble. No, I'm not likely to forget that. If anybody can take care of himself out there, it's your Zack."

"I'm much obliged to you, Royce," said Pa.

As time went on, it was almost worse not knowing. It would have been easier to deal with and get past if we had just heard he was dead. But to not know, and to have to think of him lying somewhere with an arrow in him, or frozen in a snowdrift in some ravine—that was the worst part.

The only bright spot in the last month and a half of the year was that Pa was elected to the California State Assembly. But nobody felt much like celebrating. Least of all Pa.

CHAPTER 40

SECESSION!

Christmas of 1860 was certainly not a very festive day.

Almeda and Aunt Katie tried to make it as happy as they could. There were presents and we had a nice dinner with the Rutledges at our house. But Pa felt so downcast over Zack, and everyone shared his misery.

Pa now had two things to feel guilt-ridden about—driving Zack away in the first place, and then turning back when we were there instead of going on to find him—Indian danger or not!

"If only I hadn't been such a coward," Pa said a dozen times. "I might have got to him and talked him into coming back home with me. But that handful of Indians made me hightail it outta there like a scared jackrabbit!"

"There were more than a few, Pa," I reminded him. "We both almost got ourselves good and dead."

But nothing I or anyone else said could perk up Pa's spirits. And who was I to blame him? I'd have felt terrible, too. I *did* feel terrible, but not so bad as if I'd been his father. Maybe Zack was being rebellious and independent by running off as he had. But Pa didn't have the luxury of the man in the New Testament, knowing he had been a good father and yet not being able to do anything about his son's foolish youthfulness. Maybe Pa had been a decent father to Zack; maybe he hadn't. He sure had been to me. But the fact was, he didn't think so, and he believed the accusations Zack had shouted at him the day he'd left.

So it was a lot harder on him than the father in the Bible who just had to wait patiently for his prodigal son to come to his senses.

Pa had to carry guilt along with everything else, guilt for having caused all the trouble and heartbreak himself. Now thinking that Zack was probably dead, but not knowing, and knowing he might *never* know for sure—it was just an unbearable load for poor Pa. All the rest of us could do was love him and pray for him. But we couldn't make it go away.

As always, news from the East got into our papers about two weeks after it actually happened. During that first week of the new year of 1861, we began to learn of events that did not portend good news for the future. President Buchanan still hadn't done anything to block or counter South Carolina's action. Neither had he nor anyone else made any hard attempts to resolve the crisis with a compromise of some kind. These failures led to the most serious news of all: one by one, starting with Mississippi on December 20, the rest of the southern states began to secede from the Union too. Next came Florida, then Alabama, Georgia, Louisiana, and finally later in January, Texas.

Still President Buchanan did nothing. Abraham Lincoln remained powerless until he would take office on March 3. Was nothing to be done to save the *United* States of America from becoming the *Dis*united States?

As they seceded, the southern states had taken possession of federal properties inside their borders. South Carolina could not immediately seize Fort Sumter in Charleston harbor, however, because it had no navy and because the fort was held by seventy-five Union soldiers.

But South Carolina wanted the fort. Now that the new independent little country was over a month old, it was beginning to feel itself strong and important. So a committee was sent to Washington to negotiate with the United States on behalf of the nation of South Carolina to have the fort transferred to the former state.

President Buchanan refused to give up the fort. Finally he got angry and sent an unarmed steamer down the coast to Fort Sumter with more troops and supplies. South Carolina military troops fired on the ship and forced it to turn around.

It had been the first act of war. Yet even though northerners and we in the West were shocked and astonished at what the South was doing, there was still no real sense of the danger and peril yet to come.

Even if President Buchanan had *wanted* to force South Carolina and the other states back into the Union, there would probably have been little he could have done. The regular army of the nation was only 15,000 strong, and most of those men were out West protecting settlers and wagon trains and Pony Express riders from Indians. It would have taken months to get the army back to the East—and doing so would have left the West to the Indians!

Everyone loathed what the South was doing, and said it was illegal and against the Constitution to do it. Yet no one actually wanted to *fight* to stop them from doing it.

But tempers and emotions were gradually running hotter and more violent and unpredictable.

Meanwhile, the southern states were wasting no time. As northern politicians scurried around trying to set up meetings and find compromise plans, the seven states that had seceded were busy forming a new government. From the beginning, they had planned to organize a whole new nation as soon as secession had been accomplished—a new nation based on the principle of states' rights. And it was important that they do so immediately . . . *before* Lincoln's inauguration!

Therefore, delegates from the seven states met in February in Montgomery, Alabama, and founded a new nation. They called it the Confederate States of America. And they didn't waste time with an election—the delegates themselves chose Mississippi Senator and former Secretary of War Jefferson Davis as their new president.

CHAPTER 41

A NEW PRESIDENT COMES TO WASHINGTON

The new southern nation was confident, and in early 1861 better organized and more united than the rest of the United States. All was not lost quite yet, however, because eight more slave states of the upper and border regions of the South had remained loyal to the Union and were determined to give Lincoln a chance.

All this time, President-elect Abraham Lincoln had not revealed to the country what he intended to do about the crisis. Would he attack South Carolina? If so, with what troops? Would he try to find some new compromise nobody had thought of yet? Would he just wait and let events go as Buchanan had? Or would he accept the new nation, and go on as President of just half the former country?

No one knew. So everyone in *both* countries anxiously awaited Lincoln's inaugural speech, scheduled for March 4, to find out what his new policy was going to be.

In the meantime, out in California, there was a lot of support for the South. The South Carolina fever for secession ran all the way west to the Pacific!

But for some reason, by the time it reached California, those who felt the state ought to secede didn't necessarily want to join the Confederacy. They wanted California to pull out of the Union to start a *third* independent republic. If the North and South couldn't solve their squabbles, why should California be joined with either of them?

220

A year before, former California Senator Weller had pro-
claimed: "If the wild spirit of fanaticism, which now pervades the
land, should destroy this magnificent Union, California will not
go with the South or the North, but here upon the shores of the
Pacific will found and establish a mighty new republic."

"It's plumb fool ridiculousness, Almeda!" exclaimed Pa, looking up from the newspaper.

"What is it, Drummond?" she'd asked.

"I'm just reading here in the *Standard* that this fellow Butts is
calling for a convention to found a Pacific republic. Who is he,
anyway—do you know, Corrie?"

"Judge Butts is the editor of the Sacramento *Standard*, Pa."

"Well, he's got no business interfering in politics, if you ask
me."

"You better learn to get along with him when you go to Sacramento," laughed Almeda, "or you might find yourself tarred
and feathered in that paper of his!

"It was just a month ago that you were laughing about that
proposal by John Burch proposing the formation of a Pacific republic."

"That's because I thought it was a joke—California, Oregon,
New Mexico, Washington, and Utah forming a new country! But
I think Butts is serious!"

"He is serious, Pa," I said. "The *Herald*, the *Gazette*, the
Democrat, the *Star*—they've all come out in favor of western independence."

"What about your *Alta*?"

"The *Alta*'s pro-Union all the way," I said. "You don't think
I'd keep writing for a Democratic paper, do you?"

"Well, if this one Republican has anything to say about it when
I get to Sacramento, California's gonna stay put right where it is—
in the Union, and supporting Mr. Abraham Lincoln when he gets
to be president!"

All through the elections Lincoln's opponents had made fun
of his appearance—tall, thin, and gawky, with rough features and
a big beak nose. He was said to sleep in the same shirt he gave
speeches in, and from listening to some reports I would have
thought he still lived in the backwoods log cabin where he was

raised. Even after his election he was not considered "sophisticated" enough for Washington society.

But people were in for a surprise. Lincoln might not have been handsome or cultured, but he was a strong man, a shrewd politician, and an authoritative leader—just the right man to be president at such a time, and certainly better than James Buchanan. Abraham Lincoln would not do nothing. Whatever he did, it was sure to be decisive.

Lincoln left his home in Springfield, Illinois, for Washington in late February. He traveled by train and took eleven roundabout days to get there, stopping all throughout the states of the North to visit people and make speeches and let them see their new president. Everybody wanted to know what he was going to do about the Confederacy, but he wouldn't reveal his policies yet. His speeches were light—some even thought them frivolous. People began to get the idea they had elected a simpleton to the White House. He seemed almost unaware of how serious the crisis was.

At Westfield, New York, he asked the crowd if a young girl by the name of Grace Bedell was present. She was brought up to the rear of the train where he was speaking. Then he told the listening crowd that she had written him during the campaign to tell him that he would look much handsomer if he grew some whiskers. Then he stooped down with a smile. "You see, Grace," he said, "I let these whiskers grow just for you."

When he attended the opera in New York City, he did the unthinkable by wearing black gloves instead of white. High society was aghast at the thought of having such an oafish man living in the White House and in charge of the country.

In Philadelphia a private detective named Allan Pinkerton came to the President-elect with the news that he had learned of a plot to assassinate him when he changed trains in Baltimore. Lincoln would have paid no attention, except that a little while later another report came to him of the same thing.

So Lincoln let Pinkerton take charge of getting him to Washington safely. He was put up in a sleeper that had been reserved by one of Pinkerton's female detectives for her "invalid brother." They passed through Baltimore at three in the morning and reached Washington just about daybreak.

When it was discovered what had happened and that Lincoln had at one point in the journey draped a shawl over his shoulders so as not to be recognized, all kinds of mocking and cruel stories and jokes and cartoons were printed in the newspapers, especially in the South. This was the man, they said, who was going to lead the nation! People were beginning to think he was an incompetent, ignorant clown.

But Lincoln had just been beating around the bush with his lighthearted speeches. In fact, he knew exactly how serious the crisis was. He had been planning for it for four months.

The Pony Express was gearing up to speed Lincoln's inaugural address to California the moment it was delivered. I wished Zack had been able to be part of it!

It took three days for the speech to reach St. Joseph by train from Washington. Then the Express took over at an amazing pace. The speech was brought down the Main Street of Sacramento from St. Joseph in an all-time speed record: seven days and seventeen hours. Two of the riders, trying to make up for delays, actually rode their horses to death.

The speech, which Pa read to us all from the March 17 edition of the *Alta* when it arrived in Miracle Springs on the eighteenth, was certainly not the speech of a weakling or a simpleton. It was clear right away what kind of man had been elected President, and I was glad that I'd done my part to help him win California's four electoral votes. It wasn't much, out of the 180 he'd received, but I was glad they hadn't gone to anybody else.

"The Union is older than the states," he said in his speech, "and was founded to last forever. Secession is illegal, a revolutionary act." Then the new President went on to tell what he planned to do.

He did not intend to be rash, he said, or to do anything sudden or forceful. He would proceed with patience and caution for a time. And that right there, Almeda said as we listened, was the clue that showed he had no intention of putting up with the so-called new country forever—he would be patient *for a time*.

But he *would*, he went on to say, do all in his power to enforce all federal laws in *all* the states, and he would keep firm hold of federal property. Everyone knew he meant Fort Sumter.

He was not considering any forceful retribution, and there would be no threat to the constitutional rights of the states that had left the Union. If they wished to return, they could. But the government *would* act to defend itself.

Then he brought up the horrible prospect of what would happen if the southern states *didn't* come to their senses and come back to the Union. He spoke straight to the South when he said whose fault it would be.

"In *your* hands, my dissatisfied fellow countrymen," he said, "and not in *mine*, is the momentous issue of civil war. The government will not assail *you*. You can have no conflict without being yourselves the aggressors. You have no oath registered in Heaven to destroy the government, while *I* shall have the most solemn one to *preserve, protect, and defend it.*"

The closing words of his speech showed that he still wanted to believe that the people of the South deep down felt as loyal to the country as he did. Maybe their radical leaders didn't. But surely the great masses of southerners didn't really want what was happening.

"We are not enemies," he said, "but friends. We must not be enemies. Though passion may have strained, it must not break the bonds of affection. The mystic chords of memory, stretching from every battlefield and patriot grave, to every living heart and hearthstone, all over this broad land, will yet swell the chorus of the Union, when again touched, as surely they will be, by the better angels of our nature."

CHAPTER 42

PA IN SACRAMENTO

Those were times of peril, those first few months of 1861.

The only trouble was, no one knew how dangerous they really were. No one expected what came afterward. No one knew how bad it would be. If they had, they probably would have done things differently.

As it was, time kept passing, and everybody on both sides got more and more determined *not* to give in. They all thought *they* were right and everyone else was wrong. Sometimes that may be true, but it can still be a dangerous way to look at things. Admitting you might be a little wrong yourself is hard for most folks, but it seems like the easiest way to avoid conflicts later.

Pa had gone to Sacramento to get sworn in to the new Assembly in January of 1861. He was gone a week that first time. When he came back he was so full of stories and enthusiasm he hardly stopped talking for days. I had never seen him like that! Almeda couldn't get over him; she laughed and laughed just to listen to him. It seemed such a short time ago that he'd been just an ordinary soft-spoken man trying to make a gold strike. Suddenly he had a family and a vein of wealth right on his property, a new wife and a business. Before he knew it, he was mayor of a town, then a state legislator.

"If a simple man like Abraham Lincoln can go from a log cabin to splitting wood rails to being president," said Almeda one day, "then I don't see any reason why you can't, too!"

She made the mistake of letting Alkali Jones hear her! He'd been working at the mine with Uncle Nick, Pa, and Tad, and had just walked into the house for lunch. Whenever Pa came back from Sacramento business, he worked at the mine for the next two or three days. "Makes me feel back to normal," he said, "to get wet and dirty and get my arms and back aching again. Too much sitting around talking like they do down there in the Capitol, it just ain't natural. A man's gotta sweat from hard work, at least three or four times a week, or things just get out of order. I gotta be working if I'm gonna think right!"

"Drum fer President!" cackled Mr. Jones, walking in on the tail end of what Almeda had said. "That's a good'n—hee, hee, hee! I can die in peace now, I've heard jist about every dad-burned tall tale a body could dream up! Drum fer President—hee, hee, hee!"

"You don't think I could do the job, Alkali?" said Pa seriously, giving the rest of us a wink.

"Oh, I ain't sayin' no such thing. Fer all I know, you'd march straight down t' them southern rascals an' look 'em straight in the eye and say, 'Now look here, you varmints! You're breakin' a passel of laws, an' worse'n that—you're all actin' like a bunch of dang fools. Now git back t' your homes; let your slaves be the free men they got a right t' be, and cut it out with all this blamed foolishness of tryin' t' start a country of your own. It ain't gonna work no how!' "

By now we were all in stitches from laughing so hard. Of course, that just spurred Mr. Jones all the more to keep going. There wasn't anything he loved better than being at the center of stories high on imagination and low on facts.

"Yep," he kept going, "you jist might make a president that'd git folks in this country t' stand up an' take notice of the kind of guts and grit it takes t' live out here. Drum for President—hee, hee! That's what them there fools back there need, all right—a Californian with the guts t' make them rascals back down and git off their dang high horses! Hee, hee, hee!"

"What would you do if you *were* president, Pa?" Tad asked.

Pa got a real serious expression on his face. The room grew quiet, and we all waited to see what he'd say.

"You mean about the Confederate states, boy?" he said finally.

"Yeah, Pa. How would you make them not do what they're trying to do to the country?"

"Well, I reckon the first thing I'd do is send my vice-president down to Montgomery to talk to 'em, to look 'em straight in the eye, and to horsewhip some sense into 'em."

"Who would be your vice-president, Pa?" asked Becky.

"Why, I thought you knew, girl," answered Pa. "Alkali, of course!"

"Please, Drummond," said Almeda this time, wiping the tears of laughter out of her eyes and trying to be serious. "I really am curious what you would do."

Again Pa thought long and hard.

"I don't reckon I can answer what I *would* do if I was in Washington without saying what I *am* doing right down there in Sacramento," he answered finally.

"What do you mean by that?" asked Uncle Nick, drying his hands off with a towel and walking over toward Pa.

"Just what I said, Nick. I mean, my first business is right here and right now. I tell you, there's as much foolishness coming out of some of those southern sympathizing Democrats in Sacramento as in those renegades setting themselves up as so all-fired important down in Montgomery! It makes my blood boil just to think of it. That's why I had to get back here to Miracle and swing the sledge a few times against some good hard rock."

"How you figure it, Drum?" asked Mr. Jones. I'd never taken him as one much interested in politics, but the look on his face was serious. This dispute between North and South had *everyone's* attention!

"We sat down for our first session," said Pa. "Half of the new members, like me, had no idea what was going on or what to do or how the place even worked. Then this guy named Zack Montgomery stood up. He talked half the morning about how we needed to break away from the Union ourselves. Later I heard there was a senator named Thornton doing the same thing over in the Senate room. The Democrats are trying to get California to do the same thing as South Carolina!"

"Surely it's not a serious threat?" said Almeda, in both amazement and shock.

"You gotta realize, Almeda," said Pa, "the Democrats still outnumber us Republicans in the state. Breckinridge and Douglas together got a heap more votes than Lincoln. A lot of politicians in this state think Lincoln's a buffoon, and they're not ashamed to say so.

Lots of 'em don't have that much loyalty to the Union. They figure California's the only thing that matters, so let Lincoln and the eastern states do whatever they please. Why, there's a feller named Charles Piercy who voted for Douglas—he's not a slave man, has no particular loyalties to the South. But he stood up, just a few seats away from me, and he said he'd written up what he called a resolution condemning the Republicans as altogether and solely responsible for bringing on the secession crisis. Then he walked up to the front and handed the piece of paper he was talking about to the Speaker. Then Piercy turned around to face the rest of us—and this was after Montgomery's fiery speech—and said, 'My fellow assemblymen, for this reason, I feel most strongly that we Californians will never entirely be able to support our new president. I am urging you, therefore, to stand with me in backing the formation of a mighty Pacific Republic, as advocated by our colleague, Mr. Montgomery, earlier today. Our former governor, Mr. Latham, now in the Senate in Washington, has long been in favor of such a proposition, and would no doubt return to help us in the formation of a constitution and provisional government.' "

Pa stopped, then added, "Those are probably not his exact words, but something like 'em. Speechmaking words! And ridiculous words, if you ask me!"

"What did the rest of you do?" asked Uncle Nick.

"There were some folks saying 'Hear, hear!' and agreeing with him, but others stood up when he was done and said just what I was thinking, that it was downright foolishness. One fella got up and even brought France into it."

"France?" repeated Alkali Jones. "What do them foreigners have t' do with us?"

"Well, this fella said that if we tried to set ourselves up in a new country over here, this far away from the other states, with a thousand miles of coastline and less than a million people and no army, he said we couldn't defend ourselves against anybody—especially with the North and South at each other's throats. He said Napoleon would come right in and gobble us up and make us into a Pacific France."

"Napoleon's dead, Pa," said Becky. "Mrs. Rutledge was just teaching us about him and a place called Waterloo last month, before Christmas."

228

"Napoleon the Third, Becky," I said. "He's the other Napoleon's nephew. He's the emperor of France."

"Well, whoever the varmint is, let him try t' come in here an' make trouble! We'll show him what kind of stuff Californians is made of!"

"With what, Alkali?" said Pa. "We got no army, and hardly no militia to speak of. We're barely a state, much less a country that could fight off somebody like France!"

"So what happened next, Pa?" asked Becky.

A funny look came over Pa's face. Almeda recognized it immediately. "I can tell when you're holding something in, Drummond," she said. "Now tell us, what happened?"

"Well, all of a sudden I found myself on my feet," Pa answered, as if he was embarrassed to remember it.

"Good for you, Drum!" exclaimed Uncle Nick. "You gave 'em all what for, didn't you? I knew you had it in you!"

"No I didn't give 'em what for, Nick!" Pa shot back. "What do you think, that I wanted to make enemies there my first week in the capital?"

"You must have said something," said Almeda, her eyes eager to hear what had happened.

"I reckon I did," said Pa slowly. "The second I realized what I was doing, I got afraid and wanted to sit down something fierce. But I went ahead with what I'd been thinking, and I just told 'em all that I figured since we'd elected Mr. Lincoln, he deserved for us to at least give him a chance of seeing what he could do. I said we oughta let it sit a spell. Gettin' too hasty's always a way of hangin' yourself, I said. I told 'em I'd always made a practice of trying to take important decisions slow. You don't usually get in trouble from goin' too slow, I said—that is, unless you're in a gunfight. They laughed a little when I said that," said Pa, chuckling as he remembered it. "But you *can* get yourself in a heap o' trouble by rushing into something you ought not to have done. So I finished up by saying I figured we oughta wait and give the President our loyalty, and see what happened."

The room got quiet when Pa finished.

All at once Almeda started clapping, and then the rest of us joined in, just as if we'd been sitting there in the state Assembly room actually listening to Pa's speech.

"Now cut that out—all of you!" scowled Pa. I don't think I'd ever seen his face red before, but it was then. "It wasn't no big thing!"

I glanced over at Almeda. Her face was fixed intently on Pa with a look of admiration and love, and tears stood in her eyes.

"What happened next, Pa?" asked Tad eagerly.

"Well, boy, some of the folks did just what you done—they started clapping, and I sat down pronto and wished I could just sink right down into my chair and hide. I gotta tell you, I felt a mite foolish!"

"What about the resolution, Pa?" I asked. "Did you decide anything?"

"Naw. Politics is mostly talking, Corrie. There ain't much *doing,* only yammering about everything. I reckon we'll be voting on what to do one day, but I don't know when. Most likely we'll just keep talking for a long spell, and I'll keep getting my fill of it and have to spend more time up at the mine crushing rocks just to keep from going looney from all the words that don't accomplish much of anything!"

It was quiet for a long time. Finally I asked Pa the question that had been on my mind ever since he had come back home from Sacramento.

"Did you see Mr. Burton when you were there?" I said shyly.

"As a matter of fact, I did, Corrie. He congratulated me on my getting elected, and told me to give you his fond regards. Those were his words—his fond regards. *And* he told me to give you this. I was so anxious to get up and pound them rocks in the mine that I nearly forgot."

He reached inside his coat and took out a rumpled letter, then handed it to me.

My face flushed with embarrassment, but that didn't keep me from snatching the letter and getting up to go to my room to read it.

Everybody else got up too. Just as I was going into the bedroom, I heard Alkali Jones behind me, opening the door to head back outside. He was muttering and chuckling to himself.

"Drum fer President . . . hee, hee, hee!" he was saying. "Blamed if he ain't startin' t' sound like one, at that."

CHAPTER 43

OUTBREAK!

Shortly after the inauguration, I received another letter, this one from Mr. Kemble.

You get to writing, Corrie! he said. *There's foolishness and plots and subversion afoot all over this country. The Union's in trouble, Corrie, and we've got to have a strong, supportive position. Half of California's papers are advocating everything from throwing in with the Confederacy to the Pacific Republic.*

He had enclosed a clipping from one of the other San Francisco papers, which read:

> We shall secede, with the Rocky Mountains for a line, and form an Empire of the Pacific, with Washington Territory, Oregon, and California, and we shall annex all of this side of Mexico. We don't care a straw whether you dissolve the Union or not. We just wish that the Republicans and Democrats at the Capitol would get into a fight and kill each other like the Kilkenny cats. Perhaps that would settle the hash.

Mr. Kemble finished his letter: *"It's time for the Alta to take its stand, and you along with it. The Union needs us all, Corrie!"*

He hardly needed to tell me how desperate the situation was! Every day I'd been reading, not only in the *Alta* but in other papers as well, about everything that was happening in the East. With the Pony Express making news only two weeks late, everything that was going on felt so real and urgent. I saved all the papers so I'd know just what was happening, and that when I did write things, I'd have my facts straight. If I was going to help Mr. Lincoln and the Union, I had to make sure what I wrote was right and true. I didn't want anyone to be able to complain that the young lady newswoman from California wrote nothing but female emotionalism and that she didn't know what she was talking about. So I tried to understand the events that were going on and keep track of everything as it happened.

The time to have saved the country was back in November or December of 1860. If only Mr. Lincoln had been able to become president right after he was elected! But by the time he set foot in Washington, the Confederacy was already better organized than his new administration! The Republicans had never been in power before. So Mr. Lincoln had to set up an entire executive branch of government from scratch—a cabinet, and all kinds of other appointments. While he was busy having to be an executive and an administrator, the Confederacy was growing stronger and stronger every day.

Not only was the Confederacy stronger right at first, they were confident that Lincoln and the northern states could never stand against southern might. The South had economic strength, strong ties with foreign governments because of the worldwide demand for cotton, and the best politicians in the land. Now that leadership was all in the South. Washington had a group of bumbling midwesterners and Republicans who had never governed a nation before. In addition, the South had strong financial reserves in her banks, while the North was financially strapped. Perhaps most importantly, the South had the best generals.

By the time Lincoln took office, the Confederacy had a permanent constitution, a treasury, an army, a navy, a post office, and a legal system. Its organizers had been busy. A completely functioning government had been created and was in full operation. Southern leaders had not a doubt in the world that Lincoln would be powerless to oppose them. What could he do? The Confederacy existed, and he could not undo it! If he tried to use force with the two or three thousand army troops he might muster from the northeast and midwest, the results would be laughable. The South would beat them back so fast it would make the tall, lanky railsplitter from Illinois wish he'd never run for president!

Pa returned from his next trip into Sacramento right at the end of February with serious and disturbing news. Suddenly the dispute between North and South wasn't so far away!

A plot had been discovered, he told us, by a group of southern supporters, to take control of the government of California!

"Knights of the Golden Circle, that's what they called themselves," he said. "Once they had control of Sacramento, they were going to send an armed force down into Mexico where they would seize control of Sonora."

"They could never have gotten away with it!" exclaimed Almeda.

"They had powerful men from the South behind it," said Pa. "They had 50,000 guns on the way to California by the southern route. The knights had 16,000 supporters. They might have been able to do it if we hadn't got word from Washington. They were going to set up an independent republic of the Pacific. Their first move was to grab the Presidio to hold the entrance of the Golden Gate, then the rest of San Francisco's forts, Alcatraz, the Mint, the post office, everything of the government's. Then they were going to join the Confederacy!"

"I can't believe it—in California! Who was behind it?"

"Buchanan's secretary of war, John Floyd. He left Washington, joined the Confederacy, and from what we hear had been arranging for the shipment of guns even while he was in Washington. I tell you, Almeda, it's a dangerous situation. The South has supporters everywhere!"

If 1860 had been a dangerous year in the history of the country, as I'd heard the men discussing at the celebration at the Montgomery Hotel, then 1861 was the year when that danger climaxed and exploded. It didn't take long after Mr. Lincoln's inauguration. The day after it, in fact.

On March 5, Mr. Lincoln was told that the army men at Fort Sumter were running seriously low on supplies and food. Unless they received more soon, they would have to abandon the fort. If that happened, South Carolina would take possession of it, and their victory would make the new outlaw nation seem all the more legitimate.

Mr. Lincoln determined not to let that happen. Fort Sumter was a symbol of the authority of the United States government and its army. It *had* to remain in Union hands. Even though a ship with provisions had been fired upon and turned back in January, Lincoln decided to send several ships this time, as a relief expedition.

Early in April, therefore, he informed authorities in South Carolina that the ships were on their way.

At last the leaders of the new Confederacy showed how confident they were. They didn't want to let the ships get to Fort Sumter, or else it would reduce *their* authority in the world's sight. They wanted to prove how strong they were. In their eyes, a foreign nation controlled a Confederate harbor. So they decided not to wait for the ships to get there. They would attack Fort Sumter first and take control of it before the relief force arrived. They would show whose authority was greatest!

The Confederate commander at Charleston took an order to the Union commander at the fort demanding that he surrender Fort Sumter at once. He refused.

On the morning of April 12, therefore, the Confederate commander opened fire on the fort and blasted it with cannon balls and gunfire all that day and into the night. The small detachment of Union soldiers with scant supplies was helpless. If they didn't yield, they would all eventually be killed. On the next day they gave up and surrendered.

Suddenly the North came alive. Everyone who heard the news of the attack was outraged. It was finally clear—there was no more hope of compromise!

The President and the country had been patient long enough. The honor of the flag had been flagrantly attacked; the Rebel outlaws must be punished! As with one loud unanimous voice, the public demanded retribution against the South. There could be no two separate nations! The Union must be saved. The United States of America must be preserved . . . no matter what had to be done!

The New York *Tribune* carried the news:

> Fort Sumter is lost, but freedom is saved. There is no more thought of bribing or coaxing the traitors who have dared to aim their cannon balls at the flag of the Union, and those who gave their lives to defend it. Fort Sumter is temporarily lost, but the country is saved. Long live the Republic!

News of the firing on Fort Sumter reached San Francisco on April 24, twelve days later. The very next afternoon a great crowd assembled at Portsmouth Square. Patriotic pro-Union speeches went on for a long part of the day, amid applause and cheering. It was not a day in San Francisco to express support for the South!

Immediately President Lincoln sent out a call for 75,000 volunteers, and orders went out to the regular army troops stationed at the Presidio to be sent to the East. Lincoln's message did not actually say the word. He said that the troops and additional volunteers were needed to deal with certain "combinations too powerful to be suppressed by the ordinary course of judicial proceedings." In other words, all hope of compromise was dead.

But whether he said it or not, everyone knew that the United States was now at war.

With itself.

CHAPTER 44

WHICH SIDE FOR CALIFORNIA?

Everyone expected the war to be short.

The South was so sure of a quick victory they thought all that would be necessary was for them to raise an army of volunteers and march north to take Washington, Philadelphia, and New York, and that would be the end of it. There was not even a need to sign up troops for lengthy assignments. The Confederacy made the enlistment period just twelve months. That would be more than enough time. Young men and boys throughout the South volunteered in droves. They were so feverish to join the Confederate army there weren't enough guns for them all.

Four more states promptly seceded—Virginia, Arkansas, Tennessee, and North Carolina. Although they were bound to the South in many ways, the states of Missouri, Kentucky, Maryland, and Delaware all decided to stay in the Union.

In the North, the volunteer army grew just as rapidly. More practically minded as to the true depth of the conflict, the North enlisted its young soldiers for three years. Within weeks Lincoln's request for 75,000 men had been passed. By the middle of the year, the Union's army was 500,000 strong. President Lincoln ordered a naval blockade of the whole southern coastline so that ships with provisions could not get through.

Loyalties in California were more divided than ever, now that war between the states had actually come. Pa came home from a session in Sacramento in May with what he considered good news.

"Well, we finally put all that new republic and western confederacy talk to rest," he said. "Piercy and Montgomery and all their crowd oughta be silenced for a while!"

"What happened?" asked Almeda.

"We Republicans finally got our *own* resolution on the floor— a resolution strongly supporting the Union and Mr. Lincoln's government."

"Did you speak again?"

"You bet I did! And this time I wasn't embarrassed. I got up there and I said what I had to say!"

"And it passed the vote?" I asked.

"You're doggone right it did—49 to 12. California's on the Union side of this thing once and for all, and for good!"

"What did it say?"

"Just a bunch of fancy sounding words to say, 'We're behind you, Mr. President.' "

"But·what were the actual words?"

"I'll see if I can quote them: 'The people of California are devoted to the Constitution and the Union now in the hour of trial and peril.' Some kind of political gibberish like that!"

But despite the vote in the California legislature, there still was more southern support in the state than was altogether comfortable. Many high office-holders had once been southerners. Not long after the war started, a group of San Francisco's city leaders wrote to Secretary of War Cameron in Washington about their concerns. Since he was editor of the *Alta*, Mr. Kemble was part of that group. He later let me read a copy of the letter.

A majority of our present state officers are undisguised and avowed Secessionists. . . . Every appointment made by our Governor unmistakably indicates his entire sympathy and cooperation with those plotting to sever California from her allegiance to the Union, and that, too, at the hazard of civil war.

About three-eighths of our citizens are from slave-holding states. . . . These men are never without arms, have wholly laid aside their business, and are devoting their time to plotting, scheming, and organizing. Our advices, obtained with great prudence and care, show us that there are upwards of sixteen thousand "Knights of the Golden Circle" in the state, and that they are still organizing, even in our most loyal districts.

Whether blood would ever be shed in California as a result of the North-South loyalties that were so divisive, it was still too soon to tell. We all hoped not, and hoped that the pro-Union stand of the legislature, in spite of what these men had said about Governor Downey, would ultimately influence the rest of the state to support the government of Lincoln and Hamlin instead of that of Davis and Stephens.

But in the meantime, the first major exodus *out* of California since the gold rush began to occur. Young men began making their way east to volunteer for the fighting that was sure to come, some to join the Union army, others that of the Confederacy.

CHAPTER 45

STANFORD FOR GOVERNOR

I hadn't seen Cal for quite some time, even though I hadn't stopped thinking about him. There had been letters from time to time, but it wasn't nearly the same.

Then all of a sudden one day, there he was in Miracle Springs! I was working at the Mine and Freight when the stage rolled into town. And as I stood staring blankly and absent-mindedly through the backward letters of the word P-A-R-R-I-S-H painted on the window, suddenly there he was stepping down out of the coach.

I couldn't believe my eyes! I blinked a time or two. I must have been dreaming, I thought. But when he turned momentarily in my direction, I knew there could be no mistake.

The next second I was out the door and bolting across the dirt street—not very ladylike, but I wasn't thinking of propriety at the time!

"Cal!" I called out, clomping along in my office boots, my dress flopping about behind me, and holding on to my bonnet to keep it from flying off into the dirt. "Cal. . . !"

He turned from where he had been saying something to the driver and smiled at me in greeting. Before I knew what I was doing, I'd run right up to him and almost threw my arms around him. Luckily I caught myself in time.

"Whatever are you doing here?" I exclaimed, gulping for breath.

"What else would I be doing in Miracle Springs," he said, "but visiting my favorite writer and person, Cornelia Hollister?"

Hearing my full name from his lips sent a tingle through me, and I was glad I was already flushed from the run across the street!

"But why?"

"You don't think visiting you would be enough of a reason for a man?" he said with a grin and a wink.

"Oh, Cal, don't joke with me. You must have come for some other reason. Did you come to see Pa about some Republican business?"

He laughed. "Ah, Corrie, but you are inquisitive. Well, you're right, I *did* come on Republican business—but not to see your pa. I tell you, I came to see *you!*"

"I . . . I don't understand."

"I'll tell you everything. But don't you want to wait until the dust from the stage settles? Perhaps we could have dinner together. Is there someplace—"

"Of course! You'll come home and have supper with us tonight!" I said enthusiastically. "Everybody will be happy to see you again!"

"I had in mind someplace where we might be alone," said Cal.

I blushed in earnest.

"Am I embarrassing you, Corrie? I do apologize. It's only that I have something very important to talk over with you—something I want to discuss in private, something that concerns our future."

What was he saying? My head was spinning, frantically trying to think what to say, what to suggest. Before I could get another word out, Cal spoke up again.

"Now that I think about it," he said, "I suppose it would be fitting to include your father—your whole family, in fact—in the announcement I have to make."

"Announcement, Cal . . . what announcement?" I faltered.

"Oh, you'll just have to wait to hear with the rest of them!" he laughed. "I gave you a chance to hear the good news by yourself. But now you'll just have to share it with everyone else!"

He finished his statement, then just stared at me with his blue eyes and a big grin.

"So . . . do I consider that a formal invitation to supper?" he said at length.

"Uh . . . uh, yes," I stumbled out. "Yes . . . of course."

"Tonight?"

"Yes."

"Well, then . . . I know you've probably got work to do over at the office. So I'll just keep myself busy, look around the town awhile, maybe have a drink. And Carl asked me to pay a visit to Mr. Royce as long as I was coming this way. Shall I meet you out at your house this evening?"

"Uh . . . yes," I said. "I reckon that'll be just fine."

"I'll hire a buggy and be out."

He turned and began to walk away. I was still standing there in a daze. "No . . . wait, Cal," I said, finally coming to my senses. "Ride out with me. I have Almeda's buggy here. Come over to the office around five o'clock."

"I'll be there," he said cheerily.

Still I just stood there watching him walk over to the boardwalk and then toward Mr. Royce's bank.

I wasn't much good at the office the rest of the afternoon. I couldn't concentrate on anything, and it was all I could do to keep away from Marcus and Mr. Ashton. If they took one good look at me, they'd start asking all kinds of questions about whether I was sick or something. This was one time I did *not* want two old unmarried men fussing over me. So I spent most of the afternoon in Almeda's office with the door closed. But I didn't get a single thing done!

All I could think about were Cal's words, going over and over and over again in my mind.

The announcement I have to make . . . someplace where we might be alone . . . in private . . . something that concerns our future . . . our future . . . OUR future . . .

The ride out to the claim later that day with Cal at my side was nearly torture! He was talkative and friendly, as always, but I was about as interesting as a wet dishrag! It was the longest ride home from town I'd ever had.

I wasn't any better at supper. Pa and Almeda and the others were delighted to see Cal, of course, and he was charming and friendly, laughing and nice and hospitable. He congratulated and praised Pa, saying he always knew his star was on the rise.

They talked about politics mostly, and a lot about the problem with the Confederacy and Fort Sumter.

"Do you think there'll actually be fighting, Cal?" Pa asked.

"It seems impossible to avoid it now, with both sides so dead set against any kind of giving in."

"It's just awful," said Almeda. "The thought of Americans killing Americans is horrible! It oughtn't to be happening!"

I just sat waiting, trembling inside. How could they talk about politics and the war when was Cal going to make his *announcement*?

I didn't have too much longer to wait.

"But the hostilities between North and South isn't why I've come to Miracle Springs," he said when there was a lull in the conversation. "I have some exciting news to tell you all—news that I felt merited a personal visit."

I sat staring straight down at the table, too scared to look up. Somehow I knew, though, that Cal was looking at me.

He paused, and the others waited for him to continue.

"You both know, Mr. and Mrs. Hollister," he finally went on, "how fond I am of your daughter."

I glanced up. They both nodded.

"So fond of her, in fact," Cal said, "that I knew from the very start, right from that evening we all met back in San Francisco, you remember, Mr. Hollister, just about a year ago—I knew that here was a young lady I wanted to be part of my future. I knew too that I wanted her to meet my boss, Mr. Stanford. I just had a feeling about her—a feeling which, I am happy to say, turned out to be a positive omen of things to come."

Again he stopped briefly and drew in a breath. Then he looked over at me, reached out and placed his hand gently on top of mine, and began again.

"Just a few days ago, Mr. Stanford made public his candidacy for the governorship of California. And, Corrie, he asked me to come out here to ask you personally if you would be part of his campaign—a campaign to take control of the great state of California on behalf of the pro-Union Republican party."

He stopped. His face was bright with expectation as he gazed at me. I knew he probably thought I would be overcome with gratefulness. I was overcome, all right—but with an entirely different emotion!

"That . . . that is the announcement you told me about in

town?" I asked softly, trying to keep my voice from cracking.

"Yes. Isn't it exciting, Corrie? It's the opportunity I was telling you about . . . the future. For us to be part of together, just like I was saying when we were together in Palo Alto. An exciting future full of opportunities that we can share!"

But I only heard about half his words before I was up from the table and running to my room. I lay down on my bed and sobbed quietly. How could I possibly have been so stupid?

But even as I lay there, I remembered the other time Cal had been here, and what a fool I'd made of myself, sneaking around in the woods with dirt all over me. I could *not* let something like that happen again!

I quickly jumped up off my bed, ran to my washbasin, which still had some water in it, dashed a little on my face, dried with a towel, sucked in a deep breath, and turned around to walk back out and face the music. I would be brave, and put the best face on an awkward situation I could.

I returned to the table. "I'm sorry for leaving so abruptly," I said. "I was just overcome for a minute, and had to be alone. But I'm fine now."

I sat back down and gave Cal the biggest smile I could manage to muster. I hoped my red eyes didn't betray me.

"You can tell Mr. Stanford that I'd be honored," I said. "I would very much like to do what I could to help him."

"Good . . . wonderful!" exclaimed Cal. "I know that will please him a great deal."

With the business out of the way, the conversation again drifted toward politics. It seemed that was just about the only things folks talked about these days. With a war imminent, there was a great sense of uncertainty and tension, even in far-off California.

Then the door opened and Uncle Nick walked in with his family. Cal immediately jumped up, shook Uncle Nick's hand and greeted Aunt Katie warmly. Everyone took seats and the conversation resumed.

After about five minutes, suddenly a puzzled expression came over Cal's face. "Say, where is your sister?" he asked Aunt Katie. "Edie was her name, was it not? I had hoped to see her again too."

The room was silent a moment.

"She left for the East," Katie said. Her tone reflected the sadness she and all the rest of us had felt at Edie's parting.

"When?" asked Cal.

"Right after the Sumter incident," replied Uncle Nick.

"She said she had to go—that with the South under attack, she had to be where her home would always be."

An odd look came over Cal's face. What Aunt Katie had said seemed to strike deeply into him for some reason.

"We tried to get her to stay," said Uncle Nick. "Told her it was the South doing the attacking, and that if it did come to war, there couldn't be no safer place for her than right here."

"She hardly had any family left, anyway," said Almeda. "We told her we loved her and that we'd try to be family to her now that her husband was gone. But once news about Sumter came, she changed. She was distant after that. I knew she wasn't at home here."

"Nothing we said could change her mind," said Katie, starting to cry quietly. Almeda was sitting next to her and put her arm around her to comfort her. "I asked her what if we never saw each other again. But she just kept saying she had to be with her new country. It was almost as if we were suddenly strangers."

Katie could say no more. She broke down and wept.

Cal hadn't said another word, and the faraway look remained in his eyes for some time. He seemed very thoughtful and distracted and didn't say much the rest of the evening.

The outbreak of war between the North and South was bound, it seemed, to touch everyone in the country closely, sooner or later.

Already the pain was starting to come into people's lives.

CHAPTER 46

THE CAMPAIGNS OF THE SUMMER OF 1861

Just like Abraham Lincoln, Leland Stanford faced two Democrats in running for governor—a southern Democrat and a Union Democrat. The campaign was a short one, lasting mainly just through the months of July and August.

Stanford had lots of supporters in the state besides me. Once I began to realize just how much support he did have, in fact, I wondered why he had thought of me at all.

Thomas Starr King, now a strong ally, traveled throughout the state speaking for Mr. Stanford. And as everybody was finding out, he was one of the best orators in the whole country. A group of San Francisco businessmen who were normally Democrats backed Mr. Stanford, too. Like him, they were strong supporters of the Union even if they hadn't voted for Mr. Lincoln. A man named Levi Strauss was one of the most famous of these men, and since they were all influential, a lot of people took their advice when it came time to vote.

One person who *wasn't* so enthusiastic, though it made me mad at the time he told me, was a certain individual out of my past I'd tried hard to forget—Robin T. O'Flaridy.

I had seen his byline occasionally—he called himself *R. Thomas O'Flaridy*. When we ran into each other one day in the *Alta* building, he took me aside and spoke softly to me.

"Corrie, do me a favor and take one last bit of advice from an old friend," he said.

"An old friend?" I said, laughing. "After all you've pulled on me?"

244

"All in the past, Corrie," smiled Robin. "Part of the business, you know. Surely you've forgiven me by now."

"Oh, I suppose. How could I hold a grudge against a struggling fellow writer."

"Struggling?" he repeated. "Did you see my piece on the new wharf?"

"Yes, Robin," I answered, "and a great article it was, too."

"That's better."

"So," I said, "what's the advice you have for me?"

A serious expression came over his face. For a moment it almost confused me because it was so very different than the normal Robin O'Flaridy look I had grown accustomed to.

"How much do you know about Leland Stanford?" he asked.

"I don't know . . . quite a bit, I suppose," I answered.

"I mean, how well do you *really* know him? How well do you know what kind of person he is?"

"I . . . I thought I did. I've spent time with him. I like him. He's very kind to me."

"Perhaps. But I have a hunch, Corrie, that he may just be using you for his own ends."

"What! How can you possibly say such a thing?" I was annoyed.

"He's a businessman, Corrie. I've been around this city long enough to know some things. The whole deal with the railroad— I tell you, Corrie, it's not as clean and innocent as it seems. There are huge amounts of money involved. Huge, I tell you, and your friend Stanford and his cohorts are right in the thick of it."

"What are you insinuating?" I asked coolly.

"I'm not insinuating anything other than that the railroad's not primarily about politics—it's about money. I have the feeling Stanford only wants to be governor to line his own pockets and get richer than he already is. I know about these guys, Corrie—him, Hopkins, Crocker. They're businessmen, not politicians. All they are is a new breed of fourty-niner, a new kind of gold miner. Some might even call them claim jumpers."

"How dare you, Robin? I won't even listen to you. Who would say such a thing?"

"Ever heard of Theodore Dehone Judah?"

"Of course I've heard of him."

"He might agree with me."

"I don't believe a word of it. Why are you telling me this, Robin? Are you working for the Democrats in this election?" Again the same peculiar look came over Robin's face.

"Look, Corrie," he said, "I'm only concerned for you. Believe me, I just don't want you to get hurt."

"Why do I have such a difficult time believing your sincerity?" I said sarcastically. Immediately I regretted the words. The look on his face changed to one of pain.

"I'm sorry, Robin," I said. "I didn't mean it."

"Well, Corrie, I *do* mean it. Concern for you was the only reason I said anything about it at all."

"All right, Robin . . . thank you."

"Just watch your step, Corrie. That's all. And be careful about that Burton fellow too."

"Cal?" I said.

"I'm not so sure about him either. I've heard—"

"I'll watch my step, like you said, but I won't listen to you say a word against Cal," I interrupted, getting irritated again.

Robin seemed to think better of pursuing it, and he said nothing more. But the look on his face remained with me all the rest of the day. Strange as it was to say, I had the feeling he really was sincerely thinking of me. But then, I thought he was being sincere that night when we'd escaped from Sonora together, too, and he had double-crossed me!

I didn't think much more about what he'd said, and continued working for the campaign as before. Mr. Stanford himself traveled through all the northern part of the state—through all the mining regions, from Weaverville up north on the Trinity River all the way down to Sonora in the south. Naturally he came to Miracle Springs too, where I got to stand beside him and speak to my own hometown.

I didn't really do all that much for him, but Mr. Stanford took me with him to lots of the smaller places like Miracle Springs, introduced me to people as if I were more important than he was, and always let me say a few things, either about him or about Mr. Lincoln or the need to be loyal to the Union. He treated me so

kindly, and told me—whether it was true or not—that I was helping his campaign a great deal.

The other campaign of that summer was not such a pleasant
one. It was taking place twenty-five hundred miles away—and
was not a political campaign, but a military one.

The attack on Fort Sumter had taken place in April. But for
the next two months nothing happened. Both North and South
were busy recruiting, training, and building up their armies. I
later heard that the moods of the general public were very different
during this time.

In the South, wealthy landowners and the leaders who had
organized the Confederacy were all confident—confident that
right was on their side, certain that they were doing the just and
honorable thing, confident in their strength, sure of victory. Somebody I later interviewed told me it was a self-righteous kind of
confidence. God and the Bible were on their side, so how could
they do anything but win? The young soldiers of the southern
army, though not so religious or philosophical about it, mostly
felt the same way.

But hundreds of thousands of people in the South, however,
neither leaders nor soldiers nor landowners, were shocked by what
had happened. They believed that slavery was permissible. They
believed in the ways of the South, in southern culture and their
southern heritage. But whether it was worth waging a war over,
such people had grave doubts. Surely, they thought, some more
sensible solution or compromise could be found than to have to
kill over it! Though most of these people remained loyal to the
Confederacy, many of them wondered if their own leaders—Jefferson Davis and Alexander Stephens and General Beauregard,
who had attacked and toppled Fort Sumter, and General Robert
E. Lee and Thomas Jackson, and all the political leaders who had
defected from Washington in favor of the Confederacy—weren't
doing just as much to destroy the South as the evil Yankees and
their sinister head, Abraham Lincoln. These people were scared.

As for the slaves in the South, most of the ones I talked to later
didn't have the slightest notion that all the fighting was for them.
They were at least the outward symbol of why the Civil War was
fought, but they didn't know it. *Freedom* for them might as well

have been a word in a foreign language. Even if they had freedom, they wouldn't have known what to do with it. In the meantime, their lives went on as they always had—a life of drudgery, toil, and hopelessness.

Above the Mason-Dixon Line, however, the mood was far different. People there were mad. It was time the South was put in its place, slavery put an end to, and the country made one again. The South could not be allowed to get away with attacking the very foundation of Freedom itself—the United States government. They wanted something done. They called for retribution, for punishment of the South.

Therefore, when news came that the new Confederate Congress was going to meet for the first time, and not down in Montgomery, Alabama, but up in Richmond, Virginia—only a hundred and ten miles south of Washington—the anger of the North rose to explosive heights. The call went out—the southern Congress must not be allowed to meet on July 20!

The New York *Tribune* took up the banner and repeated what it called the "Nation's War Cry" in every edition it printed: *Forward to Richmond! Forward to Richmond! The Rebel Congress must not be allowed to meet there on the twentieth of July! By that date the place must be held by the National Army!*

President Lincoln, as well as everyone on both sides, thought that the war would be short. Here was a chance, he believed, to deal a quick and decisive blow to the upstart Rebel army *and* cripple the new government of the Confederacy by taking control of its new capital—all at once!

But standing in the way, between the northern army and Richmond, were 30,000 Confederate troops. Lincoln gave the order to advance, defeat the Rebel army, and move south to take Richmond.

The battle of Bull Run near Centreville, Virginia, took place July 21.

The two armies were approximately equal in size. All kinds of maneuvering went on among the generals of both sides, trying to trick the other. But down on the fields where shots were being fired, young inexperienced boys who were hardly trained and who had never fought before were shooting guns and killing one another! Which side would panic first?

It turned out that the southern leaders were more skilled in battle tactics than those of the North. After hours of fighting on that hot summer's day, by attacks and counterattacks, they fooled the blue units of the Federal army into thinking they had more reinforcements than they really did. The boys in blue panicked and finally turned around to flee. The gray units surged forward after them.

A full retreat was on, all the way back thirty miles to Washington! The severity of the conflict was still so little understood that hundreds of northerners had ridden out toward the battle in buggies and carriages to watch. These sightseers crowded the roads, making the safe retreat of the army all the more difficult. Suddenly toward them came a streaming mass of fugitives! They turned and fled in panic too, as back to the capital rushed tens of thousands of soldiers and citizens, with the victorious and shouting Confederate army behind them!

The South had won the first major battle of the campaign. Many brave young Union soldiers had been killed.

Fortunately for the North, the southern leaders did not press the victory and keep going. Otherwise they might have taken Washington itself. For either side, Bull Run *might* have ended the contest early.

But it would not.

This was no small conflict that had any chance of being resolved politically or easily or quickly.

A full-fledged *war* had begun. The North was shocked by the southern victory. But the defeat at Bull Run only made them all the more determined. Lincoln sent out a call for more men.

Everyone was beginning to realize that this was going to be a long and difficult war.

CHAPTER 47

THE WAR IN CALIFORNIA

California wasn't the only state split over loyalties to the North and South. In June, after Virginia had joined the Confederacy, the western part of that state broke away and formed a new state, loyal to the Union, called West Virginia.

When news of it came, I found myself wondering if such a thing was bound to happen to California one day.

The election for governor, however, would serve to put the dispute to rest. It was a campaign fought not just along Republican-Democrat lines, but North-South as well. A famous lawyer named Edmond Randolph made fiery speeches against Mr. Stanford. He was outspoken in his calling for Confederate victories in the East, and after Bull Run, claimed that the South would put an end to the war any day. "If this be rebellion," he cried in a speech that I heard when I was in Sacramento with Cal and Mr. Stanford, "then I am a rebel. Do you want a traitor? Then I am a traitor."

There were far more Democrats in California than Republicans. But the split between them kept being the most important factor of all. The Democrats got almost 64,000 votes in September. Mr. Stanford got only 56,000.

But since he was running against *two* Democrats, he was elected governor even with a minority!

I expected Cal to be happier over the victory than he was. This was one of those "opportunities" he was always talking about. He was going to be personal assistant to the governor of the state! He had talked about it before with such a light in his eyes that I would have thought nothing could please him more. He had made it seem like getting to the nation's Capitol was his greatest goal, and that Mr. Stanford would be the one to take him there. But the southern victory at Bull Run seemed to shake him, and even after the election, he was still quieter than usual. We were all worried when we heard the army had been defeated and had to retreat. But Cal seemed more upset about it than I could understand.

Mr. Stanford was so behind the North, the Union, and Mr. Lincoln that the Republican victory ended once and for all any possibility that California would support the South or would withdraw from the Union to form a new republic of some kind. Talk of a third country, and even talk of splitting the state, diminished. The War Between the States was the most important thing on everyone's minds, and the Pony Express deliveries with papers from the East were anticipated eagerly to find out if any more battles had been fought or if anything else had happened. Nothing much did happen, though, throughout the whole rest of that summer and fall.

But just because Mr. Stanford was now governor did not mean support for the southern cause stopped altogether. It just meant the state would officially be pro-North. So all the supporters of the Confederacy—and there were lots of them!—had to go into hiding. They had lost their chance to take California into the Confederacy with the vote. So they turned instead to hidden and underground plots and schemes. There was news every week, it seemed, of some new threat that had been exposed, even threats of plots to take over California for the South.

All kinds of secret societies of southern sympathizers sprang up. Mr. Kemble told me there were as many as fifty thousand people involved, but I don't know if that was true. They caused mischief, but after the middle of 1861 there weren't any serious uprisings.

The debate over which side was "right" in the war continued. William Scott, the pastor of one of San Francisco's largest churches, the Calvary Presbyterian Church, openly preached his belief in the Confederate cause. He outraged many people in the state, including my editor, Mr. Kemble, who knew him personally.

Besides men, money was something the Union army needed more than anything. The North was not as economically strong as the South, and to feed, clothe, and pay an army was expensive.

California was too far away to help with any actual fighting. It was too small a state to be able to provide very many men. But there *was* one thing that California had more of than any other state in either the Union or the Confederacy.

That was gold. California *could* help President Lincoln finance the war, if nothing else.

The Unitarian pastor Thomas Starr King, who had become a good friend of Governor Stanford, turned his speaking skills and popularity in a new direction. He began to organize a fund-raising drive in California in order to send money to Washington.

Of course whenever money is involved in anything, there is always the chance of deception and robbery. Since the first gold miners had started pulling gold out of the rivers and streams of California in 1848, there had been claim jumpers and thieves. Now, with southern supporters carrying out their designs more secretively, and with their bitterness over losing California's support for the Confederate cause, there was worry that they would try to steal what Mr. King was able to raise.

According to Mr. Kemble, a quarter of all San Franciscans favored the Confederacy. There were even more down south in Los Angeles. After Mr. Stanford's election as governor, a lot of secessionists moved down there and kept calling, even then, for California to split in half, with southern California to become a slave state and join the Confederacy. The Los Angeles *Star* was so seditious and against the Union that Governor Stanford had it banned from the mail so that it couldn't even be delivered and read in the northern part of the state.

There weren't enough people in Los Angeles or the rest of southern California, however, to worry about actual trouble—all the mischief they could do was in writing. And because they had no gold, they couldn't do the Confederacy much good, either.

CHAPTER 48

A RIDER

The day was one I'll never forget. Never *could* forget!

It was late August. A hot summer's day. Hot and still. Wherever the wind from the Sierras was, it had gone to sleep that day and felt like it intended to sleep all through the afternoon. It was so still I could hear the flies buzzing about. And hot . . . so hot!

Pa had been back from Sacramento for three days. He'd been gone a week and a half, his longest stay in the capitol yet. But Tad had gone with him, and they had a wonderful time together. When he wasn't on legislative business, he showed Tad all around Sacramento, and Tad had hardly stopped talking about everything they had done together. He had gone with Pa once or twice to Assembly meetings too. When Pa first saw Alkali Jones the day after they got back, he was telling him about the trip.

"I reckon it's time you changed that motto of yours, Alkali."

"Which one's that?"

"About the presidency."

"You mean Drum fer President—hee, hee, hee!"

"That's the one. But you gotta change it now."

"How so, Drum?"

"Politics has gone and bit my son right square between the eyes. You gotta change it to *Thaddeus Hollister for President*."

Tad's face beamed at the words.

"Hee, hee . . . Tad fer President! Yep, you're right, Drum—sounds a heap more likely with his name instead of yours! Hee, hee, hee!"

But during the days since he had returned, I could see a downcast spirit coming over Pa. It had nothing to do with Tad, only that his good time with his younger son had brought back to mind the lingering doubts over the fate of his elder. We'd heard nothing about Zack all this time.

Something was different about that day besides it being so hot. There was something in the air. There was no breeze rustling the trees. But there seemed to be an invisible wind about, invisible in the way that you couldn't see it or feel it or hear it. Kind of a wind of the spirit, not a wind of the air. It was a sense, a feeling that something was coming, but you couldn't tell what.

We all felt it, I could tell. As the day wore on, I could just see a look in Almeda's and Becky's and Tad's faces that they felt it too. We found ourselves looking at one another with expressions that had no words. It was a feeling of agitation, of anticipation, as if something was at hand but nobody knew what it might be.

It was a sense of expectation, the kind of feeling people get before a big thunderstorm. Everything changes. A different kind of warmth is in the air. The breezes start kicking up, and although they don't feel too powerful, you know they are only the fingery edges of the blasts that are coming. You *feel* the storm on its way. The air smells different. Before long, the blackness begins to appear over the horizon, steadily getting larger and filling more of the sky, and you know our senses have not betrayed you.

This was a day like that. But there were no breezes, no stormy fragrances, no hints of anything in the sky other than blue going on forever in every direction.

The little breezes kicking up the leaves for a moment and then letting them settle back into place, the feeling of changes in the atmosphere . . . they were all happening inside. Every once in a while I'd catch Almeda standing at the door or window looking out, with her hand over her eyes, peering into the distance as if expecting something. Then she'd turn away with a confused expression, as if wondering herself why she'd paused to look outside, not even knowing what she was looking for.

Nobody was saying much. The day wore on, getting hotter, and everyone grew more and more quiet. Something was coming. No one knew what.

Pa tried to work at the mine some. But it was too hot. After lunch Pa went out again, walked lazily up the creek, running thin and low now in the late summer.

It was one of my times to stand at the open door looking out, with *my* hand over *my* eyes. I watched him walk up toward the mine, kicking at the rocks with his feet, one hand in his pocket. He disappeared from sight. A few minutes later I heard noises from the area of the mine. But they didn't last long.

I was still standing there, looking out aimlessly, not feeling like doing anything, when Pa came into view again, walking back down the path, this time toward the stable. Apparently he had given up on the mine again. His shirt was drenched in sweat, under his arms and down the middle of his chest. But he didn't need the work to sweat. It was plenty hot to sweat just standing doing nothing. I was sweating too, in the shade of the house and open doorway.

Closer Pa walked. It was quiet. I could hear his feet shuffling along, too tired now even to kick at the little stones along the way in front of him. Everything was so still. Only Pa's rhythmic, shuffling step broke the stillness and the silence.

I found my eyes riveted on his slow-moving feet, watching them come toward me in the distance. The soft sound of his boots along the dried dirt entered my ears in perfect cadence. *One* . . . *two* . . . *right* . . . *left* . . .

Over and over—right, left . . . thud, thud.

Still my eyes fixed themselves on the motion, but gradually I became aware that something was wrong with the sound. There were still Pa's feet walking along as before, but the rhythm had been interrupted. It had changed. There were too many sounds for only two feet. I heard the noise as of a footfall when Pa's two feet were on the ground and in the air not making any sound.

And . . . the sound itself was wrong.

It wasn't a thud, thud, thud anymore. Now I heard *clomp* . . . *clomp* . . . *clomp* mixed in with the shuffling thuds of Pa's boots.

It sounded like a horse.

I shook off my dreaming reverie and turned my eyes in the opposite direction. A horse was approaching from the direction of town. Of course, that was the other sound I'd heard.

Who could it be? I squinted my eyes . . .

"Somebody's coming," I heard Becky say from inside the house behind me.

"Who is it, Corrie?" Almeda asked from the kitchen.

I kept squinting, trying to see. I could tell it was a man, but all I could really make out was a hat and a light brown beard.

I stared. The horse plodded along as slow as Pa had been walking. But steadily he came closer.

Suddenly an incredible sense of recognition seized my heart! But . . . but it couldn't be!

I spun my head around and my eyes again sought Pa.

His slow step had become a rapid pounding of his boots along the path. He had seen the rider too! He was running toward him!

Unconsciously I started out the door. I looked toward the road. The rider was close now . . . there could be no mistake!

He was climbing down off his horse. I was running now too! "Zack!" I cried. "It's Zack!" I yelled back toward the house.

Out of the house the others came, following me as we ran as fast as we could toward the road.

Pa reached him first.

I stopped, ten yards away, weeping with happiness. I felt the others come up behind me, but I could not take my eyes off the scene of reunion being played out before my eyes. I felt Almeda's arm slip around me as she watched, too.

Zack had slipped off his horse, but he hadn't been able to take more than a step or two before Pa reached him. The father threw his big arms around the son and held him tight, weeping freely and without shame.

Slowly I saw Zack's hands stretch around Pa's back and return his close embrace.

The two stood silently holding each other for a long minute. The only sounds to be heard were the throbbing of six hearts in joy.

CHAPTER 49

WHOLE AGAIN

When the two released each other, the first words were Pa's. "Welcome home, son!" he said.

The spell of the moment was broken.

The rest of us rushed forward. For the next several minutes Zack was showered with hugs and kisses and questions and laughter. He could hardly get in a word!

"Nice beard, Zack!" said Tad.

"You little runt . . . you grew up while I was gone!" returned Zack, giving Tad a good-natured push. "And you, Becky!" he added. "When did you get to be such a beautiful, grown-up woman!"

Then Zack looked over at me. He didn't say anything at first, just gave me a long hug. Every time I tried to speak, I started crying, and all my words stuck in my throat. "Oh, Zack," I finally managed, "I'm just so glad to see you!"

"Almeda," said Zack, hugging her next.

"Oh, Zack . . . we love you so much!"

Pa had been standing back, wiping his eyes and trying to steady himself. Now he stepped up again, this time offering Zack his hand.

"How about a handshake of welcome, Zack?" he said. "A handshake between men . . . man to man!"

Zack said nothing. He just reached out and took Pa's hand. The two stood again, grasping each other firmly by the hand, gazing intently each one into the other's eyes. It was all we had hoped and prayed for! You could tell in that one moment that they

257

understood each other, and that all was forgiven.

"Why did you grow the beard, Zack?" Becky asked after a minute.

"It's a long story," said Zack, releasing Pa's hand.

"Where you been?" This time the questioner was Tad.

"Another long story!" laughed Zack.

"How did you get back?" I asked.

"That's long too, but the why of it isn't so long," he answered. Then his face turned serious, and his eyes took on a very faraway expression. In that moment he suddenly looked older, like a true man. If I hadn't known better, I would have thought he was my older brother.

"Are you going to tell us the *why*, then?" I asked.

"I'll tell you everything," he replied, "when the time is right."

"Give the man a chance to get the dust off his feet, Corrie," said Pa. "Come on, Zack, son . . . let's get that horse of yours put up. Then what do you say me and you go up and give a *howdy* to your uncle!"

"Sure, Pa . . . yeah, I'd like to see Uncle Nick too!"

The two turned and headed toward the barn. Even though Zack was an inch or two taller than Pa, Pa threw his arm up around Zack's shoulder as they went. Zack's other hand hung down at his side, lightly holding the leather reins of his horse, which followed behind.

Almeda, Tad, Becky, and I stood there watching them go.

Just then Pa stopped and turned around. "Almeda!" he called back. "You start figuring on how to fix up the best vittles we ever had! Corrie, you make up a heap o' those biscuits o' yours. We'll invite the Reverend, and Nick and Katie—I know they'll all be anxious to see Zack. We'll have us a great time!"

He turned again, and he and Zack continued on, talking as they went.

The four of us finally walked back toward the house. "Well, Tad, your brother's home," said Almeda. "What do you think?"

When I heard Tad's answer, the tone of his voice surprised me. It wasn't just the deep baritone quality of it, but rather the maturity of what he said. It was obvious Tad was a young man at peace with his place in the family and secure in where he stood with his father.

"I'm so glad for Pa," Tad said quietly. "Something's been missing for him ever since Zack left. I did what I could to help, but I reckon a man like Pa's never gonna be quite whole when one of his kids is at odds with him. 'Course I'm glad for Zack, too. He needed Pa more than he ever could admit, probably more than I needed him, because I was younger when we came here."

He paused. "Actually," he added, "I guess I'm just about as happy as I can be . . . for *both* of them!"

CHAPTER 50

UNLIKELY RESCUE

A good part of the rest of that day Pa and Zack spent together. There was a lot of getting used to each other again to get done. And of course lots to talk about. But there was time for that now, and everything didn't need to be done all at once.

I could tell when I had a couple minutes alone with Pa later in the afternoon, just from the light in his eyes, that he'd been able to tell Zack the most important thing that had been on his mind all this time—that is how sorry he was. It was obvious from one look at Pa that a huge burden had been lifted from his shoulders.

We celebrated that night to make up for the last Christmas twenty times over. There was food and laughing and singing and more of Alkali Jones's crazy stories than we could have believed in ten nights of merrymaking together, much less one.

It was so strange seeing Zack with a beard! His talk, his mannerisms, his whole bearing had changed. Being out on his own had made him more confident, more independent. Zack entered into the celebration, but when I looked intently into his eyes when he wasn't watching, I could see a certain reticence too, almost a shyness at being the center of attention, and knowing that he'd caused such a fuss. I don't know that I'd call it embarrassment exactly, but it was like embarrassment in a different sort of way. Humbleness and humiliation aren't the same, though a lot of folks mistakenly think they are because their first three letters are the same. The one is always a good thing. The other isn't bad or good in itself, but can be either depending on what you do with it, and whether you let it make you humble in the end.

It had taken real humility for Zack to come home. It would probably take him a good long time to sort through the impact that act of humility would have on his manhood. Pride doesn't die easy, but humility is the only sure weapon against it. Zack had now become man enough to draw the sword against it himself. I could see the battle in his eyes . . . and I knew he was winning it!

It was well past dark before we all managed to coax Zack into telling his story. It was clearly hard for him, because of how bitter and painful his leaving home had been. But when Pa and I told him how we'd gone looking for him and what had happened, it perked him up and gave him a good place to start his tale without having to dwell on the past.

"Well, I was riding the last two stretches of Nevada and the first Utah leg," he began, "depending on the schedule, and depending on how the others were doing."

"Pony Bob told us how unpredictable it was sometimes," I said.

"It's *always* unpredictable with Bob!" laughed Zack. "That man attracts trouble like a dog draws fleas! I never rode two or three hundred miles at a time, but there were days when you'd have to keep going to another station or two."

"Were the Indians bad?" asked Becky. "Were you afraid?"

"You bet I was scared, girl!" said Zack. "The only fellas who weren't were the crazy ones, and we had a few of those, too."

"Did you ever shoot an Indian, Zack?" asked Tad.

"I shot *at* 'em, Tad, but never shot none. You don't think I'd want to hurt somebody, do you?"

"What if they came after you?"

"They did. But the Express had the best horses in the country, and no Paiute could keep with us for five minutes. So I'd just kinda stick my Colt up over my shoulder and fire back in the air and hope it'd frighten 'em away. Even if it didn't, all I had to do was stay in the saddle five minutes and I'd be out of their sight anyway."

"What if they were in front of you?"

"Then I had a problem."

"What would you do?"

"I could turn around and make a run for it. But then the mail didn't go through. Or I could head out into the desert and try to get around them. But then they'd have the angle on me, and I might ride an extra twenty miles, only to find them still there! Or I could do like Bob Haslam did a couple of times and ride right through the middle of them and hope they didn't kill me."

"What did you do, Zack?" asked Rev. Rutledge.

"Well, I tell you, Reverend, it only happened to me once. Funny that you should be the one asking me about it, because when it did happen I thought of you."

"Me!" said an astonished Rev. Rutledge.

"Yep. I just stopped dead in my tracks. And there they were up about a hundred yards ahead of me, right in the middle of my pathway. I just sat there in my saddle, and I started praying, and that's when I thought of you. I thought back to a sermon you preached once about problems. You were saying that sometimes you gotta face your problems head-on. Then other times, circumstances were such that you had to go around your problems to get to the other side. But there was one thing you could never do, you said, and that was ignore your problems and do nothing and hope they would just go away. They never will, you said."

Everybody in the room started laughing.

"That's just what I did," Zack went on. "I couldn't help myself. Sitting there on my jittery pony, staring at twenty hostile Paiutes, I started laughing. I couldn't stop. All I could think of was that sermon of yours, and I said to myself, just like I was talking to you, 'Shoot, Rev. Rutledge, that advice of yours doesn't do me a blame bit of good! You must not have had Indians in mind when you came up with that!' "

We were all laughing so hard by now we could hardly stop. Rev. Rutledge and Harriet had tears in their eyes—they were laughing hardest of all. Alkali Jones's *hee, hee, hee!* was nearly one continuous cackle!

"I even tried what you said you couldn't do. I stopped laughing long enough to close my eyes and count to ten. I thought that just maybe they *would* go away, that it was a dream, a winter's mirage. It was so cold last December that I thought maybe my brain was frostbit. But when I opened my eyes again, they were still there. And I still had to do what you said in your sermon—either go through them or go around them. But I gotta tell you, Rev. Rutledge, I found myself wishing I'd paid better attention that day, because I thought maybe you *had* said something else that I just couldn't remember!"

"No, that was it, Zack, my boy," said Rev. Rutledge, wiping his eyes. "Through them or around them, that's all I said." He was still chuckling even as he spoke.

"Well, I'd heard of Pony Bob riding through the band of Paiutes. But for all I knew, this might be the same band! And even if it wasn't, they were sure to have heard about the incident just as sure as I had. And they certainly weren't about to let themselves be suckered into just sitting there and letting through a lone horseback-riding kid a *second* time! No, I figured my chances were about zero in a thousand of coming out the other side alive if I tried to tackle *this* problem head-on. This looked to me like a clear case of needing to go *around* the problem!"

"What did you do, Zack?" asked Almeda. She was sitting on the edge of her chair as if she was afraid for him all over again.

"It was in a mountainous area of some pretty nasty terrain. Spread out to my right was a huge flat plain, broken up by gulches and creek beds, and little ravines, mostly invisible from looking across the top from where we were. On the other side of the trail, it turned rocky and steep immediately, working its way up to a high plateau that ran parallel to the road below. So what I figured to do was hightail it out across the plain like I was trying to outrun my way clean around them. I figured they'd light out on an angle to cut me off as I started my swing around to outflank them. So my plan was to ride out into the plain a ways, then dip into a wash suddenly and get out of their line of view. I hoped that they would keep riding toward the plain and that I could double back, maybe staying low in a creek bed or wash, and get back to the road and head back up the other side and lose myself in the huge boulders of the hillside without them spotting me. Then I could work my way all the way up to the top of the ridge and ride along until I was out of danger, and then find my way back down to the trail.

"It worked perfectly at first. I lashed my horse off to the right.

They took out after me at an angle across toward the plain. I rode for thirty or forty seconds, then dipped into a creek bed, stopped, and waited. I got off the horse, and crouching down crept up to the edge. There went the band of Paiutes off into the plain, expecting me to appear again any minute still riding in the same direction. I crept back down, remounted my horse, and doubled back, staying in the lows and hollows and washes until I was almost back to the trail. Then I climbed up and out and galloped quickly across the trail and up into the mountainous terrain on the other side. Within another minute I was out of sight and safe. But I still had to work my way up to the top and around back on to the trail or else I'd run into the war party again.

"Up I went. It got steeper and steeper, more rocky and treacherous. The footing was bad. There was loose shale here and there, and wet because it had been trying to snow. I was still frightened and so was pushing the horse pretty hard, which was probably my mistake. By now I was so far away from the Indians I probably would have been safe, but I kept pushing. Both my horse and me were exhausted. And that's how the trouble came. I was just too tired. I'd already been riding six hours that day, and it was another three hours to the next station.

"I was three-quarters of the way up to the plateau, and I came to a little ledge that dropped off steep on one side but was flat enough for a trot along its surface. But it was narrow, only about a foot wide. I urged the horse into a trot, but it was so narrow, and with the cliff on one side I could tell she was spooked. It was stupid of me, but I lashed her on instead of paying attention to what she was trying to tell me. We got moving again pretty good, but then all of a sudden the ridge gave way right in front of us.

"It was only a jump of maybe four feet across to where it picked up again. On the flat at full gallop she'd have taken it so easily in stride I wouldn't even have felt a bump in my saddle. But she was tired. I urged her over it. She hesitated, then reared and stopped dead in her tracks. I was so tired I was barely hanging on, though I didn't realize how shaky I was in the saddle.

"Off her back I toppled, and I landed sideways on my leg. I felt the pain instantly, but I didn't have time to think about anything, because I'd fallen to the right, and I just kept falling, away down the slope off the ridge, over and over, banging against rocks, sliding down the moving shale. It was a long fall, I knew that, though I didn't know much else. I was only conscious of spinning and crunching and bouncing . . . and pain. Pretty soon, even as I was still rolling and falling, everything drifted into blackness, and my senses just faded away. I thought I was dead."

He stopped and took a deep breath, reliving the whole incident for the first time. Even just telling it had shaken him all over again. Little beads of perspiration were on his forehead. The rest of us were still. It was pretty late by now, and dark and quiet outside— all except for the crickets and an occasional owl somewhere.

"When next I knew anything it was still black. I woke up real slow, you know how you do sometimes, faint images, blurry sensations that don't mean anything. That's how it was. It was dark, and all I was aware of was an odor, faint at first, but something I recognized, and a sound that I couldn't figure out.

"I tried to make sense out of things. I tried to remember. Then the fall came back to me, and how I had faded out of consciousness while falling down . . . down . . . down.

"Suddenly I knew the smell. It was smoke! And the sound— it was the crackling of a fire. That was it—a fire and smoke!

"I was coming back into consciousness, but only slowly, and I was still half-dazed and confused. My first thought was, *That's it, I really did die . . . and I'm in hell! I'm in hell because of what I said to Pa, and how I left home!*"

I looked over toward Pa as Zack was talking. He was hanging on every word, as if he was living every moment of it with his son. I could tell these last words smote his heart. He winced slightly, but kept looking straight at Zack, waiting for him to continue.

"Then suddenly I felt the sharp pain in my leg. I don't know how I could have a rational thought in the state I was in, but I remember thinking, *I can't be in hell if my leg hurts, because if I was dead my body would still be lying in that ravine back there where I fell.* Then gradually my eyes started to focus, and I saw some light from the low flickering of the flames. Everything else was black. I couldn't see anything except the red orange of the flames.

"I struggled a little, then tried to sit up. 'Lay still, son,' a voice said out of the night.

"My eyes shot wide open in terror at the sound. I couldn't see who had spoken, but I know my eyes were big as a horse's! It wasn't a nice or a gentle voice, very deep, almost gravelly. And it had plenty of authority. It wasn't the kind of voice you disobeyed. Again the thought flitted through my brain about being in the fiery place. I didn't even want to ask myself who the voice might belong to!

"I did what the voice said and lay still for a long time, wondering what would happen next.

" 'What's your name, son?' said the voice again.

" 'Uh, Zack . . . Zack Hollister,' I answered. It was nice to find out *my* voice still worked. 'Where am I?'

" 'You're safe, that's where. You had a bad fall back there.'

"Now things were starting to come back to me. I remembered the Indians, the climb up the hill, and the fall. Now I knew why my leg hurt.

" 'But . . . my horse . . . the mail,' I said. 'I gotta get the mail through. Where's the horse?'

"The next thing I knew, the voice was laughing. If I thought it had been gravelly before, the laugh was a rockslide. If your cackle is mountain water tinkling over pebbles, Alkali," said Zack, turning to Mr. Jones with a grin, "then the laugh I heard out of the blackness was made out of boulders rumbling down the mountain after an earthquake. I never heard such a deep voice or such a throaty laugh.

" 'That horse and whatever mail was on it is long gone, boy,' the voice said. 'We're miles and miles from where you fell, and your horse was miles away before I got to you, anyway.'

" 'The Paiutes . . . did the Paiutes get her?' I said in alarm.

" 'Can't tell you, son. I wasn't looking for your horse. I had my hands full just dragging you back up out of that crevice you got yourself into. As for the Paiutes, they know better than to bother me. I saved enough of their lives to keep me in their good graces for fifty years to come.

" 'But . . . but where am I?' I asked.

" 'Like I said, miles from where you fell. You're safe, that's all you need to know.'

" 'But I gotta get back . . . back to my route. They'll be worried about me. I gotta see about the mail.'

"Again the deep laughter came out of the dark.

" 'Son,' the man said, 'You're not going anywhere. Your leg's broken in two places. You're miles from the Express line. And even if you had a horse and were healthy, we're snowed in.'

" 'Snowed in! Where are we? Why is it so warm?'

" 'It'll all make sense in the morning. You hungry? You oughta be—you been out for two days.'

" 'Two days! What have I been doing, just lying here?'

" 'That's right. I dragged you up here, splinted your leg, made you as comfortable as I could, and then just waited. I could tell you were a strong little rascal, and that you'd wake up. So—you hungry?'

" 'Yeah, I reckon I am,' I said.

"He handed me something in a bowl. I could hardly see, but it smelled good. I picked out some chunks of meat in a kind of gravy and started eating it. I didn't realize how hungry I was until the smell of that stew hit my nostrils and I tasted the meat. The bowl was empty inside of a minute.

" 'More?' said the man.

" 'Yeah,' I answered, handing him the bowl. 'What is it?'

" 'Rattlesnake.'

"I gagged and turned away.

"I heard the laugh again from the other side of the fire. 'What's the matter, son? You never eaten snake before?'

" 'No, and I got no intention of eating it again!' I said.

" 'You'll die if you don't. It's about all I eat most winters up here, so you better get used to it.'

" 'Where do you get them?' I asked. 'Ain't no snakes in winter.'

" 'Ah, you just have to know where to look. And I do. I find them hibernating in their dens. They're sleepy and cold. I kill ten, maybe twenty of them if I go out and spend a morning at it. Skin and gut them, cut up the meat, stash it in the snow to freeze it. Keeps me in meat all winter long. Just take out and cook whatever I need.'

" 'That's all you eat, and you stay alive all winter? This is the high desert,' I said. 'No man can stay alive out here, in summer or winter.'

"He laughed again. 'You must figure I'm a ghost then,' he said. 'I've been living off the hills here for eight years. There's food in the winter, water in the summer. Plenty for a man to live on—if the man knows how to find the provision the Maker put in the desert. No big secret to it.'

"Well, we talked a while longer, and gradually I drifted back to sleep. When I woke up again it wasn't black anymore. But it wasn't light either. There was just an eerie glow coming from one direction, and total blackness from the other.

"I shook myself awake, more quickly this time. My leg hurt, but I felt so much better. Despite how repulsed I had been at the thought of it, the snake meat had given me back some energy. I managed to pull myself up to a sitting position and look around. My host and rescuer, whoever he might be, was nowhere around.

"It was obvious to me now that I was inside a huge cave, and I heard footsteps coming from the inside of the mountain. The instant I heard the footsteps I was terrified. If he'd wanted to kill me or eat me or skin me alive to put in his rattlesnake stew, he'd had two or three days already to do it, but I was scared anyway.

" 'Sleep good, son?' he said, coming toward me and sitting down opposite me on the other side of the fire. The sound of his voice reassured me. It sounded friendlier in the light of day, if this dreary half light could be called day. But when I set eyes on the man, my first impression did not make me feel good about my future safety. This man *looked* like the kind who might skin a kid like me and freeze my meat to go along with his rattlesnake stew.

"His face was long and thin, with sunken cheeks and high cheekbones. His whole frame was slender, but not what I'd call skinny, and that's how his face was too. No fat, just muscle and bone and hardiness. He looked strong and tough, like he'd been in a few tangles and probably had given the other fellow the worst of it. He had lots of hair, going in all directions, but not as bad or as gray as yours, Alkali, and a full beard. His beard was black. I couldn't tell a bit how old he was. A beard always makes a man look older, but in the darkness of the cave, this fella could have been anywhere from thirty to fifty. He still had all his teeth, and every once in a while one of them would catch a shine from the flames.

"He tossed a log on the fire, and sparks danced up from the disturbance.

" 'Where do you get wood around here?' I asked.

" 'Spend my summers gathering wood for winter, spend my winters storing snow water down in the cave for summer. Everything you need's out here, son.'

"I looked in the other direction, toward the light. We were some thirty feet from the opening of the cave.

" 'Why is the light so pale?' I asked. 'Is the sun just coming up?'

"The deep laughter came again. 'Don't you know what you're looking at there, son?' he said. 'That's snow—solid snow! Only lets in a bit of light.'

" 'Snow?' I said. 'But why is it there?'

" 'We're snowed in! I told you that last night. There's twenty feet of snow over the whole mouth of the cave. You're not looking at daylight, son, you're looking at a snowbank . . . from the inside!'

"Well, he was right. I didn't see the real light of real day for two weeks, when we dug our way out after it had half melted down. But we got snowed in three more times before winter was over."

"We?" repeated Almeda. "How long did you stay with this man?"

"All winter and spring. Until just three weeks ago, in fact," answered Zack.

"What did you do all that time, son?" asked Pa.

"Mr. Trumbull—Hawk's what he goes by. It's a name the Paiutes gave him when he first made friends with them. Hawk Trumbull's his name.

"He never did tell me his real first name. Anyway, Hawk taught me everything he knows. He took care of me, fed me, did everything for me until I could get back on my feet, babied me like a mother hen, making sure my leg healed proper, fixing new splints for it all the time. Then when I could walk again he took me out and showed me how he lives, how to survive, where the food and water was. He taught me all about animals and the weather and the mountains, showed me where the water comes and goes above ground and below ground, showed me all his caves—"

"How many does he have?" asked Tad in astonishment.

"I don't know. I don't suppose I ever stopped to count. Eight or ten, maybe. We'd store different things in different places, use them at different times—that is, *if* a bear wasn't occupying one."

"Zack!" exclaimed Almeda.

"It only happened once," he laughed.

"What did you do, shoot it?" asked Harriet.

"No. Hawk doesn't like to kill unless he has to, unless it's life or death. No, that time we took sort of a backwards approach to your husband's advice. We stood out of the way and let the problem go past us!"

"Sounds like you owe the man your life, Zack," said Pa.

"I owe Hawk more than my life."

"How do you mean?" asked Reverend Rutledge.

"He taught me how to live, how to survive, how to see things most people never have a chance to see, and never would see even if it was stuck right in front of their noses. He's more than just a mountain man. After a while I came to realize he was almost a rough wilderness poet at heart. He was always trying to get me to look past the obvious, to look beyond what things seemed to be on the surface. That was true when we went looking for water that had disappeared into a sink somewhere. It was true when we would watch the movement of eagles up in the sky and try to detect from them what might be going on ten miles away on the ground. He was always looking *into* things, he said. Everybody had two eyes, he said, but to really live you needed *four*—two outside and two inside."

"A remarkable sounding man," said Almeda.

"Best friend I ever had," said Zack.

The house fell quiet. It had been an amazing story.

"Actually, I reckon that ain't quite true," Zack said. "He's the one who helped me see I had an even better friend than him, and had for a long time."

"Who, Zack?" asked Becky.

Zack didn't answer her directly, but just went on talking about Trumbull.

"Once he began to find out about my background, and I began to tell him about you and Miracle Springs and what my life had been before he picked me off the mountainside, he started trying to make me use my extra set of eyes to see inside myself. He helped me see a lot of things I never saw before, things about all of us, this family of ours, and—"

He stopped, hesitating. His voice had gotten quiet. It was obvious this wasn't easy for him, especially in front of so many people.

"Mostly he helped me to see," Zack went on in a minute, "a lot of things I had never seen or understood about me and Pa. Once Hawk realized how it had been when I'd left, he asked lots of questions, wanted to know how I felt about things. He probably knows you about as good as any man alive, Pa, but the two of you have never met. He told me some things about myself that weren't too pleasant to hear, even though I knew they were true. But he was a straightforward, honest man, and I knew I could trust him. So I had no choice but to believe him. And so I had to look at myself, at some of the foolish things I'd done, like running off half-cocked like I did, and blaming things on Pa that I had no right to blame on anyone.

"He made me look down inside myself, just like he made me look at things in nature. He made me look at my anger. He told me that I'd never be a man until I learned what anger was supposed to be for. And that I'd never be a man until I learned to swallow my pride and come back and say I was sorry. He said I'd never be a man till I learned to live *with* the people closest to me. 'Only takes half a man to be able to live out in nature all by yourself,' he said. 'I don't doubt that I've done a pretty fair job of teaching you that. So, Zack, my boy,' he said, 'now it's time you learned to be a whole man, a complete man. It's time you went back. Take the half of being a man you learned out here and put it to use being the other half a man. Don't make the mistake I did of never going back. I went away when I was young, and I learned a lot of things. I know how to live in the wilds. But I'm still only half a man. It's too late for me now. I've drifted for too long and too far away. And most of my people are gone now. But it's not too late for you, young Grayfox.' "

"Grayfox . . . who did he mean? Was that you, Zack?" asked Tad.

Zack smiled—a smile with worlds of unsaid words behind it.

"Yeah, Tad, it was me."

"Why'd he call you that?"

"After I'd been there a spell, that was my name up there."

"It sounds like an Indian name, Zack," said Almeda.

Again Zack smiled, the same melancholy, distant, happy, sad, full, grown-up smile he had before. "Yep," he said, slowly nodding his head. "That it was. Given to me by the Paiutes."

"Why . . . what does the name mean?"

Another long silence followed. As I watched Zack, I could tell that his memories, even for such a short time ago, went into deep regions within him that perhaps none of the rest of us would ever see. But I hoped to see into those places inside my brother—maybe even write about them someday . . . or to show him how to write about them himself.

At last he sighed deeply. "That's a long story. Maybe even longer than this one," he said. "Someday I'll tell you about it. But right now I gotta finish this one."

"You go right on ahead, son. We're all listening," said Pa, his voice full of tenderness.

"Well, Hawk and me, we talked about a lot of things," Zack continued, "and he kept on gently tugging at me, helping me to see what I needed to do. But I just couldn't bring myself to do it. I knew I needed to let somebody know I was all right. I figured that one way or another you had probably got word by then that I was missing and would be worried. But though I intended to get word to you, somehow the time passed faster than I realized, and I just never did anything about it.

"One day we decided to go down to the valley. There were a few things Hawk needed. I'd never gone down with him before. I preferred to stay up in the mountains, even after my leg had healed and after the spring thaw came. I was at peace up there, and something inside me didn't want to go back. I felt like a new person out there alone, breathing in the high mountain air, knowing that even as desolate as it was, it was a land I could call my own.

"But this time I decided to go down with him. I figured it was time I let the Express people know I was alive so they could get word to you. We rode to one of the stations, both of us on Hawk's old mule. They couldn't believe it was me, but I told them the whole story. There was even a week's back pay from months before still in an envelope with my name on it!

"They had a couple of newspapers around, extras that the guys had brought to leave off at the stations along the way to keep the stationmen up on the news. That's how I first heard about the war and everything back in the South.

"I was sitting there having something to eat. Hawk was talking to the stationman on the other side of the room. I absently picked up a copy of a Sacramento paper. I don't know what I was think-ing—maybe that I'd run across something Corrie had written.

"I just was glancing through it, I think it was a paper from May sometime, and a line caught my eye that said something about a resolution passed by the legislature supporting the Union. To tell you the truth, I don't know why I starting reading it. I didn't know anything about the conflict going on. But it had been so long since I'd read anything, I was just reading the whole paper.

"Then all of a sudden my eyes shot open and stopped dead on the page. I couldn't believe the words I'd read! *According to Assemblyman Drummond Hollister, who was interviewed briefly after the vote* . . .

"*What!* I shouted to myself inside. It couldn't be!

"But I kept reading . . . *The new legislator from the mining town of Miracle Springs, where he has served as mayor for the past four years, has been an outspoken pro-Union voice in the Assembly.* . . .

"I didn't need to read another word!

"I jumped up and ran over to Hawk, shoving the paper in his face. He didn't have a notion what I was talking about. But all I could say was, 'Look! Look . . . right there. That's my pa!'

"I was so overcome that I had to be alone. Still clutching the paper in my hand, I stumbled out the door and toward the stables and the barn where all the equipment was. I wandered inside and sat down on a bale of hay. Even here, so far away from home, I couldn't escape it. Suddenly everything I saw—every leather strap, every smell, from hay to leather to manure to wood to horseflesh—reminded me of home. Everything Hawk had been saying to me over the last two months came back to me.

"In that moment, sitting there, I saw it all so clearly—what I had done, how closed off I had been to all the love Pa had always tried to give me . . . the best friend I'd ever had, and always had, just like Hawk had told me.

"I opened up the paper again and looked down there toward the bottom where the article was. Over and over I read those words about *Assemblyman Drummond Hollister*. And all I could think was what a good man that *new legislator* was, a better man and a better father than any of those people in Sacramento could possibly realize. Better than I'd realized till right then! And the one thing I knew more than anything else was that I *had* to see him again. And I didn't want to wait! I had to see him now. I wanted to go home!

"I was crying by then. I was embarrassed at the time, but I'm not ashamed to admit it now. There were tears falling all over that newspaper page, but I couldn't take my eyes off the words."

Half the room was crying by now to hear Zack tell it—at least Almeda, Becky, Harriet, and I were. I have a feeling the men were choking back tears as well.

Zack looked over toward Pa, drew in a deep breath, and then spoke again.

"I tell you, Pa," he said, "I was so proud of you when I read those words . . . so proud of who you are! I just wanted the whole world to know you were *my* pa! And I had to tell you! I had to tell you . . . how much—I had to tell you how much . . . I love you, Pa."

Both of them were on their feet by now. This time it was Zack who approached and put his arms around Pa, bending down slightly to rest his face against Pa's shoulder, weeping like the boy-turned-man that he now was. Pa's strong gentle hands reached slowly around his son and pulled him close.

Almeda rose and went to them, followed next by Rev. Rutledge. In another minute we all stood together, weeping, hugging, sniffling, and sending up lots of silent prayers of rejoicing.

As we gradually fell away two or three minutes later, Rev. Rutledge broke the silence.

"So, what happened next, Zack?"

Zack drew in a long breath to steady himself.

"I went inside, asked if I could buy a horse for the $25 in the envelope, in up-front payment, and I'd send them the rest.

"Seeing as how it was me, the stationman said, and considering what I'd been through, he didn't figure Russell, Majors, and Waddell ought to mind too much.

"I said my goodbyes, and I had to fight back the tears again when Hawk took my hand and shook it. But within the hour I was headed west . . . and here I am!"

CHAPTER 51

THE END OF THE EXPRESS
AND A NEW OPPORTUNITY

Zack was home!

It was hard to get used to. Every time I stopped to realize it, a wave of joy swept over me.

It seemed as if life ought to stop, but it never did. There was still a war going on in the East, plots and counterplots in the West. Pa still had to keep going to Sacramento . . . and there was still Cal.

The very next morning, Pa came upon Zack with soap all over his face. "What in tarnation are you doing?" he exclaimed.

"Shaving off my beard, Pa."

"What in thunder for?"

"I figured if I'm going to come back to civilization, I ought to look civilized. Besides. I figured you'd want it off."

"Well, you figured wrong. I like it!"

"You do?"

"Sure I do. Makes you look like me when I was your age."

"You want me to keep it?"

"Well, it's up to you, son. But I sure think a man's beard looks good on you."

"Okay, Pa," said Zack with a smile. He couldn't have been more pleased!

In mid-October a letter came to me, in an envelope from the office of the governor of California. My heart skipped. I was sure it was from Cal, but I was mistaken. I can't imagine a letter from such an important person as the governor being a disappointment, but I have to admit that one was.

Dear Miss Hollister,

I apologize to seem to be always asking you favors. But when a man in my position discovers a person who is loyal and competent, with a handsomeness and intelligence to match, he does not find it easy to replace her. So I am coming to you cap in hand to once again ask for your help in a matter of extreme importance to the future of our nation. As you know, the soldiers of the Union have grave needs, and we of California are doing everything we can to help them. A major fund-raising effort is underway, led by my friend and yours, Mr. King, in order to raise and send to President Lincoln's forces as much cash and gold as possible. California, as I'm sure you can appreciate, stands in a unique position to be able to help in this regard.

It is my hope that you will consider allowing me to appoint you co-chairwoman of a new organization which is being formed to work alongside Mr. King's efforts, to be called California Women for the Union, and whose principal activity will be raising funds for the Federal troops. Your name is one that is recognized and respected among the women of this state, and your efforts on behalf of the Union will, I am certain, not go unnoticed.

I am, your humble servant,
LELAND STANFORD
Governor

A hastily added note was attached to the letter. It said, "*As always, my faithful Cal Burton has told me he will help you in this assignment in any way which might be beneficial to you. I look forward to hearing from you. LS.*"

I hardly knew what it would involve, but how could I not accept? I did want to help the Union. And when somebody as important as the governor asks for help, it seemed my patriotic duty to say yes. I wrote back the next day saying I would do it, but said that he would have to make sure somebody told me what was expected of me. I was willing, I said, but totally ignorant of what the appointment might entail.

In the meantime, another major event in the life of the country was taking place. It had nothing to do with the war, but, because of Zack, and because of what Pa and I had been through, it came a little closer to home.

The Pony Express was about to go out of business after just eighteen months in operation.

The Pony Express had never made a profit for Russell, Majors, and Waddell. They had from the beginning hoped for government financial help but never received it. Once the war began, the amount of mail had dwindled, since many army troops were transferred from the West back to the East, and the army had been a heavy user of the mail services. But on October 24, 1861, something else happened that made the eight to ten days to take news from coast to coast eight to ten days too long. Suddenly the Pony Express was no longer the fastest way to transmit news.

On that day, in Salt Lake City, two teams that had been working from California and Nebraska for six months met and joined the telegraph wires they had been stringing up across the country. The instant those wires were connected, Washington and San Francisco were able to communicate directly with each other over nearly three thousand miles—not in days but in minutes!

Unfortunately for him, Governor Stanford was away at the time. But in his place the Chief Justice of California sent this message to President Lincoln along the new telegraph wires:

> In the temporary absence of the Governor of the State, I am requested to send you the first message which will be transmitted over the wires of the telegraph line which connects the Pacific with the Atlantic states. The people of California desire to congratulate you upon the completion of this great work. They believe that it will be the means of strengthening the attachment which binds both the East and West to the Union, and they desire in this—my first message across the continent—to express their loyalty to the Union and their determination to stand by its Government in this, its day of trial. They regard that Government with affection and will adhere to it under all fortunes.

The riders of the Pony Express had ridden well over half a million miles. Only one rider had been killed by Indians, although a number of station attendants had lost their lives. Only one pack of mail was lost. Whatever its financial losses, in many other ways it had been a great success. But two days after the completion of the telegraph, the Pony Express officially discontinued its service.

All across the country, and especially in California, there were articles of praise and tribute for the Pony Express, now that it was gone. The *Alta* printed several, too. I had written a story about my experience with Pa at Tavish's station earlier, but now I wished I could have written one of these tributes. Mr. Kemble would have let me, but I wasn't a good enough writer to do the kind of articles that were being written. In November, in the Sacramento *Bee*, for example, one tribute read:

> Farewell, Pony: Farewell and forever, thou staunch, wilderness-overcoming, swift-footed messenger. Thou wert the pioneer of the continent in the rapid transmission of intelligence between its peoples, and have dragged in your train the lightning itself, which, in good time, will be followed by steam communication by rail. Rest upon your honors; be satisfied with them; your destiny has been fulfilled—a new and higher power has superseded you.
>
> This is no disgrace, for flesh and blood cannot always war against the elements. Rest, then, in peace; for thou hast run thy race, thou has followed thy course, thou has done the work that was given thee to do.

CHAPTER 52

RAISING MONEY FOR THE UNION

After the battle of Bull Run in July, there were no more battles fought in the war all the rest of that year, except for a minor skirmish here and there. Both sides now realized that the enemy was stronger than they had thought, and they spent the next six months and all winter getting their troops ready, strengthened, and trained. Both presidents and their staff of generals devised great battle plans intended to knock out the opposing forces, whatever it took.

The year 1861 had been only a beginning, the calm before the storm. It seemed that 1862 would probably be a devastating and bloody year for our country.

Therefore, fund-raising became all the more important. The Union army would need lots of money. Early in 1862, a movement was begun back in Boston to help the Union effort, and it became the focus of the nationwide effort to raise money. It was called the Sanitary Fund, although I never understood why it had such a funny name. Thomas Starr King and the other leaders in San Francisco—including me—had been raising money to send to Mr. Lincoln. We immediately organized a local branch of the Sanitary Fund.

I had a hard time thinking of myself as a leader, but I was *called* a chairwoman of the California Women For the Union. So, when the Sanitary Fund started operating in earnest, Mr. King asked me if I'd be willing to work with him as the head of the ladies' auxiliary of it. Mrs. Herndon, a woman I'd been working with on the other committee, would take that over herself. We both agreed.

As chairwoman of the Ladies' Sanitary Fund, I had to go to Sacramento and San Francisco a lot—more than Pa, in fact. He started giving me a bad time about being busier with politics than he was.

"It's you that oughta be in the legislature, Corrie," he said one day. "You spend so much time in Sacramento talking to folks about money, I oughta just turn over my seat in the Assembly to you!"

Pa sometimes had some farfetched notions, but that was about the most farfetched one I'd ever heard. The idea of a woman holding a political office like that made Almeda's running for mayor seem like nothing!

He was right, though—I was gone from Miracle Springs more than I was there, it seemed. And I hardly had any time for writing anymore—other than writing asking people to help the war effort and give whatever they could. But most of it was done in person, sitting in front of a group of people with Mr. King or one of the other men involved, listening to them give a rousing speech. They would always give me a nice introduction, saying who I was and making it sound as if I were more important than I was. And then I'd stand up and talk for three or four minutes too, urging the women especially to help out however they could.

We traveled around the northern part of the state, either by stage or in a special carriage arranged for us, or close to Sacramento by train, and spoke at lots of places. Besides being an orator who could hold people spellbound, Mr. King was a great organizer too, and he set up church meetings and town-hall gatherings and outdoor assemblies and political and patriotic festive events. Before the year was half over, San Francisco, they told me, had become the highest contributing city in the whole country to the Sanitary Fund.

We were all proud of the two hundred thousand dollars we had raised, and determined to do even better through the rest of the next year. Most of the gold was taken by ship around by Panama steamer. The stagecoach lines would have been too risky, since the Butterfield route went right through the Confederacy and was controlled by the South. Even as it was, there was always danger of the money falling into the hands of Confederate privateers.

Miss Baxter in Sacramento and Miss Bean in San Francisco each set aside a room just for me called "Corrie's room" because I stayed with them so often. Both became even better friends than before.

Cal was involved in the fund-raising too, so I saw him every time I came to the cities. We'd have dinner together most evenings when there wasn't a function to attend. More than once I turned to Miss Baxter and Miss Bean as a substitute for Almeda in trying to figure out how I felt about Cal. Neither of them had been married, but they understood about being a woman, and that was all I needed. I had never been married either, but I was finding out that I was more of a woman than I sometimes would have wished for!

Sometimes Cal would act strange, and it would worry me. I'd immediately think I had done something wrong. But if he didn't like me, why would he keep inviting me out to dinner or for a ride or walk in the evening? Often he grew quiet and distant, and his moods confused me. I would have expected him to be happy, living permanently in Sacramento, working alongside the governor, having to do with important things.

Whenever I'd ask him what was on his mind, he'd laugh and try to shrug it off lightly. But I could tell it went deeper than he was letting on. Finally I came to the conclusion that it was the war itself. The war had everybody on edge; the future was uncertain, and no matter how much money we raised, the Union might lose. Nobody liked to think it or say it out loud, but after Bull Run, we couldn't help having a gnawing worry that the South *might* win! What if Jefferson and Stephens became president and vice-president of the whole country? What if we *all* became part of the Confederacy one day? What if slavery became as common in New York and Minnesota and California and Oregon as it had been in Alabama and Mississippi?

The very thought was too horrible to dwell on!

But facts were facts. The South had won the only major battle of 1861. And as the fighting of 1862 opened, even the mighty

Union navy, which had been attempting to blockade the South, suffered a terrible defeat at the hands of the new southern ironclad warship *Merrimac*. She sank two ships her first time out, and the North's own ironclad ship, the *Monitor,* was powerless to inflict any damage upon her.

Cal had spoken about opportunity, but now that his opportunity had come and he was assistant to a governor who might run for president someday, all of a sudden it all seemed about to be destroyed. If the South won, everything would be lost for him. The Republicans—and Mr. Stanford along with them—and everything we had fought for and believed in would be destroyed. If the Union fell, so would Cal's hopes. There would be no *opportunities* left for someone like him who had so vigorously defended the Union. People like us who had worked for the Union might even be considered criminals!

As I thought about it, it became less of a mystery to me why he was downcast. I wanted him to get to have everything he'd dreamed of and hoped for. I was concerned about the outcome of the war, too, but I personally didn't have as much at stake.

I was excited when news began to reach us about Federal victories in the West along the Mississippi. It was especially exciting to hear that General Grant was leading the Union forces! I wished I could see him again.

Even after the horrible battle at Shiloh down in Tennessee in April, where neither side had been victorious, the march of Union troops toward New Orleans and Grant's control of the Mississippi River seemed to give reason for optimism. I was sure Cal's spirits would pick up.

"No, Corrie," he said, "the Mississippi's a thousand miles from the nerve center of it all. The war will be determined between Washington and Richmond, decided by who controls the two capitals. Only one president is going to emerge on top, Corrie. And right now, whatever your General Grant may be doing in the Mississippi Valley, Jackson and Robert E. Lee are threatening Washington. I tell you, Corrie, I don't expect Lincoln to last out the year!"

His voice sounded different as he spoke. Was he afraid? There was a quivering nervousness in his tone, and a light in his eye.

Through the spring of that year, as the war intensified and news continued to reach us of more battles, more bloodshed, more young lives lost, Cal grew more and more agitated. More was on his mind than just raising money for the Union, but he wouldn't say what. He didn't invite me to dinner as often either.

He seemed to be busy with other things, and often left right after our fund-raising meetings, and I wouldn't see him again for days. I didn't mind too much, but I was worried about him.

CHAPTER 53

A MOMENT BETWEEN PAST AND FUTURE

Late in May of that year, Mr. King asked me if I would be willing to travel to a few small communities and conduct some fund-raising meetings by myself.

He wanted me to go up into the foothill regions, the gold communities that I was familiar with, but not just near Miracle Springs—also down toward Placerville. I told him I'd be willing just so long as he told me what to do and arranged everything.

Railroads were much in the news that year. There had been all kinds of politics and debate; the companies had already been created, and a bill was before Congress in Washington to finance the building of a railroad from coast to coast. All the people of Sacramento, especially Governor Stanford, had been deeply involved in it for quite a while already. But California actually had only one railroad in operation—the Sacramento Valley Railroad, running out toward the foothills in the direction of Placerville.

I took the train out from Sacramento for the few meetings Mr. King arranged for me, where I spoke and got pledges from people for the Sanitary Fund. I didn't actually take any of the money back with me; it would be sent to the committee's headquarters in Sacramento later.

Traveling by train was exciting! I could hardly imagine being able to get into the passenger car behind a great black locomotive and ride right across the mountains and all the way to the East. But from the way everyone was talking, that day wasn't so far away. In fact, the route that had been decided on would go close

285

to Miracle Springs. It was called the "Dutch Flat Route" and would run in the valley just on the other side of the hills from Miracle Springs. I wondered if we'd be able to ride up on the ridge and hear it chugging along someday!

During my few days of fund-raising, after I gave my short speeches about the Union and the war and the need for money, people would come up afterward and want to talk to me. And not just women; men would come up too, asking me questions and just wanting to talk in the most friendly way.

Most of these people didn't want to talk about politics or the war, but about personal things. A lot of them had read my article about the flood, or something else I'd written, even years before, and they'd want to talk about that. Then they'd tell me what *they* were thinking about, or what was on *their* minds. Everywhere I went, women would come up and invite me to supper with their family. After the first night, I didn't have to stay in another boardinghouse for the whole trip.

If it wasn't too crowded or noisy, some of them even confided things to me, problems they were having, and one or two asked my advice and what they should do. Before long I realized that my little trip out from Sacramento had more to do with individual people and what was going on inside their hearts and lives and minds than it did with raising money for the Sanitary Fund.

The most eye-opening realization of all was that the people coming up to talk to me afterward were more interested in *me* as a person, in Corrie Belle Hollister, than they were in all the things I may have been talking about. They seemed to see in me someone they could understand and who might understand them, someone they could talk to, even confide personal things in.

I came away with lots of new ideas about how my involvement in politics might have more to do with the people I ran into than it did with the bigger issues that seemed more important at first glance. Suddenly I found myself imagining people's faces, and thinking about what I could say to them and how I might be able to help them in some way. I found myself thinking more about people than politics.

I had always tended to think of myself as young and insignificant. Even with all I was doing now, I still wasn't "important" like the men were. Yet these few days changed the way I looked at myself.

It wasn't about importance . . . it was about people. It was about looking into their eyes and seeing a friend, a person who could understand and care. I found myself wondering if perhaps that wasn't the greatest "opportunity" I could ever have, the greatest "open door" of all.

I found all these things going through my mind as I stood on the last morning waiting for the train to arrive. I had completed my final fund-raising talk the night before at a church in a small foothills town. The morning train would take me back into Sacramento, and from there I would take the stagecoach back home to Miracle Springs.

The sun was well up in the sky, and it was a bright warm spring day. As I stood there on the wooden platform, holding my leather case that Almeda ordered for me out of a catalog, I thought of the changes that had come and were coming to our country, and of course the changes that had come to my own life as a result. All my past flitted by in a few moments, and I could not help but wonder about the future—if it would hold as many changes and surprises as had the past. I remembered my talk with Pa about how circumstances sometimes take us down roads we don't anticipate.

That had certainly happened to me, even just since Pa and I had talked about it! My decision to get involved in the election two years ago *had* caused things to happen in my life that wouldn't have otherwise. Here I was, raising money for the Union! Mr. Kemble and I had talked about making a book out of some of my earlier journals, about our coming to California back in 1852. That was another change on the horizon, another opportunity, as Cal would call it.

As I stood there, hearing the whistle of the train in the distance as it began to come into the station, I felt as if I were standing between my past and future—looking back, seeing the past, and waiting for a future that nobody can ever see.

I glanced toward the slowing train as it approached. Even the train itself, and these tracks right in front of me, would before long stretch all the way out of sight to the east, over the Sierras, and beyond. The very tracks themselves seemed to symbolize to me the endless stretching out of life—going in two directions. Just like the tracks, our lives stretch out behind us, reminding us of all the places we've been, all the experiences we've lived. But it also stretches out in front, and we don't know where that train track leads! We just have to get on the train and find out.

I knew where this train was going. It would take me back into Sacramento. But where was my life headed? It had been an exciting ride up till now. But I wondered where the tracks would lead me next.

CHAPTER 54

A DISTURBING ENCOUNTER

Late summer and fall brought more bad news from the East.

The Confederate forces had scored a stunning victory in August, matching only 55,000 men against the Union's 80,000 in a battle that was called the *Second* Battle of Bull Run.

In September, General Robert E. Lee invaded the North in force, crossed the Potomac out of Virginia and into Maryland. Not only did Lee want to get the fighting out of Virginia, his home state, so as to protect the badly needed crops for the harvest season, but he also hoped that his army might make Maryland want to secede. With Maryland in the Confederacy, the Union capital of Washington would be right next door.

He did not succeed. But neither did he fail. The standoff, and resulting battle in the valley of the Antietam Creek south of Hagerstown, was the bloodiest engagement of the war. More than 22,000 young men were killed, and neither side gained an advantage.

So much blood was being shed! There was both grief and determination throughout California—determination to help the Federal forces against an increasingly hated foe. It was all so needless! And the South was held accountable for the destruction and the dreadful loss of life.

He tried not to show it, but I know this news deeply disturbed Cal. He expected the government of the North to fall any day, and his future with it.

Not long after these two battles, an appeal came to Mr. King from the Boston headquarters:

The Sanitary Fund is desperately low. Our expenses are fifty thousand dollars per month. The sick and wounded on the battlefields need our help! We can survive for three months, but not a day longer, without large support from the Pacific. Twenty-five thousand dollars a month, paid regularly while the war lasts, from California would insure that we could continue with our efforts. We would make up the other twenty-five thousand here. We have already contributed sanitary stores, of a value of seven million dollars, to all parts of the army. California has been our main support in money, and if she fails, we are lost. We beg of you all, do what you can. The Union requires our most earnest efforts.

Immediately, Mr. King, Mrs. Herndon, Cal, and I—along with a few others—met together to plan a renewed round of meetings to gather together even more funds to help save the Union.

By the end of 1862, Mr. King's efforts had been so successful that nearly $500,000, mostly in gold, had been raised for the Sanitary Fund, more than half of it from San Francisco alone. I was proud to have been a part of it!

Usually we conducted our meeting and gave speeches. Then afterward Mr. King would pass a collection box, just like at a church service, and let people give what money they could right there on the spot. But most of the money came from pledges, and then Cal and I and some of the others would go around picking them up for the next several days. We took the money to the bank we used for the Sanitary Fund, and later sent it off to Boston by steamer. Businessmen or mining companies sometimes made their contributions in actual gold or silver bars. One time I went to a prominent San Francisco banker's office, expecting to receive a check for the pledge he'd made to Mr. King. He loaded me down with twelve pounds of gold and fifteen pounds of silver, worth almost six thousand dollars!

When Cal saw me struggling out of the bank to our carriage, he burst out laughing.

"I only got a little piece of paper," he said. "We went collecting at the wrong places."

"Next time," I panted, "I'll pick up the check, and *you* go retrieve the bullion!"

In spite of my difficulty, Mr. King was pleased.

Cal, still reading every scrap of war news he could lay his hands on, was acting disturbed and fidgety. Once he got so angry after one of our meetings that he nearly came to blows.

A man I had never seen came up to him out of the crowd and started talking rudely to him.

"Got everything going your way now, eh, Burton?" said the man derisively.

"Get out of here, Jewks!" Cal answered back in an angry tone. "What business do you have here, anyway?"

"Your business is my business now, Burton—if you get my drift."

"I don't, and I don't care to!" said Cal, trying to shove his way past the man.

"Watch yourself, Burton," he said, laying a hand on Cal's shoulder.

When Cal grabbed the hand and threw it off, I was afraid they were going to start fighting! I'd never seen such a look in Cal's eyes before, and it scared me.

"Come on, Corrie," said Cal, taking my hand and pulling me along after him, "let's get out of here."

"Who was that man?" I asked once we were away from the bustle of the crowd and walking toward our carriage.

"Nobody—just a troublemaker."

"I recognized his name when you spoke to him. What was it—I've forgotten now."

"Forget it, Corrie. He's nobody, I tell you—forget you ever saw him!"

In the expression on Cal's face, I glimpsed a flash of the look he'd leveled on the man in the crowd. He'd never looked at me like that before, and I didn't like it. Neither of us spoke again right away. We still had another meeting to attend that afternoon, but there was a chill between us all day. Later that evening, Cal said he had to go someplace. When I next saw him, everything was back to normal. He took me to dinner and was even more charming and flattering than ever.

CHAPTER 55

DECEITFUL SPY

The end of 1862 approached.

I was looking forward to being home for Christmas. It had been a busy and tiring year. Besides every thing else that had happened, Mr. Kemble had gotten in touch with Mr. Macpherson, an editor from Chicago, and he *did* want to publish some of my earlier journal writing into a book. That, along with the war, Zack's homecoming, and my involvement with Mr. King and Mr. Stanford and Cal, made me ready for a good long rest. After all, I had to update my journal with a whole year of keeping track of everything that had happened!

But before that, we still had one major fund-raising gathering to conduct in Sacramento—the biggest of the year, Mr. King said. We hoped to raise as much as sixty thousand dollars for one huge donation to the Sanitary Fund at the end of the year to put us over the half million dollar mark for the twelve-month period.

The meeting was scheduled for December 13, announced all the newspapers. There was a band, and Mr. King did all he could to make it festive so hundreds and hundreds of people would come. There were brightly colored banners and patriotic posters and handbills to get people to feel loyalty and enthusiasm for helping the Union. At the last minute I overheard Cal telling Mr. King he wouldn't be able to attend. He said he had some important business to take care of, but that he would be available all the following day to help gather what had been pledged. I was standing ten feet away, but I don't even think he saw me, he was so distracted. When he left Mr. King, he walked off through the

crowd of gathering people without so much as a word to me. He
hadn't even looked around to find me.

I have to admit, my mind wasn't on the talk I would have to
give in about an hour. I couldn't help feeling hurt.

Suddenly without even thinking about what I was doing, I
hurried through the crowd in the direction Cal had gone. It didn't
occur to me that I was actually "following" him, I just found
myself leaving the assembly under the great canvas top that had
been erected for the purpose, and walking toward the business
section of Sacramento. About a hundred feet ahead of me, Cal
was walking briskly along the boardwalk.

I continued behind him, keeping alongside the buildings, stopping in front of a store window now and then. I would die if he
turned around and spotted me!

I hated myself for spying on him like I was! But I couldn't
stop. The drive inside to find out what he was doing was stronger
than my good sense.

With trembling step, and even more trembling heart, I kept
inching forward, ever closer—mesmerized with mingled fear and
agony, yet unable to tear my eyes away from the figure in front of
me.

He stopped and made motions as if to glance around.

Terrified, I ducked quickly into an open doorway.

"May I help you, Miss?" said a voice surrounded by laughter.

I looked up to discover that I hadn't walked into a store at all,
but a men's barber parlor. Immediately I felt my cheeks and neck
turning red.

"Uh . . . no, I'm sorry . . . I must have made a mistake," I
mumbled, backing out.

I glanced up the street. Cal was just disappearing inside a
building.

I ran across the street and dashed into an alley. I leaned up
against the building, then sneaked a look out and over to the other
side to try to see where he had gone.

I couldn't see through the window because of the glare of the
sun reflecting off it. But the gold lettering painted on the glass was
legible enough. WESTERN UNION it read in big letters. Underneath, in smaller script were the words "Transcontinental Telegraph Service."

I stood there waiting.

Suddenly I realized what a fix I was in! What if Cal came out and went back toward the meeting? I'd be stuck there and unable to get back without him seeing me! If the meeting started and I wasn't there, how would I explain myself?

I glanced out again. Maybe I should make a quick dash back across the street now. But it was too late—there was Cal coming out of the telegraph office!

I yanked my head back behind the building. I breathed in deeply, but couldn't get my breath. I was sure he'd know I was there and walk straight over to confront me.

What in the world are you doing here, Corrie. Spying on me, eh! No good can come of that! My mind played out the terrible possibilities.

Slowly I tried to look out around the edge of the building, not even thinking that my bonnet would lead my eye out into the open by at least six inches.

He was still there! I kept watching. Then he turned and continued on down the boardwalk the way he'd been going before. Several steps along he glanced down at a small scrap of paper he had in his hand, held it in front of him for five or ten seconds, still walking, then crumpled it up and tossed it into the street.

Suddenly I found my eyes following the wadded-up scrap instead of Cal, who walked on, rounded a corner, and disappeared.

My heart was pounding. *Did I dare?* What if he came back around the corner and saw me?

I waited another several seconds until I couldn't stand it any longer!

Suddenly I was out of the alley and running as fast as I could across the street in the direction of the Western Union office. I reached the other side. There it was! I ran the five or ten more yards, stooped down, grabbed up the piece of paper, clutched it in my hand, and sprinted back toward the meeting, hardly aware of the noise my boots were making along the boardwalk.

Faintly I heard some yells as I passed the men's parlor, but I just kept going. There was only one sound I dreaded hearing behind me—Cal's voice calling out my name!

There was the canvas tent, the grassy expanse where people

were standing and sitting. The meeting hadn't yet begun!

I slowed to a walk, breathing in huge gulps of air into my lungs. I skirted around the edge of the crowd, trying to calm myself down.

Just then the band started to play. I knew Mr. King would expect me up on the platform any minute. I breathed deeply again. I had to calm down! I would never be able to say a word about anything in the condition I was in.

I had to go join the others. But first I had to know what I had in my hand. I unclasped my fingers and unfolded the tiny piece of paper. I was trembling so violently I could hardly focus my vision on the few handwritten words that met my gaze.

The message was brief and made not the slightest bit of sense to me: F-BURG OURS STOP NO TIME TO LOSE.

"Corrie . . . Corrie, where have you been?" I heard a voice say behind me.

I nearly jumped out of my skin. Thinking it was Cal, I fumbled with my hands quickly, trying to make them disappear someplace in the folds of my dress.

"What are you so jumpy about?" asked Mr. King, walking up as I turned around. "It's not like you."

"Oh . . . oh, nothing," I faltered. "Just nervous, I suppose."

"Come, now—that's not my Corrie Hollister. We've got to be at our best. Shall we go? They'll be expecting us momentarily."

He led the way and I followed toward the platform where chairs were set out for us. I managed to get through it, but that day's speech was not one of my best. I kept thinking of the message written on that scrap of paper:

F-BURG OURS . . . NO TIME TO LOSE.

CHAPTER 56

IT CAN'T BE!

Cal never returned.

When the meeting was over, I was anxious to be out of there and get back to Miss Baxter's.

I was walking away from the platform when a man accosted me.

"Mind if I speak to you a minute, Miss?" he said. I looked up to see the man Cal had gotten so angry with a few months back. My first feeling was one of fear. He saw it.

"Don't worry, Miss Hollister. I mean you no harm."

I continued walking. I wasn't in much of a frame of mind for talking, especially to that man. But he fell in and started walking along beside me.

"Name's Jewks, Miss Hollister . . . Terrance Jewks."

I nodded.

"Where's your friend Burton?" he asked.

"I don't know. He wasn't at today's meeting," I answered.

"So I saw. How much do you know about him?" he asked.

"Enough, I suppose," I said, still on my guard.

"I hope he treats you better than he did me."

"What do you mean by that?" I asked.

"Just that he seems to take pleasure in ruining people."

"How so?"

"Only that a certain Democrat with a bright future ran into your friend and found himself in the hospital for three weeks, and with lies spreading about him the whole time. Lies enough to put an end to my political career."

"What does Cal have to do with it?" I asked, stopping to look at Mr. Jewks.

"He has everything to do with it. He was the one who did it to me."

"I don't believe you," I said.

"If it wasn't him personally, he was behind it. It may have taken me a while, but a few months ago I finally found out who it was that hired the thugs that pulled me out of my San Francisco hotel and left me for dead in an alley. That's when I came looking for him."

"Cal would never do such a thing," I said.

"Not even to win an election? Come now, Miss Hollister, you must know him better than that."

All of a sudden the conversation I had overheard between Cal and Alexander Dalton snapped into my mind. Of course—this must be *that* Terrance Jewks!

"Why are you telling me this?" I asked, finally more attentive to Mr. Jewks. "I'm a Republican and pro-Union. You're a Democrat, as I understand it."

"Perhaps I'm just concerned for a nice-looking young lady and I don't want her to get hurt like I was."

"Perhaps. But why do I have the feeling there is more to it?"

Jewks laughed. "You are a shrewd one, Miss Hollister! Honestly, I would like to keep you from trouble if it's possible. But along with that, I have two other motives. One is simple revenge for what your friend did to me. I'm sure you can understand that."

"I don't happen to think revenge a worthy motive," I said, "but I suppose I do understand it. What's the second?"

"Let's call it a change of heart."

"How do you mean?"

"I was a Douglas Democrat. Didn't care too much for Lincoln, but I was no southerner. Once the war broke out, I realized my loyalties were with the government, not with the South. I'm from Ohio originally. I voted for Douglas, and I'm still a Democrat. But the North has got to win this war or else the United States is all over—a dream of democracy that didn't work."

"I still don't see what any of this has to do with Cal . . . or me."

"A change of heart is what I called it," Mr. Jewks went on. "I had one, once the war started. And so did your friend, Mr. Burton. I've been following him, checking up on him, asking questions of people, using some of my old Democratic contacts. Spying on him, you might say, finding out things, without telling the folks exactly how I stood myself now, if you understand me."

"I'm not sure I do," I said slowly.

"Then let me put it to you plain, Miss Hollister, and you can use the information however you think best." He paused, took a breath, and went on. "I used to have lots of friends in the other camp. Breckinridge people. Once the war broke out, then especially after Stanford was elected, they all went underground. Had to keep out of sight. But I kept tabs on what was going on and didn't let my new loyalties be known. All the time I kept an eye out for who'd had me beaten up and what I might do about it. I found out the *who* several months ago, like I told you. And the *what* I might do to him, I just got to the bottom of this week."

He stopped.

I'm listening," I said.

"Miss Hollister . . . your Cal Burton is a member of the Knights—the Knights of the Columbian Star."

"But who . . . what. . . ?" I faltered.

"It's an offshoot of the Knights of the Golden Circle."

"No . . . it can't be!"

"It is, Miss Hollister. Believe me."

"But . . . I don't understand."

"It's really quite simple—your Cal Burton is a southern sympathizer."

"I don't believe it!" I finally burst out.

"I finally have the proof," Mr. Jewks added. Worse even than being a sympathizer—the man's a spy for the Confederacy!"

CHAPTER 57

CONFRONTATION, HEARTBREAK, AND BETRAYAL

The rest of that day was one of the most awful of my life.

I couldn't believe what Terrance Jewks had told me—or *wouldn't*. I was too mixed up and confused to know the difference.

I don't even know what became of the hours between my interview with Jewks and nightfall. I walked for miles, I suppose, slept in my room at Miss Baxter's, stubbornly trying to convince myself it was all a lie. Hadn't Jewks himself admitted that revenge was his motive? How better to get revenge on Cal than to turn me against him! It was a cruel hoax, an attempt to ruin Cal's reputation, and maybe even bring scandal upon Governor Stanford.

Jewks was just being a loyal Democrat. *He* was the southern spy, and his assignment had been to undermine the credibility of one of California's most loyal Unionists, the assistant to the governor himself!

It all made perfect sense! And I was Cal's weakness. They had probably been spying on me, too! I had been part of their plot all along! I had to warn Cal, and warn the governor that right here in Sacramento there were forces trying to destroy them!

But at the same time, I couldn't get rid of an uneasiness in the pit of my stomach. Cal's strange activities . . . the odd looks on his face that would come and go. I knew there must be an explanation! He would tell me everything about Jewks and set my mind at rest completely. That was the only thing to do. I had to talk to Cal tomorrow. I'd confront him with Jewks' accusations. I'd tell

299

him everything that Jewks said. He'd probably laugh the whole thing off!

Despite my attempts to reassure myself, I slept fitfully through the night. My mind told me I had nothing to be anxious about. But my stomach was quivery regardless.

The next day, the fourteenth, was a full one for all of us, contacting people, collecting money and checks and gold, confirming pledges that had been made, banking the contributions. Mr. King had called a meeting that morning to make all the arrangements and give us our assignments. It was the first time I had seen Cal since the previous afternoon. He looked and sounded like always.

We spent most of the afternoon together about the committee's work, all except for about half an hour. He knew there was something on my mind. I wasn't very good at concealing it. But we didn't have an opportunity to talk until later.

When we finally did, I just burst out and told him everything Mr. Jewks had said.

"I know it's not true, Cal," I said, nearly breaking down. "But I had to tell you so you'd know."

"Of course it's not true," he said with a lighthearted laugh. "Jewks is nothing but a two-bit politician, and a liar on top of it!" He laughed again, but the laughter sounded forced, and a little too quick on the heels of his words.

"A troublemaker, that's all he is," he added, denying the accusation too forcefully for me to feel altogether comfortable. "Probably a spy himself!" Again he laughed. But he looked straight at me as he did. I think he realized in an instant that I knew he was bluffing. I may not have been the prettiest or the smartest or the bravest person in the world, but I was able to look into someone's face and know which way the wind was blowing through their mind. I suppose up till then I hadn't made too good use of that ability with Cal. And right at that moment, I would have given anything *not* to have known what was behind his forced laughter and bravado.

Cal's laughter died away. He kept looking at me, kept watching my face for signs of what I was thinking. Then he looked away and glanced down toward the river from the little patch of grass where we were sitting. I knew him well enough to know that he was revolving things over in his mind, trying to decide what to say. Then he glanced up at me again.

Still neither of us said anything. I hadn't realized how much my face must have betrayed my doubts. But it must have, because he quit trying to deny everything. After another minute or two, a smile slowly spread across his face. A melancholy, cynical smile.

"Ah, Corrie . . . Corrie," he sighed. "You are naive."

I didn't understand his tone.

"What do you mean, Cal?" I said.

"You see the world so simply, so black and white. There's no gray for you, is there, Corrie—no in-between? Right and wrong, that's all there is."

"I . . . I don't know."

"It's a complicated, mixed-up world, Corrie. Circumstances don't always fit so neatly into black and white compartments. Sometimes there *is* gray—places where you don't know what's right and what's wrong."

"What are you trying to say, Cal?" I asked, getting alarmed by his sarcastic tone. "Mr. Jewks isn't right, is he?" I asked, still not wanting to face the truth.

"Ah, Jewks! What does he know? A low-level incompetent. If he couldn't take care of himself in this game, they should've sent somebody else!"

"Cal . . . it isn't true what he said?"

"We had to win the election. It's a rough game . . . I told you that a long time ago.

"But it's not right."

"Right? What's right? Everything has its twists and ironies. Who's to say what's right in the middle of it all?"

"What twists, Cal?" I asked. "Please . . . tell me what you mean!"

"Don't you see the irony of it? Here I am, out West, on my way up, assistant to one of California's most powerful men, when from out of nowhere my past comes back to haunt me. Suddenly the country is at war, and I am in the *wrong* place."

"What do you mean . . . what about your past?"

"I've made no secret of it, Corrie. I was born in North Carolina. You knew that. I told you about my fondness for the country, and how I admired it in you."

"Yes . . . but, what—"

"Don't you hear what I am telling you, Corrie—*North Carolina*. I'm a southerner!"

"But . . . you've been a loyal Republican. You've worked for Mr. Stanford and the Union. You left the South years ago, just like my Aunt Katie. Lots of Californians came from the South originally."

"Ah, but there's the bitter irony, Corrie. I'm not just an ordinary Californian with southern roots."

"Why?"

"Because of who I am, because of my position here. Ever since I heard about Edie leaving and returning to Virginia, I realized I had to do the same thing—not for any noble motives, but because if I didn't, everything I had worked for would be lost."

"Cal . . . what are you saying?"

"That I've got to go back too."

"Back . . . back where?"

"To the South. I have no choice."

"But . . . but *why*?" I started to cry.

"Opportunity, Corrie—remember? Suddenly all the opportunities have shifted. My golden goose, Mr. Leland Stanford, has suddenly become a millstone around my neck. My Republican affiliations, all the work I have done for the Union, even my little game with Jewks—don't you see? It will all come back to haunt me when the war's over. Men like Leland Stanford—outspoken Unionists—if they aren't in jail with Abraham Lincoln, they'll be reduced to political impotence. And unless I do something to redeem myself, something to make up for all these years when I put my money on the wrong horse—unless I do something to atone for these transgressions, as it were, I am likely to be right there with them, reduced to a life of mediocrity and meaninglessness."

"You talk as if the war is already over."

"It is . . . virtually. The North has nothing. Washington is about to fall. Lincoln could be behind bars before the year is out. Unless I make my move, and immediately, my opportunity in the new nation will be lost. Opportunity, Corrie . . . I've got to seize it while there's still time. Changing loyalties once Grant surrenders to Lee won't count for much, will it?"

"But what will you do—join the Rebel army?"

Cal laughed. "The stakes for me are just slightly higher than that, my dear naive young friend!"

"You said you always wanted to go to Washington someday."

"I wanted to get to the capital. Once the North surrenders, that will be Richmond. And I don't have to wait until someday . . . the opportunity is before me *now!*"

"I . . . I just don't see—"

"You still don't grasp it, do you, Corrie?" he said, and he sounded as though he were talking to a child. "Does the name Alexander H. Stephens mean anything to you?"

I shook my head.

"Well, he is my uncle, on my mother's side. I know I told you about him. He has been after me for some time, through discreet communications of course, to join his staff—in a very prominent position. I have simply been awaiting the most propitious time for making such a move."

I stared blankly at him.

Cal chuckled. He almost seemed to be enjoying putting me through this, seeing the confused emotions pass through me. I thought he had cared, but I had never felt so small and foolish as I did right now.

"Alexander Stephens," Cal went on, "happens to be Jefferson Davis's vice-president. When I arrive in Richmond, I won't have to wait for some distant time . . . my opportunity will have arrived! I'll be working close to the president himself!"

"There's only one President, and his name is Abraham Lincoln."

"I'm sorry, Corrie, but there is the gray again in your world of black and white. Right now there are two presidents, and before long the only one remaining in power will *not* be your friend Abraham Lincoln."

"You have made up your mind?" I said, trying desperately to be brave.

"I'm afraid I have."

"Then why did you wait until now? Why did you keep being so loyal, keep helping us raise funds for the Union, keep working for Mr. Stanford? You gave several speeches, telling people why they had to support Mr. Lincoln and the Federal troops. How could you do that, Cal, when inside you were all along planning to defect to the South?"

"Oh, I haven't been planning to defect all along. I had to keep my options alive on both sides. I have nothing intrinsically against the Union, Corrie. I told you, it's not an ethical or moral issue for me. It's opportunity, and I will go where I can climb the highest. What if I had left, and then suddenly the tide of the war turned, and Davis and my uncle were the ones being arrested for their part in the rebellion? No, Corrie—I couldn't risk that! I've had to bide my time to see how the tide of the war would go. The shifting sands of the political landscape can be treacherous if you don't watch your step. So all year I *have* been watching my step, and now that the sands are about to engulf Mr. Lincoln and General Grant and Mr. Stanford altogether, I perceive it is time for me to be off. My only difficulty will be in explaining to my good uncle, who is not a kindly disposed man, why it took me so long to come to my senses. But I'm sure I will be able to manage that."

I sat stunned. I couldn't believe all I'd heard.

"But I thought," I said at last, fighting a terrible urge to break into tears, "I thought . . . we—that is, Cal . . . you always used to talk about what *we* would do . . . about the future . . . I thought—"

I didn't know what to say. There wasn't much more to say.

"Come now, Corrie, you didn't seriously expect me to marry you, did you?"

His question was so abrupt, so stark, that I felt as if I'd been slapped in the face.

"I didn't say that."

"It's bigger than just you and me. Maybe if things had been different, who knows what might have happened? You're a great kid, Corrie. I like you. There was always something about you I admired. In fact, I always kind of figured you might be on your way up, just like me, and that we might help each other out."

"And now you don't need someone like me anymore, so that's

the end of it, is that it?" I said, my hurt turning to anger.

"Please, Corrie," said Cal, laughing slightly, "there's no need to overreact to it. It's just one of those things that happened. My uncle simply happens to have more clout than a young news writer from California, that's all. Look at it practically. But I meant every word I said—I always admired you, and I'll always wish the best for you. But this is not an opportunity I can pass up—for you, or anybody."

I sat silent again. So many thoughts and feelings were raging through me, I felt like screaming and sobbing and running and kicking something—preferably Cal Burton!

"Why don't you come with me, Corrie!" said Cal after a minute. The exuberance in his voice let me know he didn't have any idea what he'd done to me.

"Why should I?"

"Because of the opportunities there would be for you in the new government. Just think—a news writer, right at the center of power. It could put you right at the top, Corrie. You could be one of the best-known writers in the country!"

"Opportunity, is that it?" I said.

"Yes! Why not, Corrie? What's there ever going to be for you here?"

Just my family, people I love, a good home, I thought to myself. "I don't think so, Cal," I said. "Even if the Union falls, I'm still going to cast my lot with men like Abraham Lincoln."

"Have it your way. But don't ever say Cal Burton didn't give you the chance to hitch yourself to his star on its way up!"

Finally I got up off the grass and started to walk back toward the buggy. "Will you please take me back to the boardinghouse?" I said. "I'm getting cold, and I have to start thinking about getting ready to go home."

CHAPTER 58

PARTING OF THE WAYS

If I thought the last night was awful, this one was much worse. Never had I felt so isolated in my life. How desperately I wanted to feel Almeda's loving arms around me, to hear Pa's voice, to retreat to the warmth of our home!

I felt small and foolish. How could I have been so naive? Cal was exactly right—a naive kid, that's what I was, nothing more! All this time I thought I meant something to him, and now I realized it had all existed nowhere but in my own mind!

Lying on my bed at Miss Baxter's, I cried and cried, drenching the pillow with my tears.

Not until late in the evening, after my tears had temporarily dried up, did I begin to think rationally again. Should I tell somebody . . . Mr. King, Mr. Stanford?

I supposed Cal would give the governor some kind of formal resignation. We'd probably not see him again on the fund-raising platform! Now that he had decided to throw in with the South, as dreadful as it was to think it, he obviously would be hoping for the Confederacy to win as quickly as possible.

At last I concluded that it was none of my business to tell anyone. Let Cal do his own dirty work! If he was going to betray us all, let *him* tell them face-to-face. I hoped he choked on the words!

I cried some more, but managed to fall asleep around midnight. I woke up several times, suddenly remembering the ache inside my heart and longing so badly for home. Each time, however, I drifted back to sleep again, and the final time slept for several hours. When I woke up, the sunlight was streaming through the window and it was halfway into the morning.

I rose and dressed, wishing I'd gotten up early enough for the morning stage north, but it was too late now. I'd have to wait until tomorrow. The morning edition of the *Bee* had already been delivered. I greeted Miss Baxter, saw the paper lying on her table, and looked down at it. Across the top, in bold black letters, were the words: UNION SUFFERS DEVASTATING DEFEAT AT FREDERICKSBURG, MD. REBEL ARMY 40 MILES FROM CAPITAL.

I sat staring at the headlines, stunned. It was as if Cal had known yesterday.

Suddenly I ran back up the stairs, dashed into my room, and rummaged about until I found the scrap of paper Cal had thrown on the ground. I read the cryptic message again. Of course! He *had* known. The paper said the battle had taken place two days ago, on the thirteenth, the same day he had received the telegram!

But the last words of the message . . . *NO TIME TO LOSE.* What did it mean?

I stood thinking for a minute; then a terrible sense of foreboding swept over me.

Oh no! I thought. *What if. . . ?*

I couldn't even say it! With hardly a word of explanation to Miss Baxter, I ran back down the stairs and was out the door and heading toward the middle of town. I stopped at the first livery stable on the way and hired a horse. The instant it was saddled, I galloped off, and in six or eight minutes I was pulling up in front of the capitol building. I hardly stopped to think whether I was presentable or not. I just ran down the corridor toward the governor's office. It didn't take long to find out what I needed to know: Cal had not yet come in this morning.

I turned around and retraced my steps. How I wished Pa had some business in Sacramento right then! I could have used his help!

I got back on the horse, walked her quietly until I was away from the capitol, then urged her again to a gallop. Three or four minutes later, I arrived at the house where Cal lived. I had never been inside, but we had ridden by several times, and he'd pointed

308

it out. Jumping off the horse, I ran to the porch and knocked on the door.

"No, Mr. Burton isn't home," his landlady said, looking me over from head to toe with a not-so-pleasant inquisitive expression. "I don't know when to expect him, either. I didn't see him come in last night, but then I don't make it a practice to be snooping into other people's affairs."

"Did he come in last night?" I asked.

"I don't know for sure. I thought I heard him, but he might have left again later. I didn't pay too much attention. I don't like to pry, you know."

I had the distinct impression that if she had known anything more than she was saying, she might have thought twice whether to tell me or not.

I ran back and jumped up on the horse's back, wheeled around, and made for downtown.

I hoped Mr. King was still at his hotel and hadn't left for his home in San Francisco! I was at the hotel in five minutes. I dismounted in front and dashed into the lobby. From all the riding, I was sure I looked a mess.

"Is Mr. King still here?" I asked the desk clerk.

The clerk gave me a look similar to the one Cal's landlady had given me. "He is."

I knew the room. We had several meetings of the committee there. I bolted for the stairs and bounded up them two at a time.

At last I knocked on the door, completely out of breath.

"Corrie!" said Mr. King, answering it, "Come in . . . you look as if you've just ridden one of those Pony Express routes you wrote about last fall!"

"Mr. King," I panted, "have you seen Cal today?"

"Why, no, Corrie, I haven't. As a matter of fact, I was going to get in touch with you to see if *you'd* seen him. I need to talk to him about what I'm sure must simply be a clerical mistake of some kind at the bank."

"What is it?" I asked.

"So, I take it you haven't seen him this morning either?" said Mr. King.

I shook my head.

"Hmmm . . . well, we're going to have to find him sooner or later to clear this up."

"What?" I asked again.

"You and he did make the collections yesterday, did you not?"

I nodded. "Nearly all of them. Several large checks, and a big amount of gold, too. I think the total was $52,000."

"Yes, it was a marvelous day—$69,000 in pledged contributions. And you say the two of you collected over forty thousand of it?"

"That's right," I said.

"Hmmm . . . that is peculiar. When I checked with the bank this morning, it seems there wasn't a deposit made to the Sanitary Fund account yesterday. But you and Cal *did* make the deposit?"

My heart began to sink beneath a dreadful weight of doom.

"Uh . . . Cal left me for thirty minutes or so after we were through," I said. "He told me he was going to the bank and asked me to run a message over to the capitol building for him. I met him afterward."

"Hmmm," mumbled Mr. King, pondering it all. "It must be a clerical oversight of some kind. I'll go check with the bank again. In the meantime, when you see Cal, tell him to come see me. Perhaps he can clear it up."

By now I was all but certain in my own mind that Cal could indeed clear it up! Whether Mr. King would ever hear about it from his own lips, however, I was beginning to seriously doubt.

I only had one more stop—the one I hoped I wouldn't have to make. I went from the hotel to the downtown district, where I pulled up in front of the Western Union office and tied up the horse. I walked along the boardwalk and around the corner I had seen Cal disappear around after receiving the telegram. It was a street I knew well from frequent use myself. But it had never occurred to me what he was doing when I'd seen him right here the other day. Three doors down was the stage office!

I walked inside and looked up at the schedule board, then went to the window.

"Morning, Miss Corrie," he said. "You ready for your ticket now?"

"Not yet, Mr. Daws, thank you," I answered. "Only some information."

"Anything I can tell you, Miss Corrie."

"Did you have a passenger on this morning's stage, a Mr. Burton?"

"Well, not exactly," replied the stationman, with whom I'd been friendly for several years. "That is, if you're meaning the same young fella I've seen you traveling with a time or two."

"That's him," I said.

"Handsome young man, eh, Miss Corrie?"

"Yes, he is . . . but was he in? Did you sell him a ticket?"

"Yes, he was in. Came in twice, as a matter of fact. But it was yesterday, not this morning."

"He was in *twice*?"

"Yes, ma'am. First time around four, five o'clock in the afternoon—"

That was the exact time when he'd sent me to his office with the message!

"He just wanted to leave his bag right then," he said, "so he wouldn't have to keep lugging it around. Once I lifted it, I knew why! Heavy as the dickens, it was! Heaviest bag I ever recollect. 'What in tarnation you got in here?' I asked him, 'solid gold?' 'That's a good one!' he laughed. 'Taking gold by stagecoach! What kind of fool do you take me for?' he said, still laughing. Nice young man, Miss Hollister."

"And then you say he came back later? But I was sure he would be on the morning stage."

"Yep, he came back later all right—around 8 o'clock. Most curious thing I ever saw. Don't know why they never told me about it."

"About what?" I asked.

"Special stage rolled up—all outfitted and ready to go. Driver said it was government business. And your man Burton, why he was the only passenger—other than the two armed guards, that is."

"What stage line was it?"

"The Butterfield."

"Which way did they go?"

"Butterfield only goes south, Miss Corrie. Driver told me they was gonna be driving all night. Said they were heading all the way to Fort Smith, Arkansas."

"That's behind the Confederate lines."

"Yes, ma'am. I . . . I thought you knew all about it, Miss Corrie." For the first time Mr. Daws' voice lost its cheerful tone, and he began to sound concerned.

"Why did you think that?" I asked.

"Well, ma'am, on account of him mentioning you, and saying you'd be along shortly. I just . . . well, I figured you'd be taking the stage out too, one of the regular Butterfield coaches, and that, well . . . that you and he'd be meeting up somewhere, or maybe that you was going all the way back East too. The way they made it sound like government business—I figured it had something to do with you."

Cal knew that sooner or later I'd figure it out.

"He even left a message for me to give you, Miss Corrie," the stationman added. "Makes it seem kind of odd now, him doing that, and you not even knowing he'd gone."

Cal had said it himself—the world was full of ironies.

I braced myself. I didn't want to ask, but I couldn't live without knowing. "What was the message?" I asked.

"Don't make much sense now, but he said to thank you for helping him to atone for his transgressions. He said his uncle would be very grateful, and that this would help explain things very nicely. Then he said he hoped to see you when you both got where you were going."

I took a deep breath. If Zack had to learn to be a man by facing Pa with humility, I suppose today was the day when I had to learn to stand up and be a woman by facing Thomas Starr King and Leland Stanford with honesty and humility, too.

I would have to face them both, and tell them what I knew about Cal. And I would have to tell them I had known it yesterday, in time to have stopped him. I would have to apologize. I would have to admit to the two great men of California that they had entrusted too much faith in me, and that I had not been worthy of it. And I would have to beg their forgiveness for allowing over forty thousand dollars of Union contributions to be speeding along its way south toward the government of the Confederate States of America.

"So I take it you won't be wanting a ticket, after all, Miss Corrie?" said Mr. Daws.

I sighed. "I might as well buy it now," I said. "Yes, I do want one, Mr. Daws. Give me a ticket north for Miracle Springs, on tomorrow's stage."

"Round trip, Miss Corrie?"

"No, Mr. Daws. One way will be sufficient. I don't know that I will be coming back to Sacramento anytime soon."

"Your business here all done?"

Again I sighed. "Not quite. I have some very unpleasant business to attend to this afternoon," I said. "But by tomorrow, yes, my business will be done."

CHAPTER 59

HOME AGAIN

It was a lonely, tearful stagecoach ride back to Miracle Springs the next day. I kept thinking I had cried all the tears it was possible to cry, and then more would come. How many tears could a girl have, anyway? There must be an end to them somewhere!

I didn't find out where the tears ended that day. By the time I reached home I had vowed never to have anything to do with politics, writing, or men again!

The minute I walked into the house I fell into Almeda's arms. I was so glad no one else was there right at that moment. She knew from one look at my face that something was dreadfully wrong, but she just let me cry and held me tight. Gradually, through my tears, I told her everything.

"Oh, Almeda," I finally tried to say, still blubbering like a five-year-old, "how could I have been such a downright fool as to think he loved me?"

She probably had seen the whole thing coming long before I had. But if she did, she didn't say so. She just kept comforting me.

"He never cared about anything but himself. He was completely self-absorbed. How could I not have seen it?"

I had done a lot of thinking all day riding on the stage. I had wanted to talk to Almeda so badly back in Sacramento. Now that I finally had her all to myself, I gushed out with everything I'd been thinking and feeling.

"Hearts can get in the way and cloud how you see nearly everything sometimes, Corrie. It's part of life, part of growing up.

313

I wouldn't feel too badly if I were you."

"How can I not? I was so blinded by everything that was going on. Cal had no real depth—it's all so clear now! All he cared about was his own ambition. We never talked about spiritual things or what really matters in life. Oh, Almeda, I just feel so foolish!"

"Time will help you understand it more clearly. I liked Cal too, Corrie. We all did. Whether he changed after the war started or was out for what you and your father could do for him from the beginning—we may never know for sure. He seemed sincere enough. I was taken in, too."

"Besides everything else, he took the Sanitary Fund money! How can I not feel responsible? I feel as if I've betrayed both the Union and God!"

"They will both forgive you."

"But it's too late about the money—he's gone."

"You said Mr. King and Mr. Stanford immediately sent some fast horsemen after the stage."

"They did, but they didn't have much hope of catching it. They had probably over a two-hundred-mile head start and would be close to the Arizona border by the time they could reach them. Even if they did catch them, it would likely have taken bloodshed to retrieve the money, and neither Mr. King nor Mr. Stanford wanted that."

"I see. I suppose in that case it wasn't worth it."

"They were a lot more worried about information Cal had to give to the South than just the money. Working so close to an important governor like Mr. Stanford, Cal knew a lot of things about the northern war effort."

A lump formed in my throat. "Almeda, how can I not blame myself? All my writing and talk about truth and being a true person, and I can't even recognize someone who isn't true when he's standing right in front of me! How could I not have seen him for what he was?"

"*Was* he untrue right from the beginning?"

"Oh, I don't know! After the way it turned out, how can I possibly know what was there inside him to begin with?"

"I don't know either, Corrie," said Almeda. "I do know we have to learn truth in stages. It doesn't come all at once. We have to learn about truth by encountering some things along the way that aren't true. Otherwise we never learn to tell the false from the real."

"Do those things that come along always have to hurt so badly, and make me feel like such a nincompoop?"

She laughed, and I halfheartedly joined in.

"A lot of times they do," replied Almeda. "Pain is one of the world's best teachers."

"The worst of it is forgetting about God all this time. I was so absorbed in Cal and what I was doing that I thought about him only once in a while, and I hardly prayed at all. I can't believe I didn't realize it!"

"It's all part of the growing and maturing process. Perhaps this will help you remember him more in the future. You've heard the expression about being older and wiser?"

I nodded.

"Well, just consider yourself an older and wiser and more truthful young woman now, after all this. If you grow and mature from it, won't it have been worth it in the end?"

I had to stop and think about that. In my present state of mind I wasn't at all sure.

"Almeda," I said at last, "when I was waiting for God to give me a sign about his will, Cal Burton was the person who finally convinced me to get involved in this election."

"Yes?" Almeda prodded when I paused.

"Well, it's just . . . maybe . . . do you think I heard wrong from the beginning? I mean, how could it have been *right* for me to be involved when Cal was so . . . so *wrong*?"

"Corrie," Almeda said gently, taking my hand, "the Lord uses many methods to open his will to us. Apart from what's happened with Cal Burton, do you think what you've done for the election— and for the Union—has been wrong?"

I thought about it for a minute. "No, I don't. I think it was the right thing to do, but—"

"Then maybe God *did* use Cal to help you make your decision, even though Cal himself wasn't aware of being an instrument in God's hands."

"I hope you're right," I said. "Right now, that doesn't seem to help me feel much better about it."

"It will in time."

"But what about my forgetting the Lord," I went on, "and not making him part of what was happening with Cal?"

"One thing about God, Corrie, that I've learned to take comfort from, is that he never forgets us—he always keeps doing his work in us, never stops working away in our hearts and minds. We may forget him, but he never forgets us. His work down inside us doesn't depend on something so unreliable as whether we happen to be thinking of him or not. His work of maturing us goes on even when we're not conscious of it. And he won't let us remain forgetful of him—not for long, anyway. He makes sure he gets our attention again eventually when he needs to, one way or another."

"Even with an incident like I've just been through?"

"The Lord will use anything or anyone. He uses all kinds of people and all kinds of situations. He will even use people who don't know him to open doors in *our* growth, like he used Cal Burton. He will use them for us, and attempt to use us in their lives at the same time."

"I doubt if I had much impact in Cal's life."

"Oh, I disagree, Corrie! I imagine God was using you to knock on some doors in Cal's heart and mind, just like he will use Cal, even in retrospect, to accomplish some older and wiser maturing things down inside you. Nothing in life ever goes to waste when we belong to the Lord—even the times when we might think we haven't been faithful to him. He takes it all and uses it for the best and deepest purposes."

"Hmm . . . If that's true, I wonder if God was knocking at Cal's heart."

"Who knows how differently it might have turned out if he'd paid attention to the small voice of God inside him speaking through you?"

"But I wasn't saying much of anything to him about the Lord."

"Your life was speaking important things to him, Corrie. I could see that the two times he was here. Your character, your bearing, your truthfulness. You may think you were nothing but a starry-eyed young lady. But your deepest self shone through like a clear-sounding bell. Cal noticed. Yes, God was knocking at his heart through you. But he chose to ignore the voice and to go his own way. So he will have to suffer the consequences, and you will have to go on with your life and learn from it all."

Suddenly the door burst open and Pa came in.

"I thought I heard the sound of someone riding up," he said, striding toward me and scooping me nearly off the ground in his arms. "Merry Christmas, Corrie!"

I'd nearly forgotten. Christmas was only nine days away!

"Merry Christmas, Pa," I said. If only I could keep from crying again!

"You show her the letter, Almeda?"

"No!" exclaimed Almeda. "I forgot, we got so involved in talking. Corrie, you have a letter!" she cried, turning and running across the room.

"What can it be that's worth all *that* commotion?"

"Wait till you see, Corrie!" said Pa, with nearly as much excitement in his voice as Almeda's.

Almeda ran back toward me, carrying an envelope, then thrust it into my hand.

"It came five days ago, Corrie! We've all been dying of curiosity waiting for you to get home!"

I took the envelope. The return address said only: THE WHITE HOUSE, WASHINGTON, D.C.

With trembling fingers I tore open one end of it and pulled out the letter. I couldn't keep my heart from pounding as I read.

MISS CORNELIA BELLE HOLLISTER,

I have been made aware of all your work for the Republican party on behalf of my election, as well as your efforts to raise money for our Union forces in this present conflict. I want to express my deepest appreciation on behalf of the nation, and to tell you that your patriotism has not gone unnoticed. It would be my pleasure to meet you here at the White House in Washington, if circumstances would permit you to make the journey. I would very much like to give you my personal hand of gratitude, as well as ask you to help me in the war effort with a new project here in Washington.

Yours sincerely,
A. LINCOLN
President

The single sheet fell from my hand and I staggered to sit down in a chair. I sat there stunned.

"What *is* it, Corrie?" asked Almeda. "Is something wrong?"

Pa picked up the paper and read it. "Nothing wrong, Almeda," he said after a moment. "It's an invitation to visit the President!"

"The President!" she exclaimed.

"Signed right here by Abraham Lincoln himself," said Pa, handing the paper to Almeda.

"Corrie . . . that's—that's wonderful!" cried Almeda.

How could it be . . . how could I possibly accept? But how could I *not* accept? Thoughts of the war and the danger and the time and expense involved—none of that entered my mind in the first seconds that I sat there. I thought only of the face of Lincoln from a picture I had seen. The President had written to *me*!

How much time passed as I sat there in a daze, I don't know. When I first became aware of voices around me again, Becky and Tad were there too, and I vaguely heard Zack and Alkali Jones outside approaching the house. Mr. Jones was laughing and cackling over something.

In the blur of my racing brain, there was Mr. Jones on the other side of the house with Zack, both of them laughing and talking. My ears weren't working right any more than my brain. They must have been playing tricks on me from the last time when I'd heard him making jokes about the Hollister clan running for office. Because of what I *thought* I heard Mr. Jones saying was, *Corrie Fer President, hee, hee, hee!*

My mind was spinning with thoughts of the war and Mr. Lincoln and stagecoaches and trains and money, and when my eyes and ears finally cleared, the room was quiet.

The whole family surrounded me, staring straight at me as if waiting for me to say something. Not a one of them said a word. They were all just gazing expectantly at me.

"Well?" said Pa finally.

"Well, what?" I asked.

"Are you gonna answer the question we've all been asking you, or are you gonna just keep sitting there staring off like you can't see or hear anything?"

"What question?"

"Are you gonna do it, Corrie?" they all shouted. "Are you gonna go?"

At last my mind seemed to start working again. I took in a deep breath.

"Of course I'm going to do it," I said. "He's the president of our country, isn't he? I can't very well turn *him* down, now can I?"

EPILOGUE

Most of the Pony Express incidents recorded—including the breakfast incident—are true, as are all the names of the riders mentioned. Nearly all California personalities, politicians, and issues are likewise factual, and the positions, facts, and details represented, as far as can be determined, are historically accurate. Along with other sources, the following books were very helpful in researching early California history, the Pony Express, the election of 1860, and the early Civil War period:

Bartlett, Ruhl, *John C. Fremont and the Republican Party*
Hittell, Theodore, *History of California*
Lewis, Oscar, *San Francisco: Mission to Metropolis*
McAfee, Ward, *California's Railroad Era 1850–1911*
Nichols, Roy, *The Stakes of Power 1845–1977*
Reinfeld, Fred, *Pony Express*
Rolle, Andrew, *California, A History*
Roske, Ralph, *Everyman's Eden, A History of California*
Williams, Harry, *The Union Sundered*
Williams, Harry, *The Union Restored*

In addition: "The Mexican War and the Facts Behind It" by Patrick Phillips, and issue #33 of *Christian History* magazine on "The Untold Story of Christianity and the Civil War."

For all of these, as well as to Sandy Bean for the creation of Edie, the author expresses his deepest gratitude.

Into the Long Dark Night

INTO THE LONG DARK NIGHT

MICHAEL PHILLIPS

Cover by Dan Thornberg,
Bethany House Publishers staff artist.

Published by Bethany House Publishers
A Ministry of Bethany Fellowship, Inc.
6820 Auto Club Road, Minneapolis, Minnesota 55438

Printed in the United States of America

Library of Congress Cataloging-in-Publication Data

Phillips, Michael R., 1946–
    Into the long dark night / Michael Phillips
       p. cm. — (The Journals of Corrie Belle Hollister ; bk. 6)
    Sequel to: Sea to shining sea.

    I. Title. II. Series: Phillips, Michael R., 1946–
Journals of Corrie Belle Hollister ; 6.
PS356.H492I57   1992
813'.54—dc20   92–34296
ISBN 1–55661–300–8   CIP

To
Sandy Loyd Bean

CONTENTS

8

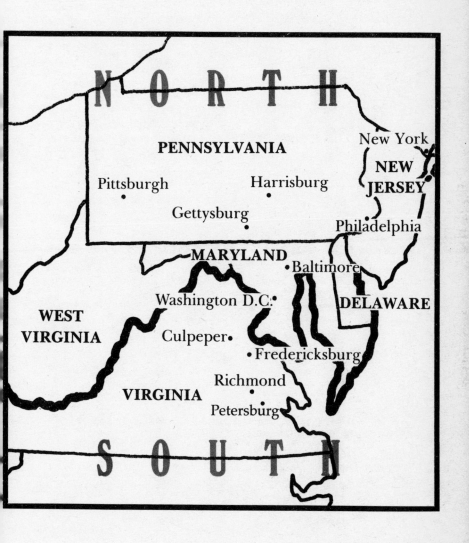

CHAPTER 1

GETTING READY TO GO EAST

"Where you bound for, Miss?" a voice rasped beside me.

I glanced up nervously. "Oh . . . the East Coast," I said. He must have gotten aboard at the last little town we stopped at. I hadn't even seen him sit down.

"Long ways for a young girl like yourself to be going," the man said. "You alone?"

I nodded. His question reminded me again just what an incredible thing this whole adventure was. I had ridden in the train around Sacramento a few times. But it was nothing compared to *this* huge, fast modern train and the locomotive pulling it.

I was about an hour east of St. Joseph, Missouri, now, and I was still pretty awestruck that I was halfway across the country and on my way to Washington, D.C.

It had been twenty-one days since I had left my family in Miracle Springs and boarded the Wells Fargo stagecoach bound for Salt Lake City. Then I changed to the Holladay Overland Mail and Stage. We mostly followed the Oregon and Mormon trails from there, over the Rockies and through Wyoming, down through Nebraska, and finally to the Missouri River and St. Joseph. After a night in a St. Joseph boardinghouse, this morning I had boarded the train to St. Louis.

I still couldn't believe it was actually happening. I was alone, on a train bound for St. Louis, Columbus, Ohio, through the Cumberland Gap of eastern Pennsylvania, and finally Washington, D.C., and the East Coast! And—the most unbelievable thing of all—in my bag I was carrying a letter from the President of the

11

United States. Abraham Lincoln himself had invited me to visit the White House, and to help him with the war effort against the Confederacy.

For a long time I thought I was dreaming. But it was all real, and here I was!

It *was* a long way for me to be going alone—the man was right about that. I glanced over at him and smiled. He had a kind face and was well-dressed, although his raspy voice reminded me of Alkali Jones.

"Well, I work for the railroad, Miss," he said. "I'm not going far, just to the next stop. But if you have any trouble, or need anything, you be sure to talk to the conductor. We're here to help you any way we can."

I thanked him, and we chatted for a few minutes more. Then he excused himself and went to talk to the conductor.

I gazed out the window, listening to the rhythmic sound of the steel wheels thrumming underneath me, and thought about the months since receiving Mr. Lincoln's letter. That had been the week just before Christmas last year, after I'd come back from Sacramento. At first I was so mixed up about Cal—feeling angry, foolish, stupid, and immature. I wanted to go out and chase him down and get back the Union's money, and make sure he wasn't able to tell his uncle or anyone else something that would hurt the northern cause. A lot of my initial thoughts weren't altogether rational!

But Pa soon talked some sense into me. It was winter, and I couldn't go just yet, not unless I wanted to risk getting snowed in somewhere on the stageline, and neither Pa nor Almeda liked that idea much. Not unless I wanted to take the Butterfield Overland stage that went through the South, as Cal had done. But I didn't want to travel through the Confederacy. There was a lot of fighting going on by now down in the region of the country the Butterfield went through—not so much during the winter months, but I didn't want to take any chances!

In the end we all decided it would be best for me to wait until spring and take the Wells Fargo and Holladay route. In the meantime, I wrote a letter to Mr. Lincoln, thanking him for his kindness and telling him I'd be proud to take him up on his offer to visit.

I said I hoped to be there sometime in late June 1863.

Besides the weather, I also had to wait several months because the first book of my journals got published in January. The whole family was so excited—especially me!

Mr. Kemble had already talked by telegraph to Mr. Mac-Pherson. In spite of all that was happening, there had already been considerable interest in the book in the East, and he wanted me to get started gathering up material from my journals to make into a second book.

None of us could believe it! I hardly had a chance to get used to the notion of being an author, and now Mr. Kemble and I had to get working on another book. I had enough stuff written in all my diaries and journals, that much was for sure. But I couldn't quite understand the idea of putting into a book what I'd written down just for myself—I still had a hard time figuring out why anyone would be interested in any of it. Of course the story of how the five of us kids got to California, and how we found Pa, might interest folks, especially because it happened in the middle of the gold rush. But the other, more personal writing—well, I didn't know.

"What parts of my journals do you want?" I had asked Mr. Kemble. "There's nothing much that seems like it'd make a book."

"Your pa's trouble with Buck Krebbs and him writing back east for Katie and Becky getting kidnapped and rescued—you don't think that's plenty exciting?"

"Sure, I guess so," I answered. "I guess I was wondering more about my private thoughts."

"Put some of that in, too. It's all interesting. It's all interesting, Corrie."

With his help, we got it all written down in a form that he thought would make a good book, and sent it off to Mr. Mac-Pherson in Chicago. Even while we were doing that, mail started coming to me from people who had read the first book about our trip west and finding Pa, and that encouraged me about the work Mr. Kemble and I were doing.

So for all these reasons, the first several months of 1863 were busy ones before I could be ready to leave for the East.

By the time I stepped onto that Wells Fargo stagecoach in the second week of May, one book about California with my name on it was being read, according to Mr. Kemble and some of the mail, all across the country, and another one was on the way. I found myself wondering if I'd someday write another book about what was happening now in the East for the people back in California.

CHAPTER 2

LOOKING BACK WITH DIFFERENT EYES

Even after the excitement of seeing the book get published and anticipating getting to visit Mr. Lincoln, still it might have been a foolhardy thing to do, heading across the country alone in the middle of all the fighting that was going on!

That just wasn't the kind of thing most ordinary young women did. But I don't suppose most folks would accuse me of being "ordinary"—in how I thought about things *or* in what I did.

Pa and Almeda both tried to talk me out of going more than once between Christmas and the middle of May when I left. I even talked myself out of it a time or two.

But they both had enough of the adventurer's blood in them to understand why I had to go. Pa and Uncle Nick had gotten into trouble, but they had their share of wanderlust when they were young, too. And after Mr. Parrish had died, Almeda had the drive and determination to do some things that other women didn't do, and to succeed at them no matter what all the men may have thought.

Ma, too, had been a mighty determined, headstrong lady before she died. The older I got the more I realized how extraordinary she must have been. Just bringing us all out across the country as she'd done was a pretty remarkable thing to do. And that was eleven years ago, when the prairie and plains were a lot less tame than they were now. And California wasn't tame, either!

Not until you grow up yourself can you see what was *inside* your ma and pa and other people around you. When you're young, you see their faces, but you don't know what they're thinking. You hear their words, but you don't understand why they said them. You see what they do, but don't know the motives causing them to do things. It takes growing up, doing a lot of thinking, and looking inside your own self, before you can understand all those *inside* things about your own ma and pa.

I was seeing that I had little bits of all of them inside me—lots of Pa and Ma, of course, but parts of Uncle Nick and Almeda, too. Sometimes I was scared, but another part of me wanted to go and see places and do things I'd never done before. I suppose I had a good share of Ma's and Almeda's strong wills too. Maybe other women hadn't done some of the things I was trying to do before. But that didn't mean I couldn't try. I might fail, but I just might succeed, too!

Pa and Almeda had both left home when they were younger than I was now. I had just turned twenty-six, and if I wasn't ready to try something out on my own by now, I figured I never would be. Life in the West had been a lot rougher and more primitive when Almeda had come around by steamer to California and when Pa and Uncle Nick had come west. Now I had a nice bright Concord stagecoach to ride in halfway—a little bumpy, perhaps, but better than a wagon train!—and now a smooth, fast train coach for the rest of the journey. This was positively luxurious compared to how they had traveled, and how it was when Ma and the five of us kids had struck out in 1852.

The only thing to worry about was the war.

It was easy to forget about that sometimes—it seemed so distant and far away. I couldn't help wondering if it was really true that the country was torn apart, with the two sides hating each other, and that thousands of boys were getting killed.

I could see the anxiety in Pa's and Almeda's faces when they waved goodbye to me in Sacramento. But we had talked and prayed it all through, and I told them that if I heard about or saw any fighting within a hundred miles, I'd jump on the fastest horse I could find, and fly due north as fast as his legs would carry me, no matter where I was at the time.

"I'm going to see President Lincoln," I said, "and to write an article or two *about* the war—who knows, maybe even part of a book. But I don't figure on getting anywhere near it myself!"

"Just don't forget it," said Pa. He smiled, but he was serious.

"We want you back," added Almeda, giving me a tight squeeze.

"You know I've got to go?" I said.

They both nodded.

"When the President himself invites you for a visit, and even to help him, there isn't anything you can do *but* go!"

So I rode off eastward on the stage, and my family all got in the big buggy they'd brought me down in and headed back north to Miracle Springs.

Who could tell how long it would be until I saw them all again? I cried quite a bit between Sacramento and Carson City. But they weren't just tears of sadness. Though I would miss my family, I was excited about the adventure ahead of me.

CHAPTER 3

AN INTERESTING JOURNEY

Stagecoach travel had to be the most intimate way imaginable of getting from one place to another. There was no escaping the close quarters. Whether you liked it or not, you were jammed in with people you didn't know for long hours every day.

Most of the Concord stagecoaches I had traveled in back in California were built to carry nine passengers—three facing forward, three to the rear, and three in a seat in the center. But between most of the stations on the trip across the country, they used smaller coaches that didn't have the middle seat. There was also room on top and beside the driver if needed. I'd read about a stage several years ago running between Sacramento and Shasta in the north of California that held thirty-five people—the largest coach I'd ever heard of. But I never saw it.

During my trip, there were between three and eight of us along various stretches of the route. When the six seats inside were filled, two other men sat on top, one beside the driver and guard, and the other on the very top with the luggage.

The seats were upholstered in nice leather and were reasonably comfortable, except where the roads were so rough that we bounced up and down all day long. Then we all got mighty sore in our hindquarters!

The most interesting fellow on the way was an Englishman by the name of Sir Jeremy Mawr. He sat opposite me all the way from Salt Lake City to St. Joseph. He spoke in the most wonderful accent and was really quite friendly, in a stuffed-up kind of way. He said he had come here to learn about the gold rush and see the

West firsthand, and was now on his way back to England. For someone interested enough to have come all that way, he did a lot of complaining about how uncivilized and uncouth everything was, although even then he made it sound appealing and attractive. Something about the voice and the accent made *everything* sound educated and full of more meaning than if an ordinary person had said it. Every once in a while he'd mumble some comment about the appalling conditions and the lack of a first-class compartment for gentlemen to ride in. His attitude was pretty uppity, but I just enjoyed listening to him talk, and didn't say anything.

One of the other passengers, a gun dealer from Denver, didn't have much patience with him. After one of Sir Jeremy's comments about the dust and bumps, the dealer said right out, "Look here, Mawr . . . if you don't like it, then get out and ride on top, or else hire yourself a horse and make the trip yourself. The West ain't for sissies, and maybe it ain't for high-falutin' Englishmen, neither!"

After that Sir Jeremy, and everyone else in the coach too, was quiet for a spell. I think the rest of us were glad when Mr. Thackery, the gun dealer, got off. Sir Jeremy's funny ways were more pleasant than Mr. Thackery's loud jokes and rudeness.

After a while I had a long talk with Sir Jeremy, and found him to be a man I really liked. He even invited me to England to visit him on his estate. I don't know if he was just being polite or not, but I found myself thinking about it a lot afterward. And when I told him what I did and about my writing, and showed him the letter from Mr. Lincoln, then he started asking *me* a lot of questions, and pretty soon the others were as well. I had been a little shy during the first few days, getting used to being away from home and being mixed in with so many people I didn't know, people who were older than I was. But once we started to find out about each other, everyone got more friendly, and I found myself more and more comfortable. By the time we'd been on the road several days, we almost felt like family.

Every station stop was interesting in its own way. The terrain kept changing, of course, but all the people tending the stations had stories to tell that kept us entertained during meals and during the nights we'd spend at the overnight stops. Some of the men reminded me of Mr. Tavish, and had stagecoaching tales about robbers and Indians just as exciting as the Pony Express stories Tavish had told.

I'd listen to the stories, and I'd also wander out to the barns and stables where they kept the horses and repaired the coaches. I talked to the hands and learned all kinds of interesting things.

The Concords were so well made that all the men who worked on them spoke with pride, almost as if they'd designed them themselves. One man got to talking so much that he showed me practically every inch of the coach and how it had been put together. He said it was built lower down to the ground than the English mail coaches so that it would be able to round the curves and handle the rough terrain of the West better. The tops were built out of thin basswood, curved at all the edges to reduce the wind resistance. Being heavier on the bottom like that enabled the coaches to take the sharp curves faster. One Concord, he told me, was being shipped from Boston to San Francisco and went down when the ship sank. But a month later, when the coach was pulled out of the water, it was put into service, and was still on the road to that day.

"Just look at them wheels, Miss," the maintenance man went on. "Why, every one of them spokes is of seasoned ash and hand-fitted to the rim and hub."

You could tell they were strong, and had to be, because the wheels were big—three feet in diameter in the front and five feet in the back. The hardwood spokes held them together and took all the weight as the wheels were spinning around.

Most of the luggage went up on the flat roof. The strongbox for valuables was stored under the driver's seat. On the back was another rack with leather over the top of it to protect everything inside from the dust that the coach kicked up. This was called the boot, and it carried extra luggage as well as tools, water buckets, and sometimes mail and other packages.

The coach body had two long, heavy leather straps underneath, running from front to back as supports. These acted as suspension, to absorb the bouncy, rutted, rocky roads. The leather worked much better than iron springs, which were used on most kinds of wagons.

We stopped every fifteen miles or so for changes of horses, and once during the day and once about nightfall at the home stations. There was still lots of snow on the ground going through the mountain passes, and the nights got cold in those small sod houses. The trip from Sacramento to the Missouri River cost over $500, which was a lot of money for Pa to part with for my sake.

I sure hoped it would turn out to be worth it!

CHAPTER 4

GROWING-UP TEARS

Every mile of the road we traveled had memories, and I was surprised at the things I recalled because I had been so young when we'd come this way before with Ma.

Ever since South Pass beyond Fort Bridger, the stage followed the same route we had come across by wagon with Captain Dixon. As I looked at the countryside passing by, I thought of Ma nearly all the time. Memories of that wagon trip kept flooding over me— the mountains . . . Fort Laramie . . . the descending plains . . . Indians . . . buffalo . . . talks we'd had . . . things Ma had said to us . . . ways she was always trying to prepare us for growing up.

And now I was grown up and on my way to St. Louis. Ma had gotten a good price on a wagon there, and had bought most of our supplies before we crossed Missouri to Independence to join Captain Dixon's wagon train. Everything was full of heart-stirring, sad, melancholy memories.

My memory of Ma dying brought me to tears a few times during the weeks of the trip. But as I saw places that stirred up the past, I felt a quiet melancholy that seemed to have nothing to do with Ma. When in the distance I saw the wooden walls of Fort Laramie, something out of another world came up from inside me, touching my heart with a significance that could not be understood by the mind, only *felt*.

As we approached the fort, I began to hear voices in my mind—Tad and Becky clamoring in the back, Emily asking questions, Zack exclaiming over the troop of soldiers escorting the wagons toward the fort, Ma trying to keep us all calm. I remember her turning, with words meant only for me, as she did so often. Even though I was only fifteen, she tried to treat me as a woman. So many voices, so much laughter, so many poignant memories . . .

Perhaps facing the past and feeling the pain of it is part of growing up. I was twenty-six, and I had a lot more growing yet to do. But the tears I cried as I traveled east somehow felt like the tears of growing up. I was experiencing emotions impossible for children to feel—the aching nostalgia of the past, and the significance of memories that ran too deep for words.

The farther east we went, the more I found myself thinking about New York and the farm where we'd lived. I wondered if it was still there, and if there might still be people there who'd known Ma and Pa, or even us kids, or any relatives, or the church.

A different feeling started to come over me. I wanted to see the place where we had lived, wanted to walk through the fields and the house, wanted to climb the oak tree again—oh, there were so many memories! I began to anticipate going there to visit.

What would it be like? Would there be anyone I'd know? Would it feel like *home*?

At the same time, I couldn't help wondering if there would be tears, and if the land and town and farm and fields and oak tree would have that sad kind of meaning, too, that couldn't be explained.

There was only one way I'd know. One way or another, I had to go back there to visit and see the place.

CHAPTER 5

INSIDES OF THINGS

Traveling all the way across the country, I had a lot of time to myself—time to think and time to write. My journal was filled with pages of thoughts and observations and feelings that didn't have much to do with where I was or what was happening around me.

I have always felt as if I were living two lives at once—one, what I was on the outside, the part of me that other people *saw*. The other, what I was on the inside, the part of me that was *thinking* all the time.

That's why I kept a journal. I had to let the thoughts out someplace, and writing them down somehow made it feel like the thoughts were completed, and then I could move on to think about something else.

One of these little thought-journeys happened just the night before we arrived in St. Joseph, and I found myself thinking about it that last day on the stagecoach. I had been talking with the wife of the stationman after supper when she said she wanted to go out to the chicken coop to check and see if there'd been any eggs laid in the last couple of hours. I went with her, and there was a big brown egg, freshly laid.

"Isn't that a beautiful big egg," she said, reaching down to pick it up. "My husband will love that for his breakfast tomorrow."

Just those few words set my mind racing. I got to thinking what it would be like if, instead of fixing the egg for breakfast, she set it up on the mantel to admire. What if it was the most beautiful egg ever seen, and she didn't want to destroy it by breaking it? So to preserve it she set it there, and took good care of it, and showed it to everyone who came through the station.

Now there's no doubt that an eggshell *is* a wonderful creation of God's. It has got a unique shape. It's strong enough to hold a little baby chick until it's ready to come out into the world.

I found myself thinking how lots of folks do that with many things—they set the shells up on the mantel to look at and admire. But they never get *inside* the shell because they're so busy looking at the outside.

But it's the inside where the life is, not the shell. The yoke of the egg becomes a baby chick, and the white feeds the chick while it's growing in its shell. An egg is no good if all you do is look at the shell. If you put it up on the mantel and leave it there, it will eventually spoil. The life in it will die if it's left there in the shell. The purpose of an eggshell is to be broken, so that the life inside can come out. The shell has no meaning all by itself. It's only a container for the life. Yet it's easy to see the outside and *think* you're seeing the egg, when really you're only seeing the shell, the husk, the container.

It almost seems as if God intentionally hides the important insides of things, surrounding them with attractive, unusual, attention-drawing outside skins. We look at and admire a tree's bark and leaves and branches and shapes, but its real *life* flows invisibly in the sap deep inside. The dirt and soil deep under the ground give life to the roots and enable plants to grow above ground where they are seen.

And people, too, have an outside shell that folks see—our body, our looks, our voice, our behavior and mannerisms, even our personalities are really part of the outside skin, our shell. But the real person is inside, in the soul. Just like the white and yolk of an egg. And like with eggs, if all we ever do is relate to the shells, the outsides of people, we'll never know the real life inside them.

After that, I found myself looking differently at people, trying to catch their eyes and seeing if I could use them like windows to see inside, past the shell into some part of their soul. I found myself listening to people differently too, watching for glimpses of the inside *real* self that might be revealed.

Why, God, I asked silently as I sat there bouncing along and thinking about the five other people in the stagecoach with me, *did you make it like this? Why did you hide the inside life of things behind shells that sometimes we can't see past?*

Then I thought of the time Jesus was telling stories to the people and trying to explain spiritual truths to them. His disciples came to him afterward, confused about what they'd heard and full of questions. Jesus said to them, "The secret of the kingdom of God has been given to you. But to those on the *outside* everything is said in parables, so that they may see but not perceive, and hear and not understand."

I was confused, too, when I thought of that. It seemed as if God were intentionally obscuring truth so that some people would be able to see and understand it, and other people wouldn't. Why would he do that? Why would the kingdom of God be a "secret"? Then I remembered another place where the Bible talked about the "mystery" of the gospel.

I thought about all this for a long time, and I kept coming back to Jesus' other words to his disciples after he'd finished telling the parables: "He who has ears to hear, let him hear." What did that mean? Did God intentionally hide the whites and yolks inside shells to keep some people from seeing where the real life was? At first that didn't sound much like God.

But then I got to thinking about God himself. He was life, the life of the whole universe! He was the one who gave *everything* else its life! If the whole universe was like an outside shell, God was inside it—like the yolk which feeds the developing chick, like a heart, like a soul, like the sap inside a tree—giving it life and energy and meaning.

But why did God make it so that the most important things are the hardest to see? I remembered one of Jesus' parables about this very question. He said the kingdom of heaven is like finding a treasure buried in a field that is so valuable you go and sell everything you have in order to get it. Buried . . . hidden . . . secretive . . . a mystery. Why did God hide himself and the truths of the kingdom of heaven? Was it because he *wanted* people to have to dig and search and look for them? Why did God show himself only through the insides of the things he made? Was it so that only those who really wanted to search and look and dig in the field for the hidden treasure would discover the hidden meaning and life? Was there something about God's being, something about truth, something about the kingdom of heaven that *required* being sought and searched after and dug for?

I never did come up with any real answers to all my questions. But I sure did find myself looking at things differently after that—looking to see where I might be able to catch a glimpse of God *inside* of something he had made.

Especially people.

CHAPTER 6

CAVERNS OF PAIN AND JOY

Clackity clack . . . clackity clack . . . The steady vibration of the engine and the cars speeding along the tracks had a sound and feel all its own. Now that I was out of St. Joseph and well across Missouri, the stagecoach part of my journey already seemed like a distant memory. This was so different than riding in the horse-drawn Concord!

The clattering and swaying of the train coach put me in a thoughtful mood, and I found it much easier to write in my journal than for the last three weeks, even though I had to be careful not to spill the ink! The sounds and rhythm were like rain on the roof, and rain had always made me thoughtful. Even though I was just getting used to it for the first time, the sound of the train hurrying along the tracks was already making me feel reflective.

The train was a remarkable invention. And it wouldn't be long before there would be trains going all the way to California! This very track I was now on would eventually take people from coast to coast!

There'd been a groundbreaking in Sacramento on January 8, just four months earlier. It was pouring rain, but that didn't stop Governor Stanford from turning the day into a great celebration. There were speeches, and then he turned over the first shovelful of dirt where the beginning of the transcontinental railroad would start toward the Sierras.

Immediately the work had started, clearing out the railbed and building bridges through the mountains between Sacramento and Nevada. But none of the actual rail for the tracks, or train engines and cars themselves arrived for a long time after that. They would all have to be brought the 18,000 miles around the Horn by ship. Nevertheless, the building of the Central Pacific Railroad had begun.

On the other side, the Union Pacific was slower to get started. They were supposed to begin laying down track westward from Omaha, Nebraska, but I hadn't heard that they had done anything yet.

Thinking about Mr. Stanford reminded me of Cal and everything that had happened. As much as I tried not to think about it, the memories were too fresh, and I couldn't help it.

I suppose that's another part of growing up—loving something or someone that gets taken away from you. Almeda said it made a person older and wiser. Sadness and pain somehow make you see things you couldn't see before, give you a clearer vision even if there's a hurt to go along with it. Any kind of pain—the loss of a good friend, a faithful dog, or horse, the disappointment of not getting something you wanted, or wanting to do something that didn't happen—all those disappointments bring with them a kind of sadness that opens a place in you that can't get opened any other way—a special place in your heart. God wants to get in so that he can live there himself, but the door to that place can be opened only by the experience of pain or sadness. It seems kind of funny that God wants to give us life and happiness and fullness and joy, but, as Rev. Rutledge often said, one of the ways he uses to do that is pain and hurt and suffering.

But I had also learned from Rev. Rutledge that God often does things in a way that seems backward to us, completely different from the way we think he should. The last time Rev. Rutledge preached about the "upside-down ways of God," he had talked about a place—he called it a cavity, a hole—that's down inside us all. This place next to the heart is where the *fullness* of God's life and joy lives.

Rev. Rutledge compared it to a big cavern, a mine. The bigger the mine, the more of God's life and joy and wisdom you can hold. He made us picture in our minds two gold mines in a hillside—one a tiny little one going in only a few feet, and the other a huge cavern that men had been working on for years that went way inside the mountain and was huge inside and where there were many different veins of gold.

"In the same way," he said, "we all have different-sized mines or caverns inside us. The bigger the cavity, the more of God's fullness we are able to hold."

But what he said next really made me think. "The way God works inside us to make the caverns bigger," he said, "is usually with painful circumstances. The trials and hurts, the bumps and bruises, the heartaches and sadnesses of life—*those* are his tools, just like the picks and shovels and sledge hammers you miners use! God has tools too, and he can't widen and deepen out our mines without using them. The greater a man's or woman's suffering, the deeper the cavern is hollowed out for holding all the more of the abundance of God's life and being and character. The greater the sadness has been, the greater potential there is for joy. The deeper the hurt, the more of God's love it is possible to feel."

I'd heard him say things like this before. But this time it struck so deep in me because I *was* feeling pain just then in my life. And I hoped it was making a place bigger inside me to be able to hold all the more of God's joy someday!

CHAPTER 7

THINKING ABOUT MARRIAGE

The hurt I felt as I rode east, wishing I could forget the events of the previous year, was more from foolishness than anything. For all my talk about growing up, I had behaved so immaturely. I had allowed myself to get swept off my feet.

I thought back to my twenty-first birthday, to the day I had ridden up the hill early in the morning and had talked to God about my future and what I hoped my life would be.

Everything had been so clear then! My heart was focused on God, and I wanted nothing but what he wanted for me. I wanted to be pure and to love him with every part of my soul. I wanted to love other people, and to tell them what was in my heart toward God.

I had even thought about marriage back then. I had envisioned the kind of man I might like to marry, *if* I ever did—sensitive, gentle, strong, open, emotional, tender. But most of all, a man who shared the desire I had in my heart to follow God with his whole heart. I had asked myself back then how a man and woman could possibly be friends and companions for a lifetime if they didn't share that most important thing of all—that inner direction of where you want to go and what you want to be in life.

All of that I had known and thought about and felt deeply and prayed to God about at the age of twenty-one. Then, only at twenty-five, I seemed to forget every word of it!

The moment that tall, handsome man with the brown hair and deep blue eyes had walked up to me in San Francisco, all my good intentions had flown out of my head like a bird leaving its perch.

31

I felt like a foolish, silly young girl! Everything Cal had said to me, and even all the happy times we had shared, totally blinded me to the one simple and most important fact of all—we *didn't* share that same desire in our hearts to follow God completely in everything.

At the beginning, I think he was being as sincere as he knew how to be—maybe as sincere as he was capable of being. He was kind and gracious, and treated me with courtesy and respect. I think he meant the nice things he said to me, and genuinely did like me for the person I was.

But a man like Cal just isn't capable of being *completely* sincere. He wasn't capable of it because he didn't have the desire to follow God down deep in his heart. Down at the very bottom, Cal was following what *he* wanted to do and be in life, nothing else. And people who are not following God with their whole hearts *will* end up just like Cal—following their own way.

I knew all these things. I had known them for a long time. I knew them before I met Cal. Yet when I *did* meet him and spent time around him, my eyes clouded over and I couldn't see things clearly. I lost sight of how important it is what someone *wants* deep down in his heart. If what he wants is for *himself*, it's going to affect everything about him.

I didn't see that in Cal. I really believed he cared about me. But when his plans and ambitions got upset, the deeper part of him that was only looking out for himself gradually started to show. I only wish I had seen it sooner. I could have saved myself a lot of the hurt.

I suppose God was using even the hurt to carve and chisel and pick the cavern inside me and make it bigger. But it still didn't feel too good!

I found myself thinking all over again about the kind of man I hoped to meet someday. I didn't really *wish* to get married. I wasn't sure that was a right and proper thing to hope for. If I had placed my life in God's hands—which I figure I had done a dozen or more times, a little deeper and more completely the older I got—then what business did I have *hoping* for something that I had committed to God?

Hoping to get married seemed to me like taking it right back out of God's hands. And hoping to get married is just about one of the surest ways to make a big mistake and either marry the wrong person or else get married too soon.

Ever since I was a little girl, I had always assumed I probably *wouldn't* marry. And even after I was older and did think about it occasionally, I only wondered *what if. . . ?* I didn't want to start hoping for something that God might not want for me. I wanted to be willing to let God make my life turn out the way he wanted it to. I would have been perfectly happy to marry or not, just so long as God had *his* way.

But thinking about it all did get my mind imagining what kind of man I would want to marry if marrying was what God had in mind for me.

Cal had viewed everything in the light of opportunity. I knew there were lots of men who looked at success in life in terms of getting rich. There were lots of people like that in California, that was for sure!

I knew, too, that some men figured they had to be tough and strong and loud, or good-looking, or able to do things other men couldn't do in order to prove how much a man they were. Those were the kinds of things most women were attracted to in a man, and I could never make much sense of that. Why would a woman want a man for what his outside shell looked like instead of looking down to the yolk and the white—the life, the real heart of who he was inside? An eggshell is a pretty durable thing. But a human being is altogether different. Our bodies get old and slow and wrinkly and fat and sick, while our souls—some people's, I should say, but not everybody's—get bigger and wiser and more full of life and love the older they get. It seemed logical that women should be looking for a wise and growing soul to fall in love with rather than just an attractive body and strong personality.

For Cal—and I suppose for lots of men—life and opportunity had to do with what benefits there were to *him*. Maybe it wasn't easy to see such a tendency in men at first. I suppose that's why women often fall in love with men who are self-centered and only out for their own gain. But the man I would look twice at in the future would be one who was constantly seeking out opportunities to do things that would benefit others.

I hoped my time with Cal had taught me this lesson once and for all—to look past the surface in men to what their souls were like. As nice as he had been to me, Cal put himself first in everything. But the Bible says that the wisest people are those who put others first. Getting and achieving was Cal's motive. He wanted to climb high in life. If I ever did have a husband, I wanted his motive to be serving others rather than striving to achieve something for himself.

Most of all, I had come to see in Cal an approach to people and relationships that originated in the question of what they could do for him. As much as I would have liked to believe that he was trying to be sincere toward me, I can't help but wonder if he didn't think that I—and maybe Pa, too—were the kind of people he wanted to associate with because he thought we might be important someday. I wondered if he would have acted as interested in us if Pa hadn't been a mayor and hadn't been asked to run for the Assembly, and if I hadn't been one of the only women newspaper writers in the state.

I think Cal was looking for opportunities for himself—in the people he met, in the conversations he was part of, in everything.

But the kind of man I'd like to meet would think about helping other people, about what he could do for them. It would never occur to him to think how he himself could use others to get ahead.

Well, that would be quite some man, whether I ever married him or not! Always thinking about truth, putting others first, doing things to benefit those around him instead of himself, looking for opportunities to help, serving however he could, trying to do good, always growing more kind and loving on the *inside* whatever the outside might look like . . . that's the kind of person I wanted to be, too!

God, I prayed, *I am so sorry for forgetting all the things you've shown me and taught me. Help me to learn and grow from what happened. Make my cavern bigger inside. Give me eyes to see people as you do, and to see into the heart of things. I pray that you would open Cal's mind and heart to you and to the truth. Forgive me for not being more aware of you last year. And whatever you have for me, whether it's being married or not, give me a thankful heart. Keep me growing, Lord, as a person whose inner life shows more and more of your life. Give me eyes to see whatever you're trying to show me and ears to hear whatever you're saying.*

CHAPTER 8

NORTH VS. SOUTH

The train passed through St. Louis in the early afternoon. We were there for two hours before starting off eastward again. Suddenly the sight of soldiers in the city brought me back to the reality that I was heading straight into a war! I had been so absorbed in my own thoughts, I had forgotten about it for long stretches at a time.

Missouri itself had long been a slaveholding state, even though it remained in the Union when war broke out. But the border of the Confederacy was pretty close. I was traveling just about a hundred and fifty miles north of it right now—a lot closer than California! In St. Louis we crossed the Mississippi River, and that brought the war close to mind too, because already there had been a lot of fighting along its shores. Both sides wanted to control the vital inland waterway.

The two best-known generals, Lee of the South and Grant of the North, were leading their troops in two completely different areas—what were called the "theaters" of the war. Lee, being a Virginian himself, was still concentrating his efforts in the north of the Confederacy toward the east. His goal was to conquer the capital at Washington, D.C., and win the war for the South that way. All the activities and battles for the last two years had taken place between the two capitals, Washington and Richmond.

The North's capital was at the very southernmost part of the Union and the South's capital was in its northernmost state of Virginia. The two cities were separated by only a little more than a hundred miles. How different the war might have been if the

35

capital of the Union had been in Maine or Massachusetts, and if the capital of the Confederacy had been located in Florida! But as it was, a lot of the fighting took place in northern Virginia and Maryland.

But another whole arena of fighting was going on at the same time, along the Tennessee and Mississippi rivers. In the same way that the South wanted to get control of Washington, the North wanted to capture New Orleans. That city controlled the mouth of the huge Mississippi River, and whoever controlled the Mississippi also controlled the Missouri, the Tennessee, the Arkansas, and the Ohio rivers too—and controlled the shipping to and from about fifteen states. When compared with New York's million or Philadelphia's half million, I don't suppose New Orleans with its 170,000 people seemed that big. But it was still by far the largest city in all the South. In fact, it was more than four times larger than any other Confederate city. Right from the beginning, Mr. Lincoln had seen its importance, and had sent troops westward to try to swing around and encircle the South from behind and get possession of the whole Mississippi.

So in one way, the war was fought over the two cities of Washington and New Orleans. And leading those two efforts were the two great generals: Lee in Virginia and Grant along the Tennessee River and later the Mississippi.

And right then, as I bounced and rode and clattered along toward the east, first by stagecoach and then by train, events were building to a climax in both places. After a whole springtime of maneuvering and minor skirmishes here and there, that summer of 1863 was predicted to be the turning point of the whole war.

And although I was absorbed in my own thoughts and writing in my journal and thinking about Cal and marriage and my family, I might be riding right into the thick of it!

Another thing that made 1863 a turning point was that the Negro people and slaves were all free now. I heard people talking about it on the train and in the stagecoach and in the cities I went through and at the boardinghouses I stayed in. How it would affect the country and what would come of Negroes and slaves being equal with white folks and being free and having the same rights, no one knew. But everyone was talking about it. There were people for and against it, even in the North and West. Some people called Mr. Lincoln a brave and courageous Christian man. Others called him a fool and said it would never work.

President Lincoln had signed and issued what was called the "Emancipation Proclamation" back in September of the previous year, but it wasn't made official until January 1 of 1863. So now all of the South's slaves were officially "free" men and women, and it was against the law to hold slaves at all. Jefferson Davis and the *Confederate* States of America didn't recognize Mr. Lincoln's new law. But if the North won the war and got us back being one country again, all the slaves would be free.

The South was already in such disarray that a lot of slaves were just leaving the plantations and heading North. As uneducated as most of the Negroes were, they had heard the news and wanted to get north of the Mason-Dixon line, where they might really have a chance to be free for the first time in their lives.

None of them had any money. But they were rugged and strong and determined, and freedom was a powerful incentive. Of course, the whites of the South wanted to prevent the Negroes from going north. They were fighting for slavery in the first place. Many of the poor black folks were killed trying to get out of the South.

President Lincoln's announcement said: "All persons held as slaves within any state—the people whereof shall then be in rebellion against the United States—shall be then, thenceforward, and forever free."

CHAPTER 9

A CONVERSATION ABOUT UNITY

About two hours after the railroad man had gotten on, the train stopped again and he got off. He walked by, sat down, and visited with me for a minute or two as the train was coming into the station, and his friendliness helped me feel relaxed and at ease for the rest of that day. It seems that God often sends somebody along like that, even if just briefly, to give you a little dose of encouragement right when you need it. And they probably never know how much their kind words mean! The coach was nearly empty, and I rode most of the next day without talking to anybody.

As we were preparing to leave Cincinnati, a lot of people had come aboard and were walking through the coaches to find seats. A Catholic nun took the seat beside me. She gave me a nice smile. I was happy for the company, and so glad not to find myself next to some of the rough-looking men who wandered through occasionally. We began talking immediately.

She introduced herself as Sister Janette, and one of the first things I noticed was the ring—it looked like a wedding ring—on her fourth finger. She was traveling back to her convent from visiting her family after the death of her father. She called her home a "cloister," and said it was in southern Pennsylvania. She was taking the train to Pittsburgh, then about halfway across Pennsylvania, to where some of her sister nuns would meet her with a wagon. I told her I was on my way to Washington, D.C., and she said she was happy to hear we'd be traveling a long way together.

I had never met a nun, but I liked her right away.

We visited a while, mostly about the ride and the scenery. Then we talked about the war. Sister Janette had grown up in Ohio and she told me about that, and of course asked about me, and so eventually I told her my story. I had always been curious about what it was like to be a nun, and I didn't know much about being a Catholic in general, so I was full of questions.

"But what do you nuns actually *do*?" I asked after she had been telling me about the small community where she lived. "I mean, besides praying and going to Mass every day. What do you do the rest of the time?"

A curious smile came over Sister Janette's face. At first I thought I might have offended her with my question, but as soon as I heard her soft voice again, I was reassured that I hadn't.

"Do you know what an *order* is, Corrie?" she asked. I shook my head.

"The Catholic church is made up of many different *orders* of priests and nuns which focus their teaching and work and worship differently. Some monasteries and convents are devoted to little more than worship and prayer. Other orders actively work to help the poor, others to establish schools. Some are devoted to nursing and medicine, some to evangelism or religious writing."

"What is the order of your convent?" I asked. Again she smiled.

"In one way, I suppose you could say we have *no* order," she answered. "Our cloister is something of an experiment. We are represented by several different orders living and working together. That's why we are called the Sisters of Unity, although that is not the name of an official order of the church."

"Why do you say it is an experiment?"

"Because it's an unusual idea—crossing the lines of your own vision and ideas and purposes and becoming involved with someone else's. At least it's unusual in the church. And it's especially unusual in the wider aspects of what I have been seeking for us to do throughout our community and area."

"Did you start the convent?" I asked in surprise. Sister Janette looked much too young for that.

"Oh no," she laughed.

"But you are in charge, then?"

"Not officially. I am not the mother superior, and as you can see I am still a young woman. But you could say that the Order of Unity is my brainchild. The convent itself is old, dating back to the early eighteenth century. But some years ago it fell upon hard times, and was eventually closed. I grew up not far away, in Lancaster, and after I decided to give my life to the church and become a nun, the thought began to grow in me to reopen the convent. After I took my vows, I spoke to the mother superior and the head abbot of the diocese in Philadelphia of my plan."

"They must have liked it," I said.

Sister Janette laughed. "No, I can hardly say they *liked* it. As I said, unity is not a particularly strong element in Catholic doctrine—especially unity with Protestants! But the older I grew, ever since I was a teenager, I found my heart open in so many ways to *all* of God's people. And it didn't seem right for us each to remain behind the walls of our own private little enclaves, never mixing, never communicating, never having anything to do with one another, pretending that no other Christians even existed."

She paused. "Well . . . there's no need to bore you with details. I'll just say that I was *very* persistent, and eventually they reluctantly agreed to reopen the convent for a temporary period to allow me to do what I could with my small new 'unofficial' order. That was six years ago, and we are twice as many in number as we were then, and so they allow us to continue. I think they are even beginning to realize that the work is valuable, although it will probably be after my lifetime that anyone will admit it!"

"Why is that?"

"Oh, the church bureaucracy is the *last* of man's institutions ever to admit they were wrong about something. You can't imagine how organizationally tied in knots the church is. We're supposed to be ministering to people's souls, and yet sometimes I think all we do is feed and perpetuate our own organization. But, be that as it may, I do love the church and at least I am able to carry on what I think is an important function among people in my little corner of it."

"How many of you are there?"

"Seventeen, mostly younger than I. I am thirty-two, the second oldest. I suppose if you had to categorize us, you might even call us a collection of misfits—sisters who love our Lord and who have given ourselves to his work and his church, but don't seem to fit very well in any of the church's more rigidly structured compartments. Slowly and gradually some of the young sisters have heard of our Unity order and have come out of other orders to join with us."

She smiled and shrugged. "The bishop looks upon us with a skeptical eye, and yet even he cannot deny the reality of the spiritual life that is among us. For some reason that is still very strange to me, it seems that those whose hearts yearn for unity among the wider spheres of God's people always find themselves dissatisfied with the existing traditions that so many are comfortable with. And it seems inevitable that when they attempt to express the yearnings of their hearts, they are looked upon as rebellious instead of full of love for the whole and complete Church of Christ. I will no doubt spend the remainder of my life trying to understand that perplexity. But that is why I say we are misfits. Yet we love one another, and we love the small community God has made of us. And we love what we do."

"What do you do?"

"Back to the question you asked in the first place! I'm sorry, I never answered you, did I?"

"I'm very interested in everything you were saying, though."

"Well, Corrie, what we really *do* is simply seek to be involved in our community, and especially with other religious groups within the vicinity of the convent."

"*Involved*.. how?"

"Oh, many different things. We might help the Amish with one of their barn raisings, or—"

"The *Amish*?"

Again Sister Janette laughed. "I forget that you are from California!" she said. "The Amish are a Protestant sect that live in great numbers in southeastern Pennsylvania. They mostly keep to themselves, and to be frank with you, they don't like Catholics much. The beginnings of their church had to do with resistance to Catholic ways several hundred years ago. But we love them in spite of it, and wherever we find an open door to help them, we walk through it. No one, even the most stubborn Protestant, can resist a smile and a helping hand."

I laughed. I couldn't help thinking of how Pa and Avery Rutledge first got on together! I wondered if what she had called a "barn raising" was anything like when the Miracle Springs church had been built.

"So you go about helping people in your community?"

"Whenever we find opportunity. But it's more than helping with a specific job or project. We try to mix in a spiritual way with other communities and sects and groups of God's people. Our desire is not merely to *do* things, although that certainly is part of it, but to share life, to break down walls of division that exist between different groups of Christians, to let people inside our hearts and get inside theirs so that we no longer look at one another as Catholic or Amish or Presbyterian or Brethren, but simply as brothers and sisters."

"How do you do that?"

"In whatever ways we can. We invite families of other church affiliations to visit us. We welcome visitors to our convent and treat them as part of our body of life, whether they are Catholic or not. Gradually word has spread that we are there to help anyone with any need he might have, and one by one people have stopped being afraid of the fact that we are Catholics and are looking upon us as friends. Some even come occasionally to our times of Bible reading and prayer."

"Do you go to other churches' meetings too?"

"Oh yes. If you want to see unity happening between Christians, you have *got* to do that. You can't wait and expect people to come to you. Unity is an active, outflowing thing. It will never happen if you expect to see it manifested in others before you do anything about it yourself. So yes, we are constantly moving out and among other Christian groups, wherever we can do so without causing offense. You should have seen it the first time four of us appeared on Sunday morning at the Amish church meeting!"

"What happened?"

Sister Janette laughed.

"I didn't know whether they were going to throw us out, or whether they might cancel the service right there on the spot! The eyes of every man, woman, and child in that little church house turned around and stared as if they were going to pop right out of their sockets!"

"Did they say anything?"

"No. There was just a long silence as they tried to figure out what four nuns dressed in Catholic habit were doing in their Amish gathering. But eventually the minister went on with the service."

"And afterward?" I asked.

"Not a word. They ignored us completely, as if we weren't even there, and we quietly left. But I wasn't offended by their silence. It takes time for people to get used to something new. We went back the next Sunday, and the next. Finally some of the children began to come up to us and ask questions. The prejudices of children don't run so deep, and their universal humanity is usually more ready to show itself. Once the children broke the ice, some of the women began to smile timidly at us. Then conversations started, until after a couple months those stiff, proud, bearded Amish men were laughing and talking with us about their crops and the weather, surprised, I think, to find out how much we knew about such things from our own experiences in our *own* fields. Since then there's been wonderful fellowship between the sisters of our convent and the dear people of that Amish community."

"And you've done the same thing with others?"

"Similar things, yes. We've attended many meetings and services all around the area—going in groups of two, three, and four. In some we've been welcomed. In others, shunned, sometimes coming into fellowship and relationship after a time, as was the case with the Amish. Sometimes the ice never thawed, and eventually we left to try elsewhere. Unity is just not something all Christians are open to."

"And when they're not?"

"You can't be obnoxious, Corrie. You can't force yourself upon those who don't want relationship with you. So eventually we have had to give up with some and move elsewhere, remaining open but not pushing. But over the years we've established contact and harmony to varying degrees with not only the Amish but also the Brethren, some Mennonites, Methodists, even a few Baptists. And yet even with those, some people are more open than others. In every church and congregation, you find those with hearts hungry and open for wider relationship with God's body, and those who are only content if they are surrounded by people just as narrow as they themselves. God's body is indeed huge and diverse!"

"And what do your own church leaders think?"

"The bishop and the others? Oh, they're still skeptical and rather aloof about the whole thing. They can't deny that we've grown, that there's enthusiasm among the sisters and the community for what we're doing, and so they tolerate our little 'order.' But to be honest, Corrie, they don't care about unity with Protestant churches and people any more than most Amish and Baptists do with Catholics. There's *so* much mistrust and suspicion on *both* sides, it's enough to make my heart break. What must the Savior think of us? I'm sure it breaks his heart even more to see his people so divided and selfish and narrow."

I didn't say anything, and a long silence followed. The conversation seemed to have reached one of those natural breaking points where both of us needed to be quiet for a while and think about everything we'd heard and said. I'd almost forgotten we were in a train. Now suddenly the bouncing and jostling came back to my senses, and we rode along for a while looking out the window, meditating to the clacking along underneath us.

CHAPTER 10

COMMUNITY OF PEOPLES

"Why did you get interested in unity?" I said after a while, turning again toward Sister Janette.

She continued staring outside, but I could tell from the look on her face that she was thinking deeply about how to answer my question. Finally she turned back toward me.

"Two reasons, I suppose, Corrie," she said. "I grew up with two childhood friends I loved very much. The three of us were inseparable. My parents were staunch Catholics, but neither of my friends was. One was from a family of unbelievers, as far as I know, and the parents of the other were Plymouth Brethren. Of course the three of us neither knew nor cared about such distinctions. We didn't even know what they meant. The two of us who came from "church" families attended church with our own parents every Sunday and never thought much about it the rest of the time. But when we began to get older, there began to be things said about the 'unsuitability' of our continued friendship, especially on the part of the parents of my Brethren friend. According to the things my friend repeated to me, Catholics were worse than atheists. In the end my friend was eventually forbidden to see me again."

"What did you do?" I asked, amazed at such a thing.

"I was devastated. I was only eleven at the time, and couldn't begin to understand. It was the most horrible thing I could imagine, not to see her anymore, and I must admit I came very near hating her parents for a time, God forgive me. But in the years since, that experience actually proved very maturing, for it deep-

45

ened within me the determination to make my life count in bringing people *together*. My friend's parents were instrumental in my life, even if in a negative way. The memory of their confining and restrictive view of Catholics has always kept before me what I *don't* want to become myself. Unfortunately, their perspective is not so unusual. Both Catholics and Protestants suffer from the disease of self-absorption. Anyway, that is the first reason I am so committed to breaking down the walls between God's people."

"And the second?" I asked.

"Just the fact of where I grew up . . . Pennsylvania."

"How do you mean—I don't understand?"

"Do you know anything about the history of Pennsylvania, Corrie?"

"Not much, I suppose. Just what we learned about the Pilgrims in school."

"The Pilgrims were actually farther north, in the New England states. Pennsylvania was settled later. And in the very beginning people came here for unity. So I guess you could say I am just following in the footsteps of Pennsylvania's founders and first inhabitants by wanting to carry on that vision today."

"Was Pennsylvania that much different from the other states? I thought all the colonies were settled for religious freedom."

Sister Janette smiled. "In one way, of course, you're exactly right. But it was a very selective kind of religious freedom the Pilgrims wanted. They were selective in just the same way as most churches and religious groups and institutions are today, selective like my childhood friend's Brethren parents, selective like my own bishop."

"*Selective* . . ." I repeated. "I don't think I quite know what you mean."

"They wanted religious freedom," Sister Janette said, "but more for themselves than anybody else. The Pilgrims first came to America in the seventeenth century to escape the persecution and intolerance they had faced in Holland and England. They sought *freedom* to view spirituality in their own way and to worship as they wanted—neither of which they had been able to do in the old countries of Europe. Yet as soon as they were settled in New England, they established an equally intolerant religious climate of their own. The very thing they had left in Europe, they brought with them and planted in the new soil of America. It wasn't long before these Puritans were persecuting those who didn't believe as they did, running dissenters out of their settlements, burning witches at the stake, rooting out those they viewed as heretics for so much as one word misspoken about one of their own narrow doctrines."

"It sounds as if they became just as bad as those they left behind in Europe," I said.

"I'm not so much talking about rightness or wrongness of what they actually believed," Sister Janette went on. "For all I know, many of the early colonists held to many true doctrines, and I have no doubt they were sincerely trying to adhere to the Scriptures. To be honest with you, I haven't studied their actual beliefs that carefully. Beliefs and doctrines and viewpoints have never really interested me as much as the *relationships* between God's people. So whatever they believed about this or that doctrinal issue, and however much truth they may have discovered, I have never been able to get beyond the fact of their extreme intolerance of others who believed differently. It seems to me they simply extended and spread still further the very sins of persecution and intolerance and disunity they had left behind in Europe."

"The history I was taught about the founding of our country never said much about that," I said.

"Of course not. Because the people writing history books try to pretend that everything about their spiritual predecessors was wonderful and perfect. But the fact is, the Puritans were at times a pretty ruthless lot, all in the name of Christ. It's been the way of many, many Christian movements. My own Catholic church was the worst of all. So many horrible atrocities have been done throughout history by Catholic leaders who, in my opinion, were no more Christians than Attila the Hun.

"But then the reformers came along, men like John Knox and John Calvin, and before you knew it, *they* were beheading and burning people at the stake and treating those who differed with them with no less cruelty than the Vatican had two centuries before. No matter what a movement's roots, it seems eventually intolerance and narrowness and persecution creep in. Jesus Christ himself began what eventually became the Roman Catholic Church. Yet look what a mockery of his teachings we made of it. Martin Luther's motivations to break with the church were pure and scripturally based. Yet look what narrow zealots like Knox and Calvin did to Luther's inspired message. The Puritans sought freedom, and yet within a hundred years they were putting people to death whom they saw as a threat to the purity of their beliefs."

She paused and looked directly into my eyes. "Wherever you look, it seems that narrowness is the eventual result of spiritual movements, churches, and organizations. I tell you, Corrie, when I look at the sorry state of what has been the history of God's people, I am mortified and dismayed. It is hardly any wonder the world pays us so little attention. We have not been faithful stewards of the message Christ gave us to proclaim—a message which has unity among his people at its very foundation."

"Why, then, are you still so committed to unity? How can you maintain your enthusiasm? Everything you said seems so discouraging."

"Because it does not *have* to be so! It is not supposed to be so! And I believe we *can* make a difference. If God's people at some time and in some place don't make unity and *tolerance* a priority, nothing about this dismal pattern will change. But it *has* to change! And I believe I, and the sisters of my convent, and you, and others like us—I believe we *can* be the kind of people Jesus wants us to be."

"What does all this have to do with Pennsylvania?" I asked.

"Now you see why my bishop has been skeptical!" laughed Sister Janette. "When I get talking like this, I'm afraid I become rather too zealous myself for my own good! He once said I sounded like a Methodist street preacher instead of a Catholic nun!"

I didn't know what a street preacher might sound like, because I'd never heard one. But I had an idea, and laughed along with her.

"To answer your question, William Penn was a man whose vision was unity, too. He saw many of these very problems I've been telling you about. The intolerance and cruelty between Christians and their sects grieved his heart just as it does mine. That's why he devoted *his* land—*Pennsylvania*, Penn's Woods—

to *all* segments of Christendom in the new world. He invited anyone to come and make a home there, no matter what his beliefs. He offered his land to be what the Pilgrims had come to New England to find but then had not extended toward anyone else— a land where spiritual freedom and unity would exist."

"What happened?"

"People *did* come. Intolerance in New England, and the continued narrowness of the followers of Calvin in Europe, led many to Pennsylvania, where they found homes and established churches, free from persecution—Baptists, Shakers, Methodists, Presbyterians, Quakers, Anabaptists, Brethren, yes, and even Pilgrims and Catholics and Calvinists and Lutherans too!"

"But what does all this have to do with *you*?"

"Just growing up in Pennsylvania, I suppose, infected me with some of William Penn's own vision. I heard about him from a young age, then later read about him. I knew what had been on his heart to accomplish with the vast woodland that was known by his name. And then there were such visible and constant reminders all around me of the reality of his vision of unity. Within thirty miles of my childhood home of Lancaster, besides the strong Amish and Mennonite influence, every one of those other Christian groups I mentioned had a church or a community. Even though my young Brethren friend was taken from me, as I grew older and began to widen my viewpoint, I saw close by such an enormous variety of expression of the Christian faith. And I could not think it to be anything but wonderful! I found welling up within my heart such a desire to know people in *all* these other sects and churches, to be part of their lives and to share my life with them.

"I happened to be a Catholic, and I wanted to remain a Catholic, but that didn't mean I didn't want to mix and interact with others who *weren't* Catholics—not to try to make them like me or to see all matters of belief as I did, but to share life with them. Oh, Corrie, don't you see how wonderful is the very idea of God's people living together in harmony?"

"Yes . . . yes, I do," I said. "But I must confess I hadn't ever thought as much about such things as you have. Back home, we have just one community church and nobody talks about all the differences. I've never even heard half the names of the groups you've told me about."

"California is young. But here in the East there are so many, many different groups. In time they will spread across this huge land, and California too will become a hodgepodge of ten or fifteen separate sects of the Christian faith."

"Has William Penn's vision of unity come about?" I asked. "Is Pennsylvania still as he hoped it would be?"

Sister Janette's face fell, and her previous enthusiasm seemed to leave her altogether.

"Oh, Corrie, it's so sad. No—Pennsylvania has become just like New England, just like every other place. From such glorious beginnings, most of the groups that came here eventually became just as isolationist in their ways of thinking as the Pilgrims before them. Even though freedom was extended to them to come here, very few actually shared William Penn's vision. They were reluctant to extend the same openness and sense of unity outward to others as had been extended to them originally when they came to Pennsylvania."

She looked out the window with a wistful gaze. "I find it so hard to imagine! It looks so double-minded to me. And yet, there they are, worshiping freely in Pennsylvania, and yet with an inwardness and skepticism and resistance toward unity with everyone else. My mind just cannot absorb the inconsistency, even the hypocrisy of it. I know that is a strong word, but that is how I feel about the matter."

"Yet you are still excited about the work of your convent?"

"Oh yes! What a perfect place for us to be—right in the midst of so many different expressions of Christianity! We could find no more perfect soil for our experiment, as the bishop calls it, than among the diversity represented in Pennsylvania. Maybe most of the groups there have lost sight of the vision that brought them there, but *we* haven't!"

Silence fell as I thought about all she had said. At last I asked Sister Janette another question, although it was far different than what we had previously been talking about.

"If unity is what your heart longs for, then this war between the Northern and Southern states must seem awful to you," I said.

"Oh yes, it's absolutely heartbreaking," sighed Sister Janette. "The other sisters and I have given as much time in prayer to the country as to all our other work. This division and strife *cannot* be God's will, no matter how much each side tries to believe God is on his side."

"How can that be?" I asked. "How can people think that God is with them, when they view things so differently?"

"Unity, Corrie . . . for the same reason that unity does not yet exist between his people."

"What do you mean?"

"Because people put their *own* self-interests above those of their neighbors, even their Christian neighbors. And then they attach God's name to those self-interests and pretend *he* originated what they believe rather than admitting that they came from their *own* biases. It's the cause of all the world's strife—putting ourselves above our neighbors. It's the very thing Jesus warned us we couldn't do without ruining all he came to do for mankind."

She sighed. "This civil war in our nation is the extreme extension of the disunity that exists between all the segments of God's people. North and South are fighting each other with guns and cannons, while the different groups of Christendom fight one another with words and doctrines and by isolating themselves and shutting out all those who do not believe as they do. But at the root, I see nothing so very different there as in this awful war we are now engaged in. In the kingdom of heaven, which lasts forever, I'm not certain that the silent strife and divisions among God's people don't have even more serious consequences than this war which is tearing our country apart."

CHAPTER 11

A DIFFERENT VIEW OF MARRIAGE

Sister Janette's words were strong ones, like nothing I'd ever heard before. Everybody has been talking about this war as if it is the most terrible thing that has ever happened in all of history. Her idea that the intolerance between Christians might even be worse was a thought that took some getting used to.

We sat quietly for most of the rest of the day, talking every once in a while but not as seriously as we had before. Late in the afternoon my eye chanced to fall on her hand again, and I suddenly remembered the question that had been raised in my mind when I first met her.

"Do you mind if I ask you about your ring?" I said. "I thought nuns weren't married, but isn't that a wedding band on your finger?"

Sister Janette looked up at me and smiled. "But we *are* married, Corrie," she answered. "When we take our vows, it is like a marriage ceremony, and afterward we wear a wedding ring."

"I . . . I don't understand."

"Not very many non-Catholics do," she said. "But when we take vows of chastity and give our lives to the church, we are not devoting ourselves to Catholicism or to a certain order or to a life of loneliness. At least it was not so for me. I gave my heart and my whole life to Jesus. I truly consider him my husband. I am married to him. The Bible speaks about God's people as the bride of Christ. And I live out the devotion of my love for him in service to his church and the people he sends me. That is why I wear a ring. My heart and my life and all that I am belong to him."

"I've never heard anything like that before," I said. "It's beautiful."

Again she smiled. "I'm glad you think so," she said. "So many people look upon women such as I—nuns, with our distinctive dress and peculiar lifestyle—and feel sorry for us. I think we are looked upon as a lonely sort, like religious spinsters who could never hope to be married and so became nuns because there is nothing else for us to do."

"Do you really believe people think that?"

She laughed lightly. "You would be surprised at the things I've heard about how Catholic sisters are looked upon! But for me, being a nun is entirely a free choice. There were some young men who paid attention to me when I was seventeen or eighteen. But I *wanted* to give my life to Jesus and him only. I could have had all sorts of marriage proposals, but it would not have changed anything. *Jesus* was my first choice as a husband. I wanted to devote my life to him and no other. And I have never been sorry—not for a minute. I made that choice, and I make it anew every day."

She looked at me with an intensity that obviously came out of deep feelings. "I love Christ, Corrie. I love his people, I love his church, I love doing his work, I love the world he made, I love his Word, the Bible, and I love being part of all he is doing in the world. I would have no other life than exactly the one I have chosen. I am a happy, contented woman, Corrie, and I wear my wedding ring with pride and a heart full of love. The life I have with him of purity and chastity gives me a fulfillment that goes beyond the mere personal satisfaction of what some might consider earthly pleasures and happiness. Some might look upon mine as a life of sacrifice and denial. But for me it is a chosen life of laying down my complete being in submission and service and devotion to him. It has *brought* me happiness, not taken it from me!"

After all the thinking I had been doing before meeting Sister Janette about Cal and marriage and my future, her words gave a whole new direction to my thoughts. Since almost before I could remember, all the way back to when Ma and I talked about my probably not being the marrying sort, marriage had always been *the* thing a young girl looked forward to. If you didn't marry, there must be something wrong with you. But now Sister Janette said that she wouldn't have married no matter how many offers she had, because she chose and *wanted* to be devoted to Christ and no one else. It was something I had never heard before.

I couldn't stop thinking about it all the rest of that day, and the next. And I couldn't help wondering what, if anything, it all might have to do with me. Was I, like Ma'd said, not the marrying sort? Or even if I was, might Jesus want me to be married to him like Sister Janette was?

I didn't know what to think of that—and I didn't know if I liked the notion or not! I didn't want to be a Catholic nun . . . or I didn't think I wanted to be. Could I be married to Christ and *not* be a nun . . . not even be a Catholic? What might "service to the church . . . service to Jesus" mean for me, a Protestant, with no convent to go to . . . no order to join?

The ideas got confused and mixed up in my mind as I considered everything she had said. I wanted to belong to Jesus, but I didn't know if that meant I shouldn't be married to someone else.

I never did get it all resolved. I tried to pray quietly, but even that was hard right then. This whole way of thinking about it was so altogether new that even prayer came hard.

Then right in the middle of my thoughts, Sister Janette's voice interrupted.

"Corrie," she said excitedly, "I've just had the most wonderful idea! Why don't you stop with me and spend a few days with the sisters at the convent? I want them to meet you, and you can see for yourself everything I've been telling you about!"

I thought about it, and the offer seemed very attractive to me. I *did* want to see Sister Janette's convent and meet the other nuns, to find out just what this new way of life was really like.

I turned the idea over in my mind. I had told President Lincoln I would be coming to Washington sometime in late June, and it was only the first week in June. Surely I could spend a few days in Pennsylvania, and then go on to Washington to meet the President.

"Thank you," I said at last. "I think I would like that."

CHAPTER 12

THE SISTERS OF UNITY

I accepted Sister Janette's offer, and in two days I found myself in as different a place from Miracle Springs as anything I could ever have imagined. Suddenly there I was, with a small community of Catholic women, most of them not much older than I was—three or four of them even younger. But they were all just as nice as Sister Janette, and immediately made me feel very much at home among them. I especially took to one of the siters whose name was Jane. She took me under her wing ad let me in on the goings-on of the place.

I had a tiny little room to myself, with only a narrow bed and a small writing desk. But after the stagecoach and train, however, it was a welcome change. After I had been at the convent for two days, they began calling it "Corrie's room."

After talking with Sister Janette on the train and listening to her enthusiasm about all they were doing among Christians of the community, I expected something quite different from what I found. I thought there would be "activity," more things *happening*. But the atmosphere around The Convent of John Seventeen was very quiet and subdued, hushed, peaceful. Sometimes I felt I was supposed to whisper all the time. It took me a day or two to get used to the change.

They had Mass every morning, which was unlike any church service I'd ever been in before. I hardly understood any of it. The nuns ate all their meals together in the large room beside the kitchen. That was a lot of fun, with talking and laughter. After lunch they went to their own rooms or to the chapel for quiet and

55

prayer and meditation. Actually, prayer and meditation went on all throughout the day, but I never could completely understand the pattern, even though Sister Janette was very good about trying to explain it all to me and make me as comfortable as she could. There were many chores, too—tending the garden and the sheep and goats and chickens and two cows, fixing meals and cleaning up afterward, laundry, and other work. They all stayed very busy all day long, besides praying and reading their Bibles and meditating, and I helped with the work as much as they'd let me.

Being part of a community of women was very different for me. The spirit of love and cooperation and unselfishness was extremely appealing. It almost made me want to stay there with them. But at the same time, it was so very *Catholic*, so different. I couldn't help feeling like a stranger.

How could Christians be so different? I wondered. But even as I asked myself the question, I realized that the Sisters of Unity were trying to lessen those differences. As totally different from them and un-catholic as I was, they accepted me among them entirely, and never once tried to make me act or behave like them. They just let me be myself, and seemed to love me as I was.

After a few days at the convent, I went with several of the sisters to an Amish barn raising. That was a day I'll never forget! The men had funny beards without mustaches, and the women wore dresses that all looked the same with little white caps over their hair. There was a sternness about them on the one hand, but, like the Catholic sisters, they made me feel as if I were one of them. And once the work started, there wasn't a second wasted! The men and teenage boys began carrying and sawing and hammering and tying big beams with heavy ropes, and in less than an hour were calling for everyone—women included—to come and pitch in together to hoist the first huge wall up off the foundation slab and into place. I found myself squeezed in between a young Amish man and one of the sisters from the convent. When the signal was given, a team of horses pulled at the ropes, the end of the wall lifted off the ground, and then we all got in underneath and lifted the wall boards up higher. In a few seconds our hands were outstretched and the great line of people standing side-by-side slowly inched forward, holding the wall above our heads, walking it gradually higher and higher, while the horses pulled the ropes attached to the top, and the strongest of the men held the bottom of the wall in place to keep it from slipping.

At last the wall reached perpendicular, another shout called off the tugging of the horses, the command was given to release the wall, and suddenly there it stood, twenty or more feet in the air, standing tall and true on its own. We all stepped back, and a great cheer of triumph went up. The first wall was in place, and the morning's dew was still not off the ground! But there wasn't a moment to lose! Even as we were shouting in our victory, half a dozen of the men were hammering diagonal boards in place at the wall's ends to hold it steady and keep it from crashing down.

I was already sweating, and the day had hardly begun! This was hard work! If the sisters from the convent made it a practice of attending barn raisings and getting their frocks dirty and their hands blistered helping with the men's work, and bringing food to help feed everyone, I could see why these Amish people could hardly help but accept them and consider them their friends. There was more unity going on in that barn raising between a handful of Catholic sisters and a small community of Amish farmers and their families than any book or sermon by an Amish pastor or a Catholic priest could ever achieve.

By the end of the day I was thoroughly exhausted! As we rode back to the convent in the back of the wagon, we were nearly falling asleep. The sun was setting over the Pennsylvania fields toward the west. Every muscle in my body ached—but what a satisfied feeling it was!

Four walls and the joists of a great roof stood where there had been nothing but a wood foundation when the sun had risen that same morning. There had been laughter and good food and many conversations throughout the day in the midst of the work. It seemed as if we'd been there a week, not just twelve hours. Not only were these women from the convent truly my sisters by this time, I now felt I had an equal number of friends among the Amish community who would welcome me into their homes just as fully.

Part of me hated to leave. My heart longed to get to know them better, and I was beginning to understand why Sister Janette was so deeply stirred when she spoke of unity. It was *love* that burned in her heart. I understood that at last, because I now felt it myself for many new people—Catholic and Amish—that I'd never even known existed a week earlier. And feeling love for them only served to stir up even deeper longings to be connected with even *more* of God's people.

I truly was beginning to feel some of the yearnings that gripped Sister Janette's heart. As we bounced along slowly in the wagon, talking and laughing and quietly recounting the events of the day with pleasure, in a deep place within me I found many thoughts and feelings I had never had before stirring into life.

Oh, how I slept that night! And the next morning when I woke up and tried to move, I discovered two hundred muscles I never knew I had—and every one of them was screaming in pain!

I crawled out of bed, only to discover that I'd slept away half the morning!

"Hard work, Corrie?" Sister Jane greeted me. I was amazed that all the sisters had been about their tasks as if yesterday's barn raising was nothing out of the ordinary.

"Yes," I answered, rubbing at my arms and shoulders. "Aren't *you* sore?"

"A little," she laughed. "Believe me, every one of us knows what you are feeling. We went through that at first, too. But we are used to it now. You'll just have to stay here long enough with us to raise two or three barns. Then you'll think nothing of it!"

I tried to laugh. But even that hurt.

But as much as the thought of raising *another* barn any time in the near future seemed an impossibility to my aching body, Sister Jane's words remained with me all that day and well into the next.

CHAPTER 13

PRAYERS OF DEDICATION UNDER AN OAK TREE

You'll just have to stay here. . . .

I couldn't get the words out of my mind. For the next few days after the barn raising, I kept to myself. I stayed in my room, resting, spent some time in the chapel praying, and went for a couple of long walks in the countryside. All the time I was thinking over and over about what Sister Jane's words might mean for me.

This was like no other place I'd ever been, and within me were thoughts like none other I'd ever had. I found myself thinking not so much about unity or about the Amish and the barn raising but about the sisters, about the life they had chosen to live. I remembered over and over what Sister Janette had said about having chosen to be married to Jesus and to serve him completely. *I am a happy, contented young woman, Corrie*, I recalled her saying. *My devotion to him has brought me happiness. . . . I would have no other life than exactly the one I have chosen.*

I had grown up for years thinking that for a young woman not to marry meant failure in life. The image of the spinster was one everybody was familiar with, and the silent dread of every girl once she got to be sixteen or seventeen. Ma had helped prepare me for it, of course, so the thought of living my life unmarried was not fearsome to me. But there was still something about being single that most folks seemed to think was unnatural. I know Uncle Nick and Pa worried about me from time to time, even though I was doing fine by myself.

But here was a whole community of women—most of them

59

young, and several of them a lot prettier than I was—who didn't even *want* to be married, who had *chosen* not to be married because there was something else they wanted even more: to be devoted servants of Jesus—devoted to him just as much as being married to him! It wouldn't be right for them to think of themselves as his wife, even though they considered him their husband. But the word I had heard them use was *handmaiden*. They were Christ's handmaidens, his servants, and he was their Master, their protector . . . their only love.

It struck a deep chord in me. This was a level of devotion and commitment and love to Jesus beyond any I had ever seen before. Faith was not something these women did just on Sunday. It was not something that concerned only their minds and what they *thought* was true about God and the Bible and spiritual things. This was real life, daily life. They had given themselves to him *completely*—minds, hearts, hands, feet . . . everything. They had given their whole lives to serve him. They had kept nothing back for themselves—not even their own clothes! They had no money. They had left their families. *Everything!* They had no future apart from him.

I thought of Almeda. She had been my closest friend, and much of what I thought, even the person I was inside, had been influenced by her. And yet even her life wasn't devoted to Jesus in the same way as I saw here. Maybe on the inside it was, but on the outside she still ran her business and thought about family things.

I didn't have any critical feelings toward Almeda. She had done more for me than I ever thought any person could do for another, and I loved her so much! But her life as a Christian was very different from the lives of the sisters at the convent.

As I thought about it, I realized that, except for Sister Janette, the sisters didn't talk as much about spiritual things as Almeda did. They just went about their work and said their prayers and had their Masses without talking too much about it. So I could see that even in living a more normal life, Almeda's openness to talk about spiritual things had helped me understand more about them than I might have been able to.

As I pondered my future and thought about Almeda, I began

to wonder what it all had to do with *me*. What kind of woman did *I* want to be? Everything I saw here in this life of separation from the world and devotion to the Lord brought out from within me deep feelings of wanting to be part of it myself.

I felt as if one part of me was considering what it would be like to *become* a nun. The question of becoming a Catholic never occurred to me, but only what it would be like to live this way, to join an order or a convent, to live with other women dedicated to God. At the same time, another part of me would remember my life back home at Miracle Springs and my family and would immediately think that the very thought of my joining a convent was absurd.

But I was twenty-six years old, after all—and perhaps it was time I found a new home. Maybe God didn't intend for me to go back to Miracle Springs. Maybe he had led me here to be part of this convent, and that's why he had kept me unmarried all this time. Could *this* be where I belonged now?

It was very confusing. I had never experienced such thoughts before. I had never thought of my life much beyond the landscape of it I could see at present. Now I was straining to look past the horizon, asking myself what purpose there might be for my future.

But even in the midst of my confusion and unsettledness, the idea held something wonderfully exciting and exhilarating. I thought about living a life *completely* in the hands of Jesus and no one else, doing nothing but *his* work, thinking nothing but *his* thoughts, being with people who were committed to the same purposes and goals. What a life that would be! What was writing, what was marriage, what even was an invitation to the White House alongside that?

The thought of the White House—and the President's invitation—drew me up short. It was already the end of June, and I had said I would be at the White House before the month's end.

Yet I was reluctant to leave the convent—to leave behind the peaceful calmness of this place, to leave the sisters, and their focus on commitment to Christ.

Could it be that God really was calling me to stay? I had to decide soon . . . but how could I know for sure?

I thought and prayed about it for two or three days. All I could think of was the single question: *Was I supposed to be part of this life I saw at the convent . . . perhaps some purpose here for me beyond just a casual visit of a few days?*

As I walked through the fields and countryside, a quiet sense of deep calm gradually stole over me as I reflected and asked God all these questions. Before long my thoughts became occupied, not just with what I ought to *do*, but with God himself. I became aware of his presence, as if Jesus himself were walking along right beside me.

Even though I was alone and far from home, and wondering about myself and my life and my future, I felt as if God had wrapped himself around me like a cloak, giving me his love and protection.

I had never been married, so I didn't know what feelings a wife might have toward her husband. But I knew what it was like to feel Pa's care and protection watching over us all, and I remembered how I felt when I was very young, lying in bed on a winter night, knowing that Ma was in the other room, tending the fire and watching over all of us.

This feeling of God's closeness was even more real than those memories. All I could think of was wanting to give more of myself to him, wanting to be totally his, wanting to be *one* with him, even in a deeper way than a wife gives herself to a husband. I could think of nothing so wonderful as being his . . . forever and completely!

Finally, on one of my long walks, I found myself a mile from the convent, walking through a little grove of trees. As I came out of the wooded area, a little clearing opened in front of me, gently rising upward toward a knoll in the distance, where a great oak tree stood. Somehow it reminded me of the hill overlooking Miracle Springs, or the mountains where I had ridden Raspberry early on the morning of my twenty-first birthday. I always felt best able to hear God when I was alone in the country, someplace high.

As I came out of that wood, and my eyes fell on that oak tree in the distance, and with my thoughts full of God's love and care for me, suddenly a great joy welled up within my heart as though I could no longer contain it. It was a happiness just in being alive, in being in God's hands, in being his daughter and knowing that he loved me and had a good life for me to live with him . . . whatever that life might be. I felt as though my heart would burst for very ecstasy!

I ran straight to the oak tree, then jumped up and grabbed its lowest branch, swinging back and forth for a minute. Then I let go and fell to the ground, laughing and panting at the same time.

I breathed in the warm afternoon air deeply and leaned my back up against the tree. A deep quiet settled over me, as I imagine Moses must have felt when looking on the burning bush. A hush descended over the whole little meadow and knoll. I heard no sound, not even a bird or a breath of wind. I sensed that the Lord himself was everywhere, calming and stilling and quieting the grass and the leaves of the tree and the very air itself.

Then from within me I found prayers rising up, and I began speaking to Jesus as if he were right there.

"God," I said, "I do so want to be yours . . . completely." The words weren't many, but they said everything that had been building up within me for days, perhaps even for years. I had prayed such prayers before, but something was different this time. Was it that I was older? Was it that I was so far from home? Was it that I was doing something I'd never dreamed of doing—going to visit the President?

Maybe it was all those things. All I know is that I had never felt such a complete abandonment to God's control, keeping nothing back for myself. And soon I found myself telling him even more of what was in my heart.

"Whatever you want for me, Lord," I said, "that is what I want. Whatever future you have for me, whether as a writer or not, whether married or not—I will be happy just to know I am with you. I will do whatever you want me to do, Father. Let me just know that I am yours, as completely as Sister Janette and Sister Jane and the others are yours. I want to be your bride as they are, and to serve your people and to work for unity as they do. Oh, God, use me and fill me with yourself, and let me be as happy and content as they are! If you want me to remain here with them, if you want me to become a nun, it would give my heart joy to do so. I am devoted to you, Lord Jesus. Let me love you and serve you. And if you want me to continue to write, speak to me about what you would have me say."

My words trailed away and finally stopped, but my thoughts did not. I found myself continuing on, talking silently with Jesus, turning first one thing, then another over and over in my mind, and then handing it to him and saying, "Here, this belongs to you now." Everything I thought about—my friendships and relationships, even things that I couldn't see yet, like this trip east and what would become of it, what I should write, whether I should marry or be single, where to live—everything, one by one, I gave to him.

I don't know how long I sat there. It might have been ten minutes, or it might have been two hours. I lost all track of time. It must have been quite a while, though, because when I again became aware of myself sitting there under the great oak, the sun was a lot farther down toward the western horizon than it was when I had left the convent.

And I found myself quiet again—quiet inside. All the words were gone, as if the well of my thoughts had run dry. I had given everything over to Jesus, and I had a quiet, almost empty feeling. But the emptiness I felt was an emptiness of *self*, not anything else. I felt marvelously *full* of his love.

When I finally rose up from the ground, I stood and took a deep breath. I had not been aware of it at the time, but my tears had been flowing as I'd been sitting there. They were certainly not tears of sadness, nor were they tears of pure happiness. Maybe there was a bit of a lonely feeling, a knowledge that my life wasn't my own anymore. Not only had I given over to the Lord the external concerns of my life, I had also given him something else. I had given him *me*, and everything I was!

As odd as it may sound, I felt almost *married* to Christ, as Sister Janette had talked about. I had given myself completely to him, as a wife does when she marries her husband, as Almeda did with Pa. I had given my heart to God, and no matter what else ever happened in my life, nothing could change that, or make me take it back. If I never married, I knew after this day that I would never be sorry about it. I also felt like a daughter feels when her father is there to take care of everything.

I got up and stood for a moment beside the great tree. All at once I became aware of a sound—a low, rumbling, thunderous noise, yet the sky was clear.

Then I saw the first rider and realized that what I had heard were horses' hooves.

He was followed not by a second rider, as in a single column, but by a massive horde of riders, all dressed in dark blue, probably ten or more abreast, and galloping hard. The thundering blue column was maybe two hundred or so yards from me, across several more fields, and they were riding west.

I stood mesmerized, watching them gallop past in the distance. Now and then a cry would go up, a yell to a horse, a commander's shout. But mostly I heard only the deep sound of hundreds of horses rumbling by. I could feel the ground shaking under my feet as I watched. One of the riders, following right behind the leader, carried a flag which waved silently in the air above him. It was the United States flag, and the blue of their uniforms was that of the Union army.

I gave a little shudder and felt suddenly cold, even though the day was a warm one.

I had never seen soldiers since the day Mr. Grant had visited Miracle Springs so many years ago. That had been a happy day. The uniforms had been bright and colorful, and the men wore them so proudly. But this day was different, and the uniforms were those of an army at war.

I watched, and then as suddenly as they had appeared, they were gone, followed by the retreating sounds of the last of the horses, until once more I was left alone in the field.

Slowly I began making my way back toward the convent, and gradually my thoughts returned to the time I had spent praying under the oak tree. Before long I had forgotten about the riders altogether, and the mood of calm serenity and peacefulness stole over me again. The noisy intrusion had not disturbed the deep sense of having abandoned myself completely to someone I loved in the depths of my being. I had the strong feeling that this was a day I would never forget, that what I'd done out there under the oak tree was something that would change my life no matter where my steps took me in future years.

CHAPTER 14

THE WAR AGAIN!

The minute I got back to the convent from my walk, things started to happen rapidly. In the midst of my quiet communion with Jesus, unanticipated events came crashing in upon me. I found myself learning again that high lofty things in your mind and heart have to get down and mix with the dirt under your feet and the work of your hands or they don't mean much in the end. The minute you have some revelation of truth in your mind, or some spiritual experience with the Lord in your heart, God throws you into something you have to do with your hands and feet. It seems he doesn't want us to spend *too* much time sitting around just thinking about him without doing something about it.

"Corrie, Corrie!" I heard a voice shouting frantically at me as I approached the convent. "Where have you been? We've been looking all over for you!"

I looked up in the middle of my reverie to see Sister Janette running toward me. Behind her I could see all the other sisters scurrying and running about. Two of them were hitching up one of the wagons. Sister Jane was just coming out of the stable with one of the horses, and all the others were carrying supplies and loading them into both wagons.

I quickened my pace and hurried toward them. "What . . . what is it?" I said as Sister Janette ran up to me.

"Word has just come to us of dreadful fighting," she said. "Some soldiers were just through here—"

"I saw hundreds riding by out where I was, too," I said.

"There were only a dozen or so who stopped here," she said.

66

"They were on their way to rejoin their regiment, but were looking for food and boots."

"What did they say?"

"That the Confederate army had invaded the North and that they had to stop them, and that terrible fighting had already started. It's not far from here—across the river, about forty miles west, outside of a little town called Gettysburg."

"What are you doing?" I asked, glancing around again at all the activity and bustle.

"We're going there," she replied. "It will take us a day to reach the battle, so we must be off without delay."

"*Going* there. . . ?" I repeated. I don't know if I was shocked or afraid, or merely surprised.

"Yes," she said, and by now we had turned back and were walking toward the others. "They are sure to need our help. There isn't a moment to lose!"

Now I saw what the nuns were piling into the wagons—blankets and water, medical supplies, bandages, alcohol, as well as food and provisions for themselves.

"What . . . what will you do?" I said, taking a handful of blankets and a doctor's kit from one of the sisters and lifting it up to Sister Janette, who had climbed up into the wagon to stow in the provisions.

"Whatever is necessary. Nuns have to do anything God sends our way, you know. We have two nurses among us—they will tell us what to do. And willing, tender hands and loving words do more sometimes to comfort the sick and wounded and dying than any amount of medical knowledge."

"The *dying*!" I gasped. I don't suppose the full reality of what Sister Janette was saying had yet sunk into me.

"There is a terrible war going on, Corrie. Many, many young men *are* dying, but perhaps we can help a few survive, and ease the final moments of others with words of hope and love. It's Christ's work, Corrie, and we must be about it, as he is always about it."

She glanced up and paused in her work for a moment. Her eyes met mine, and I could tell she knew I was shocked and bewildered and frightened by this sudden intrusion of the war so close to our lives. In that moment I felt so naive, so like a child again, and saw such a difference in Sister Janette's eyes. She was so calm, so at peace in the midst of the commotion, so unafraid of the danger, and so confident that the Lord would take care of his handmaidens. There was no fear in her voice, only the desire to be about the same work that her Master was doing to meet the needs of men.

"Sister Mary will be staying here to watch over the convent and tend the animals," she said after a brief pause. "You will be fine with her, but I wanted to see you before we left."

She paused again, then reached out and gave my hand a squeeze. "Corrie," she said, "I am so thankful to the Lord for sending you here. I am so glad to know you. I hope you will remain until our return, though it could easily be three or four days. So if you do have to continue your journey, Sister Mary will be able to make arrangements for you to meet the train."

I returned her gaze, and then without even thinking what I was saying, I found myself blurting out: "No, I'm not going to continue just yet. I'm . . . I'm going with you!"

CHAPTER 15

GETTYSBURG

The war hadn't been going as well for the South as they had hoped. At first it seemed that the Confederacy would win over the Union in a year or less. But by the middle of 1863, the tide was gradually shifting.

Only two months before, in May, the Confederate Army of Northern Virginia, under General Robert E. Lee, had struck one of their strongest victories against the Federal Army at Chancellorsville. Yet the victory greatly weakened Lee's army. And the Union forces, with far more manpower and resources to draw upon, was able to recover itself much more quickly. By summer, Lee's Virginia army was still weak, while the Union's forces in the North had recuperated from the loss.

In addition to this, in the Mississippi Valley, General Grant had laid siege to the fortress of Vicksburg ever since the end of May, and it was now clear to the leaders of the Confederacy that Vicksburg was doomed, and that very soon the Federals would control the entire Mississippi. For the South, it was a crisis of the war that could spell its final defeat. If they still hoped to win, something drastic and dramatic had to be done. Since Grant was winning the battle in the West, action had to be taken in the East—and quickly.

General Lee proposed a daring plan to invade the North. If Vicksburg was to fall, then *he* would attack and take Philadelphia and Washington! With the largest part of the Union army busy under General Grant, a successful strike against the North might, Lee hoped, force Lincoln to quit the fight. Surely, the great southern general thought, Lincoln would surrender and recognize the Confederacy's independence before allowing the capital of Washington to be destroyed.

Other factors prompted Lee's bold move, despite the continued weakness of his army. Ever since the beginning of the war, the Confederacy had sought to be recognized as a country of its own by the foreign powers of Europe, especially England and France. Lee hoped that a successful invasion of the North would secure such foreign recognition. This might mean financial aid, in exchange for cotton, which the factories of Europe needed in large supply. It might also mean pressure from England and France upon the United States—the *Union* states, that is—to recognize the *Confederate* States. Lee also thought that the presence of his army in the North would strike great fear into the people of Pennsylvania and New York and Ohio and the New England states. They were already weary of the war, and if he could destroy their morale further, it might lead to a northern surrender.

In addition, moving the battle north of the Mason-Dixon line would relieve Lee's home state of Virginia from the great strain of having to support his huge army for over two years. Many battles had been fought on Virginia soil. The fields had been ravaged, and supplies were low. Since it was probably inevitable that there would be fighting somewhere during that summer of 1863, why not move north for a time and get supplies and food and meat and leather and grain from the lush farmlands and towns of Pennsylvania? Lee wanted to let Virginia farmers grow their crops without armies trampling all over them, taking everything in sight!

The very name Robert E. Lee struck fear into the hearts of loyal northerners. He had won most of his battles, and his army seemed nearly invincible. So when news of his invasion came, many in Pennsylvania were filled with dread.

But there was one man in the Union who realized that Lee's coming into Pennsylvania might actually give the North the opportunity to turn the war in its own favor. That man was Abraham Lincoln, the man whom people had considered uneducated in military affairs. He saw the danger Lee was exposing himself to by stretching out his tired army so far from home and so far from supplies.

With Grant about to take the Mississippi Valley, if they maneuvered with skill and could cut Lee's invading army off, they could destroy it once and for all, and the war would nearly be over. President Lincoln was not afraid of Lee's reputation, for he saw what most others did not—both the weakness of Lee's army and of his plan to invade the North.

Therefore, he kept careful watch on Lee's movements throughout May and June. And when mounted Union spies brought word back that Lee's forces were moving north from Hagerstown, Maryland, into Pennsylvania toward Chambersburg and Harrisburg, Lincoln ordered the generals of his Army of the Potomac to march northwest to meet him. The climax of the war had come, though none of those involved yet knew it.

The two armies were enormous. There were approximately 77,000 southern men marching under Lee, and 85,000 Union soldiers. It was sheer accident that the two huge armies met where they did. For the whole last week of June, Lee's scouts failed him, and no reports reached him of the northern army's position. He continued his march—with his infantry divisions spread out and dispersed dangerously far behind him—thinking that the Federal troops were far away and that there was still no threat.

But on June 28, a week after I arrived at the convent with Sister Janette, Lee received word that the Union army was massed and very close. He realized instantly the danger his army was in. Immediately he sent couriers galloping off that night through the fields and along the roads of southern Pennsylvania, calling all the scattered legions and divisions together. He had to get all his troops together as a solid unit or they would be destroyed!

The orders all these couriers carried were simple enough. The Army of Northern Virginia would assemble and prepare for battle outside the little town of Gettysburg. It was close to Lee's present position, and many of the country roads led there. Once together, Lee would continue the march, depending on what the Union forces were doing.

The Federal Army didn't care about Gettysburg. It held no particular importance. They were simply scouring the countryside trying to find where Lee's army was, and Gettysburg happened to be where they found it.

As the month of June came to an end, therefore, and as I was walking about the fields and countryside thinking and praying, destiny was bringing thousands of young American soldiers across those same fields and through those same Pennsylvania woods and along the dirt roads toward Gettysburg, where their fateful and deadly collision would take place.

CHAPTER 16

ARRIVAL AT THE SCENE OF BATTLE

"Where are we going . . . what will we do?" I asked as we bounced along in the back of the wagon along the rutted dirt road. It was nearly dark. We had been riding for about two hours, and had just a little before crossed a covered wood bridge over the Susquehanna.

"There is a small convent and church in New Prospect," replied Sister Janette. "It should only be about another thirty minutes. They will put us up for the night."

"I mean when we reach Gettysburg," I said. I don't suppose I hid the lingering fear from my voice very well, because Sister Janette immediately tried to reassure me.

"We will see what the Lord will have us do," she replied. "Don't be afraid, Corrie. No harm will come to us, not when we are about his work of helping people. The fighting will no doubt be long over, though even if something should happen, nothing can take us out of God's divine care. We will not reach Gettysburg until the middle of the day tomorrow, even if we leave New Prospect before dawn. But there will be many, many wounded, and the doctors and nurses there will need all the help we can give them."

"But I know nothing about all that," I said.

"Neither do most of us," she replied. "More than anything, it takes a heart of love and a kind voice, with a dose of common sense. You'll do fine, Corrie. I'm glad you came with us."

I wasn't sure I shared her optimism. I'd nearly fainted after

73

pulling the Paiute arrow out of Tavish at the Pony Express station. I didn't know how I'd be able to keep my stomach inside me if there were wounded and dying men all around me!

We slept at the convent and were in the wagon again before the sun was up the next morning. It was about thirty miles to Gettysburg from the convent, and we reached the town about two o'clock the next afternoon.

Sister Janette had said that the fighting would be over, but we began to hear the shots of guns and cannon fire when we were still an hour away from the town. The mood of the fifteen or sixteen women in the two wagons—all nuns but me—hadn't exactly been jubilant. Everyone knew we were about serious business. Yet when we heard the dull sounds of explosions and sharp crack of gunfire off in the distance, an even greater somber mood settled over us, and hardly anything was said that whole last hour. Word had come to the convent the day before, on July 1, that the fighting had already begun. And if it was still going on as fiercely as it sounded the closer we drew to the town, it must surely have been an awful fight.

Nothing in my wildest imagination could have prepared me for what I saw. I would give almost anything to have the memory of that day and the next two erased from my mind. That brother could commit such horrible atrocities against brother—loyal Americans every one—is a crime against our country I doubt I shall ever be able to forgive the leaders of the Confederacy for. Nothing—no amount of freedom, no amount of financial or economic power, no principle they believed in, and certainly not slavery itself—could be worth having caused the horrible suffering and massive death that their rebellion against the government of our country caused. I couldn't help but think again of Cal, and it made me angry all over again, not for what he'd done to *me*, but that he could give his loyalty to the Confederacy at all. The South's cause just wasn't right!

But at the moment, there were more urgent things to think about. We had come to help, and there were plenty of innocent boys and young men—wearing *both* blue and gray—that needed tending to. And it didn't take long for us to find them. There was suffering everywhere!

Several miles outside Gettysburg we began encountering straggling groups of retreating wounded, teams of medics, sometimes officers on horseback. The closer we got, the more activity there was—moving both away from and toward the battle. Occasionally a troop of reinforcements rode swiftly by in bright, unsoiled uniforms. But those limping back in the opposite direction were dirty, torn, and blood-smeared, moving slowly, with no smiles on their faces.

Sister Jane, who was driving the lead wagon, stopped as we passed one such group and asked a man, his attire clearly identifying him as a medic or doctor of some kind, what we could all do to help.

"You see these men, Sister?" he said. "There's thousands more like them up there."

He nodded his head back over his shoulder in the direction from which he'd come, where we could hear the sounds of battle.

"Strewn out all over the place for miles. I don't know what to tell you, but if you're looking for men that need patching up or just hauling out of there, you won't have no trouble finding them. Just stay away from the front lines. The lead's flying so thick you can almost see it!"

Sister Jane thanked him and we continued on. I was already starting to feel sick to my stomach just from looking at the battle-worn men who were going away from the battle, and we weren't even there yet!

We had seen only Union soldiers, but as we entered the town of Gettysburg itself, now we began to see the gray of the Confederacy. At first the very sight of their uniforms struck fear into me, although I don't know why. There weren't many soldiers in the town at all, but there was a lot of activity just to the south. We could even see the edges of it as we came, which I later found out was a major battle going on right then for what was called Culp's Hill. The hill was held by Union forces, and they were being attacked by the Confederate soldiers between the town and the hill. So the southern commanders were doing a lot of riding back and forth between the outskirts of the town and the battle.

Sister Jane led the horses right into town and straight to the

St. Francis Xavier church. She had a feeling there would be plenty to do there, and she was right. As we approached, we could see great activity both inside and outside the church, which had already been set up as a makeshift hospital. Immediately, all the sisters jumped out of our wagons and rushed forward, talking to the nuns and one or two priests of St. Xavier's.

They were glad for the help! It was clear from one glance that they were not prepared for the deluge of wounded.

Almost before I had the chance to wonder what I should be doing in the midst of all the activity, Sister Janette was running back to me from where she'd been talking to one of the priests.

"We must get all the supplies inside first, Corrie," she said. "Why don't you get up there and start handing them down to me from the wagon."

I did so, and as Sister Janette left for the church with an armful, other sisters were there to cart in their share. Once started, I hardly had the chance to stop to think for the rest of the day. Every moment was filled with not only new experiences but awful sights and sounds, and everything so unexpected. I'd never dreamed of any of this when I started east!

I saw a doctor cut off the end of a young man's mangled arm that had been blown apart by an explosion of cannon fire. I don't mean I actually *watched*, but I knew what he was doing, and I heard the poor man's tortured screaming. I saw more blood that one day than I'd ever seen in my life—outside the church and even inside it, on the blankets where we put the wounded to lie on the floor. I saw men coming in without hands, without legs, wounded and bleeding from every part of their bodies. They'd come in from the battlefield, sometimes still bleeding from fresh wounds, or sometimes with makeshift bandages wrapped around an arm or a shoulder or even all the way around the chest, and then we'd have to unwrap them and dress the wounds.

At first I hung back, aghast at how horrible it all was. I gaped with my eyes wide and my mouth hanging open, while Sister Janette and Sister Jane and all the others rushed forward to help without seeming squeamish at any of it. They couldn't ever have seen anything like this before, yet their hearts were so full of sympathy and compassion for the poor wounded young men that they never stopped to worry about what they felt.

Even as I was carrying the last load inside from the wagon, Sister Janette called out to me from where she knelt on the other side of the church beside a boy who had just come in on a stretcher.

"Corrie, come help me for a minute," she said, glancing up at me. I rushed toward her, throwing the blankets down on the floor against the wall. "This poor lad's got a dreadful gash from his shoulder down across his chest," she said. "Would you help me bandage it up?"

I don't know what I said, but the next moment I was kneeling down on the floor beside her, the boy staring blankly up at us. I didn't realize it until later, but what Sister Janette was doing was initiating me into the role of nurse's assistant with a mild wound that wouldn't be too difficult to deal with nor would repulse me too badly. Before the next two days were over I would see so much worse. But for my first exposure to battlefield nursing, even this young boy's wound was bad enough. As she unbuttoned his tunic and peeled it away to reveal his skin, I couldn't help looking away. There was a long red gash, still bleeding a little, about eight or nine inches long. It was a clean cut and didn't look dirty, although I could hardly stand the mere thought of how painful it must be for him.

"What . . . what happened?" I found myself asking as Sister Janette dabbed alcohol on a clean white rag.

"I got thrown off my horse," he said, "and a da—"

He winced sharply in pain as Sister Janette applied the soaked cloth to the cut and gingerly cleaned the whole area of his chest.

"—a Yankee swatted down at me with his sword," the boy went on, still grimacing from the alcohol.

"That's awful!" I exclaimed.

"Nothing more'n I'd have done to him if I'd had the chance!" he said. "I'm just lucky my lieutenant shot him before he ran me through a second time."

"He shot him?"

"Yep, killed him dead in a second."

I winced and looked away, but not from the pain. I couldn't

believe how casually he spoke about another man dying. All the while Sister Janette was dabbing away at the cut.

"Did . . . did it hurt terribly?" I asked.

"Yeah, but only at first. It kinda went away. 'Course, I think I fainted for a spell, too, before I woke up here. That alcohol there, that hurts worst of all." He turned toward Sister Janette. "But I'm obliged to you, Sister," he said, "for helping me out. Don't want you to get the wrong idea."

She smiled down sweetly at him.

"Corrie," she said, turning to me. "There's some salve there in that bag just to your left. Will you get it for me? We'll dress the wound."

I found it and handed it to her.

"Now, Corrie," she went on, "get some of it out of the bottle and apply it—use your fingers—up and down the cut."

I did. There was nothing any worse about it than Claude Tavish's arrow, though I couldn't help shuddering when I first touched the open wound. The boy lay there calmly as I put the ointment on. After the alcohol, I suppose it was a relief.

"Now that roll of gauze," Sister Janette said.

I got it out and handed it to her. She unrolled several lengths, wrapping it over the wound, then up and around his shoulder, diagonally across his back, under the opposite arm, and around across his chest and over the wound again. She repeated the process several times until there were three or four thicknesses over the cut. Then she cut it off and tied it firmly in place. We would not follow that pattern too long, because there were far more wounds to treat than there were supplies. By the end of the day we were forced to be stingy with bandages and ointment. But as yet we did not know the full extent of the battle's severity.

"There you are, young man," she said cheerily. "That wound should heal just fine."

He nodded, thanked us both again, and we rose and moved away.

"You did very well, Corrie," said Sister Janette. "We will see where else we might be useful. Did everything get in from the wagons?"

"Yes," I answered.

"Good," she said, stooping down beside another wounded man, again dressed in gray, although much older this time, and with his eyes closed.

"Are you in much pain?" she asked, laying her hand gently across the man's white forehead. Slowly he opened his eyes, saw that it was a nun speaking to him, tried to force a smile, then closed them again.

"Yes, Sister," he whispered, "but nothing that will kill me. Take care of the others first. I'll live."

"Where is it?" she asked.

He nodded his head and tried to lift his hand to point. "Down there . . . my leg," he whispered.

I looked and could see instantly by the shape of his twisted leg that the bone was broken. No wonder he was so white! It was probably even more painful than the boy's saber wound, though not life-threatening.

"I see," said Sister Janette, stopping to think for a moment. "It will need a splint to set properly." She glanced around the room. "Hmm . . . I'll go find out what provisions we have. But first," she added, turning her attention back to the man, "we'll do what we can. Corrie," she said, speaking to me, "you get up by his head and hold on to his shoulders. You know what we have to do?" she said down to the man.

"Yes, ma'am," he whispered. "I'm afraid I do."

"It may hurt for a moment."

"Has to be done, Sister."

Sister Janette took a deep breath, then took hold of the dirty boot of the broken leg. "Now, Corrie, you hang on hard while I pull this leg straight and get the bone back into position."

I stretched my hands under the man's arms and held on tightly to his shoulders. Sister Janette gave a hard tug at the other end. I could feel the man crying out in pain, though hardly a sound escaped his lips. It only lasted a second or two. I felt Sister Janette's pressure at the other end relax, so I eased my hold, too. The poor man breathed out a sigh of relief. If anything his face was even whiter than before and beads of sweat were on his forehead. But one look at his leg showed that she had been successful and that it was straight again.

"There," she said, "I hope that eases the pain after a while. As long as you lie still, it will be fine until we can get it splinted."

For the rest of the afternoon, Sister Janette remained close by me, though occasionally giving me something to do alone or leaving me for a while and then returning to see how I was doing.

I can't say that I became comfortable with any of it, but I gradually got more used to it, and even ventured out on my own now and then to see where I might be able to help someone. I dressed a lot of wounds, helped attach several splints to broken arms and legs, and just talked to a lot of soldiers—most of them younger than I was, and nearly all from the South. Some were crude and angry and used foul language; others were nice and spoke gently. Some said they were from Hill's Corps and others had come back from Ewell's charge against Slocum at Culp's Hill, and others had been with Early striking up Cemetery Hill. I didn't know what any of them were talking about.

All the ones who could speak were anxious to keep talking about the various battles they'd been in, but from the sound of it, none of them had been victorious. It sounded as if nothing had yet been decided and that the battle was going to continue for some time. All during the afternoon, as we were tending to the constant flow of wounded, in the distance we could hear the sounds of guns and cannons, though after a while you quit hearing it altogether. Whenever I'd go outside the church to help unload new men from a wagon and help carry them in by stretcher, I could see smoke and fire in the distance.

People from the town were helping too, and all the churches had been set up as makeshift hospitals just like St. Xavier's. After we'd done what we could, the men who could be moved were transferred to neighboring houses where the people of Gettysburg were taking them in, or to small hospital tents that had been set up for them.

The day passed so quickly, it seemed as though we'd only just arrived when the darkness of night closed in. The fighting slowed and finally ceased, with only a few scattered spats of rifle fire now and then. We got the hundreds of wounded, in the church and outside and in nearby tents, as comfortable as possible. And then in the priests' and nuns' private quarters of the church, we took turns getting something to eat and then finding a corner to lie down in with a blanket to get some sleep. It was hot, and the floors were hard. Sleep was difficult. But I didn't realize how exhausted I was until suddenly I found myself opening my eyes to the light of morning.

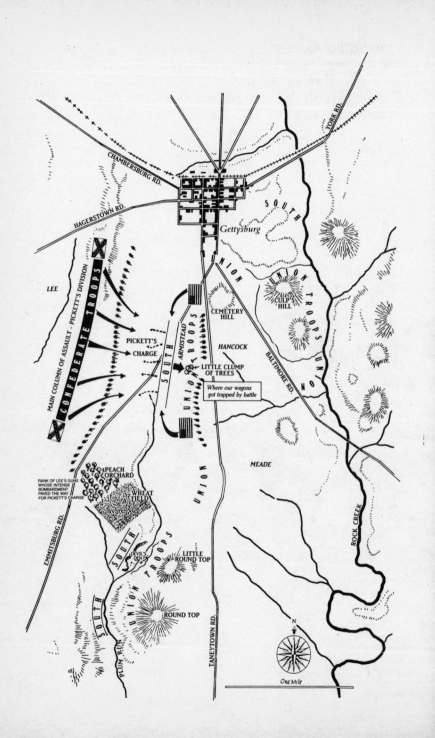

CHAPTER 17

THE FATEFUL DAY—
JULY 3, 1863

When I woke up, there were still no sounds from the battlefields. Others were already moving about. I could smell food being
prepared in the kitchen, but most of the sisters had already gone
to the church or were moving through the rows of tents outside
in the field next to the church, checking on the men, reapplying
bandages, bringing them bread and tea and milk and whatever
other provisions there were. From the relative calm, I thought
perhaps the fighting was over for good.

"Good morning, Corrie," Sister May greeted me.

I turned to see her approaching me from the kitchen.

"Are you hungry?"

"Famished," I answered.

"Some of the local women are baking bread as fast as they are
able," she went on, "both for us and for the men. I have some tea
in the kitchen, if you'd like. And Janette's next door at the Wade
home. Jennie's one of the parishioners here, and she and her sister
and mother are mixing and baking us a good supply."

"Are all the citizens helping like that?" I asked.

"A good many—although when the bullets fly too close by,
most stay in their cellars. But from what the sisters here tell me,
Jennie's never been one to be afraid of anything, and when there's
a job to do or someone in need of help, she's always there with
her sleeves rolled up."

"What should I do?" I asked.

"You could go over to the Wade home and see if they need

any help. There was talk a little while ago, too, of sending a few wagons out into the countryside to bring wounded into town."

"Is that safe?" I asked. "Is the fighting over?"

"We hope so. It's been quiet."

Even before the words were out of her mouth, a sudden eruption of gunfire rang out, very close by. Sister May and I looked at each other apprehensively, but neither of us said anything, hoping it would quickly die down.

It didn't. Gradually the sounds of ongoing fighting made it clear that the battle of Gettysburg wasn't over at all, but was now going into its third day. Within an hour, more wounded began arriving again, and the work of patching and bandaging and cleaning and nursing the casualties once more occupied every available hand.

The first few men to come in that morning with fresh wounds were talking about the reason for the renewed fighting. The Confederate troops under Ewell were making one last attempt to take Culp's Hill from Slocum's and Newton's Union troops. If they could, the men said, Ewell would be able to overrun Hancock's position on Cemetery Ridge. They could break through the Union line from the rear, while Pickett attacked frontally. Even the wounded were speaking of the brilliance of Lee's strategy, their eyes aglow, as if they fully expected to rout the Union army by the end of the day.

As I listened, I was unable to keep a great fear from rising up inside me. What if they did, indeed, smash through the Union line and continue their march to the coast and the eastern cities? I was on my way to Washington, D.C.—and so was the Rebel army of Robert E. Lee!

Maybe this *would* be a good time to become a nun, join the Convent of John Seventeen, and hide myself away from all this until the war was over!

I walked across the grass to the house next door, a two-story brick home, where Sister Janette introduced me to Jennie Wade, her mother and sister, and her sister's little three-day-old baby. I learned that this was Jennie's sister's house. Jennie and her mother had come to stay with her after the birth of the baby.

"You're baking bread besides tending to your sister?" I asked.

"My sister takes no care," laughed Jennie. "It's the baby! But idle hands are the devil's workshop, you know, Corrie. And when you and the sisters arrived yesterday, I went straight over to Sister May and told her that I would do my best to keep bread baked so you would all have plenty to eat."

"It is very kind of you," said Sister Janette.

"And delicious too, if that was your bread I ate last evening," I added.

Jennie laughed again. "It probably was. Thank you both, but really—it's the least someone like me can do. Not as important as what you and the nurses and medics do."

"If nuns and nurses and medics and helpers like Corrie don't eat," said Sister Janette, "they won't do the wounded much good. Everyone's part is just as important as the next person's."

"Thank you, Sister," Jennie replied with a smile, attacking again the large mass of dough she had been kneading.

I liked Jennie immediately. She was several years younger than I was, but so outgoing and friendly that I knew if we had the chance, we could become good friends in no time. I'd never had a close friend—a girl—my own age before, and even as Sister Janette and I walked back to St. Xavier's, I found myself thinking what it would be like to know Jennie better. A few days earlier I had been thinking about remaining at the convent and becoming a nun. Now I was thinking about wanting to stay in Gettysburg after the battle because of a new friendship with a young girl I'd only just met. I laughed at myself. I was becoming so unsettled, I didn't know *where* my future home was! Every place I went, I wanted to stay and live there. Every person I met I wanted to remain with forever. Where was my home supposed to be, anyway?

The sound of gunfire was increasing as we walked through the field. "Does it seem as if it's coming closer?" I said, half to myself.

Sister Janette must have been thinking the same thing, because she looked around with a concerned expression in her eyes, then nodded and said, "It does seem to be, doesn't it, Corrie? Yes, I think it is."

We quickened our pace, and in a couple of minutes were back inside the church building.

Within a short time, the wounded began arriving even more rapidly, and soon we were busier than we had been the day before. Steadily the sounds of the battle seemed to get louder and louder.

An hour later, I heard the rumble of perhaps a dozen horses galloping through town. Then more activity—wagons, men dragging cannons, infantrymen walking, some running . . . all Confederate soldiers. There was a lot of talk among the wounded. And from those coming in fresh from the lines, we managed to piece together the information that Ewell's Corps had failed at Culp's Hill. They had been repulsed by the Union troops and were now rapidly falling back toward the town. That accounted for all the Confederate activity. It wasn't what you'd exactly call a full retreat, and the Union army wasn't chasing them. There was no danger of Gettysburg being overrun. But the fire from Howard's Corps was following the Rebels as they fell back, and as it did the battle encroached upon the outskirts of the town itself.

I was working next to the southern wall of the church, just inside the door, when I heard a sound that sent my stomach into my throat. A dull thud sounded in the wall beside me, accompanied by the splintering of wood. A bullet had struck the church!

Suddenly a barrage of tiny whacks sounded all against the southern wall, peppering the whole church with lead slugs. A second or two later a great explosive outburst of gunfire sounded, much closer than we had heard before.

Then came the sound of breaking glass from one of the windows, and the delayed sound of gunfire echoed as the glass tinkled onto the floor below. Father Adams yelled above the din, "Everybody onto the floor!"

I dropped the gauze pads that were in my hands and in an instant was lying on my stomach, just as another window exploded into tiny pieces. The bullet ricocheted off a bell on the opposite side of the church, then thudded into a wall. Suddenly the battle had come too close for comfort!

More shots sounded, and all around the church slugs could be heard pecking the walls of wood. Then came a calm and silence.

Father Adams stood, went to the door and peered out. I don't know what he saw, but he didn't say anything. Some of the wounded men were talking, the rest of us breathing sighs of relief and rising again to our feet.

But the silence didn't last long. Suddenly gunfire erupted again. We all fell to the floor once more, but this time there were no sounds of bullets against the church. The direction of the shots had shifted. I got to my knees, listening.

Between the deafening explosions, I could hear a sound I couldn't identify at first. Then I realized it was the sound of bullets striking against a wall. But they were no longer hitting the church. It was the sound of bullets against brick—hundreds of them in rapid-fire succession. The fire had shifted and was blasting against the house next door—the home of Jennie's sister!

I had risen to my feet and unconsciously moved toward the window that looked out over the little field up in the direction of Baltimore Street. I could see dust and tiny bits of brick flying about the walls.

Sister Janette had apparently noticed the change, too, because I saw her standing at the back door of the church, a look of fear on her face as she made the sign of the cross on her chest. I had never seen her look that way before. The fearlessness she possessed with regard to herself was one thing. But now she was clearly afraid for the home of these friends of the parish. Her lips were moving in silent prayer.

Suddenly there was a scream. I glanced back out the window. It had come from the house!

I looked back toward Sister Janette. She was no longer standing at the door but was already running out across the field.

Father Adams called after her. She continued on, heedless of the danger or her own safety. Before I knew it, I was flying through the back door of the church after her.

I heard voices calling, and think I faintly heard my name. I felt a hand tugging against my arm, trying to restrain me, but I pulled away and continued outside, following Sister Janette.

My mind was a blur. I was running, though I scarcely knew why, thinking in some vague way, I suppose, of helping my new friend. There was still gunfire sounding in the distance, though it had shifted and was no longer concentrating its deathly fury in our direction. I did not know that at the time, nor care. Impulse guided my steps, not thought or reason. Neither did I hear the shouts behind me urging me to come back, nor the cries ahead from the brick home.

On I ran, following Sister Janette by ten or fifteen seconds into the house. Suddenly as I burst through the door, I stopped. My mind seemed to come once more into focus.

The room was empty. All was quiet and still. Even the gunfire had abated momentarily.

Only a second or two passed while I stood there, suddenly aware of myself. The first sensation to come to me was the smell of warm bread baking in the oven. It was such a homey smell, so deliciously fragrant, so in contrast to the horrible battle going on all around us. For an instant the smell of bread which filled the house seemed to say, *It is not so bad as it seems. Good will triumph in the end. Peace will come, and we will all enjoy life's goodness together again.*

But the feeling of tranquility was illusory. Even as I was drawing in a deep breath of the fresh aroma, I heard crying coming from the rear of the house. I headed toward the sound.

But I did not get far. Sister Janette met me, her face white and her expression somber.

Sensing the truth, I struggled to get by.

"Corrie, please—" she said.

"Let me go!" I cried. "I want to go to Jennie."

But Sister Janette restrained me. "No, come with me," she said, trying to turn me in the opposite direction and lead me back the way we both had come.

I wrestled against her, more vigorously now. "I want to see Jennie!"

"Corrie . . . Corrie, please!" she implored. "You don't want to go in there. Now, come with me."

Her voice was tender yet commanding. I continued to struggle and finally pushed my way past her.

"Corrie!" she yelled after me. "Corrie, don't go in there! Corrie, please . . . Jennie is dead."

CHAPTER 18

PICKETT'S CHARGE UP CEMETERY RIDGE

The rest of that morning is lost in a blur in my memory.

When I sat down to try to reconstruct the events to write them down in my journal, I could remember nothing for a long time after falling into Sister Janette's arms and sobbing. It was several hours before the day began to fit into a pattern that made sense to my mind again.

The gunfire ended shortly after the volley that had hit the brick house and ended poor Jennie Wade's life. Within fifteen minutes there was silence throughout the town. The fight for Culp's Hill and the retreat of Ewell's troops was over, and no more significant fighting took place for several hours. All there was for us to do was try to find room for the new wounded that kept being brought to us, even after the sharp explosions of gunfire had died away.

When my mind finally began to refocus, I was in the church, walking among the wounded, a towel draped over one arm, and a container of water in my hand. I think I had been helping Father Adams wash and clean some of the fresh wounds, because there was blood on the towel. But as I came to myself I was standing alone.

Suddenly my eyes took in the scene around me. I remembered where I was, I remembered about Jennie, and pangs of new grief shot through me. I stood there in the middle of the room—probably not for more than five or ten seconds, but it seemed like an hour—while thought after thought flooded through me like a dream.

As I glanced about at the wounded, I couldn't help but wonder why we had to be in a war at all. So much blood . . . too much fighting . . . and altogether too much dying! What was it all about . . . what was the purpose . . . why did it have to be?

I thought of Jennie, tears again rising to my eyes. I found myself wondering what it was like to die. What did Jennie *feel* at the exact moment the bullet crashed into her and she felt life slipping away? Or did she even know? Maybe she just fell asleep, and the next instant her soul was in heaven.

I continued to look around the room, wondering what was going to happen to all these poor young men lying here. I wondered if they were afraid of dying, or if they were brave like soldiers are supposed to be and had no such fears. Did any of them have a faith in God that gave hope and courage to face whatever came? I found myself thinking of their families and friends in far off places. They wouldn't even know that their sons and brothers and husbands had been wounded.

I thought of mothers worrying and praying that their sons would be safe, and asking God to bring them back safely. Many of them were Confederate mothers, and yet they were praying to the same God that I prayed to and that all the mothers in the North prayed to—everybody asking God for protection and safety, while the sons of these mothers on both sides did their best to kill one another. It didn't seem to make much sense! How could God answer the prayers on both sides?

Wondering what the parents of these soldier-sons might be thinking and praying made me think of Pa, and I thanked the Lord again for giving him back to me. I wondered what *he* was thinking right now. Did he miss me, was he anxious about me, was he praying for me? How much harder it must be for the parents of these soldiers to have their sons so far away from home, and to be so powerless to help them.

In the middle of my daydreaming, I felt a tap on my shoulder and heard Sister Agatha's voice. "You seem deep in thought, Corrie . . . are you all right?"

Startled, I came to myself and saw her standing at my side. "Yes . . . yes, I think so. I just found myself filled with more thoughts than I knew what to do with for a moment, that's all."

"Do I see some tears?"

Then I remembered. "I can't stop thinking about poor Jennie," I replied.

Sister Agatha put her arm tenderly around me. "Neither can any of us, dear."

"And then I couldn't help thinking about my family back home," I went on, "and about the parents of these wounded boys."

"Well, their parents are far away right now. So we've got to be the ones to take care of them for a while."

I sighed, then nodded.

"So would you like to help me?" she asked. "I'm about to change the dressing on a dreadful back wound, and I need another set of hands."

"Yes . . . of course."

"Good . . . you're sure you feel up to it?"

"Yes . . . I'm fine now." I drew in a deep breath. "Thank you, Sister Agatha," I said.

She smiled, then led me in the direction of the boy who had been shot in the back.

We did what we could to make the wounded comfortable throughout the morning, hearing virtually nothing from the surrounding countryside. We ate lunch, and I cried again at the sight of some of the very bread Jennie had baked the day before. Two of the sisters spent the morning with Jennie's sister and mother, helping tend the little one, and helping to get Jennie's body to the undertaker.

Around two o'clock, Father McFey suggested that, the battle seeming to be over, two of the wagons be taken out into the region south of town with supplies to see what might be done for the wounded who were farther away and had not been fortunate enough to have been carried or transported back to town.

The wagons were hitched up, supplies loaded aboard, and six or eight of the sisters piled in to accompany him.

"Corrie, what about you?" Sister Janette asked me, thinking, I suppose, that it might be good to get me busy away from the church. I had never faced having someone die like that, so close by, especially so suddenly, and from a gunshot! It was different than with Ma, who had been sick. And that was a long time ago. Sister Janette could see how shaken I was and was probably right about my needing something to occupy my hands and mind.

I nodded in agreement, and ten minutes later found myself jostling along in the back of the wagon with the others on the Taneytown Road going south.

We had gone two or three miles from town, stopping every now and then to help someone and leaving supplies at some of the makeshift tents behind the lines where some of the wounded had been taken. Around three in the afternoon, the first noises of renewed battle sounded in the distance.

It all broke loose so suddenly that we were too far into the thick of it to turn back. There was a great uproar, with smoke and fire and explosions, and within minutes the air was so thick we couldn't see more than a hundred yards ahead.

We turned the wagons around, but by then the battle had engulfed us.

CHAPTER 19

CAUGHT IN BATTLE!

There was a small clump of trees right in the middle of the Union line at the crest of the ridge, and straight toward that clump of trees Pickett's men charged.

We were on the other side, the east side of the ridge, behind the Union soldiers. But we could see the trees to our left as we attempted to go back the way we'd come. As the Confederates charged up the hill, though they fought them off, the Union line crept down toward us. And then one small detachment of Confederate troops actually broke through the Union line right near the clump of trees! For a short time there was pandemonium. Union soldiers were falling back right toward us, with shouts and orders filling the air!

In the midst of what had been a sea of dark blue uniforms, suddenly there were two or three hundred gray-clad men surging through, led by General Armistead, who had stuck his slouch hat on the end of his sword and was holding it high in the air to lead his men on. At the same time, Hancock's men tried desperately to fight them back!

Within minutes, the battle between Armistead's southerners and Hancock's northerners for control of the hill and the clump of trees had swooped down upon us!

"Everyone out of the wagons!" cried Father McFey. "Get underneath, or make for the cover of the brush behind us."

I was terrified!

Before I knew anything more, I was crouched down under the wagon, Sister Janette's hand clutching mine. All of us were praying harder than we'd ever prayed in our lives!

I had never been so close to a battle before. All the shots of guns and cannons we had heard before now had been in the distance. Now it was right beside us, all around us! And the most awful thing was seeing the actual men, so close, fighting and shooting and trying to kill one another! I smelled smoke and gunpowder. I heard the sounds of horses neighing in terror, screams of men in pain, and the constant explosions of cannons and sharp cracking reports of thousands of guns! It was so close, I could even hear, in the midst of all the noise, the groans of men who knew they had no hope, that it was just a matter of time before they bled to death.

Suddenly I became aware that Sister Janette's hand was no longer on mine. In fact, she wasn't beside me at all! I glanced around and saw her creeping out from under the wagon. She was crawling right toward the thick of the battle! A young man had fallen only about twenty feet away, and she was going to see what she might do for him—that is, if he was still alive at all!

Now most of the other sisters, as well as Father McFey, were doing the same, some crouched down, some on their hands and knees, moving out toward the fallen men in both blue and gray, who were scattered about the battlefield.

My first reaction was that I should go help them. It seemed like the right thing to do, even though I was terrified at the thought. But the impulse was just as strong to stay right where I was and protect myself! Yet in an even deeper place inside my heart, there was *another* thought. And that was the feeling that I had to obey the impulse to help instead of the impulse to keep myself safe. I may not have liked it, but I knew what I had to do—I had to get out from under the safety of the wagon and follow Sister Janette's example.

"Oh, God, help me!" I breathed, then crept out slowly toward the field of battle.

I made my way, seeing all about in every direction bodies of horses and men, some dead, some still alive. A sick feeling came over me like I had never known before. By this time all the others were working with the wounded, moving from man to man to see what could be done. But I couldn't bring myself to start. I was paralyzed—not by fear exactly, but just by the awfulness of it all.

I was still near the wagon, separated from the others. And as I stood there, the sights and sounds of the battle grew dim. Suddenly I was alone, in a cocoon, while my senses blocked out everything else but what I was thinking.

What good would it do, I thought, to help a few people? Hundreds . . . thousands of men were spread out all over these fields and hills! Some of those lying on the ground might need only a bandage to cover a wound, yet they would bleed to death because nobody was there to help them. We couldn't possibly help them all! For every one we could save, hundreds of others would die helplessly! The little good we could do—what difference would it make?

If ever I had felt like giving up completely, just lying down and crying and waiting for it all to be over, this was the moment. It all seemed so hopeless! Despair was around us—everywhere! I could find not the smallest ray of hope anywhere within me!

As I stood there, my eyes on the ground in front of me, I managed to move my head and glance about. Bodies lay everywhere. The very grass of the field was splotched with blood!

But then my eyes fell upon something else in the midst of the sickening field of death. Ten feet away, growing bravely up out of the soil, unconcerned with the chaos and noise all about it, was a little lonely flower. It was white, with touches of blue on the tops of its petals. I don't know what kind of flower it was. I had never seen one like it.

At any other time, in any other place, I might not have noticed anything of significance in the sight. Yet today it caught my attention. This little bit of purity, here, in the midst of all the death surrounding it, touched my heart. For a moment I was able to forget that only a few paces away men were killing one another. It was God's way of speaking to me, saying, *You see, Corrie, even when it doesn't look like it, and even when you can't see me, I am still here. No matter how bad it may look, I never forget my people.*

I cannot say exactly how, but somehow that flower put hope back into my heart—hope which gave me the strength to get on again with what needed to be done. Even if it were true that thousands of people were dying all around me, if I could help just a few . . . if I could help just *one*, I knew that it *would* be worth it.

If I could do but one little deed of kindness to someone here, bandaging a wound or speaking a word of comfort, I could be like the little white and blue flower in the midst of *their* despair. Who could tell—perhaps I might help someone who would go on to save others someday. No act of kindness was too small. You could never know what might come of it in the end.

All these thoughts passed through my mind in a few brief seconds. Then just as suddenly the sounds and smells and sights of the battle raging all around returned upon me. But at last I was ready to do my part in it, whatever came to me.

I breathed in deeply, then ran forward to rejoin the sisters as fast as I could.

CHAPTER 20

DEATH IN THE MIDST OF THE TUMULT

Sister Janette was nearby. I ran to her and knelt down. But she turned, then rose and motioned me away.

"It's too late for him, Corrie, God bless him. Come, there are many others who need us."

I followed her, glancing down with dumb sickening horror at the corpse lying at her feet.

I went with her, and in another minute was kneeling beside a man who was groaning in agony with what looked like a broken leg.

"Are you wounded?" asked Sister Janette, laying a tender hand on his forehead.

"No, sister. It's just my leg. It hurts something fierce!"

"If you can stand the pain, we will carry and drag you as best we can over to our wagon. I think you'll be able to lie there in safety."

"No place is safe with them bloody Rebs on the attack!" he said.

"It will be better than out here on the open field. Corrie," she said to me, "take hold of his shoulders and I'll do my best to ease the pressure on the leg."

With a great deal of effort, with groans and grimaces from the man—as well as some words I won't repeat—we finally got him into the shade underneath the wagon. Even as he was thanking us, Sister Janette hastened off again.

I ran after her, but before I had taken ten paces away from the wagon, she yelled back toward me. "Corrie . . . in that box in the wagon—bring bandages! Hurry, before this man bleeds to death!"

I spun around, found the bandages, and ran back. To my horror, I saw Sister Janette's hand literally stuck *into* the man's stomach, plugging what must have been a terrible wound. Her arm was red with blood almost up to the elbow, and her habit was smeared all over with splotches of red.

"Tear off a big piece, Corrie!" she cried. "Here . . . stick it in here. We've no time for medicine . . . he's already lost too much blood!"

The only consolation was that the man appeared unconscious and not in pain.

"Is . . . is he alive?" I asked.

"Yes . . . his heart is pumping and he's breathing well. If I can just stop—" She didn't even finish, taking the cloth from my hand and crudely attempting to fashion a makeshift bandage that would be tight enough to stop the flow. Even as I was ripping off more pieces and helping her with them, my eyes were diverted up the hill, where a horrible scene was taking place about thirty or forty yards away. Two men were fencing fiercely. One was an officer in the Confederate army, and appeared to be about forty-five. The other, dressed in the dark blue of the Union, was a foot soldier, much younger.

The awful thought swept through my mind that within a few short minutes, one of these proud soldiers would probably be lying on the ground, either dead or in unimaginable pain. But then my attention was again brought back to the young man lying unconscious in front of me.

When I glanced up again, suddenly the Yankee lunged forward with his blade. The gruesome scene was too much for me, and I hid my eyes.

When I again dared to look up, the old soldier was sprawled out on the ground. His slayer was nowhere to be seen.

I was no longer thinking about Sister Janette and the man whose life she was trying to save. Suddenly I was on my feet. I darted toward the wounded man, hardly conscious that I was running straight toward the little clump of trees!

The poor man's shabby gray uniform had a big red spot on

the left side of the chest. The blood glistened in the sun, still wet, the wound obviously fresh. I thought he was dead. I stooped down. Then I saw him half open one eye.

"What's . . . what's a girl like—"

He struggled to speak, but his voice came out only in a faint raspy whisper.

I took out some of the strips of bandage I was still carrying, then reached out and placed them over the hole in his chest.

"What is your name?" I asked him, looking into his face contorted with pain.

When he answered his voice was weak. "Lieutenant Isaac Tomlinson," he replied, uttering the name with pride.

"Would you like some water?" I said.

"Just . . . just wet my face . . . I'm—I'm so hot."

I dabbled some drops from the canteen I was carrying onto a cloth and spread it across his forehead and cheeks.

"That feels good . . . are you an angel? What are you doing here?"

"I'm just someone who got caught in the battle like you," I said.

"I didn't just get caught, girl. I joined up . . . to get the Yankees for what they done. I—I used to own a large plantation in New Orleans. It was a good life . . . but then they came . . . and the slaves all up and left, some of us were burned out . . . they killed my wife. So I went to war with my son."

His voice was still soft, but full of passion at the memory. He seemed to be using his last ounce of strength, even if it was with words instead of his sword, against the hated northerners.

"Where is your son?" I asked.

"He was killed last month."

"I'm sorry."

"Thank you, but . . . but don't—don't worry. . . ." His words were filled with pain for his son rather than himself. "Now I have nothing . . . nothing more to live for. Death will not be hard to bear."

"You are not going to die," I said, wiping his face again and doing my best to keep my tears away.

"No, girl. You do not..how can you understand? Death . . .

it is close at hand . . . I can feel it closing in. . . ."

I didn't know what to say. He seemed to be giving up. How could I convince him that life was worth living, worth fighting for?

"At last my sorrowful life will be ended . . . I will not be sorry to leave it behind."

I struggled to find words of consolation for this wounded, bitter man. "But God—" I began.

"Yes," he mocked. "God. You think there could be a God who would take everything from me, and . . . and then leave me here to die?" His voice, still gravelly and labored, had suddenly turned its bitterness away from the Yankees who had killed his wife and son, blaming God instead for the tragic circumstances that had befallen him.

His words made my heart sick! I *had* to find a way to make him see that God *loved* him and was not at all like he thought! "Perhaps . . . he was just trying to reach you."

"Well, he certainly went about it the wrong way." His words were accompanied by a sharp look of pain that swept over his face.

"He loves everybody," I said. "Even in the midst of all this, you mustn't forget that. He is sometimes all we have left to hang on to."

"I used to believe all that. My wife . . . my wife and I . . . we used to—" He grimaced in agony and took in a quick breath or two. "We used to go to church . . . every Sunday . . . believed all that. But when she—"

"We mustn't blame God for what men do," I said in desperation.

But no more words from the Confederate soldier came back in reply. I looked down into his face, waiting for an answer.

But no answer came. He had shut his eyes for the final time. Lieutenant Isaac Tomlinson was dead.

I could not hold back the tears. In a rush they suddenly flowed from my eyes, and with them came a sense of dejection and failure. I had not been able to help the poor man either physically *or* spiritually! If I had had just a few more minutes with him . . .

But I could not think that way. I could not let my spirit be broken in the same way as his had been. I had told him he could not blame God. Neither could *I* blame myself.

I stood, tears still streaming down my cheeks, and looked down at the dead man. Peace was on his face. For that much I could be grateful. I could not understand how he could be glad to leave this earth. But he did not understand the true reason for living, so how could he possibly understand the true meaning of dying? "Oh, God . . . take care of him!" was all I could pray.

I returned to Sister Janette and helped with other men fallen in battle. I suppose I did help to save others that day. But the face and words of Lt. Tomlinson stayed with me.

CHAPTER 21

LIFE IN THE MIDST OF DEATH

The next two hours passed like five minutes! And yet as I try to recall the events, the time stretches out in my mind as if it were five days. I saw more death, more hand-to-hand fighting, and heard what must have been a million shots of gunfire. But in the midst of the smoke and tumultuous din, we were able to help a few men here and there who might not have survived the day otherwise.

The surge of General Armistead's Confederate troops didn't succeed in dislodging the strong Union position along the ridge. After breaking through temporarily, Hancock's men once again closed ranks, and eventually succeeded in killing or taking prisoner nearly every one of Armistead's men. It was probably the most dramatic moment, the high-water mark of the Confederate attack. And it came close to winning the day for General Robert E. Lee, who was observing from the opposite ridge behind Pickett's charge.

Prior to the outbreak of the war, the regular army of the United States had been rather small. Most of the high-ranking officers knew one another professionally, and many lasting friendships went back to shared experiences at West Point and years of service together in various forts and posts of the army. When the country suddenly broke apart, some of these officers remained with the Union, others took up command positions in the Confederacy. Suddenly friends and former comrades found themselves fighting *against* one another!

Even California came in for its share of this heartbreak. Back in 1861, as the Union was splitting up and the officers of the old army were forced to choose sides, a farewell party was held in the officers' quarters of a little army post outside of Los Angeles. The host was Captain Winfield Hancock, and he was giving the party in honor of his companions and fellow officers who were resigning in order to join the Southern army. One of those present was another captain by the name of Lewis Armistead, one of Hancock's close friends. When the party was over, Armistead shook Hancock's hand with tears in his eyes. "You'll never know," he said, "what grief this decision has cost me. Goodbye, my friend."

He and Hancock would not see each other again. Now they were generals in opposing armies. And Armistead led the spearhead of Pickett's charge up Cemetery Ridge, straight toward the little clump of trees, and straight toward his old friend Hancock, who was waiting for him at the top with his huge battery of Federal forces.

The fighting was fierce, and the smoke so thick that sometimes the soldiers could hardly tell their own comrades from the enemy. Riding up into the middle of the fray to make sure the hole in his lines had been plugged, General Hancock was shot from his horse. He was immediately carried back to the rear of the fighting, seriously wounded but still alive. At nearly the same time, on the southern side, General Armistead kept waving his black felt hat, but the tip of his sword had pierced through and now the hat had slipped all the way down to the hilt. Then suddenly a bullet slammed into his body and he, too, fell. Both generals had now fallen, yet still the battle raged on.

As much horror as I had seen, the most awful moment of the day was yet to come. It had been probably an hour since I had seen Sister Janette. All the sisters and Father McFey and I were scattered so widely over the battlefield, we only seemed to meet occasionally when one or more of us would be running back to fetch something from the wagons, or when one of us needed another's help. By this time twenty or thirty men had been dragged or carried back to the relative safety of our wagons. At one of these times I ran into Sister Janette.

"Corrie," she called out when she saw me, "could you help me? There's a fellow I can't budge by myself."

I looked up toward her voice and saw her running toward me. She was an absolute mess—blood all over her habit, her face blotched with sweat and dirt. She looked exhausted, but as full of life as ever. I ran immediately to join her.

"He's a huge man," she went on, leading me up the slope in the direction of the fighting. "I'm afraid for him if he stays where he is, but I can't move him an inch by myself, even though he still has one good leg."

In another minute we were at the man's side and Sister Janette was helping him to a sitting position. Then she stood behind him, grabbing at his broad shoulders and grunting and lifting, trying to help the man get his strong leg underneath him. She was right about his size . . . he must have weighed three hundred pounds! His left leg was badly shattered and bleeding.

I got under one of his arms, and with his weight on both of us, he pulled himself up by using the butt of his rifle as a cane. Eventually the three of us managed to struggle to our feet. We turned and, with the man hobbling along with the two of us on either side helping to prop him up, we slowly staggered down the hill away from the fighting.

I never heard the shot. They say you never hear the gun that kills you because the bullet gets to you before the sound of the gunfire. And there was so much fighting and gunfire filling the air that it was impossible to distinguish one shot from any of the other thousand shots going off every second. But the first thing I knew, I was toppling over onto the ground beside the big man. He swore a little, and cried out from the pain as his wounded leg crumpled beneath him.

At first I thought we'd lost our balance. I scrambled out from amidst our tangled arms and legs to see what could be done to get the motley trio back on our feet. The man grunted and swore and got himself back to a sitting position. I jumped up and took my position again under one of his arms.

Then suddenly I noticed Sister Janette lying face down on the ground on the other side of him. She wasn't moving. The back of her shoulder was covered with blood—and not the blood of those she had been helping.

"Sister Janette!" I screamed, rushing around the big girth of the man to her. "Oh, God . . . no . . . God, please!" I cried, gingerly turning her body over. Her eyes were closed, her face a ghastly pale white.

I forgot about the wounded man completely, although there was nothing more I could do to move him by myself. Without even thinking what I was doing, I found myself lifting the limp body into my arms, unconscious of the blood of my dear friend spilling all over my own arms and chest. I hardly even felt the weight, even though Sister Janette was a larger woman than I was. With one of my arms under her knees, and the other under her shoulders, and with her head dangling back lifelessly, I staggered and half-ran the rest of the way down the slope and across the field to the wagons.

I was completely out of breath when I arrived. Immediately the other sisters were at my side, sensing that a crisis was at hand that touched us all more closely than anything we had yet encountered.

They took her from my arms, and before I could even catch my breath, had laid her gently in the wagon. The two sisters who were nurses were working frantically and talking between themselves.

"Is she . . . is she—?"

"No, Corrie," replied one, "she is not dead. She has lost a lot of blood, but it appears that the bullet passed all the way through her arm. You probably saved her life by getting her to us so quickly. We have already managed to stop the bleeding."

I felt no relief at her words, but rather a numbness. Before I knew it, I was wandering away from the scene. I had tried to help others, but I guess I knew Sister Janette had the best care she could get right now, and I didn't want to be in the way.

I was walking almost aimlessly. I should have gotten someone else to go back and help me with the heavy man with the wounded leg, but I'm ashamed to say I had already forgotten about him. Not even knowing it, I went off in a different direction altogether, and then found myself almost stumbling over a man lying on the ground. He wore a Union uniform.

"What are you doing out in the middle of all this, Miss?" he said.

I glanced toward the voice, then stopped and knelt down beside him.

"Trying to help, whenever I can," I replied. "What can I do for you?"

"I ain't hurt too bad. I think the bullet broke the bone in my arm. I couldn't hold my gun no more, so I figured I might as well sit myself down before I got myself killed outright. What's your name?"

"Corrie Hollister," I answered, looking his arm over and pulling out some bandages I had shoved into the pocket of my dress when Sister Janette and I had begun lifting the big man. The fellow was right—his arm did look broken. But besides that, his ribs were pretty badly shot up, too. "What's yours?" I said.

"Alan Smith." As friendly as he was, his voice was soft and he was in obvious pain. He wore a beard that was probably a week old, his clothes were scruffy, and he looked to be in his early twenties.

"Where are you from?" I asked.

"Texas."

"But Texas is a slave state. And your uniform. . . ?"

"Oh, I'm in the Union army, all right. But I live in Texas. My pa was a friend of Sam Houston's. When they kicked Sam out of the governorship of the state 'cause he didn't want slavery and wouldn't go along with the Confederacy, why he up and left the state and came north. My pa and some of Sam's other followers came with him, and I came with my pa, 'cause I ain't no friend of Jefferson Davis neither. So I joined up with the Union army. Maybe I'll go back when it's all over, who knows? I reckon I'll always be a Texan at heart, and I sure don't consider myself a traitor to Texas. Why, shoot, I'm on the side of the tallest Texan ever, on the same side as Sam Houston. By the way, where you from?"

"California," I answered.

All of a sudden a sharp pain seemed to come over his face. He closed his eyes and lay still. I was scared. I thought maybe he'd died. But then gradually he opened them again and started to breathe more easily. The jovial look he'd had just a moment before was completely gone. He seemed to have something much different than Texas on his mind.

"How do you feel?" I asked him.

"It ain't the pain I mind so much, Miss . . . what did you say your name was?"

"Corrie," I said.

"It ain't so much the pain, Miss Corrie," he went on, "although that last one was a real doozer. I thought I might be done for all over again. But the worst of it is realizing how close I come to dying back there without never really being prepared for it. What I'm trying to say is, I never really thought about what's to become of anyone when they die."

"You're pretty young to be thinking about dying," I said. "If it hadn't been for my ma, I'd probably never have thought much about it either."

"Your ma?"

"She died when I was fifteen."

"How old are you now?"

"Twenty-six," I said.

"Well, I'm twenty-three. But I'm a soldier, and it don't seem too smart for someone like me to go twenty-three years of his life never thinking about what might become of me later, after this life. Especially for a soldier. But the minute I was hit a little while back, suddenly I realized I'd faced what might have been a certain death if the bullet had been a couple inches one way or the other. I *still* might die of this thing!"

"I think you'll be fine, Mr. Smith," I said. He was certainly in better shape than most of the other wounded men I'd seen.

"What if you can't stop the bleeding? What if I get shot again! You know what I'm getting at, Miss? What's to happen? You understand what I'm trying to say?"

"I think so," I answered. "You're wondering if there really is a heaven to go to after you die, is that it?"

"I reckon that's just about the size of the question exactly," he said. "Or a hell too, for that matter. Heaven ain't guaranteed for fellows like me that ain't been all they maybe ought to have been!"

"I certainly believe there is," I said.

"A heaven and hell?"

"I don't think too much about hell. But I know there's a heaven because Jesus said so, and I believe in him more than I believe in anything."

"In Jesus? How do you mean that you *believe* in him?"

"I mean he lives in my heart—his Spirit, I mean, not his actual bodily self that lived back so long ago in history."

"That don't sound altogether reasonable. I mean, it don't make no sense that somebody could live inside somebody else like that. That ain't exactly what I meant about believing in God and heaven and hell."

"But that's what God means by believing. Jesus said that his Spirit—his real deepest self, the part of him that was God's Son—he said that part of him would live on and would come and dwell in the hearts of anybody that wanted to share life with him. He talked about it in the Bible a lot. That's why he rose from the dead, so he could share life like that with us—in our hearts. That's what he said belief was, and that's why I know I'll go to heaven when I die—because that's his home, and he promised to take us there to live with him."

"That's a heap more than I ever heard about in church when I was a kid! How do you know it's all true?"

"Because the Bible says so, and Jesus said so. And that's enough for me to believe it. I reckon that's what faith is too, just believing because God says something."

"But how do you know?"

"I guess because Jesus is my friend, too. I've been sharing things with him in my mind and heart for long enough that I know I can trust him."

He didn't say anything for a minute, and seemed to be real thoughtful.

"I reckon it's like this," he said at length. "If anything *should* happen to me, like I was saying, like if I was to die or something, well, I want to make sure that I do go to be with God. I ain't never thought about all this before. I always just took life as it came. To tell you the truth, Miss, I can't even say as I know there's a God at all."

"I don't suppose I can answer every doubt you have," I said. "I've had doubts from time to time myself, but I still know that God's love for me is as real as anything there is in the world. And his love for you is just as real."

Again Alan was quiet for a while.

"What about all my buddies who died?" he asked. "People like Sergeant Thomas and Corporal Harry—what if they never make it to heaven? One thing I know for sure, and that is that they weren't Christians! Are they all doomed? I ain't sure I'd want to go to heaven if none of my buddies are there."

"But if God *is* real, and if he's the one that made you, and if he does love you like I say, then wouldn't you rather be with him?"

"I don't know. I never thought much about what being with God would be like."

"I don't know what to tell you about your friends, Alan," I said. "I don't know what happens to people like them. But I know that God knows. And I also know that he knows what is best, and that he will be completely fair and just and loving in everything he does. We're not supposed to know everything about him. And where we don't know, we can trust him to do whatever is best."

There was a long silence.

"Well, I do reckon there's a lot of sense in what you're saying," he said at last. "And the way you put it, a person'd be a fool not to want to know God better, especially if it's all you say it is."

"Oh, it is," I said, "and even more."

"Well then, how do you get to be Jesus' friend, like you said? How do you get to believing him like you talked about, you know—with him in your heart and all that? What do you have to do?"

"Just pray to him," I said, "and tell him you want to be his friend, and that you *want* him to live inside you."

"That's all . . . ain't nothing more to it than that?"

"That's all."

"Sounds too simple."

"It is simple. All it takes is someone who wants to be friends with Jesus, because he's more anxious to live with us and help us through life than we can even imagine. It's just that most folks don't want his company."

"Well, maybe it's high time I quit being that way myself. So you just go ahead and tell me what I gotta do."

"Just pray to him and tell him just what you're telling me. He'll do the rest. Would you like me to pray for you?"

"Would you? I'd be much obliged."

I closed my eyes and put my arm around Alan's shoulder. "Lord," I prayed, "I thank you for leading my steps here to my new friend, Alan Smith. I ask you to come into his heart and be his friend, and to live with him for the rest of his days. Take care of him, Lord Jesus. Heal him of these wounds he got today. Make him strong again, and protect him throughout the rest of this war. And most of all, show him what you are like. Show him how much you love him. And make every little part of his life such that he'll want to share it all with you. Thank you, Lord, for giving us *both* your life and your love inside us. Amen."

I looked over at Alan. His eyes were still closed, but I could see a tear or two escaping out from under the lids. I knew that he had indeed opened his heart to the presence of Jesus. *Oh, Father, I breathed silently, thank you . . . thank you so much for this dear new life!*

When I opened my eyes again, Alan was looking at me, a bright smile on his rough, dirty, unshaven face.

CHAPTER 22

THE MORNING AFTER

From their advantage on top of Cemetery Ridge, the Union army had held their line together, repelling the enormous wave of Confederate troops. The fighting had been so fierce, and the day so hot and still, that the smoke from the guns and the dust from fifty thousand human and hoofed feet clung in the air like a vapor from the pits of hell, burning the eyes and choking the lungs . . . and smelling of death.

Eventually the Confederate charge began to break down. The formations fell apart. The tight assault, designed to break the Union line in half, frayed and splintered. And before the afternoon was over, thousands of gray-uniformed southerners began drifting back down the long slope, not in outright retreat but in a slow return to their position of the morning.

The Union army made no attempt to follow them down the hill to try to turn its victory into a slaughter. They had successfully beaten back the supreme effort Lee's army could muster, and they were satisfied with the victory. Besides, they were exhausted, too, and were content just to see the enemy backing away down the hill.

Lee's invasion of the North had been stopped, right there on Cemetery Ridge, during those two hours of fighting. Philadelphia and Washington, D.C., were safe from the Confederate army!

Behind the line, Union General Meade rode forward from his headquarters and was told that his soldiers had won a great victory. For a moment it looked as though he were going to give a huge shout of triumph. But then he simply took off his hat and said quietly, "Thank God!"

A mile away to the west, General Lee rode among the men of Pickett's Corps who had made the charge, trying to encourage them, telling them that he was proud of their efforts, and adding, "It is all my fault."

Probably one of the most poignant and ironic moments of all came not far from where we'd been. After most of the fighting had stopped, and after all the Confederate soldiers under General Armistead had either retreated, been killed, or taken prisoner, Union medics found the southern general himself, barely alive, lying amid the dead on the battlefield. He had only the strength left to whisper a last message for them to take to his old friend Hancock before he died. Not yet knowing his friend's fate, General Hancock himself had been carried from the field bleeding from his wound, but he would survive to serve his country again.

Though the Confederate army had been defeated in their attempt, and was certainly crippled, it was far from broken. The Union army had lost nearly as many men, and the Rebels were ready to take the battle of Gettysburg into a fourth day if the Yankees tried to attack. They had failed in their own attack, but they were still confident they could smash any offensive General Meade might try.

It was evening when we arrived back in town at the church—exhausted, dirty, bloody . . . and silent. We had seen things no human being ought to see. We had been part of something God never intended the humans of his creation to do—fighting and killing one another.

It was a day none of us would ever forget . . . *could* ever forget!

As night fell, ending July 3, it was silent in every direction in the fields surrounding Gettysburg. But none of us knew whether there might not be still more fighting to be resumed the next day.

My thoughts were nearly entirely occupied with trying to make Sister Janette comfortable. My heart had been turned inside-out and upside-down so many times in the last two days that I scarcely was thinking now, just going through the motions of doing what had to be done. Everyone was concerned about Sister Janette, yet there were so many others to look after, too, that most of the nuns kept busy with the soldiers—redressing wounds, feeding, washing, taking water around. I remained mostly at Sister Janette's side. Whenever she regained consciousness, even if only for a moment, I wanted to be there to hear what she might say or to get anything for her she might want.

Shortly after dark a man suddenly strode into the church. His boots echoed heavily on the wood floor, and every head immediately turned in his direction. His gray uniform immediately identified him as a Confederate officer.

"We're pulling out, men!" he called out. "All of you that can travel, wagons'll be coming through town for you in less than an hour."

"We surrendering, Captain?" asked one of the wounded.

"No, we ain't surrendering!" he shot back angrily. "We're just getting you men out of here and back to Virginia."

A few whoops and hollers sounded at the mention of their home state, but mostly it remained quiet. The captain turned and left as quickly as he had come.

About forty minutes later, the sounds of several wagons approached along the street outside. They had been combing through the fields for wounded, and had already stopped at the tent hospital nearby, so a good many men had been loaded up. Half a dozen men walked in with stretchers and began transporting the wounded out of the church. We helped those who could walk or hobble. In half an hour the place was nearly deserted, and the wagons disappeared down the street and out of town to the west. Only three men remained, all unconscious, whom the medics didn't expect to live. I didn't know then what happened to all the dead, though I hardly wondered about it at the time.

All through that night, General Lee pulled his men together from their scattered positions—those around the town who had fought for Culp's Hill, Longstreet's Corps down at the peach orchard and Devil's Den opposite the Little Round Top. Most of the night Confederate wagons began making their way toward the South Mountain gaps before swinging south for the crossing over the Potomac.

The next day dawned quiet. It was July 4. But it was a somber and dreadful national anniversary. No one was thinking happy thoughts.

I went out early for a walk. I wouldn't have dared to do so the day before, but something about this day was different. There was a stillness you could not only hear, but could *feel*. The troops who had been around for a day or two as part of Ewell's Corps were all gone. A lot of the southern wounded had been taken, and their wagons were now far away. Smoke from a few fires still rose quietly into the warm morning air. Outside of town, a tent village for the wounded showed signs of activity.

I walked south, along the very road we had taken yesterday. The only soldiers I saw now were dressed in the dark blue of the Union army, but they didn't pay much attention to me.

As awful as the previous day had been, there was something even worse about what I saw that morning. The farther from town I went, the greater were the indescribable horrors—dead horses and dead men lying everywhere, some of them barefoot, their boots pulled off by survivors in desperate need of new footwear. Now I knew what had been done with all the dead—nothing! Bodies clad in both blue and gray were strewn everywhere.

There would probably be huge mass graves dug, and townspeople and medics and church people and the soldiers themselves would all eventually come to remove the evidence of battle—corpses and broken wagons and shattered weapons and discarded supplies. But for now, on this morning so soon after the smoke had settled, all the horrible scars of destruction and violence and death lay everywhere for all eyes to see.

As I was gazing out over a field into the distance, my careless steps stumbled, and I nearly fell. I pulled my eyes back in front of me and looked down. I had nearly toppled right onto a corpse.

Aghast, I stepped back, but not before I saw the dreadful look of the dead boy's eyes staring straight up at me. A look of anguished fear remained on his face, caught there and preserved at the very moment of death! I would never get it out of my mind as long as I lived. I felt as though he were looking at me, from the other side of the curtain of death, still asking—asking me!—what all the nonsense of killing was supposed to be about, asking why *he* had had to die.

Suddenly my stomach churned. Choking, and my eyes stinging with tears, I backed away from the body, then turned and began to run. Faster and faster I flew, and ran the entire distance back to the church, crying all the way.

CHAPTER 23

THE TRAIN AGAIN

The fighting did not resume.

Most of that time the two great armies watched each other warily, each wondering if the other was going to attack. Neither did. The Confederates half expected Meade to come after them, but when he didn't, Lee finally made the decision to call off his hoped-for invasion and to retreat back into northern Virginia. He gave the order, his army began the long retreat the way they had come, and General Meade followed at a distance. Lee was still dangerous, and Meade wanted to make sure the general did indeed go back to Virginia.

The great battle of Gettysburg was over. Lee had tried to invade the North and had failed. But he had also made good his escape, even if in defeat.

Those of us from the Convent of John Seventeen remained another two days in Gettysburg. By then Sister Janette had recovered sufficiently to travel, although she remained very weak.

Gettysburg was the bloodiest battle of the whole war. Over 50,000 men were killed—23,000 from the North, 28,000 from the South! The dead lay everywhere surrounding the town. And once the armies departed, the 2,400 inhabitants were left with ten times that number of wounded to do their best to care for. The wounded were brought into homes, even as graves were being dug for the dead, and the town's churches did even more than they had been able to do during the fighting to help care for them. Carpets and walls and floorboards and blankets and pillows and books used for pillows—all were saturated with blood! The U.S. Sanitary

Commission, for whom I'd helped raise money at the start of the war, sent in doctors and nurses and supplies to help with the effort, too. They erected many more tents outside town, which eventually relieved the burden on the townspeople.

Several of the sisters, including the two who were nurses, remained behind in Gettysburg. But now that General Lee's invasion had been stopped, I felt I ought to continue on to Washington. And I did not want to leave Sister Janette's side. We again spent the night in East Prospect, and then arrived back at the convent late the following day.

Whatever my future held as far as marriage or being single, becoming a nun or joining a convent, writing or not writing, of one thing I *was* certain. I needed to continue on to see President Lincoln before anything. It was for that reason I had come, and I had to follow through. He had asked for my help with the war effort, and now more than ever I wanted to do whatever I could.

Now I had been part of what the Sanitary Commission did and saw how valuable and necessary their work was in caring for the wounded. I had seen firsthand where the money raised for the Sanitary Fund went. And if I could help with that again, perhaps I could do more good in that way than I'd been able to do with actual bandages and medicine in my hands.

Four days later, therefore, I found myself back on the train and again heading northeastward toward Harrisburg, where I could connect with another train to take me south to the nation's capital.

What an unbelievable three weeks it had been since I'd met Sister Janette on the train and decided to get off with her and visit the convent!

It would be a long time before I'd know which had effected my life the most—my talks with her, being with the Sisters of Unity, or witnessing the battle of Gettysburg. How could I ever be the same again? All three experiences had enlarged the world of my mind. Never had I encountered so many new things to think about in such a short time.

I sat in the train all that first day, staring blankly out the window, unable to focus my thoughts. All the enthusiasm and jubilation of the earlier part of my journey was gone. I felt very isolated and alone. A huge dark cloud settled over my spirit, and I couldn't get out from under its oppression. I had felt so cared for, so safe, so at home with the sisters at the convent. Why I hadn't felt lonely before meeting Sister Janette I didn't know. Nothing had changed. This had been my plan all along. Yet now that I *had* met her, met them all—everything was different. I had left a part of myself behind, a piece of my heart. And now I didn't feel altogether whole because a part of me had remained with them.

Even the thought of seeing President Lincoln was no longer exciting in the same way. What is meeting the President of the United States alongside a friendship that stirs deep bonds of attachment and love inside your heart? I felt as if I'd left home all over again. In fact, I felt more sadness in my spirit now than I had felt leaving Miracle Springs.

I pulled from my pocket a small silver cross the sister had given me the night before. It was a simple little token of friendship, yet merely holding it in my palm and gazing on it with my eyes sent stabs of painful longing deep into my heart.

I turned it over. There on the reverse, in letters so tiny I could just barely make them out, were the words: Sisters of Unity, New Providence, Pennsylvania. I read them over and over, three more times. Would this, I wondered almost wistfully, one day be my home too? Why did I feel such a longing to remain there at the convent? Was it their life of dedication to Jesus that had penetrated so deeply into my soul, or merely the friendship of other young women whose spirits hungered for the same kind of life I did?

Perhaps it had to do with what had taken place at Gettysburg. Perhaps what I felt was a melancholy lingering from Jennie Wade's death and watching Sister Janette fall to the ground with a bullet in her shoulder—seeing the face of death so close all around me.

Whatever the reason, part of me didn't want to be on this train anymore. I wanted to turn around and go back . . . back to the convent . . . even all the way back to Miracle Springs.

But I knew I couldn't turn around. I had to finish what I'd started out to do.

Sister Janette's final words of parting came back to me. "You will always have a home here with us, Corrie," she had said. "And you will always occupy a special place in my own heart. You are a dear friend. I thank God for allowing our paths to cross, and I shall pray for the day when I see you once more."

I looked out the window at the passing countryside. Everything seemed gray and dreary. I tried to take in a deep breath, but it was no use. I choked on the very air, and my eyes filled with tears of sadness.

CHAPTER 24

WASHINGTON, D.C.

I arrived at the Capital early in the afternoon. The station was in the center of town. I left my bags there and walked straight to the White House.

There were soldiers and guards all around, I suppose on account of the war and the danger there could be to the President. Something was going on, but I couldn't make out what. There seemed to be an unusual amount of scurrying around, and then all of a sudden I saw three policemen come out of a gate holding on to a handcuffed man. They shoved him into a waiting enclosed carriage, got in after him, and the driver called to the two horses, and they lurched off down the street.

Once all the hubbub had settled, I remembered what I was doing there. I asked one of the guards in front near one of the fences surrounding the grounds where the gate was where I could get in. He gave me a funny look, but then directed me around to the side.

I walked around toward where he had pointed and came to a gate where there were even more guards. People were coming and going into the grounds. It was the same gate the three policemen had just come out of. There was a little guardhouse where two men with guns were in charge of opening and shutting the gate and letting people go through, and there still was quite a bit of activity and bustle after the incident I had just witnessed.

I walked up to the men standing in front of the guardhouse. "I would like to see Mr. Lincoln," I said.

One of the men eyed me carefully, then answered roughly,

120

"Beat it, little girl. No one sees the President, especially not to-day."

"But I've—"

"Scram, you hear me!"

He made a menacing move toward me and I immediately backed away. There was enough of a crowd around that I quickly found myself surrounded by people and moving away from the gate. But after a minute or two I stopped and glanced back at the man who had spoken so harshly to me.

He was still watching me—and not with a friendly look, either. I was sick inside. What was I going to do?

I turned again and stumbled along, following the leisurely crowd of people wandering around the White House. My mind was swimming. I didn't know what to do. Maybe there was another entrance, somebody else I could talk to. I kept moving along the walkway, eventually walking around the entire perimeter of the White House grounds, until I found myself back at the guard-house. There was that same mean-looking man standing there, holding a rifle!

I walked away again, this time back in the general direction of the train station. I didn't have anywhere else to go, though what I intended to do there, I'm not sure. I wanted to run away and hide, to get on the first westbound train and go back to the convent in Pennsylvania.

I felt so alone and so foolish. What had I thought, that I would just walk up to the White House and walk in as if it were the house next door? How could I have been so naive? That was where the President of the United States lived! Who was I to think I could just walk up and knock on the door? He probably wouldn't remember me at all. He probably wrote nice notes like that to hundreds of people, never expecting them to do anything so outlandish as actually come to the White House and try to see him! It was all so clear now! He had never intended me to visit him at all. It was just his way of being nice and expressing his gratitude, and I had misunderstood the whole thing by thinking of it as an actual invitation.

Oh, I felt like such a stupid fool! I had come all this way for nothing! And what was I to do now? I was three thousand miles from California. I didn't even know where home was anymore! What should I do?

If a train had been available right then to take me back where I'd come from, I would have bought a ticket and boarded it at once. I was so discouraged I could not even think clearly! But after checking the schedule, I found that there *weren't* any trains leaving until the next day. So I would be stuck in Washington at least overnight. I'd have to find someplace to stay, and then I'd leave the city the following afternoon.

I retrieved my bags and asked the man behind the window about boardinghouses nearby. He told me of one just down the street and around the corner.

"You want me to get you a cab, ma'am?" he asked.

"Yes . . . yes, I suppose so. Thank you," I replied.

He signaled to one of the boys around the place, and when a twelve- or thirteen-year-old boy ran up to take me to where a horse-drawn cab was waiting, I couldn't help thinking of the first time I saw Robin O'Flaridy in the lobby of the Oriental Hotel. This little fellow had exactly Robin's flair and manner. He led me to the cab with all the confidence of a street-wise grown man, and when I gave him a quarter as I climbed into the carriage, he flashed me a bright smile, kissed the coin, and ran back inside the station.

Ten minutes later I was inside the boardinghouse making arrangements for the night.

The lady whose house it was wasn't as friendly as either Miss Baxter or Miss Bean, and the house wasn't as clean or as nice either. She looked me over a minute, as if wondering why I would want a room. Finally she agreed to let me stay the night, acting as if she were doing *me* a favor. She took me to the room and told me that dinner, if I wanted it, was served promptly at six o'clock.

"Don't be late," she added. "I don't have time to be keeping things warm or serving any longer than I have to."

And with those words she shut the door behind me and I found myself alone. I set my bags down on the floor and glanced around. The room was small and plain, and from the looks of it I judged that mostly men stayed here. It wasn't very clean, and not at all homey. The blanket on the bed was a plain, drab olive green, and the curtains on the windows were so faded and threadbare they looked as if they'd been up for fifteen years.

I walked to the window and pulled back the curtain. Dust fell from it and settled to the sill. Outside, the only view was the back of the station, train tracks, and parked train cars. I hadn't needed the cab. I could have walked from the station.

I turned again back to the room. As I took everything in, the room was even smaller and uglier than I had first realized. I sighed, thinking to myself that I ought to try to make the best of a bad situation.

But my heart wasn't really in it, and before I knew it I had flopped across the bed and was crying from sheer loneliness.

CHAPTER 25

A LONELY DAY

I didn't have the energy or desire to make use of the rest of the day to see anything in the city. All I could think of was getting out and away from there!

I cried for a while, then fell asleep. When I woke up my stark surroundings seemed even more dingy than they had earlier. I got up off the bed and washed my face, put on some fresh clothes, and went out for a walk, hoping that would raise my spirits.

But it didn't.

I just walked around for a while in the vicinity of the train station. It was not a pretty part of the city. I should have taken a cab to see some of the buildings and monuments, but I just didn't have the heart to go back toward the Capitol or White House. Anything, though, would have been better than the smelly slaughterhouses and sooty brick buildings where I found myself. There were even what looked to have been slave-auctioning platforms, now in disuse. I was too depressed in my own thoughts to be afraid, although perhaps I should have been. The people I passed looked none too friendly.

I forced myself to look into people's faces. Once you saw someone's eyes, really saw *into* them, and knew they had seen you as well, people usually stopped seeming so fearsome. I began to see in the faces of people I didn't know a look that I can only describe as *vulnerable*. I could see that they were lonely, sometimes sad, but in deeper ways than they wanted others to detect. When I caught their eyes, some smiled, but others sort of stared right through me, and I saw the aloneness. They could cover and shield and guard their inner selves in the way they walked or dressed or spoke or conducted themselves. But not in their eyes. Once I made contact there, even if only for a second, it was like a window opened into a deeper part of their being.

At times my heart went out to such people, and I found myself wanting to touch them with more than just a look, just a passing glance, or just a brief smile. Yet I didn't know what to do. How do you touch another person, someone you don't even know, when all you're doing is passing by for a second or two? I found myself wondering how it was when Jesus caught people's eyes? What did he do, what did he say to them?

And then in the midst of my thoughts, a stab of renewed pain went through my heart. I was lonely, too. I was vulnerable and exposed and isolated, just like everyone else.

The sad melancholy I had felt before deepened all the more. I was almost glad for the rain that started pouring down. It fit the dreary loneliness of my mood perfectly, and the drops falling down over my face helped to hide the fresh tears spilling from my eyes.

By the time I reached the boardinghouse again, I was soaked nearly to the skin. I just had time to change into dry clothes before making my appearance in the dining room a minute or two after six.

"I told you six, prompt, young lady," said the landlady abruptly.

"I'm sorry," I said. "I'm afraid I got caught in the rain."

"Makes no never mind to me what happened. Just don't be late again."

"I won't be here tomorrow," I said. "I'm leaving town on tomorrow's train."

"Just as well," said the woman grumpily, serving a plate with potatoes and a slice of meat and handing it to me. She certainly didn't seem very appreciative of having my room occupied! All the other guests were men. No one said a word throughout the whole meal except one of them, who seemed as if he just might have a bit of friendliness to him.

"Don't be too hard on her, Marge," he said, giving me a smile. "Can't you see she's new in town?"

"I got my rules, Mac," she replied to him, no more friendly

in spite of the fact that they obviously knew each other. "They've got to apply to young ladies traveling through where maybe they oughtn't to be, just as well as to you working men. Besides, how I treat my guests is my own affair, so keep your nose out of it."

"I'm your guest too, Marge," he said, grinning at one of the other men.

"If you don't like the service, Mac," she grumbled, "then find yourself another place!"

Mac apparently thought better of any further exchange with the surly landlady, and his momentary speaking out on my behalf didn't lead to any more friendliness on his part. He and the other men continued to fill themselves with enormous quantities of Marge's bland dinner. She served them all seconds, and scarcely another word around the table was said. She took no more notice of me and offered me nothing further, although I had trouble enough finishing even the meager first portion. Finally I excused myself and went back to my room.

It was too early to go to bed, but I was too depressed to do much of anything else. I lay down on the bed and cried some more. All I could think of were the people I loved so dearly and missed so painfully.

Under normal circumstances, the people around the edges of our lives come and go, and we hardly notice. Then suddenly when we're lonely, they all come back into our memories, making us aware of the huge tapestry of relationships into which our lives have been woven.

Of all people, I found myself thinking of Mr. Ashton at the Mine and Freight office, missing his smile and kind, "Good morning, Corrie," he always greeted me with. Even more surprising, I thought of Mr. Royce. It would be wonderful even to see *him* right now! I'd probably give him a huge hug and scare him half out of his wits! Robin O'Flaridy . . . Mr. Kemble . . . Patrick Shaw . . . the Wards . . . oh, and dear Marcus Weber! I would have traded everything I owned right then for just a glimpse of any one of them! I felt so alone, so far away!

I thought of the sisters at the convent. I wondered how Sister Janette was doing, and if she was up and around again, if her shoulder hurt. I would see them all again . . . and soon! They weren't so far away, and it didn't hurt quite so deeply to imagine all the faces at the convent. I would get back on the train tomorrow, and before another two days were gone, I *would* be with them again. This time I would stay as long as I pleased! I would relish being with them, sharing life with them, and working alongside them. Maybe there would be another barn raising! I could help with their garden and the animals and other work around the convent. And such talks we would have!

There was so much I wanted to ask them about their life, to find out if it was the kind of life I wanted to live. Oh, I did want to be not just God's daughter but his woman! Completely his . . . married to him . . . devoted to him . . . serving him with all my life and everything I did!

Perhaps the convent was the place for me to begin. Perhaps I would stay . . . for a time. If I didn't become a nun exactly, well . . . maybe I could be *like* a nun! Were there such things as *Protestant* nuns? I didn't know, but I could find out! They probably weren't called nuns. But whatever they were called, that's what I would become—a woman devoted in service to God in every way, with time to pray and to read and study and contemplate everything about my Father in heaven.

And then I would write . . . yes, I would keep writing, and would write not just newspaper articles and stories but about my life of devotion to God.

I closed my eyes, and images started to crowd into my mind. My thoughts were racing now—with the faces of everyone I knew. I could even hear their voices, but couldn't exactly tell what they were saying. Everybody seemed to be saying something different, calling to me, urging me to do something . . . but I couldn't tell quite what.

Corrie . . . Corrie . . . I thought I heard them calling, but then as soon as my name faded from their lips, the words all became jumbled and confused, as if they were speaking in a foreign language. But it wasn't a foreign language! They were speaking English, and I knew the words, but I couldn't understand what they were saying.

Of course . . . that was the problem! They were all speaking at once, and so all the multitude of words tumbled over each other, confusing and garbling everything. There were too many voices, too many people calling my name, trying to say things to me.

Why wouldn't they all just speak one at a time? Why didn't they stop shouting and interrupting each other so I could make out their words? If only they would just slow down a little! I could see their lips moving . . . I could hear the words . . . they just didn't quite make sense. The meaning was so close . . . I could almost—if I could just listen a little more intently. . . .

"Corrie . . . Corrie . . ." The voice was distant, almost in a wail, as if calling me to come back from someplace far away.

Suddenly Mr. Ashton's face loomed huge right in front of me. He had been calling to me. "Corrie . . . Corrie," I heard him say again, "Corrie . . . you're late for work . . . there's an order that has to be written up for Chase and Baxter in Colfax."

"I . . . I'll . . ." I struggled to find the words to tell him I was on my way to the office, but the words wouldn't come.

Even as I was trying to answer him, all of a sudden there was Mr. Kemble. His voice was even more insistent. "Corrie . . . you've got to get in here to talk to me about . . ."

But his voice faded away, and I couldn't hear him finish. I opened my mouth to try to say something, but then it was Sister Janette's voice speaking softly to me.

"Corrie . . . Corrie," she said, "you have to stay here with us."

Over and over came the words: *"stay here with us . . . stay here with us . . . come, Corrie, stay here with us . . . don't leave . . . don't go away . . . come back, stay here with us . . . come back, Corrie . . . come back . . . come back. . . ."*

The words began to fade. I tried desperately to cling to the sound of Sister Janette's voice. As it drifted into the distance, a terrible pang of loss stabbed through my heart. Suddenly Jennie Wade's pretty young face appeared! She opened her mouth to speak, but no words were there. A look of pain instantly came into her eyes, but then they slowly closed. She was dying!

"Jennie . . . Jennie!" I tried to cry out, but my mouth opened with the same silent impotence as hers. I could feel my lips moving, but they were mute and soundless. *Jennie . . . no . . . Jennie, don't die. . . !* But they were only thoughts, not words. I could not make her hear me! Oh, dear God . . . horror of horrors! All of a sudden, a tiny red splotch appeared on Jennie' s forehead, just above her left eye! It grew in size, and began to drip down over her eyebrow into her eye. *God . . . oh, God . . . no!*

I tried to look away, but could not move my head! Then Jennie's face faded away, along with Sister Janette's . . . and in another second both were gone.

The faces from the battlefield began to haunt me—young Alan Smith in dark blue and Lt. Tomlinson in his red-stained gray . . . all the faces in the church, and the men I'd seen lying on the ground . . . passing through my memory in a second or two. I seemed to relive every moment of the awfulness of Gettysburg. Then before me was the grotesque face of the dead soldier I'd stumbled over the day after the battle, his eyes wide open, staring into my heart, though I knew he was dead and could see nothing!

God, take away the memory of that face! I tried to cry out, I tried to pray, I tried to run, but I couldn't move. I could feel the dead soldier's body against my feet. I tried to step over him . . . I tried to turn around, to get away . . . but it was useless! Suddenly I felt myself stumbling and starting to fall . . . I fell and fell . . . tumbling down and down . . . falling right on top of the hideous corpse!

But as I fell, all of a sudden there I was in my bed back at the house in Miracle Springs, and the next thing I heard were the playful musical voices of my brothers and sisters. They were young again! There they all were—Zack, Emily, Becky, and Tad—calling to me, trying to get me out of bed, urging me to get up and play with them.

"Corrie . . . Corrie . . . get up!" they all cried in unison. "The sun's been in the sky for hours. Come play with us, Corrie . . . please, get up . . . come . . . what's the matter, Corrie? . . . why won't you come with us? . . . come back, Corrie. . . ."

Tad was so young, and Zack was still a boy with a high-pitched voice, and Becky was giggling in her happiest way, and Emily was still young and innocent. All four were imploring me to join them, tugging at my arms and legs. But I couldn't get out of bed. And try as I might, I couldn't answer them, though my heart was filled with such longings of love that I couldn't stand it.

Then another voice intruded over the din, and from behind them I heard Pa approaching.

"Come on now, Corrie Belle," he said. "You've been away from us too long . . . I know you got lots of notions and ideas in that writer's mind of yours, but it's high time you came back to the real world where your family—"

Oh, Pa . . . Pa . . . I want to come back! I tried to say.

His tender face was looking over me now, full in my mind's eye. Oh, how dearly I loved him! What a good man! How thankful I was that God had given him back to me!

"Come, Corrie . . . I tell you, it's time you was back where you belong—"

His voice was interrupted by a sound from the room.

"Hee . . . hee . . . hee . . . tell her we ain't gonna put up with her gallivanting much longer . . . tell her that from Alkali, Drum, hee, hee, hee!"

Still Pa's face loomed before me. He had tears in his eyes . . . and I knew they were there because he loved me.

Pa . . . Pa . . . I love . . . I love—

But I couldn't get the words out. I loved him, but I couldn't make him hear . . . I couldn't make him understand!

His face began to grow pale and distant.

Pa, please . . . don't go away, Pa . . . don't leave me again. Pa, I want to come back . . . help me, I don't know which way to go . . . Pa. . . .

The next voice I heard was soothing and comforting.

"The Lord is with you, Corrie." It was a man's voice . . . it was Avery Rutledge!

Oh, Rev. Rutledge. I've . . . I've been away, and I don't know what the Lord wants me—

"Yes, Corrie, I know all about it. He has heard your prayers, and you need have no worries."

But . . . but I don't know what he wants me to do . . . there's so much I don't understand, and—

"He will make sure you know when the time comes."

But . . . but I—

Suddenly Almeda was at my bedside, sitting beside me, stroking my forehead. I could still hear the children clamoring outside for me to join them, but a great sigh of relief washed through my whole being at Almeda's soft voice.

"There, there, Corrie," she said tenderly, "I am here now. You've been ill . . . your mind has been wandering. . . ."

Oh, Almeda . . . it was so dreadful . . . there were boys younger than Zack . . . they were dying all around me!

"It's all right now, Corrie. Dr. Shoemaker says the fever has passed, and that you will be yourself again in twenty-four hours."

It was so awful . . . I didn't know if I'd . . . oh, Almeda, I was so afraid . . . so lonely . . . I missed you so much. . . .

"Yes, dear. You were talking in your sleep about the train and the nuns and a battle you were in, and about someone named Jennie—"

Oh, Almeda . . . it was so awful . . . there was so much blood and death!

"Just relax, Corrie . . . everything will be all right now. It was all a dreadful dream . . . from the fever. You are with us again now . . . you are with us . . . you don't ever need to leave us again."

I started to cry. *Thank you . . . thank you! You can't imagine how alone I felt! I wanted to be with you so much!*

"But you are not alone now. I am here with you, dear Corrie."

She stretched out her arms to embrace me. Her touch felt so warm and good. I was still crying, for sheer joy, to feel Almeda's arms around me.

I struggled to lift my own arms from the bed. I had tried so desperately to speak to everyone else who had come into my mind. But I hadn't been able to open my mouth . . . I hadn't been able to move . . . I had been powerless and silent.

But now, with a groaning of agony, I forced myself to raise my arms. Slowly I felt them leave my side. I stretched them upward and encircled Almeda's waist, returning her warm embrace.

It felt so good to have her there at my bedside, to send the dark cloud of loneliness away with her loving presence.

I squeezed her tightly, crying freely now for joy. But why wouldn't she return the pressure? I felt her arms around me and her hands on my back, but they seemed weak and limp.

A sudden chill swept through my body. Why was I suddenly

so cold? But . . . but . . . of course, that was the reason . . .
Almeda's arms had grown cold . . . that was what I felt.

I hugged her tightly, but then felt her arms fall from around
me lifelessly. I glanced up into her face.

Oh, God . . . God . . . no!

It wasn't Almeda's face at all! My arms were clutched around
Jennie's cold, dead body, where she lay, eyes closed, in a wooden
coffin somewhere.

I tried to jump back, aghast. But once again I couldn't move.
My arms were locked in an embrace around the corpse that had
once contained the life of young Jennie Wade!

But my head did move. I glanced to the right and left. All
around me, stretching for as far as I could see in every direction,
lay coffins . . . coffins . . . with the bodies of the dead. . . .

With sickening horror I realized I knew every face! There were
the soldiers—Smith and Tomlinson, the lieutenant, with the
sword that had killed him sticking morbidly out of his body . . .
there was the dead face with open eyes . . . *Oh, God, no it can't
be!* . . . there lay Sister Janette! She had died from the wound in
her shoulder!

I shut my eyes and tried to scream. I couldn't look at another
single coffin—it was too terrifying. I was afraid that in one of them
I'd see my own face, and that the moment my eyes fell upon it
. . . I'd be dead.

I squeezed my eyes shut, but could not stop the flow of tears.
Still my arms clung to the cold body in the coffin. I could not pull
them away.

I felt tears pouring out from under my closed lids and falling
down onto the body beneath me.

Some inner compulsion forced my eyes to open. But I
squeezed them tight . . . I didn't want to look!

The cold was now beyond endurance. My arms felt as though
they were wrapped around an iceberg. Slowly my eyes opened.

There, just inches from my face, my arms about the body her
soul had once called home, was the white, pale, dead face of my
mother.

Oh, Ma! I wailed in forlorn and bitter agony.

The cry of my own voice woke me suddenly. I jumped up with

a start, glancing around wildly in the middle of the darkened room. My lungs were heaving, my body drenched with sweat. My arms were clasped around a pillow that was wet from my weeping.

For five or six seconds I stared into the darkness, bewildered and disoriented. As wakefulness gradually stole back over me, I remembered where I was.

The reality was nearly as bad as the dream. For with the return of consciousness the acrid reality of my aloneness returned as well. I slumped back onto the pillow and wept once more.

CHAPTER 26

NIGHTTIME THOUGHTS

Sleep did not return for a long while.

I cried, at first from the renewed despondency of finding myself again so far removed from all those I loved, and then for a while from nothing more than a sorrowful sadness over my plight and the disappointment of the day before. Then I relived my dream, trying to sort through everything it caused me to think about. It was a long, dark night.

I didn't have any idea what time it was, but finally I crawled off the bed. I was still wearing my clothes from the previous evening. I felt around for a match, lit the kerosene lantern, and once again beheld my dingy little quarters. The dress I had worn in the rain still hung damp over the wardrobe door. Outside I heard the continuing sounds of rainfall.

Slowly I undressed and changed into my bedclothes, then lay back down. Somehow the dream and the crying had taken my loneliness through the deepest valley of despair. And now as my tears began to dry, I found myself taking a few deep breaths of air, and with them drawing in the first breeze of a reviving hope.

I turned the wet pillow over, then stretched out on my back, staring up at the ceiling. I was here, I thought. I couldn't leave just yet. The soonest I could leave would be tomorrow afternoon. Why not at least try again to make the best of it? Even if I missed tomorrow's train, what would be the real harm to me? If worse came to worst and I had to remain another night, I could endure the sour disposition of the landlady through one more mealtime. And I'd be sure to be on time!

She was lonely too, I thought. Lonely and growing old . . . her husband was probably dead, or maybe she'd never married at all. What business did I have to be so absorbed in my own self-pity that I would ignore one of God's children in such obvious need of graciousness and love as this lady?

I determined that I *would* stay another day, and that I *would* find an opportunity to return the landlady's grumpiness with as much good cheer as I could muster! Maybe I *was* homesick, but that was no excuse for not doing what Jesus told me to do. And he said to do good and be kind and to treat others as I wanted to be treated. So I would make an effort to do just that tomorrow . . . at the first opportunity that presented itself, which would be at breakfast. I would be there at 7:29, with a smile and a kind word for every one of her cranky ones!

After that . . . well, who could tell? I would determine to make it a better day than the one just past. Even if circumstances didn't go right—even if they all went miserably—I would make it a better day by my attitude toward it. I would be thankful for all things that came my way, for every person who crossed my path, and for every word that was spoken to me!

I found myself thinking about the White House again and what had happened there. I don't suppose I should have expected anything different. Who was I, anyway, to be given an audience with President Abraham Lincoln? But, I thought further, *had* I indeed mistaken his meaning? I had been so sure that coming to Washington was what I was supposed to do. Where had I misunderstood?

I jumped off the bed, went to my suitcase, and pulled out the letter. I opened it and read it again, though I hardly know why—I'd already read it enough times to have memorized it ten times over!

MISS CORNELIA BELLE HOLLISTER,

   I have been made aware of all your work for the Republican party on behalf of my election, as well as your efforts to raise money for our Union forces in this present conflict. I want to express my deepest appreciation on behalf of the nation, to tell you that your patriotism has not gone unnoticed. It would be my pleasure to meet you here at the White House in Washington, if circumstances would permit you to make the journey. I would very much like to give you my personal hand of gratitude, as well as ask you to help me in the war effort with a new project here in Washington.

Yours sincerely,
A. LINCOLN
President

How *could* there be a mistake? What could I possibly have misread about his words? *It would be my pleasure to meet you here at the White House. . . . I would very much like to give you my personal hand of gratitude . . . as well as ask you to help. . . .* Surely, if the man at the White House gate knew what the President had said, he would realize his mistake.

I had to try again! I wouldn't be so easily discouraged this time. I would tell them that I was *supposed* to see Mr. Lincoln . . . that he'd invited me. How could everyone around the grounds be expected to know everything the President said or did? I should have expected them to turn me away. I had been completely unprepared. But I wouldn't be next time.

Making a mental resolve is the quickest way out of an emotional valley. Engaging your will and deciding to *do* something, however small a thing it may be, is the surest method for battling feelings of discouragement. And now that I'd decided upon two things I was going to *do* the next morning—smile and be nice to the landlady, and go back to the White House—I felt a great deal better.

I still didn't know what I'd do the day after tomorrow. But one day was enough to worry about, and usually paved the way well enough for the next.

It was probably only an hour or two before dawn, but with a considerably lighter heart, I finally fell asleep.

CHAPTER 27

THE WHITE HOUSE AGAIN

The next morning, despite the rough night and lack of sleep, I appeared in the dining room at 7:28. The other men were already there. A couple of them nodded at me as I entered. We sat down, and the lady called Marge served us. There wasn't much more conversation than the previous evening, but I tried to smile whenever I could catch anyone's eye.

When I was through, as the men were finishing up, I stood, picked up a couple of the dishes from the table, and followed the landlady as she was heading back into the kitchen.

"Would you like some help?"

She hesitated briefly, looked at me from under a suspicious bushy black eyebrow, then replied, "If you want to."

I followed her the rest of the way in, deposited my load on a sideboard, then turned to go back out to the dining room.

"I'll get the rest of them," I said. She didn't reply, but she didn't follow me back out, and when I returned to the kitchen again she had begun washing the other dishes, and let me continue until the men had gone and the table in the dining room was clean.

It was a rather silent affair, but I remained a while longer, found a dish towel, dried the dishes as she washed them, and then finally excused myself.

"If it won't be too much trouble," I said, "I have decided that I would like to remain at least one more night, maybe two."

"Suit yourself," she said. "I got nobody else for the room."

"Oh, thank you," I said. "I'll probably be gone all day," I added.

She said nothing.

"I hope you have a pleasant day," I said. "I'll see you tonight."

I turned and left. It wasn't much of a conversation, I'll admit, but at least I felt better for having tried.

I went back upstairs, got my bonnet, and set off again for the city. Forty minutes later I was approaching the White House. I went straight around to the east gate where I had gone yesterday, greatly relieved *not* to see the man who had been gruff to me before. Two men, both with guns, stood there letting people in and out. It seemed considerably calmer and more orderly than it had been yesterday.

I walked up to them.

"I'm here to see the President," I said as cheerfully as I could.

One of the men stared rather blankly at me, looked over at his partner with the hint of a grin, then back at me.

"The President," he repeated. "President *Lincoln?*"

"Yes," I nodded. "The President."

Again he glanced at his partner, this time with a definite grin. I didn't altogether like his expression.

"She says she wants to see the President," he said, and it was obvious from his tone he was mocking me.

"Look, Miss," said the other man to me, "we can't let just anybody who wants to see the President in here." At least his tone was more friendly.

"Why, there was a crazy man just yesterday who got over the fence, had a gun, and was trying to shoot the President. Luckily we nabbed him in time. But there are constant threats, and protecting him is our job. I'm sorry."

Everything he said made perfect sense, and now I understood what I'd seen yesterday. But as he spoke I found myself forgetting everything I'd planned to say.

"But I've been traveling for a long time, just to see him," I said.

"I'm sorry. Those are our orders. That's why we're here—to *keep* people from getting in."

My face fell. I tried to collect my shattered thoughts so I could think. But before I had much of a chance to, the first man spoke again, and at least he wasn't teasing me anymore.

"How far did you come, Miss?" he asked.

"From California," I answered.

Both men looked at each other with wide expressions of surprise. "That is some distance. We ever had anyone come that far, Joe?" he asked the other guard. "Private citizen, I mean?"

"Not that I can recall."

"Please, I've just got to see him!" I interrupted, suddenly seeing a ray of hope.

"Suppose we ought to tell Hank?" said one of the men.

"Couldn't hurt," replied the one called Joe.

He turned and began walking toward the building behind him, while his partner, acting very nice and friendly now, spoke to me again.

"I'm sorry, Miss. We don't mean to be gruff with you. But with the war on, and with the battles of Gettysburg and Vicksburg just over with, it's been mighty tense around here. Lots of comings and goings—generals and couriers. There have always been lots of warnings of possible danger to the President. But then after yesterday, suddenly everything tensed up a whole lot more. I'm sure you can understand."

"I was at Gettysburg," I said.

"I thought you said you came from California."

"I did. But on the way I was at Gettysburg, right during the battle."

The man looked at me with an expression of mild interest and surprise. But after a couple of seconds, he apparently decided against whatever he had been thinking, and said with finality. "I'm sorry, Miss, but we're under orders not to let *anybody* in without a thorough check."

I nodded.

"We just don't get many visitors from quite as far away as you've come. Most folks write the President first. He does get lots of mail."

"Oh, but I *did* write him!" I said, suddenly remembering the letter.

"Oh?" One of his eyebrows raised slightly. "Did you receive a reply?"

"No," I answered. "I was replying to *him*."

"Who?"

"The President."

"President Lincoln?"

"Yes."

"He wrote *you* a letter?"

"Yes, and my letter was in reply to that, telling him I'd come."

"That you'd come where?"

"Here . . . to visit him, just like he asked."

"The President wrote you, inviting you here . . . for a visit?" By now the man's voice was incredulous.

"Yes, that's why I'm here." I pulled the letter out of my pocket. "Here it is," I said, handing it to the guard.

He didn't look at it long enough to read it, only long enough to see the signature at the bottom.

"Hey, Joe!" he called out to the other man, who was just entering the building across the wide walkway. "Wait a minute . . . come back. I don't think we need to bother Hank about this."

Joe turned and came part of the way back to the guardhouse, while the man I had been talking to thought a moment.

"I think you'd better go call Mr. Hay."

Joe hesitated. "You sure you know what you're doing?"

"I think so. And I think once he meets Miss Hollister here, he's going to ask us why we didn't call him down immediately."

Joe turned and went into the building. When he returned, the other man led me inside to a waiting room, where I sat down. In less than ten minutes I was talking with John Hay, Mr. Lincoln's private secretary. I showed him the letter I had received. He read it over carefully.

"Well, Miss Hollister," he said at last, "you certainly have come a long way to see our President."

"Yes, sir," I replied nervously. "I would have been here sooner—in June, as my letter stated. But I got caught up in the fighting at Gettysburg, and it seemed like the right thing to stay and help out with the wounded."

"Certainly," he said. "We're very grateful for your help." He paused. "We, uh . . . we would like to speak with you, of course, but you must understand—not knowing exactly when you would arrive—it will be a matter of fitting you into the President's schedule."

"Yes . . . I understand."

"And after that terrible business yesterday, things are in a bit of a stir around here. The President is out of town. We got him out of the city to safety immediately, just in case there was a larger plot afoot—there have been some nasty rumors floating about, and we just can't be too cautious about the President's safety."

I nodded.

"He will be out of town, we think, until the day after tomorrow. Might you be available, let me see—"

He glanced down at a notebook in his hand, turning the pages, then pausing.

"The day after that. Friday, that would be . . . how would that work out for you, Miss Hollister?"

"That will be fine," I said.

"Shall we pencil it in for three o'clock in the afternoon?"

"Yes, sir."

"Fine—very good!" He rose, then shook my hand. "Where are you staying, Miss Hollister, just in the event I should find it necessary to reach you for any reason?"

I gave him the address of the boardinghouse.

"Why, that's old Marge Surratt's place!"

"I believe that's correct."

"Nobody but railroaders and hobos stay there!"

"It's not so bad," I said, trying to put the best construction on it.

"Not so bad? It's a dreadful place! Marge Surratt is the surliest, nastiest landlady in this town. Everybody knows her . . . and stays away from her!"

"Do *you* know her, Mr. Hay?" I asked.

"Sure. Like I said, nearly everyone in town does."

"Where do you know her from if everybody tries to avoid her?"

"Oh, it wasn't always this way with Marge. She used to be quite the political dilettante. She was married to a senator, and the two of them hobnobbed with all of Washington's society. Why, Marge has been right here in the White House dozens of times."

"What happened to her?" I asked.

"Nobody knows quite the whole story in detail," answered Mr. Hay, "least of all me. There were rumors of trouble even before the election, to the effect that Surratt was in league with some big-money fellows from the South—you've probably never heard of Senator Goldwin?"

The very name suddenly filled my mind with memories of Derrick Gregory and my daring ride to Sonora and the whole plot against John Fremont. But it was too long a story to tell Mr. Hay about!

So I merely nodded. "Yes . . . yes, I have heard of him," I answered.

"And you know what kind of man *he* is?"

"I think so."

"Well, as I said, rumors started flying, including some that said there was trouble between Surratt and his wife—that's Marge. Surratt was defeated in fifty-eight. He went back to Ohio, but Marge stayed on. Word had it that she was still in league with Goldwin. If you ask me, she just couldn't stand to suddenly be cast adrift after years in the limelight. I suppose she thought that if she remained in Washington, the glow of power and prestige would linger about her life. Then he died the next year."

"And did it?"

"No. She never set foot in the White House again, as I understand it. Even James Buchanan, southern sympathizer and ineffective as he was, was shrewd enough to realize that having her anywhere near his administration would tarnish his already shaky reputation. After her husband died there were reports of all manner of nefarious things Marge was mixed up in. Probably more than half of them aren't true, but once people began to talk about her in connection with slave-selling and gold-running, and even more serious plots on behalf of Goldwin and the southern cause, she became a pariah among the honest and upright politicians in the city.

"Once Mr. Lincoln was elected and the war broke out, Marge faced three choices: go back to Ohio where she was from, go South and join the Confederacy, or stay here. By then, I think, Goldwin had no more use for her. With the war on, he had bigger problems than the fading star of an aging woman in the North. For whatever reasons, she remained here, broken, embittered, and angry at the whole world. She opened that run-down, dilapidated boardinghouse and has been there ever since."

"And she's no longer involved in politics or anything like that?"

Mr. Hay laughed with a curious expression. "Politics . . . no," he said. "But as to *anything like that,* it is hard to say. There continue to be persistent rumors that float about from time to time about what Marge is associated with. Gutter stuff, mostly, but sometimes more serious."

"What kind of things?"

"Well, you can imagine her feelings of antipathy toward the North, with her years of southern connections. She hates Mr. Lincoln with a passion rivaled only on the streets of Atlanta or Montgomery! Nothing against her has ever been proven, but as I said, rumors persist of her association with low causes that would stir up trouble for the Union, and especially with people intent on the President's defeat and the victory of the Confederate cause."

I was silent. Mr. Hay had certainly given me a great deal to think about. I had wanted something more tangible to pray for the landlady about, and some insight into her that might make it easier for me to be nice to her. Now all at once I knew *too* much about her! Knowing how she felt about Mr. Lincoln, whom I admired, and about the Union cause, which I supported, would make it harder, not easier, to love her in a Christian way! And yet it still seemed that that was what I had to try to do. She wasn't exactly my "enemy," but when Jesus said to love your enemies, it probably applied to situations like this as well.

"In any event, Miss Hollister," Mr. Hay went on, "we can't have you staying at Marge's place. Whatever may or may not be true about Marge herself, the boardinghouse itself is rundown and dirty, and certainly not suitable for a young lady such as you."

"It's really not so bad," I said.

"Hmm . . . well, let's see . . . we shall have to make some other arrangements for you. Something closer by would be good."

"I . . . it isn't necessary for you to go to any trouble . . . not for me," I said.

"Nonsense, Miss Hollister," said Mr. Hay. "You just wait here for a few minutes. I will arrange for a carriage for you, and I will have one of the women on the staff accompany you and see what can be done. I'm sure after the letter the President sent, he would not take it kindly if we did not do everything possible to make your stay in Washington comfortable. You will be the President's guest . . . we will see to everything."

There was a slight pause, then he rose. I didn't want to be stubborn. After all, he could take it wrong. He might even suspect *my* loyalty and cancel my appointment on Friday. But something inside told me I had to do it anyway. I had prayed for an opportunity, and now that I had one, I couldn't let the offer of more plush quarters make me selfishly lose sight of it.

"I'm sorry. I don't mean to be difficult," I said, "but I really feel I need to stay where I am, for another night or two at least. I told her I would be back."

"It's nothing but a flea trap, Miss Hollister!"

"I'm sorry. It's just . . . well, I feel I wasn't altogether as gracious to . . . to Mrs. Surratt as I ought to have been."

"Gracious . . . heavens! That's the last word I would ever associate with Marge! She hasn't a gracious bone in her body, and certainly would not return any graciousness she was shown."

"Nevertheless, it's *my* duty to be gracious to her, whether she returns it or not."

At length Mr. Hay shook his head in consternation.

"Have it your own way, Miss Hollister," he said, "although it makes not an ounce of sense to me! You won't object, will you, to my arranging the carriage for you?"

"No, sir," I replied. "You're very kind, and I appreciate it."

"Nor to the White House, and paying the tab for your expenses? You are the President's guest, wherever you choose to stay."

"That will be fine. Thank you again."

"And when you have discharged what you feel is your duty to Mrs. Surratt, you *will* allow me to put you up in a more suitable place?"

"Yes, sir, I will," I said with a smile.

CHAPTER 28

MARGE SURRATT

How could I possibly make Mr. Hay understand my feelings about Marge Surratt? I had prayed for some kind of a chink to open into her crusty, crabby, lonely heart. And now that I knew something about her, I couldn't just turn my back and walk away. But how could he understand? All he could see was that it was a dingy place and that I might have a much nicer room somewhere else. For me, however, it was a matter of the heart, not how nice the linens and blankets might be, or what kind of curtains hung in the window.

Maybe nothing would come of it. Marge Surratt could just as easily take offense at my trying to be nice to her as receive it kindly. Still, I had to try.

But Mr. Hay was very kind in every other way. He arranged for a carriage to take me back, and the lady who took me spent several hours with me, showing me around Washington. I saw the Capitol building, where the big dome for the top was in the middle of construction, the Washington monument, and some of the other important buildings. When she left me I had plenty to occupy my attention, and I spent the rest of the day walking.

Just the day before I had thought the whole thing a terrible mistake. But now I was gradually warming up to the city and thought maybe I did like it here, after all.

My opportunity to talk to Mrs. Surratt didn't come till the following evening.

After all the dinner dishes had been washed and put away, I tentatively left my room and walked downstairs, then knocked softly on her sitting room door.

145

"Who's there?" I heard from inside.

"Corrie . . . Corrie Hollister," I said.

I opened the door a crack and looked in. "I wondered if you'd mind if I talked to you for a minute," I said.

"Yes, I *would* mind," she answered irritably. "What is it?"

I opened the door enough to step across the threshold. As I did so I went on, hoping not to give her the chance to throw me out.

"I was at the White House yesterday," I said quickly, "and Mr. Hay said he knew you, that you used to be at the White House a lot, and that you knew President Buchanan."

"Yeah, that's right, a regular politician I was! What of it? And what were you doing with John Hay, anyway?"

I didn't want to tell her that I'd come to see President Lincoln, if it was true she hated him.

"What was it like to know a President so well?" I asked. For the first time since I'd knocked on the door, she looked up at me. She eyed me cautiously for a moment or two. I couldn't tell what she was thinking. But if it bothered her that I hadn't answered her question, she didn't show it, because finally she answered mine.

"Aw, it wasn't much. It was my husband who knew him. That was the only reason we got invited to the White House."

Her voice betrayed the hint of pain at the memory. It was the first time she'd let down the tough mask she was wearing, letting out just a thin beam of light from her inner self.

"Your husband?"

"Yeah, he was a senator."

"Where from?"

"Ohio."

"So you were a senator's wife!" I said.

"Yeah, yeah, it wasn't no big thing."

"It seems pretty important to me."

"Don't seem to mean much now, does it?" she said, then laughed bitterly at the irony, glancing around at the poverty of her surroundings.

The laugh contained no joy, but through it I glimpsed a little deeper place in her heart.

"What happened? Did he—"

"He got himself defeated, that's what. Then he went back to Ohio and died."

"But you wanted to stay here?"

"Look around for yourself. Can't you see that I stayed?"

"Why did you?" I asked, inching still farther into the room.

For the first time she seemed to grow thoughtful for a passing moment. A look came over her face that was more than hurt. It was a pensive kind of pain, as if she were wondering whether she had done the right thing. Finally she spoke, but her words didn't have an enthusiastic ring to them.

"I had friends, professional associates, things I didn't want to leave behind. That fool of a husband of mine was going back to Ohio to retire, right when everything was getting interesting and when they needed us more than ever. So I figured I'd start a business and stay."

"Who needed you?"

"Never mind who—it's none of your concern."

"I'm sorry. I didn't mean to pry."

"Aw, forget it, dearie. It's just that there's too many loose tongues and long ears in this town—especially now. Someone like me who used to know important people—people on the other side of the fence, if you get my meaning—someone like me's got to be careful every minute."

I was dying to ask what she meant, but didn't dare.

"Well, you have your business, anyway," I said.

She laughed sardonically. "Yeah, some business!"

"It's a nice place," I said, trying to be positive, "and you seem to be busy with plenty of people."

She glared at me and didn't respond. "So what do you want?" she asked at last. "You said you wanted to talk to me."

"Oh, nothing in particular. I'm a long way from home, and I don't know anyone in Washington, and I just wanted to visit with you."

"Visit . . . with me?"

"Yes—you know, just get to know you a little better."

The laugh she gave at my words sounded like a grunt of disbelief, as if the idea of someone wanting to get to know *her* was too preposterous to even be thinkable.

"Well, suit yourself," she said. "And you might as well sit yourself down instead of standing there like that," she added. I think she was as surprised as I was to hear coming out of her mouth words that were *almost* an invitation to join her. From her look and tone, I don't think anybody had ever sat down with her right here in her sitting room just to chat.

I took the chance while I had it, and grabbed the nearest chair to the door.

We talked for a while longer. The conversation didn't get lively, and she didn't warm up much to the idea. But at least she put up with it, although I was hard pressed to find things to ask her, and she remained as tight-lipped as ever. So I told her a little about my life and about Miracle Springs. She didn't seem particularly interested in anything, but listened.

Finally I could tell I had stretched it about as far as I could. I had hoped to find some way to get in where I could touch the real human soul of the woman, but the fences she had up around her heart were too thick and too high. Still, I hoped it was a beginning and that more might come of it. In the meantime, I intended to pray for Marge Surratt that God would soften her crusty exterior enough so that he might find a way in.

I stood up and thanked her for letting me spend the time with her.

She nodded an acknowledgment, but said nothing.

"Well," I added, "I hope you have a pleasant evening and a good sleep. Good-night."

She grunted again, and I left, closing the door quietly behind me, wondering what the poor lonely lady was thinking.

CHAPTER 29

A WINDY, CLEANSING WALK

My talk with Marge Surratt had an unsettling effect on me. And as I lay down that night to go to sleep, lots of anxieties gnawed at me.

I slept all right, but when I awoke it was still with a sense of inner agitation. It was Thursday. I had another twenty-four hours to wait before my appointment with President Lincoln. As much as I hoped for another chance to find some opportunity to speak with the landlady, I didn't much like the prospect of spending the whole day cooped up in my tiny room. So after breakfast I went out.

A storm had blown in as I'd slept, and the day was windy and blustery, with a fitful shower now and then. The rain would pour down, then stop suddenly. But it was warm, and when it was not raining, it felt comfortable. The smell was somehow different than the storms at home. Maybe it had something to do with the Atlantic, or with the fact that it was a summer storm. There was never rain in Miracle Springs during the summer.

I enjoyed the warm wind and the wetness in the air, and when the downpours came, I found the protection of some building to take shelter in until it passed. During one of the particularly long showers early in the afternoon, I wandered through the halls of the Capitol, and found myself wondering how Pa was doing in Sacramento, and even entertaining the fanciful notion of him coming *here* to Washington, D.C., someday. Yet as the thought came, I knew he'd never do such a thing, even with an engraved invitation from the President himself. He loved the West and California, especially Miracle Springs, far too much ever to leave it!

I went outside again, walking for miles, it seemed.

Part of me couldn't help feeling small, lonely, and insignificant in the midst of all the important things that Washington, D.C., represented. Moments would sweep over me, as they had two nights earlier, when I thought I had made a mistake in interpreting God's intention that I come here. Who was I? . . . what did I matter to the country, to the President . . . to anything? Then I'd remember the loneliness and the people I missed, and would feel sad and isolated and far away again.

But such feelings didn't usually stay with me for too long. Mostly I found thoughts of deep reflection that were directed at *me*—what kind of person I was becoming through all this. There was a certain melancholy to it, and yet something that felt good at the same time. I found myself taking in deep breaths of the warm, stormy air, almost as a symbol of taking in the thoughts and experiences and conversations I'd had since leaving Miracle Springs.

I suppose if I tried to put it into words, I was struggling with the deeper reality of what it meant for me to be growing fully into an adult—for me to be becoming someone completely *my own*, disconnected from home and Pa and my family and everything that had come before. Of course I would never *really* be disconnected. Yet being so far away from home was forcing me to step into a new level of individuality. I was meeting people and getting into situations as *me*. Not as Corrie Belle *Hollister*—my father's daughter and part of his family. Not as Corrie *Belle* Hollister, who was associated with Ma and Uncle Nick and the past generations of my family name. Here I was *Corrie*, a person of my very own. Myself . . . alone . . . God's daughter . . . an adult . . . with no one but myself to fall back on. It was a scary sensation, but it was strengthening at the same time.

The security of home was far away. I thought a lot about my life. I had had many adventures, but compared to being so far away, as I was now—somehow my early life seemed almost protected. Now the person I had become had to stand up to the test of whatever I might face—every day! There was no comfortable nest to return to at night, no secure arms to rest in, no shoulders to cry on. It was time for me to find out what kind of fiber I was made of, what kind of person I was down at the deepest parts of my being, my soul.

I thought about all the encounters I'd had with people thus far. Even the Englishman in the stagecoach, for all his pomp, had character and personality. Did I? Sister Janette and the rest of the nuns . . . their lives seemed to contain so much purpose and significance. Did mine? Lt. Tomlinson and Alan Smith and all the soldiers at Gettysburg had fought for their beliefs. Would I be willing to do that?

Everything I had been through had gone much deeper into me than I realized at the time of each encounter. I found myself comparing my life all over again to the Sisters of Unity, wondering anew if there was something for me there.

Who had I been? . . . who was I now? . . . who would I be a year from now? Was there any significance to my life, my being, to the person I was—any significance alongside the lives of Sister Janette and Jennie Wade and Alan Smith and even Abraham Lincoln? Toward what purpose in life had God been leading me?

I was going to see the President of the United States tomorrow! Why me? Who was *I* that he would care to see me? Why not one of the nuns, one of the soldiers wounded in battle—*anyone* but me?

And yet . . . *my* name was written down in his secretary's book for tomorrow afternoon at three o'clock!

And where did God fit into the whole maze of questions?

I *knew* where he fit. *He* was the force behind everything, the fountain of my life and everything in it, the one who had led me into every encounter I'd had, the one to whom I'd given my life, the one who directed my steps even when I didn't know it. If my life was a story, a progression of events and situations, then *he* was the author!

And if I didn't know what the next chapter held, or even if I didn't know what the chapter just written meant, it didn't matter. I was just a character on the page. But it was *his* book, not mine! And as long as *he* knew what the past meant and where the future was going, then all was well.

Did I possess the fiber, the character, the strength, the wisdom, the integrity to walk as a mature adult—as a *woman* of God at the same time as I was his daughter?

I didn't know. Perhaps I wasn't supposed to know just yet. But *he* knew. And if I didn't, well, he would see to it in his good time. He knew how the story of my life was supposed to progress, and who was I to worry about it?

As my swirling thoughts finally began to settle, I realized again that what I hungered for more than anything—a need which went deeper than people or experiences, beyond ideas and ambitions and dreams and goals, that settled fears and questions and uncertainties—was simply for more of God in my life. That hunger swallowed up all other desires. Intimacy with God absorbed and gave meaning to every other relationship. And being part of God's story gave purpose and direction and significance to all other of life's passing events, large and small. In God's story, my few moments with Alan Smith on the field behind Cemetery Ridge might be more significant than the time I hoped to spend with President Lincoln tomorrow. I did not need to fret in any way about *any* of these questions that had occupied my mind all day as I'd walked.

The presence and nearness of God . . . *that* is what mattered more than any significance my life might have, more than what I understood or didn't understand, more than whether I was strong or weak, mature or immature, more than whether I was a "woman" or still in many ways only a little girl.

"God, stay near me," I prayed, "and put in my heart a trust in you to take care of *everything* else."

CHAPTER 30

THE PRESIDENT

The moment I stepped into the room where Mr. Lincoln was waiting, a great sense of awe came over me.

He was tall and thin, his face tired and his voice soft. Everything about him, from his black suit to the familiar beard, was exactly like the pictures I'd seen. And yet no picture could capture the aura of what it was like to be in the presence of a man of such stature and dignity.

His secretary introduced me.

The President came forward slowly, then extended his hand. I shook it, trying not to act as timid as I felt. At the touch of his grip, a thrilling surge of thrill passed through me. All over again it hit me—*this is the President of the United States. This is Abraham Lincoln himself!*

"Miss Hollister," he said softly. "I am so pleased to finally meet you, and pleased that you wanted to make the long trip here to Washington."

I swallowed and tried to say something, but couldn't get anything out!

"As I told you in my letter," he went on, "I'm most appreciative of how you helped with my election, and with raising money on behalf of the Union and the Sanitary Fund. It is important work they do, especially now with so many wounded, and of course they need money to continue their humanitarian operations. It is people such as you that the country has to thank for allowing such a work to continue. So when I tell you thank you, it is from the bottom of my heart."

It was clear he really meant what he said. I was humbled for him to speak so graciously to me, but at last I managed to find my own tongue.

"I . . . I saw some of the Sanitary Commission's people at Gettysburg." I said. My voice sounded so small! I felt like a tiny little fly in the presence of the President.

"Yes, I did hear from one of our guards, through Mr. Hay, that you *were* at Gettysburg. I would like to know more about it. Surely you weren't near the actual fighting?" As he spoke, Mr. Lincoln took a chair, motioning me to sit down opposite him. I did so.

"It was dreadful," I said.

"The fighting itself?" he said. "Were you near enough to actually see what was going on?"

"Oh yes . . . everything about it was terrible! And yes, we were very close."

"We?"

"I was with some Catholic nuns. We were helping the wounded however we could. Although with as much dying as there was, our efforts didn't seem to amount to much."

He asked how we came to be there, and I told him the whole story.

Mr. Lincoln listened quietly and patiently, and, it seemed, with great interest and thoughtfulness, asking me a question now and then, but mostly just letting me tell him about everything. I almost forgot where I was, and who *he* was! When I stopped, he was quiet for a minute, just thinking about what he'd heard. At length he let out a long sigh, then rose from the chair he'd been sitting in and walked slowly to the window and gazed out. When he turned back to the room, anguish and heartache were evident in every line of his face.

"Ah, Corrie," he said, "this is indeed a dark night for our country. Perhaps the darkest hour we have ever faced as a nation."

He paused briefly, then went on, more as if thinking aloud than talking to me. I almost felt as if I were intruding into some private place in his mind.

"Will we endure it? That is the question," he said. "And if we do, what will be the cost? Is freedom for the Negroes and keeping this nation united as one—is it worth the terrible price we have paid? Will this nation survive, or will the fallen have died in vain? Will freedom survive . . . or will this noble experiment we call the United States of America one day perish from the earth?"

Again he paused, and I was surprised to hear my own voice speaking in response.

"It *will* survive, Mr. President," I said. "It *has* to . . . I am sure of it."

"But again the question—at what price?" he replied. "How much longer will the night of conflict last? Oh, that the dawn would soon break through!"

It was the first time the great passion locked away inside his large frame had revealed itself. He was obviously very moved.

"Wasn't Gettysburg a great victory?" I said. "Perhaps the end of the war will come soon. Perhaps it *is* nearly over," I added hopefully.

"Perhaps," he said, nodding his head thoughtfully. "And Vicksburg."

"Vicksburg?" I repeated.

"The huge bastion of the Confederacy on the Mississippi. General Grant finally took it the day after Gettysburg, on the fourth."

"That's wonderful news!" I said.

"Yes . . . yes, I suppose it is."

I told him of seeing Mr. Grant long ago in California.

"My, but you have seen a great deal for one so young—the gold rush, Ulysses Grant, two national election campaigns, Gettysburg. . . ."

"I am more honored to be able to meet *you*, Mr. Lincoln," I said, "than all the rest of it."

He gave a slight chuckle at my words, and I was immediately embarrassed.

"Do you think, then, that the war will be over quickly," I asked, "now that the southern army has been defeated both at Vicksburg and Gettysburg?"

"We can only hope so," he replied. "Yes, the war in the West has culminated and it would appear the Mississippi Valley is at last ours for good. I doubt they will give us more serious trouble in that region. Their supplies and troops are thinning badly, from the reports I have. But—"

He stopped abruptly and suddenly an altogether different look than I had yet seen came over his face.

"But Lee," he went on after a moment, "is a skilled and crafty officer. I fear we let him off too easily."

I didn't understand what he meant. Lee's army had been turned back and his invasion of the North stopped. I thought it had been a great Union victory.

About that same time, Mr. Hay came back into the room.

"Excuse me, Mr. President," he said, "but this telegram just came in from General Meade. I thought you should see it. He is still following Lee's retreat."

Mr. Lincoln took the paper from his secretary, scanned it briefly, then replied heatedly.

"Lee has crossed back into Virginia and is in full retreat toward the south, he says! He rejoices that he has been driven away from *our soil*, as he puts it!"

He tossed the telegram onto his desk behind him, then slammed the fist of his right hand into the open palm of his left. His face was red, and he didn't look tired anymore.

"Will our generals never get that idea out of their heads!" he exclaimed angrily. "The whole country is our soil! The Union has been endangered for three years, not merely because Lee attempted an invasion of Pennsylvania. His army moving north of the Potomac isn't the threat, but rather that Lee's army exists in the first place!"

Mr. Hay excused himself. Mr. Lincoln gradually calmed, then looked back to where I was sitting, still wondering what I was doing listening to such talk between the most important man in the country and his private secretary!

"I'm sorry you had to witness that, Miss Hollister," he said. "But, you see, that is exactly the point I was trying to make to you before. When word came to me from Gettysburg, calling it a great triumph, I found myself seriously displeased rather than enthusiastic."

"Why, sir? I'm not sure I understand."

"Because it was our opportunity to destroy Lee's army completely. Once Lee cut his ties with Virginia and marched his men deep into the North, he was isolated. We could have compelled him to surrender, or perhaps to destroy himself if he tried to escape. We should *never* have allowed him to escape! But Meade didn't pursue him, and now the wounded lion will live to fight against us another day—mark my words."

It was surprising to hear him talk so ruthlessly about destroying General Lee. I had always taken him for a peaceful and gentle man.

"But surely you wouldn't want to have seen *more* men killed?" I said.

"Of course not. But there *will* be more killing, and the war will be prolonged now, I fear. You must understand, the ruthless pursuit of Lee I was advocating would have, I am convinced, shortened the war. We might have exacted a surrender at any moment. But now, alas, Lee will rebuild his army, the senseless killing will go on, and the war may drag out for another year."

"I think I understand now."

"We may have won the battle, yet we had an opportunity to end the war, and *that* mission we did not accomplish. I hate the killing! Yet sometimes to get to the light at the end of a tunnel, we must go through a long darkness first. Every day reports come to me of more death, more killing, more destruction of our nation, and every time it breaks my heart to realize the means by which we are being forced to obtain freedom for all our people—white *and* black, North *and* South."

"Do you think that aim is worth a war—freedom, I mean?" I asked.

Mr. Lincoln sighed deeply. "Ah, you've asked the question of my life, Corrie," he replied, his voice soft again and far away. "I shall go to my grave trying to find the answer. I know that when I became President, it looked to many as though I had run for this office just to start a war. You cannot imagine how such talk grieves my heart. Yes, we are engaged in a dreadful conflict—but not because I *wanted* it. There are two reasons. One, to keep these United States whole without being divided, and second, to declare to all the world that all men *are* created equal. That is, of course, the question of slavery."

Suddenly he seemed to catch himself. He stopped, gave a little chuckle, then added, "I'm sorry. I still have an old lawyer's habit of thinking out loud. I'm sure you didn't come here to hear an old man ramble on about his woes."

I was shocked to hear him refer to himself as an old man. But I didn't say anything, and when he spoke again it was in a different vein altogether.

"As I told you earlier, Corrie," he said, "I am grateful for your help in the past. And now that I have met you face-to-face and heard of your experiences at Gettysburg, I am doubly glad for inviting you here and that you were willing to come. I think you may indeed be able to help the Union cause."

"I would, of course, be happy to do anything I could . . . but I don't see how . . ."

"Don't you see how your testimony of having actually been on the battlefield could galvanize the citizens of the Union? You could tell of the crying need for supplies and volunteers and money on behalf of the Sanitary Commission. As long as this war continues, there will be more bloodshed, more wounded, and more need for volunteers to help with them, just as you and the sisters from the convent did. You can help us make this crying need known."

"I might be able to write an article about the battle," I suggested, "telling people how important it is they contribute to the Sanitary Fund."

"Exactly. It could be telegraphed back to your home state of California, and we might arrange for several of the eastern papers to run it as well. Yes, I think that is a splendid idea!"

Even as he was finishing his statement, Mr. Hay walked into the room again.

"Mr. President," he said, "I'm sorry to interrupt, but there's your four o'clock appointment with the French Ambassador."

"Ah, yes . . . has he arrived?"

"Yes, sir, he's waiting down in the east parlor."

"Miss Hollister . . . Corrie . . . I am sorry to have to cut our visit short like this," Mr. Lincoln said, turning toward me again. "I have so enjoyed talking with you."

"Thank you," I replied, standing up. He approached and shook my hand again, very affectionately, I thought.

"I meant every word," he said. "I sincerely hope you will be able to help in some of the ways we discussed. I'll leave you and Mr. Hay here to make the arrangements for the remainder of your time in Washington. Good-day, Corrie, and thank you again for a fine visit."

CHAPTER 31

MR. HAY'S BIG PLANS

President Lincoln had been gracious, humble, and at the same time so honest and down-to-earth. Even though I had been in his presence, and even though now his face still filled my memory along with everything he'd said, it would be a long time later before I'd really comprehend what I had just experienced. And when it began to dawn on me what a unique and treasured encounter this had been, I found myself thinking that America would surely remember Abraham Lincoln, for years to come, as one of the nation's greatest Presidents ever.

And I had actually spent an hour with him! He had listened to me talk. He had seemed interested. And he had, just as in his letter, asked me to help the country and the cause of the war! All my doubts and reservations about coming East suddenly evaporated. I walked out of the White House more full of enthusiasm and a sense of purpose than I had for months. I said goodbye to the two guards at the gate, Joe and Al, who were now very friendly to me every time I passed, and fairly skipped on down the street.

Mr. Hay asked me to come back and see him the following day, even though it was Saturday. When I did, he made arrangements for all kinds of things for me to do. He was very business-like, but not like Almeda and Mr. Ashton. White House business was a lot different than Miracle Springs gold-country business!

When I left after my interview with the President's secretary, I had a list of things a whole page long to do. I just hoped I'd remember everything!

There wasn't much chance of my forgetting, of course, because

Mr. Hay had written down the same list and had said he'd take care of everything.

There were many people he wanted me to meet, he said, beginning on Monday. Mrs. Harding, a nurse who had been out on the field, was now recruiting and training volunteers for the Sanitary Commission to send them out behind the troops where battles were anticipated. Mr. Vargo, the Sanitary Commission chairman in Washington, was primarily in charge of fund raising.

Both of them, Mr. Hay said, would have plenty for me to do. Once Mrs. Harding heard what I'd been through in Gettysburg, he said, she would be putting me up in front of women's and church groups all over the North to tell about it and to encourage others to help them save lives.

"And Vargo, too," he went on, "will be anxious to enlist your support on behalf of his financial efforts, especially once he learns that you already have experience in that sort of thing out in California."

I was starting to get tired just listening to him make plans for me. It sounded like a busy schedule!

"How long did you plan to be in Washington, Miss Hollister?" he asked me.

"I . . . I didn't really have specific plans," I replied. "I don't know, a few weeks perhaps. . . ."

"Hmm," thought Mr. Hay, "two or three weeks . . . that doesn't give us much time. We'll have to make use of every minute we can."

"Mr. Lincoln mentioned something about writing, too," I reminded him.

I was willing to talk to people if the subject was something I believed in enough and could talk naturally about. But "speechmaking," as I had heard politicians do plenty of times, was not something I *could* do, or *wanted* to do. Besides, I felt more comfortable expressing my thoughts on paper.

So I didn't want Mr. Hay to forget what the President had said about article-writing. I had already become excited about writing something to be telegraphed back to the West Coast. Wouldn't Mr. Kemble and Robin O'Flaridy come out of their chairs when it came across the wire!

I could just see them! Robin would be jealous, but he'd try not to let it show. Mr. Kemble would try to pretend that it wasn't anything so out of the ordinary, as if his reporters went to Washington and talked to people in the White House all the time! But then when he was alone, he'd mutter something like, "C.B. Hollister . . . I can hardly believe it! I didn't think you had it in you . . . but you've done all right, Corrie!" If I were there in his office, though, his next words would probably be, "But don't you go getting a swelled sense of your own importance to this newspaper . . . I'm *still* only going to pay you six dollars for the article, even if you are supposedly a friend of Abraham Lincoln's!"

I laughed at the thought. I didn't care if he paid me a cent! *This article's on me, Mr. Kemble!* I thought.

And when everybody in Miracle Springs got the paper and saw an article from the National Capital with *my* name on it, what a day that would be! The thought brought a great lump to my chest, and I wanted to burst out laughing and crying both at once! I didn't know if I could stand not being there with them all when that happened!

"Look . . . look here! It's Corrie!"

"Why didn't she tell us. . . ?"

"How could she have told us, Drum? She's all the way back—"

"Why, if that don't beat all! Miz Corrie's done met Mister Lincoln himself. . . ."

"Let me look at it!"

"Hold your horses, Tad, son—we'll all get a chance to read it."

"We're all gonna be famous now, hee, hee, hee!"

"Aw, nobody's gonna be nothin', Alkali, you old goat!"

"Don't be so sure, Nick. . . . Corrie might put Miracle Springs on the map yet."

Voices and faces crowded into my mind all at once . . . laughing, grabbing at the *Alta* . . . all talking about me, and yet with me not there with them.

All these thoughts about writing and home flew swiftly through my mind in two or three seconds, even as Mr. Hay was nodding his head and replying to what I'd said.

"Yes . . . hmm, that's right," he said. "He spoke to me about that when we were discussing you this morning."

"I want to do whatever I can, but writing's what I do best."

"And indeed, we want you to do it. Are you still set on staying at the Surratt woman's place? It doesn't seem that the atmosphere would be terribly conducive to what you have in mind."

"I suppose you're right. . . . There isn't even a desk in the room."

"There, you see! It's imperative that you let me make arrangements for more suitable quarters. Why, you're practically working for the President now, Miss Hollister!"

"Yes, I see the practicality in what you're saying. Just give me another couple of days, and then I'll be happy for you to put me anywhere you like."

"Fine! Early in the week I'll have everything arranged! And in the meantime, I'll have your itinerary set as well. Why don't you come see me again on Tuesday morning? We'll send someone over to pick up your things, get you settled in one of the better boardinghouses close by—*with* a desk!—and by noon you can be hard at work on your first article. How does that sound?"

"Just fine, Mr. Hay," I replied, "but I . . . uh, I don't know if I can . . . that is, I don't have a great deal of money, and until the articles—"

"Miss Hollister," he interrupted, "I told you before, don't worry a thing about it. As I said, you are our guest. We will see to all your expenses—lodging, meals, cabs, whatever else you might need. And if the newspapers pay you for your articles besides, keep the remuneration with our blessings."

"That's awfully kind of you."

"The President was quite taken with you. He's counting on you to help him in this fight to preserve the Union. He feels it's the least he can do in return."

CHAPTER 32

MY FIRST ASSIGNMENT

The next few days I spent mostly at the boardinghouse, either in my room or trying to find opportunities to visit with Mrs. Surratt. Neither was particularly fruitful. Mr. Hay had certainly been right—it was not a place where I could work very well. And even with all the friendliness I could muster, Mrs. Surratt remained distant and untalkative.

Actually, my greatest worry became one of making a pest of myself. Something about the poor, lonely old lady had gone into my heart. It would be exaggerating to say that I *loved* her. Jesus told us to love people, especially those who were difficult to love, those who treated us badly, and even our neighbors. I doubt he meant we were to feel the same kinds of things for those kinds of people as we did our family and friends and the folks we called our *loved ones*. Yet he still said we were supposed to *love* them.

I found myself wondering exactly what he did mean when he told us that. It seemed like a contradiction to tell us to love people we don't, and maybe even *couldn't* love in the way we think of the word. All I could figure out was that he must have been telling us either to *try* to love them, or else to *do* nice things for them and to be kind to them no matter what we felt. In either case, it was still confusing.

But confusing or not, Jesus didn't leave much room for doubt about the matter. He said we *were* to do it—whatever it meant. We *had* to love people—enemies, friends, people we liked, and people we didn't like. So that meant I had to love Marge Surratt, whether I liked her or not. And I figured that meant I had to do my best to *try* to love her by being kind and nice and looking out for opportunities to help her or speak kindly to her, however I could. I didn't know if that was all Jesus meant, but it's all I could lay hold of for the time being, and I knew I'd better do that much.

So I puttered around the boardinghouse, and I'm afraid *did* make kind of a nuisance of myself. Nothing much came of it. She still spoke harshly to me. But we did have some more conversations, and she didn't object when I helped her with the meals from then on. And she seemed halfway interested when I told her what I was going to be doing, and even asked a question or two. I made sure I didn't get into things when we were talking that would have turned into an argument over different viewpoints about the country or the war or Mr. Lincoln or anything like that. If she really had been for the South, as Mr. Hay said, and if she disliked Mr. Lincoln as much as he'd said, then I knew there could be nothing worse than getting on different sides of issues like that. Arguing or talking about things you disagreed about was the *worst* thing you could do if you were trying to love somebody as Jesus commanded.

When Tuesday came and it was time for me to leave, she gave me a halfway sort of smile and said I'd be welcome back anytime. My heart jumped inside me, and I almost felt like telling Mr. Hay I'd changed my mind and I was going to keep staying with Marge Surratt! One of the interesting things I learned from my time with her was that when you do try to do what Jesus said, whether you love somebody or not, eventually something starts to happen inside your *own* heart just from the effort, and by and by you *do* find yourself starting to love them. I was surprised to find myself a little regretful about leaving her. I had already grown more fond of her than I realized.

Yet I knew there were other important things I had to do. So I packed up my things as planned and said goodbye to Marge Surratt, but told her I'd be back to see her sometime.

I did have to admit, though, that the new boardinghouse where Mr. Hay'd arranged a room for me was so much nicer. Not that niceness all by itself mattered so much. Some of the soundest sleeps I'd enjoyed had been around a campfire with Zack or Pa, and even a time or two by myself, on hard ground with nothing for company but the crickets and owls and distant coyote howls. So it wasn't the large bed with pretty yellow and white quilt, or the ruffly curtains, or looking out from my second floor room right out on the White House half a mile away . . . it wasn't those things alone that made the new boardinghouse so perfect. But the room had a nice desk where I could work, and it was quiet, without the sounds of trains coming and going. And seeing the White House out the window as I sat there at my writing table helped keep me inspired about why I was there and how important it was that I do a good job at what Mr. Lincoln had asked of me.

And I did get right to work as soon as I had my things put away in the wardrobe. It had been a long time since I had actually sat down with pen and paper and ink in front of me. Once I started, I realized how much I'd missed writing.

When I did start, something happened that I'd never felt before in any of the articles I'd done. I don't know if it was being so far away from home, or because of what I was writing about, or because of the importance of it—Mr. Lincoln had stressed that people needed to understand about what being at war really meant and how urgent was the need for money and help and supplies and medicine and volunteers. Maybe it was all those things together. But I found myself thinking more "personally" about what I was writing, and imagining myself talking to *real* people as I was doing it, as if I were standing up talking to them. I felt as if I were talking especially to the people in California—just as if I were writing a letter home.

It certainly didn't feel as if I were writing an "article." Before I knew it, I'd written what I'd seen at Gettysburg and what I'd thought and felt, too. I showed it to Mr. Hay the next day. He showed it to the President and some of the Washington newspaper editors, and by the following week what I'd written was appearing in the papers of Washington, Philadelphia, Boston, and Chicago. Mr. Hay said he'd wired it to Mr. Kemble at the *Alta* as well, and then told me to get working on another.

"But I thought—" I started to say.

"Never mind what you thought," said Mr. Hay. "I thought perhaps one article and a speech or two might be all we'd need. But the President says what you wrote about Gettysburg is better and more to the heart of the matter than three fourths of the war journalism he's seen so far. I have to tell you, Miss Hollister, he likes what you've done very much. This is a man who's seen a great deal and is not easily impressed or swayed. 'A breath of fresh air,' that's what he called your story. And he wants more of the same. He says you're just what the war effort in the North has needed to rouse the people out of their complacency and to strengthen their resolve once again to fight on to preserve the Union."

"It pleases me that he liked it," I said.

"Liked it!" Mr. Hay exclaimed. "I should say he liked it! Now you get your mind and your pen busy. In the meantime, I am lining up some things for you with Mrs. Harding and Mr. Vargo."

The moment I saw the actual article in the paper, I had to laugh. What *would* Mr. Kemble say when he saw it? However it came to him over the telegraph, once he actually *saw* the printed copy in the *Post* and the *Mirror* and the *Globe* when they came to him later, he was sure to make some exclamation. There were the words in black and white! I could hardly believe them myself, even as I read them:

By Corrie Belle Hollister, reporter for the California Alta, *on special assignment with the White House.*

What a byline for a girl who'd started writing just to keep a journal, and whose first articles were about leaves, trees, and snow! I almost didn't believe it myself . . . but there it was! What had Almeda begun by giving me a journal and then by running for mayor? She'd gotten me writing, then interested in politics, and look where it had led!

I settled back in the chair and began to read the article. Even though *I* had written it, somehow it was different to read it once it was actually in the paper. They always made a few changes, of course, and I wanted to see those. But most of all I wanted to read my words as if I were a reader myself, seeing them for the first time. I'd written *When I came . . . ,* but they changed the first sentence to the third person. I was glad they let me get onto the page as *myself* a little farther on.

When this reporter came east from California, she had no intention of getting involved in the war up close. But war seems to have a nasty way of intruding into life in ways that aren't always expected. And that is certainly what happened to me as I was traveling by train through Pennsylvania.

I had never heard of Gettysburg. Probably neither had most of you a month ago. It used to be just a sleepy little farming community in the rich heartland of southern Pennsylvania. But ever after this, whenever the name of that place is heard—that place where the fate of North and South collided—the very word will call to mind images in my memory that will bring tears to my eyes and a wrenching feeling of hurtful loss to my heart. For I will never hear the word *Gettysburg* without seeing in my mind's eye the faces of friends I knew there, some of whom I shall never see again.

I then went on to tell about how I had come to be at Gettysburg, and about Jennie Wade, Isaac Tomlinson, Alan Smith, and Sister Janette.

One was on the side of the North, the other fought for the South. The two women did not fight at all. Their only involvement was in trying to help. None of the four were bad people. They had all been swept up into events larger than their own lives. None deserved to die.

Yet today, only two of them are alive. The other two—an aging southerner and an innocent citizen of Gettysburg—are dead. The two who live are still, even as these words are written, nursing serious wounds, and their recoveries may never be complete.

Yes, war always intrudes into life when we least expect it. And its intrusions are always cruel. For war takes life.

But even in the midst of war, people can *give* life. Wars are fought about large issues of national importance, and perhaps individuals like you and me—as well as Jennie and Alan and Isaac and Sister Janette—cannot stop them from coming. The terrible civil war that is tearing at the very fabric of this nation is perhaps one that must be fought so that the liberties and freedoms upon which the Constitution is based might be preserved. But if it must be fought, we must nevertheless save life wherever opportunity is given us.

I then explained about the Sanitary Commission's work of caring for the wounded, and about what we'd done at St. Xavier's, and told everyone how desperate was the need for help. Whether they could actually help someone face-to-face or not, there was plenty they could do to make sure the Commission and other such agencies had everything they needed. Mr. Hay helped me add a few things that they wanted to make sure people knew.

Then I said a few words just to my fellow Californians, reminding them of things Mr. King and I had said, and encouraging them to continue giving aid however they could. A sickening feeling of guilt crept in when I thought of the money Cal stole. But it just made me all the more determined to make up for it now!

As I put the paper down, I smiled to myself. All I could think was what it was going to be like around the house when Pa and Almeda and the others opened the paper and saw *me* there.

The very thought made me cry. When I sat down at my writing table again fifteen minutes later, it was not to write anything for the papers, but to begin a long overdue letter home.

CHAPTER 33

A TIRING AGENDA

Before I knew it I was writing more articles and traveling around with Mr. Vargo to fund-raising events on behalf of the Sanitary Commission, and with Mrs. Harding to help her get people to become part of the volunteer "army of helpers," as she called it.

When I was introduced to Mr. Vargo, he shook my hand with a momentary puzzled look on his face.

"This isn't *the* Corrie Belle Hollister?" he said, glancing toward Mr. Hay.

"I'm not sure what you mean," replied Mr. Hay. "She *is* Corrie Hollister, of that much I am certain."

"But are you the Corrie Belle Hollister who writes . . . are you the author?" he said, to me this time.

"She writes for the *Alta* . . . in San Francisco," said Mr. Hay.

"But the book—are you the young lady who wrote the book about the little town in California . . . about the gold rush and your coming across the desert and the cave falling in on the young boy?"

I nodded sheepishly.

Mr. Hay looked puzzled. He hadn't known anything about my journals.

"My wife read your book, Miss Hollister," Mr. Vargo went on. "It is such a pleasure to meet you! She told me all about it! She has a friend in Chicago who sent it to her. She will be very excited when I tell her you are here in Washington and are going to be working with me."

Mr. Hay asked a few more questions, and Mr. Vargo told him what he had heard about me from his wife. I must say it was dreadfully awkward and embarrassing to hear the two men talking to each other . . . about *me*!

My days were taken up with so many activities that I scarcely had time to sit down and do much more writing. I did, however, manage to keep a regular series of articles appearing and being sent back to California. By then it was clear to me that I might be in the East for quite some time. I began writing letters home, too, so they would know more about what I was doing than they would find out from reading the stories in the paper.

I had to laugh when Mr. Hay brought me a copy of the *Alta* with that first story in it about Gettysburg. Mr. Kemble had changed the byline. Above it, and with every article that appeared later, were the words *By the* Alta's *own Corrie Belle Hollister, on special assignment in Washington to cover the war effort*. It was obvious he wanted everyone to think *he'd* sent me himself!

There wasn't any more fighting anywhere close by all the rest of that summer. The battles of Vicksburg and Gettysburg had exhausted both armies, and they spent the following months recuperating. Word did begin to come to us, however, about movements in and around Tennessee, the last great Confederate stronghold now that the North and West were securely in Union hands.

President Lincoln continued to be frustrated by General Meade's allowing Lee to escape so easily after Gettysburg. As Lee retreated southward, Meade followed but made no attempt to inflict any further damage. When Lee came to the Potomac River, he found it swollen from heavy rains and he was unable to cross. Meade caught up and found the Confederate army trapped. Once again he could have overcome Lee and possibly ended the war for good. But he did nothing. The water level fell, and Lee got his army across to safety.

Mr. Lincoln was furious. It almost seemed as though his own general had been trying to *help* Lee survive so that he could regain his strength and try still another invasion of the North! Later in August, General Meade came to the Capital for a meeting with Lincoln. I happened to be in Philadelphia at the time with Mrs. Harding and Mr. Vargo and several young nurses of the Sanitary

Commission. But Mr. Hay told me about their meeting later.

Mr. Lincoln had said to the general who'd won the battle of Gettysburg, "Do you know, General, what your attitude toward Lee for a week after the battle reminded me of?" Meade said he didn't. "I'll be hanged," the President told him, "if I could think of anything other than an old woman trying to shoo her geese across a creek!"

I made enough friends that I had people to talk to and to keep from being too lonely. I even began to feel at home in Washington. The landlady at the boardinghouse, Annabelle Richards, really did make me feel as if I were coming home every time I returned after I'd been away for a few days. After a while I didn't think of myself as being a "boarder" but rather that her house was where I lived. I did go back to visit Mrs. Surratt from time to time, though she continued to try my resolve. There just didn't seem to be any way to get "inside" her and establish any kind of a friendship. I continued to pray for her.

I wrote to the convent and was so happy to get word back that Sister Janette was recovering nicely and was nearly returned to full strength. They invited me to come back soon, and all the sisters signed the letter and added personal words of their own. Every letter from California made me cry, and so did the one from the convent. I did think often about the time I'd spent there. I still couldn't help but wonder if God might someday want me to follow that same life myself. Part of me hoped so.

In the meantime, I knew such a life wasn't for me *yet*. Right now I had enough to occupy my time just keeping pace with the tiring agenda that had been set before me. I did take a week off from the Commission work in early September to go back north to visit the Convent of John Seventeen and the Sisters of Unity. They treated me like one of them, making me even more homesick for the sense of belonging I had known when I was with them.

But I returned to Washington, and then visited the headquarters of the Sanitary Commission in Boston later in September. I traveled there by train with Mrs. Harding and Eliza Ireland, a nurse who supervised much of the training of the volunteers and who had become quite a good friend.

In Boston, I first saw Dorothea Dix. I'd heard plenty about

her and was frightened at the prospect of her seeing me and maybe even telling Mrs. Harding to get rid of me. She had volunteered her services to the Union just five days after Fort Sumter fell and was put in charge of all female nurses used by the Union. She was tireless but autocratic and unbending—so much so that eventually she began to be called "Dragon Dix."

She was especially hard on young women wanting to help the war effort because it seemed like a romantic, adventurous thing to do—which was the mentality of many of the young men who joined up, too. I don't suppose that was so much of a problem after the war had been going awhile, but from everything I'd heard of her, she even turned down nuns sometimes. "No woman under thirty years need apply to serve in government hospitals," she had always maintained. "They are required to be very plain-looking women. Their dresses must be brown or black, with no bows, no curls, no jewelry, and no hoop skirts."

She didn't actually work for the Sanitary Commission but for the army itself. She was in Boston for the same planning and training sessions as I was attending. So even if she'd wanted to, I don't suppose she could have had me thrown out. After we were introduced, she looked me over from head to foot without a smile, without so much as a word. When Mrs. Harding mentioned that I was a writer who'd written a book and several articles on behalf of the war effort, the dragon lady's only remark was a noncommittal "Hmmph." It wasn't hard to tell that she thought I was too young to be doing what I was doing and if she had her way I wouldn't do it anymore.

Far more pleasant was my meeting with Mary Ann Bickerdyke, a Quaker widow who *was* a Sanitary Commission agent. She had traveled with the Union army for over three years, through sixteen battles. After Gettysburg, she said, she wanted to take some time in the North to round up more support, to encourage the volunteers, and to assist Mr. Vargo in raising desperately needed funds. As soon as she was able, she said she intended to be back with the soldiers on the front lines where she could do the most good. She had visited with President Lincoln too, and laughed when telling me that he'd heard of her nickname and had called her "Mother Bickerdyke," just like the boys in the hospitals all did.

The most widely circulated story about Mrs. Bickerdyke related her response when a surgeon she was helping asked her on whose authority she was acting. She answered, "On the authority of the Lord God Almighty. Have you anything that outranks that?" She was the only woman General Sherman allowed in his camps. When he was asked why he allowed *her,* he replied, "I make the exception in her case for one simple reason: She outranks me."

The trip to Boston was the only time I ever saw Dorothea Dix. Our paths never crossed again, much to my relief. But I did see a great deal more of Mother Bickerdyke. Several times we spoke in Washington together on behalf of the Commission. And because we both were working for the Sanitary Commission, we remained in loose touch with each other through Mrs. Harding and Mr. Vargo, even after she returned to the front lines.

We spent two weeks in Boston before returning to Washington via New York, Philadelphia, and Baltimore, where we held meetings featuring Mrs. Bickerdyke. While in Boston I wrote Almeda a long letter that took me several nights by candlelight after the others had gone to sleep. Being in her home city of Boston had turned my thoughts toward her in a deeper way than ever before. My heart filled with such volumes of love for all she had been in my life, and I had to try to tell her.

I realized too that it was time I tried to say to her, as one adult woman to another, how deeply appreciative I was of everything she had built into me spiritually—with her patience and her love and her understanding and the many long talks we had had together. She had been a mother to me after Ma's death. Much of my own relationship with God I owed to her loving nurturing of me as I grew from girlhood into adulthood. Not until you're older do you realize how deeply people have affected you as you've grown. I needed to tell her again, even though I had told her some of my feelings before. I wanted to tell her, too, how much it had meant to me that she'd shared so openly about her past and about Mr. Parrish and how she'd come to know about God's love for her. Being in Boston reminded me of that all over again and carved out new depths in my love for her.

When I was in Boston I also wrote to Mr. King to tell him what I was doing. I sent the letter to Governor Stanford's office in Sacramento. Mr. King had been involved in many activities in and around Boston before he had come to California, and I thought he'd like to know that his work with me in 1860 had led me back to his old home.

CHAPTER 34

THOUGHTS OF FARAWAY PLACES

The temperature began to cool steadily, and it became obvious that fall was approaching.

Still I was busily involved, meeting more and more people, traveling to new places, seeing cities I'd never dreamed of being able to visit. And somehow the time continued to pass. I wasn't consciously thinking of staying on the East Coast, but the days slipped by, then weeks . . . then months. Whenever anyone would ask me where I was from, I'd immediately answer, "California." I never stopped to think about actually *living* somewhere else. And yet I was growing older, and my writing *was* paying enough that I could support myself and wouldn't *have* to go back to California if I didn't want to.

It always took me off guard, but more and more I would encounter people who recognized my name. "Oh, I read your article about such-and-such," they might say. Some knew me from political articles, others from gold rush stories. I even met one lady who remembered my story about Katie coming from Virginia and the little apple seedling. And the book was making its way to the East Coast from Chicago too, and the few people who knew about it and had read it were always so nice about what they said.

We usually don't see big bends and forks in the road of our lives until we're past them. No matter how much we plan, things still have a way of sneaking up on us and sliding past without our noticing. I doubt General Lee or General Meade realized how decisive the battle of Gettysburg would be on June 29 as they were approaching the town from opposite directions. Gettysburg itself wasn't part of anyone's strategy—it just happened to be there in the way, and then people looked back later, as they were doing this fall, and said that stopping Lee had been a major turning point.

Well, now it *was* fall, and it had been over four months since I had said goodbye to my family in Miracle Springs. And when in every one of their letters they'd ask me when I was coming back, I'd read the words lightly, not thinking about them too much. Without knowing it, I suppose I was gradually working my way around one of those bends in the road that I didn't even know was there. If very much more time went by, I'd have to start realizing that I was *living* and *working* in the East, not just "visiting" for a short time. Because I felt a great purpose in what I was doing, I knew it was important. And to be truthful, I *wasn't* thinking of returning just yet. There was still so much more to be done, and I felt I needed to be part of it.

This was especially true once reports began to come to us that General Lee's army was, as Mr. Lincoln had feared, rebuilding itself to full strength. And once the fighting flared up seriously again, it would cause terrible casualties and increase the need for medical care.

All the while, I was writing and was being paid for my stories. Several years earlier, Mr. Kemble had been sending my stories about California and the gold rush and west coast politics to the East so folks here would know more about the West. Now I was writing about the East and about the civil war, and the articles were being sent back to California so folks *there* would know what was happening through the eyes of one of their own—me!

Then came a day, in early October, when suddenly all this dawned on me in a flash.

"What am I doing here?" I thought to myself. "How long am I going to stay . . . how long will the war last . . . what will I do when it's over . . . where *is* my home now?"

As significant as the questions were with regard to my future, even more significant was the fact that I knew I didn't have the answers. I didn't know.

Would I return to the convent? If I did, would it be the same, or had the experience struck so deeply in me simply because of how and when it had come? If I did go back to Miracle Springs, what then? What would I do—live forever with Pa and Almeda, writing and working at the Mine and Freight?

Or did my future hold something I still couldn't see, around bends in the road of my life that I hadn't even come to yet?

Then I realized that writing was something you could do anywhere. It paid enough for me to rent a room and pay for board anywhere, and the government was taking care of my expenses now, so I could save my article-money. For all these reasons, it suddenly dawned on me that if I wanted to, I could go *anywhere* to live and keep writing.

Just think . . . anywhere! Now that there were telegraph lines all across the country, and now that Mr. Stanford and his men were working so hard to get a railroad line built all the way from the Pacific to the Atlantic, I could stay in touch with my family and Mr. Kemble and even President Lincoln from just about anywhere on the whole continent.

The thought was staggering!

Women didn't usually have the opportunity to mark their own path any way they chose. But it seemed that I *could*! How could I be so fortunate? Why had God so blessed me as to give me a freedom that so few people knew? Ma certainly had never known anything like it. She had had to work hard just to keep us five kids alive! And now here I was, her eldest, experiencing a freedom she could not even have imagined.

It all made me feel humble and thankful, adventurous and bold and daring—all at once!

I could go to Alaska or Colorado and write stories about the new gold rushes there, or to Canada or Oregon . . . maybe I could even travel to Europe someday!

But the very next afternoon my thoughts took an altogether different and equally unexpected turn.

CHAPTER 35

A SURPRISE LETTER

The moment my eyes fell on the envelope that Mrs. Richards handed me, I recognized my sister Emily's handwriting.

I had heard from every one of my other brothers and sisters, but not Emily. The only news of her I'd received had come from Almeda, and that wasn't much.

It was not a long letter, but pleasant and newsy, and it was so good to hear that she and Mike were doing well, that she was happy, and that she saw the rest of the family once a month or so.

But the most important reason she'd written, she said, didn't come till the last of the three pages of her letter.

You'll never believe it, Corrie, but guess what—I'm going to have a baby. I just found out from the doctor two weeks ago—sometime in the spring, he says. Oh, Mike and I are so happy, and I wanted to tell you first of all. I haven't even told Becky or Almeda or Katie yet. Nobody else except Mike, that is. Of course he knows!

You've always been the best sister a girl could have. You took care of us, you were always so patient with us, and though we didn't know it at the time, you were practically both Ma and Pa to all four of us there for a while. I don't suppose I ever said it enough to you, and I'm sorry I waited so long. But knowing there's new life inside me has awakened me to lots of things I never realized before.

So I wanted you, my older sister, to know before anyone. You are so special to me, and I'm so proud of you! Every time I see something of yours in the newspaper, my heart just gets big inside and I can't help but smile on account of my famous sister, the friend of the President!

Oh, Corrie, I love you so much, and I hope and pray you'll someday know the joy I feel right now of being able to bring a new life into the world.

God bless you, my dear sister,
EMILY

I was sobbing long before I was through reading.

I laid the letter down on the bed and went outside. I had to have some fresh air, and walk.

Why had her words of happiness stung me so deeply? Why couldn't I rejoice and laugh with her?

I knew why. And it made the tears streaming down my cheeks all the more difficult to ignore, because Emily's letter had come immediately after my enthusiasm about going wherever I wanted to.

Perhaps I *could* go to faraway places. Perhaps I *had* shaken President Lincoln's hand and written newspaper articles, and perhaps even a few people recognized my name when they heard it.

But what did all that matter? What difference would that make if my life wasn't complete?

That was the hardest question of all to face—one that I now wondered if I'd always been afraid to look at. *Could* a woman's life be complete without being married? Ma had always tried to prepare me to not be married, but I could tell from her tone that it was a sorry pass for a young woman to come to, and somehow we ought to be making plans to make the best of it. I had always just accepted it as my fate that I wouldn't be married, and I even began to like the idea.

But maybe my experience with Cal had wounded me more deeply than I wanted to admit. The way I'd gotten my hopes up about him showed me that down deep I *wanted* to be married just like everyone else.

During my time with Sister Janette at the convent, I thought I had put the question to rest once and for all. I felt as if I truly understood for the first time that the *deepest* meaning a woman's life could have, and the most eternally significant, was to be devoted to Jesus in as complete a way as if married to him. I had been excited about that prospect, eager to give myself and all the rest of my life to him with that abandoned totality.

Why, then, did Emily's words bring tears of anguish and loss to my eyes? *I hope you'll someday know the joy I feel. . . .*

But I never would know it! And why should it make me cry? Why should I feel saddened by it? Sister Janette wouldn't. She had chosen to live a life that would never bring the things Emily was speaking of. I thought I had wanted to make that choice, too. And yet . . . Emily's words rubbed something raw within me.

I *did* want to know the joy she spoke of! I couldn't deny it! I wanted to know what it felt like to have a man's arms wrapped around me, to hear the words spoken in my ear, "Corrie . . . I love you!"

Oh, God, I'm sorry, I thought. *I want to love you and serve you and be content that YOU love me. I'm so sorry . . . but I do wish that someday I might know the love of a man, too.*

But I would never know it. I was too old already, and I didn't know any young men, and I wasn't pretty . . . worst of all, I wasn't the marrying kind—just like Ma had said. I wasn't fun and lively. I was a reading, thinking kind of person, not the kind of girl any young man would ever look twice at. And I wasn't interested in doing nothing but making a home for a man and having ten children. What man would want to marry a woman who was always doing man-things, like writing and making speeches? None of any of that mattered anyway. I was twenty-six, and that was too old. Ma'd said I wasn't the marrying sort clear back when I was ten or twelve, and I guess she was as right about that as she was about most things.

I wiped my sleeve across my eyes as I walked, but I couldn't stop the tears from coming.

I hope you'll know the joy I feel right now of being able to bring a new life into the world. . . .

No, Emily, I thought to myself, *I'm afraid I never will know what it's like to love a man, to be loved in return, or to have a baby and to be a mother.*

How much did being a woman depend on such things? Would I be complete without them? *Could* a woman be complete and yet remain alone?

I don't know if it was wrong to think it, but I couldn't help wondering right then what it was like to be intimate with a man. What did it *feel* like in your heart to be that deeply bonded with another human being? What was it like to love someone that much?

I began to think of Emily and what it would be like for her. What was childbirth like? Was it as painful and yet as joyous as women said? How could it be both excruciating and exhilarating at the same time? What was it like to hold in your arms a newborn son or daughter, the child of your own womb?

I couldn't imagine how wondrous a thing it must be! And I couldn't keep my tears from starting up all over again.

What was it like to be a parent, to watch that son or daughter grow and learn to walk and talk and begin becoming a person with individuality and character all its own? What were the emotions that a mother's heart would feel?

I had been so close to Ma, and now felt so close to Almeda. And yet for the first time I realized what a huge gulf there had always been between us . . . and always would be. Emily had bridged that gap already in many ways, and in another six months or so she would share womanhood with Ma and Almeda in a complete way—a completeness I would never be able to enter into.

The realization was too painful for me to think of further. I turned and walked briskly back to Mrs. Richards' boardinghouse, still crying but determined not to sink any further into the despondency that was threatening to overwhelm me altogether.

CHAPTER 36

FORGETFULNESS AND REMEMBRANCE

I didn't do very well at keeping the tears and self-pity away. Both remained with me the rest of the day.

I *couldn't* go down to dinner looking the way I did. As soon as the other guests were served, Mrs. Richards came to my room and knocked on the door to see if I was coming.

"No, I don't think I'll be down tonight," I said through the door. I'd never missed supper the whole time I'd been there.

"Corrie . . . are you all right?" she said.

"Yes . . . I'm fine," I answered, knowing I wasn't being truthful. "I'm just not feeling too well."

"What can I do for you, child?"

"I'll—please, I'll . . . I'll be fine in the morning. It's just a headache, and . . . I'm not hungry."

"You'll tell me if there's something I can do?"

"Yes . . . yes, I will. Thank you, Mrs. Richards."

She went downstairs to the dining room, and I lay back on the bed and started crying all over again. Oh, I would have given anything to have Almeda at my side right then! I was miserable!

But I just couldn't stand to be such a victim of my moods. One minute I was happy and excited about life, and everything looked so bright. Then the next I would find myself knocked off my feet and knee-deep in a slough of despair and hopelessness. Pa had said to me more than once, "All that thinking's bound to tie your brain in knots now and then, Corrie. Just take life as it comes, and don't cogitate so much on it."

183

But I couldn't help thinking about everything. Besides, I didn't *want* to just take life as it came. I wanted to have a hand in the process. I figured I knew better than anyone else—anyone except the Lord, that is—what I did and didn't want to be doing.

But if thinking was part of looking your life in the face and getting on with it, and if up-and-down feelings went along with thinking about things, then I suppose I was stuck with it.

Uncle Nick always said, "Aw, that's just the way women are. Men are the *doers,* but women are always gettin' all emotional about everything. If there weren't no men, why you women'd make one fine pickle of it, and you'd never get nothin' done!"

Even while Alkali Jones's cackle was sounding through the room, I could see Aunt Katie biting her lip to keep quiet!

Almeda had a different explanation, and she and I had talked about it plenty of times. "Yes, Corrie, we women do have a more sensitive emotional nature. And we're prone to violent fits of unpredictability now and then—usually about once a month!"

We both laughed.

"Men think they're so smart, but they don't know anything about how a woman's body and mind and emotions all work in a delicate balance. And neither do they know how much a mess of things *they'd* make if we weren't quietly holding everything in *their* lives together. Though don't ever expect a man to realize that . . . or to say it, if he did!"

I smiled through my tears as I recalled the conversation. Yet I wasn't willing to accept that answer for my moods either, that I was just a victim of how women happened to be made and I couldn't help it.

I *wanted* to help it! Whatever explanation there might be to account for it, I didn't like it. I wanted to be more consistent and steady, and yet here I was again, suffering through a terrible case of the doldrums!

The following morning an open-air meeting had been scheduled on the lawn surrounding the Washington Monument. I was going to talk for about five minutes on the importance of people volunteering to help with the recent fighting down in Tennessee, even if they knew absolutely nothing about doctoring or nursing, telling how I was able to be of some use to the sisters at Gettysburg, although I'd had not a minute of preparation ahead of time.

I awoke early and decided to go out before breakfast to try to clear my brain of yesterday's cobwebs and depression. Maybe I wouldn't ever marry or know real intimacy or experience childbirth or know what motherhood was like, but now was not the time to worry about it. I had responsibilities, and I couldn't neglect them by wallowing around in the hole I'd dug for myself as a result of Emily's letter.

The air was crisp and chilly. Fall was definitely in the wind. There would probably be rain by evening.

I walked and walked, trying to be stoic and strong and brave and not give in to those womanly "emotions" that had knocked me to the ground yesterday. I would fight them, whatever their source. If it was my destiny, my fate, my lot in life to remain single and alone, then I would be brave about it. I would endure it like . . . well, not exactly "like a man," but like a strong woman, anyway! Nobody ever promised that life would be everything we might want. People faced lots of hardships many times worse than I ever had. Hundreds of thousands of boys were dying in this terrible war. And hadn't I just realized two days ago how blessed I was? What business did I have thinking otherwise?

I was walking along, breathing in deeply, keeping a stiff upper lip about all my troubles of the day before, and I never thought of God once. I didn't pray, I didn't talk to him about any of it, I didn't ask him what I ought to do or think. Worst of all, I didn't even realize it. I hadn't thought of him once since reading Emily's letter! I was just determining within *myself*, with no help from him, to be strong. I never realized that when you're trying to summon up strength *only* from within yourself, there's no strength there. There is no weaker position for a man or a woman—for anybody—than standing alone. Yet that's what I was trying to do, deceiving myself that I was being strong.

All of a sudden I remembered God. I remembered that he was there, that Jesus was walking right beside me, that he had never left me. I remembered that he had been there all through yesterday too, that he was beside me in the room as I'd read Emily's letter, and had been with me all night as I slept, and even through the hour I'd been walking this morning, even though I hadn't been aware of his presence for so much as a second.

A new wave of heartbreak swept over me. This time it was not the despair of self-pity but rather the mortification of what I'd done, that I had forgotten him so completely.

All the strength I'd been trying to summon up only a moment before evaporated in less than a second. I felt so small, so weak, as if I'd betrayed him, even though he had been good to me and had never left me.

Tears filled my eyes—tears not of self-motivated sadness but of remorse and grief.

"Oh, Lord . . . I am so sorry!" I whispered.

There was nothing else to pray, no more to say. I felt so low. How could I have doubted that he would take care of me, that he knew what was best, and that he would do the very best for me in every way? How *could* I forget? Yet I had.

My heart heaved with wave upon wave of unspoken and faulted attempts to convey my sorrow over forgetting to trust him and doubting that my life was utterly in his hands. But no words escaped my lips.

Then, just as suddenly as I had remembered the Lord's presence with me, I remembered something else—my own words, words I had prayed while at the convent:

. . . *Whatever future you have for me, whether married or not, I will be happy just to know I am with you. Let me just know that I am only yours. I want to be your bride. . . . Oh, God, use me and fill me with yourself. I want to be yours completely.*

How could I have forgotten so quickly?

I had given myself in marriage to Jesus. I had given him my heart and my future. I had meant every word of those earlier prayers . . . and I knew that I still did.

"I *do* want to be yours, Lord," I said softly through my tears. "I am sorry I am so weak. Help me . . . help me to be strong—strong as you would make me strong, not trying to be strong by myself without you. Please, Lord, help me! I don't have that kind of strength alone."

Asking for his help calmed me some, and gradually I was able to breathe in deeply and stop crying.

By now I was walking back toward Mrs. Richards'. I felt

drained, both emotionally and physically. I was aware of the Lord's presence with me, but was too spent to be able to articulate the prayers my heart was feeling. Then a new realization came upon me. And I know he put it into my mind in answer to the pain and questions that had engulfed me from Emily's words.

Corrie, I will *make of you a complete woman. You need have no fear of anything missing from your life from being married or being a mother or not. Complete womanhood comes from joining yourself to me, and in no other way. There are many wives and mothers who are incomplete, broken, lonely women. They will never know the completeness of their womanhood until they join their hearts to mine and allow me to make them complete. I alone can raise up my daughters into the fullness of their being, their personhood, their womanhood. None but* my *daughters will become true women, and they must become my daughters before all else.*

"But why, Lord," I found myself saying, "why can't I remember? Why is this so hard for me when my heart truly does yearn to be only yours?"

I have allowed you to suffer these things, Corrie, I felt I heard him saying, *so that you will know the cost, and know the worth of womanhood as my daughter*—full *womanhood as you yourself long for*—*so that you will be able to speak of these truths to others of my daughters.*

My thoughts were silent. My heart was still at last, and at peace.

CHAPTER 37

ANOTHER PRESIDENTIAL INVITATION

Late in October, one evening when I arrived back at the boardinghouse—which by now I had begun calling "home"—there was an envelope awaiting me. It had no stamp, however. It had been hand delivered, Mrs. Richards said, by John Hay himself. It bore the insignia of the presidential seal.

I opened it hurriedly.

Dear Miss Hollister,

President Lincoln would like to see you again. Please come by the White House tomorrow. Ask for me, and we will set up a time as soon as possible. Thank you.

> I remain,
> Sincerely yours,
> JOHN HAY,
> Secretary to the President

I went the next morning, and Mr. Hay asked me to come back that afternoon at 1:45. Shortly before two, I was shown into the presence of Mr. Lincoln.

He was just as kind as the first time, and I think I was no less awestruck.

"Miss Hollister . . . Corrie," he said, shaking my hand warmly. "Thank you for coming to see me again."

"Of course, sir," I answered.

"Mr. Hay has kept me apprised of your work here in Washington, and I have read some of your articles. Again, as I attempted to express before, I am most appreciative."

"Thank you."

"I have another request to make of you," he went on, "although this one is in a slightly different vein."

"Anything," I said.

"I am planning a visit to Gettysburg in about three weeks, to dedicate a new Union cemetery there. I am hoping to be able to talk you into accompanying me, along with the rest of the ever-present presidential retinue."

He *hoped* to "talk me into it"! As if I were so busy I'd have to think twice and consult my schedule to see if I had room to squeeze Abraham Lincoln in! I was speechless!

Somehow I heard the words coming out of my mouth, "I'd be honored, Mr. President."

"Good, I am delighted to hear it. We will travel by train, of course. Mr. Hay will fill you in on the details. The day's schedule is not finalized yet, as I understand it, but I hope there will be an opportunity for you to say a few words. I trust you would have no objection?"

"Not if that is what you would like, sir," I said.

"I knew I could count on you."

The President looked tired and dejected. At my last interview with him in July, despite his irritation over how things had gone at Gettysburg, he had been full of life, and his eyes had glowed, even with anger at times, as he'd spoken of the possibility of ending the war.

Indeed, a quick end to the war now seemed as remote as ever. Robert E. Lee was rebuilding his strength, and Mr. Lincoln continued to have trouble with his generals being timid about dealing the death-blow to the Confederate army. It seemed the North had the most courageous president, while the South had the shrewdest general. Lee's hands were tied by an ineffectual President Jefferson Davis, while Lincoln's decisive military strength was blunted by hesitant generals who did not share the scope of his vision. The two greatest military minds in the country—Lincoln and Lee— were fighting on opposite sides of the conflict, and their mutual skill and determination only extended the killing in a prolonged stalemate. Time, of course, favored Mr. Lincoln because of sheer numbers of men and quantities of supplies. But in the meantime, the South fought bravely and determinedly on, with the result of a *huge* loss of lives.

The hoped-for end of the war following Gettysburg and Vicksburg faded through that fall of 1863. The Confederacy was not dead yet! In September they routed Union forces in the small Georgia town of Chickamauga in one of the bloodiest battles of the war. Lincoln was not only frustrated with his commanders, but sorrowful personally as well. His wife's brother-in-law, Confederate Brigadier General Ben Hardin Helm, was killed in the battle. Mrs. Lincoln wept but was overheard to say to a friend that she wished *all* her Confederate relatives would be killed. "Any one of them would kill my husband in an instant if given half the chance," she said, "and completely destroy our government."

I'm sure the war was on his mind a great deal when I saw him in October. Oppression seemed to hang about his countenance. I also learned that just a few days earlier he had taken the bold step of naming General Grant commander of all Union forces between the Appalachians and the Mississippi. Here was a general who would follow his President's orders, who was brave and a shrewd tactician of nearly Robert E. Lee's caliber, and who could hopefully unite the Federal effort.

And I was a little more than fond of him for the simple reason that he had once been to Miracle Springs! That was a long time ago, of course, and how could he possibly remember? Yet in my secret heart I hoped that *someday* maybe I'd have a chance to meet him again.

I was glad when I heard the President and Mrs. Lincoln had gone to the theater a week before we were scheduled to go to Gettysburg. I hoped it might be a sign he was feeling better and that the stress I'd seen on his face was perhaps lessening. He had gone to see a play called *The Marble Heart*.

"It's got to be young Booth playing in it," remarked Mrs. Richards.

"I don't know anything about it," I replied. "And who's Booth?"

"Oh, a young actor, John Booth. Not as good as his father, Junius Brutus Booth, or even his brother Edwin for that matter. But he's young and ambitious and on the rise. Who knows, the world may hear of young John Wilkes yet."

CHAPTER 38

GETTYSBURG . . . AGAIN

The train ride to Gettysburg was certainly nothing like coming across the country alone. There were newspaper people and reporters and politicians and military men. Gettysburg was a town of only about two thousand people, but they expected a crowd of some six thousand. And a lot of them were on the train with us!

I sat next to a man who was a correspondent for the London *Times*, living in the United States to cover the war. We had a lively talk, although I'm not sure what he thought of a young woman calling herself a reporter as if I were on *his* level. Neither did he seem to think very highly of Mr. Lincoln, which annoyed me. I told him I happened to think Abraham Lincoln the greatest man on the continent and that I was going to Gettysburg to speak along with him, at the President's *personal* invitation. I don't suppose it was altogether humble of me, but I just couldn't tolerate people criticizing the President after all he'd stood for, and being the great man he was. I suppose he wasn't impressed with the backward colonies that still had slavery, after it had been banned in the British Empire for over twenty years. I don't think the fellow believed a word I'd said about being invited there to speak.

Mr. Lincoln sat in the back of the same coach I was in. Mr. Hay was beside him, and every so often they would exchange a word or two, but mostly the President kept to himself. He seemed distracted, thoughtful. He spent a lot of time looking out the window, after which he'd scribble down notes on the back of an envelope. Later I found out that he was actually writing down his speech as we bounced and clattered along!

His mind was probably on General Grant, too. However much the purpose of our trip was to commemorate a battle whose echoes had long since died away, the fact of the matter was that even then, at that very moment, huge troop movements were amassing tens of thousands of soldiers in Tennessee in what would prove to be Ulysses Grant's first test of generalship since his promotion a month earlier.

The date was November 19, 1863. It is a day I shall never forget, and I doubt the citizens of Gettysburg will forget it, either.

The huge mass of people assembled in town, then walked and rode in a great procession to the new cemetery. Mr. Lincoln and other dignitaries rode horses, some rode in carriages, most walked. I was pleased to see some of my friends from St. Xavier's, and I rode with Father McFey, along with Jennie Wade's mother and sister, in a large black-draped carriage.

Everyone was dressed in black—the men in suits and tall black top hats, the women either in black dresses or draped with black shawls. Even though the mood was solemn, on the outskirts of town local entrepreneurs, some of them only ten or twelve years old, had set up tables and were selling drinks and cookies and battlefield relics they'd collected—even dried wildflowers, which had grown up since July.

Most everyone stood. Some of the women and families from town had brought blankets to spread out and sit on. A wooden stand had been built for the speakers so they could be seen. Several dozen chairs stood just below the speaker's stand, where I sat next to Mr. Hay. I was the only woman among those seated in front, and I felt more than a little conspicuous!

The main speaker of the day was Edward Everett, a noted pastor, diplomat, and politician, who had served as governor of Massachusetts. He was now seventy years old and mostly traveled about the Union giving stirring, patriotic orations.

He was introduced, stood up, and began the longest speech I have ever heard in my life—before or since! It's a good thing it wasn't as hot as it had been during the actual battle, or the death toll might have mounted still further among those in attendance. As it was, they didn't drop from the heat but gradually sank to the ground from sheer boredom! After an hour, most of the listeners who had begun on their feet were seated on the ground. And he was only half through!

Finally Mr. Hay leaned over to me.

"Corrie," he whispered into my ear, "I'm afraid we are going to have to eliminate your remarks from the agenda. If Everett doesn't sit down pretty soon, everyone will be asleep and even the President won't be able to speak!"

I smiled and nodded. Actually it was a great relief.

Occasionally during Mr. Everett's speech, the President had continued to write on the envelope he had been scribbling on during the train ride.

At long last, Mr. Everett began winding down his passionate oratory, and then finally stopped—just a minute or two short of two hours since he'd begun—and took his seat next to President Lincoln. There was scattered applause—mostly because the speech was finally over, not because of anything Mr. Everett had said.

Then President Lincoln stood up. A great silence descended upon the crowd. The words that came from his mouth were so brief, and yet so powerfully forceful—especially to my ears, because I had actually *seen* this battle—that I could not keep tears from coming to my eyes. Every face from these terrible days came back to me—Jennie Wade's, Alan Smith's, Isaac Tomlinson's, as well as faces of the dead whose names I had never known and whose voices I had never heard. I cry every time I remember Mr. Lincoln's words, some of the most magnificent words ever spoken:

> Fourscore and seven years ago our fathers brought forth on this continent a new nation, conceived in Liberty, and dedicated to the proposition that all men are created equal.
>
> Now we are engaged in a great civil war, testing whether that nation, or any nation so conceived and so dedicated, can long endure. We are met on a great battlefield of that war. We have come to dedicate a portion of that field as a final resting place of those who here gave their lives that that nation might live. It is altogether fitting and proper that we should do this.
>
> But in a larger sense we can not dedicate—we can not consecrate—we can not hallow—this ground. The brave men, living and dead, who struggled here, have consecrated it, far above our poor power to add or detract. The world will little

note, nor long remember what we say here, but it can never forget what they did here. It is for us, the living, rather, to be dedicated here to the unfinished work which they who fought here have thus far so nobly advanced. It is rather for us to be here dedicated to the great task remaining before us—that from these honored dead we take increased devotion to that cause for which they gave the last full measure of devotion—that we highly resolve that these dead shall not have died in vain—that this nation, under God, shall have a new birth of freedom—and that government of the people, by the people, and for the people, shall not perish from the earth.

He turned and went back to his seat. People were still shifting around trying to get comfortable, and his short address was finished.

Not much more happened. Afterward Mr. Lincoln was introduced to Jennie Wade's family, to whom he gave his regards. He'd heard about Jennie before, as the only citizen of the town to be killed as a result of the fighting.

On the train ride back to Washington I saw the *Times* man again.

"I had a feeling you were trying to pull my English leg, telling me you were going to take to the podium with your President," he said.

"I told you the truth," I insisted. "But after Mr. Everett had gone on for an hour, they decided they should shorten the program, and mine was the one they eliminated."

He shrugged as though he halfway believed me but still wasn't sure. "Whatever you say. Might have made it a more memorable day though."

"How do you mean?" I asked.

"Not hardly worth our coming all this way for, wouldn't you agree?"

"I wouldn't have missed it!"

"I could have found ten more useful ways to spend the day. Your President was an abject failure. It's a wonder to me you Americans have managed to keep your country from blowing apart all this time, considering the mediocre men you thrust up into leadership from the most unqualified of backgrounds."

I couldn't believe what I was hearing. The gall of him to say such things about Mr. Lincoln!

"It was the most wonderful speech I've ever listened to!" I said.

"Ha! It will be forgotten by next week!"

The article he sent back to be printed in his own London *Times* was circulated through the papers of Washington and New York, too. About Gettysburg he wrote: "The ceremony was rendered ludicrous by the sallies of that poor President Lincoln, whose ridiculously brief remarks were hardly fitting for so momentous an occasion. Anyone more dull and commonplace it would not be easy to produce."

I was furious when I read them.

I hoped Mr. Lincoln never saw the disparaging words. There was at last some good news for him from the South. His appointment of General Grant had paid off! Just six days after his speech at Gettysburg, the two-day battle of Chattanooga began. When it was over, Ulysses Grant had scored another brilliant Union victory.

Three great turning points of the war had come during 1863— Gettysburg, which beat back Lee's invasion of the North. Vicksburg, which gave the Union control of the Mississippi. And now Chattanooga, which solidified General Grant's leadership and gave the entire Tennessee line into the control of the Federal army.

As the fateful year ended, it seemed impossible that the South could hope to win the war militarily. All the advantages were with the Union.

Yet still the stubborn Confederacy refused to yield. And as a result, thousands more would have to die. . . .

CHAPTER 39

A NIGHT TO REMEMBER

Christmas of that year was one of the loneliest times I had ever known. Christmas was always such a special day in our family, and I was so far away! All I could think of was what they were doing, and I couldn't help feeling sorry for myself. But even if I did want to go back, once winter set in, travel across the country was no longer possible. I would be in the East at least until the spring—maybe longer. As long as the war lasted, nothing was certain.

But I didn't have to spend the day alone. I enjoyed a nice morning with Mrs. Richards and some of her family. The afternoon I spent with Mrs. Harding and some of the other Commission people. We had planned several Christmas events at both Harewood Army Hospital and the Armory Square Hospital. We'd arranged for decorations and what extra food the citizens of Washington could donate. We had a small band to play Christmas carols and a choir of nursing volunteers to sing to the men.

By evening I was too tired to remember that I was lonely. None of the wounded men or the soldiers in the field could be with their families for Christmas, either. It was a time of sacrifice for everyone, and mine was hardly to be compared with all the suffering and misery I'd seen.

A little over two months later, in the first week of March, 1864, President Lincoln announced that he had promoted General Grant again, above brigadier general, placing him at the head of *all* Union armies. Grant would be coming to Washington to personally receive from the President the specially created rank of lieutenant general. No one since George Washington had held such a high military rank.

I was thrilled to receive an invitation to attend a reception at the White House on the evening of March 8, at which General Grant would be honored!

I immediately made plans to take some of my article money out of the bank, and asked Mrs. Richards if she would help me select a new dress for the occasion.

When the day came I was so excited I could hardly wait till evening. What a birthday present this was—even if it was two weeks early—to be invited to a fancy reception at the Executive Mansion *and* to see General Grant!

He was just as I remembered him—older, of course, and now with some gray in his hair and beard, but short, strong-looking, stocky, with piercing eyes.

After Grant left California, he had resigned from the army altogether. He'd done lots of things since, but had failed at all of them—farming, selling property, peddling firewood on the streets, bill collecting. Finally he went to work as a clerk in the family leather store, working for his brother in Galena, Illinois. That's where he was when the war broke out.

He reentered the army, was put in charge of a small band of volunteers, and gradually began to be noticed by Union leaders when he started winning battles while most of the northern generals were suffering humiliating defeats. Within two years he was in command of the whole Mississippi theater of the war.

The instant he walked into the room, all the guests began applauding. The President immediately approached him, took his hand, and vigorously pumped it up and down. "Why, here is General Grant!" he exclaimed. "This is a great pleasure, having you here, General, I assure you."

Everyone was pressing around to see him and greet him, but he could hardly *be* seen because of his height. There was Mr. Lincoln, easy enough to see above most of the heads. But Mr. Grant was eight inches shorter than the President. Most of the women were taller than he was!

All at once, from near the back where I was standing, I suddenly saw the general's head appear—taller even than the President's. He had stepped up onto a crimson-covered sofa where he could be seen. And there he stood for over an hour, shaking hands with everyone in the room.

What a sight it was! For once the President of the United States was *not* the central figure, but stood back while all the attention was directed toward this apprehensive man who disliked crowds, disliked Washington, D.C., and who even then, he confessed later, was eager to get out of all the hubbub and back to battle. But then he stood on a sofa while the most important people in the National Capital treated him like a hero.

And, in a way, I suppose he was. He was the first general, at least, that President Lincoln was entirely pleased with. And to have the confidence of a man like Abraham Lincoln was no small accomplishment for *any* man.

I waited patiently in the stream of people moving steadily toward the crimson sofa.

When at last the moment came, and I found my hand in his and his piercing eyes looking down into mine, it was all I could do to find my voice.

"I'm happy to see you again, General," I said. "I saw you out in California in 1853."

"Where was that?" he asked.

"North of Sacramento. You stopped by in our little town to see your friend Simon Rafferty."

His eyes brightened. "Yes . . . yes, of course. I do recall the day."

"You were on your way up to Eureka."

"Ah, yes . . . Fort Humboldt—a dreadful place. Drove me to the bottle and straight out of the army!" He laughed.

"I'm glad to see you didn't stay out," I said.

"Under the circumstances, so am I, young lady, although if I do ever catch up with Robert E. Lee, I may live to regret my decision." He paused, then bent down a little and added softly, "but don't tell the President what I just said!"

"No, sir, not a word."

I moved on, but he stopped me. "Wait, young lady," he said, "you forgot to tell me your name."

I turned back toward him. "Corrie Hollister," I said, "Corrie Belle Hollister."

"I'll try to remember it," he said. "I hope our paths may cross another day, Miss Hollister."

"Thank you, Mr. Grant," I said. An instant later I was past him, and he was busy greeting someone else.

Ulysses Grant had not only come to Washington to receive his new rank from the President, he had come quite literally to take charge of the Union army of the North—which had until then been led by General Meade—and to do what no other northern general had been able to do—advance upon the Confederate capital of Richmond. Five different generals had attempted it. All had been repelled by Robert E. Lee, who was already being called the greatest general of the war—on either side.

But now it was time for the greatest Union general to take on Lee's army face-to-face. It seemed almost inevitable that one day the two men would square off and do battle against each other. It was fitting, I suppose, that the war would culminate in such a way. The Union controlled every other major front—the seas, the Mississippi, Tennessee, and Georgia. The only area the Union could not gain control of was northern Virginia and the Rebel capital of Richmond.

Only Robert E. Lee stood between the Confederacy and utter defeat.

And at last the moment had arrived for Ulysses S. Grant to take firm command of the armies that had been placed under him, and march south to meet Lee.

In April General Grant reviewed his new troops, then retired to confer with General Meade and discuss strategy for the planned campaign. As they met, members of his staff told of his great exploits and triumphs in the West and at Vicksburg. The veteran soldiers of the Army of the Potomac were not impressed.

"Everything you say may be true," one man said. "But you never met Bobbie Lee and his boys. Grant'll have his match in him, and that's the truth."

CHAPTER 40

FOLLOWING GRANT INTO THE WILDERNESS

For months I had been talking and writing about helping the war's wounded and donating money and supplies to the Sanitary Fund. I had helped Mrs. Harding recruit and train people, and worked at the organizational duties of the Commission. Then one day it dawned on me that I hadn't really *done* any of the work I was telling other people *they* ought to do. What had happened at Gettysburg had come upon me almost by chance. I just suddenly found myself in the midst of it. I began to wonder what business I had saying what I said to others when I had done only two days of it myself.

The very next day I went to see Mr. Hay, then I talked to Mr. Vargo, and finally I discussed my plan with Mrs. Harding. I told them all the same thing—that I thought it was time I joined the Commission volunteers myself, and put the nursing and medical training I'd been giving into practice on the actual battlefield again. I told them that I was going to go south with the Commission brigade that was getting ready right then to follow General Grant's movements as he marched toward Richmond. I would continue to help them in any way possible, I said. I would continue to write articles and send them back to Mr. Hay. But in the meantime, I felt I needed to be near to offer any *real* help that I might be able to give.

They all said they would be sorry to see me go, and that they would miss me, but they understood.

I wrote to Pa and Almeda about my plans too, although I didn't tell them how close to the actual fighting the Commission tents sometimes were. I figured they would probably worry enough without my adding to their troubles by talking about the potential danger.

General Grant launched his move into the wilderness of northern Virginia during the first week of May. He hoped to force Lee into a showdown that would end the war quickly. The Confederate capital was only seventy-five miles away, but General Grant could not take Richmond. Supreme general faced supreme general. Neither would give up, neither would retreat, both continued to wage skillful and canny warfare—Grant offensively, Lee defensively. Neither could defeat the other.

It was the military chess game of all time. There had never, in all the years of the war before this, been such a period of sustained, day-after-day, unrelenting savage fighting. Over 90,000 men were killed in the first month alone. All Americans, all young . . . all dead. And still the war was no closer to being over.

The Confederacy could not possibly achieve a victory now. The numbers against them were too strong. Yet Lee fought on, determined, it seemed, not to lay down arms as long as a single boy wearing gray was left alive. In truth, the South's greatest general also cost the South countless lives and great destruction of property. How many Rebel boys could have gone on living had Robert Lee not been so stubborn to continue after defeat was inevitable?

Lee's strategy was not to defeat Grant. He knew he could never do that. To make up for Grant's superior numbers, his strategy was to fight a skillful defensive game, making Grant attack him at the worst possible positions, and make the cost of Union losses so high that eventually the northern public would turn against the war effort and sue for peace. If he could just stall Grant's march until November, until the presidential election, thought Lee, and if he could inflict enough damage on Grant's army, Lincoln's prestige would be hurt and he would be defeated in the election. With Lincoln gone, Lee was sure the North would eventually tire of the war and decide to let the South go her own way.

But if that was Lee's hope, Grant's determination to win a decisive victory for his President was just as strong. Some called him ruthless, others called him brutal. But Lincoln had made him the President's supreme commander because of the general's willingness to fight. And fight he did!

Through the summer, into the fall, and toward the end of the year, the great and terrible bloody standoff between Lee and Grant continued. Richmond still remained in Confederate hands, with Jefferson Davis still President of a rebel nation.

The same week when Grant had plunged into the wilderness after Lee, General Sherman in the South left Chattanooga for Atlanta. This was the second objective in the North's final two-pronged offensive to end the war. Once Atlanta and Richmond were in Union hands, the end of the war would not be long behind.

But neither was easy to gain. The fighting on both fronts lasted all summer.

When I left Washington with the Commission brigade, I envisioned being gone for months and perhaps traveling hundreds of miles. But the battle was so tightly confined that we were able to transport many of the wounded back to the Washington hospitals, and to travel back regularly ourselves for needed supplies. We never went more than a hundred and fifty miles from the Capital.

Nevertheless, the wounded came faster than we could nurse them—two thousand a day for a month! The atrocities of war are too horrible to describe. I will spend the rest of my days on earth praying to God to erase those images from my memory.

I saw huge mass graves filled with bodies. I had to walk across battlefield trenches strewn with so many corpses that I could scarcely make my way without stepping on them. I literally stumbled over the bones of the unburied dead from a year earlier while trying to make my way through the dense woods of the wilderness. I witnessed amputations, saw crates piled high with hands and feet and whole legs, waiting to be carted outside the camp and piled atop the mound from the previous day.

I held men in my arms the moment they died. I prayed for the mercy of death to overtake some who couldn't die. I listened to the screams for death while holding down panicked and demented men with all my strength, in the fiercest heat of battle. And I even had to take the knife in my own hand to cut away tissue down to the bone, making it ready for the surgeon.

More than once I remember thinking it was the lucky ones who lay there dead. Ordeals more horrible and appalling awaited the wounded in the hospitals and our makeshift wards than they had encountered in the thick of enemy fire.

Sometimes there was more peace among the dying than among the living. When the cannon fire and shelling would stop for a while, the doctors and surgeons and medics, if they could be spared, would go out onto the field of recent battle to see what could be done for the freshly wounded. Accompanying them was never pleasant, for despite all I had seen, I feared some new horror that was more awful yet.

Following the doctors a few paces behind, we came upon the poor men the moment after the doctor had seen there was no hope and had moved on. Usually by this time the pain was past and life was quickly ebbing away. Sometimes fear filled their eyes, and they looked to us beseechingly, imploring us to do what the surgeon could not. Most seemed to show no fear. All had forced themselves to accept the inevitability of death, and to accept that it could come to them any day. Those who could do so usually mouthed only two words, "How long?"

It was no good lying to them. Everyone knew what was coming.

"Twenty minutes," a doctor might say. "Soon . . . not long, son, be brave . . . only another fifteen minutes. . . ."

And then to those of us who followed came the task of looking into those same eyes and communicating in those final moments something that said to them that life had been good. Mine was often the last human face a young man would ever see, mine the last eyes he would gaze into, mine the last voice his ears would hear.

Not mother, not sister, not wife, not father . . . but *me* . . . me—a girl he didn't know, had never seen before. And yet here I was, kneeling at his side, having to be the wife and mother and sister that he would never see again.

In those few brief, awful seconds, with but a look into the eyes, how can you speak of love, of hope, of *life*? How can you tell a boy whose life is draining out of him and soaking into the dirt beneath him about a Father in heaven who loves him?

Never was my faith so tested as in that furnace of terrible affliction when I followed the army of General Ulysses S. Grant into the wilderness of Virginia. I knew it had to be done. The war had to be won. But I hated it. I hated the death, even as I tried to give life in the midst of it.

Usually there were no words—only a look from my eyes into theirs. After a while the tears even quit coming, and for that I was sad. My heart wept, but for a time after that awful summer of 1864 my eyes were dry.

And then I would move on . . . to the next boy who perhaps could be saved and about whom the doctor was already giving me instructions . . . or on to the next pair of waiting eyes, and lips murmuring, "How long. . . ?"

We "fixed" the corpses by pinning the toes of their stockings together after their boots were taken off. That way, when they hardened from the rigor mortis, their legs were straight and more bodies could be laid out and more easily carried off to burial.

One boy the doctor had just passed looked up into my eyes as I knelt for a moment beside him. There was no fear in his face. Just a pale, white calm, the peace of knowing that it was nearly over.

"Fix me," he said softly to me.

My heart tried to rise up into my mouth, and I stifled a great cry of anguish.

Then he crossed his arms over his chest as he knew we did with corpses, and with the last strength of his legs managed to pull his feet together and touch his toes. I pulled off his boots, laid them beside him, then pinned his stockings together. He smiled thinly, then closed his eyes, looking so pleasantly at rest I thought him asleep.

I leaned over and gently kissed his forehead.

Not a muscle twitched as my lips met the grime-encrusted skin of his boyish forehead. He was so young!

I stood up, looking down again at his face. I knew he was dead.

CHAPTER 41

CLARA BARTON

In the wilderness of Virginia, behind the trenches and fortifications and siege works of Grant's army, in our mobile field hospitals where we moved about doing what we could to alleviate the massive suffering, I met Clara Barton.

I had heard of her, of course. Everyone involved in the medical and nursing aspect of the war knew of the bravery she had already demonstrated. When I suddenly found myself working beside her one day in a hastily erected tent, my first thought was not that I was meeting someone well known but that here was the first person I'd ever met who was like me! When we had the chance later, we talked about what had brought us here, and discovered so many similarities that we became fast friends at once.

She was in her early forties and, unmarried like me, had gone through almost all the same quandaries and doubts and frustrations over that very thing—being unmarried and working and living alone, when everyone except nuns seemed to think it a completely unnatural thing. We had a good laugh and several long talks about that.

She kept a journal, too, and that was as nice as finding out that she wasn't married. My only regret was our meeting like this, in the midst of battle, where it was impossible to find enough time to talk. She was so sweet and pleasant, always with a kind word to the men, always smiling, it was no wonder she had come to be known as the angel of the battlefield.

"How did you get started in all this?" I asked her one day when our hands were sharing a pot of warm water, scrubbing at the clothes that had been taken from the dead to use for bandages and slings.

"I was a clerk in the Patent Office in Washington when the war began, Corrie. Actually, I am from Massachusetts. My first exposure to the troops came when I met some boys who were down from my home state. I'd visit them and talk to them and try to help ease their homesickness."

"I'm sure they were glad to see such a pretty, smiling face," I said.

"Pretty? Corrie . . . come now. If you and I are going to be friends, we mustn't lie to each other!"

I laughed. It was easy to see from the twinkle in her eye that she was teasing me.

"Well, you're as pretty as I am, anyway," I said.

"Then I'll take your words as a compliment!"

"Now who is stretching the truth?" I said back.

It was time for both of us to laugh. It felt good to joke and laugh for a change in the midst of all the blood and death. These days there weren't too many opportunities to see the bright side of anything.

We were both silent a minute. Then a very thoughtful look came over Clara's face.

"Corrie," she said seriously, "I don't know what it's like in California, if it's anything like Massachusetts or Washington, but—"

She paused, trying to find the right words.

"Do you ever feel *odd*," she went on, "strange, out of step with the rest of the world, because, you know—because you're not married? Especially, do you think people look at you and think you a bit peculiar because you *want* to do other things in your life besides just marrying and having a family?"

I nodded, relieved to find someone at last who understood my predicament.

"You asked how I got started," she said. "As soon as I began meeting those poor, homesick men, I *wanted* to do something for them. How do you explain that kind of thing to someone whose only thought is to have a little place to call home, where they can stay for their whole life, always cooking over the same stove, always going to sleep in the same bed at night? There's nothing wrong with any of that, but I wanted to *do* something more than just go back to my boardinghouse every evening after my work at the Patent Office. . . . Corrie, I don't even know *where* I would call home now . . . do you understand me?"

How well I understood! After this last year, living in boardinghouses and traveling all around the North and visiting new cities and staying with people I'd never met before, and now here, following the fighting and sleeping outside under the stars or wherever there was room in one of the tents . . . I didn't know where to call home, either.

"So I started collecting things to take to the men—nothing much . . . soap and candies, tobacco and brandy when I could get it, lemons, supplies for sewing, homemade jellies. Oh, but you should have seen their faces! They were so appreciative.

"And then came Bull Run, and the wounded poured into the Washington hospitals. Before I knew it I was doing more than just helping with homesickness with little treats. That's when I began trying to help with nursing and assisting with the wounded in the hospitals, although at first I knew nothing whatever about it or what to do."

I thought of my own experience at Gettysburg. "When the blood is pouring out before your very eyes, I don't suppose it takes long to learn where to put the bandage," I said.

"I remained in Washington for a time," Clara went on. "I wanted to do more. I so hungered to help save lives, whether I knew anything about nursing or not. But I was afraid to follow the troops. I didn't want to be seen as a camp follower. I'm sure you understand, Corrie. I knew what they'd all think—the surgeons and officers and commanders, and even the regular army nurses like old Dotty Dix—they'd all think I was after nothing more than a husband."

I smiled. "I have a very dear uncle who thinks like that too," I said.

"I don't want a husband, Corrie. There's too much to be done, and a lot of it takes a woman to do it, not a man. Nobody questions Mary Ann Bickerdyke—have you met her?"

I told her I had.

"A dear, isn't she?"

"Yes."

"But she's older and a widow," Clara went on, "so nobody thinks it strange of her to be involved. And Dotty Dix—how about that woman?—have you met her?"

"Yes, but I don't think she thought too much of me."

"She doesn't want women like us around," laughed Clara. "That's exactly what I mean—even she, one of our own kind, thinks all we have on our mind before we're fifty years old is marriage, and it's just not right."

"You don't call her Dragon Dix?" I asked.

"Not that I haven't wanted to a few times," replied Clara. "I've been around her enough to know why she earned the title. And frankly, it's not that far wrong! But I owe her the courtesy of treating her more nicely than she treated me."

Neither of us said anything for a while. It was time to rinse out the trousers and shirts and change the water. Fortunately this was one occasion when we *had* fresh water to begin a new batch with. In another ten minutes we were back scrubbing in the pot again, with white, wrinkled fingers and palms.

"Have you ever thought about becoming a nun?" I asked her.

"I'm not Catholic."

"Neither am I, but I still find myself thinking about it." I told her briefly about my time at the Convent of John Seventeen.

Clara was quiet a long time. Finally she spoke. "You know, it's funny you should ask that," she said. "I'd nearly forgotten about it, but now that you remind me it comes back to my mind that I *did* think about it for a time back when I was nineteen or twenty and didn't know what a young, unmarried girl ought to do with herself. But then I went to Washington and later got involved in the war and found nursing more to my liking than praying and Bible reading."

"I don't know if I could make a lifetime of being around blood," I said.

"You seem to be doing fine here."

"It's what's needed, and there aren't enough hands. But I don't think I could ever get used to it. My stomach is always in knots. Are *you* used to the blood, the death, the screams, the pain?"

"Used to it—no," replied Clara. "I hope I never become *used* to it. It's unnatural, wrong. War is an evil thing. But the blood doesn't bother me any more than lots of things. When there's fighting, young men are wounded and need tending to. I suppose it's something I feel called to do, why God put me on the earth. It's when I feel most . . . I don't know what to say exactly, most— *myself* . . . most at peace with who I am supposed to be . . . and least concerned with what anyone else—Dotty Dix or the generals who don't think women ought to be near the fighting, or anyone else who thinks someone like me should be finding a husband and living a quiet life as somebody's wife—might think. My place, Corrie, is anywhere between the bullet and the battlefield. I'm happy here. It's what I want to do. It's what I know I was meant to do."

She stopped, and her hands stilled for a moment. She looked across at me, then asked, "When are you most yourself, Corrie? When are you most at peace with what you want to be doing?"

It was a hard question to answer. I had been trying to figure it out ever since meeting Sister Janette.

"I suppose when I'm writing," I said at length. "I love to think about ideas and try to put them on paper."

"What kind of ideas?"

"Anything . . . all kinds. Things about God, mostly—how the truths in the Bible give meaning to life, how God speaks and moves and is involved in what we do. But I like to write about anything— describing how something looks, or telling about people I've met. When I get the time, I'm writing right now about what it's like trying to help the wounded. I may even write something about you!"

Clara laughed. "And then what will you do with what you have written?"

"Give it to the newspapers, send it to my editor back in San Francisco to be printed there. To me it's important that people are told how things are, what it's like. And when I'm doing that— whether I'm telling about the war or describing something I've seen or even telling what I'm thinking and feeling inside—I suppose *that's* when I feel, as you called it, most *myself*."

"I write in my journal whenever I have the chance, but I've

never thought of writing for a newspaper. Women aren't suppose to *do* that."

"Neither are they supposed to be on the battlefield during a war!" I said.

"You're right," laughed Clara. "And I suppose as long as women like you and I have it in our heads to be doing things that women don't do, and have it in our hearts that we want to spend our lives doing them because we feel it's right that we do, I don't suppose we can ever get away from folks thinking of us as just a bit peculiar!"

I joined in her laughter. It was nice to have a companion who shared some of the same feelings and could understand. For once, even if briefly, I didn't mind being different than other young women my age.

CHAPTER 42

LINCOLN VS. McCLELLAN

George McClellan was one of the Union generals with whom President Lincoln had grown extremely frustrated early in the war, long before the star of Ulysses Grant began to rise so brilliantly onto the horizon. He had been the President's top general early in the war, and had led the first Union assault on Richmond back in 1862. Had Grant been in charge then instead, the war might have ended quickly. But McClellan was cautious, fearful, and indecisive. Rather than an all-out attack, he waited and probed timidly, sending message after message back to Washington for more troops, more supplies, more guns, more horses.

His hesitation gave Lee the time he needed: time to defeat McClellan and prolong the war for several more years. President Lincoln had put up with his failure to lead a decisive way long enough. Finally, in October of 1862, in frustration and anger, he relieved McClellan of his command for good.

The general was embittered, always felt he had been judged harshly and unjustly, and never forgave his Commander in Chief. When 1864 arrived, he ran for president, won the Democratic nomination, and thus was pitted head to head against his old rival, whom he still hated—Republican President Abraham Lincoln.

It was an ugly, bitter campaign throughout the late summer and fall months. Republicans accused the Democrats of treason because many of them were calling for peace even above the preservation of the Union. Even McClellan did not go quite that far, although he did agree with the stinging democratic editorialists who charged that the true objective of the "Negro-loving, Negro-hugging worshipers of old Abe" was miscegenation, a new word coined for the mixing and blending of white and black. Whatever the North as a whole may have thought about slavery itself, and however willing its people were to fight the South to outlaw slavery, it was clear that prejudice against the Negro race was as deeply ingrained in the cities of the Union as in those of the Confederacy. The election of 1864 proved it.

The South was elated at McClellan's nomination. Confederate Vice-President Alexander Stephens called it "the first real ray of light since the war began." If McClellan could defeat Lincoln, they were confident, the war could be brought to a swift end, and terms of peace could be arrived at which would insure the continuation of the Confederacy as a separate nation. The people of the North were ready for the war to end. Only Abraham Lincoln stubbornly insisted on prolonging it, the southerners thought. If Lincoln could be defeated, slavery and the Confederacy could both be preserved.

Such was Robert E. Lee's hope. Such was the hope of all loyal southerners, every one of whom hated Abraham Lincoln passionately. Every white man and woman, that is. To the slaves, he was the liberator.

At its core, the election was a struggle not between ideologies but between two men—one a President, the other a scorned general, still resentful over his dismissal from command. McClellan publicly called Lincoln "the original gorilla."

It did not look good for Mr. Lincoln. There had never before been an election for a nation in the midst of a civil war. No President since Andrew Jackson had served a second term, and the public mood in the North did not bode well for reversing the trend.

In August, President Lincoln said, "I am going to be *beaten*." Then he added, "And unless some great change takes place, *badly* beaten."

His only hopes seemed to lie with his two generals, Grant and Sherman, now engaged in the final fight to bring the Confederacy to its knees, hopefully before November.

CHAPTER 43

ANOTHER LETTER

While Lee and Grant slugged it out in Virginia, without noticeable success for either side, General Sherman was making more progress in the South. He and his 100,000 men made it to the vicinity of Atlanta in early August.

The siege lasted a month. But finally he hurled everything he had at the starving, beleaguered city, forcing the Confederate army out once and for all.

Sherman moved in to occupy it for the Union, then sent telegrams north to both his President and his friend and commander, Ulysses Grant: *Atlanta is ours and fairly won.*

But Atlanta was only half of Grant's final objective. The fall of the great "Gate City of the South" and second most important manufacturing center of the Confederacy could not alone seal the victory for the Union. There was still Richmond to be won. Sherman's victory, however, did boost morale in the northern states, so that President Lincoln's election prospects began to brighten.

And Lincoln, Grant, and Sherman had all learned the lesson of Gettysburg—that the enemy army must be destroyed so that it could not rise to fight again. Mead and McClellan were not commanding this time, but rather two determined fighters—Grant and Sherman. And they would insure that the victory at Atlanta completely destroyed the Confederacy's will to continue the struggle. Once Atlanta was secure, Sherman proposed to march his troops to the sea to take Savannah, then to drive northward, vanquishing the South entirely, until he met up with Grant in Virginia. It was a bold plan that would surely bring an end to the war. The South *refused* to lay down its arms, so it would have to be forced to do so.

It the meantime, a break came from the field hospital where I had been working, and I suddenly found myself traveling back to the Capital.

The message that had come to me was as unexpected as was the stir it caused in our camp. Only moments after the courier had arrived with newspapers and letters and a few supplies, Mother Bickerdyke came hurrying toward me.

"Corrie . . . Corrie," she said, "here's something for you—it looks important!"

As I took the small envelope from her hand, I couldn't imagine who could be writing to me here—or what could be so important. I was hardly aware of the other nurses and assistants following right behind her with looks of wonder and anticipation on their faces. It didn't dawn on me that they were all following her on account of *me*, and to see what the letter could possibly contain.

"The courier said there were two important messages from the President," Mrs. Bickerdyke went on as I took the envelope from her. " 'One of 'em's in here,' he said as he threw down the hospital pouch onto the ground. 'The other's marked *Urgent*, and it's for General Grant!' Then he galloped off on his horse toward the front lines."

"Hurry, Corrie," said one of the nurses. "Open it. We're dying to see!"

I fumbled with the edges of it and finally succeeded in pulling out the paper inside. I couldn't help glancing immediately to the familiar signature at the bottom, and it took me two or three readings to absorb the words that preceded it.

MISS HOLLISTER,

The reports reaching us here tell me you and Mrs. Bickerdyke and Miss Barton and all the other faithful servants of the Union are doing a brave and courageous job of healing in the midst of terrible suffering and anguish. I commend you, and all your colleagues of the Sanitary Commission and other agencies involved in the relief and medical efforts, and would ask you to personally convey my appreciation to all those with you there on the battlefields of Virginia. I only hope the brave soldiers under General Grant can sustain their valor under the terrible conditions of this mighty battle for freedom.

As I read the words aloud, I paused and glanced around. A few shouts and cheers and whoops and clapping broke out at the President's words, which they all knew had been addressed to them as well as me. How could we not be encouraged and uplifted to know that Mr. Lincoln had heard of and appreciated our efforts!

Sadly, I too am facing a mighty battle—this one political in nature. It appears more than likely that I will be defeated for reelection in November, and I fear such a result bodes extremely ill for the future of the nation, and could mean defeat for everything we have been fighting for.

Loathe as I am to remove you from such important work as you are doing, there are many capable hands who can carry it on. There is, however, only yourself who has the experience, both in politics and in reporting, to assist my campaign in the unique manner of which you are capable. You have campaigned on my behalf before, with good result, and I would like to call upon your assistance once again. Your experience on the battlefield will only add to the estimation in which you are already held by the growing readership in this nation, which recognizes your name as one they can trust.

I look forward to a speedy reply from you, and trust it will be an affirmative one. Please make an appointment to see me immediately upon your return to the Capital, and we will discuss our mutual ideas to insure a victory in November.

As always, I am indebted to you for your help, Miss Hollister.

I remain,
Sincerely yours,
A. LINCOLN

All the friends who were gathered around listening as I read began talking and congratulating me the moment I was through. So many things were flitting through my mind. Then I heard Clara's voice beside me.

"It would seem your writing *is* what you are to be doing," she said, "just as you told me. President Lincoln seems to think it is even more important for you to do than helping here with the wounded. It looks as if you're going to have the chance again to do what you *like* to do as well as helping the country."

"Just like you," I said, looking at her with a smile.

"I'll help with bandages, you with words from your pen."

CHAPTER 44

BACK IN WASHINGTON

I left the rear line of the camp the next day for Washington. General Grant's army had been stuck for more than two months outside Petersburg, south of Richmond, and it did not appear likely the Confederate capital was about to fall anytime soon. I went north, but the siege for the two vital cities went on.

After the front lines of fighting and the terrible condition of our camp hospitals, even the drab room at Marge Surratt's place would have seemed spacious and clean. But when I walked into my former room at Mrs. Richards' and set down my bag and looked around, I truly thought myself in a palace! Everything looked the same, and yet it seemed almost tinged with a heavenly cleanliness and purity.

Clean sheets! I can hardly describe what it felt like that first night to slide down between them and pull the quilt up and snuggle it in between my shoulders and neck, stretching my legs back and forth and knowing everything was *clean!*

And the quiet during the night! No moaning, no distant cannon fire, no sudden screams from a waking amputee who was feeling about for his hand or foot or leg in the night and suddenly realizing it wasn't there. No foul smells of smoke or gunpowder or wet hay, no smell of men coming in after months without a bath. No mud . . . no rain . . . no dirt and blood . . . no death.

Even with the quietness, I slept fitfully my first few nights back in the city. I could not rest comfortably and peacefully. Part of me somehow felt that I still ought to be back there in the hospital tents with the others whom I now considered my friends, helping

217

with the work that was always more than we could possibly do. And in truth, part of me still *was* there with them, even if only in my heart and my prayers. I would never forget . . . *could* never forget the experience. I felt that I would never be completely whole, completely at rest or at peace again after the things I had seen and heard and been part of.

But there was work for me to do here too—important work, after talking with the President.

His campaign was in trouble, he said. Sherman's victory in Atlanta had helped, but McClellan was still traveling about the North claiming to be the only man who could succeed in putting the war-ravaged country back together. He wanted me to write— to write as fast as I could and as much as I could—to tell where I'd been and what I'd seen, and to write as openly as I cared to, expressing my support for the President and my conviction that his reelection was vital to the country.

"You mustn't underestimate the mighty power of your pen, Corrie," he said. "Women can't vote for me, but they are the morale booster throughout the whole country. Without their hands we would have no stockings, no shirts, no trousers, no uniforms for our soldiers. You know as well as I do that without the women of the Union, there would be no Sanitary Commission, fewer nurses, fewer hospitals, fewer lives saved. Your words have a wide audience among women *and* men, and I'm counting on you to speak—with your pen and your mouth—to help those others who are engaged in like effort to rally the spirits of our people to persevere in this fight to the end, which is nearly at hand. McClellan must not be elected. It would mean doom to the Union, and, I fear, permanency to the Confederacy."

"Will the papers publish my articles if they're obviously and blatantly political?" I asked.

"We'll make sure they do!" interjected Mr. Hay.

"We have a very shrewd man on our staff who manages affairs with the press," added Mr. Lincoln. "You write what you can, Corrie. The Democratic papers, of course, won't touch it. But there are enough who are on our side that your words will be read in all the major cities."

"And California?" I asked.

"Yes, there too, and Oregon as well. Your own paper—what's your editor's name?"

"Mr. Kemble," I said.

"Yes, Kemble—well *they'll* print your articles, surely, and I'll make a note to him personally, asking him to circulate them around the state."

"To the competition?" I asked.

"I'll make a personal request. And . . . well, if he's not in agreement, you can tell him we'll file your articles with *another* of the major California papers."

"I'm sure he'll be happy to do as you ask," I said, smiling.

"What do you say, Corrie? Are you with me in this? Will you write . . . for the Union cause . . . and for *me*—to help us with this reelection?"

"Of course, Mr. President."

"Do I still detect some hesitancy?"

"Oh no, not about you, or my belief in the country or your presidency. It's only that I don't suppose I'm as confident as you seem to be that anything I say or do will make that much difference."

"You leave that to us," said Mr. Hay. "We have many skillful people hard at work on the election. We have enlisted the support of a number of other known reporters—men, of course. There will be many people speaking on behalf of the President. And all of it together, including what you will be able to do, *will* carry the day. You mustn't worry about results. Do what *you* do best, and we will do what *we* do best."

CHAPTER 45

MY THIRD PRESIDENTIAL CAMPAIGN

I began immediately to do what Mr. Lincoln and Mr. Hay had asked. I didn't know what result it might have, but I could and would write about what I'd seen, about what I thought, and about the importance to the country of Mr. Lincoln getting reelected.

Everything now was so different than the two previous times I had been involved in campaigns—for Mr. Fremont in 1856 and for Mr. Lincoln in 1860. I'd never really stopped to think about whether I ought to be a Republican or a Democrat. But I had supported the Republican candidate for three elections in a row because of the men themselves and because of the slavery question.

That very afternoon I sat down to try to begin a new article about the war and the election and Mr. Lincoln.

In 1860 I supported a man I'd never met for President of this great country we call the United States of America. I didn't know Abraham Lincoln, but I believed slavery to be wrong, and I felt strongly that we needed a President who would seek to rid our nation of it and would stand up for the truth that our country was founded on—freedom.

So when they asked me to help, to speak out on behalf of his election, I agreed, even though I was young and timid. Mr. Lincoln was elected. My home state of California voted for Mr. Lincoln, as did most of the rest of the states of the Union.

Now, four years later, a lot has changed for all of us. We've been fighting a terrible civil war almost since the last election. Hundreds of thousands of our sons and friends and brothers have been killed. Mr. Lincoln has freed the slaves and declared slavery illegal.

But the most important thing that has changed is that we are now *two* countries instead of one. As important as the question of slavery is, we are fighting now to preserve the United States of America as *one* nation. And after all this fighting and all this killing, we are still a country at war, and the South is still unwilling to come back and be part of the Union it should never have left.

If we quit now, these last four years will have been for nothing. At Gettysburg ten months ago, Mr. Lincoln delivered a dedication speech for the young men who had died there. He said that we had to resolve that they did not die in vain. He said that we had to dedicate ourselves to the great task before us of *finishing* the work that they began.

That work is the preservation of freedom. That is what they fought for, and died for. And for us to give up now will mean that all who have given their lives these last four years will have given them for no result. For nothing will have been gained.

If we give up now, the things we have been fighting for will not come to pass. We will remain *two* nations—the Union and the Confederacy. Slavery will remain in the South, and the dream of freedom for all men and women will vanish.

Four years ago I supported a man I did not know because I believed in what he believed in. Today I support a man whom I *do* know because he is the only man who can lead this nation forward—this *entire* nation—into the full measure of the freedom we are fighting for, and into the full stature of nationhood that is the destiny of this land. To turn our back now on Mr. Lincoln and all he has stood for on our behalf will be to invalidate the lives of all those who have sacrificed for the cause of freedom and unity.

I urge you all, men who can vote and even women who cannot, to continue supporting our President, Mr. Abraham Lincoln, until this battle, now drawing to an end, is fully won and freedom is restored throughout our *whole* land.

"That's it exactly!" exclaimed Mr. Hay when he had read the two sheets I'd handed him. "Yes, Miss Hollister . . . yes, this is wonderful—the President will be most pleased!"

I couldn't help being a little embarrassed. He continued to look over what I'd written with an expression of surprise, but also with a smile.

"The President might want to use some of your phrases himself—*the full stature of nationhood . . . the destiny . . .* you've really touched upon some remarkable concepts, Miss Hollister—*invalidate the lives of those who have sacrificed . . .* yes, I'm certain some of this will find its way into the President's own remarks. Very well done!"

"I'm happy you like it," I said.

"It is perfect—just what we were after. Within a week we will have this running in as many of the papers sympathetic to our cause as we can."

"And the *Alta*?" I reminded him.

"Of course. I'll arrange to have it wired to San Francisco, too. Now, Miss Hollister, do you have other ideas for more such pieces?"

"I . . . I suppose—that is, yes, I always have ideas, but I never know exactly what's going to come out until I sit down and start writing."

"Well, however you do it, you get to work on some more of it! If *this* is what comes out when you put your hand to the paper, I would like to see, perhaps, a new article once a week—or even more often, if possible. With Sherman's victory and your articles and the President's campaigning, I think we may turn this election around yet. If only Grant can keep Lee from running him out of Virginia. A Lee victory now would be a devastating blow to our whole effort."

He rose and led me to the door.

"So, Miss Hollister," he said, "continue just as you have been doing. Bring me whatever you come up with. And in the meantime, I'll also be contacting you about making some campaign appearances."

"You mean . . . speaking?" I said.

"Somewhat, perhaps. But don't be anxious. I've heard that you are a fine speaker."

"I do better with my pen."

"Well, we'll see. But just be ready—I may want to call on you to accompany either the President or one of our Republican senators on a campaign swing or two—Ohio, New York, Pennsylvania, New Jersey . . . these are states we must not let McClellan win."

"I'm sure nobody would pay much attention to—"

"Come, come, Miss Hollister. I know better than that, even if you do not. There have been reports, even from as far away as California, about some of the appearances you made on the President's behalf four years ago. I happen to know that you are very effective on the stump as well as at a desk."

I could feel my face turn red. How could I convince him that I really disliked standing up in front of a crowd of people?

"Besides," he went on, "you won't always have to *say* anything at all. Your mere presence says something too—a woman sharing the platform with the politicians, a woman whose name people recognize, a woman who has been on the front lines where the fighting is, and now who is writing and appearing on behalf of the President—not to mention that your book about California when you were younger is beginning to circulate a bit. It all speaks very well for the President."

"I'll do whatever you would like me to," I said finally.

"Then you keep writing articles and editorials for President Lincoln, and I will be in contact with you."

He shook my hand and I left.

CHAPTER 46

ON THE CAMPAIGN TRAIL

I did as Mr. Hay wanted, and kept writing. Ideas kept coming to me, and I wrote them down. Sometimes they turned out to be an article that was printed, sometimes not, but I sat down at my writing desk every day to see what I might be able to say. I wrote about Mr. Lincoln, about how I saw the country, about some of my personal experiences both at Gettysburg and recently in Virginia, and even now and then about something relating to California, because there were voters back on the West Coast too, and they had to vote for Mr. Lincoln as well as those closer by.

A week and a half after my return to Washington, Mr. Hay asked me to accompany several congressmen and their wives, two senators, and the vice-presidential candidate, Mr. Johnson, on a train trip to campaign in Pennsylvania and Ohio, then back through Buffalo, New York, and south to Philadelphia before returning to Washington.

"There will be other women along," he said. "All arrangements for lodging and the like will be taken care of. You'll have a wonderful time, and we hope it will be a very effective opportunity to sway the vote in these crucial states."

"Do you want me to stop writing articles?" I asked.

"Oh no. You should still have time to continue that work as well. You will not have to speak more than a few times. We simply want to be able to introduce you and let people see your face. But we want fresh new articles to continue to appear as well. The President himself will be joining the party in Philadelphia for two major campaign addresses."

I agreed, and told Mrs. Richards of my plans. Since we'd be gone three or four weeks, I told her I'd move my things to one side of the wardrobe and the bottom drawers of the dresser so that she would be able to rent out the room to other travelers or visitors to the city in my absence.

The very morning we left, a letter arrived from Clara Barton. I waited until we were on the train north to Baltimore and then Harrisburg before reading it.

Everyone here sends you greetings. We all miss you, though we are glad you do not have to see the suffering for a while, and we know the work you are doing for the President may help the war end sooner.

But oh, Corrie, the suffering is so dreadful. With every new attempt at Petersburg, more men are killed and wounded. Where will it all end? The battle is a tactical one, with standoff after standoff. There have even been reports of spies in our midst, even plots against Generals Grant and Meade. Yet our work in the hospitals goes on much as it was when you were with us. We have had to continue to move with the army, making use of homes and buildings in the surrounding towns whenever we can. Yet the means we have of helping is woefully inadequate!

I saw, crowded into one old sunken hotel, lying upon its bare, wet, bloody floors, five hundred fainting men holding up their cold, weak, dingy hands as I passed, and beg in heaven's name for a cracker to keep them from starving (and I had none); or to give them a cup that they might have something to drink water from, if they could get it (and I had no cup and could get none). As much as comes to us daily from the faithful women of the northern states who labor making bandages and supplies, we have so much less than is needed.

I saw two hundred six-mule army wagons in a line, stretching down the street to headquarters, and reaching so far out on the Wilderness Road that I never found the end of it; every wagon crowded with wounded men, stopped, standing in the rain and mud, wrenched back and forth by the restless, hungry animals all night. Dark spots in the mud under many a wagon told all too plainly where some poor fellow's life had dripped out in those dreadful hours.

A man came through the camp just last night, following

the battle with his wagon, an itinerant embalmer. Oh, just to read the words of his dreadful flyer made my flesh crawl: "Persons at a distance, desiring to have the bodies of their deceased friends disinterred, embalmed, disinfected, or prepared and sent home, and have it promptly attended to, apply to the office of Simon Garland, 35 South 13th Street, Philadelphia. No zinc, arsenic or alcohol is used. Perfect satisfaction guaranteed."

To think of human death being reduced to such a grisly business! He was prowling about the hospital looking for the bodies of those he had been hired to fix. It was all too terrible to think about!

Do whatever you can, dear Corrie. Tell our President, tell the people of the country, how awful it truly is. This cannot go on . . . it *must* end! The killing and destruction must be put to a stop. Tell them, Corrie—from all of us!

I was wiping away tears even before finishing her words. I determined then and there to somehow find a way to include some of what Clara had said in my very next article. In fact, within ten minutes I had pulled out my pen and paper and began right there on the train, as best I could without spilling the ink.

The trip was long and tiring, yet exhilarating too. I met many new people and saw places I'd never seen before. Our first major stop was in Pittsburgh, then on to Columbus, then north to Akron, Cleveland, Erie, Buffalo, and Rochester before heading south. When I stood up to speak for the first time, I tried to remember what I'd said the first time I was on the platform in Sacramento four years earlier. Afterward, people came up to talk to me, especially women, and a lot of them had read either my book or some of the articles, and they were all so nice and kind with their words. After that it began to get easier, just as it had when I'd traveled with Mr. King, although I still preferred when the congressmen and Mr. Johnson did the speechmaking and only introduced me or said something about my articles.

I did manage to find time to keep writing, although it wasn't quite as easy as if I'd been back at Mrs. Richards'. During the campaign trip, I sent four articles back to Mr. Hay. One of them appeared in the Buffalo paper the day we arrived. One of the senator's wives came excitedly into my room of the hotel where we were staying, carrying it in her hand.

"Corrie, look," she said, "here's the article you sent back to John Hay when we were in Pittsburgh. I've brought you a copy of the paper."

"Thank you," I replied.

I glanced at it, but was embarrassed to read any of it just then.

Later that night, after I was alone and ready for bed, I opened the paper up to the second page and read what I'd written on the train as we'd traveled across Pennsylvania. As we'd gone through Harrisburg and Gettysburg, so many things were in my mind. I thought a great deal about Sister Janette and all she'd told me about Pennsylvania and William Penn and others of the early leaders of the country. Then I began thinking of the founding of our nation as a whole and of the men who had written the Constitution and organized our government. And I thought about slavery and what part it had played in our country right from the beginning.

When the fathers of our country wrote the Declaration of Independence, they said, "We hold these truths to be self-evident—that all men are created equal; that they are endowed by their Creator with certain inalienable rights; that among these are life, liberty, and the pursuit of happiness." When they later wrote the Constitution, by which we've been governed ever since, they again spoke of "the blessings of liberty" as the reason why the Constitution had to be written.

These documents have been the very foundations of this nation ever since. Yet what was the *liberty* they spoke of? What did they mean when they wrote *all men are created equal*? Who were the *all men* they spoke of?

Many of the very men themselves who signed the Declaration of Independence and the Constitution owned slaves. Five of the original thirteen states were from what is today the Confederacy. Four of our first five presidents were from Virginia, what we call today a "slave state."

These men, our very founding fathers whom we revere, obviously didn't think there was anything wrong with slavery. So what are we to make of their words *liberty* for *all men* and *created equal*?

As I read, I could not help but be reminded of Miss Stansberry, now Mrs. Rutledge, and how she had drilled us from our history books, making us memorize the first part of the Declaration of Independence and the Preamble to the Constitution, as well as the names of all the Presidents. Zack had hated it, but I was glad now for all the hard study she'd made us do.

If our nation truly was founded on "liberty" and "equality" for "all men," why are we now engaged in this terrible war?

Perhaps something was wrong from the very beginning, something that the founding fathers didn't know was wrong, but something that was eventually going to have to be fixed. Perhaps Abraham Lincoln is the man who has taken upon himself the task of completing what the founding fathers only began.

This great nation was founded and built upon principles known to few other nations on earth—principles of liberty and freedom and justice. And yet perhaps there has been a crack in that foundation, a crack barely visible, and indeed *invisible* to many, a crack which has from the very beginning of our nationhood weakened the structure of the nation we have been trying to build. That crack is the existence of slavery.

Why has there been a crack? Why has the foundation been weak?

Because something was established as a truth in the foundation of the country which *wasn't* a truth in the way things actually were. The Constitution and Declaration of Independence spoke of equality and liberty, and yet the laws of the land permitted slavery and inequality. Two opposite and contradictory things have been allowed to exist in this country all this time. Yet we still talk about this nation as the land of the free. But it has never been truly and completely a land of freedom.

Four years ago, our brave President said, "It is time to fix this crack of inconsistency . . . it is time that we at last make what have been truths in principle truths in fact . . . it is time we make *all* people in this land we call a land of freedom—it is time we make *all* people free at last."

Now we are fighting a dreadful and awful war over whether this crack is worth fixing. We must find out what kind of a nation we really are, and what kind of a people we really are. Do freedom, and justice, and equality really matter, or will this nation be satisfied to say that our government is founded upon such principles but in fact deny those very rights to a large number of people because of the color of their skin? Do we *really* believe that "all men are created equal"?

I think we *do* believe that. I know I do, and I think most northerners, and probably a lot of southerners do, too. Therefore, we must continue to support President Lincoln. The crack is nearly healed. If we do not return him to the presidency now, it will be to give up when we are so close to making our land truly a land of freedom to all, when we have paid such a great price and fought such a great battle to do so.

We must now complete building what the founding fathers only began. And to insure that the foundation is strongly built and that its cracks are completely healed, we *must* reelect President Lincoln to another term of office.

CHAPTER 47

A FATEFUL NIGHT

For the rest of the campaign trip, everyone seemed to treat me just a little differently. Something about the article made them look at me almost with a look of astonishment. The women complimented me on what I'd written and said they'd never read anything like that before from me. They asked how I knew all those things to say and how I'd thought of it and how I knew so much history. But the men seemed to wonder to themselves if I was really the person writing those articles. In person I probably seemed shy and didn't say too much. And then when they read what I'd written, it didn't sound at all like the same person.

I suppose I had changed some. Being around Washington and important people, and listening and talking to them, I suppose I didn't sound quite so much like a little girl from the backwoods, as I once had. My writing was getting a little better too, at least people told me so. I wondered sometimes what Mr. Kemble and Mr. Macpherson—who always said he liked my "homespun" style!—thought of it now. Maybe they didn't like it as much as before!

Afterward it seemed that this article, more than any other, was one people remembered reading. In Philadelphia, they introduced me as the young woman who wrote "so eloquently about the crack in our nation's foundation." Everyone had been nice until then. But after Buffalo, people treated me with greater courtesy and respect. Maybe for the first time some of them realized what Mr. Hay had been saying to me all along, that the written word was just as able to influence people as speechmaking.

Our itinerary had been somewhat uncertain. President Lincoln joined us in Philadelphia for two speeches; then he and Mr. Johnson and two of the senators went on to New York, while the rest of us returned to Washington. I hadn't been able to let Mrs. Richards know when I would be returning, and as a result, my room was occupied on the evening when I arrived back in the Capital. She offered to find me a place for the night in her own part of the house, but after thinking about it briefly, I realized that this might be an opportunity sent by the Lord for some purpose. So I told her not to worry about me and that I'd see her the following afternoon.

Thus I found myself again knocking on the door of Marge Surratt's boardinghouse.

After everything I'd been through down in Virginia, and now after three weeks on trains and at meetings and in hotels, I was almost eager to see her. Hers wasn't exactly a friendly face, but there is something unique and special about laying eyes on someone you've been praying for. The moment I saw her, the most remarkable little stab of genuine feeling for the lady sprang up within my heart. I suppose praying for *her* had worked changes within *me*. But I thought I saw the beginnings of a smile as she saw me standing there in front of her.

"Hello, Mrs. Surratt," I said. "I need a room for tonight. Do you have anything available?"

"Turned you out, did they?"

"No, I just got back earlier than I anticipated."

"Well, you might as well come in, now that you're here. You can go to the same room as before. Supper's still at six."

"I remember," I replied with a smile. "Six sharp."

She almost smiled. I took my bag and went up to the room. Even its drab colors and ugly curtains didn't look half so bad this time.

Supper was uneventful. The men around the table were all faces I'd never seen before, and no more talkative than the others had been earlier. I helped her clean up afterward and tried to talk. But it wasn't much use. She seemed distracted and fidgety, looking toward the door and out the window as if she were expecting someone. Eventually I excused myself and went back to my room. If I was going to get anywhere with her, it would have to wait still longer.

I was tired and went to bed immediately. It was probably no later than eight o'clock when I lay down, and I think I was asleep within five minutes.

Dreams intruded into my consciousness. There were faces I didn't recognize, although they were familiar and I knew I should know them. A feeling of oppression came over me, but the dreams were fuzzy and undefined. There was more feeling to them than sights and activity—feelings of dread, of danger, and around and behind it a feeling of hurt and pain. I wanted to cry, but no tears would come. I had been hurt. I could feel it, but I didn't know why. And with it came the feeling that more hurt was coming, that danger was somewhere close at hand.

But where? I couldn't see it, couldn't find it. Danger to whom? I wasn't the one who was in danger. It was someone else . . . someone important. Who could it be? I had to warn them . . . then came again the hurt, the stab of pain in my own heart.

Visions of the battlefield began to distort everything . . . blood and screams . . . broken bodies lying everywhere, explosions of gunfire . . . mangled limbs and hands and feet . . . red bandages and blood dripping from them. Then came nurses all dressed in white. There was Clara and Mrs. Bickerdyke. They were talking in hushed tones. . . . Then again came the pain— were they talking about me? Had I done something they disapproved of? Why were they talking. . . . I couldn't quite hear them, couldn't make out their voice . . . if I could just listen more intently. . . .

The white figures disappeared, and there were two men, leaders, commanding men, standing in front of thousands, trying to speak, but no words would come from their lips. I thought I recognized the two men, but why could they not speak? Why were such looks of sadness and pain upon their faces?

Then I did hear voices again . . . softly this time. Still the two bearded leaders moved their lips, but I knew the voices were not theirs. There were other voices, speaking in hushed tones . . . not wanting to be heard . . . speaking evil things.

They were talking *about* the men in beards, whispering so as not to be heard.

And still over it all was such a feeling of dread . . . of pain . . . of suffering to come. But I couldn't hear them . . . I couldn't make out the words . . . if only I could. . . .

CHAPTER 48

VOICES IN THE NIGHT

Suddenly I was awake!

The room was dark. It was the middle of the night. I couldn't even guess the time.

And there *were* voices!

Not voices from a dream, but *real* voices—speaking in subdued and hushed tones, yet above a whisper. Through the thin walls I could hear them plainly, although I could not make out the thread of the conversation. The discussion was fervent, but not exactly an argument.

I listened for several seconds in the blackness. Then all the feelings of oppression and dread and fear and hurt from out of my dream blanketed me all over again. But this time it was real! Now I knew why my dreaming consciousness had felt such pain at the sound of the voice that had intruded through the walls and into my sleeping brain.

My heart pounded, and my whole body broke into an instant sweat. Along with the pain, a new emotion rose up within me— anger! I was filled with such a tumult of feelings that I almost began to wonder if I really *was* awake!

I threw back the covers and sprang to my feet. In the darkness I sought a drinking glass that I'd set on the nightstand. It was still half full of the water I'd brought to the room with me. Hastily I put it to my lips and swallowed it in two gulps.

I tiptoed silently to the wall near my bed from which the sounds were coming. With great care I placed the open end of the glass against the wall, then rested my right ear against the other end.

Again I strained to listen, and I could hear the voices in the next room clearly.

There was no mistaking it. I *did* know the voice. It was Cal Burton!

I couldn't believe my ears! How could it be? Yet I *knew* it was him!

" . . . That may be, Surratt," he was saying, "but I don't think even your contacts could get you in that close."

"There are times when the protection breaks down. It only takes a second and the deed is done." The speaker must have been Mrs. Surratt's son.

Cal laughed. "And one more second for you to be killed too," he said.

"Kidnapping is the best plan," interjected another voice. "Then we could exchange him for every Confederate prisoner they're holding."

"That's still the wrong target, Booth," said Cal. "You're all a bunch of crazy malcontents—"

He was interrupted by a German voice I could barely make out, "Watch what you be saying, Burton, you swine, or I kill *you* first."

"Atzerodt's right, Cal," chuckled the fellow he had called Booth. "We outnumber you three to one."

"In everything but brains," rejoined Cal. "Look at the prac- ticalities of this, Booth. When you aim too high and miss, you've wasted your chance and you won't get it back. The kidnapping scheme's foolhardy. It would never work, and would only rally people around him all the more. I know you think you've been cowardly all this time for not joining up, and I know you dream of being a spy like our friend Surratt here—"

"Be careful of the insults, Burton, or I'll give my German friend leave to wring your neck."

"Are you going to deny what I've said?"

Booth was silent.

"Then like I said, look at the practicalities. No foolhardy deed of heroic daring is going to do the Confederacy any good. If we want to turn the tide of the war, we can't make a martyr of the old gorilla. It's Grant we've got to concentrate on, I tell you. If he's not stopped, he'll eventually push Lee back and overrun Richmond and all will be lost."

"And what do you propose?" asked the man called Surratt.

"That we focus our efforts there, on Grant. If we can eliminate him, the will of his army will collapse."

"And are *you* going to infiltrate his camp?" asked a skeptical Booth.

"Of course not. I'm no assassin."

"Who then?"

"I have someone high up in his command whom I am confident can be persuaded to see that there's an accident."

"You can get closer than you think I could?" said Surratt.

"Not me personally. One of Grant's officers. If you can lay your hands on the sum of money you spoke of, and one of the two of you, either you or Booth, can get it to me in Richmond, I have ways of contacting my friend, the lieutenant. He will do it for us, I'm certain. Then none of you will face the gallows."

"Or you," added the German voice.

"I have no intention of getting so close myself that my hands get blood on them."

"I don't know whether I trust you or not, Burton," said Booth, "but your scheme has a ring of sense to it. But believe me, if it fails, we will have to look to stronger measures."

"Have it your way, Booth," laughed Cal. "You and your demons of greatness! You would make the world your stage if only given half the chance. I, on the other hand, only believe in taking what opportunities are presented. Pragmatism, Booth. It's probably not a word you are familiar with. But I tell you, Grant is the target that *is* within our reach, and which will serve the Confederacy just as well."

"We will go along with you . . . for now."

"Good. Then meet me in Richmond. Will four days be enough, Surratt?"

The other mumbled something, but I could not make it out.

"We'll make it five then. You be in Richmond on Wednesday next. At noon, say. I'll meet you at Winder Supply. I'm on good terms with the owner. He'll have a room we can use."

"I don't know the place."

"Down the hill from the State House, on the river, about a hundred yards along the waterfront."

"I'll find it."

"Wednesday," repeated Cal. Then I heard him rise and leave the house.

CHAPTER 49

MIDNIGHT FLIGHT

What could it be but a plot to kill General Grant?

My mind was racing a thousand directions at once. Even all the old anger and pain over what had happened with Cal disappeared. I temporarily forgot about the money he'd stolen. He had obviously gotten mixed up with some evil-sounding men and was still willing to do just about anything for the sake of his own personal gain. And it sounded, too, as if his allegiance to the Confederacy had grown considerably. Maybe he had become one of the South's important men, just as he'd wanted.

But killing? I could hardly believe that . . . even from Cal! Yet I'd heard what I'd heard, and by now I was wide awake—so wide awake I was shivering both from the cold and from the fearful things I had overheard. I was remembering, too, things Mr. Hay had said about the Surratts. I felt very alone and exposed and isolated.

And suddenly I felt very unsafe in this house!

I had to get away and somehow get word to General Grant of the danger. Should I notify the President? No, he was still in Philadelphia. Mr. Hay was there with him.

Whom could I tell? Who would *believe* me? If I went to the police or the army headquarters, I would sound like some crazy lunatic. They wouldn't know me, wouldn't know my connections with the President. And what difference did those connections make, anyway? Who would believe such an insane story?

As my mind raced over it all, my hands fumbled about in the darkness for my clothes. In a few minutes I was dressed.

Should I leave immediately? What if they heard me?

I hadn't heard the front door open or close. What if they were all staying here tonight? What if Cal himself were in the next room? If they heard so much as a peep out of me, they'd pounce on me in a second.

But how could I wait till morning?

There wasn't a moment to lose. One way or another, I wasn't going to wait for them to find me, and then do whatever awful things they might do to me!

I had already been stuffing my things into my leather bag, and now squeezed it shut and cinched up the leather straps. It was still dark, but I dared not light a candle. I was confident I could make it down the stairs in the dark and to the safety of the street outside.

I picked up my bag and tiptoed softly to the door. I didn't care how threadbare it might be, I was happy enough for the old rug on the floor to keep my feet silent.

Slowly I grasped the latch. With hardly a squeak it turned. I pulled the door open. It gave no sound and I breathed a silent sigh of relief. I stepped out onto the bare wood floor. Neither the landing nor the stairs were carpeted.

I swung the door closed behind me, then took two or three small steps across the landing, feeling about with my foot for the edge of the first step.

I found it, paused, then gingerly began making my way down the narrow flight. My heart was pounding so rapidly I thought it would wake the entire house!

Slowly, one step at a time, feeling my way with cautious steps, I inched down the stairs . . . one step . . . two . . . three. If only I could remember how many there were! Six . . . seven.

It seemed there were twelve or thirteen, maybe sixteen in all! . . . Nine . . . ten . . . I had to be over halfway. Any moment my foot would find the bottom landing and the outside door.

. . . Thirteen . . . fourteen . . .

Suddenly what sounded like an ear-splitting *creak* gave way under my foot. I'd forgotten how terribly the bottom three stairs squeaked! I remembered noticing it almost every time I climbed them!

I froze in sheer panic. The only sound in the blackened hallway was the beating in my chest! Maybe no one had heard it. I would wait, then would stretch my leg all the way to the bottom and avoid the first two offending slabs of loosened wood.

I remained stock-still.

"Who's there?' suddenly came from somewhere upstairs behind me.

My heart jumped into my throat!

"Who's there, I say?" It was Mrs. Surratt's voice. I heard the sound of her footsteps trudging across the floor of her room. "John, is that you? George? Who's there?"

For another moment I was paralyzed. Then I heard her hand on the latch. It was all I needed to jolt my legs into activity once more. Even as the light from her candle entered the hallway above and sent its inquiring rays down the stairs, I flew down the remaining steps, heedless now of either the squeaks of the wood or the echo of my footfall, and raced across the entryway to the door. My free hand found the latch and turned it hard. It was locked.

Behind me I now heard Mrs. Surratt's hastening feet and angry voice. "John," she cried to her son, "John . . . get out here now, I tell you!"

I had dropped my bag and was now fumbling with the bolt and latch of the door with frantic and sweating fingers, paying no more attention to the noise I was making. The metallic sounds echoed badly in the still night!

The door swung open! I grabbed up my bag again and the next instant was through and onto the porch. The cold night air slapped me in the face, but I was hardly aware of it. Behind me Mrs. Surratt's muffled feet were followed by the thick clomping of boots down the stairs.

"After her, John!" cried Mrs. Surratt.

I was running now, clumsily carrying my bag. The night was black. How thankful I was there was no moon!

I crossed the street in seconds, then ran to the left, staying on the dirt of the street rather than pounding loudly along the wooden walk. I sprinted as fast as my legs would carry me. It seemed like an eternity, but must have been only two or three seconds.

I heard the bolt and latch open behind me from where I had

just come. That same instant I threw myself into an alley that appeared on my right, stopped, and leaned against the side wall of a feed store, out of sight of the boardinghouse.

I heard John Surratt take several steps across the porch and onto the street.

"Hey . . . what do you think you're doing?" I heard him call out into the night. "Come back here . . . come back, or I'll have to hurt you . . . you hear me!"

My lungs heaved up and down. My mouth was wide open, trying to gulp down the air as silently as I could. My chest burned with pain. I stood absolutely still, not moving a muscle.

I could hear Surratt's boots walking slowly across the street. Then the sound ceased.

In terror I listened for the next sound. I knew he was looking up and down, trying to figure out which way I had gone. At any moment he could appear at the entrance of the alleyway beside me. Then his hands would grab me and close around my neck!

"Come back, and I won't hurt you," he called out again.

The sound was still some distance away. Then he began slowly running again along the street. His footsteps receded. He was going the other direction!

I let out a long breath. When he was about a block away, I slowly stuck my head out from behind the edge of the wall. The door to Mrs. Surratt's was closed. At least she had not followed him outside. I craned my neck out a bit more to see if I could see her son in the distance.

It was too dark to see him, but I could still hear his booted feet. They were even farther away than before.

I crept out of the alley and back into the street. If I couldn't see him, neither could he see me from the same distance!

As rapidly as I was able without breaking into a noisy run, I began walking along the street in the opposite direction. I walked the rest of the way to the next street, took it to the right, and, now that I was well away from the boardinghouse, eased again into a gentle run.

I went on for two or three more blocks, turning several times.

All at once I realized I had arrived at the railroad yard.

I was still too close to the boardinghouse! Where could I hide?

I glanced around. Everything was still and quiet and mysterious. The vague shadows and outlines of the silent trains and buildings gave a spooky and frightening look to the night.

I listened behind me, sure that at any moment I would hear John Surratt's heavy feet chasing after me!

I had to get out of sight, out of the open. I had to conceal myself somehow!

I kept moving slowly, without direction or a plan, across the yards, stumbling across the huge iron tracks.

Suddenly looming before me were the huge boxcars of an immobile freight train. I squinted into the darkness. One of the cars appeared empty, its great sliding door standing open.

I approached slowly, trying to quiet my feet on the rocky surface below.

"Is . . . is anybody in there?" I whispered up into the car as loudly as I dared.

No sound came back through the night.

"Hello . . . anybody?" I repeated.

Still there was no answer.

I hoisted my bag up onto the floor of the car, then felt about for an abrupt edge or a hook or anything to get my hands on. In another few seconds I was scrambling up into the freight car. In another second or two, I had my bag beside me and was safely hidden away in the blackness inside.

John Surratt would never find me now!

I leaned back against the wall of the car, finally aware of my exhaustion, breathed deeply, and closed my eyes.

CHAPTER 50

UNCERTAIN THOUGHTS

When I next came to myself, the gray of dawn had spread over the city of Washington.

How long I had been there I could hardly guess. I stretched the kinks out of my muscles and tried to rearrange myself, then glanced about. The car was empty.

I stood up and poked my head out.

The freight yard was still silent, and the city still slept. But I could hear a few voices and clanking sounds in the distance. Morning was approaching, and I knew there would be a great deal of activity around here within an hour as the trains were readied for their various destinations.

I sat back down inside. I had to think.

Cal had said five days. Now there were only four. Yesterday was—what was it? We'd arrived back in the Capital on Thursday afternoon . . . that made today Saturday . . . no, that was only yesterday. Today was Friday!

There were *still* five days!

Five days to get word to General Grant!

There must be someone else I should tell! I couldn't go chasing off as I'd done two or three times in the past. I was older now, not so impulsive and foolhardy, as Pa had called me then. I'd been lucky that everything had turned out so well when I'd ridden off to Sonora after Derrick Gregory. But now there was danger to more people than just me. I had to settle down and think through what would be the wisest thing to do!

I could go to Mrs. Richards' house as soon as the sun was up. I could talk to her about—

No, I thought to myself. By now they would know it was me who had left in the night. Mrs. Surratt had probably rummaged through my room within minutes of my flight. They would suspect I had overheard, with my room right next to the parlor. I had mentioned to her earlier where I was staying.

No, her son—or even Cal or that mean-sounding German fellow!—was probably hiding somewhere nearby, watching for my return, waiting to nab me!

And if they did know it was me, and suspected what I was planning to do, might they accelerate the timetable? Maybe they wouldn't wait the five days after all! That is, if Cal was still there . . . or if they could get word to him.

There could be no delay! The danger to Mr. Grant might now be ever closer than next Wednesday.

Should I telegraph him?

They would be sure to think it a hoax! He would never remember my name. I could send it anonymously! No . . . that would be even worse. They would think it a Confederate plot to distract him and cause him to change his plans.

Worse still, any message I tried to get to him, by telegraph or through somebody else, could easily be intercepted before it got to the general, either by the lieutenant spy Cal was talking about, or by somebody else who didn't think the message valid enough to bother the general about.

No . . . somehow I had to see General Grant myself. . . . I had to tell him face-to-face. Otherwise he wouldn't know how serious it was if I didn't tell him what I knew of Cal and how high up his Confederate connections were. It was the only way. . . . I had to get back to Petersburg and the front lines!

But how?

I'd have to go by horse. But first I had to get out of the city. The train would be the safest and quickest. The lines behind General Grant's army were safely in Union hands. I could take the train as far as Culpeper, then rent or buy a horse there and ride behind the lines the rest of the way south to Petersburg.

I sat down on my case. I couldn't do anything for several hours, until the station opened. I was certain a train would be heading south out of Washington before noon.

As my thoughts cleared, my body began to remind me that it had been a long night. I needed to find either an outhouse or a clump of trees before the sun came up and too many people were about! If only there was someplace I could wash my face and comb my hair. The hunger pangs in my stomach didn't bother me. Food I could do without for a while, if I had to.

Again I peered out of the car. The yard nearby was still completely deserted. It was probably not later than five-thirty or six. Leaving my bag where it was, I carefully jumped down.

CHAPTER 51

BOXCAR ACCOMMODATIONS

When I got back and had once again climbed aboard the car where I had spent the night, I sat down to wait as patiently as my stirred-up mind would let me for morning to come.

It wasn't long before another thought struck me. If they knew who I was—which they did—and they suspected I'd overheard their plot—which I was sure they did—and if they were looking for me at Mrs. Richards' . . . then they were just as likely to look for me at the train station too!

Even if Cal had left the house before I had, there would still be two of them, and they would be sure to be searching for me wherever they thought likely. And where more likely than the train station?

No, I couldn't just walk in and ask the attendant for a ticket. One of them was sure to be hanging about the place—maybe even Mrs. Surratt herself, if she was in on it too.

If I was going to take the train, I would have to find some other way to do it. I'd have to find an open boxcar like this one going south, at least until I was out of the city.

I got up and went to the door again. This time when I climbed down I took my bag with me. The car was on a side track and was clearly going nowhere anytime soon. I began walking toward the back of the station, keeping behind other cars and buildings so as to stay out of sight as best I could.

I thought I knew which tracks were northbound and which southbound. In the central part of the yard, I saw men loading several cars about two-thirds of the way back in a long line of cars.

The engine at the front I was positive was pointing south. *Of course,* I thought. The southbound train would be taking provisions to General Grant's army. It would have come in mostly empty or else bearing wounded to Washington's hospitals, and it would return with supplies. There would likely not be many passengers traveling *toward* the fighting.

I inched my way closer, keeping out of sight.

Before long I began to hear the voices more plainly. I got as close as I dared, then stopped to wait.

"This one be full," a man called out two cars down from where I was standing on the back side of the train opposite from where the doors opened toward the loading yard.

I bent down and looked underneath through the wheels. I saw a man's feet walking away from me. Then he stopped at the next car and joined another man there. I walked slowly down until I was at the back of the car he'd just finished loading, then stood directly behind one of the huge iron wheels so they wouldn't be able to see my legs even if they should look under the train.

In another fifteen or twenty minutes I heard them move on down the line to the next car. I stooped down and glanced underneath again. They were walking back to the building where the supplies had been brought, while a third man jumped up on the board of the wagon from which they'd been unloading, and from the sound of it yelled a command to a horse to head back to the supply building for another wagonload.

Now was my chance! They all were sure to be looking the other way. I crouched down, got on my hands and knees, and, dragging my case along behind me, crawled under the car and peered out the other side. The two men were just entering the building about thirty yards away. I looked the other way, squinting into the sun, which was just coming up in the east. That way was also clear.

I crawled out from under the train, stood up, threw my bag up into the open door of the boxcar, scrambled up behind it as fast as I could, and in another few seconds was safely inside and crouched behind sacks of flour, a bunch of wooden barrels, and crates marked "Explosives." There could be no doubt left that this train was heading south toward the war!

I got as far toward the back and out of sight as I could manage, then hid down as low as I could, trying to find a way to make myself halfway comfortable.

Two hours later, from the sounds of the voices outside I gathered that all the cars were loaded. I heard footsteps approaching, then saw the shadow of a figure beside the door of the car I was in. I held my breath. The next instant a loud clanging crash echoed through my ears from the heavy wood door being pulled shut on its clamp with a slam.

Suddenly I was left in the darkness. The only light came through in tiny gleaming shafts through the board and the edge of the door. For a moment a new fear surged through me. What if I was locked in and *couldn't* get out! As long as the train was going in the right direction, I suppose it wouldn't matter. We were sure to get someplace before I starved to death.

I continued to wait. About an hour later I heard the sounds of the engine starting up. By this time many voices filled the yard outside. Another thirty minutes went by. Then the unmistakable jerking motions and clanking and creaking all indicated that the train was getting underway. Gradually it picked up speed.

After some ten or fifteen minutes, once we were safely out of the station and I thought probably out of the city as well, I got to my feet and worked my way over the sacks of flour to the door. In the dim light I located a lever that looked as if it would unhook the latch from the inside. I put both my hands against the end of it and shoved upward with all my might. It didn't budge. I tried again, harder this time. I felt it give slightly. Encouraged I gave it one more huge effort.

All at once the lever flew upward, the latch unhooked, and the sliding door sprang back and opened two or three inches.

Now I could shove the door open on its bottom rail at will. I did so, opening it to a space of six to nine inches. We were still not up to full speed, but had left the city. The rising sun of the morning was looking straight in the opening at me as we moved to the right. We were heading south!

Relieved, I took a seat closer to the opening and sat down on one of the canvas sacks. I had a long ride ahead of me and I might as well make myself comfortable. It was too dreary and spooky in the darkness, however, so I left the door open as it was.

I didn't know when or where the train would stop, but Culpeper was, I thought, some sixty miles away. We were sure to be there sometime that afternoon.

CHAPTER 52

CULPEPER . . . AND SOUTH

The train rumbled on slowly for several hours without a stop. I didn't exactly know the route or where we were bound, but as long as it continued south, I was moving in the direction I needed to go. There was no direct rail link yet between Washington and Richmond. Now that the Army of the Potomac under Grant had been dug in for so long in a wide swath arching down from Spotsylvania and Fredericksburg down through Cold Harbor and to Petersburg, most of the supplies were sent to them by ship down through the Chesapeake Bay and up the mouths of the Rappahannock, the York, or the James. Where this trainload of supplies was headed I wasn't sure, but it couldn't go much past Culpeper without getting dangerously close to being exposed to the rear lines of the Confederate troops and General Lee's position. I assumed it was bound for the northernmost of the Union troops flanked out between Culpeper and Fredericksburg. If I could get a horse there and ride around behind the lines, it would still be another hundred and fifty miles, through rough terrain, to the siege position of the army outside Petersburg.

At the first town where I felt the train starting to slow, I managed to close the door and latch it again so as not to be seen. We stopped briefly twice. I listened, but was unable to hear anything that indicated where we were. But the third stop, which must have been somewhere around two or three in the afternoon, had to be Culpeper. Moments after we'd pulled in, the engine let out a huge and final-sounding burst of steam, and I knew we'd arrived at our destination. Down the line I heard the boxcar doors being opened.

There wasn't anything they could do to me for stowing a ride now, so I decided to just jump down and be off. If someone tried to question me, I'd make a run for it.

In fact, why should I wait until they opened the door at all? After all, they might take *me* for a Confederate spy!

I got my bag right beside me—wishing by now I'd left it and whatever it had in it to the dubious care of Marge Surratt and her cohorts!—then gave the door lever a mighty shove. It gave way. I pushed against the door with my shoulder, got it open about two feet, grabbed my bag, and jumped down.

"Hey . . . what the—" exclaimed a voice only about five feet away.

Out of the corner of my eye I saw a large Negro man with a crate hoisted over his shoulder. He couldn't have chased me even if he'd wanted to, with that heavy load. But I didn't wait to answer his unfinished question. My feet hit the ground running and I bolted straight away from the train.

Nobody else seemed close by, although I heard a couple more cries that sounded as if they were meant for me. But I didn't look back, and I heard no footsteps giving chase. In less than a minute I was out of sight of the station. I slowed to a walk and tried to take stock of my surroundings.

The poor little town looked as if it had been ravaged by the war and had come nowhere near recovering. The only men were recent arrivals and wore the dark blue of the Union. The only natives of the place that were left were women, children, and the elderly. No one smiled.

There were two hotels in town. One looked pretty badly shot apart and was boarded up. The other was still open, though who traveled this way now in the vacuum created by the armies I didn't know. I went inside, found a table, sat down, and enjoyed three cups of water before ordering an early supper that, judging from the woman's expression, was far too much food for a young lady of my size to be eating. She said nothing, however, beyond many curious looks and glances, and I offered few words in return.

When I was through I asked her if there was a livery stable nearby. She directed me up the street, the curiosity on her face turning to outright suspicion. I determined that I had better make haste away from this place!

It was a good thing I had some money with me when I'd made my escape out of Washington. The old man at the stable was only too glad to part with one of his horses for hard Yankee cash, and threw in a sorry old saddle for five more dollars. The horse looked as tired as the town, but once I got him used to my voice and to the idea of carrying me on his back, he did just fine. I missed Raspberry more than ever, but this sturdy fellow ought to get me there in one piece.

I asked the man for a couple of long straps of leather, tied my clumsy bag onto the back of my saddle where it would rest on the horse's rump, bought a canteen and a bag of feed, and after about forty minutes of transacting business and making all the impromptu preparations I could think of, I thanked him and sped down the street on my way.

I glanced back and saw him wiping his forehead with his sleeve, holding his crumpled, dirty hat in one hand, with an expression of bewilderment on his face.

I figured I had a good three hours of daylight left, maybe four.

I took the road due south out of town. Having no idea how close I was to the very spot where fierce fighting had taken place back in May, and how close I was, in fact, to where I had earlier been when helping behind the lines, within an hour I was crossing the Rapidan River.

Fredericksburg and the safety of the Union position lay southeast of Culpeper. But somehow I missed the Fredericksburg road and continued south.

Danger was closer than I knew.

CHAPTER 53

INTO THE WRONG CAMP!

My first inkling of my predicament came too late for me to avoid it. Suddenly I found myself riding straight into a Confederate camp!

My first reaction was fright. If I'd had time, I would have wheeled the horse around and galloped back the way I'd come. But I was past the sentry before I knew it, and it was suddenly too late. My heart leaped up into my mouth.

"Well, hey there, little lady," drawled the lookout, standing up from his post. Within a second or two I was surrounded by six or eight others.

"Where y'all bound?"

"Uh . . . south," I said.

"No need to be afraid, we ain't aimin' to hurt you none," said one.

"If you be headin' south, ma'am, then you're among friends now. Get off your horse and stop a spell. Y'all both look like you could use it."

The others all laughed good-naturedly. By now the group had grown to ten or twelve, and I realized I was right in the middle of a whole unit, not just a handful of men.

My first reaction was: *This is the enemy!* I'd been involved with the North and the election and Mr. Lincoln and the whole point of view that we were "at war" with the Confederacy for so long that I forgot that these men clustering about me were Americans just like me. There was no difference between us. I had come only a few miles into Virginia. This was George Washington's home state! And yet I was looking at them as if they were from some foreign country! When I later realized all this, I hated all the more what this awful war did to us. The unity that was the whole purpose of the Convent of John Seventeen was being trampled to death every day on the battlefields of this war—and I had succumbed to it, too!

I sat there on my horse too terrified to move, or even to speak, but trying desperately not to show it. If they found out what I was doing, what awful things might they do to me? I was, after all, a spy—trying to outspy Cal and Surratt and the others with their scheme!

I had heard they shot spies on sight, or hanged them, without even a trial!

And I knew they must be able to read all over my face every single thing I was thinking!

"It's nigh on to nightfall, ma'am. You'd best get down and join us. We got us some beans an' biscuits you'd be welcome to."

"Join us for the night!" shouted out somebody from the back, and the comments from a few of his companions were too awful to think about. I had to get out of here before they took me prisoner!

"I . . . I, uh—I have to keep going," I said lamely.

"Ain't no place *to* go, ma'am," said one of the gray-clad men who was being nice and courteous. "We're the rearguard unit, and if you was to keep on this way, you're gonna get yourself all tangled up in the rest of our army. There's some nasty fighting going on down that way. You tryin' to get to Richmond?"

"Uh . . . yeah," I nodded.

"It ain't safe down there, ma'am."

"I . . . I reckon I took a wrong road back a ways," I said, trying to put on a southern accent. It sounded ridiculous in my own ears, but none of the men seemed to notice.

"Spend the night here, little lady," called out the man who had said it before. "*We'll* help ya find your way, all right!"

"I . . . I have to go back," I said. "I've got to get to Fredericksburg."

"Fredericksburg! Why, ma'am, the blame Yankees has got Fredericksburg! Ain't you heard? We got a war on—and you're right in the middle of it!"

One of the men, who looked a little older and might have been an officer, now walked around, eyed my big brown leather case strapped behind me, patted it once with his hand, then asked, "Where you come from anyway, Miss?"

"Uh . . . Culpeper."

"You don't sound very convinced."

"I came from Culpeper all right," I repeated.

"Well, the corporal here's right. It *is* nearly nightfall, and we *do* have food left, and you'd be welcome and safe here. I can promise you that none of these louts will bother you in the least . . . and neither will the Yanks. You'll be as safe here as anywhere for miles."

There was a slight pause. I didn't know *what* to do! If I did stay, I'd never be able to sneak out of *here* in the middle of the night! They kept sentries posted all the time, and if they saw me trying to make a run for it, then I would *really* be in for it!

Meanwhile, the man's hand was still resting on my bag. "What you got in here anyway?" he asked.

"My clothes," I answered, feeling myself starting to sweat. What if they opened it? My letters from Mr. Lincoln were in there, copies of several articles I'd written in *northern* newspapers, and notes for new articles . . . not to mention my journal. They would hang me for sure if they found all that!

"Mighty big bag for coming down just from Culpeper," he said. I didn't at all like the suspicious sound in his voice.

Just then, from farther into the camp, a man approached who looked even more important yet. Some of the men fell away to make room for him, and he came straight on toward me.

"What's going on here, Lieutenant?" he said to the man who had been talking to me. Then he glanced up at me where I still sat on the horse, tipped his head slightly, and added, "Ma'am." Then he looked back to the lieutenant.

"This young lady just came riding in here like she was in a pretty big hurry," the lieutenant said to him. "She says she's from Culpeper, Major, and bound for Richmond. But she's not altogether making sense. Then she said she's got to get to Fredericksburg, which the Yankees got now. I don't know, sir, she just seems a mite confused. And then there's this bag of hers," he said, patting it a couple more times.

The major glanced up at me.

"You confused, young lady?" he said. "Or maybe just frightened?"

I nodded, and whatever else may have been said, he knew I was telling the truth about that!

"Well, I'll tell you one thing, these men of mine may be a hard-fighting and a rough-tongued bunch. But if there's one thing we southerners know, it's how to treat a lady. I promise you, you have nothing to be afraid of."

He paused, then added in a more serious tone, "But these are dangerous times, ma'am. I'm sure you're aware of that. There's Yankees and spies and patrols and marauders prowling around through these woods for miles in every direction. So you see, we've got to be mighty careful, and we've got to know where you're going and where you come from, and what your business is. We're under orders from General Lee himself to let no one past us on this road here. No one. So you see why my men are asking you all these questions. We got our orders, ma'am. And besides, we can't just let a young woman like you be riding out loose any old place you want. Why, you might run into a patrol of Yankees and get yourself killed! They're a ruthless lot, and we'd never forgive ourselves if we let something happen to you."

"Let us open up her bag, Major," called out the man whose sound I didn't like. "It's been a long time since we seen any *women's* duds! We'll find out what she's up to all right!" He gave a terrible and suggestive laugh.

Suddenly I found my voice, though I was shocked to hear what came out of my mouth.

"I was just trying to get some warm things down to my husband before winter!" I cried. "I haven't seen him in four months, and I was desperate to get word to him that we was going to have a baby!"

I burst out crying, yanked back on the reins, spun the horse quickly around, and without waiting for another word from any of them, kicked at the horse and galloped off as fast as I could northward along the road I'd come in on.

The last thing I saw out of the corner of my eyes was the group of gray-clad Rebel soldiers standing where I left them.

I heard a few comments and some laughter. But just as I rounded a turn and was nearly out of earshot, I thought I heard the major say, "Well, Lieutenant, you'd better go after her. Make sure she gets headed back to Culpeper all right."

CHAPTER 54

RETRACING MY STEPS

I rode the poor tired horse as fast as he would go, but it wasn't near as fast as I wanted him to go! Oh, for Raspberry right then!

It was five or ten minutes before I heard hoofbeats behind me. My mount had slowed noticeably. The moment I heard him I knew it was no use. I reined in and let the rider behind me catch up. He galloped up alongside, then eased to a gentle canter beside me. I glanced over to see the southern lieutenant.

"Whoa . . . whoa there!" he said, as much to me as to my horse. We both slowed to a stop.

"You really didn't have to chase outta there like that," he said. "None of us meant you any harm."

"I know," I said. "I was just nervous and scared."

"Well, now that we all understand, the major wanted me to ride along with you awhile, just to make sure you was going to be all right."

"I can find my way," I said.

"And I'll just make sure of it." He eased his horse forward. Mine followed.

"Are . . . are you going to ride with me all the way . . . to Culpeper?" I asked.

The lieutenant laughed.

"No, missy," he said. "Culpeper may be in Virginia, but that's Yankee territory now. No, I'll get back to my unit before this night's well settled in, as long as I know you're safely on your way. The clouds have lifted and the moon should be out. I think you'll make it before it's been dark more than an hour or two."

"It's very kind of you to be so concerned about me," I said.

"Like the major said, we southerners know how to treat a lady. Being a Virginian yourself, ma'am, I wouldn't think you'd be surprised."

I said nothing. What he'd said reminded me of Katie and Edie. I wondered where Edie was right now, and if she was safe.

"And I still can't rightly see why you was so jittery back there," he went on. "Us southerners gotta stick together, not be afraid of each other."

Still I didn't reply. I was getting all the more uncomfortable having him think things about me that weren't true!

He rode along with me for about another thirty minutes. We talked some, but I felt so awkward that I don't suppose I exactly encouraged a lively conversation. Finally he turned his horse around.

"You just keep straight on this road, ma'am," he said. "It'll take you straight into Culpeper. If you meet any Yanks, don't tell 'em nothin' about your husband or you'll never know what they might do to you. Just tell 'em you lost your way, or tell them anything. And if they do try to start bothering you, like Yanks'll sometimes do to women, well, you just tell 'em, you know, ma'am . . . tell 'em as how you're in a family way. Even them brutal Yanks won't bother a woman that's carrying a child."

I thanked him again for his concern, and told him to thank his major for me, too. Then the minute he was out of sight, I dug my heels into the horse's sides again. He'd had far too long a rest. And I had urgent business I had to get back to!

I had no intention of riding all the way back to Culpeper. The thought of a night in that hotel with that suspicious lady wondering about me was not one I relished.

Within another thirty minutes I came to a crossroad. It didn't look like much, but it was running east and west. It was nearly dark by now, but I saw a small hand-painted wooden sign a little off the road. I moved up beside it, leaned forward in the saddle and squinted. I could just barely make out the words *Locust Grove* and beneath it *Fredericksburg*.

That was all I needed to see. I wheeled my tired but trust-worthy steed to the right and off through the wooded thicket along what wasn't much more than a wide path. I'd ride as long as I could be certain of my way, then find some place to hide out of sight and sleep until dawn. It didn't cross my mind until later that I was in the very vicinity of the battle back in December of 1862, which Cal had received the telegram about when I was following him in Sacramento. It had been the Confederate victory at Fredericksburg that had convinced him to defect to the South's cause. Now here the two armies were again, nearly in the same place, with the outcome of the entire war hanging in the balance.

CHAPTER 55

GENERAL ULYSSES S. GRANT

I made it the rest of the way without incident.

After I'd settled onto the softest grass I could find for the night, using some of my clothes as bedding and blankets as best I could, I found myself reflecting on the events of the day.

Suddenly it occurred to me what I'd done an hour and a half earlier. I'd *lied* to get away from the Confederate soldiers! Not only had I lied, I'd done it naturally, without even thinking about it.

A part of me tried to justify it, but without much success.

Whatever the result, even though I had gotten safely away, I *had* done wrong. If I hadn't told the lie, perhaps God would have found some other way to get me out of there. Or maybe he *did* have some other way in mind, just waiting to perform, and then I snatched it out of his hands. Perhaps I had *prevented* him from helping me by helping myself instead!

By the time I finally fell asleep, I was feeling bad for not trusting him enough to know that he would have protected me. But I was too tired to be miserable about it. And I did trust him enough to know that he would forgive me and would keep taking care of me from now on, if I would let him.

"I'm sorry, Lord," I said finally. "I got so caught up in what was happening that I didn't think to pray and ask for your help. Forgive me for lying. Help me to remember your presence. Wherever my steps go from here in this thing, please guide me and keep me exactly where you want me to be."

The night passed tolerably. By early afternoon the next day I was in Fredericksburg, where I got food, water, and a new supply of feed for the horse. A few suspicious looks came my way, but I paid no attention, took care of my business, and headed south, confident now that I was well behind the stretched out line of *Union* troops. By taking my way southward in an arc behind them, I would eventually arrive at the southern position outside Petersburg, where the intense fighting was still going on. That's where I was certain I'd find General Grant.

It took me a day and a half more to reach the front lines. It was evening when I rode into the hospital camp. I was amazed to find it virtually unmoved from where it had been when I'd left well over a month before. The siege of Petersburg and Richmond hadn't had much result. Most of my friends from the Commission were still there, although the fighting had abated considerably and many of the wounded had been transferred to hospitals in the North, so it wasn't nearly so horrid as before. I was surprised to find Clara Barton still there. Even before I left, she had been talking of going down to Atlanta, where there had also been a great amount of bloodshed.

I went immediately to the army doctor who was in charge of the hospital and medical units.

"How far are we from the field headquarters?" I asked.

"You mean General Grant's quarters?"

"Yes. I have to see him."

The captain could not help laughing. "*You* want to do *what*?" he asked.

"I've got to see him," I repeated. "It's extremely urgent. How far away is it . . . could I get there tonight?"

"I don't know, Miss Hollister," he said, still chuckling. "I'd say it's three or four miles. But at night, with all those trenches, unless you had an escort, it could be a mite risky."

"Could you take me?" I said.

"Me?"

"Yes. I need to get there, I tell you."

"I suppose I could," he answered slowly. "But not tonight. I wouldn't go out there toward the front in the dark. They're liable to take you for a Reb patrol and shoot you dead before you had the chance to say a word."

I thought to myself a few seconds. This was only Sunday night. There was still plenty of time.

"How about at dawn, then?" I said after a pause. "Will you take me there first thing in the morning?"

"Maybe I could. Say, what's this about, anyway?"

"I can't say. I've just got to see the general, that's all."

"He'll throw you out. You're never going to get close to him . . . at *any* time of the day."

"Will you take me?"

"All right, all right! You've patched up enough wounded around here, I guess you're entitled. But I tell you, you're not about to get inside General Grant's tent."

"Let me worry about that," I said. "I'll be here at sunup."

I turned and left his tent and returned to the nurses' quarters, where I spent the night.

The next morning I was saddled and ready to go just as the sun's first rays were coming over the ridge in the east.

True to his word, the captain was also ready. We set off westward toward the front lines, passing through the regiments and units of thousands of Union soldiers. General Grant's army had been encamped here so long that everything had a look of permanency. Along with hundreds of tents and campfires, there were even a few small buildings that had been constructed, stables for the animals, blacksmith shops. In places it resembled a real town—except that there were no women or children, and everyone wore blue and carried guns. In a way it *was* a city—a mobile city of eighty or ninety thousand men . . . a city whose only purpose was to wage war on the Confederate capital.

There had been no fighting the day before, and none was expected today. Guards and cooks were about, of course, but many of the men still slept or else were just rousing themselves. Everywhere the white smoke of campfires lazily filtered upward into the still frosty morning air, but it was a far calmer scene than I might have expected when riding through the middle of the Army of the Potomac.

Occasional stares followed us as we passed, now and then a salute to the captain. But these men had seen more already than a lifetime would allow them to forget, and the sight of a woman riding through camp, even when they were just getting dressed for the day, was hardly enough to surprise them. Most hardly seemed to notice me at all.

At length we came to a collection of larger tents, two or three buildings, and a farmhouse that had been commandeered, and I knew we had arrived at our destination. In the distance I could see the edges of the maze of trenches that had been dug around Petersburg where the men in the front stayed.

We rode up to the house. "We're here to see General Grant, Sergeant," the captain said.

"I don't know if the general is up yet, Captain."

"Then find out, Sergeant. We'll wait."

The sergeant disappeared inside, then returned about a minute later. He was followed by a major.

"What's this all about, Captain?"

"Only that we have to see the general."

"The general is barely out of bed," replied the major, "and is not seeing anyone all morning."

The captain glanced over at me—apologetically, yet with an I-told-you-so look.

"I'm afraid you're stuck, Miss Hollister," he said. "I brought you here, but like I said, they don't let just anyone into the general's headquarters."

"Especially not before 7:00 A.M.," added the major curtly. "Good-day, Captain." He turned and began walking back toward the house.

I was off my horse and after him in an instant.

"Wait . . . wait, please, Major!" I called, running after him and grabbing his arm. "I've *got* to see General Grant! It can't wait . . . it's *very* important!"

He stopped and spun around, pulling his arm away from my grasp and casting down a look of extreme annoyance at me. He bored into me with his eyes for several seconds. Then, apparently not thinking I deserved so much as a word in reply, he turned again and with deliberate step began walking again to the house.

Once more I hurried after him, grabbed his arm and held on tightly.

"I've *got* to see him!" I repeated.

The major spun around and glared at the captain still sitting on his horse watching the scene. "If this is your idea of a prank, Captain," he spat, "it has gone far enough! You get her out of here or I'll have you court-martialed. The affections of this schoolgirl for the general hardly befit your commission, Sergeant!"

But I was not about to be hauled away by the major and the guard. And by now I was more than a little upset myself! *Schoolgirl affections!* I was trying to save the general's life!

I let go my hold on the major's arm and dashed for the door. I was onto the porch before he realized it, and now he sprang after me. But by the time he had a chance to grab me, I threw open the door and bolted inside.

"I must see General Grant!" I cried. "Won't anybody listen to me? The general is in danger!"

There were two or three other men inside what looked to be a parlor or sitting room just inside. They glanced up, but before anyone could say a word, the major burst through the door after me and had hold of me in a vise-grip within seconds. I tried to scream out again, but felt his large hand clamp tightly over my mouth. Then he dragged me toward the door.

This was awful! I was going to be sent off, probably to a stockade. If I didn't do something drastic—and soon—the general would never hear of the plot against him.

The major's strong right hand was over my mouth, and his left clutched me around my midsection. But one of my arms was halfway loose. With a great heaving effort I lifted my right arm and slammed my elbow into the major's stomach. I don't suppose it hurt him much, but the jolt of it took him by surprise and he lost his breath momentarily.

It was all I needed! I kicked at his legs, struggled free, and again bolted away, this time for a closed door on the opposite side of the room. I heard shouts and curses behind me, as well as the major's running feet.

Just as I reached it, the door opened, and I suddenly found myself running straight into a man's chest, and then toppling to the floor at his feet.

The steps of the major behind me stopped instantly, and the shouting ceased.

"I apologize for this most bothersome intrusion, General," the major said. "I assure you, this tramp and the man who brought her here will be punished severely."

I looked up from the floor. There, towering above me, his fingers still fiddling with the suspenders over his long underwear, stood General Ulysses Grant himself!

CHAPTER 56

AN EARLY MORNING FRACAS

Again I felt the major's hands grab me. He yanked me to my feet and away from the general.

"General . . . General, please!" I cried in desperation, "I *must* talk to you . . . it's extremely urgent! I came all the way—"

"Shut up, little girl!" cried the major, and once more his huge paw closed down over my mouth. I struggled to try to bite it, but he pressed down all the tighter.

"Major!" commanded General Grant, and it was the first time he had spoken. "That is hardly the way to treat a young lady."

"She has disregarded my every command, General. There's only one thing no-goods like this understand!"

I was furious, and was struggling and twisting fiercely to get free. "Hey, one of you men—Sergeant—" the major was saying, "help me with this contemptuous little vixen. She's as feisty and strong—"

"Major," came the general's voice again. "Major . . . let her go."

I stopped struggling. The major stopped dragging me across the floor, but did not loosen his hold over my mouth.

"I said let her go," the general repeated.

"But, sir, she has—"

"Major."

"Yes, sir," said the major. His grip loosened. The instant I was free I sprang from him and ran across the room, nearly crashing into the general again. Now that I was standing instead of looking at him from on the floor, I was almost shocked to find that I was as tall as he was.

"General Grant, please," I implored him, "please listen to me before you have them throw me out!"

He eyed me intently, looking over my face.

"I'm sorry," I went on. "I know I had no right to storm in here like this, but I didn't know how else to see you! It is extremely important, General!"

Still he was looking me over, unconcerned about being only half-dressed, and not nearly so worried about the early hour or the incongruity of the situation as the men of his staff.

"Don't I know you, young lady?" he asked after another moment's pause.

"Corrie . . . Corrie Hollister," I said, trying to make myself as calm and presentable as I could. "We spoke a little at the White House earlier this year." I took a breath and made the attempt to look mature.

Suddenly his face broke out in recognition. "Of course . . . yes, I do remember you, Miss Hollister."

At almost the same instant, he looked past me to the major and his face turned stern.

"Don't you know who this is, you fool?" he barked.

"She never identified herself, sir."

"Did you give her half a chance, Major?" rejoined the general. The major stood silently.

"I just happen to have spoken to her at the White House," the general went on. "This young lady happens to be a well-known writer for the Union cause, and is working personally for the President on his reelection campaign. Now, do I hear any more words about no-good tramps?"

His booming voice filled the room. When the echo died down, only the silence of the morning was left.

"Now . . . what's this all about, Miss Hollister?"

"A matter of great urgency, General Grant," I answered. "I've come all the way from Washington."

"Did the President send you?"

"No, sir. I'm afraid he knows nothing about it. He was out of town when I heard, and I didn't know what else to do but come straight to you."

"Heard what?"

"That's what I must talk to you about."

"Go on."

"Not here, please, sir," I said. "I think we ought to talk in private."

General Grant's face indicated that he was ruminating on it for a moment; then he nodded slightly.

"Fair enough," he said. "You don't mind if I finish dressing first?"

"No, sir," I said, smiling.

"Good!" he laughed. "I'm happy to hear it isn't *that* urgent."

He turned to the other men in the room. "Is the coffee on yet?"

"Yes, sir," barked out one of the sergeants who had been silently observing the drama.

"Good . . . good! Get me a good strong cup ready, and see if Miss Hollister here wants anything. She is my guest, and I want no more of what went on earlier, is that clear?"

Without another word, General Grant turned and disappeared again into the room from which he had come. When the door had closed behind him, the sergeant left for the kitchen.

CHAPTER 57

A FRIGHTENING PLAN

Fifteen minutes later I was seated in General Grant's office in another room of the farmhouse. The door was closed. We were alone.

He was completely attired in his dark blue uniform and boots, although not wearing his hat. He took a long swallow of his coffee, then turned his eyes upon me.

"All right, Miss Hollister," he said. "You've got your private hearing. Tell me what was so urgent you had to bring it to me direct from Washington personally?"

I recounted the events of three nights earlier, repeating everything I had heard.

"And you say you know this fellow Burton?"

"Yes, sir. We worked together closely back in California before the war broke out and in the first months of it."

"And you say he defected to the South?"

I told him as much of the story as I felt I needed to. He listened to the whole thing very patiently. If he looked worried about his life, he didn't show a trace of it, though his expression was certainly serious.

"And the other fellow's name again?"

"Surratt," I replied. "I think it's *John* Surratt."

"Hmm . . . Surratt," mused the general. "It has a vague ring of familiarity to it. I seem to recall the name in connection with an intelligence report about southern spies our people had identified."

"They said they would meet on Wednesday, General. It's Monday now—you've got to *do* something, sir! They're going to try to kill you. They said one of your own lieutenants—"

"Right . . . yes, I heard everything you said, Miss Hollister," said the general. "And I see why you insisted on seeing me alone. Hmm . . . ," he muttered again, obviously thinking very hard, "it could be any of a hundred men . . . there's no way to find out the identity without—"

He stopped abruptly. His eyes were wide open and his face animated. Even behind the beard, I could tell he was hatching some plan to undermine the plot against him.

"Hmm . . . yep, there's no other alternative . . . what we're going to have to do is nab your friend and bring him back here. If I've got a Reb in the ranks of my command, I've got to find out who it is!"

Before I could reply, he was on his feet. He strode quickly to the door and opened it.

"Sergeant!" he called.

A moment later one of the men I'd seen in the house before appeared at the door.

"Get me Captain Dyles."

The sergeant disappeared as quickly as he had come and again I was alone with the general.

"We have a man on the staff who's been infiltrating the Confederate ranks the whole time. He's been with me since Fort Henry. I'd trust him with my very life—which, I suppose, is what I'm doing now! He's from Alabama, talks with as thick a southern drawl as you please, but loyal to the Union as I am. I've sent him behind enemy lines a dozen times. He's never failed me yet. And a scrappy fighter when push comes to shove. You won't be safer with anyone."

I didn't know what he meant, but he kept talking, and before I had the chance to ask, a knock on the door came, and a moment later he was introducing me to Captain Geoffrey Dyles, who was dressed in plain clothes instead of a uniform.

"Geoff, we've got to get into Richmond," General Grant said. "Gotta get in and back out again safely . . . and soon. Before Wednesday. Can you do it?"

"I reckon so, General," replied Dyles. It was indeed one of

the strongest southern accents I'd ever heard—perfect for a Union spy.

"You'd have forty-eight hours."

"I can manage it."

"You got another man or two you can trust?"

"The more men the more danger, General. You think I gotta have more men?"

"You're going to have to grab a high-placed Rebel agent—nephew of their vice-president, no less—and bring him back here. I doubt he'll take too much a shine to the notion, so I figured it might take more than one of you."

"I'll take Crabtree."

"The Negro?"

"Plays as good a compliant slave as there is. I've used him before."

"Big man, isn't he?"

"Huge, General," laughed Dyles. "Three hundred pounds, if he ain't eaten for a week. More if he has! A better man in a pinch I couldn't have. Saved my life half a dozen times."

"Doesn't he call too much attention to himself?"

"As long as I treat him like a slave, and he keeps his head lowered, all we get is comments about his size. That way, nobody pays me the least attention. Best cover I could have."

"Can you smuggle in a gun?"

"Crabtree's so big, General, I've smuggled whole cannons stuffed inside his clothes past the stupid Confederate sentries!"

"Good. You might need a cannon to kidnap this fellow. It'll be broad daylight—what time did you say the meeting was, Miss Hollister?" said the general, turning to me.

"Noon," I answered.

"Hmm . . . yep—broad daylight. And you say in a scrap, Crabtree's a good man?"

"As good as four others!"

"Good. I want to make sure nothing happens to this lady. I may owe her my life."

Both Captain Dyles and I looked up at General Grant with looks of amazement. The captain's was one of question, but mine was one of fear!

"You want her going into Richmond with us?" he asked.

"Of course."

"But it's behind enemy lines."

"That's why I want to make sure she's safe."

"She'll slow us down and add to the danger, General."

In reply, General Grant just smiled. "Don't bet your horse on it, Geoff," he said with a knowing grin. "This lady's been through some scrapes of her own. From what I hear, she can take care of herself."

All this time I was listening to their exchange with mingled astonishment and terror. *Me* . . . go *with* Dyles and Crabtree . . . into the middle of the Confederate capital?

"But why, Sam?" asked Captain Dyles. I'd never heard anyone use the general's nickname before, but I noticed that there were no other officers around.

"How else you gonna know the man?"

Dyles shrugged. "I figured I'd have some description."

"It's too risky. Time's short, and we have to be sure. Miss Hollister here's the only one who knows this Burton on sight. There's no other way to do it but to have her there to put you onto the right fellow. Then you bring him back to me, and we'll make sure he gives us the name of the spy who's infiltrated my command."

CHAPTER 58

INTO THE CONFEDERATE CAPITAL

Two mornings later, at dawn on Wednesday, I sat on the board of a rickety old wagon, dressed in rags intended to make me look more southern than I had before. Beside me sat a plain-dressed Geoffrey Dyles. The wagon, pulled along by a tired old work-horse, entered the outskirts of Richmond, Virginia, along the road from Lynchburg and the east. Jacob Crabtree sat behind us on a load of hay, ropes tied around his feet. There were also several large wooden barrels in the back, and another horse clomped along behind us, tied to the back of the wagon.

Captain Dyles had spent all Monday morning devising his plan and getting together everything necessary—the horses, the wagon, our clothes, and the barrels. After lunch, the three of us had left the Union camp on a course due south, which would take us below Petersburg, away from the positions of both armies. It took us the rest of the day to work our way down to Stony Creek, where we made camp. Tuesday morning we headed westward to McKenney.

Only a few people gave so much as a second look at us, and anyone we did chance to meet, Captain Dyles talked to like a friendly southerner trying to get his wife and slave away from the fighting, all the while cursing the Yankees who were trying to take all his land. No one thought a thing about it. Neither Jacob nor I said a word, and we just kept on moving.

By Tuesday evening we had come up on the rear of the Confederate lines holding the perimeter around Petersburg and Richmond. This was the touchier part of Dyles' plan. Most of the southern flank, however, was concentrated between Richmond and Petersburg, so he hoped by getting far enough to the west we would be able to move into the city without opposition.

We were nearly to the city before anyone said more than a few words to us. But as we drew to within sight of Richmond, we approached a unit of Confederate soldiers guarding the main road. They were stopping everyone.

We inched our way forward.

"What's your business in Richmond?" the soldier asked Captain Dyles when our turn came.

"Can't y'all see?" drawled Captain Dyles lazily. "We got us a horse to deliver."

"I see the horse all right," rejoined the soldier. "Looks like a nag to me."

"You mightn't oughtta let th' genrul hear you say that, son," drawled Dyles.

"What general?"

"*The* genrul. How many genruls we got us left? Genrul Lee, of course."

"What's he got to do with you?"

"That's what I been trying to tell you, son. This here's his horse."

"General Lee's! I don't believe you. It's just an old nag!"

Dyles started laughing, slowly and calmly at first, then gradually rising for effect. Finally he seemed to be struggling to stop and get control of himself.

"What's your name, son?" he asked, still laughing.

For the first time the soldier looked a little uneasy.

"Uh, Gibb . . . Lieutenant Jacobson Gibb."

"Well, Lieutenant Gibb, nag or no nag, Bob Lee bought this horse offen me last week, down t' my farm where I raise nags like this. Why, he's been getting horses from me for years. Afore the war I took 'em all the way up to him at his place at Arlington. You have heard of Genrul Lee's fondness for horseflesh now, ain't you, Gibb?"

"Yes, sir . . . yes, I have."

"And you want me to tell Bobbie Lee that it was one Lieutenant Jacobson Gibb who held me up when I was trying to deliver his latest purchase?" Captain Dyles wasn't laughing now, but eyed him sternly.

"No . . . no, sir."

"You want me to convey to th' genrul what you think of his nag?" Dyles asked.

"No, sir. I'm sorry, sir. You're free to move through."

I breathed a sigh of relief, and was surprised when the captain kept sitting there and made no move to go on.

"Ain't you gonna ask me about the hay and the barrels?" he said.

By now Lieutenant Gibb was so flustered he didn't know what to do! I don't know if it was hearing General Lee spoken of with such familiarity or the captain's commanding tone that was more upsetting for him.

"I, uh . . ."

"You want me to tell the genrul you let us through without a proper search? That's as bad as calling his horse a nag. For all you know I'm a no-good Yankee lying to you. Why, Gibb, I might have me a spy in them barrels back thayere."

"Yes, sir. Tell me, sir, what's the hay for? And what's in the barrels?"

"I thought you said you knew horses, Gibb! You ain't as bright as you look, son! The hay and feed in the barrels is for the horse, what else you thank they'd be for? Bob Lee always orders a wagon of hay and two barrels of my special mixed feed so the horse feels at home in his new surroundings. That make sense to that feeble brain of yours, Gibb?"

"Yes, sir."

"Hey, you ornery galoot," Dyles shouted, turning around to Jacob in the back of the wagon, "open up one of them barrels and show the lieutenant here th' special mix of grain."

"Yes, massah," replied the big black man in his laziest and most compliant tone. He took the lid off the barrel he'd been sitting on, plunged his thick hand inside, and lifted it high, with the grain pouring through his fingers.

Jacob sat back down on the barrel.

Once again Lieutenant Gibb motioned for us to pass.

"Ain't you gonna ask to see the bill of sale for that nag, Gibb?"

drawled Dyles. "You wasn't planning to let us through without proof, was you?"

"No, sir."

"Well, here 'tis." Dyles pulled a sheet of rumpled paper from his coat and shoved it toward the lieutenant. He eyed it briefly, then nodded.

"What about her?" he said, nodding his head toward me.

"What about her?" said Dyles.

"Why's she along?"

"Why, Gibb, she's more important than the horse! What do you thank she's got under that towel there. More feed for the horses? My wife *always* bakes the genrul a fresh huckleberry pie to go along with the horses he buys! And she insists on delivering it personal, war or no war!"

Suddenly Captain Dyles clicked his tongue and flicked the rein and we jerked into motion, leaving a bewildered and relieved Lieutenant Jacobson Gibb standing alongside the road watching us go.

Slowly we continued along until we were out of sight. Then from behind me I heard a gradual rumble of low laughter coming from Jacob, which grew and grew until he could no longer contain it. I glanced over at the captain. His eyes were sparkling and he could hardly contain himself either. I had been terrified every second, but it was obvious both of them enjoyed this!

Captain Dyles glanced back at his large black friend, then started laughing himself.

"That poor lame-brained Rebel kid! Why, he was about to let us go without even having to use the bill of sale!"

"Why didn't you just go?" I asked. "What difference did it make, after all that?"

"Why, Miss Hollister," Captain Dyles replied. "I *had* to show him the paper! General Grant's orders."

"General Grant? Why . . . I don't understand."

"General Grant's been practicing ol' Bob Lee's signature for two years waiting for a chance to try it out. He told me just before we left to make sure I had a chance to show this to somebody. If we got captured and they hanged us, then he said he'd know he had to practice a little harder!"

Jacob roared with laughter.

I didn't think it was so funny. At the word *hanged,* a shiver of dread shot through me.

"Hey, quiet back there," Dyles said back to Jacob. "We're coming into the city. These folks around here don't much like their colored folk looking like they's having fun."

"Yes, massah . . . anything you say, massah."

A faint chuckle followed his words.

CHAPTER 59

WINDER SUPPLY

By the time we reached the middle of Richmond it was about nine in the morning.

Captain Dyles drove the wagon to the street along the waterfront, and after about a mile I saw ahead of us a building with the words "Winder Supply" painted on it. He seemed to know Richmond pretty well. I wondered if he had been here before.

We went slowly past the building, the captain eyeing it carefully, then around the corner onto the adjacent street.

"You say they said there was a *room* here they were going to use?" he said to me. "But nothing about where it was?"

"No, all I heard was 'he's got a room we can use,' " I replied.

"Probably in back somewhere. There's bound to be another door back here we can get in."

He took the wagon along the side street, glancing about, looking over the side and rear of Winder Supply, which stood on the corner and then extended down the adjacent street as well.

We went past the end of the building, down to the next street, then turned and headed back toward the river. He reined the horse in at the back of the supply building, glancing around. Several men were carrying bags in and out of a small warehouse, and two others were loading up a wagon.

"Probably in the main building someplace," Captain Dyles mumbled to himself. "But we can't stay here too long or we'll attract their notice."

He flipped the reins and we began moving again.

"Where you figure to ditch the hay and feed and the nag, Geoff?" asked Jacob behind me.

279

"Don't know. We gotta keep it long enough so we're not just driving around in an empty wagon and attracting notice."

"Gotta be rid of it before that fool Gibb sees us again," added Jacob.

"We'll ditch the stuff. Hate to cut the horse loose, though— nag or no nag," said Dyles.

"I reckon the general figured one horse was a small price to roust out a traitor."

"Reckon he's right at that."

We were still riding along slowly as they talked, and I could tell the captain was thinking at the same time.

After two or three minutes, a look of resolve came over his face. "I've got it!" he said, and immediately pulled at the reins and began leading the horse back around yet again. This time when we approached the rear of the Supply Company building, he pulled the wagon to the side of the street, then stopped, in full view of the men and workers who were about. We sat there and waited.

A few minutes later a man came sauntering our way.

"Anything I can do for you?" he asked.

"We's just waitin' on master Jim," answered Captain Dyles, this time with the sound of an ignorant field hand.

"Jim who?" asked the man.

"Master James T. Bow*reee*guard," said Captain Dyles, stretching the name out slowly. "Master Jim, he done tell me to hitch up the horses an' take the darkie an' meet me at Winder Supply an' he'd be there directly, maybe sometime 'bout noon."

"It's three hours till noon."

"He done tol' me t' wait for him no matter how long he was. He said we had a heap o' stuff t' get."

"What about the woman?"

"She's powerful strong for her size," said Dyles. "We kinda short o' darkies now, what with all of 'em leavin' t' fight or go North. Master Jim, he tol' me t' bring her along t' help with the loadin'."

Apparently satisfied, the man turned and began walking back to the supply building. "Just keep this area clear," he said. "We've got a lot of loading that'll be going on this morning."

"Yes, suh," replied Dyles, following his retreating figure with eyes that were shrewdly taking in everything about the place in spite of his backward-sounding tongue. It was becoming more and more obvious to me all the time why General Grant had sent him on this mission. He was adept at playing just about any role.

As the thought of his acting came into my mind, so did the name *Booth*. Suddenly I made the connection between the actor Mrs. Richards had told me about and the name I'd heard in conversation with Cal. Was it the same man? I wondered what a well-known actor was doing mixed up with Cal and John Surratt.

My thoughts were interrupted by the voice of Captain Dyles beside me. "Time's come, Miss Hollister," he said. "You up to your part in this little charade we're playing?"

"I'll try, Captain," I said.

"Then here's what I want you to do. We'll stay here, but we can't see the front door of the place from here. I want you to walk up the street, and cross over there by the river. Find yourself someplace to sit down where you can see the front door and me at the same time. Then you sit there and look bored and tired, and if anybody comes around you put on as thick a drawl as you can. You keep your eyes peeled for your friend. I reckon he'll use the front, but there's no telling. But keep your head down underneath that bonnet so he can't see your face."

"He'll never expect to see me here," I said.

"Keep the brim of that bonnet over your eyes regardless. When you see him, you take off the bonnet and give me a little wave—that is, *after* he's gone inside. Then you get back here to me."

"What will we do then?"

"I don't know. Reckon we'll have to go inside, find 'em, and then do a little improvising."

I got down, but then Captain Dyles spoke up again.

"One more thing, Miss Hollister," he said thoughtfully, still running options through his mind. "Tell me about your friend."

"He's not my friend," I said.

"No matter. I want to know . . . is he likely to fight? Is he a hero or a coward? With a gun in his gut, is he bound to do what we say or risk his life for his cause?"

It didn't take much reflection for me to answer.

"Unless he's changed, Captain," I said, "under those conditions, I'd say he'd do whatever you tell him. Cal Burton's only cause is himself. I can't see him risking his life for anybody."

CHAPTER 60

KIDNAP

Late in the year as it was, after more than two hours sitting in the sun, I was hot, tired, and sweating.

But when I first saw Cal striding up the street, suddenly all my senses jerked to attention. My heart started pounding and I could feel my whole body tense up. I hadn't actually laid eyes on him since the end of 1862. All the same emotions I'd felt five nights earlier were suddenly back—but this time even stronger! I was angry, afraid, and hurt. But I managed to keep it all inside instead of jumping up and running over and yelling all the things I was thinking. I kept my head down, and watched as he approached and then went inside the front door of Winder Supply.

The next instant I took off my bonnet, gave it a little wave in the direction of the wagon, then stood and walked hurriedly back in that direction myself.

By the time I got there, Captain Dyles and Jacob were out of the wagon and moving toward the back door of the place. I joined them, and we walked inside. None of the other people around paid us much heed, and I didn't see the fellow who had questioned us before.

We walked in. It was dark and smelled of grain and hay and boxes and wood and leather. Gradually my eyes became accustomed to the dim light. There were people around. Some of them glanced at us, but no one said anything.

I was afraid, but both Captain Dyles and Jacob acted as if they belonged there, and we didn't seem to attract any notice.

Suddenly I spotted Cal at the other end of the large room. He was coming straight toward us.

283

"That's him!" I whispered to the captain, then turned sideways and bent down my face to the floor. I was so glad it was dark!

We kept shuffling along. Cal was talking to another man and brushed right beside me. I could have grabbed at his arm, he was so close. As he went by, the captain followed him out of the corner of his eye. Cal and the other man entered what looked like a storage room off the large one we were in. The door closed behind them.

"You recognize the other one?" the captain whispered down to me.

"Surratt?" I replied. "I only heard him, but never saw his face."

"We'll have to get a listen, then."

Dyles turned and began sauntering aimlessly in the direction Cal had gone. I stuck as close to him as I could. We edged toward the closed door. He motioned to me to get up next to it and listen.

"Is it him?" he whispered.

"I can't tell . . . I think so."

Dyles thought a moment. "Doesn't matter if it's him, anyway. All we need is your Burton fellow. You ready, Jacob?"

The big Negro nodded.

"We gotta get the both of 'em before they can yell out, so we gotta be quick."

Jacob nodded again.

"Then let's go. Hollister," he said to me, "you follow us in and get the door shut pronto so nobody hears nothing."

Even as the words were coming from his mouth, he opened the door and he and Jacob burst through. I was right behind them.

Cal Burton glanced up, and his eyes fell straight on me. A shocked look filled his eyes and a pallor spread over his face. It was almost worth everything I'd been through to finally see the tables turned on him.

"Corrie—" he breathed. But it was the last word he spoke. Jacob's huge hand clamped down across his mouth. Cal's struggle was momentary. One look told him he was no match for Jacob. At the same time, Captain Dyles had overpowered the man I took for John Surratt.

"That him, Hollister?" said the captain, nodding his head toward Jacob's prey.

I nodded, feeling suddenly sick to my stomach. Despite what Cal had done to me, I felt all at once like Judas!

"Then get that rag outta my pocket," he said.

I found the pocket of his coat and pulled out a length of rag.

"Stuff it in this swine's mouth," he said.

I moved toward them. The captain slowly moved his hand aside. But before I could get the rag in, Surratt started to cry out. A slap across the side of his head from the captain silenced him again.

"You try that again and I won't be so gentle! Now, Hollister, get it in there!"

"I'll get you for this, little lady," growled Surratt through clenched teeth. "You may have gotten away that night in the street, but I'll—"

I jammed the rag in between his teeth and lips. He tried to spit it out, but I shoved it in tighter. Suddenly he chomped down on rag and fingers together and bit me hard.

"Ouch!" I cried, jumping back.

The next instant Surratt lay on the floor unconscious from another blow from Captain Dyles' fist.

"I warned the varmint," he muttered. He stooped down, took another length of rag from his coat, and tied it so tightly around Surratt's mouth I thought his lips were going to bleed. Then hastily he pulled out some rope and quickly bound Surratt's hands and feet, leaving him lying in a heap on the wood floor. Then he got up and turned his attention to Cal.

"Now, Burton," he said, "you can make this hard on yourself or you can make it easy. You've seen what I can do when I'm crossed. But Jacob here ain't half so nice a feller as me. Besides, Jacob's got a gun in your ribs too—Jacob, be so good as to show Mr. Burton what you got aimed at his heart."

Jacob brought around his left hand, which cradled a small revolver, in front of Cal's face.

"Now then, Jacob's gonna let you go. You make so much as a peep, and you'll feel his hand again. You make any ruckus when we're outside, and you'll feel the bullet from his gun, and it'll be the last thing you ever feel. Now move!"

Jacob removed his hand from Cal's mouth, then grabbed him

by the arm and pulled him toward the door.

"We're going for a little walk, Burton. And like I said, if you know what's good for you, keep quiet."

Cal threw me a look of mingled fear and disbelief at my betrayal of him. All I could think of was what I'd felt in Sacramento to discover him gone—but it didn't help me feel any better.

Dyles opened the door, and with Cal between the two of them, he and Jacob made their way out into the large warehouse and immediately began walking toward the doorway through which we had come. Jacob stuck so close to him that the gun was invisible, but every once in a while I saw him jab Cal in the ribs as a reminder. I followed behind them.

The moment we were outside and in the sunlight, Captain Dyles ran nearly headlong into the Supply Company man who had questioned him before.

"We found Master Jim," the captain said, slackening his pace but continuing on.

"Everything in order, Beauregard?" he asked, looking straight at Cal.

I saw him wincing as the steel pressed against the back of his rib cage.

Cal nodded and, encouraged by Jacob's bulk next to him, continued moving.

The man eyed our small entourage with a question in his eyes. Yet what could be wrong in a well-dressed southern gentleman accompanied by two poor white field hands and his Negro slave? We kept walking. I went past him, and we all moved straight to where the wagon was still sitting. The man continued to watch us.

"Tell us to load in some bags of oat feed," whispered Dyles to Cal.

Cal was silent.

"You heard the man," growled Jacob, again reminding Cal of the gun.

"You . . . you men get some oats in there," Cal said half-heartedly.

"Louder, Cal," I said. "I think he wants the man to hear you."

"You heard me," he said, louder this time. "Get those oats loaded."

Dyles and Jacob stood shuffling around the wagon another moment or two. I glanced back at the man who'd been watching us. Finally he turned and headed back toward the building.

"He's gone!" I whispered.

"Into the back, Burton!" said Jacob, practically throwing Cal up and onto the hay as he spoke. The next instant he was beside him.

Captain Dyles sprang up on the board, and I scrambled up to the seat next to him. He flicked the reins, and we bounded into motion.

I glanced back. Cal lay on his back on the floor of the wagon, hay strewn all around him, with Jacob's boot against his chest, and the gun in his hand pointed toward his head.

Captain Dyles urged the horse as fast as he dared, first up the street to the riverfront, then left, and then along the same route we had followed into the city a few hours earlier.

CHAPTER 61

THE SCHEME IS UNDONE

Now that we had actually kidnapped Cal and were making our escape through the Confederate capital, I was assaulted by many thoughts and feelings.

Mainly, I was just plain scared! What if Cal shouted out? What if someone thought we looked suspicious—which it seemed to me we did—and stopped us? What if we ran into a unit of Rebel soldiers? They were all around Richmond in the outlying districts! What if someone from Winder Supply followed us? What if Surratt got loose and suddenly all of Richmond was on the lookout for us!?

But mostly I felt an awful feeling in the pit of my stomach about what I'd done. Somehow it didn't matter that they were trying to kill General Grant, or even that Cal had stolen the money in California and had done what he'd done to me. None of that mattered right then. All I could think of was that I had betrayed another human being, someone I had once cared about! I had *betrayed* him!

It was no lingering and misplaced loyalty to Cal I was feeling. He was a rat in my eyes. Even worse—he was a spy and a criminal against the Union and a participant in a murder plot. I had no feelings left other than anger for what kind of man he'd allowed himself to become.

Yet what was even more despicable than a spy and murderer? The stool pigeon, the traitor . . . the Judas! How could I have stooped so low! *Was* this justified to save a man's life? Was it forgivable to betray a traitor?

288

And then, right in the middle of my thoughts, I heard Cal's voice.

"Corrie," he said behind me, "I'm surprised at you. All that religious talk . . . I thought you were different."

His words stung me. But any tears I had left for Cal Burton had been wept and were dried up long ago. And the patronizing, disdainful tone of his voice snapped me out of my self-recriminations. Cal had, indeed, changed! His voice was cold—hard, callous, and biting. If I'd thought he might have repented of what he'd done, I could not have been more wrong! The sound of his voice told me that he had continued his downward slide, and that perhaps he had become a man even capable of murder if it suited his selfish purposes.

I turned around and looked down at him where he lay. Seeing him so vulnerable and helpless filled me with a sudden sense of pity. All the pain from the past was gone.

"I'm sorry, Cal," I said sincerely. "I haven't changed . . . it's *you* who has changed. And whatever you may think of me, I couldn't let you kill General Grant. The future of this country is too important to me."

"Bah, Corrie, who are you trying to kid?" he spat back. "There are no noble causes. It's every man for himself in this world!"

"I don't happen to agree, Cal. I think the future of this country *is* a noble cause, and I intend to keep fighting for it, whatever you may think."

"You always were a starry-eyed idealist."

"I'll still take my ideals over your principles, Cal."

"Do *your* principles include betraying a friend?"

"A *friend*, Cal? After what you did to me, after what you have tried to do to the Union? Whose friend are you, Cal—anyone's but your own?"

"You're a fool, Corrie, if you think—"

But Jacob had had enough of his derision, and the rude coarseness of his tone toward me.

"Shut up, you!" he snarled, jabbing Cal with his boot.

"You big ox," Cal snapped back. "You're not going to shoot me in the middle of town. A shot would bring soldiers down on you like a swarm!"

"You'd be just as dead though, wouldn't you, *Massah Cal*? But before it comes to that, I'll stuff your mouth full of hay and tie it shut like your slimy friend back there. So shut your mouth, or I'll get down there and start feeding you like I do my hogs back home!"

Apparently Cal believed the threat and said no more.

We went on a while longer in silence. Beside me I could see Captain Dyles glancing furtively about, his eyes scanning the streets and buildings, looking for any signs of threat or trouble. At the same time, I knew him well enough by now to know he was thinking about how we were going to get out of town, through the sentries watching the roads, and safely back to the Union encampment on the other side of Petersburg with our kidnapped quarry. Even though we had Cal, the hardest part of the whole plan might still be ahead of us!

"We gotta get rid of this stuff back here before long, Geoff," said Jacob at length, as if reading both my mind and that of the captain at the same time.

Dyles nodded. "Yeah . . . I'm thinking. We still got about a mile to go."

The houses and buildings of Richmond were thinning and we were reaching the outskirts of the city.

"You'll never get away with it," said Cal. "They search every wagon in and out of the city!" His voice was cocky; I wondered if *anything* would ever humble him!

"I told you to shut up," said Jacob, grabbing a handful of hay and throwing it in Cal's face. "One more word, and I'll make it so that mouth of yours can't utter a peep!"

We bumped along another few minutes; then the captain noticed a barn off to the right side of the road that looked unused. At least there was nobody anywhere nearby, and the fields next to it were vacant of cows or horses. Immediately he pulled at the reins and steered our wagon toward it. He drove around to the back side, stopped, handed me the reins, then jumped to the ground.

The great door had no lock. He swung it open and nodded to me; I flicked the reins and the horse pulled us inside. The moment the trailing horse was through, Captain Dyles closed the door behind us, then jumped back up onto the wagon.

"Miss Corrie," said Jacob, handing me the gun. "If he makes a move, shoot him."

I knew my eyes widened and my heart started beating hard. I was glad for the darkness of the barn. I didn't want Cal to know I was afraid.

"Nobody'll hear it now, Burton," he added to Cal.

"She'd never have the guts!" shouted Cal, given new boldness by seeing the gun in my hand.

"You don't have to kill him, Miss Corrie," said Jacob. "Just a bullet in his leg someplace'll be fine."

Already the captain and Jacob were struggling with the barrels. Jacob popped the lid off the first. The next moment I heard the *swish* of the grain falling onto the floor. Then they did the same with the second, and within two minutes we were ready to leave the barn and be back on our way.

Again I was at the reins and Captain Dyles began to open the large rear door of the barn.

Suddenly he stopped.

"Hold on, Miss Hollister," he said.

I pulled back and stopped the wagon.

"I just don't like the idea of leaving a good animal for the Rebs," he said, looking back into the barn at the horse he had untied from the back of the wagon. "Not to mention your safety being a mite worrisome to me . . ."

He thought a few seconds more.

"There just might be a way . . ." he mumbled to himself. "Yep . . . it might work." Then he glanced up at me. "I haven't been too comfortable with your part in this, Hollister. If anything was to happen to you . . . well, there's got to be some way to insure that if anything goes wrong, you can get safely away. Yep, it just might work. . . ."

Even as he was talking to me I could tell he was still thinking about what we might do.

"That's what we'll do," he said finally, with a sound of resolve, closing the door again. "Get down from there, Miss Hollister and unhitch that mare. We're going to swap her for Lee's nag."

Having no idea what he meant to do, I obeyed. Jacob remained where he was watching over his charge in the back of the wagon.

Five minutes later we were set to go again. This time, however, I wasn't sitting next to Captain Dyles on the board of the wagon, but was on the bare back of the mare that had pulled us faithfully all the way from Petersburg.

"Okay, let's be off," said the captain, flipping the reins and leading the wagon through the open door of the barn. I followed on the mare.

"I hate to leave behind the pie the sergeant made us," Jacob said, laughing.

"It'll make some Reb farmer happy when he finds it," said Dyles. "And we don't need it now. It won't do us no good, but the horse still might."

A few minutes later we were back on the road. Half a mile farther on, the soldiers from the guard unit appeared up ahead of us. I inched the mare up alongside the wagon.

"You stick close, Miss Hollister," said Captain Dyles, "but keep to that side of me so the Reb don't get too good a look. We can't have him recognize that white star on the mare's forehead."

"I'll try to keep her nose turned away from him," I said.

"If anything goes wrong, you save your own neck."

"Nothing will go wrong," I replied, wishing I felt as confident as my words.

"You hear me, Miss Hollister—you don't worry about us if anything happens. You get that mare back to General Grant in one piece, and yourself along with her. That's an order. That's why I put you on her . . . just in case."

"Yes, sir," I said.

Five minutes later we approached the gray-clad Confederate guard.

"Howdy theyere, Lieutenant Gibb," drawled Dyles in such a heavy accent that I almost had to laugh. "We're on our way back to th' farm."

"General Lee like his new horse?" said the friendly sentry with a smile.

"Shore did. *He* didn't think it was no nag, neither."

Just then I heard a faint groan and a kicking sound from the back of the wagon. I glanced over and saw Jacob kicking against an empty barrel lying on its side—rolling it back and forth to drown out the sound of Cal kicking against the inside of the other.

Poor Cal! Jacob had finally stuffed his mouth full of hay, tied a rag around it, put him inside the empty grain barrel, replaced the lid, and sat down on top of it himself. No one would be able to budge it with Jacob's weight holding it down.

Both Dyles and the guard glanced over at the sound. The captain barked out angrily at his black friend.

"If you can't keep that empty barrel from rollin' round back theyere while I'm talkin' to the lieutenant, I'll whip your hide when we get home, boy!"

"Yessuh, massah," mumbled Jacob, casting his eyes down, but managing to keep making enough noise to cover Cal's.

"What's she doing?" asked the guard, glancing over at me.

"My wife?"

"Where'd that horse come from?" he asked, eyeing my mount carefully, then looking at the one hitched to the reins the captain held in his hand. He seemed to be turning over something in his mind, but it hadn't quite occurred to him that we'd just switched the two.

"Why, that there's the genrul's old horse. We was tradin' the two of 'em."

"Why's she riding it?" he asked, now beginning to look back and forth between the two horses.

"Genrul Lee wanted it that way."

I didn't like the suspicious look in Lieutenant Gibb's eye. But before I had a chance to worry about it further, Captain Dyles spoke again, to me this time.

"You might as well get goin', dear," he said. "We'll catch up with you in a minute or two." With his eyes he motioned me to go. I saw that he was worried.

Out of the corner of my eye, I could see the guard starting to object. I think it might have suddenly dawned on him that we still had the same two horses as we'd gone into the city with that morning. But I wasn't about to look at him. Instead, I urged my horse on and moved gently forward in front of the wagon and along the road leading out of town.

Then suddenly everything started to happen fast.

I heard Lieutenant Gibb's voice yelling at me to stop. And I heard more ruckus than ever coming from the back of the wagon. I knew Cal was kicking at the barrel where he was crumpled up underneath Jacob's weight, and I knew Jacob was kicking and rolling the empty barrel about to keep Cal from being heard.

But a third sound seemed to mingle with the sound of my horse's hoofs on the dirt road, Cal's kicking and the barrel rumbling about, and the sentry's shouts.

Unconsciously I began to quicken my pace.

The noise increased . . . there was more shouting . . . the sound of galloping hooves!

I glanced back.

A rider was approaching from the city, galloping hard, shouting, calling out to the guard.

The sound of his voice sent a chill of fear up my spine. Still turned, I squinted to see if I could make out the figure atop the fast-approaching horse.

It was John Surratt!

In panic I hesitated, then stopped. *What should I do?*

My question was answered the next second. Seeing my uncertainty and that I had stopped, Captain Dyles shouted above the din.

"Go, Hollister . . . I gave you an order . . . now ride!"

Already I could see that Lieutenant Gibb had his rifle aimed at the captain and Jacob, and that one of his men was helping Cal out of his temporary imprisonment.

A cloud of dust from Surratt's approaching horse swept over the scene as he reined in to a frantic stop amid more shouts.

Everything was a confusion. *"Union spies!"* Someone shouted, *"After her! Don't let her get away!"* But my mind and arms and legs all seemed paralyzed, and images of jail cells and gallows flitted through my imagination like a dreadful nightmare come to life.

Then the sound of Jacob's enormous booming voice raised louder than all the rest echoed thunderously through the air.

"Get out of here, Miss Corrie!" he cried, and I don't think ever a voice sounded so commanding or penetrated so deep into my bones. "Ride like the wind, and don't—"

His voice was cut short. The butt of Surratt's rifle clubbed him alongside the head, and he slumped to the ground unconscious.

It was all I needed. Suddenly I was awake again!

I spun around on the mare's back, dug my heels into her sides, and galloped away, my eyes filling with tears for Jacob and the captain.

Behind me I heard more voices and shouts. Then came a shot from Surratt's rifle!

Still riding, I glanced back. He was mounting his horse to follow me. I heard Cal's voice calling after him. "Let her go . . . she's of no more use to us."

"I've got a score to settle with the lady, Burton!"

I was well down the road now, probably two hundred yards away and riding with a desperation I'd never known.

Another shot came! Though I heard nothing, somehow I knew the bullet had whizzed by me not more than inches away.

"Stop, Surratt!" I heard Cal's voice faintly in the distance.

There was no answer, only the sound of Surratt's horse, now galloping after me. I knew he was making up the distance rapidly.

Another shot . . . closer yet!

This poor mare was no match for whatever Surratt had under him! I could feel his approach with terror.

Suddenly I felt a slamming sensation in my back. My right arm went limp and dropped to my side. The pain was different than anything I'd ever felt before.

The explosion of sound which followed the bullet seemed hazy and slow and dreamlike, as though it were coming ten minutes after the impact. My fading consciousness somehow was still alert enough to realize that the sound and the bullet had left Surratt's rifle at the same time, and my confused mind tried to make sense of the contradiction . . . but couldn't.

The pain lasted but a moment. Then followed only numbness.

All sounds began to fade.

I heard several more shots; then I heard nothing more of Surratt's hoofbeats. I could not even hear my own horse . . . all was quiet and still.

Still I rode, though I hardly knew it. Vaguely I was aware of my hair flying out behind me.

I was slumped over the mare's neck, struggling to maintain my grasp of her mane, trying to stay on her back.

I only knew there was danger behind me. I had to get away . . . had to keep riding. Why was it so quiet? Was I asleep? And if so, why did this dream seem so real?

Let me sleep a few minutes more, Almeda . . . be up soon . . . had the strangest dream . . . about a war . . . men dressed in black . . . they both have beards . . . they are in danger. . . .

I'll be awake soon . . . Ma . . . what are you making for breakfast . . . strange dream, Ma . . . I thought I saw Pa . . . he was somewhere far away . . . we were all with him, Ma . . . all except you . . . I didn't see you there, Ma. . . .

The quiet of the dream grew quieter . . . all was still . . . nothing but silence . . . peace . . . no pain . . . everything was white . . . bright. . . .

Then even the silence faded into nothingness.

Slowly the brilliant whiteness turned pale, then ashen . . . then gray . . . and finally gave way to blackness.

EPILOGUE

When I next woke up, I found myself staring into a face I had never seen before.

How much time had passed, I didn't know. The room was clean and white, and I was lying in bed. The first sensation I felt was a slight pain in the back of my shoulder. It didn't occur to me immediately that it was from the wound where I'd been shot.

This, however, was not the biggest surprise of all. That was the simple fact that when I woke up and looked around, I couldn't remember who I was!

But that is another whole story, and I'll have to tell you about it later!

St. Francis Xavier Catholic Church in Gettysburg, used as a hospital for wounded during and after the battle.

From: *Gettysburg, The National Shrine*, Pictoral Edition Guidebook, Copyright by N.A. Meligakes, 1948, Gettysburg, Pa.

JENNIE WADE—The only citizen of Gettysburg who was killed during the battle. Miss Jennie Wade, 20 years old, was struck by a sharpshooter's bullet in a little brick house on Baltimore Street, near the National Cemetery. She and her mother were taking care of her sister, who had given birth only three days before the battle started. Jennie and her mother were compelled to remain in the house for her sister's sake; nearly all of the citizens of Gettysburg were in their cellars. On the morning of the third day she was in the rear room baking bread, and was killed instantly by a bullet, which passed through two doors before striking her. The others in the house escaped without injury. The house, still standing, shows the marks of several hundred bullets.

People Making A Difference

Family Bookshelf offers the finest in good wholesome Christian literature, written by best-selling authors. All books are recommended by an Advisory Board of distinguished writers and editors.

We are also a vital part of a compassionate outreach called **Bowery Mission Ministries**. Our evangelical mission is devoted to helping the destitute of the inner city.

Our ministries date back more than a century and began by aiding homeless men lost in alcoholism. Now we also offer hope and Gospel strength to homeless, inner-city women and children. Our goal, in fact, is to end homelessness by teaching these deprived people how to be independent with the Lord by their side.

Downtrodden, homeless men are fed and clothed and may enter a discipleship program of one-on-one professional counseling, nutrition therapy and Bible study. This same Christian care is provided at our women and children's shelter.

We also welcome nearly 1,000 underprivileged children each summer at our Mont Lawn Camp located in Pennsylvania's beautiful Poconos. Here, impoverished youngsters enjoy the serenity of nature and an opportunity to receive the teachings of Jesus Christ. We also provide year-round assistance through teen activities, tutoring in reading and writing, Bible study, family counseling, college scholarships and vocational training.

During the spring, fall and winter months, our children's camp becomes a lovely retreat for religious gatherings of up to 200. Excellent accommodations include heated cabins, chapel, country-style meals and recreational facilities. Write to Paradise Lake Retreat Center, Box 252, Bushkill, PA 18324 or call: (717) 588-6067.

Bowery Mission Ministries are supported by voluntary contributions of individuals and bequests. Contributions are tax deductible. Checks should be made payable to Bowery Mission.

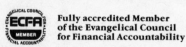

**Fully accredited Member
of the Evangelical Council
for Financial Accountability**

Every Monday morning, our ministries staff joins together in prayer. If you have a prayer request for yourself or a loved one, simply write to us.

**Administrative Office:
40 Overlook Drive, Chappaqua,
New York 10514 Telephone: (914) 769-9000**